Valorian's
Children

Valorian's Children

Dark Horse
Lightning's Daughter

MARY H. HERBERT

Contents

Valorian's Children

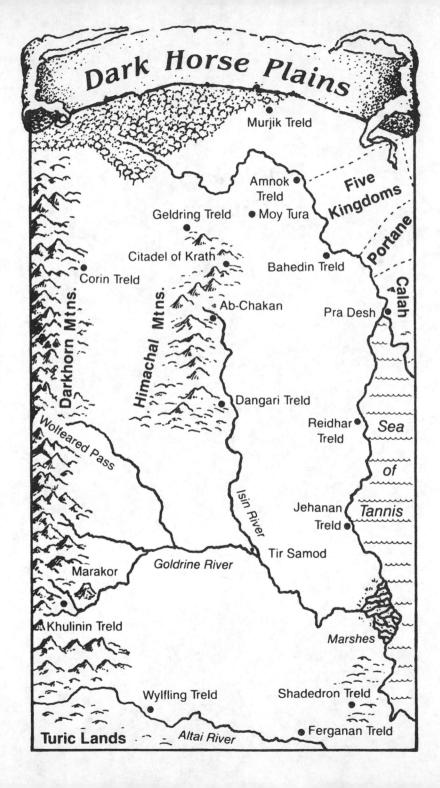

Dark Horse

1

Gabria paused and leaned wearily against her walking staff. She could not go on much longer like this. Her ankle ached from a bad fall and her shoulders were rubbed raw by the unaccustomed pack. The wind, which blew cold from the icy passes of the mountains, cut through her woolen cloak and chilled her to the bone. She had not eaten since fleeing from her home at Corin Treld two days before.

The girl sat down on a rock and threw her pack to the ground. There was some dried meat and trail bread in the old pack, but Gabria had no idea how much longer she would have to walk and food was difficult to find on the plains this early in the spring. It was better to save her rations until she was desperate. At any rate, she had no desire for food now. Her body was too numb with grief and despair.

Gabria wearily examined her boots. The soles were almost worn through from the sharp shale she had struggled over. Ragged boots, the sign of an exile. Her breath suddenly caught in her throat and, for a moment, she nearly surrendered to the anguish that tore at her resolve like starving vultures. No! she cried silently. I cannot weep. Not yet.

Gabria pounded her knee with her fist while her other hand convulsively gripped the short sword at her belt. Her body trembled violently as she fought to regain control of her despair. There was no time for grief now. Nor did she have the strength to waste on self-pity. Her family and her clan had been massacred at their winter camp at Corin Treld. She was the only one left to claim their weir-geld, recompense for the blood of her family that stained the grass of their home. She would seek her revenge and then she could weep.

Gabria closed her mind to all but her grim resolve. It was the only way she could survive. It gave her a strength and a purpose in the face of a debilitating loneliness and fear. She was an exile now and therefore dead to her people unless another clan accepted her. She was a wanderer and an untouchable. Somehow, she had to find a clan that would take her in. Somehow, she would claim her vengeance.

Slowly her trembling eased and the emotions that threatened to devour her were forced into a deep prison. She remembered that her father had once told her that strong emotions were a power to be harnessed and used like a weapon. She stood up and smiled a feral grimace, like the snarl of a wolf. To the north, the direction from which she had come, a line of clouds lay along the horizon. It seemed to her that a pall of smoke still hung over her home.

"My grief for you will be used, Father," Gabria said aloud. "Our enemy will die."

Out of habit, she reached up to brush a strand of flaxen hair out of her face, only to touch the rough-cut stubble on her head. The girl sighed, remembering the pain she had felt when she had cut her hair and burned it with the bodies of her four brothers, including her twin, Gabran. Her brothers had been so proud of her long, thick hair. But she gave it to them as a gift of mourning and in return she took her twin's identity. His clothes now covered her body and his weapons were in her hand. She would no longer be a girl. For the sake of survival, she would become a boy, Gabran.

It was clan law that no woman could claim weir-geld alone; she had to be championed by a male member of her family. To make matters worse for Gabria, the clans usually did not accept an exiled woman unless she was of exceptional beauty or talent. Gabria knew she had little chance of being accepted on her own merits. On the other hand, she was slim and strong and had been raised with four boisterous boys who often forgot she was only a girl. With luck and careful attention, she thought she could pass well enough as a boy. The deception could bring her death, but it could also give her a greater chance for survival and revenge.

Ignoring the jab of pain in her ankle, Gabria shouldered her pack once more and limped southward across the hillside. She was in the Hornguard, the low, barren foothills that lay like a crumpled robe at the foot of the Darkhorn Mountains. Somewhere in one of the sheltered valleys to the south, she hoped to find the Khulinin, her mother's clan, led by Lord Savaric. She hoped her kinship with the Khulinin would overcome the stigma of exile. Gabria prayed it would, for even driven by the strength of her desire for revenge, she knew she would not be able to go far. The Khulinin were still many days distant and either her twisted ankle or her food would fail long before she could find another clan.

Gabria hurried on, forcing her legs to move. It was almost twilight and she wanted to find shelter before dark.

Then, above the wind, she heard the howling of wolves. Hungry and insistent, the cries sang through the dusk like wild music. Gabria shuddered and gripped her staff tighter as the feral hunting calls sounded again. The wolves were not after her, she realized. They were upwind of her and deeper in the hills. Still, that was too close. Alone and virtually defenseless against a pack, Gabria had no desire to meet the vicious marauders. She stopped and listened, following the progress of the hunt.

The howling continued for several minutes. The animals were moving south, running parallel to her. Then the cries grew louder, for whatever the wolves were chasing seemed to be trying to reach the open ground of the plains. Gabria tensed and her eyes searched the hills for the approaching pack. But the howling stopped abruptly, and the wolves broke into yowls of glee and triumph. The girl sighed with relief. The wolves had caught their prey and would not hunt again for a while.

She was about to move on when she heard another sound that froze her heart: the enraged squeal of an embattled horse. "Oh, Mother of All," she breathed. "No!"

Before she could consider her choices, she limped toward the sound even as the echoes faded. The howling burst out, sharp with rage and frustration. Gabria ran faster, forcing her sore legs to navigate the rugged, brush-covered hillsides, while the pain stabbed through her ankle and the heavy pack slammed against her back. She knew it was utterly stupid to think of challenging a pack of killers for their chosen prey, but this prey was different. Horses were special to her, to all her people. They were the very existence of the clans, the chosen of the goddess, Amara, and the children of the plains. No clansman ever turned his back on a horse, no matter what the danger.

The yowling abruptly increased and the horse's screams took on a note of fury and desperation. Gabria pushed on until her breath came in ragged gasps and her legs were heavy with pain. For a moment, she despaired reaching the stricken horse before it was brought down. The sounds became louder, but the distance seemed so much greater than she had expected. She dropped her pack, then pulled off her cloak and wrapped it around her arm as she ran.

Suddenly the sounds ceased. Gabria faltered when she lost the guidance of the cries. She stopped and listened again, trying to locate the attack. The wind whistled around her, carrying the smell of an old winter as the hills dimmed in the approaching night. Beyond the grasslands, the full moon was rising.

"Oh, Mother," Gabria gasped. "Where are they?"

As if in answer to her plea, another furious squeal came out of the growing darkness and the howling rose in response. This time, the sounds were quite close, perhaps in the next valley.

Breathing a silent prayer of thanks, Gabria broke into a run. She topped one hill, plunged into a valley, and toiled up the next slope. At the crest she stopped and peered down the hill. The land at her feet sheered off into a deep gully between three hills, where several runoffs emptied into a bowl-like depression. After the last thaw, melted snow had gathered in the center, creating a pool of mud and standing water rimmed with ice.

In the midst of the pool, now churned to a filthy mire, stood a huge horse, very angry and very much alive. Gabria's eyes widened in astonishment and excitement when she recognized the animal. It was a Hunnuli, the greatest of all the horse breeds. They were the legendary steeds of the ancient magic-wielders, and, even though their masters had been destroyed by hate and jealousy, the horses themselves were revered above all others. Their numbers were few and wild, and when they deigned to be ridden, they only accepted the men of the clans. It was said that the first Hunnuli was sired by a storm on the first mare of the world; a streak of lightning was left indelibly printed on their descendants' shoulders to prove it.

Gabria had never seen one of these magnificent animals before, but there was no mistaking this was a Hunnuli. Even in the twilight, Gabria could see the jagged white streak that marked the black hide at its shoulder. She simply could not believe one of those horses had been brought to bay by eight or nine wolves.

She moved behind a scrub pine to where she could see without being detected. The wolves were still there, slinking around the edge of the mire and keeping their distance from the wicked teeth of the horse. The horse itself was obviously exhausted, and steam rose from its heaving flanks.

Suddenly the Hunnuli lunged, squealing in fury as it tried to lash out at a sneaking wolf. The girl knew then why the horse had not run, for it was trapped in the clinging mud. Its back legs were sunk to the haunches in the freezing mire and its front legs pawed desperately for purchase on the slippery edge of the pool. It could only use its teeth to fight the wolves for fear of sinking deeper into the mud.

The horse settled back warily and snorted. Two wolves then made a feint for the horse's head to draw its attention while a third leaped from behind to slash at the unprotected tendons in the horse's back legs.

Gabria screamed and the horse whipped its head around and slammed the leaping wolf into the mire. Like a snake, the Hunnuli flung back and snapped viciously at the other two beasts. One wolf screeched in agony and fell back with its leg hanging in bloody splinters. The second was more successful. It caught the horse by the neck and left a gaping slash dangerously close to the jugular. The other wolves yipped and snarled.

Gabria's mouth went dry and her legs were shaking. She wished fervently for her bow and some arrows to bring down the wolves, but the bow lay in the ashes of her tent, and she did not trust her skill with the sword that hung by her side. All she had was her staff. She hefted it and swallowed hard. If she waited to think any longer, all would be lost. The horse was weakening rapidly and the wolves were growing bolder.

With a wild yell, the girl sprinted down the slope, lurching on her injured ankle. The wolves whirled in surprise to face this new threat and the horse neighed another challenge. Before the hunters realized their danger, Gabria was upon them, swinging her staff like a scythe. The wolves snapped and lunged at her, and she fought them back with a strength born of desperation. One wolf fell, its back broken. Another lay whimpering with smashed ribs. A third leaped away and was caught by the teeth of the great horse, which flung it high in the air. Using her cloak as a guard for her arm and her staff like a double-edged sword, Gabria drove the wolves away from the pool. At the foot of the enclosing hills, they broke and ran.

Gabria watched them disappear over the rim of the hill, then she turned to gaze with some surprise at the bodies lying in the gully. Something seemed to snap inside her and she sagged on her staff, feeling utterly exhausted and aching from head to toe. She stood there for a while, panting for breath, sweating and trembling with dizziness.

The girl glanced blearily at the wild horse and wondered what to do next. The big animal stood immobile and watched her quietly. She was relieved to see its ears were swiveled toward her rather than flattened on its head. The horse seemed to realize she was not an enemy.

The evening had dimmed to night and the full moon swelled above the plains; its silver light flooded into the gully and gleamed on the standing water. Gabria limped to the edge of the mudhole and sat down to rest while she studied the horse. Even mired in the mud, she could see the animal was enormous. It probably stood about eighteen hands at the shoulder, and Gabria mentally cringed at the thought of moving such a massive animal out of its trap. Yet she obviously could not leave the Hunnuli. The wolves could return and the horse was in no condition to free itself. Somehow she would have to devise a way to free it. But how? She had no tools, no rope, and very little strength. Of course, its size gave the Hunnuli incredible power, but if it struggled too much against the heavy mud it would wear itself into deadly exhaustion.

The girl shook her head. At least the horse did not appear to be sinking deeper. Gabria hoped that meant the ground was frozen below the mud and would support the horse through the night. There was nothing more she could do now. She was too weary, beyond thought and beyond effort, to do anything else that night.

Gabria stood up, feeling slightly better, and walked slowly around the pool. She stared at the horse, her face wrinkled in a frown. There was something odd about this horse that she could not quite discern in the moonlight. Its glossy black hide was filthy with muck, and blood oozed from the gash on its neck, making a slick rivulet down its withers. But the blood was not the problem. There was something else . . . something unusual for a seemingly healthy horse. Then she realized what it was.

Oh, no, Gabria thought. So that is why the Hunnuli was trapped so easily. She is a mare and heavy with foal.

There was no alternative now. Gabria knew she would have to extricate the Hunnuli or die trying. She glanced up at the horse's head and saw the mare staring intently at her. Their eyes met and the meeting was so intense Gabria was rocked back on her heels. Never had she seen such eyes in any creature. They were like orbs of illuminated night, sparkling with starlight and brimming with incredible intelligence. They were gazing at her with a mixture of surprise, suspicion, and an almost human glint of impatience.

"How did *you* get caught like this?" Gabria breathed softly, her voice mingled with awe.

The mare snorted in disgust.

"I'm sorry, it was unfair of me to ask. I'm going to find firewood. I'll return."

It was normal for her to talk to a horse like another human being, but this time the girl had the oddest feeling the mare understood.

Gabria put her cloak around her shoulders, for the air was turning bitterly cold, and went to find her pack. She found a dead tree on her way back and broke off enough wood to last the night. As an afterthought, she dragged the dead wolves out of the gully and left them downwind of her camp.

She lit a small fire in the shelter of the cliff wall, where the horse could see her, and set most of the fuel aside for an emergency. There was only stale bread and dried meat for a meal, but Gabria ate it gratefully. For the first time since she fled the devastation at Corin Treld, she was hungry.

She sat silently for a while, staring at the horse. In the darkness, it loomed as an even darker obscurity on the edge of the firelight. Every now and then it would shift slightly and the flames would reflect in its eyes. Gabria shuddered. The blackness in her mind began to creep insidiously over her thoughts. Fires licked in her memory and the phantoms of things remembered grew out of the shadows. The flames rose and fell and ran with blood. There was blood everywhere. Her hands, her clothes, and even her scarlet cloak was stained with blood and reeked of death.

The girl stared at her hands, at the stains she could not remove. Her hands would never be clean. She frantically wiped her palms on her leggings and moaned like a wounded animal. The tears burned in her head, but her eyes remained dry as she stared glassily at the ground. Her shoulders shook with silent sobs.

"Father, I'm sorry," she cried. Above her, the moon followed its unseeing path and a damp, chill wind swept through the hills. Beyond the gully came the sounds of bickering wolves from where they were tearing at the bodies of their dead.

After a long while, the fire died down and the phantoms faded from Gabria's mind. Moving like an old woman, she stoked the fire, then curled up in her cloak. She fell asleep, borne under by the weight of utter exhaustion.

A horse neighed, strident and demanding, above the hoofbeats that thundered over the frozen ground. Half-seen forms of mounted men careened past to set their torches to the felt tents. Swords flashed in the rising flames as the attackers cut down the people, and scream after scream reverberated in the mist, until they blended into one agonized wail.

Gabria started awake, her heart pounding as the cry died on her lips. She clutched her cloak tighter and shivered at the dream that still clouded her thoughts. A horse neighed again, angrily. The unexpected sound dispelled the nightmare and brought the girl fully awake. This sound was no dream. She stiffly sat up and blinked at the Hunnuli. The mare was watching her with obvious impatience. Gabria realized the sun was already riding above the plains, though its warming light had not yet dipped into the gully. The chill of the night still clung to shadows, and frost flowered everywhere, even on the mud-encrusted mane of the trapped mare.

Gabria sighed, grateful the night was gone and the wolves had not attacked again. With infinite care, she eased to her feet, convinced she would shatter at any moment. Every muscle felt as if it were petrified.

"I'm sorry," she said to the horse. "I did not mean to sleep so long. But I feel better." She gently stretched to work out the kinks in her joints. "Perhaps I can help you now."

The mare whinnied as if to say "I should think so," and a wisp of a smile drifted over the girl's face. For a moment the smile lit her pale green eyes, then it was gone and the pain that had dulled her expression for three days returned.

Sitting by a newly built fire, Gabria emptied her pack onto the ground. There was very little in it that would help her to dig a gigantic horse out of the mud trap: only a bag of food, a few pots of salve, a dagger of fine steel that had been her father's prized possession, an extra tunic, and a few odds and ends she had salvaged from her family's burned tent. At the moment, she would have traded it all for a stout length of rope and a digging tool.

She sat for a time, totally at a loss over what to do next. Finally, she walked around the pool and considered every possibility, while the mare kept a cautious eye on her. In the daylight, Gabria could see the mare had none of the fine-boned grace of the Harachan horses Gabria was accustomed to. The Hunnuli's head was small in comparison to her immense neck, which curved down regally to a wide back. Her chest was broad and muscular and her shoulders were an image of power. There was granite in her bones, steel in her muscles, and fire in her blood.

"Well," said Gabria at last, hands on hips. "There's only one thing I can think of now. Food."

She laid the contents of her pack on her cloak, rolled it up, and set it aside. Then, with her knife and empty pack, she went in search of grass. On the hilltop she paused to watch the sun climb the flawless sky. It was going to be a lovely day despite the early season. The wind had died, and a fresh smell of new growth rose from the warming land. A few patches of stubborn snow clung to the sheltered hillsides, but most of the winter's snowfall was gone.

Before her the foothills fell away into the valley of the Hornguard, a broad, lush river valley and the favorite wintering place of her rival clan, the Geldring. The land rose again beyond the river's domain into the Himachal Mountains. The small range of rugged peaks sat like an afterthought in the midst of the grasslands. From their feet the vast steppeland of Ramtharin flowed for leagues to the seas of the eastern kings. This was the land of the twelve clans of Valorian and the realm of the Harachan horses, the fleet, smaller cousins of the Hunnuli. The steppes were hot in the summer, cold in the winter, dry most of the year, and merciless to those who did not respect them. They offered little to a people beyond the wind and the immense solitude of their rolling hills, but their grass was rich and the polished dome of the sky was a greater treasure to the clans than all the palaces of the east.

Behind Gabria, the mountains of Darkhorn marched south, then bent away to the west. Somewhere beyond the curve was the valley of the Goldrine River and the Khulinin clan's winter encampment. She looked southward, hoping to see something that would encourage her, but the landmarks she knew were lost in the purple haze. She bit her lip, thinking of the miles she still had to travel, and bent to her task.

Gabria soon had a pack full of dried grass for the mare and a few half-frozen winterberries for herself. Although the fare was meager for a horse of that size, the old prairie grass was well cured by last year's summer sun and was rich enough. The Hunnuli would survive for a while.

The horse was watching intently for the girl to return and greeted Gabria with a resounding neigh.

"This is all I have for now," Gabria told her. "I will bring more later." Cautiously she laid the grass within reach of the horse. The mare tore voraciously at the proffered food, bobbing her head in her efforts to swallow quickly.

Meanwhile, Gabria tried to decide what to do next. She examined every possibility that came to mind no matter how ridiculous, but there seemed to be only one hopeful course—and the very idea of that nearly defeated her. She would have to dig the mare out.

Fortunately, the standing water had run off during the night, leaving only the deep, thick mire. The properties that made the mud so treacherous might help her in its removal. It was so thick, it stuck everywhere. Nevertheless, if the Hunnuli thrashed about or tried to fight her off, it would be impossible to get close enough to do anything.

Gabria shrugged and picked up her empty pack. She could only hope the mare would understand her attempts to help. She walked up one of the eroded stream beds that ran into the gully and soon found what she needed. There was an abundance of loose gravel and broken shale lying in bars along the dry bed. Quickly the girl filled her pack and returned to the pool. After several trips, she had a large pile of rock close to the mudhole.

Next, she went to collect broken branches, fallen logs, twigs, dead scrub, and anything that would suit her plan. In a nearby stand of pine, she cut boughts of springy needles and hauled them to the growing heap. Finally, she was ready.

Panting slightly, she spoke to the mare. "I know I have not earned the privilege to be your friend," she said. "But you must trust me. I am going to dig you out and I cannot spend my time avoiding your teeth."

The Hunnuli dipped her head and snorted. Taking that as a positive sign, Gabria eased to the mare's front legs and watched the ears that flicked toward her. The mare remained still; her ears stayed perked.

Gabria knelt in front of the horse. With a long, flat rock, she began scraping the mud away from the mare's legs. The muck was not deep by the edge and Gabria was able to reach frozen earth in several places.

"I'm going to make a ramp here for you," she said to the horse. "So you can stand without slipping." The Hunnuli remained still, apparently waiting.

By late morning, Gabria was drenched with sweat, and mud covered her like a second layer of clothes. She stood up, wiped her hands on her tunic, and surveyed her work. She felt a moment of pride. The mare's front quarters were free of the clinging mud and her front hooves rested on a short ramp of logs embedded in the mud and banked on either side with rock and dead brush. The horse's belly and hindquarters were still firmly mired, but Gabria felt a little relief and a twinge of hope.

The girl ate a quick meal and returned to work. First, she laid a narrow platform in the mud around the horse so she could work without fighting the mire herself. Scraping and digging with her rock shovel and her bare hands, she cleared away the mud from the Hunnuli's sides, then packed in handfuls of gravel and shale to keep the walls from slipping in. It was agonizing work. Gabria's back was soon a band of pain and her hands were sore and blistered. The mare watched her constantly, remaining motionless except for the occasional swing of her head. Only her tail twitching in the mud betrayed her controlled impatience.

The first stars were glimmering in the darkening sky when Gabria stopped digging. She looked at the trapped mare in dismay and said, "I'm sorry, it will be another day before I can get you out." She groaned and staggered to her feet. "The digging's going so much slower than I expected."

In the long afternoon's work, she had only cleared away a distressingly small area of mud surrounding the huge horse. At the pace she was going, it might be several days before the mare was free. Weary and depressed, Gabria collected more grass for the horse and rubbed down her front legs to stave off swelling. She was rewarded with a soft nicker.

She looked at the Hunnuli in wonder. The mare returned her gaze calmly, her eyes glowing like black pearls. Impulsively, Gabria leaned over and buried her face in the Hunnuli's thick mane. It did not seem possible she could feel something after the destruction of her home and family. She thought every emotion had withered within her when she looked on the mutilated bodies of her brothers. Only revenge had remained to hold her together and fill her heart. Yet, this trapped horse awoke a feeling of kinship in her, and the battered remnants of her old self reached out desperately for comfort. Perhaps, she thought with a frantic yearning, this great horse would accept her as a friend. If so, that friendship was worth a lifetime of labor.

But after a while she stood up and rubbed her face, chiding herself for her fantasies. Hunnuli only accepted warriors and old sorcerers, not exiled girls. It was ridiculous to even imagine. She cleaned herself off as best she could and rekindled her fire. She ate some bread and was asleep before the flames died to embers.

The next morning came with a dismal dawn and a brief but heavy snow. The mountains were veiled behind a raiment of gray and silver clouds, and the wind gusted through the valleys. Gabria woke with a groan. She was badly chilled and so sore she could barely move without pain stabbing somewhere in her body. Her shoulders and back ached and her arms felt petrified from her exertions of the day before. Closer inspection showed her ankle was still swollen. She moaned irritably and pulled her boot back on. Much more of this, she thought, shaking the snow off her cloak, and the wolves will have two meals.

She decided to wrap her ankle for better support and hoped the rest of her abused body would gradually lose its kinks.

The Hunnuli was watching her as she ate her meal, showing none of the impatience of the previous day. The snowfall had patterned the horse's black coat like a bank of stars in a midnight sky, yet she did not bother to shake it off. Gabria glanced at her worriedly and wondered if something was wrong. The wild horse seemed abnormally subdued.

The girl became more alarmed when the Hunnuli ignored a fresh armload of grass. The horse's eyes were withdrawn and dull, as if the light of their glance was turned inward.

"Please, tell me it's not true," Gabria said, sick at the realization that dawned on her. The mare moved restlessly in the mire and turned to nose at her belly. It was difficult to tell under all the mud, but some of the signs were apparent. If Gabria was right, the mare would foal soon. The trauma of the attack and the two days in the mudhole had probably triggered the labor prematurely. Gabria looked at the mare's bulging sides and wondered how far along she actually was.

Desperately, Gabria went to work. The digging she thought she could do in two days now had to be finished in one. Some of the mud had slipped back during the night, but most of the walls had held. Extending these deeper, Gabria dug along the mare's stomach and down her haunches. She could see how the foal had dropped, and she hoped it would be an easy labor. The mare was stiff and weakened from her imprisonment and was in no condition to fight a difficult birth.

The morning passed slowly, broken by intermittent snow and moments of warm sun. Gabria stopped several times to collect more shale and brush, then continued on as fast as her complaining body allowed. Once, she had to stop to wrap the bleeding blisters and lacerations on her hands.

By late afternoon, Gabria was nearing the end of her strength. Only her intense desire to free the mare and the unborn foal gave her the energy to keep digging. Her movements became automatic: scoop out the mud, throw it aside, and pack in the rock. The aches in her arms and back united into one massive hurt, then faded as she pushed herself to the edges of endurance. After a time, it became easy to ignore the melting snow that trickled through her clothes. She only concentrated on fighting her growing lassitude.

The mare became agitated. Faint tremors rippled along her flanks, and she tossed her head in annoyance. Finally, in an effort to calm the horse and keep herself moving, Gabria began to talk aloud.

"I'm sorry, beautiful one, to be taking so long. I will have you out before your time, I promise. I just wasn't prepared for something like this." She laughed bitterly and flung a handful of mud behind her.

"Do you know how much is left when an encampment is burned? Very, very little. A few bits of charred rope, some blackened metal, and heaps and heaps of ashes. Many bodies, too . . . stabbed and slashed, or shot with arrows, or crushed by horses' hooves, or burned. But dead. All dead. Even the children. The horses and livestock are gone. There is nothing. Only death and emptiness and stench."

The Hunnuli quieted and was watching Gabria with an uncanny look of understanding and sympathy, but the girl was bent over her task and did not see the horse's eyes.

"It has never happened before, you know. Oh, we fight often. There is nothing a clansman likes more than a good fight. But not like this. Nothing like this. It was a massacre!" She fiercely wiped her eyes.

"I found my brothers together," Gabria continued dully. "They fought back to back and their enemies' blood flowed. I saw it. The murderers took their dead with them, but they left a great deal of blood behind. My brothers must have been too much for them, though. In the end, the cowards ran my brothers through with lances instead of fighting them like men. Father died before his hall and his hearthguard, his chosen warriors, defended him to the last man. There is no one else left."

For a time, Gabria was silent, and the ghosts of her dead clan haunted her memories. Even the pain of her body could not mask the aching loneliness that terrified her soul.

"I'm the only one," she snapped. "I was not there when they needed me. I ran off like a spoiled child because my father said I was to be married. When I came back to apologize for my heated words, he was dead. I am justly punished." She paused for a moment, then continued.

"I must earn the right to be a clansman now. I am neither man nor woman: I am an exile!" Gabria slammed a handful of gravel into the mud. "That is what is so ironic, Hunnuli. It was a band of exiles, renegades, that ambushed my clan. Exiles sent by that foul dung, Lord Medb.

"Oh, but he will pay the weir-geld for this, Hunnuli. He thinks no one is alive who knows. But I know, and I know, too, that Lord Medb will die. I, Gabria of Clan Corin, am going to take my weir-geld in his blood. He does not realize that I am still alive, but he will know soon.

May his heart tremble at the thought of his treachery being shouted to the clans and the world."

Without warning, dizziness shook Gabria's head and she fell against the mare. The girl lay panting on the horse's warm back while her whole body trembled with rage and fatigue. "I must hold on." Her voice rasped in her throat.

The Hunnuli remained still, letting the girl rest until her muscles slowly relaxed and her violent trembling eased. At last, Gabria sat back on her heels. Her face held no expression except for the rigid line to her jaw, the only mark of her hard won control.

It was getting dark and another light snow was falling. Despite her own weariness, Gabria noticed the mare was getting more uncomfortable. Her worry increased, for if the mare went into labor now, she would not be able to pull herself out of the mud. It was time to get the Hunnuli out.

Her legs sore from kneeling, Gabria painfully worked her way off the log platform to the bank. The mare neighed irritably. Her eyes rolled in distress.

"Yes, I think I'm finished," Gabria said. "But I do wish I had some rope." She quickly threw more gravel on the ramp to give the mare added traction.

Much of the mud had been cleared away in a crude circle around the horse, but the heavy mire still clung tenaciously to her hind legs and a great mass lay under her belly. Gabria hoped with the log ramp beneath the Hunnuli's hooves, the horse could utilize her massive strength to pull herself out. There was nothing more Gabria could do.

"It's up to you now," she said to the horse.

The Hunnuli understood. She stilled and closed her eyes. Her muscles began to bulge as if she were concentrating all of her power into one gigantic upheaval. Her neck bowed and trembled in her effort. Her nostrils flared as her breath steamed like the vent of a volcano. Then, without warning, the mare lunged forward, her entire being straining against the confining mud. Her muscles bunched in cords of black along her neck and rump. Her sinews stretched until Gabria thought they would surely snap. Her huge hooves planted on the log ramp, the mare heaved upward, fighting for every inch of freedom.

Gabria sank to her knees, enthralled by the horse's struggle. She felt helpless just watching, but she knew she would only be in the way if she tried to help. There was no place for her puny efforts beside the colossal exertion of the black horse.

Slowly, the mud began to relinquish its hold. The mare's front legs jumped a step forward, driving the logs deeper into the earth. She pulled her back legs inch by inch toward the bank. Her stomach cleared the mire, clumps of mud clinging to her underbelly and to the distended milk bag. With one final effort, the mare threw herself upward. One hind leg lifted out and touched the ramp, then the other. She heaved out of the mudhole with a neigh of triumph that echoed through the gully. Gabria scrambled to her feet, crying with relief. They had done it! She threw her digging rock as far as she could and shouted again when she heard it hit the ground.

Immediately she went still. The Hunnuli was standing in front of her, her black form towering above Gabria's head and her neck arched proudly. Before Gabria knew what was happening, the horse reared. Despite her sluggish body and aching legs, the mare threw her head back and rose up on her hind legs in the Hunnuli's ancient obeisance of respect and honor. Then the mare leaped away and cantered out of the gully. Her hoofbeats faded in the darkness.

Gabria's head began to whirl. A Hunnuli had reared to her—a mere girl, an exile. No one could claim mastery over a Hunnuli; what they gave was freely given. That one would pay her such an honor was more than she could believe.

She stared numbly at the mire where the mud was slowly falling back in place. Her eyes dimmed and the hills swayed around her. Her muscles seemed to freeze, and, before she could stop herself, Gabria collapsed to the ground and emptiness closed her mind.

2

Help me! a voice cried in her dreams. *Help me, Gabria.*

She turned away from the insistent voice, wishing it would go away. The voice was strange, almost inhuman, and some sense told her it was female, but she did not care. Gabria just wanted to be left alone. She was so cold, she did not want to know who it was. Something warm nudged her cheek. She feebly pushed it away and wondered vaguely why her arm was so unwieldy. Not that it mattered; it was too much effort to find out. Sleep was more comfortable.

The thing shoved at her again with more force.

"Leave me alone," she mumbled.

Suddenly, something heavy slammed down beside her head. The girl flinched and slowly pried her eyes open. The moon had long set, and the sky was overcast. The darkness was almost total. It was impossible to see more than a few feet beyond her outstretched hand. Groggy and chilled, Gabria rolled over and tried to sit up. It was then that she saw a gigantic black shadow looming over her. Fear shocked through her. She screamed, threw her arms up, and jerked away from the terrifying apparition.

Help me, the voice came again, pleading in her mind. Gabria crouched, staring about wildly. She had not heard a sound other than her own pounding heart. Where had that voice come from? The black shape had not moved, but stood, looking at her, its eyes glimmering with a pale, spectral light. It nickered softly, urgently.

Gabria's breath expelled in a loud gasp of relief. "Hunnuli?" she asked.

She stood up, shivering uncontrollably, and stared at the horse in surprise. Something was terribly wrong. Gabria's fear for herself evaporated. She fumbled to the horse's side and was horrified to find the animal trembling violently and sweating despite the cold wind.

Gabria groped her way to her small camp and renewed her fire into a roaring blaze. The flames illuminated the Hunnuli and, in the unsteady firelight, Gabria saw her worst fears were confirmed. The mare was deep into labor; from the droop of her proud head and the tremors that rippled her mud-spattered coat, she had been for some time. Her hide was drenched in sweat and her ears wavered back in anxiety.

Slowly, so as not to startle her, Gabria stroked the horse's neck and carefully moved along her side to her tail. She had never delivered a foal alone, but she had helped her father with stricken mares and knew well enough what to look for. The horse stood immobile, panting hoarsely as Gabria examined her.

"Poor Hunnuli," said the girl. "What a time you've had. Your foal is so big. He may even be twisted inside." She prayed fervently it was not a breech birth. The mare's waters had broken some time before and her birth canal was painfully dry. If the foal was twisted inside, Gabria knew she did not have the strength to push the foal back against the natural contractions of the mare, straighten it, and pull it out again. She could only hope there was something else that was preventing an easy birth. She did not even know if the foal was alive, but something had to be done quickly if she was going to save it or the mare.

Rapidly, Gabria scraped some snow into her small water bag and set it near the fire. She sorted through her few possessions and picked out a pot of salve and her extra tunic. Then, working with all haste, she tore strips from the tunic and tied them with tiny knots into a soft rope with a noose fashioned at one end. As soon as the snow melted in the skin bag, she used the water to wash her hands and one arm clean. She took a liberal dab of creamy salve and rubbed it over her forearm and hand.

The girl picked up her rope, careful to keep it clean, and moved to the mare's side. What she had to do next was going to be uncomfortable for the mare and herself, so she hoped the horse was too exhausted to complain. Using the utmost care, she eased her hand, holding the noose, into the mare's birth canal. The horse tossed her head, but she offered no resistance.

Gabria soon found the foal's front legs. She inched the noose around the tiny hooves and pulled it tight, then she pushed her arm deeper past the foal's knees, struggling against the mare's contractions, which squeezed her hand with crushing force. When she found the foal's head, she sighed with relief, for the baby was not breech. Only its head was twisted, jamming it tightly against the pelvic bone.

Gabria's relief was pushed away by a feeling of dread. As she edged her fingers down the foal's cheek, her heart sank. The body was very unyielding and had none of the wiggling, warm movements of a live foal. In despair, she straightened the head and withdrew her arm. The mare, as if sensing her release, lay down while Gabria took the rope. With each contraction the girl pulled steadily, softly talking to soothe the mare and hide her own fear.

At last the foal was born. It lay on the cold ground, its birthing sac wrapped around it, its eyes glazed in death. Gabria removed the sac and the afterbirth, and cleaned the foal's nostrils, although she knew her efforts were futile. The tiny horse had suffocated during the prolonged labor.

The girl sat down abruptly and stared at the dead foal. It was not fair, her heart cried. Why was she always too late? The baby was a stud colt of perfect proportions, with a streak of white on its black shoulder. Gabria's eyes filled with tears. If only she had not failed again, the colt would now be discovering its new life.

The mare lay motionless, half-dead with exhaustion. She made no move to examine her baby, as if she knew it was already beyond her help. Her eyes settled shut and her ragged breathing eased. Gabria sat with her arms on her knees and her head sunk in grief.

The fire slowly died to embers and its light was replaced by the glow of the rising sun. Night's gloom faded. A bird piped from a nearby clump of gorse. The clouds withdrew from the mountains, leaving the peaks in a dazzling coverlet of snow. On the steppes, the air was clean and brilliant.

It was the sun that finally roused Gabria. Its warmth seeped into her chilled limbs and nestled on the back of her neck until she raised her head. She took a deep breath of the passing breeze and stretched out the stiffness in her aching muscles.

The sun felt delicious. It was so good to just sit in its warmth. But the heat on her back reminded Gabria of a possible danger. The mountain snows would begin to melt soon in this heat and the water would fill every available stream and wash. The last thaw that had formed the mudhole in the gully had only touched the foothills. Should the mountain run-off come down the eroded valleys, the gully she and the mare were in could be flooded. The water would take a little time to gather, but she did not want to dawdle. She had spent too much time here as it was. Her food supply and her strength were dwindling rapidly.

Gabria picked up a pebble and flicked it away. Was it really worth the effort to leave? She was so tired. She knew that on foot it would take her perhaps fifteen days to reach Khulinin Treld and then only if she were in good condition. She shook her head. It was impossible. She had never walked that far in her life. Her feet were already blistered and her boots were worn just from the two-day journey from Corin Treld. Her ankle, which was still swollen and weak, would never heal under the strain of constant walking. Her muscles were already strained, her hands were badly lacerated, and her stomach was empty. She would trade almost anything for a warm bed and a hot breakfast.

Then Gabria sighed and stood up. It did not really matter how many problems she could list. She knew in her heart she was not going to give up. She was the last Corin and she would never give Lord Medb the satisfaction of her death in a muddy gully.

Gabria gazed at the dead foal and planned her next move. The colt would have to be buried, she decided. She could not bear the thought of its small body torn by wolves and kites. The mare appeared to be sleeping, so Gabria lifted the colt and carried it to the hilltop. It was surprisingly light, even for a newborn foal, but its body was unwieldy and the hill was slippery with thawed mud. Gabria was limping badly by the time she reached the crest.

Sadly, she placed her burden at the foot of an outcropping of stone and there she built a cairn over the body. As she worked, she sang the death song she had sung when the flames devoured her brothers' bodies. When she was finished, she sat back and gave in to the desolation in her heart.

"Oh, Mother," she cried, "giver of all life, I am tired of this. Is this what I have come to? Burying everything that means something to me?"

Do not mourn for my son, a voice said.

Gabria jumped, startled out of her misery. It was the same voice she remembered from her dreams, a voice she could not hear. She gripped her arms, afraid to speak. The words had been spoken in her mind, and she knew of no mortal, except for the ancient sorcerers, who had telepathic ability.

The voice came again. *My son is dead, but perhaps he will return to me after another mating.*

"Who are you?" Gabria demanded, terrified by the invasion of her mind.

My true name is unpronounceable to your tongue. You may call me Nara.

In a flash of understanding, Gabria realized who was speaking to her. Dumbfounded, she closed her eyes and turned around. When she opened them, she saw the Hunnuli standing a few feet away.

"It *is* you!" she breathed.

Of course. The mare was filthy with muck and dried blood, her mane and tail were matted, yet her proud spirit had revived; her eyes glowed with a depth of wisdom that stunned Gabria. *We do not often communicate with humans. Only a chosen few.*

Gabria leaned against the outcropping for support. Her knees felt like melting wax. "Why?"

It is too difficult. Human minds are too confusing to us. With some, though, it is worthwhile.

Gabria gestured weakly at herself. "No. Why me?"

I owe you a life. The voice became softer. *And you need my help.*

"Can you read my thoughts?"

No. I can only give you mine.

"If you could, you would know that I am unworthy of your help or even your offer. I am in exile."

The mare ducked her head and looked at the girl sideways with her full black eye. *I know what you are and what has happened. I understand much about you that you cannot see yet.* The mare snorted. *I am Nara. I am Hunnuli, daughter of the Storm Father. I choose whom I will.*

"I am not worthy of you."

You are stubborn. Forget worthy. You are my friend.

Gabria glanced away. Her green eyes brimmed with tears. "I could not save your foal."

My son was dead before I came to you. In my pride, I wished to bear my first-born alone, but I was too weak.

"I'm sorry," the girl said, feeling the inadequacy of the words.

There will be others. For now, I will go with you.

Gabria wanted to argue further. She was mortified that a Hunnuli, a creature of the legends she had grown up with, had offered her friendship. How could she accept it? She was an outcast with no clan to support her, no family to defend her, and no future. Her life was like a clay pot that someone had thrown carelessly away, so there was nothing left of the familiar, comforting shape but fragments and shards, and the memory of what it had been. What did she have to offer one such as the Hunnuli? Only fear, uncertainty, suspicion, and death.

No. No matter how she might wish for such a fantastic thing, she could not consent to Nara's offer.

Gabria's stomach felt leaden, and she shivered with a chill that was not caused by the wind. "Nara, I do not think there is anything left in me that can return your friendship. I am so empty."

If that were true, I would not have come back.

"I am seeking only revenge. After that . . ." Her voice failed. Gabria could not think beyond that goal. Although she did not care to admit it, she was terrified. Many had tried to kill Lord Medb, both in battle and duel, but he was a skilled and ferocious warrior. It was also said he was protected by forbidden magic. If that were true, and battle-skilled men failed against him, how could she succeed? Her pride and grief would never free her from her duty, but she had no illusions about the future.

Nara dipped her nose until it was a hairsbreadth from Gabria's face. The mare inhaled deeply as a horse will do to acquaint itself with another creature. Gabria could smell the mare's warm, comforting scent that was a mixture of grass, sun, and the distinctive sweetness that was purely horse. The familiarity of the scent comforted her wounded spirit. Her objections faded to insignificance.

When Nara told her, *Let the days come as they will. I am going with you*, Gabria merely nodded, unable to speak.

In a daze, the girl limped down the hillside to her camp. She ate a quick meal and returned her belongings to her pack. Her torn tunic was useless and she threw it away. Her remaining tunic was as filthy as she was, and she thought how nice it would be for a bath. It might be the last one she would have in peace for a long time to come.

"Is there a stream or pool nearby?" she asked the mare, who was waiting patiently for her.

Yes. But farther from here are hot springs.

"Hot water?" Gabria breathed, unable to believe her luck. "What direction is it?"

Beneath the horned peak.

Gabria looked toward the line of peaks and smiled with relief. That had to be Wolfeared Pass, a strangely formed mountain with twin summits that stood to the south of the gully. She picked up her pack and her staff and threw her cloak over her shoulders.

"Lead on, Nara," she said, pointing with her staff.

The mare glanced at her with a glint of amusement in her brilliant eyes. *Do you not think it would be faster to ride me?*

Gabria's jaw dropped. "You would let me ride?" Her voice rose higher with each word.

You can ride, can you not?

"Of course, I just—"

I am not going to plod all day, waiting for you to keep pace. Besides—Her telepathic thought turned wistful—*I would like warm water, too.*

Gabria was stunned. She had never imagined this! "But Nara, women may not ride a Hunnuli."

The mare whickered in a way that surprised Gabria. It sounded much like laughter. *Could that be a tale spread by men who fear the ambitions of their women?*

The girl laughed and a great load of worry fell from her shoulders. She threw her walking staff away and climbed up a large rock. From that added height, she clambered onto Nara's broad back. Gabria was astonished by the heat of the Hunnuli's body; it was the vibrant, glowing warmth of a fire barely dampened. She reached out to touch the horse's ebony, arched neck and marveled at the power and intensity that flowed beneath the slick hide. It was as though the lightning bolt emblazoned on Nara's shoulder hid in reality within the horse's form.

Nara trotted out of the gully, and, once onto the treeless hills, she moved into an easy, mile-eating canter.

Gabria held onto a fistful of mane, not for support, but merely for something to do with her hands. She did not need to find her balance or even use her legs, as the mare moved with a surprising fluidity and grace for a horse so large. She felt herself mold into the movement of the horse as if they had been fused together by the heat of Nara's being. The girl settled back, letting the wind brush through her hair and the sunlight flow over her face. She began to relax in the delight of the ride.

They swept over the land as one, like the shadows of clouds pushed by the wind, until the gully in the Hornguard became a memory and the southern peaks of Darkhorn reared like sentinels in their path. Perhaps, Gabria thought for a fleeting moment, there was a little hope.

They made camp that night in a small valley of thermal pools and mineral springs. To Gabria, it was an eerie place of shifting vapors, strange smells, and pools that bubbled with odd colors and noises. But Nara, unperturbed by the strange landscape, found a water hole formed by the run-off of an erupting mineral spring. There they bathed and soaked away the aches of the past days. Before long, Gabria had forgotten her dislike of the valley in the bliss of the relaxing water.

They stayed in the valley for several days while their bodies mended. Gabria used her salve to dress Nara's neck wound from the wolf attack, as well as the other cuts and scrapes they both had. Nara, in return, gave the girl the rich, nourishing milk that had been meant for the foal. Gabria had heard stories of the effects of Hunnuli milk on humans, but her stomach had a stronger voice than the vague hints from old legends, so she drank the milk gratefully and attributed her fast recovery to the reviving waters of the spring.

When two days had passed, Nara sensed the coming of another spring storm. Reluctantly, Gabria packed her gear and mounted the mare for the final journey south. The Hunnuli and her rider cantered for three days through the foothills hugging the Darkhorn's towering ramparts. The country slowly changed as the air became warmer and more arid. The trees retreated up the mountain flanks, giving way to tougher shrubs and grasses. The hills, worn by wind and erosion, lost their sharp outlines until, to Gabria's eye, they looked like a soft, rumpled carpet. The Himachal Mountains on her left fell behind, and the eastern horizon flowed away on the endless rim of the steppes.

Sooner than Gabria imagined, the mountains began to veer west. She could hardly believe they had come so far in such a brief time. Visitors from Khulinin Treld to Corin Treld usually needed seven days on horseback, yet Nara had covered most of that distance in three.

On the evening of the third day, they came to Marakor, the Wind Watcher, the isolated, cone-shaped peak that guarded the northern entrance into the valley of the Goldrine River.

Behind Marakor, the mountains strode westward, then swung around in a great arch to return to their southward trek into the desert wastelands. There, in the crescent valley where the Goldrine River spilled from its deep gorge, the Khulinin clan had its wintering camp. For generations, the Khulinin clan had roamed the steppes in the summer, pasturing their herds on the richest fields, and every winter they returned to the sanctuary of the valley. In the shelter of Marakor and Krindir, the twin peak to the south, they lived and danced and celebrated the Foaling as their fathers had done for countless years.

From where Gabria and Nara stood—on a crest just below Marakor—they could see black tents spread out like huge butterflies and the encampment's few permanent buildings. Gabria was stunned by the size of the treld. She had never seen all the Khulinin together in one place and, in spite of the dim tales she remembered her mother telling her, she was not prepared for the camp's sprawling size. Her clan had been small; they barely numbered a hundred. But this! There had to be many hundreds of people in the valley below.

She tore her fascinated gaze away from the encampment and looked at the pastures where the animals grazed. The number of horses and livestock was an indication of a clan's wealth, and Gabria could tell from the size of the herds that grazed along the river that the Khulinin were rich indeed.

As she made camp that night in a copse of trees, Gabria tried to recall every detail she knew of Savaric, chieftain of the Khulinin. There were not many. Although he was chief of her mother's clan, Gabria had only seen him a few times at the summer clan gatherings and she had been too busy then to notice very much. What she did remember was an image of a dark-haired, bearded man who constantly carried a falcon on his arm.

She knew her father had liked and respected Savaric. The two men had been close friends in boyhood, but Gabria did not know how far their friendship had extended or whether it would have any influence on Savaric's decision to accept her.

She wished she could learn more about Savaric before venturing into his domain. How was he going to react to the sole survivor of a massacred clan dropping the horrors and problems of her continuing existence at his feet? If he did not see through her disguise, would he accept her into his werod? He had ample food and wealth to support many warriors, even one as poor and inadequate as herself, but in all likelihood, he had as many warriors as he needed. Besides, Savaric probably would not want to risk taking such a dangerous exile into his clan.

Still, Gabria thought as she ate her evening meal, the fact that my mother was of Clan Khulinin, coupled with my father's friendship, might sway Savaric's mind. And of course, there was the Hunnuli. So few men rode the magnificent horses, Savaric would think twice before denying Gabria's plea and ignoring the honor Nara would bring to his people.

On the other hand, if he discovered her true sex, the question of her acceptance would be meaningless. Clan law strictly forbade any female from becoming a warrior. The chieftain would have to have Gabria killed immediately for masquerading as a boy and trying to join his werod.

She could only hope he would not find out, for she had no other chance for acceptance—and no chance of gaining her revenge against Lord Medb without the Khulinin's help. She would have to trust to luck and the guidance of the goddess, Amara, when she rode into Savaric's camp tomorrow. Until then, she decided to ignore her anxiety. Curling up under her cloak, she tried to rest, but it was a long while before she drifted off to sleep.

Gabria was awakened at dawn by the echoing, sonorous summons of a horn. The eastern stars were dimmed by a pale light that gleamed on the sharp ridges of the mountains. The horn sounded again, swelling through the valley with an urgent appeal to the sun. Gabria scrambled to her feet and walked to the rim of the hill.

Far below her, at the entrance to Khulinin Treld, an outrider of the dawn watch sat on a light-colored horse and lifted his horn to his lips for the third time. Darkness faded and the colors of day intensified. A red-gold sliver of fire pierced the dark horizon and painted the earth with its glow. The meager light of the stars was banished.

They do well to welcome the sun.

Gabria glanced at the mare standing beside her. "I went out on the dawn watch once with my twin brother, Gabran," she said slowly. "Father did not know or he would have whipped me for going with the outriders. But I begged and pleaded and Gabran finally let me come. We stood on the hill above the treld, and he blew such a blast of eagerness and joy, his horn burst. To me he looked like an image of our hero, Valorian, the Lord Chieftain, calling his people to war."

I know of Valorian. He taught the Hunnuli to speak.

Gabria nodded absently, her gaze lost in the memories of other mornings. In the valley, the outrider returned to the herds and the treld came alive with activity. The girl continued to stare where the rider had been, her face grim and her jaw clenched. A tear crept unheeded down her cheek.

Nara nudged Gabria's shoulder gently and broke her reverie. Gabria sniffed, then laughed. She wiped her cheeks with her sleeve and laid her fingers on the healing slash on the mare's neck.

"It is time to begin this game, Nara. You have brought me this far, but I do not expect you to go farther."

Nara snorted and dipped her head to give Gabria a sidelong look through her thick forelock. *This game began long ago. I would like to see how it is played.*

The girl laughed and, for a moment, she leaned gratefully against the mare's strong shoulder.

They returned to their camp, and Gabria added the final touch to her disguise. She had not washed her clothes, so they were still filthy with mud, sweat, and dried blood. She wrinkled her nose as she slipped on the black tunic. It smelled horrible and three days had not inured her nose to the stink. She rubbed dirt onto her face and hands and into her hair. If all went well, no one would look past the filth to realize she was not a boy. Later, she would have to devise another trick to hide her face until the clansmen became used to her. She did not want to remain filthy forever.

She fastened her short sword to the leather belt around her waist. Her father's dagger, with its silver hilt encrusted with garnets, was thrust into her boot. She picked up her pack, threw her cloak over her shoulder, and took a deep breath.

Nara sprang to the top of the ridge and neighed a bold, resounding call of greeting. The Hunnuli's call pealed through the pastures of Khulinin Treld and echoed from the far hills. Every horse below raised its head, and Nara's cry was greeted by the clarion neigh of a stallion.

The game had begun.

3

The stranger rode into the treld at morning, just as the horns were recalling the dawn watch. He was flanked by two outriders, who kept a wary and respectful distance from the Hunnuli mare which dwarfed the Harachan stallions they rode. The people froze, appalled, as he passed by, and they stared at his back in utter dismay. The news spread quickly through the tents. Men and women, whispering in fearful speculation, gathered behind the three riders and followed them up the main road through the encampment.

The stranger appeared to be a boy of fourteen or fifteen years with a lithe figure and features obscured by a mask of dirt. His light gold hair was chopped shorter than normal for a boy his age and was just as filthy as his face. He sat on the Hunnuli easily, his body relaxed, but his face was tense and he stared fixedly ahead, ignoring the crowd behind him. On his shoulders, like a blazon of fire and death, was a scarlet cloak.

The cloak was nothing unusual. Every clansman of the steppes wore one, but only one small clan, the Corin, wore cloaks of blood red. According to recent messengers, that clan had been completely massacred only twelve days before. Some said by sorcery.

Who was this strange boy who wore the cloak of a murdered clan? And to ride a Hunnuli! Not even in the tales told by the bards had anyone known of a boy taming a wild Hunnuli, especially one as magnificent as this mare. She shone like black lacquer overlaid on silver and walked with the tense, wary pride of a war horse. She wore no trappings and would tolerate none. The observers could not help but marvel how a boy, not even a warrior yet, had won the friendship of one such as she. That tale alone would be worth the listening.

By the time the three riders reached the circular gathering place before the werod hall, most of the clan had gathered and were waiting. The boy and his escort dismounted. No words were spoken and the silence was heavy. Then five men, their swords drawn and their golden cloaks rippling down their backs, appeared in the arched doorway of the hall and gestured to the boy. They took his sword and pack and, with a curt command, ordered him to attend the chieftain. The outriders followed.

The Hunnuli moved to stand by herself and snorted menacingly at the clanspeople. They understood well to leave her strictly alone. They settled into noisy, talking groups and waited patiently for the meeting's outcome.

Unlike many of the clans' wintering camps, Khulinin Treld had been established centuries ago. Generations of Khulinin had returned to the natural protection of the valley until it became instilled in the clan as the symbol of home. For the seminomadic people, the valley was their place of permanence and stability—a settlement they could return to year after year. Because of their pride in the ancient traditions of the treld, the Khulinin had built a permanent hall for clan gatherings, a building that would survive until the last hoofbeats dwindled from the valley.

The hall delved into the flank of a towering hill near the falls of the Goldrine River. From the massive arched entrance, the sentinels who stood on either side could look out over the open commons to the encampment that spread like a motionless landslide down to the valley floor. The Khulinin banners of gold swayed in the breeze above the door.

Inside, the main room of the hall ran deep into the hill. Wooden columns, hauled from the mountains, marched in two files down the long chamber. Torches burned from brackets on every column and golden lamps hung from the vaulted ceiling beams. A fire burned in a large stone pit in the center of the hall. Its flames danced in a vain attempt to follow the smoke through the ventilation shafts. Trestle tables, a rarity in an encampment, were piled against a wall in readiness for feasts and celebrations, and several tapped casks of wine and mead stood beside them. Tapestries and weapons taken in battle hung on the whitewashed walls.

At the far end of the hall, the chieftain sat on a dais of dark stone. He watched thoughtfully, his dark eyes veiled behind half-drawn lids, as the stranger was brought before him. Behind him, in a semicircle, stood his personal retainers, the warriors of the hearthguard.

The men shifted uneasily as the boy walked toward them. Savaric could feel their angered tenseness. It was little wonder they were ill at ease, for they all had been disturbed by the rumors of sorcery and the horrors of the massacre at Corin Treld. Such a thing had never happened to the clans before. The reverberations of this hideous deed might never end, and the gods alone knew what aftershocks this boy was bringing.

Savaric masked his own concerns for the sake of the boy, but he knew the others were openly wary. Even Savaric's son, Athlone, who stood at the chief's right hand, was watching the boy with unconcealed suspicion.

Four paces before the warrior-lord, the boy knelt and extended his left hand in a salute. "Hail, Lord Savaric. I bring you greetings from my dead father." His voice was low and forced.

Savaric frowned slightly and leaned forward. "Who is your father, boy? Who greets me from the grave?"

"Dathlar, my lord, chieftain of the ghost clan of Corin."

"We have heard of the tragedy that befell that clan. But who are you and how is it you have survived if you are indeed Dathlar's son?"

Gabria felt a spasm of pain. She had expected the question of her survival to be raised, but she still could not answer without guilt. She hung her head to hide her face, which burned with her inner shame.

"Are you ill?" Savaric asked sharply.

"No, Lord," Gabria replied, keeping her eyes downcast. "My eyes are not used to the shade of this hall." That part at least was true. After the bright morning sun, the gloom of the hall made it difficult for her to see. "It is my greatest shame that I am alive. I am Gabran, youngest son of Dathlar. I was in the hills hunting eagles when I became lost in the fog."

"Fog?" Athlone broke in sardonically. Murmurs of astonishment and skepticism from the watching warriors echoed his disbelief.

Gabria glared at Athlone, seeing him clearly for the first time. He was different from the men around him, for he was taller, of heavier build, and fairer in skin. His brown hair was chopped short, and a thick mustache softened the hard lines of his mouth. There was a natural assumption of authority in Athlone's manner, and an unquestionable capability. Since he wore the belt of a wer-tain, a commander of the warriors, he could pose more of a threat to her than Savaric. Savaric was chieftain, but as wer-tain, Athlone was captain of the werod. If Gabria were accepted, she would be under his direct command. That thought unnerved her, for he came across as a man of power rather than charm, resolution rather than patience. He could be a formidable opponent.

Still, the way Athlone looked at Gabria irritated her. The man's brown eyes were narrowed in distrust, looking as cold as frozen earth. His hand was clenched on his belt, a hairsbreadth away from the hilt of a short sword.

"Yes, fog!" She snapped the word at Athlone, daring him to doubt the truth of it again. "You know we do not have fog in the afternoon of a cool spring day. But it came! Because of it, the outriders brought in the herds, and the women and children stayed in the tents." Except me, she thought bitterly. She had become lost in the fog on her way home and would never forget its dank smell.

"That fog was cold and thick, and when the attack came from every direction, there was no warning. They slaughtered everyone and combed the woods to ensure no one escaped. When they finished, they drove off the horses, scattered the livestock, and burned the tents." Gabria turned back to Savaric, her head tilted angrily. "It was well planned, Lord. It was an intentional massacre, done by men with no desire to plunder or steal. I know who is responsible. I am going to claim weir-geld."

"I see." Savaric sat back in his seat and drummed his fingers slowly on his knee. The chieftain was as handsome as Gabria remembered, of medium height with a dark, neatly trimmed beard and eyes as black and glitteringly dangerous as a hawk's. His face was weathered by years of sun and harsh wind and bore the marks of numerous battles. His right hand was missing the little finger.

He sat now, studying Gabria, waiting for a weakness or a slip of the tongue. He recognized a family resemblance in the boy, but oddly Gabran reminded him more of the mother, Samara, than his friend, Dathlar. Savaric was inclined to believe the boy's story, as incredible as it was. The chief's instincts told him that the boy was not treacherous and his instincts were always right. Still, he had to satisfy his warriors before he considered taking the boy into the clan.

"You have the red cloak of your clan, Gabran, and your story fits what little we know of the ambush. But I have no obvious proof that you are who you say you are."

Gabria bit back an angry retort. It was only to be expected that they would not accept her tale immediately. Rumors of war had been growing since last autumn, and, after the annihilation of an entire clan, every chieftain of the plains would be cautious.

She removed her cloak and swept it onto the floor before her. Its brilliant color drew every eye and held them like a spell. "My father was Dathlar of Clan Corin. He married Samara, a Khulinin, twenty-five years ago. They had four sons and one daughter." She spoke slowly as if repeating her history by rote.

"My mother was beautiful, as fair as you are dark. She could play the lyre and the pipes, and she wore a gold brooch of buttercups. She died ten years ago. My father was your friend. He told me of you many times. In token of that friendship, you gave him this." She pulled the silver dagger out of her boot and threw it on the cloak. It lay on the scarlet fabric, a silent messenger, its red gems glowing in the light like drops of blood.

Savaric stood up and reached out to pick up the dagger. "My guards are growing careless," he said quietly. He stared at the shining blade and turned it over in his hands. "If you are truly the son of Dathlar and he was slain in treachery, then I must also seek weir-geld for my blood brother."

Gabria was stunned. Blood brother! She had not expected this. If Savaric believed her and the garbled news he had received about the massacre, he was bound by his oath of friendship to Dathlar to settle the debt owed to Dathlar's family—what was left of it. Blood friendship was as binding as a blood relationship and carried the same responsibilities. The fact that Gabria was an exile was now irrelevant to Savaric. She had only to convince him that she was telling the truth and, most difficult of all, that she really did know who was responsible for the killing. Then he would do everything possible to help her.

"Lord Savaric," she said. "By the Hunnuli that bears me and the gods that nourish us, I am the child of Dathlar and I *know* who had my clan murdered." She spoke forcefully, her eyes matching Savaric's black gaze.

Savaric sat down again, still holding the dagger, examining it as if it bore a vestige of the man who had once carried it. "If nothing else, the Hunnuli is the strongest plea in your favor. She alone vouches for your character."

Athlone stepped to his father's side. "Hunnuli or no, there was sorcery at Corin Treld. We cannot accept this boy's word so easily." He leaned over and grasped the cloak. "Anyone with a little ingenuity could obtain a scarlet cloak and an interesting tale."

Gabria snatched the cloak out of his hands and held it tightly to her breast. Fury blazed in her eyes. "Yes, sorcery formed the fog at Corin Treld, sorcery spun by the hand of Lord Medb. Not I!"

It was the first time Lord Medb had been mentioned, and the

significance of his name was not lost on the watching warriors. They muttered uneasily among themselves and no one looked surprised at her accusation. Athlone was not surprised either, and he made no attempt to hide his suspicions of Lord Medb's rumored heresies.

"Perhaps not. But you could be a servant sent by Medb to spy on us. Certainly you could not have survived the massacre or obtained a Hunnuli mare without help," Athlone replied with deliberate derision.

"Certainly not," Gabria retorted. "Since you are convinced it cannot be done."

"I know it is not possible for a mere boy to earn a Hunnuli's respect. I ride a Hunnuli stallion and taming him was no task for a child."

"I can see why it was so difficult for you," Gabria noted with heavy sarcasm. "The Hunnuli are good judges of character."

Several of the guardsmen laughed. Savaric crossed his arms, watching the exchange with interest. The boy had pride and courage to stand up to a wer-tain. He certainly learned that from his father.

Athlone shrugged. "Then you accomplished it the simple way, with sorcery or coercion, knowing a Hunnuli could help you worm your way into our clan. How can we not think you are an impostor?"

"Why do you think that?" Savaric interrupted conversationally.

"Impostor!" Gabria nearly shrieked, cutting him off. She cringed at the high note her voice had hit and quickly lowered it again, hoping no one had noticed its feminine tone. She knew Athlone was deliberately baiting her, but she had had enough of him and his arrogant accusations. He did not realize how close he was to the truth. "You faceless, dirt-eating, dung shoveler . . ."

She continued on at length, richly describing Athlone's habits and character with every appellation she had heard her brothers use, until the men around her began to choke with ill-concealed laughter. Even Savaric was taken aback. Athlone's face began to turn red and his mouth hardened to a granite slash. Finally, before his son's temper exploded, Savaric cut Gabria off with a curt word.

"Now," he said to Athlone in the sudden silence. "I would like to know why you think this boy could be an impostor."

Athlone stood by the dais, his body rigid. There was something wrong about this boy—he could sense it. But he could not recognize what it was. Incredible as the boy's story sounded, it was plausible. Athlone knew full well that the Hunnuli could not be won by coercion or treachery. Yet a niggling little warning disturbed him. The boy was not telling the truth about something.

He stared hard at Gabria, at a loss to explain his suspicion.
"Medb would like to have an informer in our camp. Why not a boy
with a story of kinship to Dathlar?" He curled his lip. "Or maybe he is
just a miserable exile using a stolen cloak to gain acceptance."

"I *am* an exile," Gabria cried. "Medb made me one. Because of
him my clan no longer exists." A bitter sadness seeped into her heart,
stifling her outrage. "I came to ask for a place in the Khulinin, to seek
aid against Lord Medb, for he is too powerful for me alone. There was
no magic in my coming to you, or treachery. Only blood ties. There
was only pain and hard work in winning the Hunnuli." She held out
her hands, palms up, and the men saw the raw cuts for the first time.

The cold left Athlone's eyes and his anger receded under the pain
he saw in Gabria's face. He glanced at his father and briefly nodded.

Savaric stood up and the hearthguard moved to his side. "I would
gladly accept you into this clan and do everything I can to help you
attain your rightful blood debt. To my eyes, you are Dathlar's son, and
to my heart, you are honest and very courageous. However, it is the
clan that must sustain you. In this case, I will let them speak. Come."

He walked to the entrance, followed by Athlone, Gabria, and the
others. Nara, seeing the girl surrounded by the guardsmen, firmly
pushed between them and Gabria until the men drew off to a respectful distance. Gabria reached up and twined her fingers into the horse's
glossy black mane.

You are well? Nara asked.

Gabria nodded, her face turned to the watching clansmen. The
people were quiet as Savaric told them Gabria's tale and her reasons
for seeking the Khulinin. They listened intently. The men, in warm
woolen jackets, baggy pants, and boots, stood to the front of the
crowd. The women, dressed in long skirts and tunics of bright colors,
stood as a brilliant backdrop behind their men. Many faces were expressionless, despite the fear that pervaded the encampment.

When Savaric was finished speaking, several men detached themselves from the crowd and conversed together for a few minutes.
Gabria recognized them as the elders of the clan, Savaric's advisors.
One wore the emblem of the herd-master, the head stockman, and
one was a priest of Valorian. No one else from the throng offered a
word. The decision, it seemed, rested on the elders.

The herd-master finally approached Savaric and said reluctantly,
"Lord, we do not want to endanger our clan with the evil and taint of
sorcery this boy brings, but there are too many sides to this tale to
refuse him outright. He does ride a Hunnuli, and to turn the mare

away might bring the gods' displeasure. If you agree, we feel it would be just to allow him a time of trial. If he serves you well and follows the laws of the clan, then let him be accepted. If he does not, then he is truly exiled."

Savaric nodded in satisfaction. "Gabran, you may stay with the clan. You and the Hunnuli are welcome . . . for now." He smiled at her as the clanspeople slowly dispersed. "Athlone will be your mentor," he said, ignoring Gabria's horrified look. "When you have washed and had some food, I would like to continue this conversation about Medb and how you won your Hunnuli."

Gabria leaned against Nara and said weakly, "Yes, Lord."

The dazed young girl was too drained to even react when Nara said in her mind, *The first contest is yours.*

4

How can you be so certain it was Lord Medb who ordered the massacre?" Lord Savaric asked as he leaned back on his fur-draped seat. "You have not given us sufficient proof to believe your accusation."

Gabria slumped in frustration. "I have told you everything I can."

"It is not enough. You are bringing serious charges against a clan chieftain. How can you know what happened at the encampment? Or that it was an exile band that slaughtered the clan? You say you were not there."

"No, I was not there during the killing, but I know! I can read the signs of battle and I know what led up to the massacre," she cried.

Gabria was sitting before the dais, facing Savaric, Athlone, and the clan's elders, who were seated in a semicircle before her. They had been interrogating her for several hours, and she had told them repeatedly everything she could remember of that awful day at Corin Treld and the days following. Still they were not satisfied.

Behind her, the men of the werod had gathered to hear her story. They clustered in silent groups around the fire pit. Gabria was very self-conscious sitting before this large crowd of men. It seemed as if any second, one of them would see through her disguise. They were so quiet and watchful. If she turned her head slightly she could see them, their dark, muscular faces regarding her with a mixture of surprise, disbelief, and speculation. A flagon of wine was being passed around, but few of the warriors were enjoying it.

The girl wished they would finish this inquisition. It was night and getting quite late. During the day she had had a chance to eat, clean off a little of the dirt, and rest. But now she was getting tired. Gabria had refused to part with her cloak and sat with it bunched up on her lap.

"Can't you understand?" she asked sadly. "Lord Medb needed my father's cooperation. Our clan was small, but we were the first he had attempted to win to his favor. The other chieftains in the north respected Father. With his support, Medb would have had some control in the northwest."

Savaric nodded to himself. He had been following Medb's plots for some time, but even he was shocked by how far the chieftain seemed willing to go. "And your father refused these overtures of friendship?"

"Violently." She laughed bitterly, remembering her father's exact words. "Medb only made one offer. When that was rejected, he resorted to coercion and threats and finally an ultimatum."

Athlone was sitting on a leather stool near his father. His hand idly scratched the ears of a large deer hound as his eyes watched Gabria and the reactions of the men around him. "What sort of ultimatum?" he demanded.

Gabria spoke slowly, stressing each word. "Lord Medb made it clear that he wants to be overlord of the clans. To that end, he offered Father the lordship of all the northern lands. If Father refused, our clan would die."

The men burst out in a loud clamor of outrage. Whispers of Medb's bid for absolute power over all the clans had been blown from one encampment to another all winter, but the idea of a sole monarch was so far-fetched to the clansmen that few people had paid close attention.

"No!" The herd-master's voice cut through the noise. "I cannot believe this. No chieftain would have such audacity. How can he offer power that is not his to give?"

"The power is not his yet," Gabria interjected. "But he made good his threat to my father."

The master turned to Savaric, who was watching Gabria thoughtfully. "Lord, how can you listen to this. Lord Medb's clan is many days' ride from the Corin range. It would be senseless for him to look so far afield."

"Yet, you agree he is looking," Savaric replied.

The man shifted uneasily. "We have all heard the rumors of Medb's growing ambitions. But this is absurd."

Savaric stood up and paced in front of the dais. "Is it?" He posed the question to all the men. "Think about it. Medb needs allies to help him hold the vital regions of the grasslands. The Corin were a perfect choice. If Dathlar had agreed to his offer, Medb would have held a valuable hammer in the north, a hammer he could have used with his clan in the south to crush us in the middle. But," Savaric said as he gestured at Gabria, "when the Corin refused, Medb used them as an example to the other clans. He is proving he is deadly serious."

The warriors' voices quieted and even the herd-master looked pensive as the full impact of Savaric's words sank in. The chieftain stood by the stone seat, momentarily lost in his own thoughts.

Gabria closed her eyes and let her head droop. The chief seemed to understand after all, and if he did, that was all that mattered. She was too exhausted to worry about the others. Sleep was all she wanted now. The girl felt her body sag and her head seemed to grow heavier. She heard Athlone get to his feet and say something to his father.

Then someone dropped a cup on the floor, and the metal rang dully as it struck the hard-packed earth. The clang caught Gabria's attention like the distant clash of swords. She dragged open her eyes. Her glance fell into the fire burning in the center of the hearth. Everything was silent; she could feel the eyes of the men upon her, but she could not see them. She could only see the flames. The girl began to breathe faster and her heart raced.

In the back of her mind Gabria heard a faint thunder, like hoofbeats, that mingled with the crackle and roar of the fire. She tried to move as the sound grew louder, to escape the noise and the terror that came with it, but the thunder engulfed her and swept her into the light of the fire. The flames bounded high, burning away her self-awareness. The men, the hall, even the fire faded into obscurity while her consciousness fell helplessly through the lurid gloom and touched a dying link with Gabran, her twin brother. Born together, they had always shared a special bond, and now, like the touch of a dead hand, his presence coalesced out of the chaos and led her back to the paths of Corin Treld.

Her vision cleared and the familiar encampment lay before her, shrouded in a veil of thickening mist. "Fog," she mumbled. "Fog is coming in. Where did it come from?" Her voice changed and seemed to take on another personality.

Athlone tapped Savaric's arm and nodded at the girl. The chieftain suddenly frowned and stepped forward, motioning his men to keep silent.

Gabria swayed, her eyes pinned in the fire. "The herds are in. Everyone is here, but . . . wait. What is that noise? Taleon, get Father. I must find Gabria. There are horses coming. It sounds like a large troop." Her words came faster and her face drained like a pale corpse. The men about her watched in fascination.

"Oh, my gods, they are attacking us!" she shouted and stood up, gesturing wildly. "They are burning the tents. We must get to Father. Where is Gabria? Who are these men?"

Abruptly her voice went heavy with grief and rage. "No! Father is down. We must stand and fight. The women and children run, but it is too late. We are surrounded by horsemen. Fire everywhere. We cannot see in this smoke and fog.

"Oh, gods. I know that man with the scar. These men are exiles! Medb sent them. He swore to kill us and he has. The cowards, they are bringing lances. Oh, Gabria, be safe . . ."

The words rose to a cry of agony and instantly died into a silence of emptiness and despair. Gabria's link with her brother snapped and the vision was gone. She trembled violently, then crumpled to the floor. A sigh, like a suppressed breath, wavered through the listening men.

For a long moment, Savaric stood staring into the fire. Finally he said, "Take him to the healer. We have heard enough for tonight."

Without a word, Athlone and another man wrapped Gabria in the scarlet cloak and carried her from the hall.

The healer, a tall, wiry man in a pale rose robe, touched Gabria's forehead with a cool hand and glanced at Savaric. "Forgive me, Lord, but you pushed him too hard. The boy is exhausted."

"I know, Piers, but I had to find out what he would tell us."

"Couldn't it have waited?"

"Perhaps." Savaric gestured to the prostrate form, still wrapped in the red cloak, sleeping on a pallet. "The boy hid it well. He is strong. I did not realize how worn he was until it was too late."

The healer's mouth twisted into a smile. "An hour or two of questioning before the clan elders would tire a lion. You mentioned a vision?"

"Hmmm." Savaric poured wine into two horn cups and took a swallow from one before he answered. "He seemed to be reliving the massacre at his treld—through someone else's eyes. Is it possible he could have fabricated what he told us? Or did he truly see a vision of what happened at the encampment?"

Piers sat down on a low stool and picked up his wine cup. Savaric leaned against the center pole of the tent. "A terrible shock and exhaustion can do strange things," Piers said thoughtfully. "He may have been dreaming what he imagined happened, or . . ." The healer shrugged, his thin shoulders shifting slightly beneath his loose robe. "I do not know. Medb is a cruel man and his powers are strange. Maybe this tale was planted in the boy's mind to confuse us, or maybe he did have a vision. It's been known to happen before."

Savaric gave him a wry grin. "You are not much help." He looked at the healer curiously. "What makes you think Medb had anything to do with this?"

"Word spreads fast, Lord. Besides, only Medb has the capacity and the ambition to destroy an entire clan," Piers replied.

"You don't think it was a band of renegades or marauders?" asked Savaric.

"I doubt it. Raiders like that take women and plunder. This attack was total destruction. No, I think the boy was right, and if he is, then Medb is getting bolder."

Savaric nodded, the worry plain on his face. "And stronger. We have ignored Medb's ploys for power for too long, Piers. If we do not break him soon, he will become too strong for any of us."

Piers's mouth hardened. "You are talking war, you know. A war that could destroy the clans."

"Medb will destroy us if he becomes overlord. I would rather die a free chieftain than live as his underling."

Piers drained his cup and poured more of the light, fragrant wine he loved. He took a long swallow, then said, "They say Medb is reviving the black arts."

Savaric glanced at the sleeping form under the cloak, then back at Piers. "They say many things about him, but that fact I find hard to swallow. His clan would not tolerate their chief practicing magic. It would mean dishonor for all the Wylfling."

"Not if they were already under his thumb. Magic can be used for other things besides creating fog."

"So you heard about that already, too." Savaric chuckled. "Was there anything you missed?"

The healer stared at the tiny fire in his hearth for some time before he answered. "Have you had any word from Cantrell or Pazric?"

"No. I am not worried about Cantrell. The bard has been gathering information for me for a long time. He can take care of himself, even in Medb's camp. But Pazric should have been back from the south by now. It does not take this long to negotiate a trade with the Turic tribes."

Piers nodded. The men were quiet for a while, each wandering in his own thoughts. Their silence was companionable, born of a long friendship and respect.

Finally, Piers said, "That boy is an enigma. Perhaps he holds a key you can use to unlock Medb's doom."

Savaric shook his head and straightened. "That is very unlikely. Even grown men can't kill Medb." He walked to the entrance. "But take care of him, Piers, or you will have an angry Hunnuli trampling your tent."

"Did this mere lad truly rescue a Hunnuli?"

"He certainly did."

Piers raised his wine cup in a mock salute. "Then he shall be treated like a hero."

Savaric matched his salute and left the tent.

Gabria slept through the night and most of the next day, lying motionless beneath her cloak, too weak to move even in sleep. Piers watched her anxiously, and several times he checked her to be sure she was still breathing. Outside the healer's tent, Nara waited patiently. Savaric visited once to check the boy's progress, but Gabria made no sound and still lay as if lifeless.

In the late afternoon, Piers was giving Gabria a sip of mild tea between her slack lips when, without warning, she began writhing and lashing out at him. Her face was twisted in hatred and her breath rasped in her throat. "No!" she cried hoarsely. "You can't have me, too."

"Easy, boy, easy." The healer held Gabria down and soothed her until the dream passed. With its end came a slow awakening to consciousness. Gabria's body relaxed, her breathing eased, and her eyes crept open until she was staring into the healer's concerned face.

"I don't know you," she whispered.

Piers sat back on his heels at the edge of the pallet and allowed himself a rare smile. The boy was obviously on the way to recovery, for there was no fear or hesitancy in his voice.

"I am the healer of the Khulinin. Piers Arganosta."

"That is a strange name for a clansman," Gabria said. Her voice was stronger and color was returning to her skin.

Piers was relieved to see the boy was not withdrawn or dwelling on his grief. Savaric was right: the lad was very strong. "I am not a clansman," he explained. "I am from the city of Pra Desh."

"What are you doing on the plains?" she asked curiously.

"Amongst the barbarians?" he asked with a touch of irony. "The city lost favor with me."

Gabria bristled at the word "barbarian" until she realized that Piers was not being insulting; he was merely repeating a phrase he had heard too often. His face was rather pleasant, she thought, if a little sad, and his pale eyes reminded her of mica: smoky and opaque. There was nothing pretentious about him, a characteristic she did not expect from a man from Pra Desh, the greatest of the eastern cities. In fact, he seemed to deliberately avoid drawing attention to himself. There was little bright color about him, nothing to draw the eye. He was pale with light skin and fair hair cut short.

His tent was plain and simply furnished with a portable medicine chest, a few light pieces of furniture, and an undyed carpet. Hangings of cream-colored wool hung on the walls of the tent, and another curtain hid his sleeping area. The soft rose of his healer's robe was the only extravagant color Gabria could see.

"I have never been to Pra Desh," Gabria said as the man stood up and fetched a bowl of soup from the small pot on his hearth.

"Then you are very blessed."

Gabria was unexpectedly irritated. How dare he say something like that. He knew nothing about her. "I have not been blessed," she snapped. "By anything."

"You are alive, boy. Enjoy that," Piers exclaimed.

"I have no right to be. My place was with my clan."

"Your place was where the gods chose to put you." He handed her the bowl, but she ignored it and glared at the open tent flap, where the afternoon sun was slanting through.

"You are a stranger. What can you know of our gods and their ways?" she retorted.

"I do know self-recrimination is useless. It does not bring back the dead, so do not waste your gift of life on guilt or lost opportunities."

Gabria continued to stare outside. "May I get up now? It must be late."

Piers sighed. Obviously, his advice was being ignored. "If you feel like it. The Hunnuli is waiting for you, and I am sure you can find food in the hall."

"Thank you, Piers," she said coolly.

"You are welcome, Gabran."

The girl flinched at the name he used and wondered if she would ever grow used to the pain that clung to it. She stiffly climbed to her feet. Immediately, she wished she had not. Her muscles trembled, her head whirled, and dizziness shook her like an ague. She took a few faltering steps, then her ears roared and her stomach threatened to rebel. Piers wordlessly handed her a stool. She sank down gratefully and rested her head on her hands before the nausea overcame her.

"What is wrong with me?" Gabria groaned.

"Do you expect to go through all you have and not pay for it? You have used your body beyond its limits. And you have hardly eaten a thing. Give yourself time to snap back." He gave her the soup. "Now, eat this."

She took the bowl and sipped the meaty broth. "Thank you," she said again, this time with more sincerity.

Piers stepped to the tent flap and summoned a passing warrior. "Tell Lord Savaric the boy is awake." The man hurried away and within minutes, Savaric entered the tent. He was caked with dust and sweat, and a large falcon gripped his padded shoulder where his golden cloak had been pushed aside.

"The hunting was fair today, Piers," the chieftain said, his eyes on Gabria.

She sat on her stool, staring into the distance. Lost in thought, she had forgotten her precarious disguise and did not rise to give her chieftain a warrior's salute of fealty. Just then Gabria realized the men were looking at her and she sprang to her feet, spilling the hot soup over her leg.

"Forgive me, Lord," she stammered.

Savaric waved off her apology. "Your forgetfulness hardly matters here. But do not lose your memory before my other warriors."

Gabria nodded and sat down, chagrined. Her face reddened with embarrassment. Piers gave her a rag to clean the spilled soup and refilled her bowl.

"Your newest warrior will soon be ready to assume his duties," the healer said to Savaric. "He will be tender for a day or two, but he will toughen."

"Good. The boy will need all the strength he can muster."

"I understand Athlone is to be Gabran's mentor," the healer said.

Savaric chuckled. "Of course. Athlone wished to personally handle the boy's training."

"Athlone can go jump in a swamp," Gabria muttered.

The chief turned to her, his expression hard. "What did you say, boy?"

Gabria winced. She had not meant to speak so freely. She had to remember she was no longer with her own family. Her face blushed even brighter, and she stared at the ground speechlessly.

"Keep a civil tongue, Gabran," Savaric ordered, hiding a smile as Piers winked at him. "Tomorrow, if you can ride, you will begin your duties."

"Yes, Lord," Gabria mumbled as Savaric strode out. She sagged on her stool and gripped her bowl to still her trembling hands.

I am an idiot! she thought to herself. First I forget to salute the chief, and then I scorn the wer-tain in front of his father. Careless mistakes like those could draw unwanted attention and expose the weaknesses of my disguise. There were too many other things to remember about behaving like a boy to be caught in some dull-witted error. I have to be more careful! Glancing sideways at Piers, Gabria stretched out her legs in a masculine manner and rested her elbows on her knees as she finished her soup.

"Your Hunnuli has been waiting. Perhaps you might walk out and reassure her," Piers suggested when Gabria returned the bowl.

The girl nodded and stood up, waiting for the dizziness that struck before. This time, the soup steadied her and she found she was able to walk without shaking. Nara was by the tent's entrance and nickered in delight when the girl came out.

I feared you might be ill.

"No, just weary," Gabria said. She wound her fingers through Nara's ebony mane. "Have you had any food?"

No, I have been waiting for you.

"Then let's go down by the river. I need to think."

They walked side by side through the encampment, ignoring the faces that turned to watch them and the fingers that pointed their way. No one greeted them or offered them hospitality, and no one came near. Gabria was relieved when she and Nara left the tents behind and reached the banks of the river. It was difficult to hide her weakness and walk like a Corin past the staring clansmen. Her legs were trembling again and she felt lightheaded by the time Nara found a secluded place by the water.

Gabria gratefully sat down in the long, lush grass of the treeless bank while Nara began to graze. The girl leaned back, letting the wind touch her face and tufts of grass tickle her neck as she listened to the rippling music of the river.

We are being watched.

Nara's thought was a rude awakening. The mare still grazed in apparent disregard, but she faced away from the girl toward a bare hillock, where a lone horse stood, its head turned toward them.

Gabria glared at the distant horse, then turned away in disgust. "I'm not surprised. Where is the rider?"

There is none. That is a Hunnuli stallion.

"Athlone, the wer-tain." Gabria pitched a pebble in the water and watched as the circles were overwhelmed by the flow of the stream. "He sent his Hunnuli to watch us so he could be sure we do not try to contact Medb—or do anything else suspicious," she said sarcastically.

The man is cautious and has a need to be, the mare pointed out with mild reproof. *He is to be trusted.*

"Trusted!" Gabria cried. "He would kill me if he ever found my secret. One mistake, one little slip of my disguise, and he will spear me as neatly as a jackal." She pulled her cloak closer and added, "Women are not permitted to be warriors among our people. But I must try to be one. Death is the only thing I can trust to receive from Athlone if I fail."

It is too bad you feel that way. He would be a powerful ally.

"You are the only ally I need. You, my sword, and the good will of the gods."

They remained by the river for a long time while Nara ate her fill of the rich grass and Gabria watched the meadowlarks dip above the grazing livestock. They both ignored the watching stallion.

But Gabria found that her peace had fled her. She could not relax or let her mind wander while the Hunnuli stallion guarded her every move. She was not accustomed to such distrust or being treated with dislike. In all of her seventeen years, she had never felt so alone, for Gabran, her family, and her clan had always been with her. Nothing had prepared her for the endless confusion and emptiness that had dogged her steps since the day of the massacre. She was not a Khulinin and she never would be, but she wished someone would accept her with open arms. She wanted to be warm and comfortable and welcome, not pushed out in the shadows like a thieving beggar.

The evening was growing cold when Gabria and the mare returned to the treld. Nara led the way to the healer's tent. Piers was gone when Gabria entered, yet she found another bowl of soup warming by the fire and her pack lying on the sleeping pallet. Everything in the bag had been cleaned and mended, and a new tunic of soft linen had been added. Sleepy again, Gabria finished the soup, curled up in her cloak, and sank into another motionless sleep.

Athlone came for Gabria at dawn, when the echoes of the morning horn were fading. Astride his towering stallion, he shouted at her to come, for her apprenticeship was about to begin. She barely had time to grab a warm bun from Piers's table, pin on her cloak, and dash out of the tent before the wer-tain was cantering off toward the meadows. Groggily, she clambered onto Nara's back and followed, her irritation wide awake.

"Come on, boy, your duties start at sunrise," Athlone said when Gabria had finally caught up with him. "And don't let me catch you shirking."

He led her to a practice field where several targets and makeshift figures were set up. "Before I can begin your training," he stated, sliding off his horse, "I need to know what you can do." His tone implied that he did not expect much. Then, his eyes hardened to stone. "Where are your sword and bow?"

Gabria felt her stomach fall to her knees. The day had barely begun and already she had made a careless error. No warrior left his tent without his weapons; she had not even brought her dagger. "Wertain, I'm sorry," she gasped. "I do not have a bow and I . . . left my sword . . . in the tent."

Athlone walked deliberately around the horses until he stood by Gabria's foot. The silence crackled. "You what?" he snarled with withering scorn. "If such carelessness is characteristic of your clan, it is little wonder they were wiped out."

Gabria stiffened as if he had struck her. Her face went livid and her hand flew to her empty belt.

Careful, Nara warned, sidling away. *Keep still*.

"Return with your sword," Athlone ordered. "If you know what one looks like."

Before Gabria could reply, Nara wheeled and cantered back to the treld. Once they were out of earshot, Gabria clenched her hands in the Hunnuli's black mane. "That dog!" she screamed. "Insufferable pig! He just insulted an entire clan and I can do nothing."

They came to Piers's tent. Gabria stormed in and retrieved her short sword, the one she had taken from Gabran's hand.

"Trust him, you said!" she raged as she flung herself back on the mare. "I'd sooner trust a viper."

Nara deigned to ignore her. She carried the fuming girl back to the field where Athlone waited impatiently. Gabria spent the next few hours keeping her misery and anger tightly leashed. Athlone worked her at swordplay and hand-to-hand fighting. They began on horseback, where Athlone's stallion, Boreas, could help Nara with complicated maneuvers. Then they moved to the ground. Athlone pressed Gabria to the limit of her strength and skill.

A thousand times Gabria blessed her brothers for teaching her the rudiments of their weapons. She was no match for the wer-tain, but she could keep her borrowed identity from suspicion as she fought Athlone through each of his testing exercises. No woman should have known the fighting skills Gabria used.

Athlone worked her hard, both mentally and physically, and he watched Gabria's every move, waiting for her to slip from anger or carelessness. He deliberately taunted her, shot orders at her, and gave her no rest. When he finally stopped, late in the morning, she fell to her knees, panting and drenched with sweat. He stood back and studied her. The nagging little warning in his head was ringing madly, yet he still could not put a reason to his suspicions. The boy could hold a sword and he knew most of the basic moves, but there were some important details he did not know about swordplay that he should have. There was also a hesitancy in his attacks that belied a normal boy's experience with weapons.

Athlone sheathed his sword and whistled to Boreas. Whatever the boy's secret was, it was obvious from the past few hours that he had a great deal of determination. That was something in his favor.

"Keep practicing the last three parries I showed you," the wertain ordered. "Remember to keep your weight balanced or you will find yourself in the dust. I will take you to the saddler later." He vaulted onto the stallion's back.

Gabria glared at him, too tired to move. Without thinking, she said, "What for? I do not need a saddle."

"No," Athlone replied sarcastically. "Nara will keep you mounted. But you will need the other trappings befitting a warrior."

Gabria bit her lip as the stallion cantered away. She had done it again. She had walked into that blunder like a child. This acting was much more difficult than she had anticipated. When she had thought of this scheme, Gabria had imagined herself drifting easily into the fringe of Savaric's clan and playing the part of a boy with little concentration and great ease until she found the right time to challenge Lord Medb. If she could handle a bow and a sword, she could pretend to be a boy for as long as necessary.

But Gabria had never fully appreciated the countless differences between a male and a female, not only physically and mentally, but socially as well. A boy would never have questioned the wer-tain about the saddler, for a boy would have already learned what was intended. A woman, on the other hand, made her own leather goods. She had no need to visit the saddler, who was the warriors' craftsman for saddles, harnesses, and leather accoutrements—things a woman had little use for.

In the clans, a woman was expected to keep her place in the tent. She was protected by the men in her family or her husband's family, and in return, the men demanded obedience. Despite their restrictive lives, the clanswomen were intelligent, efficient, and often fierce, but they understood and believed in the social mores of the clans and followed them by habit. No woman was allowed into the werod, the council, or any of the important ranks of the clan. Only the priestess of Amara and the wife and daughters of the chief had any status and esteem.

As the daughter of Dathlar, Gabria had had status in her clan, and as the only girl in a family of five men, she had been raised with love, respect, and a measure of equality. Her family had given her more freedom and responsibility than many clanswomen had, and she had been happy and content. Before the massacre, Gabria would never have dreamed of pretending to be a boy, or joining a werod, or challenging a chieftain for weir-geld.

However, her life was drastically different now, and she was forced to make some radical decisions. Gabria had chosen this plan of deception because she thought she had enough self-confidence and a great enough understanding of males to pull it off. Now, she was not so sure. There were too many details to constantly remember and so many ramifications she had no experience with. It was so confusing!

Gabria was still deep in her musings when Nara came to her side and brushed the girl's cheek with a velvety nose. *Are you going to sit in the dirt all day?*

Gabria shook her head, smiled, and stood up, her sword hanging limply in her hand. The girl knew it was too late to alter her course now. She could imagine some impending difficulties with her disguise, and there would be other problems she could not expect, but she would just have to handle the pitfalls as they came and hope for a great deal of good fortune. Gabria rubbed Nara's neck affectionately, and together they went in search of a midday meal.

Later that afternoon, Athlone took Gabria to the saddler. The girl had to be completely outfitted with a shield, belt, boots, leather jerkin, helmet, and a quiver for arrows. The old craftsman promised to have the items finished within a few days and he gave Gabria a used, restrung bow he had no use for.

Gabria also found an old, wide-brimmed hat in a pile of scraps the saddler had planned to throw away. The old man laughingly gave it to her and threw in a leather thong to tie the hat down on her head. The girl pulled the brim down low over her eyes and tried to look casual as she leaned against a post and waited for Athlone.

Athlone was still speaking to the saddler when a boy arrived and gave him a message from Savaric. The wer-tain quickly ended the conversation and, without a word to Gabria, hurried her to the clan hall.

Savaric was waiting for them in the main room of the hall. He stood beside a tall perch, feeding tidbits to his falcon and talking to two of his warriors. The two men saluted as Athlone and Gabria approached, then the men quickly left the hall.

"I'm glad you could come now," the chieftain told Gabria and Athlone as he moved to the dais. "I have just received word that a messenger has arrived. I would like you both to stay and listen."

Gabria sat down on the stone rim of the fire pit and tried to be inconspicuous. She wondered if the news the messenger brought concerned her in some way. She had made no effort to hide her trail at Corin Treld, and it was possible that someone had realized there could have been a survivor and spread the word. Enough time had passed for the news to reach the farthest clans.

"Gabran," Savaric said, jolting her out of her thoughts. "Remove your cloak and keep it out of sight."

"Yes, Lord." She unpinned the red cloak, folded it into a cushion, and sat on it. She should have remembered it herself. Her anonymity would be lost if another clan learned of her presence with the Khulinin, and, without some cover to protect her until she was ready to challenge Medb, her life would not be worth a slave's wage.

While she waited, the girl watched the chieftain and the wer-tain as they talked quietly. She marveled at the rapport that existed between the two men. Both men were strong individuals with very different personalities and yet their respect and love for each other was unmistakable. Many chieftains would have feared an intelligent, strong-willed son like Athlone when the question of clan control came into contention, but as far as Gabria knew, that question had never been raised between these two men. They worked together to rule the large and powerful Khulinin.

In other circumstances, Gabria might have grown to like Athlone, as much as she liked the chief. Nara was right: the wer-tain would make a potent ally, but Gabria and the wer-tain clashed from the beginning and their relationship was slipping from bad to worse. He grated on her already battered confidence. His arrogance, his caustic contempt, and his probing suspicions made it impossible for her to accept him as only a man. He hung over her consciousness like a great storm cloud, blinding her to other dangers and overwhelming her with his potentially deadly vigilance. Around Athlone, Gabria was constantly on guard and afraid. It was little wonder she acted like a bungling fool whenever he was with her.

She was still staring at the two men when the messenger, wearing the green cloak of the Geldring clan, was escorted into Savaric's hall. Gabria, seeing the messenger's cloak, edged farther into the shadows of a pillar and hoped he would ignore her. The Corin argued frequently with the Geldring and there had been much interaction between the two clans. It was possible the man would recognize her if he had seen her or Gabran in the past.

But the messenger only gave her a cursory glance as he passed, for his mind was on the news he brought. He bowed before Savaric and offered his chieftain's greetings. "Lord Branth bids me tell you—"

Savaric straightened in amazement. "Branth! When did he become chieftain?"

"Just before the massacre at Corin Treld. Lord Justar died quite suddenly of a heart ailment," the messenger said.

"Did a dagger cause his 'heart ailment'?" Savaric asked dryly.

The messenger looked uncomfortable, as if that thought had occurred to him before. "I do not know, Lord Savaric. Only his wife and Branth were with him when he died and his body was prepared for the pyre by his wife's hands."

Athlone and Savaric exchanged glances of silent speculation. Gabria was relieved she had not tried to seek refuge with the Geldring. Lord Justar had respected her father, but Branth hated the Corin with a passion. If she had gone to him, he would have turned her over to Medb. It was well known he supported the Wylfling chief.

Savaric shrugged slightly. "All right. Continue."

"We found Corin Treld two days after the killing, and we spent some time reading the signs of the battle. We discovered there may be a survivor, but we do not know who or what that person was or where he went."

"How do you know this?" Athlone asked.

"There was a makeshift funeral pyre near the ruins and five bodies had been burned. One, by the shield and helmet, was Dathlar. No enemy who slaughtered the clan like that would have afforded the chief such honor. We also found foot tracks leading out of the treld. They went south, then we lost them in a storm. Lord Branth feels we should search the foothills and send word to every clan to seek this survivor."

"Absolutely," Savaric agreed with the right amount of enthusiasm. "This survivor could be the last Corin."

Athlone shot a quick look at Gabria, who was sitting motionless, as if carved from stone.

"The rest of the information was not clear either." The messenger hesitated as if unsure how to continue. "But it appears that a large band of exiles attacked the treld."

The reaction the Geldring was expecting did not come. Savaric merely raised an eyebrow and said, "Indeed."

"You may not believe me," the messenger replied stiffly, "but Lord Branth believes it to be true. The hoofprints were those of unshod horses, and we found several broken arrows with colorless feathers. The attackers took or burned their dead."

Savaric drummed his fingers on his knee and looked thoughtful. "Branth is a minion of Lord Medb's, is he not?" he asked casually.

The Geldring started at the unexpected question and his hand came to rest on his sword. "I do not know, Lord."

Savaric raised his hand to reassure the man. "Forgive me. That was not a fair question to you. I merely wished to know if there were other reasons besides my ignorance to warn me of the exiles' infamy."

"I only report what I am told." The Geldring paused. "But you are not surprised about the exiles banding together and carrying weapons? It could mean more death and pillage for us all."

"Did they pillage the treld?" Athlone inquired.

Surprise overcame the young man's face as the realization dawned on him. "No. No, they did not. They burned everything and drove off the animals."

"There were other motives for the attack besides the greed of a few brigands." Savaric suddenly looked tired. "If that is all your news, then please rest yourself and take Lord Branth my greetings."

The messenger bowed again and left. A silence dropped in the hall. In the doorway, the guards stood in the sunlight that streamed down from the west.

Finally, Savaric stirred and rose slowly to his feet. He looked as if his mind were still grappling with the meaning of the Geldring's news. "Gabran," he said at last.

Gabria glanced up at Savaric's face. For a moment he seemed so old, as though the growing flames of tragedy and deceit that burned among the clans were more than he wanted to deal with. Then the look passed, the weariness and defeat were gone, and his eyes glittered.

Unconsciously, Gabria straightened her shoulders. "Yes, Lord?"

"It seems that your story is falling into place. You were careless, though. Medb will soon know his bandits were not thorough."

"I expected he would find out one way or another, Lord."

The chieftain smiled humorlessly. "True. But we must be more circumspect. You will wear the Khulinin cloak from now on. I do not wish to startle any guests."

Gabria nodded. She wanted to keep her cloak with her. It was her only link to her past and the happiness she had known. Nevertheless, she understood that wearing it would be unsafe, as well as an insult to the Khulinin who had tentatively accepted her. She would obey. For now.

"Also," Savaric continued, "you have the choice of sleeping with the other bachelors in this hall or with Athlone in his tent. He has no woman, but it would be more comfortable than the hall."

Gabria did not even consider the choice. "I will sleep in the hall."

Savaric chuckled. It was Athlone's duty to care for his apprentice, but if the boy chose to be on his own, then so be it. The chieftain stretched his legs as he stepped off the dais. "You will ride with the evening outriders for now."

"Yes, Lord."

"And, boy, be careful. You *are* the last Corin."

5

The smells of cooking food for the evening meal were warming the treld when Athlone took Gabria to the leader of the clan's outriders and left her in his charge. The man, a pleasant-faced warrior of thirty some years, wore his black hair bound in an intricate knot and had several gold armbands on his right arm.

He gave Gabria a pleasant smile. "My name is Jorlan. I am pleased to have the Hunnuli with us. I hope she does not mind such menial tasks as guard duty."

Nara nickered her impression of laughter and rubbed her nose on Gabria's back.

With Athlone gone, Gabria relaxed a little and enjoyed the leader's unexpected friendliness. It made it easier to ignore the hostile glances of the other outriders and the blatant gestures they made to ward off evil.

"She does not mind at all. Besides, she has to do something to earn all the grass she eats," Gabria said.

Jorlan laughed. He sent his men to their tasks, then mounted his bay horse and gestured to the meadows where the clan's herds grazed. "You will be riding with the brood mares tonight. They are due to foal soon."

Gabria was surprised. No wonder the outriders had been so hostile. The brood mares were the most coveted herd to guard and the duty was usually given to the favored warriors in the werod. She, as the newest warrior-in-training, should have been sent to the farthest fringes of the valley to stand sentry duty.

On the other hand, if she considered the leader's point of view, it was excellent sense to put the Hunnuli mare and her rider with the valuable brood mares. Nara was the best possible protector, combining the speed, strength, and senses of several men and their mounts. The duty was not given as a reward but for expediency.

"Right now, I will take you to the meadows to meet the meara," Jorlan added.

They followed the well-worn track down the hill to the extensive meadows that filled the valley. To the north, where the fields were protected from the winter winds by the backbone of Marakor, the Harachan horses were divided into several herds, each led by a stallion or mare of high rank. The largest herd was the work horses, the second was the yearlings and young horses in training, and the third was the brood mares.

Over all reigned the meara, the greatest stallion in eminence and rank. Each clan had a meara, which was chosen from their herds for the finest blood and ability, and these stallions were the pride and heart of their clans. No man dared lay a hand on one, save the chieftain, and to kill a meara was a crime punishable by the most hideous death. In the summer, the meara fought for his rank against selected males. If he was victorious, he was honored for another year; if he failed, he was returned with gratitude to the goddess, Amara, and the new meara ruled the herds.

The Khulinin meara was named Vayer. He was standing on a small hillock near the river, a mounted outrider with him. Even from a distance, Gabria would have recognized the horse as the meara. She had never seen a Harachan stallion to compare with him in form, beauty, or strength. He was a large chestnut with a golden mane falling from his high arched neck, and the gleam of fire in his hide. Although the Harachan horses did not have the size or intelligence of the Hunnuli, this stallion was wise from years of experience, and he carried his nobility like he carried his tail, as boldly as a king's banner in battle.

When Jorlan and Gabria reached the hillock, Vayer neighed a greeting. As Jorlan spoke to him, Gabria looked closer and saw the horse's muzzle was hoary with age, and scars from many battles marred his red hide. Still, his muscles were solid and his regal courage blazed in his golden eyes.

Vayer gravely sniffed Nara and snorted. She neighed imperiously in answer. The stallion, obviously satisfied, nickered to the men and trotted away. The outriders watched him go.

Jorlan and the rider talked for a moment longer, while Gabria looked over the herd of young horses nearby. They were a strong and healthy group, and they had wintered well. Their long coats had not shed yet and were still thick and shaggy. It would be a few more weeks before their sleek beauty was revealed.

The colts reminded Gabria of the Corin's horses. She wondered what had become of the brood mares, the yearlings, and the stallions. Had the exiles stolen most of them, or had the horses wandered onto the steppes and been taken into wild herds? Perhaps some of them had found their way to other clans. One horse she would have liked to have back was the Corin meara, Balor. He had been her father's pride and joy.

"We had a good yearling herd this year," Jorlan commented to Gabria.

Gabria nodded absently, her mind still on the lost stallion. "Amara should bless you with another rich Foaling," she said.

Both warriors stared at her in angry astonishment. Men did not speak of Amara and the Foaling in the same breath for fear of incurring bad luck. Amara was a woman's deity.

"Your fortunes have been bad," Jorlan snapped. "Do not cast any of it on us."

Gabria winced at the reproof. It was well deserved, for she had spoken thoughtlessly.

I should keep my mouth shut, Gabria decided, but it was too easy for her to slip back into her old habits. To make matters worse, she had forgotten what Jorlan reminded her of: she still carried the stigma of exile and death. Most people would refuse to look beyond that, and if anything unfortunate happened, especially a poor Foaling, they would find some way to blame her. She was an easy scapegoat—particularly if the clan discovered she was not a boy.

Jorlan said no more to Gabria and, after bidding farewell to the outrider, guided her to the brood mare herd.

The mares were pastured in a small valley at the edge of the mountains, where a creek flowed out of the hills to join the Goldrine River. Cottonwood, willow, and birch shaded the creek banks, and grass, herbs, and shrubs grew thick on the valley floor.

Spring was not well advanced, but already the fodder was green and lush, and the trees were bursting with budding leaves. There was a delicate, almost tangible essence of anticipation in the valley, as if the rising life in the trees and grasses and the stream had combined with the sunlight to bless the mares and their unborn foals. Almost fifty horses grazed contentedly among the trees, while the lead mare, Halle, kept a close watch on them all.

Nara whinnied a greeting when Jorlan led them into the valley. Halle returned her call and every mare close by replied with a ringing cry of welcome. The mares trotted over to greet the Hunnuli. Their bellies were distended and they moved ponderously, yet their heads swung gracefully as they sniffed the Hunnuli and her rider.

Another rider hailed Jorlan from the creek and came splashing down the stream to meet them. "Ye gods, she is a beauty," he called. His mount bounded up the bank. "I heard there was a Hunnuli in the treld, but I could not believe it." He ignored Gabria and stared at the great black horse. He was a tall, deceptively languid man with muddy eyes and an unconscious curl in his lip.

Gabria disliked him immediately.

"Cor," Jorlan called over the heads of the mares. "This is Gabran. He and the Hunnuli will be riding with you tonight."

The young warrior's pleasure abruptly vanished and anger darkened his face. "No, Jorlan. That boy is an exile. He cannot ride with the mares or his evil will destroy the foals."

Gabria clenched her hands on her thighs and stared unhappily at the ground.

"As you so aptly noticed, the boy rides a Hunnuli. You know full well the mare would tolerate no evil near her," Jorlan replied. His voice was edged with sarcasm and irritation, and Gabria wondered if he, too, had doubts about her effect on the mares.

Cor shook his head forcefully. "I will not ride with him. Let me have the Hunnuli. I can handle her. But the exile must go."

"Cor, I appreciate your concern, but the boy and the Hunnuli will stay."

Cor pushed his horse closer to Jorlan's mount and shouted, "Why should that boy be allowed to ride guard on the mares just because he has a Hunnuli? Why can't he earn the duty like the rest of us?"

Jorlan's patience was at an end. "One more outburst from you," he said tightly, "and you will be relieved. Your disobedience and insolence are intolerable. I have warned you before about your behavior."

Cor's face paled and the muscles around his eyes tightened in anger. "Sir, the exile will blight the mares. It's not right!"

"He is a member of the clan, not an exile."

The outrider slammed his fist on the scabbard of his sword. He wanted to say more, but the look on Jorlan's face stopped him.

"Return to your duties," Jorlan snarled, His tone left no room for argument

Something swirled in the silty depths of Cor's eyes like the flick of a pike's tail. He snapped a look of fury at Gabria, reined his horse away, and sullenly rode back up the valley.

"Sir . . . ," Gabria started to say.

"Gabran, you will learn that I will not tolerate such arrogance or questioning of my orders."

"You do not believe I will bring evil luck to the mares?"

"What I believe does not matter. Lord Savaric gave me his orders." Then Jorlan glanced at Gabria's face and his tone softened. "Do not be concerned about Cor. He has received several warnings about his vindictiveness and bad temper. If he gets warned again, he loses his duty as outrider. He is probably more worried about himself than the mares."

Gabria glanced at him in gratitude. It was a relief to know Cor's attitude was not entirely her fault.

Jorlan whistled sharply and two large hounds bounded through the undergrowth. He tossed them some meat scraps from a small bag at his belt.

"The Hunnuli can guard the herd better than our men, but stay close to these dogs. The hunters found signs of a lion in the hills nearby." Jorlan started to leave, then came back. "If you need help, there is a horn hanging in that tree by the creek. Your replacement will be here about midnight." Jorlan left, cantering his horse back toward the treld.

Gabria was relieved to be left alone with Nara and the mares for a while. She could relax in their undemanding company and enjoy the peace of the evening. The evening was a lovely one, clear and mild, and the twilight gently lingered into night. The wind was cool and the stars glittered overhead in glorious sprays. The night was full of sounds familiar to Gabria: the ripple of the creek, the rustle of the trees, and the sounds of contented horses. She hummed a tune to herself while she rode Nara along the creek and scouted the surrounding hills, keeping watch for a mare in trouble or a hunting predator. The hounds padded silently beside her.

She only saw Cor a few times in the course of their duty. He remained near the head of the little valley and stayed to himself.

The moon, now waning, rose near the end of Gabria's watch. She and Nara stood under the trees at the mouth of the valley with the mare, Halle. The night was quiet; the dogs sprawled on the ground, panting.

Suddenly, Nara tensed. Her head came up and her nostrils flared. *Gabria, there is trouble.*

A stray breeze wafted down from the hills, disturbing the mares. Halle stamped nervously and whinnied a warning. The dogs sprang to their feet. Gabria reached for the horn that hung close by.

All at once, a blood-chilling squeal tore through the night. The mares panicked. Like a storm breaking, Nara bolted up the creek, the dogs fast on her heels. Gabria hung on desperately to the Hunnuli and clutched the horn to her chest. Shouting and wild whinnying broke out ahead. Terrified mares galloped down the valley away from some horror. Nara had to swerve violently to avoid them.

The small valley narrowed, and trees crowded around the stream, making it difficult for Nara to run. The dogs surged ahead. They scrabbled over a gravel bank, came around a curve, and leaped a fallen tree into a clearing. Cor was already there, on his feet, his sword drawn, watching a cave lion crouched over the body of a dead mare. Faint moonlight gleamed on the lion's fangs and on the white blaze on the dead horse's face.

The tableau seemed to freeze for a moment as Nara and the dogs burst into the clearing, then everything shattered into a chaos of noise and motion. The dogs leaped at the snarling cat from either side and Nara drove her front hooves into the lion's head. The cat was knocked off the dead horse into a tumbling pile of snapping dogs. Gabria lifted the horn and blew peal after peal of strident notes.

During the furor, Gabria forgot about Cor. He slunk back to the trees' shadows and watched the fight, making no move to help. He studied everything for a moment, then a calculating smile tightened his thin mouth. Without a word, he faded into the darkness.

Before long, the lion had had enough. It fought its way out from under the dogs and bolted into the underbrush with a squall of pain and rage. The dogs were about to follow when a whistle brought them to heel. Mounted men bearing torches and spears crowded into the clearing behind Jorlan. Their faces were grim as they looked over both the dead mare and the boy on his Hunnuli. Several men stooped over the body and studied the tracks of the lion, then they disappeared into the brush on the cat's trail.

Jorlan looked up at Gabria. "Report, Outrider."

Gabria explained as best she could what had happened. It was then she realized that Cor was gone. Her heart sank. It was horrible enough that this hideous killing had happened during her first night as an outrider, but without Cor to collaborate her story, the clansmen would heap the blame, undeserved or not, upon her. The lion had found the straying mare near Cor's position, and even Nara had not discovered its presence in time. But those were merely excuses. The Khulinin would never forgive her for the loss of the precious mare.

Gabria could see the men's faces in the flickering torchlight; it was obvious what they were thinking. Only Jorlan seemed puzzled. He had dismounted and was walking carefully around the clearing, scanning the ground.

Nara neighed as Cor walked out of the trees. He was leading his limping horse. His clothes were torn and dirty. He tried to look surprised and horrified as he saluted Jorlan.

"This was your guard position, Cor. Where were you?" the leader demanded.

"My horse bolted a while ago and fell into a gully north of here. He hurt his foreleg, as you can see. I had a rough time getting us out of there." Cor sounded unhappy, but he could not completely hide the smugness in his voice.

Nara snorted in contempt.

Jorlan crossed his arms and raked the man with a furious glare. "While you were so conveniently absent, the cat killed a daughter of Vayer."

Cor shook his fist at Gabria. "It is the exile! His curse has brought this down on us. I tried to warn you."

The other men looked at their leader uncertainly. All of them were unsure how to deal with this strange boy and the complicated twists of his destiny. It was easy to dump the blame for this tragedy at the Corin's feet, but the men knew Cor well and they sensed something was not quite right about his story.

Jorlan refused to respond to Cor's feigned anger. "The boy told me you were here before him, on foot, and that you made no effort to help."

"He lies!" Cor shouted.

"I don't believe so," Jorlan said. "I have seen your tracks."

Cor looked sideways at Gabria and realized he had made a serious mistake. He licked his lips. "The exile should not have been guarding the mares. It is his fault this happened." He paused, sensing he was losing his credibility. The other warriors were muttering among themselves, and Jorlan was staring at the dead mare. Gabria was watching Cor from the back of the Hunnuli, as if waiting for him to trip himself. Cor's anger and embarrassment suddenly overwhelmed his common sense and he threw his sword at the Hunnuli. It missed and landed at her feet.

"All right, I was here," he shouted furiously. "My horse threw me.

But that sorcerer's servant was the cause of this. He drew the lion here and was going to leave me to be killed, too. We cannot let him stay in this clan! He will doom us, just like the Corin."

Jorlan strode forward, struck Cor to the ground, and stood over him. "You are a disgrace. You are relieved of all duties as an outrider and your behavior will be reported to the chieftain for further punishment." Jorlan's voice was cold with disgust.

Cor looked wildly around the dark clearing for some sign of support from the other warriors. When he saw only the disdain on their faces, he jumped to his feet and ran into the trees. No one moved to stop him.

Gabria spent the last hour of her duty in a blur. She was badly shaken by the lion's attack and by the hatred she had seen in Cor's eyes. It was all she could do to stop her hands from trembling while she helped the men bury the dead mare in the clearing. The women would come later to bless the mound and send the dead mare's spirit to Amara, but Gabria paused long enough to whisper a quiet prayer of peace. The familiar, comforting words in her head eased her own pain a little, and when her replacement came at midnight, Gabria was able to bid good-night to the remaining men and leave the valley with a straight back.

The ride across the fields to the treld was the last quiet moment she had for the rest of the night. News of the attack had spread rapidly through the encampment and the clan was in an uproar. A hunting party was being organized. Groups of men clustered around the tents, discussing the import of the news while the women wept for the mare and her unborn foal. Cor had stormed into the hall and, after gulping down a flask of wine, was cursing Gabria and Jorlan at the top of his lungs, protesting his own innocence. Jorlan and most of his outriders had already returned and reported to Savaric.

Gabria and Nara stopped at the edge of the treld and watched the activity for several minutes. Gabria slid off the horse, and the Hunnuli dipped her head and gently rubbed her nose along the girl's chest. Gabria scratched Nara's ears. The girl wished she could borrow some of the mare's vast energy to bolster her own flagging strength. She was exhausted now, but she would have to sleep in the hall tonight with the unmarried men. She doubted she would have much rest.

I am going to the meadow. If you need me, I will come.

Gabria nodded and gave the horse a final pat. When Nara trotted away, the girl pulled her now golden cloak tighter about her and walked wearily to the camp. The light from the torches and campfires danced around her. The black tents sat like noisy, humped creatures with their backs turned against her. The clanspeople were busy preparing to hunt the lion, and, to Gabria's relief, no one noticed her. She passed by, a sad shadow in all the hubbub, unseen by all but one.

Athlone stood in the darkened entrance of his tent and watched as Gabria came up the path. His handsome face was hooded in darkness, so she did not see him as she went by. He waited until she was past the guards at the hall before he turned to fetch his spear from his tent.

Something still bothered him about that boy. The nagging suspicion would not stop. Why? The Corin showed spirit and courage despite his grief, and his determination seemed unshakable. Jorlan had reported favorably about the boy and his actions during the lion attack. Neither these attributes nor his unmistakable love for the Hunnuli were the usual characteristics of an exile on the run or a spy for an ambitious chieftain.

The mare was another curious aspect of the boy. The Hunnuli had accepted him, and the horses of that breed were impeccable judges of character. Even Boreas liked the Corin, although the big horse found something humorous about the mare and her rider. If the boy was treacherous or wicked, no Hunnuli would come within smelling distance of him.

Athlone had heard very recently that Lord Medb had tried to win a Hunnuli by capturing it and keeping it penned in a box canyon. As he understood the story, the horse had nearly killed Medb before throwing itself over a cliff, preferring death to serving the lord of the Wylfling clan. Athlone did not know how true the rumors were of Medb's injuries, but he was greatly saddened and not at all surprised by the Hunnuli's death.

Nevertheless, Athlone could not reconcile himself to Gabran's presence. Something was not right with the boy. There were too many little details in speech and movement that did not fit. What was he?

For a fleeting second, Athlone remembered the Shape Changers, the sorcerers of ancient legend who had learned shape changing to avoid punishment for practicing magic. He shuddered. But that was long ago. The heretical magic was dead and its followers died with it. It did not matter, though. The boy was no magician, simply a clansman with a secret that might prove dangerous to all.

Athlone found his spear and walked out of his tent to join the hunt for the lion. He could only hope that he would discover what the boy's secret was before it proved fatal for someone in the clan.

* * *

The huge doors of the hall were still open when Gabria returned from the fields. She entered the hall reluctantly and stood blinking at the sudden light. A fire was burning low in the pit and a few lamps still glowed from the ceiling beams. As she became accustomed to the light, the girl saw her pack and the new bow lying by the nearest pillar. Looking up, she saw several men already asleep on blankets and furs along the right-hand wall, beneath the colorful tapestries of Valorian's adventures. The storerooms were closed and the heavy curtain was drawn over the entrance to Savaric's private quarters. Four other men were sitting on the opposite side of the fire at a trestle table. Two were playing chess, one was watching, and the fourth was slumped over a wine flask.

Every clansman was entitled to a tent of his own once he reached manhood. The huge, black felt tents were made by the man's family and presented to him at the initiation of his warrior status. However, the tents were difficult to maintain, and it was usually the women who kept the fires burning, patched the holes, and kept the tents neat and pleasant. Most bachelors, therefore, chose to sleep in the hall. It was warm, relatively comfortable, and did not have to be packed every time they moved. They could eat there and entertain themselves long into the night without disturbing the treld.

Yet, despite the freedom and convenience of the hall, most men did not stay there long. Marriage and the tents, even with their numerous problems, were preferable to the conditions of bachelorhood. A man needed a woman, his own hearth, and the privacy of the felt walls. The clans survived because of unity and cooperation, but they retained their identity because each man valued his own individuality and the strength drawn from his home, even one that was packed into a cart every summer.

Gabria certainly did not feel at home in the strange, pillared hall. She was nervous being with these men in such close and intimate quarters. She could see at least one of the sleeping men was wearing nothing beneath his blankets. With her own family that would not have bothered her, for she was used to seeing men in various stages of undress. But here she had no brothers to defend her, no chieftain's quarters for security, and no protection as the chief's daughter. She had nothing but a disguise—and a flimsy one at that

Quietly, she slipped along to the right-hand wall to the gloomiest corner, away from the sleeping men. Gabria fervently hoped no one would notice her. If she could curl up in the blanket Piers had given her, perhaps they would not realize she was there.

"We have a new member in our illustrious ranks," a voice called out in a raucous tone. "Take note of him, men, a boy who has barely left his mother's breast and already he has lost his clan and killed our mares."

Gabria cringed at the words. Slowly she turned and stared at the speaker. It was Cor. He was sitting at the table, waving a wine cup in her direction. The other three men had previously ignored him, but now they watched in anticipation of some entertainment. Gabria turned her back on them and tried to disregard Cor's sniggers. Cor was swaying gently, but his voice was not broken or slurred.

"He sits on his great black horse and spits on us while he deafens the lords with his whining and pleas of innocence." Cor staggered toward the girl as the others watched in interest. Gabria listened apprehensively.

"But I know you. I can see what you keep hidden beneath your bold face."

Gabria stiffened and her eyes widened.

"You are a coward!" he hissed. He was so close to Gabria, his breath brushed her neck. "A spineless pile of sheep dung who fled his clan instead of standing and fighting. Or did you lead the attackers to the camp? You are so brave when you are sitting on that black horse, but how brave are you, worm, when you are low to the ground on two puny legs?" Viciously, Cor grabbed Gabria's shoulder and spun her around.

The girl stepped back against the wall, too terrified by the drunken rage that distorted Cor's features to run. The other warriors cheered them both and taunted Cor with bets and jibes. No one moved to help Gabria. Disgruntled yells came from the men who had been awakened. The shouts, jeers, and insults crashed together into an unnerving cacophony. Gabria threw her head back.

"Stop it!" she shouted. "Leave me alone."

"Leave me alone," Cor mocked. "Poor little worm is not so brave after all. He needs his mama. But she's dead and rotting with the other Corin." He rocked back and forth in front of Gabria, exuding wine fumes. His muscles seemed to bunch beneath his tunic.

Without warning, Cor slapped her. Gabria gazed at him speechlessly. "You brought the lion. It is your fault the mare died and I lost my duty. No one would listen to me . . . but you will. You are going to listen to me until you are crushed beneath my boot." He chuckled

at himself. Getting no reaction from Gabria, Cor hit her again savagely. She tried to avoid it, but she was too late. The blow sent her
reeling, and blood spattered her tunic from her split lip. The other
men looked on, neither helping nor hindering. Cor came at her again.

"Stop it!" Gabria cried, stumbling away from him. "Go away."

"Go away," he sneered. "Not for a while, my little man, not until
you crawl at my feet and plead for my forgiveness." He swung at her
again and smashed her in the face. Gabria crashed into the wall and
collapsed on the floor, her head ringing with pain, blood pouring from
her nose.

"Crawl, worm," Cor shouted gleefully. He kicked her in the side.
Waving to the others in victory, Cor stood over Gabria like a con-
queror, gloating at his prize. He reached down for her again.

Gabria was lying still, panting in shock and fear. Then she saw
Cor's hand coming. Deep within her emotional prisons, the frustration
and anxiety she had suffered the past few days fused together in a
furious surge of power. Unbeknownst to her, an aura began to glow
faintly around her hands as the white-hot energy of her emotions
burst outward to every muscle and nerve ending, overcoming her pain
and weakness. The power ignited in her eyes. She screamed like a cat.

Without a conscious thought, Gabria reached behind her shoulder
and grasped her new bow. The unseen aura in her hands flowed up
the weapon. Before Cor could react, she rolled off the bow and, with
both hands, swung it upward between his legs. The stave caught him
neatly in the groin. Just for a second, there was a burst of pale blue
sparks.

Cor howled in agony and doubled over. Gabria rolled away, stood
up, and crouched, her bow held before her like an axe. But Cor could
barely move. He slowly toppled to the ground and lay curled in a ball,
moaning. As the warriors moved to him, Gabria backed into the corner, still gripping her bow and trembling with rage. Her green eyes
glinted dangerously.

"Nicely swung, boy," one of the warriors said with a grin.

"Cor won't be riding for a day or two," added another man. "Especially the wenches." They all laughed uproariously.

Gabria stared at them speechlessly. The warriors shook their
heads and left her alone while they picked up their whimpering companion and tossed him unceremoniously on his blanket. Then, the
sleepers returned to sleep, the chess players continued their game,
and a subdued quiet settled over the hall—all as if nothing had hap-

pened. Only Cor's soft moaning was out of place in the illusion of friendly peace.

Gabria stood in her corner without moving. Her anger and the pale blue aura that no one had noticed subsided, leaving her drained and empty. She dared not move for fear of disturbing the fragile peace.

Gabria knew fist fights and brawls happened constantly in the hall, often just for the fun of competition. But the violence and hatred of Cor's attack was not part of the camaraderie. He blamed his disgrace on her and wanted his revenge. Gabria glanced at Cor, as if he might jump on her again, but he remained curled like an infant, whimpering and weeping. She dreaded to think what Cor would do when he recovered. He did not have the manner of a man who forgave readily.

Gabria shuddered and sank to her knees. Maybe she should accept Athlone's tent. At least he would not beat her. No, she reminded herself sharply, he will kill me if I reveal my identity, and it will be much more difficult to hide in the confines of a tent. But is it safer here with more ears to listen and eyes to watch? Safer with Cor's dagger within easy reach of my heart? Oh, gods, what am I going to do? Either choice could mean death.

The girl clutched her blanket about her shoulders, thankful for its warm comfort, and huddled into the corner. Her face felt horrible—swollen and caked with blood—but she was not going to move from her corner. She was safe there, for the night at least. Perhaps she could decide what to do tomorrow. Cor might decide to leave her alone, although she doubted it, or perhaps her goddess would provide a way to protect her. Amara had always been with her. Gabria took solace in that, and, after a long while, when the fire had died down, she fell asleep.

Gabria awoke long before dawn. In the deepest hour of the night, she dreamed of a blue fire in the core of her mind. She tried to banish it, but it was a part of her and it would not be denied. It grew in intensity and surged outward from her hands, taking the form of a lightning bolt that seared a path through the surrounding darkness and burned with the vengeance of a dying star. Unerring, it struck a half-seen figure of a man and burst him into countless flaming fragments.

Gabria bolted awake in horror. She knew without question what that deadly flare had been. Sorcery. She cringed as she gazed at her hands in the dim light of the single lamp that still burned. She vaguely expected to see a glow of blue still on her fingers where the bolt had sprung.

How could it be? Why had she dreamed of magic? She knew nothing about the arcane except the half-truths of legends and the clan strictures that forbade its profane use. Sorcery had been eradicated generations ago and anyone guilty of trying to resurrect it was put to immediate death. So where had that dream sprung from? Gabria had never considered using such power, and she did not think wielding magic was an inherent ability.

Since birth, Gabria had been taught that sorcery was an evil heresy. The priests claimed sorcery was an abominable sham of the gods' power, an insult to the deities and the cause of hideous retribution upon anyone who tried to use it.

Gabria shuddered at the memory of her dream. It was impossible that she could create that blue fire herself. She did not have the knowledge or desire to do so. Yet why had she dreamed of that power now? She sat frozen in a crouch, musing over the fading images of her dream, very afraid of falling asleep and dreaming again.

When the horn of morning faintly echoed in the hall, Gabria was still awake. The warriors rose from sleep, laughing, yawning, and grumbling. They rolled their gear out of sight, into a storeroom behind a tapestry, and prepared themselves for another day. A serving girl brought cups of steaming wine and heaps of meat-stuffed rolls. Gabria remained still.

Athlone, back from the night's hunt, found her as she had been most of the night, hunched in the corner beneath her blanket, her eyes fixed on something in the distance. The wer-tain breezed into the room, smelling of morning dew and horse's sweat, and greeted the men. He saw Gabria in the corner and anger pulled at his mouth. Muttering a curse, he ripped off the blanket and yanked her to her feet.

"I warned you about shirking . . ." His voice trailed off as she slumped against him and he saw the bruises and dried blood on her battered face. She feebly pushed against him and tried to stand alone, but a searing pain melted her ankle. With a moan she could not stop, she fell to the floor. Sometime during the fight with Cor, she had wrenched her barely healed ankle again.

"What happened?" A look of pity intruded into Athlone's stony eyes.

"I fell down the steps last night," Gabria answered listlessly. She shoved against the wall and painfully levered herself to a standing position. She teetered on one foot, glaring at the wer-tain, daring him to gainsay her.

The pity faded and Athlone turned to the warriors who were watching as they ate. "What happened?" he repeated harshly.

One man jerked a thumb at Cor, who was still lying curled on his bed, apparently asleep. Athlone's brow lifted, and he strode over to the recumbent warrior. He leaned over to shake Cor's shoulder. At the first touch, his hand leaped back as if scorched.

"Good gods," Athlone said in astonishment. "This man is burning with fever. Tabran, call the healer quickly." Then he remembered Gabria standing in the corner with blood on her face, and his nagging suspicions turned to a noisy warning. But he still was not sure why.

"The rest of you men get to your duties," Athlone ordered. "Now."

The men glanced at each other uneasily, and fetching their weapons, filed out the door. Athlone stayed by Cor. The wer-tain's face was bleak and his body was tense with his unnamed suspicions.

"I am going to ask you again," he said without turning around. "What happened?"

Gabria heard the change in his voice immediately. He suspected something strange had happened between her and Cor. "I hit him with a bow," she snapped.

"Why?"

"I should think that is obvious, Wer-tain." Piers's voice came from the entrance. "Just look at him. The boy was being beaten."

Athlone and Gabria turned to the healer as he came into the hall. "I asked the boy," Athlone said, rankled by the man's immediate defense of Gabria. "I want to know what happened to Cor."

"I know what you meant." Piers's pale eyes were like the clouds of a winter storm as he helped Gabria to the fire pit and made her sit on the stone rim.

Gabria watched the two men surreptitiously. Even through her listlessness and pain, she could recognize the signs of a long-lived dislike between the healer and the wer-tain. Piers's movements were hurried and brusque. It was as if he could not wait to be away from Athlone's demanding presence. Athlone, on the other hand, seemed to be edgy and impatient dealing with the quiet foreigner. Gabria found Athlone's discomfort interesting, and she drew closer to Piers's supporting arm.

Athlone glared at them both, annoyed that the boy had found

such a quick ally in the healer. "The boy will live. I called you here to
see to Cor."

"If Gabran lives, it will not be because of your efforts. I asked you
to go easy on him yesterday until he recovered, but you deliberately
ran him into the ground." Piers squeezed Gabria's shoulder and went
to examine the unconscious warrior. The healer's mouth opened
slightly in surprise when he touched Cor. He quickly straightened out
the man's body and checked him over carefully.

"How strange. I have never seen anything quite like this," Piers
said worriedly. "What did you say happened to him?"

Athlone gestured to Gabria. "He hit him with a bow."

"Certainly a mere blow could not have caused this." Piers checked
Cor again, and a small frown creased his forehead. "Hmmm. I wonder
. . . have some men take him to my tent."

Athlone called the guard and gave his orders. He asked Piers,
"What is wrong with him?"

"I am not sure. He has a high fever, among other things, but this
is something quite unusual. Gabran, you had better come, too."

"He has work to do," Athlone said flatly.

The healer shook his head. "Not today. Not in his condition."

"Your defense of him is misplaced, Healer. He can obviously care
for himself," Athlone stated as he picked up Gabria's fallen bow.

Gabria could not look at Cor. She stared at the floor, and the
memory of her dream returned like a hidden shame. A pang of guilt
made her shiver, but she could not believe it was possible that the
dream held any truth. She had only hit Cor with a wooden bow, not
magic. There was something else wrong with him, something very easy
to explain.

"The healer is right, Athlone," a woman's voice came from the
back of the hall.

"Good morning, Mother." Athlone smiled at the small, fair-
haired woman standing by the curtain to the chieftain's quarters.

"Good morning, son, Piers, and you, Gabran. I am Tungoli, lady
of Lord Savaric."

Gabria returned her greeting and, for the first time since she
came to Khulinin Treld, she felt that she was meeting a friend.
Tungoli's eyes were as open and as green as summer, and her expression was warm and smiling. She was a comely woman whose true age
was hidden by a gentle beauty that grew old with grace and radiated
from her contentment within. Her hair was braided and wound with a
dark gold veil. Her hands were slender, yet strong and confident. She

walked toward them with a loose-jointed stride that swirled her green skirt about her feet.

"The boy needs rest," Tungoli said to Athlone. "There is no sense having two warriors ill. But," she added soothingly, cutting off Athlone's next words, "if you insist he stay busy, I have a few things he can help me with." She slipped her arm through Athlone's and led him aside, continuing to talk to him all the while.

Piers sighed, an audible sound Gabria barely caught, and he shook his head. "Tungoli and Savaric are the only ones Athlone bows to," he said softly to Gabria. "Tread carefully around him."

Several men arrived then and helped Piers lift Cor's body onto a makeshift stretcher. The healer said, "Wait here, Gabran. I'll send them back for you."

In the corner of her eye, Gabria saw Athlone watching them, and her pride dragged her to her feet. The pain sucked the breath through her teeth. "No. I'll come now," she managed to gasp.

"Do not be long about it," Athlone demanded.

Tungoli lifted her eyes to her son in mild reproof. "Athlone, your thoughtlessness is atrocious. Gabran, let them come for you. When the healer is through with you, come to see me."

"Mother, you are interfering again."

"I know. But if I do not, who will? The entire treld is terrified of you," she said, laughter in her voice.

Gabria collapsed on the stone rim again and gazed at the woman thankfully. Tungoli reminded Gabria of her own mother, in a vague, comforting way, and it would be delightful to spend some time with this lady and be out from under Athlone's iron hand.

Piers nodded to Gabria and followed the stretcher bearers out the door. Gabria did not respond, for she was too engrossed watching Tungoli and Athlone. The small woman looked so incongruous standing up to the tall, muscular warrior, but Gabria was certain the mother won most of their battles. In her own gentle way, Tungoli was just as stubborn as Athlone.

"All right, all right. The boy is yours for as long as you need him. Just don't spoil him," Athlone exclaimed.

Tungoli crossed her arms and nodded. "Of course."

Gabria felt as if a great weight had been taken from her shoulders. She was free from Athlone for a time and she was free of Cor long enough to gather her wits. Gabria still had to decide where she was going to sleep in the future, and she wanted to consider her dream. Perhaps Piers could help her understand. Being from Pra

Desh, he would not have the horror of sorcery any clansman would. Maybe the healer would talk to her and give her some reassurance that her dream had been only a figment of her imagination.

Gabria still felt unreasonably guilty for Cor's sudden illness. Although she was certain it was not her fault, she could not forget the flare of blue power that struck from her hands with such deadly swiftness, or the nameless fear in her heart that there was a connection between the fight and her dream.

"Come on, boy." Athlone walked to her side. "I'll get you to the healer and back before my mother starts on another speech."

To Gabria's surprise, he slipped her arm over his shoulder and helped her up. Gabria was too stunned by his move to object. Speechless, she looked at Athlone from a few inches away. He met her eyes and, for the first time, his brown eyes did not clash with her green. The wer-tain gave her a sketchy smile, and they moved out the door.

6

Rain was falling when Athlone and Gabria left the hall, a cold, steady drizzle that soaked through clothes in minutes and chilled everything into a lethargy. The low-slung clouds moved sluggishly over the mountains, as if they too were reluctant to hurry on. Gabria closed her eyes, not wanting to see the dismal dawn, and leaned wearily into Athlone.

His gesture of help surprised her. She would have expected him to urge her out with the flat of his sword rather than the strength of his arm.

"The healer was right. Cor beat you badly," Athlone said, looking at Gabria from only a headspan away.

The girl quickly turned her face away. If he was this close and watching her so intently, he could notice details she did not want him to see, like the smoothness of her cheek. There was no dirt to disguise her skin and not enough tan to hide the softness of her face at such a close range. The bruises helped, but the wer-tain was beginning to look puzzled.

Gabria deliberately stumbled and slammed into Athlone's calves as she fell. He lost his balance, tripped over a tent rope, and fell on top of her. Gabria froze in fright. His weight crushed her into the mud, but it was nothing compared to the fear of what he might discover as he lay on top of her. She had not meant to bring him down like this!

"I'm sorry, Wer-tain," she blurted from under a tangle of cloaks and swords. Athlone moved off her. Every bruise and ache in Gabria's body complained. It took all the willpower she had to control a cry of pain. The warrior stood up and offered a hand to her. Once again the wer-tain surprised her—he was laughing.

She staggered up and looked down at herself ruefully. Athlone would never cease to amaze her. Instead of berating her for her clumsiness, he was laughing like it was a joke. They were both covered with mud—at least she did not have to worry about her face for the moment—yet he was not angry. Thank the gods he had not put his hands in the wrong places.

"Keep this up, boy, and you will not live long enough to claim your weir-geld," Athlone said.

She smiled shakily at him and replied, "I will have my revenge if I have to crawl to Medb and stab him in the knees."

"No one has tried that yet." Athlone took her weight again and his humor disappeared. "You are the most stubborn whelp I have known. That trait is infuriating, but it can be a good advantage." He lapsed into silence, and they crossed the distance to Piers's tent in thoughtful quiet.

The healer's eyes widened as they came in, whether in surprise at Athlone's action or at their appearance, Gabria could not guess, for he only motioned to a water skin and bent back over his patient.

Gabria felt an unexpected warmth for the wer-tain at her side. It was the first sign of friendship he had offered since she had arrived, and the coldness in her heart retreated a pace as Athlone sat her down on the low stool, poured a bowl of water, and handed it to her with a rag.

Athlone paused at the tent flap before he left. A streak of mud creased his face and dyed half of his mustache. More mud was smeared on his gold cloak and down his legs. His soft boots were caked. "When you are through here, go to the Lady Tungoli. But do not expect to be coddled by her for long. I will be waiting for you." The wer-tain's voice turned glacial again. The veiled threats had returned.

Gabria stared after the warrior as the dark flap closed behind him. It was as if their moment of companionship had never happened. The wer-tain's suspicions closed around her again like a trap. The girl shivered. For just a moment, she had nourished a hope that he would leave her alone or maybe help her as Nara suggested. But his confusing manipulations leaped ahead of her and blocked her speculation like a granite cliff.

"The wer-tain is an interesting man," Piers said.

Gabria tore her gaze from the entrance and watched the healer as he worked swiftly over Cor. "Do you always know what I am thinking?"

"It does not take a mindreader to interpret that look on your face. You are overwhelmed by the good chieftain's son." He shook his head. "You are not the only one."

"I noticed you are not comfortable with him," Gabria noted dryly.

"No. Athlone has a strong presence. Savaric rules the clan, but Athlone is its mettle. Where he goes, the werod follows. Not even Pazric, the second wer-tain, wields the immediate obedience of the riders."

Gabria stretched her legs out to ease her ankle to a more comfortable position and dabbed half-heartedly at the mud on her face, considering Piers's words all the while. Cor was lying motionless on the mat she had slept on, his face still captured in pain. Piers was wrapping the warrior's body in warm blankets.

"Who is Pazric?" she asked when the silence had gone on too long.

"He is Athlone's second in command," Piers replied.

"I do not remember him."

"He is in the south, meeting with one of the Turic caravans."

"Does the werod always follow Athlone without question?" Gabria asked. She was trying to think of some way to lead the conversation around to her dream and Cor's condition. As repugnant as the answer might be, she had to know if there was any connection. The dream was such a strange coincidence, and only Piers would have the openness of mind to help her understand it.

"I realize you and Athlone do not approve of each other. It takes time to know him." Piers shrugged as he stood up. "Even that may not help. But don't ever go against his authority, or the entire werod will tear you to pieces." The healer removed some items from his chest of medicines and poured a small heap of dark gray grains into a mortar. As he ground the grains, a pungent smell filled the tent. It reminded Gabria of cloves, and she inhaled deeply.

Piers worked for several minutes before he spoke again. "What happened between Cor and you? May I assume he started it?"

"I don't know," Gabria muttered, feeling guilty again. "He wanted a fight with me, for what happened in the fields last night."

Piers added a few dried leaves to his powder and continued grinding, his robe swaying gently with his movements. "You are not accustomed to fighting, are you?"

Gabria stiffened. "What do you mean?" she asked carefully.

"It's obvious. You are beaten bloody and he does not have a mark on him. You won by luck . . . or something else." When Gabria did not answer, he laid the pestle down and turned to face her. His pale eyes were sad, but his face had a strange look of wariness. "Do you know what is wrong with this man?" His words were soft, but edged with steel.

Gabria felt as if her mind would shrivel into dust. A cold fear clenched her stomach and her breath failed even as she drew it. Piers obviously thought Cor's condition was not just a simple illness. All the terrors of her dream surged back in the face of his unspoken accusation. "No," she whispered. The word escaped her lips and leaped at his silence. "What have I done to him?" she cried, clenching her fists to her sides.

"So you admit this injury was caused by you."

Gabria stared at the healer miserably. "I don't know what I caused. I only hit him with a bow . . . but later I had a dream of a blue flame that sprang from my hands and struck a man. I don't know why I would dream of something like that. All I did was hit Cor to make him stop beating me." She suddenly stopped the flood of words, then took a deep breath and asked, "What is wrong with him?"

"I am not certain either," Piers said quietly. "I have a very good idea, if I can only believe it."

Gabria hunched over as if a pain stabbed her stomach. "What?"

"He has suffered a severe shock. He has a high fever and rapid heart beat. Unusual symptoms for a mere blow to the groin."

"Will you just tell me?" Gabria cried.

"No." Piers strode over to her side and leaned over her, no longer hiding his anger. "You tell me, Gabran. You only hit him with a wooden bow, you say, but this man has been wounded by an arcane power called the Trymian Force. Where did it come from?" Abruptly, his hands dug into her shoulder, and he hauled her to her feet. She swayed, staring at him in dumb dismay. "That man may die, and I want to know why. Did your power come from Medb?"

The sound of that name galvanized Gabria like a shock. She wrenched away from the healer and grasped the center tent pole for support. "I received nothing from Lord Medb but death, and that is all he will receive from me," Gabria gasped, shaking with anger.

Piers eyed her dubiously, his arms crossed. He wanted to believe the boy was not an agent of Medb, yet the Wylfling lord was the only one rumored to be delving into sorcery and Gabran was the only one

Piers knew of who had struck Cor in the past day. "Then how is it that Cor suffers from the Trymian Force?"

"I don't know! I don't even know what you are talking about." She leaned into the pole, her eyes beseeching him. "I didn't want to hurt him. I just wanted him to leave me alone."

Piers watched her expressions and was satisfied. The boy was telling the truth about this at least. After years at the court in Pra Desh, he had learned to recognize truth and deceit hidden in people's faces. The green eyes that met his were free of guile. Piers saw only bewilderment and a desperate plea to be believed.

The healer sighed as he stared into those eyes. Before, Piers could not have said what color they were; now he knew they were as green as the sea with the same subtle lights and the same feeling of power. He shook his head, surprised by the depth of Gabria's gaze. It seemed to the healer that even if the boy did not have a talent for magic, he certainly had the inner strength to wield it.

"All right, sit down," he ordered. He poured a cup of warm wine into which he added a small dose of poppy extract. "Here, drink this."

Gabria glared at him and did not move. "What is it, a truth drug?"

"No, boy. Now sit down. It will dull the pain so I can examine your ankle."

Gabria hesitantly accepted the cup and returned to the stool. Piers's attitude had changed. The suspicion was gone from his voice and had been replaced by a tone of resignation. She wondered what conclusion he had reached. It was difficult to read this city-bred man, for he kept himself behind an unbreakable facade—motionless features, still eyes, and a modest manner. He had none of the unrestrained character of the steppe clans. The endless, wild, easily given emotions of the clanspeople were alien to Piers's way of life. Nevertheless, the healer had abandoned his lifestyle and sought a new life on the plains. Whether he did this to forget his past or to find a new existence, Gabria did not know, but she wished she knew what had made him leave Pra Desh. The answer might explain much.

Gabria left her drink on the table for the moment and watched as Piers continued grinding the powder. Neither spoke. The healer seemed content to let the problem settle for a while and rationality return before taking the next leap. Gabria was relieved by his silence. The acknowledgment of the possibility of sorcery was made. But now that it was said, she was not sure she wanted to know if she was the source of that magic. It was enough to have to bear the weight of her grief and the need for revenge, without the fearsome burden of a heretical power she did not even want. No, she implored silently, gripping her hands. It had to be impossible. Sorcery was learned, not an inherent talent.

Piers laid aside the bowl and opened his medicine chest again. The large wooden chest, the only thing he had brought from Pra Desh, was filled with a myriad of drawers and trays. Gabria noticed each one was crammed with packets, bags, vials, bottles, boxes, wrapped bundles, and scraps of paper, all clearly labeled. The healer poked through several drawers, then, from one of the smaller trays, he drew out a smooth red stone the size of an eagle's egg. He juggled it several times before he spoke.

"Forty years ago, when I was an apprentice to the senior physician of the fon of Pra Desh, I met an old man in the market square. He claimed he was the son of a clansman and had been exiled because he accidentally murdered a cousin with sorcery. He had escaped death only by fleeing before anyone caught him."

Gabria stared at the stone in the healer's hand. "Why are you telling me this?"

"Because the man was a Corin."

She came alert. "You lie," the girl snapped, though she said it with more hope than conviction.

Piers shook his head. "My master was a fancier of magic and studied the history of its use. He thoroughly examined this man and confirmed the truth. The Corin, who had no training and had never witnessed a performance of sorcery, had been born with a talent to call the powers to his bidding."

Gabria felt numb. Whether she wanted it or not, the truth was coming out. Somewhere she would have to find the strength to face the awful possibility that she could be a sorceress. "What is the Trymian Force?" she asked. The fear in her voice threatened to spill into tears.

Piers saw the tense lines that altered the boy's face. There was a stubborn dimension to that face that showed his strength and will to survive. He had noticed it before, and now it was very apparent in the clenched jaw, the tight muscles around the mouth, and in the way the boy did not hide from the truth. It was good. Gabran would need every advantage to live to the next wintering. The healer knelt by Cor and stared at the warrior. A tremor moved beneath Cor's jaw where the blood raced under the skin, and the heat of his fever beaded into sweat on his forehead.

"The spell," Piers said slowly, as if remembering a long forgotten passage, "is the marshaling of the different flows of energy that constitute magic into one destructive force that can penetrate most defenses. It often appears as a blue flame. It is only as strong as the person who wields it, but if it is not controlled, it can appear as an automatic reflex in times of intense emotion."

"I do not understand. Do you believe this force came from me?" Gabria asked quietly.

"It's possible that it originated from someone else in the room, but that is unlikely," he replied.

"Piers, I know nothing about this sorcery. How could I have cast a spell of any kind?"

Piers looked straight at Gabria and said, "There are only two ways. If Medb did not give the ability to you, then your ancestors did."

"No, it cannot be," Gabria cried, her voice edged with fear.

Piers gripped the stone and rubbed his chin with his free hand. "I am a stubborn old man, Gabran. I see something I do not understand and I try to force an answer because I am afraid. You are the only answer I see. If you did not use the Trymian Force, even inadvertently, than the alternative is beyond my understanding. I am not certain there was sorcery. Only this can tell us." He held up the stone to the firelight and watched the warm glow of color spread over his hands like blood.

"My master told me once the steppe clans long ago produced the greatest sorcerers because they were empathetic to the primal forces that govern magic. He believed wholeheartedly that the ability to draw on that power was an inherited talent." He paused and then said, "Unfortunately, the legends of those years are hazy with time and prejudice. After the destruction of the city of Moy Tura and the persecution of the sorcerers, no one wanted to remember where the talent came from."

In Piers's hand, the large stone began to flare suddenly. For a moment, Gabria thought it was just the flicker of firelight reflected in the gem's opaque interior. But the radiance brightened, driving out the opacity until the stone shone with a scarlet luminosity and crowded out the light of day and fire. The entire tent filled with the ruddy gleam.

"Now we know. Fasten the tent flap," Piers ordered. He held the stone gingerly over Cor's face as brilliant flashes flared out of the stone in radial bursts.

Gabria limped to obey and tied the fastenings tight with trembling fingers. She moved to the healer's side and watched in fearful awe. The rays of light from the stone seemed to probe into the warrior's head. "What does that stone do? What is it?" she whispered.

Piers answered slowly. "I do not know exactly what it is, only what it does." A weak smile touched his mouth. "I have never had to use it before."

"Will it help him?"

"I hope so. My old master gave it to me before he died. He said it was a healing stone that could only be activated by the presence of magic. The stone is supposed to remove all traces of magic from an injured person."

Piers laid the stone on Cor's forehead, and they watched in silence. The direction of the light beams focused into a downward spray that danced over Cor's face. Gabria noticed in amazement that the rays did not illuminate his skin, but sank into it like bright needles. She felt she ought to be horrified by this display of blatant heresy and leave before she was tainted further, but she held back and watched the light with an unacknowledged fascination.

The stone was beautiful and, if it could heal, it was a positive good—a denial of everything she had been led to believe about magic. Maybe sorcery was more complicated and multifaceted than she had imagined, with aspects both good and evil and every shade in between. Her mind boggled at such a revelation. Sorcery was supposed to be totally evil, a dark power that corrupted men into acts of hideous cruelty and depravity. It hardly seemed possible magic could also be helpful. She pushed the uncomfortable thoughts away and wondered instead how a healer could tell when the stone had finished its work.

As if to answer her question, a blue haze—the remnants of the Trymian Force in Cor's body—began to form around the warrior's head. The glow was pale at first, as indistinct as cold breath, then it brightened and thickened. The red stone blazed fiercely. The bloody light spread out over the blue haze and immobilized it in a prison of beams. Gradually, the red light began to recede into the stone's core, pulling the haze with it. The blue force seemed to struggle, bursting through its bonds with tiny blasts of purple. The red light grew stronger, and it finally dragged the last tendrils of the blue haze into the stone. There was a flash of violet and the light snapped out. The stone rested, dull and opaque, on Cor's forehead. His body shuddered and relaxed into sleep, and the grimace of pain on his face slackened into peace. Piers picked up the stone and gently wiped the sweat from his patient's skin.

"What happened?" Gabria breathed. She was shaken by the display. Until that moment, magic had been so vague to her, something obscure, something she could only guess at. Now, it was a tangible truth. Its power, whether good or evil, did exist.

"The stone seems to have worked," Piers replied. He could not hide his intense relief. "Cor is resting peacefully. His fever is down, too."

Gabria abruptly sat down on the stool. She could hardly believe what had just taken place. Her throat was dry, and, without thinking, she gulped down the contents of the wine cup on the table. In just a moment, a dull heat crept out of her stomach and slowly seeped into her limbs. She grew very sleepy. She had forgotten about the poppy extract.

The girl squinted woozily at Piers. "Will Cor be all right?" she asked thickly.

"He should recover. What he needs now is sleep." Piers returned the stone to its wrapping and placed it back in the chest. "I hope I never have to use that again." He did not look at Gabria, but gathered the contents of his mortar into a small bowl and added hot water to make a tea. He gently spooned the liquid down Cor's throat. When he was satisfied with the warrior's comfort, he opened his tent flap and turned to Gabria.

Piers was surprised to see her sitting on the stool again, leaning against the center tent pole. Her legs were thrust out in front of her and her eyes were dulled with drug and exhaustion. Without speaking, the healer eased the laces on her boot and carefully removed it. He tried not to jar the puffy flesh of her injured ankle. The joint was purple and red, and still tainted green from the original injury. He twisted it slowly, feeling the tendons and torn muscles beneath the soft skin.

Piers glanced up at his patient's face. The drug had relaxed Gabria's muscles, so her expression was slack and unwary. At that moment, the sun came out from behind the clouds, and the bright light poured through the open tent flap and illuminated her face.

Piers's hands froze; his body stiffened. Unbelieving, he wrenched his eyes from the face to the slim ankle in his hands, and the realization hit him like a blow. Gabria was gazing into the distance and did not see his horrified recognition. The medicine had dimmed her awareness and was carrying her to sleep. She did not even remember he was there.

Piers rocked back on his heels and wondered why he, of all people, had not seen it before. This enigmatic "boy" with the uncanny talent for magic and the companionship of a Hunnuli, was now even more inexplicable. A thousand questions hid her background, and Piers was only now beginning to understand a fraction of them. He thought back upon some of their previous conversations and the information he had heard from other clan members. He marveled at her skill in acting. It was a miracle of the gods' hands, if he cared to admit it, that this girl had survived so long undetected.

The healer considered telling Savaric, even though he knew the penalty for the girl's transgressions would be death. Gabran, or whatever her name was, had committed one of the most serious crimes in clan law by entering a werod in disguise, and, if the incident of sorcery were to be known, there would be no mercy. As a Pra Deshian, however, Piers did not share the clans' hatred for magic. Nevertheless, he had lived with the clans for ten years and their laws and customs were his. If he failed to reveal this girl's crimes, he would be just as guilty as she and would suffer the same punishment.

Piers began to move toward the tent flap. There would be warriors nearby who could fetch Savaric. In a few moments it would be over. With luck, Gabran would die before the poppy wore off. Then, the Corin would be gone, the Hunnuli would leave, and the magic would be ended. Piers's duty to his people would be fulfilled. The healer's hand felt for the opening.

"Father?" a weak voice whispered.

Piers stopped, and he realized with surprise that he was shaking.

"Father, don't go. I'm so afraid." The voice came again like a frightened child. A familiar echo of grief and despair woke memories Piers thought he had banished. Aching, he turned around, half expecting to see another girl with long blond hair and pale blue eyes, instead of a tall, dirty figure slumped on the stool. Gabria's eyes were closed and her head had fallen forward. Her cloak was on the floor, and her bare foot looked incongruous against the rest of her clothing. She was shivering.

"Father, what is all this blood?" she whimpered. Her fingers twitched as if she had touched something repulsive. "It is all over everything. Father, please don't leave me!"

Piers picked up the cloak and wrapped it around her shoulders. She cuddled into it and sighed. "I'm so cold. Where is Gabran?"

The healer listened sadly as she mumbled on about her family and the scenes she remembered of their murders. The images of their deaths mingled with his own memories of another painful death. Long ago he had run away from Pra Desh, carrying his unpurged grief and rage with him—and the guilt that he had failed his own daughter. He looked down at the girl, the last Corin in the clans, and wondered if he was being given a chance to atone for his failures. Ten years ago, he had been weak and had followed his lord's command, against his better judgment. As a result, his daughter had died, and he had done nothing to save her. Now he had a chance to save this girl.

He picked her up and laid her gently on his mat behind the curtains. He bound her ankle in cold cloths and went to heat water for a hot pack. Piers could understand why the Khulinin had accepted the exile, despite their reluctance. There were too many conflicting sides to the Corin's tale. Now, he added his own motives. The girl was an outcast, like himself, yet she had survived so much with courage and intelligence. She deserved a chance, not a betrayal. He would simply take his chances with Savaric's wrath if—no, *when*—the Khulinin discovered the girl's secret.

It was late in the afternoon when Gabria awoke. She lay on the warm bed, feeling more comfortable and peaceful than she had in many days.

Then she heard pots rattling, and she opened her eyes. Cream curtains met her startled gaze. The memories of the past days returned in a deluge. It was all true—the massacre, the search for the Khulinin, Nara, the death of the mare, and the fight with Cor were all painfully real. She sighed.

"Piers?" Gabria called.

The curtains were thrown back and the healer stood beside her. "Good afternoon, Gabran," Piers said, his face carefully masked.

Gabria's eyes widened. "Afternoon? How long have I slept?"

"Only a few hours."

"Oh, no. Lady Tungoli—"

"She is the one who ordered me to let you sleep as long as necessary. Athlone led another hunting party after the lion."

Gabria carefully sat up and gingerly moved her ankle. It was tightly bound, but the swelling was noticeably less and she could move it some without pain. Piers gave her a hand and she stood up. She hobbled to the stool. The healer gave her soup, bread, and cheese. The girl inhaled the rich smell of the soup and suddenly realized how hungry she was.

When Gabria was finished eating, she pushed the plates away and relaxed with a full stomach. She looked over to the pallet to see Cor still sleeping comfortably under the blankets. His face seemed free of pain, and there was no sign of the incredible magic that had invaded his body.

"How is Cor?" she finally asked.

Piers was cutting a slice of bread for himself and he glanced over at the warrior. "I am sure he will live, but he will never take a wife." He felt pity for the young man. The blow from Gabran's bow and the arcane force had probably ruined Cor's sexual manhood. The man was an ill-tempered fool, but he did not deserve the stigma of impotency.

Gabria stared at the ground for a long while. She had so many thoughts and memories and emotions raging inside her mind, she could not think. She had no idea what to do next.

After a time, Piers came over and sat on another stool by the table. Gabria looked up at him. "What will you tell Savaric?" she asked, trying to keep her voice level.

The healer's long hands played with a crust of bread. His face looked old and tired. "I have been trying to think all afternoon of what I will say."

Gabria was pale, for she knew at this moment her life was in the healer's hands. By law, Piers must accuse her of sorcery to the clan chieftain and leave her fate to the chief and his elders. But if he did so, Piers would risk himself, for he had used the magic in the healing stone. It was a ticklish decision, and Gabria could not even guess what the healer would do. "Have you thought of something?" she inquired as calmly as possible.

"At the moment, I will simply tell him Cor was ill from complications of his injury from the fight, but that he is recovering now." Piers lifted an eyebrow. "Will that be sufficient?"

A faint sigh escaped Gabria's lips. She nodded quickly. "Thank you."

Piers leaned forward, his hands on the table edge. "But we still have to face the fact that Cor was struck by a magic power."

Gabria tensed. "I know!" she said. "I agree he was injured by something more than my bow. But you have no proof I did it! I do not know where the power came from and neither do you."

"I know, but—"

Gabria jumped up, knocking over the stool. Her fears and emotions crowded in on her until she wanted to scream. She had to get out of the tent, go somewhere and collect her wits. She had to think. "No. Enough. Whatever happened, it will never happen again."

Piers came around the table and grasped her arm. "You don't

know that," he exclaimed. "If you have this talent for sorcery, it will
not go away. It will always be there, waiting for some spark to set it off
again."

"*If.* You only say *if,*" Gabria shouted. "You do not know for certain. Even if I had this ability, what could I do about it?" She limped
to the entrance, hoping to escape before the healer could say any
more.

"Gabran," Piers said quietly.

Gabria cut him short. "Thank you for your help, Healer. I am
grateful." Then she ducked out and fled.

The rain had stopped some time earlier, and the clouds were
breaking into huge, fluffy islands. The sun poured through every rent
and covered the hills with moving patches of light and shadow. A fresh
breeze blew up to Gabria from the steppes beyond Khulinin Treld.
She took a deep breath. The invigorating coolness relaxed her a little
and helped her sort out her thoughts enough to know what she wanted
to do that moment. She wanted to find Nara.

The girl pushed her shorn hair back and hobbled down the path
between the big tents, toward the far pastures. Nara was probably out
there, grazing, and Gabria wanted desperately to be near the comforting strength of the Hunnuli.

Most of the men were gone from the treld, hunting the lion, but
many of the women were out of the tents, enjoying the bright sun. No
one acknowledged Gabria as she passed, so she hurried on, trying not
to feel the loneliness and self-pity that reared up inside of her.

By the time she reached the picket lines at the edge of the treld,
she was limping badly again. She stopped to rest. In the fields before
her, several men were training young horses. Another group of warriors was practicing archery. Gabria balked at the thought of crossing
to the pastures, because she would need agility and speed to pass
through all of the activity without getting in the way. At the moment,
she had neither.

She watched the archers for a moment as they sent their mounts
in a full gallop across the grass. As one, they roared a ferocious cry,
wheeled their horses, fired a barrage of arrows over their backs at a
target, and retreated, whooping with glee, to the starting point. Gabria
watched the strange maneuver in surprise. It was a difficult one, re-
quiring skill with horse and bow, and timing. The warriors had performed it flawlessly, and the target was riddled, witnessing to their
accuracy.

"They are getting good," someone said behind her.

Gabria turned her head and saw Jorlan, the night commander of the outriders, standing beside the farrier's tent a few paces away. He was holding the halter of a snappish filly. The farrier, a burly man with huge hands, had the filly's foreleg clamped between his thighs and was trimming a hoof.

"Where did they learn to do that?" she asked.

"It is part of some new tactics Athlone is teaching. He learned it from the Turic raiders, who are masters of the hit and run," Jorlan replied.

Gabria glanced back at the archers who were lining up for another run. "Why should a clan this size have to worry about raiding tactics?"

Jorlan pursed his lips and patted the filly's neck. "Lord Medb is growing very powerful. He is pulling other clans to him or dealing with them as he did the Corin. We are not invincible. Before summer is out, I believe there will be war."

The farrier snorted, a sound not unlike his horses'. "Lord Medb is a fool. He cannot hope to control the entire grasslands or the clans. He will burn out soon."

"Maybe," Jorlan said thoughtfully. "As long as he does not scorch us in his passing."

The farrier laughed, startling the filly. "Stand still, you girl," he soothed. "You fret more than my wife."

"Have you seen the Hunnuli?" Gabria asked. She did not want to discuss Medb. The treld was closing in on her and she wanted to run.

Jorlan gestured to the river. "I think she is by the river. You did well last night. I am sorry about Cor," he added as an afterthought.

"So am I," Gabria shot back, irritated by the reminder of that incident. She did not want to think about last night until she was clear of the treld. She swung around, put her fingers to her lips, and gave a piercing whistle. She waited for a moment, wondering if Nara had heard.

Then came a thundering neigh in answer to her summons. The call reverberated through Khulinin Treld like the horns of a battle charge. Everyone in the treld paused in their tasks and listened again for the neigh of joy and pride. Movement ceased in the fields. Men and horses alike watched as Nara appeared on the crest of a distant hill. She neighed again, this time in greeting, and Gabria, feeling the mare's delight, laughed in pleasure.

The girl whistled once more. Nara leaped down the hill, her tail unfurled, and galloped toward the treld. Her mane whipped out like grass before a tornado; her hooves flashed as she flung her legs forward. Like a black comet, she burst onto the crowded field and swept through the men and horses. They parted before her power and grandeur. She thundered up the slope and skidded to a halt, inches away from Gabria. The mare snorted delicately.

Gabria laughed again, hearing the excited shouts of the men around her. She grabbed for the Hunnuli's mane and hauled herself up. "Go, please!" Nara spun around and ran to find the wind on the plains.

Jorlan watched them disappear and grinned. "I would give my best mares to do that."

The mare carried Gabria along the banks of the Goldrine River to the entrance of the valley, and swiftly passed between the two guardian peaks to the plains.

Beyond Marakor and its twin, the foothills fell away to the steppelands of Ramtharin. The semi-arid grasslands rolled out of the mountain's shadow and away into a dusky horizon. The plains were endless leagues of land that awed men by their sheer vastness and a subtle intensity, traits not found anywhere else in the land inhabited by the clans. The character of the high steppes was found in the ceaseless winds that shaped the rocks and bent the long grass, in the rough colors that blended in a myriad of shades, in the pungent aroma of the tough shrubs that grew in every gully, and in the bitterness of a winter blizzard or the heat of a summer drought. The steppes were an empty land that did not invite easy acceptance, yet the land suited the clans and their restless herds, and was beloved by them.

Nara galloped east, following the Goldrine River. She sensed something was worrying Gabria, but she kept her thoughts to herself and waited for her rider to speak of it.

When Marakor dwindled behind them and Gabria could no longer feel the eyes of the Khulinin watching her, she relaxed and settled down on Nara's broad back. The Hunnuli slowed to a walk, and they wandered quietly along the shallows of the broad river. The wind breezed by them, cool from the morning rain and heavy with the smell of wet land. Ducks paddled in the backwater and several antelope watched them curiously from a safe distance.

Gabria breathed a long sigh. "He accused me of sorcery, Nara," she said at last.

Who?

"The healer. He thinks I used some form of power to strike down

Cor in a fight last night. The worst of it is, I do not know if Piers is right."

Why did the healer think you had used magic?

Gabria shook her head despairingly. "Cor was injured by this power called the Trymian Force. Piers says I was the only one who could have struck the man. He feels I have an inherited ability to use magic . . . but he has no proof." She was silent for a while, then added, "I did have a dream last night. It was horrible."

About sorcery?

"Yes. Oh, Nara, I have been told since I was born that magic was something foul and corrupting. But I am not like that. I can't be," Gabria flung her arms around the Hunnuli's neck and held on. The girl wanted to believe in herself, in the inherent good that was a part of her and her beloved family. If she did have a talent for sorcery, she hoped that her beliefs about magic were wrong, for she could never accept that she was evil.

Nara stopped. She swiveled her head so her lustrous black eyes were staring into Gabria's unhappy face. *How do you think the Hunnuli became as they are?*

Gabria's throat tightened. "They were created by the gods. Amara shaped the first mare, and Surgart, in the shape of a storm, bred her." She spoke hesitantly, as if uncertain.

That part is true, but our creation goes farther. In the dawn of the world, we and the Harachan horses were as one.

Gabria took a deep breath. She felt as though she was standing on the edge of a crevasse. To her back lay her life, its basic beliefs and morals unchanged. Before her lay new concepts and strange truths, the strangest of which being the idea that magic was not an evil power. All she had to do was jump the crevasse and ask the Hunnuli the rest of the unspoken question. The girl already divined the gist of the answer, but the unknown realms that the knowledge might lead her to frightened her more than anything she had ever faced. It could mean a total disruption of her entire way of thinking and living. It could mean that, for two hundred years, the clans had believed in a lie.

Nara remained still, her gaze compassionate, while she waited for Gabria to speak. Gabria slowly traced her finger along the white lightning mark on Nara's shoulder and tried to find the courage to even form the words of the question in her mind.

The jagged streak, she thought, was the mark of the gods on an animal they, too, loved. The Harachan did not have the lightning mark, yet Nara said they and the Hunnuli were born from the same source. So why did the Hunnuli have the mark of favor and the Harachan did not?

"What happened?" she whispered so softly even Nara barely heard it.

But the Hunnuli understood the depth of the question. *In your legends, you have a tale of Valorian in which he rescues the crown of Amara from the demons of Sorh. In his escape he was helped by a black stallion. The horse was badly wounded by a bolt of fire, and, after Valorian returned the crown to the goddess, he nursed the horse back to health. In gratitude for his help, the goddess decreed the stallion would forever be Valorian's mount and that his offspring would always bear the white scar to honor him. After that, Valorian taught the horse to communicate and to protect him. He made the stallion invulnerable to magic and to evil. With his sorcery, the hero gave the Hunnuli a new existence.*

The chasm had been leaped. Gabria felt her body grow hot and her hands began to shake. "Valorian was a sorcerer?"

There are many things your priests neglect to tell.

"Nara, I think I want to go back to the treld."

The Hunnuli nickered softly and complied. She trotted easily back to the encampment to give Gabria time to consider the information that was now shaking her belief. It would take days before the girl could fully accept the magic that was a part of her—Nara had known the truth from the first day she had seen Gabria—and many more days before she would understand the reality of her power. But it would happen. Gabria would have to break her bonds of prejudice and accept her talent to wield magic if she hoped to fight Lord Medb and survive.

On the edge of the treld, Gabria slid off and stood for a moment, fighting back the tears that balanced on her lids. She rubbed her fingers over the ebony hair on Nara's withers. "I have despised sorcery all my life." She paused and swallowed hard. "You tell me you are a creature of magic, but I can't hate you. You are my friend." Gabria clenched her jaw and marched up the hill to the hall. Nara watched her for a moment, then she neighed and returned to the quiet pastures on the outskirts of Khulinin Treld.

7

The rains of early spring fell heavy that year. The water filled the streams and rivers, and drowned the low valleys. The rain fell for days in a fitful downpour, until the tents began to rot and the animals sickened and tempers frayed. The Goldrine washed over its banks and threatened the brood mare herd in the valley, so the horses had to be moved to shelters within the encampment. The work fields became a quagmire, and the paths through the treld turned to treacherous gumbo.

Before long, the hall was the only dry place in Khulinin Treld and the floor was crowded with people seeking relief. Around the fires at night, the clansmen drained the last of the wine and whispered of Medb's heretical practice of sorcery. Could it be, they wondered, that Medb had grown so powerful he could control the weather? Did he hope to demoralize the clans by endangering their herds, ruining their tents, and spoiling their food? Was he trying to prove the strength of his power?

The whispers spread as far as the distant clans, whose chieftains were little concerned with Medb's plans for dominance. Medb's name was in every mind, and the influence of his deeds, real or rumored, spread like a thickening mist. The tale of the massacre at Corin Treld was passed from clan to clan. The first horror and outrage sparked by the news was eventually dampened with excuses. People listened, but no one wanted to accept the fact that the Corin had been slaughtered. Clan fighting was a normal pastime for entertainment, revenge, or profit. But for a clansman to deliberately annihilate an entire clan was inconceivable.

Yet the massacre was a reality, and the chieftains knew in their hearts that something like it could happen again. Unfortunately, no one was certain why the Corin had been murdered in the first place. It was common knowledge that Dathlar loathed Medb. Perhaps the Corin chieftain had angered the Wylfling lord once too often and had received the full force of Medb's wrath. Several chiefs thought that, if this were true, it would be wise to avoid Medb's displeasure. Secretly, they began to accept the Wylfling emissaries and to listen to the promises of wealth and power that could be theirs in exchange for alliance.

Lord Branth of the Geldring waited only until the period of mourning for Lord Justar was over before he married the dead chief's widow and swore allegiance to Lord Medb. Meanwhile, scores of exiles—banded together, well armed, and mounted—began to ride the steppes like marauders. No violence occurred, but often livestock was found slain or horses were missing after the band swept through a clan's territory. The clansmen were left furious and alarmed by the depredation, but the band was so large and moved so swiftly, there was little the individual clans could do against them. Only the council of lords who met at the clan gathering each summer would be able to instigate any united action against the exiles. Unfortunately, the council did not meet for another three months.

In his huge hall near the southern fringes of the steppes, Medb gathered the news from spies and messengers and watched with growing pleasure as the fruits of his plans began to fall into his lap. At night, he retired to a hidden chamber and pored over the fragile pages of an ancient tome he had bought from a beggar in Pra Desh. He was still shaken that the fabled *Book of Matrah* had fallen into his hands. Matrah, the greatest of the clan sorcerers, had died in the destruction of Moy Tura, but despite years of searching, no one had ever found his manuscript. His book held references to three hundred years of arcane study, and many men had coveted its priceless contents. Now, after all this time, the manuscript had been discovered by a ragged man poking through the ruins of the sorcerer's city, and delivered to Medb as if by divine providence. The book could have so easily been destroyed or given to another man. Instead, it had come to Medb. Now, he had the means to overcome his crippling injuries—caused by an enraged Hunnuli—and the power to fulfill his dreams. No man or army could stand against him while the forces of magic lay within his grasp. An empire would be his.

To Medb's great amusement, the heavy rains were not of his making, but they fell like another link in the chain of events that was leading irrevocably to his victory. The destruction and unrest caused

by the weather further undermined the confidence of the clans, and
the constant storms kept them separated while Medb strengthened his
hand. Before long, he would be ready to launch the next part of his
plan.

In late spring, the rains finally ended. The Khulinin gratefully set
to work repairing the rotted tents, clearing the flood debris, gathering
the first fresh food of the season, and caring for the livestock. Many of
the shaggy, long-legged goats had sickened in the wet, and too many
of the newborn kids died. Days passed before the last goat recovered
and the losses were counted. The brood mares fared a little better
and, as their valley dried out, they were released to graze on the
verdant grass that sprang from the mud like a carpet.

Cor recovered and returned to duty, although it was clear to everyone that Gabria's blow had destroyed more than his chances for
fatherhood. He was surly and withdrawn and nursed a hatred that ate
at his soul. When the hills finally dried enough to resume the hunt for
the lion, he went out alone and after five days returned with the lion's
body slung across his saddle. He ignored the cheers and congratula-
tions and Savaric's gifts of thanks, and dumped the dead cat at
Gabria's feet.

"Your servant," he snarled at her and stalked away.

Gabria did not need to look in his eyes to know this was not the
last word she would hear from him. She was only relieved that Cor
had moved his belongings out of the hall to his father's tent and, for
the time, was leaving her alone.

Life slowly returned to normal. The goats were sheared and new
felt mats were made for new tents. The women spun and wove. The
men and horses returned to training. There was too much for every
person to do to worry about phantoms. Medb dwindled to a distant
irritation and the thought of war was pushed aside by the demands of
life.

The only blight in the pleasure of spring was Pazric's disappearance. The second wer-tain had not returned from the desert, and
Savaric worried about his absence. It was not like Pazric to not send a
message or be gone so long. Still, the clan had other things to worry
about. The Foaling time was coming and all had to be prepared. Excitement grew with the length of the days. Many people silently prayed
to the gods that the Corin's had fortune would not affect the coming
event.

Then, one night, Nara sensed the stirring among the mares.

Gabria woke the clan, and by morning the first foal was born. Wet and clumsy, he struggled to his feet while the Khulinin watched in silent awe and thanksgiving. By all the signs, the Foaling would be good: the firstborn was a bay colt as strong as a lion.

As if to make up for the disastrous rains, the following days were gorgeously warm and dry. The brood mares responded eagerly and a night did not pass without the birth of a foal or two. In the burgeoning meadows, the babies capered by their dams' sides, little knowing they were the continuation of the clan's existence.

Gabria took little joy in the time of Foaling. Her heart was wrapped in her own thoughts and desires as she grappled with her changing belief in magic. The growth of the Khulinin herd meant little to her, except for the lessening animosity toward her. She was glad for Savaric's sake, because she had become fond of him, but the affairs of the clan seemed distant and unimportant to her at the time.

Athlone, still suspicious of the Corin, sensed her detachment and kept a close watch on her. Their training times grew longer and more strenuous as Athlone sought to break her guard. Gabria disliked him intensely, and it frustrated her endlessly that she could do nothing to avoid him.

In spite of Athlone's temper, Gabria had to admit that he taught her well. The wer-tain was quick to find fault, but he was highly skilled and fair in his judgment. The girl understood why he earned the un-hesitating loyalty of the werod. Athlone was fiercely proud, coura-geous, and dedicated, and he received in full measure what he gave.

By the time early summer came, Gabria felt a grudging respect for the wer-tain. Because of his meticulous training, her muscles were tough, her balance and coordination were improved, and she could wield her sword like an extension of her arm. He gave her no mercy— and she knew Medb would have none—nor friendship. Rarely, Athlone would give her brief encouragement, urging her on to greater efforts. Gabria knew that she would never have attained such profi-ciency as a warrior without his help. If only he would forget his suspi-cions.

Gabria had little time for relaxation during the Foaling and even less as the Birthright approached. The Birthright was the celebration of thanks to the forces in the spiritual world that bestowed fertility on the clans and their herds. The predominating spirit of life was Amara, the mother goddess. It was for her that the Birthright was celebrated. She was the giver of life, the power that preserved it, and the guardian of the clans' continuance.

However, Amara was only half of a greater whole. While Amara was the positive side of life, her sister, the goddess Krath, was the dark side. Krath was the ruler of unbridled passion and secrecy, violence and jealousy. She had the power to destroy, not as her brothers, the two gods of man who commanded the forces of war, but in subtle ways that were slow and unnoticeable. Together Krath and Amara formed a whole that was embodied by the clanswomen.

Paradoxically, women were considered physically inferior to men. But because women had the ability to sustain life, they were endowed with potentially more spiritual power. The clansmen believed that a woman's smaller, weaker form was a compensating balance for the inner strength the life force gave her. Therefore, it was only natural that the women, the true beneficiaries of Amara's grace, should perform the ritual of thanksgiving in the Birthright.

Before the massacre, Gabria had enjoyed the Birthright. The secret rites of the fertility ceremony and the prayers for the herds were the first words she had learned, and the joyous celebrations that lasted through the night were the happiest times of her year. But this year she dared not even hum the chants. When the last foal was born and the procession of red-robed women gathered by the hall, Gabria hid in Piers's tent. She could not risk the slightest slip of the tongue this night.

While the women walked silently to the clan burial mounds, far from the treld, to perform the rituals in the presence of their ancestors, the men remained behind, waiting for the full moon to reach its zenith and the rituals to end. They were apprehensive of the mysteries of the Birthright, but they enjoyed the wild abandon of the celebrations after the rites. As long as the goddess blessed the clan, the women could do as they pleased this one night.

It was a beautiful evening for the Birthright. The moon hung like a pearl on the breast of night. The music of drums and pipes grew louder as the breeze died, and the torches danced around the distant mounds. A silence intense with expectation held the encampment. Even the animals were quiet. The horses watched the flickering flames warily, and the dogs stayed close to their masters.

In Piers's tent, Gabria heard the music crest the silence of the camp like the wind over the earth. It tugged at her mind, urging her to move, to sing the familiar words. The drumbeat lured her memories back to Corin's field, where she had drunk the wine of fertility and danced to please the goddess. The girl clasped her arms around her knees as the chants sang in her mind. It took every cord of her willpower to hold her body still and to stay seated at the fire like a disinterested boy. Piers was gone, but he could return at any time, and she would not betray herself now.

When the music reached its climax and the women shouted in triumph, Gabria sighed deeply. The final words of the ritual's benediction ran through her mind. It was over. Now the women would return to bless the herds and the firstborn colt would be sent to Amara with gratitude. Soon the clan would celebrate.

Gabria could already hear the musicians warming their instruments and the excited talk of the waiting men. For a while she considered joining them, but now she was as tired as if she had just completed the ritual herself. She did not want to face the boisterous gaiety. Instead, she curled up in a blanket and stared at the flames of the dying fire in Piers's hearth. The girl sensed rather than heard his coming. She was instantly alert.

"You are welcome to join us," Athlone said softly from the entrance.

Gabria looked at his shadowy form standing on the edge of the firelight. Like Nara, she thought with surprise, that night in the gully. Even his eyes gleamed in the flickering light as he watched her, wary but not threatening.

"I cannot," she said, hoping he would understand and leave.

The wer-tain was quiet for a breath, then he said, "You have served my father well these past days. Continue to do so." The tent flap settled back and he was gone.

Gabria stared at the black wall long after he left.

By dawn the clan was asleep, tired and content with the Birthright. Gabria woke early and slipped out of Piers's tent. The healer had come in very late, reeking of wine, and had collapsed on his bed. She doubted he had seen her. The encampment was quiet for this hour of the morning, and Gabria was relieved to see no sign of Athlone. The sun was barely above the horizon, but already the heat was building and the flies were starting to stir.

She decided to snatch the opportunity and spend some time alone. Solitude was a rare gift in a large treld, and Gabria did not want to lose this chance. She found Nara and they slipped out of camp and cantered into the mountains. Only Nara was aware that they were being followed.

High above Khulinin Treld, Nara found a stream that fell tumbling at her feet into the gorge and the Goldrine River. She started upstream. The mare forced her way through the heavy underbrush, following trails only she could see, past tiny marshes and through thickets of brambles and deer brush. Gradually, the low growth gave way to scattered trees and copses, and the water's voice was stronger as it fell over its rocky path. Nara climbed higher and deeper into the mountains as the sun warmed Gabria's back.

Finally, the mare was stopped by a steep rock wall over which the stream spilled in a cascading spray. Jutting rocks, cushioned with dark green moss, separated the falling water into thin streams veiled in mist and bejeweled by beams of sunlight. The water was collected in a deep, foaming pool before it continued down to meet the river. Moist gray-green lichen draped the pine and juniper that grew nearby. A thin undergrowth of grass, herbs, and wildflowers carpeted the sun-dappled ground. A squirrel chattered above them, and a dragonfly skimmed the water.

Gabria slid off the mare and dabbled her fingers in the cool water. "I am going for a swim," she said, looking at the pool happily.

Nara glanced back the way they had come. Her nostrils flickered in a gentle whicker. *Be careful. I will be back soon.*

Gabria started. "Wait. Where are . . ." But Nara was already gone. The girl was rather surprised by the Hunnuli's quick departure, but maybe the mare wanted to graze in a nearby meadow. Gabria shrugged. All that mattered now was the cold, glassy water that waited for her beneath the sparkling mist.

She tore off her clothes—the boy's pants, tunic, and the leather hat she had come to loathe—and dove naked into the pool. It was delicious. She swirled through the water like an otter. The bubbles tickled her skin, and the water flowed over her body like a sensuous massage, washing away tension and weariness. Gabria scrubbed off the dust and sweat, and combed her fingers through her hair, then she relaxed and basked in the mottled sunlight.

It was so good to forget about everything, to be herself without the guilt or the duplicity to encumber her. There were no eyes constantly watching her, no evil, no pretending, no remembering. She was a woman again. Gabria giggled as a water weed brushed her thigh, then she stretched luxuriously and swam to the waterfall.

Suddenly, over the noise of the fall, Gabria heard a Hunnuli neigh. Nara. Then another answered and her heart stopped. There was only one other Hunnuli . . .

"Oh, gods," she muttered and started to stand up.

"Hello, Gabran."

Fear jolted through Gabria's stomach. She fell back into the water and edged against the rock wall by the falls. Athlone stood on the bank by her clothes. Lazily, he nudged her sword with his foot and removed his own sword belt.

"How is the water?" he asked casually.

She only stared at him in wordless horror. He pulled off his tunic and unlaced his boots. "I followed you to be sure you did not have any trouble. These mountains can be treacherous." His pants joined the heap of clothes, and he stretched in the warm sunlight. His body was lean and muscular and traced with white scars. "A swim is an excellent idea. I think I will join you."

Gabria watched him dive into the pool and buried her face in the moss. "Oh, goddess," she pleaded. "Help me now."

While he swam toward her, the Corin bolted away toward the opposite bank in the vain hope that she could hide before the wer-tain saw her body. But the crystal water betrayed her. There was nothing to hide her curved hips or the swell of her breasts.

Athlone abruptly stopped dead in the water. He stared at her, and his eyes froze in astonishment and stunned realization.

Gabria stopped swimming, stood up in the shallow water, and faced him, her chin tilted up and the water running down her breasts. "Now what, Wer-tain?" she challenged.

Without warning, he lunged at her and his hands clamped her arms before she could move. Her eyes were pinned by his gaze of erupting fury. "By the gods," he snarled. He dropped her in the water, grabbed her hair with one hand and felt her breasts as if he could not believe his eyes. Gabria's skin crawled at his touch, and she closed her eyes. He shook her, nearly snapping her neck.

"A woman," he spat. "Are you Medb's little spy?" He pushed her underwater and held her, struggling, until her lungs burned, then he hauled her out like a gasping fish. "Who are you?" Athlone thrust her under again without waiting for an answer.

Gabria's fingers tore at his wrists, but she could not loosen his grip on her hair. She would have given almost anything for her sword at that moment. Inexplicably, she began to feel more anger than fear, and resentment surged through her.

Once more Athlone dragged her head out of the water. "Defiling pig!" he cried. "Who sent you to spread your lies in my father's treld?"

Gabria shrieked in fury and lashed out at his stomach. He dodged and shoved her under for the third time. She fought his merciless hold with frantic strength until her lungs were bursting and the blood pounded behind her eyes. Despite her training, she was no match for the wer-tain in unarmed combat. He was stronger, heavier, and more skilled. But maybe she could surprise him.

Unexpectedly, the girl went limp and let a few bubbles trail out of her mouth. Her head hurt horribly, but she concentrated on relaxing every muscle and floating as if dead. Athlone loosened his grip on her hair. As she felt his hands relax, Gabria drew her legs up, shoved violently against the bottom of the pool, and rammed her head into Athlone's stomach. He doubled over, cursing and gasping. Gabria fled for the bank. She scrambled over the damp rocks and moss as he came after her. The girl glanced back and saw the wer-tain plunging through the water like a furious stallion, his face twisted in rage and his eyes murderously dark. Frantically, Gabria ran for her clothes. Her fingers found her dagger, and she whirled to face Athlone as he lunged out of the pool.

"Keep away, Wer-tain," she cried, backing toward a tree.

Athlone paused for a moment, his eyes on her face. "Show your tooth, viper. Even Medb's snakes can be stepped on." He edged nearer.

Gabria's eyes flared with green fire, but she stayed with her back to the tree.

"Medb's whore," he taunted. "Is that how you survived the Corin's massacre? Did you spread your legs for him—and his exiles, too?"

A searing rage tore away Gabria's sensibilities and, like a catalyst, sparked the blue fire of her arcane power. "Curse you!" she stormed, unaware of the magic building within her. "You know nothing. You are as bad as Medb, rooting through corpses for a shred of self-esteem. You snap and snarl like a toothless dog."

Athlone laughed. "Far better to be an equal of Medb's than his whining cast-off. Will you grovel in the dirt to save your life again?"

Gabria leaped at the warrior like a cornered lioness. Her attack was so fast it took him by surprise and, when she stabbed at him, her dagger found the hollow of his left shoulder. The blade went deep, embedding in the muscle and ligaments. Even as the dagger sank in, the blue aura rose from Gabria's hand and raced down the jeweled hilt and silver blade into Athlone's body.

Her force was stronger this time and would have killed the wer-tain, except that the magic met a strange resistance. Instead of destroying Athlone, the attack only weakened him.

He gasped and went pale. He flung her violently away and stood rigid, staring stupefied at the blood that trailed down his chest. The warrior hissed, "Sorceress! What have you done to me?" Then his strength failed and he collapsed unconscious.

Gabria stood for a long time, her body shuddering in the release of her rage. She closed her eyes and forcibly controlled her wild panting. The beast. He deserves to die, she thought triumphantly. How dare he call her Medb's whore. She leaned over and wrenched her dagger loose. The blood surged out of the wound and flowed down the wer-tain's side.

Gabria held the point of the weapon against the hollow of his throat, where life lay just below the skin. It would be so easy. One simple thrust. Then the wer-tain would be dead and his suspicions with him. It would be the first time she killed a man, but it would be wonderful to start with this one. She could still feel his hands pawing her body and hear his unspeakable insults. The knife dug into the skin as her anger rekindled. A bead of blood glistened on the dagger point.

Kill him, her mind said. He's dangerous. He will betray you if he lives. The blade eased deeper. More scarlet beads welled up. Red, Gabria mused as she watched the blood stain the tan of Athlone's neck. As red as the blood on the grass at Corin Treld.

In disgust, Gabria threw down the dagger and squatted on the grass beside him. She hated herself for her weakness, but she could not kill Athlone in cold blood. She had seen enough blood to last a lifetime, and, as her rage cooled, she realized that she did not really want the wer-tain's murder on her hands. Besides, he did not deserve to die like this. His wound was payment enough for his insults.

However, that still left the monumental problem of what Athlone would do to her if he recovered. Gabria had little doubt he would expose her disguise and have her killed immediately. But maybe, just maybe, he would wait long enough to talk to her. Perhaps she could convince the wer-tain to help her. Nara did tell her Athlone could be trusted. Gabria hoped the mare was right—it was Gabria's only chance.

The girl sighed irritably. If Athlone was going to live, she would have to bind his wound and take him to Piers quickly. But what would she tell Savaric? Unhappily, she dressed and cleaned the wer-tain's wound and bound it with strips from his own tunic.

Just as she finished clothing him, Nara and Boreas trotted through the trees to the pool. Gabria backed away, eyeing the huge stallion warily. She wondered if he would be angry at her for his master's injury.

Boreas sniffed Athlone and snorted softly. *I see you two have settled your differences.* His thoughts, lower and more masculine than Nara's, rang richly in her head. Gabria stared at him.

Nara nickered, obviously pleased. *We waited for this, Gabria. You need him.*

"I need him like a broken leg," she said vehemently. "Where were you two?"

Boreas nuzzled Nara's neck, and she nipped playfully at him. *We were occupied.*

"Why did you leave me alone?" Gabria demanded. "You knew Athlone would find me."

Of course, Nara told her.

Athlone is bleeding. We must take him to the healer. Boreas nudged Gabria.

The girl glared at them both, feeling furious, hurt, and annoyed. Nara had left her intentionally, knowing Athlone would come to the pool. Why? The mare knew that the wer-tain was dangerous. Although the Hunnuli accepted him, how could Nara risk leaving her rider to face Athlone alone and virtually defenseless? In his rage, Athlone had nearly killed Gabria, and it was only through luck she had escaped. Yet both Nara and Boreas had anticipated the outcome of the confrontation.

Hesitantly, Gabria picked up Athlone's gold belt and weighed the heavy metal in her hands. There must have been something that told the Hunnuli that Athlone would not or could not kill her at that time. Her hands tightened around the belt. Perhaps their intuition had something to do with the incident with Cor. Gabria had tried to forget the fight, her dream, and Piers's accusations, but the memories replayed in her mind time and again.

A sickening feeling grew in her stomach. This incident with the wer-tain was too horribly familiar. Oh, gods, she thought, looking at Athlone, what if I have done it again? Maybe the Hunnuli knew she had a hidden defense, one that could defeat even Athlone.

That idea was more than Gabria wanted to think about then, so, for the moment, she pushed aside the fears forming in her mind and wordlessly helped Nara lift the wer-tain onto Boreas's back. Gabria wrapped the golden cloak around Athlone's bare back and threw away the remains of his tunic.

They traveled slowly back down the mountain, Boreas stepping carefully to keep Athlone balanced. Gabria spent the time thinking of something to tell Savaric. She wondered if she should flee before Athlone regained consciousness. Even slow starvation would be better than the death Savaric would give her for impersonating a warrior and attacking a wer-tain. Her life could be over the moment Athlone recovered, and no power on earth could save her.

But where could she go? Gabria would be permanently exiled and marked for death. Any clansman who saw her would be obligated to kill her. She would have no clan, no honor, no hope to kill Medb. Yet if she stayed, she was risking her life on the insights of two Hunnuli. Somehow, Nara and Boreas had realized that Athlone was not a danger to her. Otherwise they would not let her return to the treld. Nara had said Athlone could be her best ally. Maybe it was true.

Perhaps if Nara and Boreas supported her, she could convince Athlone to help her. The wer-tain's willing skill and influence would be invaluable in the battle against Lord Medb. Gabria was beginning to realize that there was far more to killing a chieftain like Medb than a simple challenge and a duel. Athlone's help would greatly improve her chances. Unfortunately, she doubted she would be able to convince the wer-tain before he exposed her to Savaric. The wer-tain's rage would undoubtedly wake with him.

Give him time to think, Boreas told her, breaking her preoccupation.

Gabria started. She had the uncomfortable feeling that the Hunnuli could understand her thoughts, despite what Nara told her. "What?" she asked.

The man is not always impetuous. Give him time and he will understand.

"May I stake my life on that?" Gabria asked hopefully.

Yes. The stallion was adamant.

Gabria rubbed her hand down Nara's neck and sighed. "I hope you will move fast if Savaric orders me killed."

Nara shook her mane. *There will be no need.*

An outrider saw them as they walked down the hill, and he galloped back to the treld to find Piers. Gabria watched him disappear among the distant tents and steeled herself to meet Savaric. She would have to control her every movement and reaction for fear of the chieftain seeing through her feeble story. She just hoped he would not look too carefully at Athlone's wound beneath the makeshift bandages.

A crowd met them at the edge of the treld, and gentle hands lifted Athlone down and carried him to Piers's tent. Gabria did not try to hide her relief. But other clansmen watched her with open hostility. The hearthguard came and unobtrusively circled around her. Savaric stood before her with his arms crossed. His face was expressionless.

"How did this happen?" the chief demanded.

Gabria dismounted and met his gaze levelly. "Athlone followed me this morning when I went for a swim in the stream above the Goldrine. While Nara and Boreas were grazing, he climbed a rock wall by the pool and fell on a broken branch."

"Why?" The word was an accusation.

"I don't know," she said as innocently as possible. "Maybe the rocks were slippery. I only saw him fall."

"Why did he follow you?"

She glanced at Boreas and patted the horse's neck. Too many details could sound contrived, so she replied, "I guess he wanted to go riding."

The chieftain looked at the two Hunnuli standing protectively beside the girl and then considered her for an excruciating moment. She could feel the eyes of the other warriors boring into her back as everyone waited for Savaric to guide them. A minute passed and Gabria quelled the desire to bolt for Nara's back.

"Thank you for bringing him back," Savaric said at last.

The ring of men visibly relaxed. The watching clansmen began to drift away, but Gabria still stood her ground. "It was my duty."

Savaric smiled, a knowing lift of his thin lips that held no humor. "Sometimes duty is not taken into account." He turned on his heel and left her, gesturing to his warriors to follow.

When she was alone with the horses, Gabria leaned back on Nara's shoulder and took a deep breath. "That is a dangerous man. Savaric sees many things people try to hide. Even Medb would do well to stay out of his way."

Savaric is no longer a match for the sorcerer, Nara told her.

"What?" Gabria was stunned. "That is impossible."

Medb has powers now even he does not understand. But he is learning fast.

Gabria ground her heel into the dirt and said, "I am such a fool to think I can kill him."

Boreas flicked an ear at her. *Yet you do not give up.*

"I cannot. By clan law, he owes me recompense." She looked at both horses. "I admit, though, I need help. Will you and Boreas support my plea to Athlone?"

Nara answered, *Of course. But we do not think you will need us.*

The two Hunnuli trotted off to the pastures, and Gabria walked up the path toward the hall. The encampment was swarming with activity as the women began the monumental task of packing and the men made preparations for the summer trek. All signs of the celebration were gone. The Birthright was over, gone with the rain and snow of the winter. Now the plains beckoned to the camp-weary clan and the sun burned hot on their backs. They would be leaving soon for the clan gathering at the Tir Samod, the meeting place of the Isin and the Goldrine rivers.

Lord Medb and the Wylfling clan would be there, as well as Lord Branth and his Geldring and the other clans who vacillated under Medb's increasing influence. Gabria thought that Medb would probably make a move at the council, when the chiefs of the clans were all together. One decisive attack could do irreparable damage to clan unity and reinforce his bid for supreme rule. But Gabria hoped to ruin his plan, whatever it might be, by challenging the chief to a duel. A duel to the death was her right under the rules of the weir-geld. Even if she could not kill Medb, maybe she could spoil his plots before he plunged the clans into war.

"Gabran!" Piers's voice stopped her cold. She saw him standing by his tent and her heart lurched. His face was grim, his hand gripped the tent pole like a crutch, and his pale eyes spoke to her as clearly as his words.

Wordlessly, she followed him into the tent. Piers said quietly, "This is the second time."

He moved aside and she saw Athlone lying unconscious on the pallet. His wound had not been tended yet, and the bloody bandages lay like dark stains on his skin. She started to say something when she noticed the healing stone resting on the wer-tain's forehead. A stray gleam of purple still flickered in the core.

"Oh, Piers," she breathed.

"Athlone has been struck with the Trymian Force," Piers said with controlled calm. "And this time you were the only one with him."

"You still cannot prove that. How do you know I did not find him like this?" Gabria demanded. She was grasping at straws and they both knew it.

"You said you were with him."

"Not the entire time."

"You were not there?" Piers picked up the red stone from Athlone's forehead and put it back in its wrappings.

Gabria shifted nervously. "I brought him home."

The healer returned the stone to its tray and slammed the chest door shut, then turned back to Gabria. "Granted. But should I tell Savaric the injury in his son's shoulder is a knife wound?"

Gabria stared at the healer in alarm. She had forgotten that Piers would recognize the cause of the wer-tain's injury. If the healer told Savaric the truth, no one would believe it was only self-defense. Savaric would kill her. Of course, if Athlone's rage recovered with him, her fate would be the same.

"Tell me the truth, Gabran," Piers prompted. "I think you did this, however unintentionally."

"It was a misunderstanding," she mumbled.

"And the Trymian Force?"

Suddenly, Athlone's last words began to pound in Gabria's head. "Sorceress, what have you done to me?" He had felt it! Somehow he had realized that she had struck him with something more than a dagger. Her fear and confusion closed in as the truth came crashing down around her.

"But I don't know how to cast a spell," she cried.

"You have to face the truth, Gabran," Piers demanded. "You have the power and Athlone nearly died of it. The next time, you might kill someone."

"You are wrong. I am not a sorceress!" She flung the last word at him and fled from the tent. She ran furiously through the treld, dodging dogs and children, but the word followed her like a curse. Sorceress. A creature despised. It could not be true. She had never felt this arcane power and, the gods knew, she did not want it. Piers has to be wrong, Gabria concluded desperately. He's only a foreigner and knows nothing about me.

Gabria nearly slammed into an old woman carrying an armload of newly dyed wool before she regained her composure. With a quick apology, she helped the woman with the heavy wool, then she walked tiredly to the hall. Sorceress or not, it would hardly matter if Piers or Athlone revealed the truth. Her punishment for any one of her crimes would be irrevocable.

The cool gloom of the hall was comforting, and, luckily, the long room was empty. Gabria poured a cup of wine and sat in a corner by the main door to wait. There was nowhere else to go.

8

The wind died down at twilight, and the dust settled in the fields. One after another the cooking fires were lit, and the weary women prepared the evening meal. The men gratefully set aside their work and came home, until all but the outriders were comfortably settled by their hearths. In the hall, Lady Tungoli and her women lit the lamps and torches, then served the bachelors from a pot of simmering stew.

Through the noise and activity of hungry, raucous men, Gabria sat in her corner in stony silence. She ignored their questions and offers of food, and stared at the entrance, waiting for one man to walk through and accuse her. But Savaric never came. His place at the table remained empty. After a while, the others forgot her and she was left alone in her self-imposed solitude. The fire was allowed to burn low in the central hearth since the weather was warm. Most of the warriors wandered outside to take advantage of the pleasant evening. Gabria still sat in tense expectation, wondering how Savaric would feel to learn the truth about Dathlar's "son."

Moonlight was flooding through the open doors when a young warrior slipped into the hall. Many of the men had returned for the night, and he squinted at the sleeping forms as if looking for someone. Finally he moved next to Gabria.

"Gabran," he whispered loudly.

Gabria stood up stiffly. So, Savaric had sent a messenger. The girl was surprised he had not come himself or sent the hearthguard, but perhaps he felt she did not deserve the honor.

The warrior waved her over. "Come on, hurry up. The wer-tain wants to see you."

She paused in surprise. Athlone. Not Savaric? "The wer-tain?" she repeated.

"Yes, now. He woke up a while ago and moved back to his own tent," the warrior said impatiently.

He led Gabria down the paths to Athlone's tent and left her by the entrance. Her knees felt weak and, for a moment, she had to stop. The night air was cool and refreshing, and the sounds of the camp were pleasantly familiar. If she closed her eyes, she could feel the similarity to Corin Treld, even to the smell of wood smoke and the barking of a dog. The thought gave her comfort, just as the memories of her clan gave her strength. Gabria leaned on that strength now as she pushed the tent flap aside. She wondered why Athlone had requested her presence, but she realized that he probably just wanted her there when he revealed her lies to his father.

Resolutely, she stepped inside. The only light in the large tent was from a lamp burning on the center tent pole. On the edge of its glow, she could see Athlone lying on a low bed. The sleeping curtain was pulled back and he was watching her in the flickering shadows. To her astonishment, they were alone and his sword was propped against a chest, too far away to be easily reached. She stayed by the tent flap, keeping the light between them, and stared at him through the flame. They stayed silent and eyed each other like two wolves on a narrow path.

Athlone gingerly sat up. He waved to a stool, then poured two cups of wine. "Sit down," he ordered. He tasted his wine and set the other cup on the floor for her.

Her heart in her throat, Gabria obeyed. She took a quick swallow of wine to ease the dryness in her mouth and let the liquid warm her stomach before she spoke. "You have not told Savaric."

He grunted. He was still very weak and any movement was an effort. "Not yet. I have some questions I want answered."

"Why haven't you?"

With an ironic grimace, he pointed to the cut on his throat. "First you tried to kill me, then you changed your mind and brought me back. Why?"

"Nara said I should trust you," Gabria replied.

"She puts much faith in me."

"Too much."

Athlone cocked an eyebrow much like his father. "Yet you did not kill me, even though I could sentence you to death."

Gabria looked away and her fingers tightened around the cup. "It was a chance I had to take. I need your help."

"Blunt. After nearly killing me, you ask for my aid." He took a drink and considered her. "Remove your hat."

Surprised, Gabria pulled off the leather hat and shook her head. Her hair had grown out a little since she cut it at Corin Treld, and it curled in uneven waves around her neck.

"Who are you?" Athlone muttered as if debating the answer himself. His eyes were no longer suspicious, only puzzled, and he leaned toward her, ignoring the pain in his wounded shoulder.

"Gabran's twin sister," she said, her voice hesitant. "I am Gabria."

He snorted. "Gabria? Doesn't your name mean buttercup? What an ill-matched name for a lioness. At least you are a child of Dathlar, that is obvious. You have his stubbornness." He paused. "How did you escape?"

Gabria bit her lip. It still shamed her to remember that disgraceful argument with her father, but she was not going to lie about it now. "I had a disagreement with Father and I ran away to be alone."

Athlone refilled his cup. "What about?"

"Marriage," she said angrily. She took another gulp of wine to hide the flush that burned on her cheek.

The wer-tain laughed outright and nearly spilled his wine. It was the first time Gabria had seen Athlone laugh, and she was amazed by the pleasant change. The hard lines of his face relaxed and his eyes warmed to a rich, dark amber.

"I am sorry," Athlone finally apologized. "I just cannot imagine any man taming you. You are much like your Hunnuli."

Gabria was relieved by his compliment, however undeserved, and her hope grew. Perhaps Athlone would keep her secret. His rage from their earlier confrontation seemed to be cooled, and, if he could laugh at her and apologize, he was not planning to have her head removed immediately.

"Why did you come to us?" the wer-tain asked, returning to seriousness.

"For the reasons I told your father," Gabria answered.

"To claim weir-geld against Lord Medb?" He shook his head. "You don't have a chance. The man is a chieftain and a reputed sorcerer." Suddenly Athlone stumbled over his words and stared at Gabria as if something had jogged his memory.

The girl slammed her cup down and said too quickly, "Yes, I want weir-geld. I am the only Corin left to claim it, and man or woman, I am entitled to revenge. That chieftain—" She spat the word contemptuously. "—is responsible for the murder of an entire clan!"

"And for your revenge, you want Medb's death?" Athlone asked slowly. He was taken aback by this girl's vehemence and was uncertain how to deal with her incredible behavior. And yet, she fascinated him like nothing he had ever known.

"Of course."

"Even if you break clan law to obtain your revenge."

Gabria's face hardened. "I will do what I must to see Lord Medb dead."

"He will destroy you."

She nodded. "Maybe. But I have to try. And, Wer-tain, I will use any means or any person to attain my vengeance. Even you."

For a long moment Athlone was silent, and, as he stared into the flame of the lamp, his eyes seemed to soften and his body sagged back on the pallet. The last of his indignation and hesitation vanished. "Warning accepted," he said at last. "Despite my earlier temper, I have not told Savaric yet that a woman is a warrior in his werod. You intrigue me. Your will and persistence go a long way to balancing your deceits."

"Will you tell him?" Gabria asked.

"You didn't leave me in the mountains to die. I owe you that at least. I won't tell him, but know also I will do nothing to save you if he discovers your secret from someone else."

Gabria nodded. That was fair. She was beginning to understand why Nara and Boreas trusted Athlone. He was a man of honor and, as long as one stayed within his boundaries, he would do everything to keep his word. She only hoped he had forgotten any suspicions of sorcery he might have. Gabria had seen the glint of speculation in his eyes when he mentioned sorcerers. The gods only knew what fantastic ideas he might have about her connection with it.

"If I'm not to be executed," she said, "what now?"

"You are still in training. If you insist on fighting Medb, you'll have to know more than the simple tactics of the practice field. Your dagger attack was atrocious."

Gabria nodded and replaced her hat. She stood up and saluted him with boundless relief. "Thank you, Wer-tain," she said gratefully.

He smiled wearily. "I hate Medb almost as much as you do. Perhaps between the two of us we can at least discomfort him." Gabria had turned to go when he added, "You have been courting disaster sleeping in the hall. Move to either my tent or Piers's."

Gabria was jolted by the mention of the healer. "Piers. He knows I stabbed you."

Athlone lay back and laughed softly. "He knows more than that. He has kept your secret for some time."

"What?" she gasped. "How could he have known?"

"A healer learns many things. You should ask him why he did not expose you."

She walked dazedly to the tent door. "Good night, Wer-tain. Nara was right."

As the flap closed behind her, Athlone sighed and murmured, "So was Boreas."

Piers was drying herbs when Gabria stalked into his tent and dropped her belongings on the floor. She stood in the middle of the pile and crossed her arms as if daring him to challenge her presence there. The felt tent was steeped with earthy smells of mint, hazel, and wild rose. Piles of freshly cut plants lay on the wooden table.

At the sound of the weapons and bundles hitting the carpeted floor, Piers glanced over his shoulder. "Good evening, Gabran. There is a pallet for you over there." He pointed to the sleeping area and turned back to his work.

Gabria saw another cream curtain already dividing the sleeping room in half and a wool-stuffed mat and several furs and blankets waiting for her. After the heated words of the afternoon, Gabria was not certain Piers would want her as a guest, but he had obviously already thought of it. Nevertheless, the girl did not want him to feel pressured into being a reluctant host. She wanted the arrangement to be acceptable to him as well.

"You were expecting me?" Gabria asked, surprised.

Piers hung another bundle of herbs on his drying rack. "It is safer for you to move out of the hall; I am the older of two bad choices." Gabria still had not moved, and the healer smiled briefly when he turned and saw her standing in her heap of clothes and weapons. "You are most welcome to stay," he added gently. "I had a long talk with the wer-tain this afternoon. We thought you would choose my tent." He paused, then added, "In case you were wondering, Athlone does not remember much about the stabbing except that you did it."

Gabria was relieved to hear that news. She studied the healer for a moment and thought about their earlier argument on magic. She was relieved that she could move out of the hall, but living with Athlone was out of the question. Staying with the healer who called her a sorceress was almost as objectionable. On the other hand, Piers had not betrayed her. Gabria's curiosity prompted her to give him a chance.

"How long have you known about my disguise?" she asked.

Piers chuckled and came over to help pick up her belongings. "From the day I bound your ankle."

"Then why didn't you tell Savaric?"

His brief humor faded and was replaced by an abiding sorrow. "I will just say you reminded me of someone."

"That is quite an excuse for risking your life for a stranger."

Piers picked up the girl's blanket and cloak. "It was enough." He helped her pack her clothes in a small leather chest ornamented with brass. She hung her weapons on the tent supports.

As they worked silently, Gabria wondered if this someone the healer mentioned was responsible for him leaving Pra Desh. A sadness was still in his face, and his mind seemed to be years away.

"Did this person resemble me or just pretend to be a boy?" Gabria asked the question lightly to draw him back to the present.

Piers did not answer at first. He stored his fresh herbs in a damp cloth, then poured a cup of wine and sat staring into its depths for a long while. Gabria had decided he was not going to answer when he said, "I drink too much of this. Before she died, I never touched wine."

"She?" Gabria prompted. There was a bitterness and grief in Piers that echoed her own. This shared pain, whatever had caused it, began to dispel her anger toward him.

He continued as if he had not heard her. "You resemble her in a vague way: fair hair, young. But you are stronger. She was pretty and delicate like silk. When she married the fon's youngest son, I did nothing to stop her."

"Who was she? What happened to her?"

Piers stood up. His reverie was reaching into places he wanted to forget. "It doesn't matter now," he said curtly. "She is dead. But I want to keep you alive, so get some rest." He went to his own pallet and drew the curtain.

Gabria sighed and sat down. She had not meant to push him so hard. Whoever this girl was, she must have been very close to Piers to kindle such a response. The mysterious girl's influence was still quite strong if she were the only reason for Piers not telling Savaric of

Gabria's disguise. Maybe later the healer would reveal the rest of his tale. Until then, she would accept Piers's hospitality, whatever his motives were.

After a while, Gabria blew out the lamps and sat in the darkness of the tent, considering the day. With the stroke of an ill-aimed dagger she had found two allies, three if she could add Boreas, and by her reckoning she was no longer an exile.

By clan law, an exile was a man or woman who committed a criminal offense or who, for some unusual reason, was totally separated from a clan. Until that person was accepted by another clan, he or she was considered an untouchable, an outcast. Gabria had been accepted temporarily by the Khulinin, but she knew that they had agreed only on the merit of her disguise and the Hunnuli. Therefore, in her own mind, she was still an exile.

Tonight, though, Piers and Athlone had acknowledged her for herself and, by their acceptance, erased the stigma of rejection in her mind. Piers, by his own admission, had become her protector, and Athlone was her mentor. With the help of these two men, Gabria knew she would survive, at least until the clan gathering.

Only Piers's accusation of sorcery bothered her. Gabria still could not completely accept the idea that she had an inherent talent for sorcery. Cor's injury and the dream, Nara's revelations and now Athlone's collapse were not enough to overcome all of Gabria's prejudices. A part of her still hoped the growing evidence was nothing more than strange coincidence. So far, she only had a single dream and Piers's word for proof that she was the source of the magic involved. It was possible the dream was only a part of her imagination and Piers was wrong. Gabria hoped that nothing else would occur and she could put the whole ugly problem aside like a bad dream.

Gabria yawned and realized the night was getting late. She had been chasing her thoughts around for too long. The girl made her way to her sleeping area, removed her pants and boots, and sat down on the comfortable pallet. After living with the constant noise in the hall at night, Gabria was relieved to hear only Piers's soft snoring. Before long she was lulled to sleep.

But like any ugly problems, the question of sorcery refused to be ignored. Deep in the night, when Gabria was asleep, she dreamed of a blue fire that rose from her being and grew in strength like a storm. It fed on her emotions, drawing its power from her until it burned in every vein. Then the fire flared in her hands and exploded outward as a bolt of lightning. Again it struck and burned a half-seen figure of a man, only this time the man wore a golden belt.

Gabria jolted awake and lay shivering in the darkness. It was another coincidence, she told herself. It had to be. She dreamed of the blue force because she had argued with Piers about it that day. That was the only reason. For the rest of the night Gabria tried to convince herself that the dream was not important and she needed sleep, but when the horn sounded at dawn, she was still wide awake.

To Savaric's amazement, he learned the next morning that Gabran had moved out of the hall and into Piers's tent. The healer had been alone for so long that the chieftain found it difficult to believe the man had asked the boy to share his tent. On the other hand, they shared a bond of two uprooted people, and perhaps they were drawn together by similar needs. If that was the case, Savaric was pleased. He was fond of them both and felt they deserved friendship.

Savaric received another surprise after the morning meal, when he rode past the practice fields and found his son teaching Gabran dueling exercises with the short sword. Dueling was a frequently practiced method of ending blood feuds, settling arguments, or claiming weir-geld. The rules were strict and rigidly adhered to, and, because it was fought solely with swords, dueling was restricted to skilled, initiated warriors of a werod. With no mail or shield for protection, a man needed every advantage to survive. Boys Gabran's age could not hope to best an older warrior in personal combat, so Savaric saw no reason for Athlone's training.

But when he questioned the wer-tain, Athlone merely shrugged and replied that the boy was determined to challenge Medb and there was no harm in humoring him. Savaric eyed them both doubtfully, but he trusted his son, so the chief only shook his head and cantered off with his men to hunt.

Meanwhile, Athlone turned back to Gabria. His arm was in a sling and his face was strained from weakness, but he held his sword as if it were a feather and watched Gabria's efforts with a sharp eye.

"One thing puzzles me," he said during a rest. "Where did you learn to use a sword?"

Gabria smiled. Since Athlone's acceptance of her true sex, she felt like a wasting illness had suddenly vanished from her mind. He still distrusted her, and Gabria noted that the vestiges of his anger and resontment would probably never disappear—at least as long as she wore pants and carried a sword—but his suspicions were gone. She found it easier to assume her role as a boy and to keep her mind concentrated on the details of survival.

"My brothers liked to pretend I was a boy," she answered with some humor.

Athlone examined her critically from head to toe. "If you looked then as you do now, your brothers did not have to pretend very hard."

Unconsciously, her hand crept to her short hair beneath the ever-present leather hat. "If I had been pretty, I would be lying in a cold grave now instead of keeping warm with light work," she said mildly.

"Light work! Impudent wench, I'll show you work." Athlone lifted his sword, and their blades clashed. He fought her hard, showing her tricks with the flick of the wrist or the turn of the blade. The short sword, generally used in melees on horseback, had a flat, broad blade that was better suited to slashing and hacking. Gabria had difficulty adjusting to the more polished form of swordplay used in dueling. But Athlone was a master swordsman and, by the end of the morning, Gabria was beginning to understand this new method of fighting.

"Remember," Athlone told her, "in dueling, the sword is the only protection you have. It must be your shield as well as your weapon."

He would have continued the training, but by noon the strenuous work had caught up with him. Athlone was exhausted. His skin was gray and blood stained the bandage on his shoulder. He returned to his tent for the rest of the day, promising to continue Gabria's lessons the next morning.

Gabria was left to her own devices. She went in search of Lady Tungoli. She found the chieftain's wife in one of the hall's storerooms, supervising the distribution of the remaining foodstuffs for the trek to the clan gathering.

Stacks of cheeses and cloth bags of dried fruit lay in heaps around Tungoli's feet, and huge earthen jars of grain were being emptied by other women into sacks for easier transportation. The Khulinin produced most of their own food through their herds, hunting, and some gardening. Many things, however, were traded for at the gathering with other clans and merchants from the south and east. Delicacies such as figs, fruit, honey, or dried fish, as well as necessities such as salt and grain, were taken in exchange for furs, goats, woven rugs, cloth, felt, saddles, and occasionally horses. To the competitive clansmen, the bartering was half the fun.

When Gabria walked into the storeroom, Tungoli gave her a smile and gestured to the piles of food. "If you would like to help, you are just in time."

Gabria was quickly put to work lifting the filled grain sacks into a pile by the main entrance, where several strong boys carried them to various families. After months of Athlone's training, Gabria was pleased to find the sacks easy to move. The last time she had done a task like this her brothers had had to help.

People bustled in and out of the storeroom, shouting, talking, and calling questions, while the stores slowly disappeared. Tungoli stood in the middle of the chaos and hummed softly as she sorted the bags and bundles. The women worked for several hours in companionable chatter until the room was nearly empty. Gabria was happy to work quietly, listening to the voices and relishing the company.

At last only Tungoli remained, along with the final stores. The busy crowd had moved on to other jobs, leaving Gabria and Tungoli in the storeroom in a backwash of peace. There was still one jar left to empty when Tungoli was called to another task; she left Gabria to finish the last bags. By that time, the girl was pleased to be alone in the cool, quiet storeroom. The tapestry over the doorway was pulled back to admit the afternoon light, and she could hear other people passing back and forth in the main hall. Gabria worked unhurriedly and became lost in her own thoughts. She didn't notice when everyone left the hall and two men entered.

Gabria was scooping the last grains into the leather bag when she heard a horribly familiar voice. Her body froze. The jar, balanced on her hip, slipped from her fingers and dropped to the floor. Its fall was muffled by the filled bag and Gabria managed to grab the jar's edge before it struck the ground. She shakily set the jar upright and leaned against the wall, trying to regain her breath. Like her heart, her lungs seemed to have stopped at the sound of that voice: the voice with the slight lisp that came from the throat of Medb's most trusted emissary.

The last time she had heard that hateful voice had been in her father's tent when the Wylfling delivered Medb's ultimatum. Now he was here, soliciting Lord Savaric's aid. She realized that the chieftain and the envoy did not know she was in the storeroom. Gabria thanked all the gods that she had been out of sight when the Wylfling arrived, for he had seen her several times at Corin Treld and could have recognized her.

Gabria slipped quietly to the door and flattened against the wall in the shadows, where she could see the two men. Savaric was seated on his chair, watching the short, brown-cloaked man who was standing before him. The Wylfling had his back to Gabria, but she knew the figure immediately, and in her mind she saw his face. The emissary's face was not easy to forget: it was hollow like a wind-eroded rock, and its clean-shaven skin was as immobile and as pallid as limestone. The envoy reminded her of a statue.

She wondered what message he had for Savaric. It was difficult to read the chief's reactions. Surely the emissary was not offering Savaric the same bribes and threats that Medb had offered her father. That would be a mistake with a clan this big. Perhaps the Wylfling had been here before.

"The Khulinin is a powerful clan," the man was saying. "And a large one. It is well known your tents lap the edges of the valley and your herds overgraze the meadows before you leave each summer. Soon your young men will be pressing for tents of their own and there will be nowhere to go. You need more land, perhaps new valleys, to begin holdings for another encampment before the Khulinin burst apart."

"I was not aware the Wylfling were paying so much attention to our problems. I am honored. I suppose you have a solution?" Savaric asked with barely concealed sarcasm.

"Oh, not I, Lord," the emissary purred. "But Lord Medb. He feels the lands to the south of Marakor should be relinquished to you and your heirs for a second, even a third holding. He would be willing to endorse your petition to the council for the formation of another holding."

"That is most generous of him, but I doubt the tribes of Turic would appreciate my claims to their holy land."

The emissary waved aside the notion. "You would have nothing to fear from that rabble. They will come to heel when they see the combined swords of Wylfling and Khulinin."

"Combined?" Savaric asked, his eyes glittering.

"Of course. After all, our clan holdings border the Turic's land as well. They would be trapped between two enemies. My Lord Medb is so pleased with the idea he is willing to aid you in your claim on the southern hills."

"In return for what?"

The man shrugged eloquently. "A small tribute—once a year, perhaps—to help feed our growing werod. We, too, are pushing the limits of our winter holdings."

"I see." Savaric raised an eyebrow and asked thoughtfully, "Why does Medb concern himself with the welfare of other clans? If he wants use of the Turic lands, he could take them himself."

"It is no secret that Lord Medb's ambitions exceed the position of chieftain. He needs strong, loyal allies, and he is willing to pay well for them. His generosity can be endless."

"With lands and favors that are not his to give," Savaric said with deceptive mildness.

The emissary's manner shifted subtly from ingratiating to a self-confident superiority, the arrogance of a man assured of his future position. "The lands will be his soon. Lord Medb's hand is growing stronger and if you do not accept his proffered friendship . . ."

"We will end our days in smoking ruins like the Corin," Savaric finished for him.

The man's eyes narrowed. "Possibly."

"May I have time to consider this generous offer?"

Gabria smiled to herself and regretted her father had not taken the same tack. Perhaps if Dathlar had controlled his temper and not thrown the emissary out, they would have had time to escape Medb's wrath.

The emissary was taken aback. He had not expected any cooperation from the obstinate Khulinin; he assumed even the vain hope of gaining the rich grasslands to the south would not sway them to Medb's rank. Perhaps the Corin massacre had affected the clans more than the Wylfling imagined.

The emissary hid his surprise and smiled coolly. "Of course. You may tell Lord Medb in person at the gathering." The man hoped that would discomfit the chieftain, since it was very difficult to say no to Medb's face.

Savaric only leaned back and nodded. "Fine. I will do that. Was there anything else?"

"Yes, Lord. My master asked that I give you this as a small token of his esteem." The emissary drew a small bag out of his belt and dropped something onto his palm. Gabria craned her neck around the door to see what it was as the man handed the object to Savaric. The chief held the thing up to the light, and Gabria gasped when a flash lanced through the hall with brilliant beams of color. It was a gem called a fallen star, a rare and very precious stone once loved by the sorcerers.

"The stone is a flawless blue taken from one of Lord Medb's mines in the hills. He wants you to have it as a reminder," the man said blandly.

Savaric's brows rose together. "Indeed. This is quite a reminder."

He sat back in his seat and nodded toward the door. "Tell your master I will think about his offer."

The emissary accepted Savaric's abrupt dismissal with ill-concealed irritation. He bowed and left. The chieftain sat for a moment, juggling the gem in his hand as he stared at the floor.

Gabria wondered what Savaric was thinking. She knew the chief well enough to know that he was not seriously considering Medb's offer, but she did not understand why he had accepted the stone. Medb's gifts were always double-edged.

The girl was about to return to her work when Lady Tungoli called to Savaric from their private chambers. The chief tucked the jewel under his cloak, which was lying on the dais, and went to talk to his wife, drawing the tapestry closed behind him. The hall was empty. Gabria knew she should not pry into the chieftain's business, but her curiosity got the better of her. She waited a full minute, listening for voices or footsteps, then she slipped to the dais and pulled aside the gold fabric. The gem was set in a cloak brooch of finely woven gold, and it glittered on the dark fur of the seat like its namesake, the star. It was an unusual gift to give a chief such as Savaric. The offer of land was a far better bribe to the lord of the Khulinin. Why had Medb sent it? He had offered no gifts like this to her father, and Gabria could not believe that Medb was giving a fallen star to Savaric out of the generosity of his heart.

Gabria picked up the gem. A strange tingling touched her fingers. Surprised, she dropped the brooch and the tingling stopped. What's this, she thought. She gently touched the gem and the sensation happened again, like the distant vibration of a faint pulse of power. Gabria was inexplicably reminded of Piers's healing stone. She had not touched the red stone, but she sensed intuitively that this gem and Piers's stone would have the same feeling of power.

Gingerly, Gabria picked up the gem again and held it up to the light from the hall's entrance. The jewel tingled between her fingers. She looked into the gem's brilliant, scintillating interior and wondered if this strange pulse was caused by magic. The gem had come from Medb, so it was possible he had put a spell on it.

The thought of Medb's magic frightened her. She was about to drop the jewel back on the fur when suddenly an image began to form in the center of the stone. She watched horrified as the image wavered, then coalesced into an eye.

Not a simple human eye, but a dark orb of piercing intensity that stared into the distance with malicious intelligence. Gabria shuddered.

The eye's pupil was dilated. Looking into its center felt like falling into a bottomless hole.

"Gabran! What are you doing?"

Gabria leaped back, startled out of her wits. The image vanished. The gem fell out of her hands, bounced off the stone step, and rolled to Savaric's feet. He leaned over to pick it up.

"No," she cried abruptly. "Don't touch it."

Savaric's hand halted in midair, and he glared at her, his black eyes menacing. "Why not, boy?"

Gabria stumbled over her words and her face flushed with guilt. She backed away from the dais, still shaken by the memory of the eye in the stone.

Savaric straightened, and the gem sparkled by his foot. "Why not?" he repeated harshly.

"It came from Medb. It's dangerous," she mumbled.

"How do you know where it came from?" the chief demanded.

She glanced back at the storeroom, then down at the floor. "I overheard the Wylfling emissary."

"I see. And why do you think this gift is dangerous?"

Gabria swallowed. Her throat was very dry. What could she say? That she had felt the power embedded in the stone and saw the image of an eye in its center? She could hardly believe that herself. But she was certain of the danger the gem posed and the damage it could do if Savaric was not warned.

"I, uh . . . it is not exactly dangerous," Gabria replied, stumbling over her words. "But it is . . . I have heard Medb is learning sorcery. I thought he may have tampered with the gem. It feels strange when you touch it."

"I noticed nothing strange about the gem." Savaric crossed his arms and stared at the girl. His face was dark with anger. "But you felt free to see for yourself."

"I am sorry, Lord. I should not have touched your gift, but . . ." She paused and from somewhere in her memory, she remembered an old story her father liked to tell about a jealous sorcerer and a seeing stone. "Father told me a tale sometimes," she said, looking up at Savaric, "about a sorcerer who kept watch on his wife through a jewel with a spell on it. It was a spell of surveillance, and it enabled the man to see and hear everything the lady was doing."

The anger on Savaric's face cleared a little. "I have heard that tale, too," he said thoughtfully. "What made you think Medb may have done something similar to this brooch?"

Gabria clasped her hands behind her back to hide their shaking. "The Khulinin are dangerous. Medb needs to keep close watch on you and a spy would be too obvious. This gift just seemed overly generous."

Savaric picked up the gem and turned it over in his hands. He slowly relaxed and, when he finally spoke, his voice was no longer caustic. "I thought there was a hook in this gift, but I never imagined something like a seeing spell." The chief gestured toward the door. "Did you know the Wylfling?"

Gabria sighed with relief, for it seemed Savaric had accepted her explanation. She considered the lord's question and her lip curled. "He delivered several messages to Father. Has he been here before?"

Savaric was about to answer when something occurred to him. With a deft motion he folded his cloak and wrapped the jewel in the thick material. "If you are right about this," he said, tucking the bundle under his arm, "we don't need to announce your presence to Medb."

Gabria drew a long breath. She had not even thought of that. "What will you do with the jewel?" she asked.

"Since I have chosen to trust you, I would like to see if your suspicion is right. The gods knew where you got this idea, but if it is true, perhaps we can use the gem to our advantage. I might try a little test. It would brighten Medb's day if he thought the Khulinin would accept his offer."

"He would be most pleased," Gabria said with a small smile.

"For a while. He will have a rude awakening at the gathering." He stopped and studied her intently. "Do you seriously intend to claim weir-geld by challenging Medb to a duel?"

"Yes. It must be a Corin who takes the payment."

"It may not be possible."

Gabria stiffened and her eyes met Savaric's stern gaze. The chief was not going to dissuade her from challenging Medb. She had trained her body and prepared her mind for battle against her clan's killer and no man, no matter how close in kinship or strict in lordship, was going to divert her. She would fight the Wylfling lord against her chief's direct order if need be. "I will make it so," she stated flatly.

Savaric walked to Gabria's side and put his hands on her shoulders. His dark eyes glittered like jet, but beneath the cold glints was a warmth of sympathy. "I know you have your will set to fight Medb alone, and I will honor that as best I may. But there are other factors you do not know about that may influence your decision. When the council is held, remember who is your chief."

Gabria nodded. She was relieved that Savaric seemed to accept her resolution and her obsession for vengeance. What bothered her, though, was his reference to "other factors." There could be nothing that would stand between Gabria and her vengeance on Medb.

Savaric's hands dropped and amusement eased the hardness in his face. "The emissary will be here for another day or two, presumably to rest before he returns to Wylfling Treld. I will see if Athlone is fit enough to argue with his father over the rule of the clan. Medb would be fascinated to think a rift was developing in the Khulinin."

Gabria smiled. "And will you wear your new cloak brooch, my lord?"

Savaric chuckled. "Of course. You had better stay out of sight." He shifted the folded cloak to a more casual position and walked purposefully out of the hall.

Gabria watched him go and noted with a pang of familiarity the way his stride lengthened and his body tensed as he prepared for some important activity. Her brother, Gabran, used to radiate that kind of energy, a concentration of thought and power that boded ill for anyone who tried to thwart him. It was a calculating, tightly controlled strength that had helped him defeat many opponents in chess or swordplay. She had seen the same energy in Savaric before.

Gabria knew now that Savaric was concentrating on the jewel and his plan to test her warning about the seeing spell. If all went well, Medb would fall for Savaric's ruse and reveal his hand. Gabria knew the gem had been tampered with, and she was certain of the purpose of the spell. But how had she known? Savaric had not noticed anything strange about the gem. Only she had felt the power in the stone and saw the image of the eye. After the incident with Athlone the day before and her second dream, this encounter with sorcery was too coincidental to be ignored.

Something was happening to her, and she did not like it. Medb was a sorcerer, not she. Yet she was the one who was accused of striking two men with an ancient arcane power. She was the one who recognized the spell on the brooch. If what Piers said were true, then she was the same as Medb: a profaning heretic.

Footsteps sounded lightly behind the girl, breaking her distraction, and she whirled in alarm to come face to face with Tungull. The lady's arms were full of rugs. "Gabran, I am sorry to startle you. Jorlan is looking for you."

Gabria's eyes flew to the doors where the evening sun was setting beyond the rim of the plain. "Oh! I didn't know it was so late." She dashed to the entrance, thankfully leaving her thoughts behind. "Thank you, Lady," she called and was gone.

9

Gabria rode guard duty that night and, after she had bid good-night to Nara, trudged to Piers's tent for some welcome sleep. Savaric visited them briefly and told her that the "argument" had gone as planned, with Athlone playing the impatient, disgruntled heir. The next morning passed uneventfully while the clan continued to pack for their summer trek. Savaric acted the congenial host to Medb's emissary, and Gabria stayed out of sight in Piers's tent. The chieftain made no mention of the mock disagreement with his son to anyone to be sure that Medb could have only learned of it through the stone—providing Gabria was right about the spell.

At nightfall, Gabria left for her duties. When she returned, Piers told her that Athlone had requested her for another game in his tent. She went with a curious foreboding in her heart and a chill in her fingers. She found Athlone and Savaric both waiting for her. From the quiet triumph on their faces, she knew she had been right.

"Come in, boy," Savaric said. "You have not only proved to me that Medb is resurrecting sorcery, but your quick wits have saved us much grief."

Gabria sat down heavily on a stool and hugged her knees. She was horribly afraid her wits had nothing to do with it.

Athlone removed the sling from his arm and paced back and forth across the deep carpets. He grinned. "Medb heard our fight, every last word of it, and he went for it like a weasel after a mouse."

"Good," Gabria said, trying to sound enthusiastic. "Is he trying to unseat you?"

Her question was to Savaric, and he answered with a dry laugh. "He offered the world to Athlone in return for my death and the loyalty of the second most powerful clan." He lapsed into silence and stared at the floor.

Gabria realized that Savaric had moved into a deeper concentration. He was absorbed in his thoughts and his muscles wasted no effort in pacing or excess motion. Only a part of his mind was answering her, while the greater part wrestled with the problems posed by Medb.

"The world is a large order, even for Medb. Will Athlone be able to control that much holding?" Gabria asked with mild sarcasm.

"Medb plans not, I am sure," Athlone replied. "We are too close to Wylfling Treld for Medb's comfort. He will probably try to dispatch both Father and me. Then, with Pazric missing, Medb could put a man of his own over the Khulinin. Only then will his back be safe."

The three of them fell silent, busy with their own thoughts. Savaric sat on his stool like a priest in contemplation, while Athlone paced noiselessly and Gabria twisted the light fabric of her pants between her fingers and imagined Medb in his tent, congratulating himself for putting a wedge into the all-powerful Khulinin.

Gabria shook her head. This feigned division of father and son was the only leverage they had at the moment, and it was a poor one, for it would only last until Medb put pressure on the Khulinin to accept his rule or he discovered Savaric's deception. Gabria had found the secret of the jewel, and the gem might help them mislead Medb for a while to gain time, but it would not tell Savaric and Athlone how the other clans received Medb's ploys or how strong the Wylfling werod was—or how powerful Medb's arcane skills had grown. The stone would not help Savaric many days hence when the Khulinin were given their ultimatum and had their backs to a cliff.

Gabria knew, as surely as Savaric must, that the clans were being swept into war. Like a game master, Medb had leashed each clan and was drawing them into a confrontation that would tear them apart. If Medb forged his empire, the clans as they had endured for centuries would cease to exist. Instead of autonomous entities of a similar tradition and ancestry, they would become scattered pieces of a monarchy, ruled by one man and bound by one man's desires.

Yet, even if the clans defeated Medb, Gabria realized that the clanspeople would still lose a great deal. In a war between brothers, complacency dies fast, fury burns hot and the flames take longer to cool. The girl couldn't imagine how the clans would survive the conflagration of this war or what their lives would be like when peace fell on the steppes. She sighed softly, regretting the changes that were coming.

Savaric heard Gabria's almost soundless breath and raised his gaze to her face. Their eyes met and locked in understanding. Like Piers before him, Savaric recognized the strength behind Gabria's look. Until that moment, he had only considered his friend's child to be a stubborn boy, who, like any young, hot-tempered adolescent, demanded to fight for his clan's revenge because of an overdeveloped sense of outrage. But as he looked into those green eyes, Savaric suddenly understood that Gabria's determination went far beyond adolescent eagerness, to a calculated, controlled obsession. He knew without a doubt that "Gabran" would do anything to bring down Lord Medb. Inexplicably, the thought frightened him. He was not certain what a boy could do against a chieftain and a professed sorcerer, yet it occurred to him with a great deal of surprise that "Gabran" might succeed. Savaric remembered Piers's words the night the boy rode into camp and set the clan back on its ear. The healer said that the boy might be the key to unlocking Medb's doom. Maybe he was right.

"Well, Father," Athlone said, startling both the girl and the chieftain. "Now, at least, we know the rumors of Medb's heresies are true." He glanced oddly at Gabria, but continued. "What do we do now that we have him on the wrong trail?"

Savaric broke off his stare and looked at his son. "Keep him there for as long as we can. It will not hurt us to let him think the Khulinin will fall into his grasp."

"What did he offer you, Wer-tain?" Gabria asked. She was feeling very tired and wanted to return to Piers's tent, but she wondered what the Khulinin were worth to Medb.

"That crow of an agent came to see me this evening." Athlone paused and looked thoughtful. "I would like to know how Medb contacted him so fast. Maybe he has a seeing stone, too. He offered me, in Medb's name, men, gold, land, and the chieftainship in return for obedience and my father's head."

Savaric chuckled. "I hope you will not be too free with either."

"Nothing is worth that price."

Gabria listened to the brief exchange with a little envy. Despite their differences, the two men were devoted as a father and son and even closer as friends. Only her brother, Gabran, had been that close to Gabria, and his death left a void that would never be filled. Nara helped heal some of the wounds in her soul, but there were a few hollows no one would ever find, hollows still filled with unshed tears. Gabria closed her eyes and turned away. It was still too soon to cry.

Savaric noticed her movement and said, "Daylight will be here soon and we have much to do."

They said good-night, and the chieftain walked with Gabria as far as Piers's tent. He hesitated as if he were going to speak, then he changed his mind, nodded, and left. Gabria watched Savaric until he disappeared between the tents. She felt closer to him that night than ever before, and she had the impression something had altered his thoughts about her. The way he looked at her in Athlone's tent—it was as if he had stripped away everything but her basic strengths and weaknesses and had accepted what he found. She was pleased by his understanding and relieved, too. She had no living family left, and she was beginning to appreciate how much Savaric and his family meant to her. Gabria closed the tent flap behind her. With a prayer to Amara, she fell asleep.

Like huge butterflies, the black tents of the treld began to fold their wings and disappear. Wrapped around their poles and ropes, the tents were bundled onto large, brightly painted wagons pulled by oxen or horses. Each family's possessions were packed beneath the tents and protected by carpets. After generations of practice, a clan could often dismantle their treld in a few days and their trail camp in a few hours. Packing the encampment was a fine art, and the women prided themselves on their expertise and speed.

The morning the Khulinin left their treld, the day dawned cloudless and hot. The faint dew quickly dried in the breeze and dust billowed everywhere. The first breaking of camp always took longer than usual, so the clan rose before sunrise to bring down the remaining tents, close the hall, saddle the horses, and bid farewell to those few who elected to remain behind. When the horn sounded at dawn, the caravan was already forming in the work field as each family took its position. The old people, the sick, and those who remained to care for the empty treld watched sadly and helped as best they could to send the clan on its way. The bachelors of the werod gathered the livestock. The three Harachan herds were mingled into one since mating would begin soon, and those horses that were not being ridden or worked were moved to the entrance of the valley. The mares, foals, and yearlings trotted about excitedly, but the stallion, Vayer, stood at the foot of Marakor and sniffed the wind that blew from the steppes and listened quietly for the signal of the horns.

Savaric himself closed the great doors of his hall and took down the golden banner. He passed it on to Athlone, who held it high and

galloped Boreas down the path to the fields where the caravan waited.
A shout of joy rose from every throat and echoed through the valley.
Horses neighed in reply; the dogs barked frantically in excitement.
The chaos of people and animals slowly shifted into a vague pattern of
order. Forgotten items were retrieved, last minute good-byes were
said, wandering children were found, and the ropes on the carts and
pack animals were checked and rechecked.

Finally, when all was ready, two outriders carrying horns rode to
the mouth of the valley. A silence of anticipation fell over the caravan.
Then, in unison, each horn bearer lifted his horn to his lips and blew a
great note of music that soared out over the empty plains like a cry of
triumph and welcome. The clanspeople roared their approval. Savaric,
riding beneath the huge golden banner, lifted his sword to the sky as
Vayer neighed.

Like a giant snake, the caravan crawled forward. Gabria sat on
Nara's back and watched with awe-tinged respect as the Khulinin
moved out of their valley. It was a sight she would always remember.

From the moment Valorian taught the first clansman the joy of
mounting a horse, the clans had been nomads with the wind of the
steppes in their faces and the dust of the trail on their clothes. Although the clans had slowed down over many generations and were
unknowingly growing roots in the places they had chosen for winter
camps, they were still nomads at heart. Wintering was fine for the cold
months when the blizzards froze the land, but when the freshness of
spring gave way to summer, the clans returned to the old ways and left
the trelds behind.

For Gabria and her clan, the packing and preparations for the
trek had always been simple. With only twenty-five families, the Corin
had been able to move often and with little fuss. They had been more
nomadic than the Khulinin and sometimes never bothered to winter in
their treld. But this trek fascinated Gabria. The Khulinin, with their
numerous families, huge herds, and powerful werod, moved ponderously out of the treld in a wondrously noisy cavalcade.

At the head of the caravan rode the hearthguard and the chieftain. Behind them was the main body of the clan in a procession of
wagons, carts, pack animals, people on horseback or on foot, and a
vociferous crowd of excited dogs and children. The livestock came
next, and in the rear was another troop of warriors. The werod was
spread out along the flanks of the caravan, and five outriders kept the
horse herd off to the side to prevent mishaps. Gabria marveled at the
organization that kept each man in his place and prevented tempers

from exploding, but she could not help but wonder how the tremendous caravan traveled very far in a day. At the rate they were moving now, the gathering would be long over before the Khulinin arrived.

To her surprise, the caravan slowly increased its momentum until it was moving at a fair pace along the banks of the river. Before long, the rich green foliage of the foothills' brush and trees was left behind. Instead, deep-rooted herbs and grasses, already maturing to a golden green, stretched to the horizon. Old, thickly matted growth cushioned the travelers' steps as the caravan wove across the grasslands. Beside them, the Goldrine River grew from a foaming, bouncing headstream to a staid, contemplative river that meandered through gravel bars and basked silently in the sun. Ahead of the clan, several outriders rode the point to keep watch for marauders or game. Raiders rarely bothered a clan the size of the Khulinin, but this year Savaric took no chances.

Medb's emissary rode with them, having blandly explained that the Wylfling were already on their way to the gathering; he would meet them just as fast as if he traveled with Savaric's clan. Both Athlone and Savaric knew the real reason the agent stayed, and they made a point of waging frequent arguments while Savaric wore the star brooch. Because of the man's presence, Gabria was forced to ride with the outriders in the caravan's rearguard.

The days passed quickly under the open skies as the clan traveled east to the gathering at the Tir Samod, the holy meeting of the Goldrine and the Isin rivers. Breaking camp became a habit again and muscles adapted to walking and riding. The heavy winter cloaks were exchanged for lighter, linen cloaks with long hoods that were worn as the occasion demanded: either draped around the head for protection against the sun and wind, or drawn across the face for battle. Clouds rarely marred the boundless expanse of the sky, except for an occasional afternoon thunderstorm.

The summer heat increased and with it, as the time to the gathering shortened, the tensions in the clan grew heavier. Savaric's eyes constantly roved the horizon as if he were expecting a yelling horde to sweep over his caravan. Arguments flared among the warriors, and even Medb's emissary lost his aplomb at times and was snappish to the men he was supposed to charm. Messengers, who were usually numerous as the clans grew closer together, were strangely absent this year. No word came from anyone.

Athlone had Gabria relieved of her duties and spent the warm evenings sharpening her skills with the sword, out of sight of the clan.

Most of the warriors ignored Athlone's curious attention to the outsider, but Cor still nursed his hatred for Gabria. Before the trek, he
had been too busy to deal with her as he wanted. Now, he followed
her constantly, looking for excuses to report her to Jorlan or humiliat-
ing and insulting her before other clansmen. He pulled petty tricks on
her and dogged her like a jackal waiting for a meal. He avoided her
when Athlone was near, but the wer-tain was constantly occupied during the day and Gabria was too proud to tell him of the wretched
man's tormenting. She began to detest the sight of Cor.

Gabria tried to reconcile herself to Cor's hateful presence since
she could not avoid him, but his murky eyes and his twisted sneer
grated on her and his jibes cut with increasing irritation. There was
nowhere she could go during the day to escape him. At night she
dreamed of his rude laugh. She slipped around the camp, looking over
her shoulder and wincing every time someone laughed. Even with
Athlone, she was distracted and nervous. She could only hope to ignore Cor until they reached the gathering. Then, everyone would have
more on their minds than petty vendettas.

As the day approached when she would meet Lord Medb face to
face, Gabria was beginning to understand more of the ramifications of
her demand for weir-geld. One night she was sitting with Athlone in
Piers's tent, listening to the two men discuss the coming council meeting. The healer and the wer-tain had found a common ground in their
shared knowledge of Gabria's secret and had become tentative
friends. It dawned on Gabria, as she considered their words, that her
claim to Medb was only a small portion of the charges against him.
Although she was the only survivor of her clan and could give evidence of Medb's complicity in the massacre, the other chieftains
would probably not allow her to fight him. They had too many other
matters to settle with him besides her desires for revenge. Even the
destruction of an entire clan paled in the light of Medb's revival of the
forbidden arts of sorcery. She doubted even Savaric would have an
influence over the council's decisions.

The thought that her struggles would be worthless was almost
more than Gabria could bear. She was so close, yet Medb could still
slip through her fingers. A specter rose unbidden in her mind of the
smoking, charred ruins of Corin Treld, and a small moan escaped her.
The men's voices stopped. She glanced up, her eyes bright with unshed tears, and saw Piers and Athlone looking at her strangely. Without a word, she bolted from the tent. Gabria ran blindly through the
tents and wagons, pursued by the black phantoms of her memory.

All at once a figure leaped out of a shadow, grabbed Gabria's arm, and whirled her around. She caught the smell of old leather and wine when the man began to shake her violently.

"It is the wer-tain's favorite," Cor's voice hissed. "And where are you going in such a rush, my pretty little boy?"

Gabria twisted fiercely in his grasp, but his fingers crushed into her elbows.

"Not so fast, Corin. You and I have things to talk about." Cor dragged Gabria into the shadow of a tent and pushed his face close to hers. His breath reeked of liquor.

"I have nothing to say to you," Gabria snapped. Her tears were threatening to spill over. She fought him, frantic to escape.

Cor grinned wickedly. "Now, now. Is that any way to treat a friend? I know someone who might be interested in meeting you."

The mocking triumph in his voice chilled her and she stopped struggling. "What do you mean?" she whispered.

"That's better. You'll like this man. I heard he was a close friend of your father."

Gabria stared at him in growing alarm. There was only one man in this camp Cor would be pleased to take her to and that was the one man she desperately wanted to avoid. "No. Let me go, Cor. I'm busy."

"Busy," he sneered. "Running errands for your precious wer-tain? This will only take a minute."

Suddenly, Gabria was furious. With a curse, she wrenched away from Cor and swung her fist into his stomach. Then she bolted into the darkness, leaving him doubled over and swearing in futile pain.

She wove through the camp like a fleeing animal, to the dark fields and the comfort of the Hunnuli. Nara came before she whistled. Together they walked along the banks of the river until long after the moon rose. But even the company of the mare did not ease Gabria's fear and depression. Voices and memories came to haunt her, and Cor's rude laugh echoed in her mind. She was still frustrated and angry when she went back to camp, her tears unshed. To her surprise, Athlone was waiting for her.

He fell into step beside her as she walked past his tent. "I do not want you disappearing like that," he said.

Gabria glanced up at him irritably and was amazed to see his face showed worry. "Surely you were not concerned about me. My loss would hardly be noticed." Her voice was full of bitterness.

"Oh, I don't know," he said dryly. "Cor would be so bored without you."

She came to a stop. "You know about him?"

"He is one of my men." Athlone leaned back against a tent pole and watched her in the dim moonlight. Somewhere nearby, a woman was playing a lap harp and singing softly. Her music filled the darkness around them like a distant lullaby. "Why didn't you tell me?" he asked softly.

"Cor is my problem."

"He is a self-serving, weak bully who is harassing and distracting one of my warriors from training. That makes him my problem," Athlone replied tightly.

Gabria crossed her arms and said, "I am not one of your warriors."

"While I train you, you are."

Unexpectedly, Gabria laughed. "Do you realize what a strange remark that is to say to me?"

Athlone was about to say more, but he changed his mind and laughed with her. "I never believed I would be telling a girl this, but you are getting quite good with your sword."

Gabria laughed again, this time with resentment and anger. "Little good it will do me, Wer-tain. I will not be able to fight Medb. The chieftains will not let me near him. There will be too long a line."

"Perhaps you're right. But watch and wait. Your opportunity may come when you least expect it. Just continue your training."

"May I practice on Cor?" Gabria asked irritably.

Athlone glanced at her, a strange, thoughtful look in his eyes. "Maybe you already have."

Her fingers clenched at her sides and she took a deep breath. What did he know? She searched his face for any indication of his thoughts, but his features were impassive and his dark eyes glimmered without guile.

Athlone returned her look. He was intrigued by the play of shadows on her face. Fascinated, he reached out and pulled off her leather hat. The shadows vanished, and her visage was bathed in moonlight. He wished he had not done that, for the moon stole the colors from her face and transformed her into a pale ghost. There was nothing to show the deep feelings and desires that moved beneath the surface of that pallid flesh. Her skin looked so cold in the silver gleam, he wanted to touch her cheek to see if it was soft. His hand twitched, but he held it out of sight.

This girl was unreal to him. She had more determination and courage than many of his warriors and a way of meeting one's eyes that was disconcerting. She did not meekly submit to the laws governing women, nor did she bow to the devastating events that changed her life. Although Athlone did not admit it aloud, he was glad she was not submissive. Her stubbornness and strength of character made her unique.

Briefly, Athlone tried to imagine her as his lover. He did not remember very much of their fight at the pool, yet he did recall her body was too shapely to be called boyish. Nevertheless, he could not reconcile the image of a warm, passionate woman with this stiff-backed, sword-wielding, fierce-eyed girl. He decided that she would probably never make any man a good wife—if she lived long enough for any man to offer.

Unexpectedly, the thought of Gabria dead made Athlone queasy. He had grown to like her, despite her strange behavior, and he was horrified when he fully recognized what the consequences of her actions would probably be. Even if the council refused her challenge to Medb, the Wylfling lord would mark her for death. If she fought him, the end would be the same, for Gabria had no chance to kill Medb in a fair duel.

Bitterly, Athlone tossed her hat to the ground. If the girl chose to revenge the murder of her clan, then so be it; he honored that choice. But that did not mean he had to like the price of her decision. He brushed past her without another word and went back to his tent.

Gabria stared at her crumpled hat in dismay. Something had upset Athlone. She thought back over their conversation to see if she had said something to anger him. She picked up the cap. It could have been her remark about practicing on Cor. Maybe Piers had told Athlone of Cor's injury and the healing powers of the red stone. Maybe Athlone, too, thought she was a sorceress and was trying to dissuade himself. Or perhaps he just did not appreciate her remark.

She hoped that was all it was. Gabria desperately needed the wertain to continue her training and further her cause at the council. She also didn't know if Cor was serious about taking her to the Wylfling emissary, but she would take no chances. She would tell Savaric about Cor's threat in the morning so the chief could keep the emissary distracted with other matters.

Gabria crumpled her hat in her hand and moved slowly back to Piers's tent. For the first time in her life, she prayed to Surgart, the warriors' deity, to guard her and give her strength for the challenges that lay ahead.

*   *   *

Five days later, the Khulinin reached the junction of the two rivers. By this time, the Goldrine had widened into a broad waterway. It wound through a wide, level valley and converged with the Isin, which flowed down from the north. An arrow-shaped island, named the Tir Samod, had formed long ago at the junction of the two rivers. On the island, in a circle of standing stones, was the only sacred shrine dedicated to all four of the immortal deities. It was a holy place, filled with the magic of spirits and the powers of the gods who protected it. Even in the years of heavy rains or snowfall, the shrine had never been flooded. Only priests and priestesses were allowed to set foot within the circle of stones. But on the last night of the gathering, every man, woman, and child came to the island to worship in a ceremony of thanksgiving to all the gods.

Around the island, on the banks of both rivers, gathered the clans. The gathering was the only place and time in the span of the seasons when all the clans were together. In that short time, the business of many thousands of people was dealt with.

The clans as a whole had no leader. Each clan was led by an independent ruler who was accustomed to being a law unto himself. These men did not easily yield to a greater authority, save tradition and the laws of the gods. But the clans liked to maintain their ties and traditions, and so once a year the chieftains met in council. The council had the power to alter laws, punish certain criminals, settle arguments or feuds between clans, establish new holdings, accept new chiefs, and continue the traditions handed down from their fathers.

Clan gatherings were also a time to reestablish old acquaintances, see relatives from other clans, and exchange gossip, stories, and songs that would enliven many cold winter nights to follow. Young people, unable to find mates within their own clans, vied for each other's attentions. Games and contests were held, horses compared, and races run every day on the flat stretch of the valley.

Merchants from the five kingdoms to the east and the desert tribes to the south arrived early and quickly set up shop to trade with the enthusiastic clanspeople. A huge bazaar sprang up even before the last clan arrived. There, people could barter for anything their hearts desired: rich wines from Pra Desh, fruits, nuts, grain, salt, honey, sweets, figs, jewelry, perfumes, silks from the south, salted fish, pearls, metals of all grades, medicines, livestock, and rare spices. Besides the foreign merchants, each clan fostered its own group of artisans who specialized in particular crafts and always displayed their work at the gathering. The foreign merchants had a ready market for the clan wares and bartered hotly for everything they could get.

When the Khulinin arrived at the Tir Samod late in the afternoon, four clans—the Geldring, the Dangari, the Amnok, and the Jehanan—had already encamped along the rivers. After countless gatherings, the clans had unwritten rights to their preferred areas. These grounds were blessed with the clan's particular tokens and were considered inviolate. The Khulinin's place was on the west bank of the Goldrine, not far from the site of the giant council tent.

But this year, as the head of the Khulinin caravan crested the ridge that overlooked the valley, Savaric saw the green banner of the Geldring floating above Lord Branth's tent in the place where Savaric's tent should be. Savagely, he reined his horse to a halt and stared down at the offending clan in astonished fury. The hearthguard and several outriders gathered about him, their outrage plain on their faces. The caravan ground to a halt. No one behind Savaric could see over the hill, but word of the Geldring's insult flew down the line of wagons until the warriors in the rear began to edge toward the hilltop.

Gabria watched Athlone gallop Boreas to Savaric's side and, even from her distant position, she could see him explode in anger. Watching his Hunnuli prance in agitation, she wondered worriedly what he might do. If Athlone had his way, the Khulinin could sweep down on the Geldring and begin a war before Medb arrived. Savaric might even decide to turn the caravan around and leave the gathering in a fit of honor. Lord Branth's move was a grave insult, but there were more important problems brewing at the gathering that required the Khulinin's presence.

Gabria pulled her hat low over her forehead and urged Nara up the slope. A short way behind the warriors, she slipped off the Hunnuli and ran the last few yards into the crowd of milling riders. The chieftain, Athlone, the Wylfling emissary, and the guards were all watching the encampments below, where warriors were suddenly swarming at the sight of the Khulinin. With a cautious look at the emissary, Gabria squeezed among the horses and heard Athlone's disgusted voice.

"If that conniving snake thinks he can do this . . ."

"Obviously, he already has," the emissary interrupted, trying to hide his amusement.

Athlone drew his sword and crowded near the Wylfling. "One more word, and I will relieve you of your duties as the Mouth of Medb."

The emissary shrank away from the sword poised near his throat and glared fearfully at the wer-tain. "My master will hear of this."

Savaric glanced down at the brooch on his cloak. "He probably already has," he said resignedly.

The emissary froze. His eyes narrowed to slashes, and his face seemed to shrink around his skull as he analyzed the meaning of Savaric's remark. He was shaken, but he rearranged his demeanor and hoped he had misunderstood the chieftain. "I am sure word has already reached my master of Lord Branth's petty attempt at insult. However, it appears it is too late to do anything but accept the situation. The council must convene."

Athlone slammed his sword back into its scabbard. "I will see Branth dead before he gets away with this."

Savaric shook his head. His initial wrath was cooling and tempering into a more devious anger. "He will not get away with anything. But now we have to move carefully. He is testing us. Somehow, we need to draw his teeth without drawing our swords."

Gabria smiled to herself. She had misjudged Savaric. She knew that she should stay behind the men and out of sight, but she was curious to see the camps. She wriggled past a guard's horse and stood by Athlone's heel, where Boreas's bulk hid her from the emissary.

Gabria looked down at the two rivers, where the tents of the four clans lay stretched out like dark birds. To the north of the island, in a wide, quiet bend of the Isin, was the ground where her clan would settle. The area was far from the bazaar and the council tent, and rather isolated from the rest of the encampments, but the Corin had always used it, preferring the convenience of water and pasture. Now it was empty, and Gabria knew that the other clans would avoid it like a curse. If the Khulinin took it, they would pay an honor to the dead clan as well as irritate Medb's faction. She grinned at her idea.

The Khulinin men were deep in consideration of their next move. No one knew she was there. "You could camp on the Corin's land," Gabria suggested into the tense quiet.

Athlone turned furiously, taken by surprise. "Get back to the caravan. Now!" The emissary was looking curiously over his shoulder so Athlone nudged Boreas into his way.

"What did you say, boy?" Savaric was more startled by her suggestion than her presence.

"Why don't you camp in the Corin's place?" Gabria repeated.

A slow, devious smile curled Savaric's mouth, and he chuckled appreciatively at the thought of the other chiefs' reactions. He said, as if to himself, "Dathlar would be pleased."

The wer-tain leaned over and hissed at Gabria, "Get out of sight, you fool!" She ducked behind a guard's horse just as the emissary pushed around Boreas.

"Who was that boy?" the agent asked suspiciously.

Savaric replied blandly, "My brother's son. He sometimes forgets his place. Athlone, what do you think of his suggestion?"

"It has merit," the wer-tain said, studiously ignoring the emissary's frown.

"I agree." Savaric turned to his men. "Jorlan, we will camp by the Isin where the Corin once camped." The chieftain disregarded the astonished looks of the riders and added, "There will be no reprisals against the Geldring. We will behave as if nothing has happened. Is that understood?"

Jorlan and the warriors saluted. They were appalled at the whole notion, but their lord's word was law. Jorlan, who was filling in as second wer-tain, gave the necessary orders, and the caravan began to move reluctantly down the hill. Gabria ran back to Nara and returned to the end of the procession. It had been foolish to risk exposing herself to the emissary, but it had been worth it. She released Nara to run with the other horses and went to hide in Piers's wagon until the clan was settled.

The outriders moved the herds to the distant pastures while the wagons rumbled down the hill. A few shouts of welcome met the caravan, and clansmen rode out to escort them. Yet few of the greeters showed their usual excitement. They were waiting nervously to witness the Khulinin's reply to the Geldring's insolence. A few Geldring, too, were watching from the edge of their camp; the rest were out of sight.

Then the clansmen stilled and gazed at the Khulinin, astounded at what they were seeing. The wagons turned off the main path and crossed the Isin, coming to a stop at the wide, grassy bend everyone had hitherto fearfully ignored. The other clans had expected anything but this. Savaric, as he watched the carts unloaded and the tents lovingly constructed, smiled to himself. He wished that he could see the look on Medb's face when the Wylfling saw the Khulinin camp on the Corin's land.

10

The Shadedron and the Ferganan clans arrived that evening amid shouts of welcome and a flurry of speculations. The clansmen were stunned by Savaric's move to the Corin's ground. The Khulinin were intentionally reminding the other clans of the massacre and were honoring the dead clan at the same time. The Wylfling had not yet come, and the chieftains wondered how Medb would react to Savaric's taunt. They were also taken aback by the Khulinin's disregard of the Geldring's insult.

Normally such a flagrant offense would precipitate a challenge or a violent protest at the very least. But the Khulinin merely set up their tents by the river and mingled with the other people, blatantly ignoring the Geldring. No one could decide if Savaric was bowing to Branth, and therefore Medb's superiority, or if he just felt that Branth was beneath his notice. Savaric gave no indication of his feelings.

Intrigue and gossip spread like wildfire through the camps. Rumors blossomed everywhere. The chieftains, when they were not puzzling over the Khulinin, studied each other warily, guessing who supported Medb. Branth strutted through the bazaar like a mating grouse in full feather, secure in his coming authority and power. Tensions, worries, and whispers spread through the encampments like smoke.

When the clanspeople discovered the Khulinin had a second Hunnuli, the smoke thickened. They tried every means to discover the rider, but no one could find the mysterious man who had tamed the spectacular mare, and the Khulinin were surprisingly tight-lipped about the horse and her rider. The black mare remained grazing with Athlone's stallion, unconcerned by the people who came to stare at her and the conjectures that crowded around her. Meanwhile, her rider stayed out of sight in the healer's tent.

Late that evening, three chiefs came to give Savaric the customary welcome, then declined his hospitality and quickly left, for they were uncomfortable on the Corin land. Lord Branth avoided Savaric altogether. Only Lord Koshyn, chieftain of Clan Dangari, stayed to share a cup of wine.

The young chief wore his light hair short in the manner of his clan and had a pattern of blue dots tattooed on his forehead. His eyes matched the indigo of his cloak.

Koshyn smiled infectiously and made himself comfortable on the cushions. "You certainly know how to make an impression." He accepted the cup Tungoli handed him and saluted his companion.

Savaric returned his toast. He liked the younger man and hoped the Dangari would not accept Medb's bribes. "Dathlar was my friend," he said simply.

"Yes. I think Branth was secretly relieved to find that you did not make an issue of his choice of camping places."

"I doubt it was his idea."

Koshyn stared out the open tent flap for a while, tasting his wine. "Care to make a wager?" he asked, his face crinkling in humor.

"What sort of wager?"

"I'd bet five mares that Medb leaves this gathering with the council in his complete control."

"Cynical, aren't you?" Savaric replied.

"I was offered a rich prize if I aided his bid for power. I am not the only one."

"I know. But what will be stronger: greed, fear, or independence?" Savaric paused. "All right, I accept." He looked frankly at the Dangari. "Are you going to ally with the Wylfling?"

Koshyn laughed. "That might give away the wager." He drained his cup, held it up for more, and gave Savaric a long look while the Khulinin refilled the cup. "Was there any truth to the rumor that someone survived the Corin massacre?"

Savaric only lifted an eyebrow and repeated, "That might give away the wager."

By the next afternoon, three other clans, the Reidhar, the Murjik, and the Bahedin from the north, had set up their camps along the rivers. The gathering went into full swing, and everyone tried to pretend this year was like every other. But the atmosphere among the camps was electric. Although the clansmen tried to appear casual, details, barely noticeable, gave away every person's true feelings. Hands stayed close to dagger or sword, faces strained into smiles, and chieftains were quick to break up arguments. The women, who knew everything despite the men's efforts to keep the problems quiet, remained closer to their tents. Even the merchants were nervous and kept most of their goods packed. Two days had passed and the Wylfling still had not arrived. They were the last. Every eye surreptitiously watched the south for any sign of the late clan.

Medb, it seemed, was delaying his arrival to let the clans stew. When the huge caravan of the Wylfling was finally spotted early that evening, every man ran or rode out to witness Medb's coming. It was exactly what he wanted. The Wylfling were the largest and wealthiest clan; they claimed the best land at the gathering for their camp and the richest pasture for their herds. When his caravan rolled into the valley, Medb arrayed his people to remind the clans of his power and might.

Wearing his long, brown cloak to hide his crippled legs and the rope that held him in the saddle, Medb rode at the head of his werod like a monarch. The warriors, over fifteen hundred strong, rode with their lances pointed to the sky and the chain mail of their long-coats polished to a bronze gleam. Their brown hoods covered their leather helmets, and the long, tasseled ends draped over their shoulders. Behind them were the wagons. Countless carts, wagons, animals, and people moved in an orderly procession toward encampments. Another troop of warriors followed, and a vast herd of horses and livestock took up the rear.

The clans greeted the Wylfling with none of their usual enthusiasm. They watched warily as each cart rolled by, and they silently counted each warrior. In a short year's time, Medb's clan had ceased to be a part of the whole. It was now a threatening force that loomed over them all and foreboded changes that few welcomed.

Savaric and Athlone stood at the edge of the encampment and nodded civilly when Medb rode by.

"Medb has had a most prosperous year," Koshyn said, coming up beside them.

Savaric nodded, his face bleak. "The Wylfling women have been most prolific. His werod has increased by several hundreds in a mere winter."

"The sun must be hotter in the south this summer, too. Did you observe a few of his outriders?" Athlone remarked.

"Even dust and distance cannot hide dark skins," Koshyn said.

Athlone shaded his eyes against the sinking sun and watched the riders maneuver the Wylfling herds to pastures across the Goldrine. "Turic mercenaries. I've seen one of them before."

Savaric followed his son's gaze and studied the distant horsemen. "Interesting."

"Care to increase the wager?" Koshyn suggested.

"Seven mares," Savaric replied.

Koshyn grinned. "Savaric, I believe you are hiding something."

The Khulinin chief tried to look astonished. "What have I got to hide?" he asked.

"How about a rider for that Hunnuli mare?"

"Oh, him," Savaric said casually, scratching his head. "He's ill."

Koshyn did not believe him for a moment. "How sad. May he recover soon."

"He will."

"I'm sure. Well, whoever he is, this unknown man cannot be the rumored Corin survivor. None of them had a Hunnuli. If there was a survivor, he was probably lost in that spring blizzard."

"Probably," Athlone said blandly. He was finding it difficult to keep his expression innocent.

Koshyn shot him a quick look, then shrugged. "Seven mares it is. I'll be interested to see who wins. Medb is going to move fast, so if you're going to pull the rug out from under him, you had better start soon." He walked off.

"Seven mares?" Athlone asked.

Savaric clapped the wer-tain on the shoulder. "The Dangari have the swiftest horses in the clans. Our stock needs new blood."

"What if you lose?"

The chief smiled, a slow lift of his mouth that belied the sadness in his eyes. "If I lose, I doubt I will live long enough to regret my debt."

Athlone chose not to comment on that. Instead he said, "I had heard recently that Medb was injured by a Hunnuli. Did you notice he was tied to his saddle?"

"Hmmm. Medb's injuries must have been crippling," Savaric noted. "That puts a different slant on things."

"I was glad to see it."

The chief knew what his son meant. "Yes. Gabran's duel becomes impossible now."

They walked back toward their own camp, keeping their heads close and their voices low.

"Why hasn't Medb tried to heal himself?" Athlone asked. "I thought sorcery could change anything."

"I doubt he has reached his full strength yet, so he may not want to reveal his power." Savaric slapped his scabbard. "And that, my boy, is our hope. Most of the clansmen do not know for certain that Medb has resurrected sorcery. This is his one chance to gain control of the council, so we must stop him while we can."

"But even with the mercenaries and the Geldring, he does not have enough men to overpower the rest of us."

Savaric jabbed a finger in the air. "He does as long as we stay separated."

"You mean unite the clans?" Athlone was skeptical. "Has it ever been done?"

"Not to my knowledge."

"How are you going to pull them together? It would take nothing short of a cataclysm to make these chiefs unite against Medb."

"How about the truth?" Savaric said mildly. "An irrefutable revelation of Medb's sorcery? In front of all the chiefs."

Athlone stopped dead. He immediately understood what his father was suggesting. "No! You cannot do it."

"It is the only way the chiefs will recognize their danger." Savaric stopped, too.

"They will recognize it well enough! They'll see you goad Medb's power and die in a blast of arcane fire, then they will run screaming back to their holdings, where Medb will be able to take them at his leisure." Athlone started walking again, his hands working in agitation. "Father, be reasonable. If you try to force Medb to reveal his sorcery, he'll kill you. You are the only one who could possibly hold these clans together against him."

Savaric caught up with his son and took Athlone's arm. The chief's eyes burned. "I have to try this. You said 'nothing short of a cataclysm.' "

Athlone stared at the chieftain for a long moment. He knew the determination that showed on Savaric's face would not be shaken. They had no real proof that Medb was a sorcerer, nothing tangible to show the council. Now Savaric wanted to provide the council with proof at the risk of his own life. Athlone doubted it would serve to unite the clans. They had been independent too long to see the sense of standing together, even in the face of the resurrection of sorcery. But maybe one or two would join the Khulinin to fight Medb.

"Will you at least talk to the others first?" Athlone asked, although he knew that talking would probably be useless.

Savaric's eyes softened. "Of course. I do not relish incurring Medb's wrath."

"We'll do that anyway," Athlone said, "when he finds out I have no intention of bringing the Khulinin to his heel."

Savaric suddenly laughed. "Then we have nothing to lose."

With the eleven clans together at last, the priests crossed to the island that evening and, from a secret cavern, brought out the gigantic council tent. In a large space on the bank of the Goldrine, under a few trees that grew by the water, the tent was raised with the help of men from every clan. Ten supporting poles on each side stretched the tan material over enough space to accommodate fifty men. Rich carpets were spread over the ground, and a fire pit was unearthed. Sections of the wall were rolled up to allow the breeze off the rivers to cool the interior. Cushions and stools were brought for the men's comfort.

Early the next morning, the banners of the eleven clans were hung outside the council tent. Dark gold, blue, green, brown, gray, black, purple, yellow, orange, dark blue, and maroon, they unfurled in the wind like flames. Only the scarlet of Clan Corin was missing. Everyone tried to disregard the banners around the tent, but the scene was strange and foreboding without the familiar splash of red. Time and again, men caught their glance wandering to the poles of the huge tent.

At noon the horns were blown, calling the chieftains to council. Forty-four men—eleven chieftains with their sons, wer-tains, elders, and priests—gathered within the cool, breezy tent. Women passed around flagons of wine and ale, and set bowls of fruit within reach, then they silently withdrew, for no woman was permitted to attend the council. Malech, chief of the Shadedron, called the men to order and the high priest blessed the gathering. The council began.

The first day the men only discussed minor problems. Savaric asked for information about Pazric's disappearance but received no news. Lord Branth was welcomed into the council, and the damage caused by the spring rains was discussed. Every man avoided looking at Medb, who sat ominously quiet with seven of his men. Few outside the Wylfling clan had known the extent of Medb's crippling injuries and no man dared comment. Crippled or no, it was obvious that Medb still had full control of his clan and his power.

Nor did anyone mention the issues that were uppermost on every man's mind: the Corin massacre, Medb's unlawful bribes to the chiefs, the banding of the exiles, and the rumors of Medb's heretical practice of sorcery. The men were not ready yet to broach those explosive subjects. Instead, they talked of everyday events and watched each other, waiting for someone else to make the first move.

Medb said nothing. He sat on his litter within the half-circle of his most trusted guards and watched the chiefs with hooded eyes, like a lion eyeing his prey. They had nowhere else to go but down his path and they knew it. Let them leap and feint away. In the end they would come to him. Then his crippled legs would make no difference; when he unleashed the full power of his magic, every man would fall to the earth and worship him—or die.

When the council ended for the day, the men thankfully quit the tent to go to their own camps. After a night of feasting and dancing, in which the Wylfling took no part, the council reconvened the following morning.

The meeting was the same as the day before. Yearly business was transacted, a few major punishments were meted out, and several grievances were smoothed over. Again Medb sat in his place and said little. The tensions mounted like a tightly lidded pot set too near the fire.

Savaric wore his star brooch to the council on both days, although he said nothing to Medb about an alliance, and he covertly watched the responses of his companions. The stone drew many looks and comments, some envious, some admiring, but it was obvious where the stone had originated and many men wondered what Savaric had done to earn it.

Yet the Khulinin chief said little to anyone at the council. He watched and waited with the rest of the chiefs. Savaric was biding his time. He was waiting for the right moment, when the tensions were at their highest, before he made his move.

When the second day's council was over, Savaric nodded to Athlone. "Tomorrow," the chief said. "Tell the boy."

"What boy?" Lord Koshyn asked as he stepped up beside the Khulinin. He grinned at Savaric and Athlone. "Is your mystery man finally going to make an appearance?"

Savaric picked up his cloak from the cushion he had been sitting on. "The Hunnuli's rider has recovered from his illness," he replied.

Just then, Lord Sha Umar, chief of Clan Jehanan, strode over to join the three men. The frustration was plain on his handsome face. "Savaric," he said with annoyance, "the council cannot go on avoiding Medb's criminal behavior. Someone has to prod these chiefs into action."

Koshyn nodded. "We were just discussing that. I believe the Khulinin have a plan under their cloaks."

Sha Umar looked relieved. "I don't mind telling you, Savaric, Medb scares me. He is a menace to us all."

The Khulinin chief looked at the Jehanan thoughtfully. "Are you thinking of allying with him?"

Sha Umar snorted. "I am frightened, but I'm not stupid. I would rather have my clan die as the Corin did than live under his rule." He glanced at the entrance where Medb's men were carrying the chief's litter out of the tent. The three other men followed his gaze.

"We have to deal with him," Savaric said quietly. "Before he grows too strong."

"I'm glad to hear you say that. You can count on me to help." Sha Umar nodded to the men and left with his warriors.

"Do you want to change your wager?" Savaric asked Koshyn.

The younger man shook his head. "It would be worth seven mares just to be wrong. I will be looking forward to tomorrow." He, too, left the tent.

Savaric and Athlone, and their accompanying guards, walked back to the Khulinin camp. Neither man had much to say, for their thoughts were on the coming morning. When they reached the camp, Savaric retired to his tent and Athlone went to talk to Gabria.

During the two days of council meetings, Gabria had been fretting in Piers's tent. The waiting was interminable. Savaric had ordered the girl to remain out of sight, and Gabria knew that his plans would be destroyed if she were recognized prematurely. But this did little to alleviate her frustration. That hard-won, longed for moment, when she could confront Medb and fling his crimes in his face, was so close. Soon, she would see him broken and bleeding, dying in pain—as her family had at the treld.

Gabria savored the image. Oh, she might die in the attempt, but now death had no fear for her. She would be victorious and her clan would live forever in the glorious tales that would be told about her. Nothing would stop her. Gabria might wait now and cooperate with the chief's plan, but when the time came, she would fight Medb with every weapon she had. Not even the council would be able to stop her. The weir-geld *would* be paid.

Gabria's moods shifted restlessly from boundless rage to nervousness to irritation and impatience. She could not stand still. Her hands fretted at everything, and her body flinched at sudden noises. To make matters worse, Cor had taken to lounging outside the tent. When he was not working or eating, he was lolling in the shade of a tree near the healer's tent, making crude comments about Gabria to anyone who would listen, or taunting her through the felt walls. Gabria didn't know what Cor would do if she stormed out and confronted him, but both of them knew Savaric had forbidden her to leave the tent. Cor was making the most of it.

Piers tried time and again to force him to leave, but Cor kept returning to sit under the tree and taunt the Corin. Gabria tried to ignore Cor, for his disembodied voice sounded eerie in the dim interior and his insults only added to her agitation. In the brief silences when he was gone, she tried to calm her taut nerves. But very little helped. Cor's voice would soon abruptly cut through the quiet of the tent and send her clawing at the walls.

By sunset of the second day, Gabria was nearly out of her wits with tension and frustration. When Athlone strode in to talk to her, he startled her. She grabbed a knife and nearly stabbed him before she recognized him in the half-light of evening.

"I'm sorry," she said shakily. "I thought you were Cor."

Athlone took the knife out of her hands and set it on Piers's medicine chest. "He is elsewhere. I apologize to you. I should have dealt with Cor sooner." He watched as she paced back and forth on the rugs. "Father plans to take you to the council tomorrow," he said at last.

Gabria glanced up and her lips curled in a feral smile. "I will be ready."

"Gabria, don't get your hopes up," Athlone tried to explain. "There are too many things you do not know about."

The girl shook her head. "Do not worry about me, Wer-tain. I am fine."

Athlone watched her and knew she was not, but there was nothing more he could do then. No one had had the heart, or the courage, to tell Gabria that Medb was too crippled to fight a personal duel. No one knew how she would react or if she would even accept the truth. Athlone started to tell her, then he decided not to. In her frame of mind, she would never believe him.

The warrior bid her good-night and went outside. Piers met him near the tent. The healer was carrying a full wine skin and a blanket.

Piers held up the skin and shook the contents. "Would you believe it's water?" he asked. "I don't think I will sleep well tonight. Would you care to join me?"

Athlone agreed and the two men made themselves comfortable under the nearby tree. Together, they sat guard on the tent and its seething occupant through the night. Cor stayed well away.

Gabria slept badly that night. The shadows that haunted her after the massacre returned in strength and hovered around her as she drifted in and out of sleep. Her frustration from the two days of waiting boiled in her stomach, and her throat was tight with unshed tears. Tomorrow it will be over, she kept reminding herself. In the morning, she was going to the council with Savaric and, by sunset, the ordeal would be ended. As if to mock her ignorance, her dreams crowded in and the circling phantoms laughed at her with the voices of her brothers. Soundlessly, she cried out to them.

Then, from the void of ghosts and memories, came a dream as clear as the vision she had seen in the fire that night in the Khulinin hall. Corin Treld. Gabria saw herself standing on a hill, looking down at the remains of the once busy camp. The sun was high and warm, and grass grew thick in the empty pastures. Weeds sprawled over the moldering ashes and covered the wreckage with a green coverlet. A large mound encircled with spears lay to one side, its new dirt just now sprouting grass. The darkness of her grief receded a little when she saw the burial mound. Someone had cared and had shown their respect by burying the clan with honor. It was an act she had been unable to do, and she gave her thanks to whoever had buried the Corin.

All at once the dream vanished and Gabria came awake. She lay on her pallet, staring at the darkness and wondering if the dream had been a true vision or merely her own wishful imagination. Then again, the source of the dream did not really matter. The image of the burial mound gave her peace and remained with her through the darkest hours of the night, helping to ease her terrible tension.

By the time the light of dawn leaked through the tent, Gabria was composed. The shadowy phantoms were gone; her nervousness had passed. The tension had drained from her mind and body. There was nothing left but a single, clear flame of resolution. Only the memory of the burial mound remained to remind her of her duty.

Gabria straightened her clothes and drew on her boots. Her

weapons, now a part of her, were gently laid aside for the time they would be needed. The sword was already honed to a killing edge and her father's dagger glistened from constant rubbing. She folded her gold cloak and surprised herself by running a regretful finger over the light linen. She had grown comfortable with the Khulinin. It would be hard if, for some reason, she had to leave them, too.

Turning her back on the gold cloak, Gabria drew her scarlet cloak out of a leather chest and shook out the folds. The red wool cascaded to the ground. Such a true color, she mused, clear and pure like a gemstone; not muddied like blood. She swung the cloak over her shoulders and pinned it in place with the brooch her mother had given her. She smiled to herself. Medb was in for a surprise.

Piers watched her worriedly as she finished dressing. He wanted to say something to ease his own tension, but he could find no words. The healer recognized the look of intensity that altered Gabria's face. Her eyes glowed with an untarnished light, and the dark circles that ringed her eyes made them look enormous. Her skin was flushed, and her movements were brief, as if she were preserving all her strength. Piers wanted to tell her, to warn her that her hopes of fighting Medb were in vain, but when he looked into her face, he could not find his voice. The girl was too withdrawn to listen. Only the sight of Medb and his crippled legs would convince her that her challenge for a duel was impossible.

Piers hoped that the realization would not break her. Gabria had survived so much and planned for so long to destroy the Wylfling lord in a duel that it might be difficult for her to see other possibilities for revenge.

When Gabria was ready, she sat silently with Piers and waited. The council was to begin at midday, so she had some time before Savaric came for her. She could not eat and she tried not to think, so she detached herself from everything except her resolution. Piers respected her solitude and simply sat with her in wordless support.

Earlier that morning, Savaric and Athlone had risen before the dawn. A messenger found them as the moon was setting and he bid them follow. To their astonishment, he carried a thin, long whip with a silver death's head crowning the butt. Only one small group of men bore such strange weapons and they had not come to the gathering for untold years.

Bridling their curiosity, the two Khulinin belted on their swords and walked soundlessly past the guards, toward the two rivers and the sacred island. The flow of the rivers made the only sound in the cool night, and a short breeze tugged at their clothes. The messenger stopped them at the water's edge and whistled softly. Three figures detached themselves from the shadows of the standing stones and waded across the rapids. Each wore no cloak, only a simple tunic and an ankle-length robe belted with leather. They carried no visible weapons except for whips, which hung curled at their waists. Behind them, the dark gray stones waited like sentinels, watching but not listening. Athlone shivered under their gaze.

One of the men came to Savaric and held up his hand in a gesture of peace. "Good hunting, Brother," he said. He was the same height as the Khulinin, and they eyed each other for several minutes.

Savaric tilted his head to one side. A slow smile spread across his face. "Seth. You are most welcome."

The strangers with the newcomer seemed to relax. They remained as stiff as statues, but they tucked their hands into the sleeves of their robes and moved back to give the chief and his brother more room.

Seth nodded imperceptibly. "I am glad to hear you say that. Does your hospitality extend to us all?"

The chieftain's glance swept over the four men, then returned to his brother's face. "Are all of you here?"

"No. Only the four of us. We need your help."

Savaric's eyebrows lifted. "Since when do the men of the lash need help?"

"Since the clans named us Oathbreakers. We wish to attend the council."

"What?" Athlone gasped.

Seth raised an eyebrow much like his brother. "What is the matter, Nephew? Has the council passed a law forbidding us entry to the gathering?"

Savaric put his hand on Athlone's shoulder. He shared his son's surprise. The men of the religious cult of the goddess Krath had shunned the gatherings for generations. Savaric wondered why, of all times, the men of the lash chose this year to come. Then he remembered that they were in sight of the guards and the camps, and he gestured to his brother. "Perhaps it would be better if we talked in my tent."

Seth agreed. He said something in a low voice to his companions and they disappeared into the darkness.

Savaric, Athlone, and Seth skirted the encampment and slipped into the chieftain's tent unseen. Tungoli was waiting for her husband and she nodded politely, barely hiding her surprise, as Seth entered.

She fetched wine before retreating behind the sleeping curtain. The three men squatted by a small lamp and watched each other thoughtfully. In the dim light, Athlone recognized a strong resemblance between the two brothers.

The Oathbreaker was younger than the chieftain, but years of rigorous training, self-denial, and life in wild lands had aged him. His skin was dark beneath his thick beard. His eyes were carefully deadpan. It was said the followers of Krath could look into men's hearts and reveal the hidden evils that lurked there; they pried into secrets and opened guarded hatreds that were buried beneath facades. Because of this, few men dared to look an Oathbreaker in the eye and they themselves kept their eyelids half-closed as if to contain the horrors they had seen.

Savaric was the first to break the silence. "Maybe now you will tell us why you have come."

Seth leaned back on his heels and wrapped his robe carefully around his knee. "Medb."

"I did not realize he took an interest in Krath's cult," Savaric said.

"He has the *Book of Matrah*."

Athlone and Savaric were badly shaken. The wer-tain paled. He looked at his father, for the first time showing real fear.

"We suspected that he was reviving the black arts, but we never imagined he had such help." The chieftain stared into the flame of the lamp, his face grim.

"He asked us to translate passages for him," Seth continued. "The library in the Citadel of Krath contains the only sources available for such an undertaking."

"What was your answer?" Athlone's voice was harsh.

A glint of irritation escaped Seth's eyes and his mouth tightened. "We said no."

Savaric looked up. "I'm surprised. I thought Krath would have appreciated Lord Medb's methods."

"Our ways may be different from the men of horses and iron, but we do not sit lightly by when threatened by the likes of a miserable *chieftain*."

Savaric ignored the insult. Despite his blood kinship to an Oathbreaker, he could not understand what turned a man from the ways of the clans to the dark secrets of a bloodthirsty goddess. Seth was beyond his comprehension, and, because of that, Savaric took a perverse pleasure in cracking his brother's shell whenever possible. "You're skittish tonight, Seth," he retorted.

The Oathbreaker's expression went deadpan again. Even after years of training, he still could not maintain complete control before his brother. "We need you to take us to the council. Clan sentiment has never been with us and, without your endorsement, we would not be permitted to enter the council," he said in strict formality.

Athlone slammed his wine cup down. "You still haven't told us why."

"Medb promised to destroy our citadel if we do not help him."

"And you want our help defending that nest of assassins?" Athlone cried.

Seth stiffened. The mask in his eyes slipped slightly and, for a moment, Athlone fancied he saw the glow of a raging inferno in the depths of those black orbs. The wer-tain tore his gaze away and stared at the floor.

"You would do well to learn tact, Athlone. You are stirring embers that are best left alone." Seth paused. "We came to warn the council of Medb's book and his growing powers—and to ensure that he does not threaten us again."

Savaric nodded. Only the men of Krath's cult knew what was in the library of their citadel, but if the Oathbreakers wanted to break their self-imposed exile to warn the clans, it would be best if someone listened. "You may come." He paused and smiled at Athlone. "We will have several surprises for Medb in the morning."

"I hope he has none for us," Athlone muttered. "Father, you are not going to go through with your plan after hearing this."

"We will see. Perhaps, with the right bait, Medb will trap himself."

Seth drained his wine and said, "Only fools believe in an easy road."

11

At midmorning, Nara appeared by Piers's tent to fetch Gabria. Savaric decided for appearance as well as safety to let her ride the Hunnuli. The effect would be worth a thousand words when they came to the council.

When Gabria walked out with the healer, she saw Savaric, Athlone, several of the hearthguard warriors, and the four Oathbreakers already waiting for her. She was surprised by the presence of the men of the lash, but she only gave Seth and his companions a cursory glance. Seth, on the other hand, exchanged looks with his men, and, when Nara pranced to Gabria's side, he gave his brother an appreciative shake of his head.

Athlone helped the girl mount Nara's broad back. He looked into her drawn face and recognized the fires burning her within. He squeezed her knee. When she glanced down at him, her eyes were bright and distant.

"Keep a guard on your tongue. Do not do anything to risk the lives of this party. Do you hear me?" Athlone demanded.

His emphatic tone drew her back to the present. She nodded with some surprise.

The Hunnuli nudged her thoughts. *He is right, Gabria. Do not challenge the man yet. You are not ready.*

Gabria was watching Athlone talk to his father. "I am more than ready. My sword thirsts for his blood," she snapped.

I do not mean swordplay.

Gabria was jolted. "What do you mean?"

But the mare said nothing more, for Savaric was gesturing at them to lead the group. Gabria did not pursue the answer. Her mind was already set on her course of action and she did not want Nara dissuading her for any reason.

The Hunnuli tilted her nose down, arching her neck into curved ebony. She snorted.

"Are you ready, Gabran? It is time," Savaric said.

In answer for her rider, Nara threw her head high and neighed a challenge that reverberated through the camps. Boreas answered her from a distant meadow, and other horses neighed in return until the meadow echoed. The mare pranced forward, and the men fell in behind her. Gabria straightened her back. The girl flipped the edges of her cloak back until it lay neatly over the Hunnuli's haunches and flowed in a crimson tide to her boots. Behind her, the men walked, silently admiring the horse and her rider. Clan Khulinin gathered to watch them leave.

Gabria knew the effect the red cloak would have on people who did not know a Corin still existed, but she was not prepared for the impact her arrival made on the volatile atmosphere of the gathering. Nara's neigh had stirred the camps like a stick in a wasp nest. Hundreds of people were crowding the riverbank, staring toward the Khulinin tents. The chieftains, who were waiting for Savaric at the council tent, went outside as word of the Corin's coming spread through the gathering.

When the Hunnuli and her escort crossed the Isin, a babble of voices broke out. A wall of clansmen stood on the riverbank, blocking the way to the council tent. For a moment, Gabria wondered if they would let her pass. Confusion, fear, and amazement were on every face. The crowd shifted and grew. There were many people she recognized, but they seemed like strangers to her. Several people shouted at her; a few cursed her. Everyone now realized one Corin still remained, and they were bitterly reminded of their own negligence in honoring the memory of Clan Corin. Gabria ignored them all and raised her eyes to the banners flying above the council tent.

They reached the edge of the crowd. For the space of a breath, no one moved. Then Nara neighed again, imperiously. Immediately, the mob's attention focused on the mare, and a sigh drifted through the press. They moved aside, forming a corridor. Nara pranced forward, just as a short gust of wind unfurled Gabria's scarlet cloak like a chieftain's banner. Every eye followed the horse and her rider. Few noticed the Khulinin chieftain behind the Hunnuli, or the Oathbreakers who walked beside him. When Nara came to the council tent, Gabria dismounted. The chieftains met her at the entrance. Only Medb remained inside.

"My lords." She bowed to the other nine chiefs as Savaric joined her. "You may not remember me: I am Gabran of the Clan Corin. I would like permission to attend the council."

The nine looked at one another uneasily. Koshyn caught Savaric's eye and smiled with a twist of irony.

Malech, the Shadedron chief, said dubiously, "No uninitiated warrior is permitted to enter without his chieftain."

"I am the son of Dathlar and the only Corin, so by rights of survival, I *am* chieftain," Gabria said coolly.

Athlone choked at her audacity and looked away. The lords talked among themselves for a moment, and Savaric held back to allow the chiefs to make their own choice. Around the tent, men from every clan watched and waited and held their own council.

Finally, Malech nodded and gestured to the tent. "You may join us, Gabran."

Before anyone moved, Savaric stepped forward. "Lords, I have given permission for a high priest and three members of the Cult of the Lash to attend the council as my guests. They have several important matters to discuss with us."

The chieftains suddenly noticed the four strangers with the Khulinin. Noise broke out anew as the men presented themselves. Several chiefs blanched and every clansman seemed to move back, away from the hated black whips.

"Treacherous filth," Caurus, the red-haired chieftain of the Reidhar, snapped. "Leave this gathering at once."

The others murmured in agreement. The members of the cult had forsaken their vows of fealty to the clans and the chiefs, rightly earning the title "Oathbreakers." They were not specifically banned from the gathering, but they were certainly not welcome.

A dark cloak of fear hung on the Oathbreakers' shoulders, a fear born of whispered rumors and stories of heinous deeds. Few men knew the secrets of Krath's followers because few survived who broached the confines of the Citadel of Krath. Only the Oathbreakers' reputation as highly trained killers and their aversion to metal were known to all. Because they used no metal, their only weapons were their bodies, their whips, and their finely crafted killing instruments of leather or stone. It was said an Oathbreaker could snap a man's neck with bare hands or remove a head with a flick of a vicious black whip.

Their religious goal was to perform the perfect kill in the service of their demanding mistress.

But it was not the cult's bloodlust the clansmen despised, it was the subterfuge its members practiced. The stealth in the dark night, the garrotte in the throat, the subtle poisons, and the furtive killings were incomprehensible to a clansman. No one knew when an Oathbreaker would strike. There was never any warning.

And now they wanted to join the council.

Lord Branth pushed his way forward and stared down at Seth. "How dare you return here."

Seth's cold eyes shriveled Branth's brashness to dust. "Medb dared us," he said in a voice sharpened with malice.

Branth fell back a step, and the other chiefs looked upset. Medb's involvement with the Cult of the Lash was something they had not considered. The tension built like a storm.

"You have my word that my brother and his men will not disrupt the council. They are here under my protection," Savaric said soothingly.

Malech's mouth tightened. "They must leave their weapons outside and may only speak on the matter that brought them here."

Seth agreed, and the four men piled their whips by the entrance, knowing no man would dare touch them. The chiefs and their men filed into the council tent.

Nara nudged Gabria. *Remember.*

The girl nodded and moved numbly after Savaric. Inside, Medb was waiting for her. Her determination burned whiter; her fingers itched for the feel of a sword. She tried not to crowd Savaric through the entrance, but craned over his shoulder for her first glimpse of the Wylfling lord. Gabria had never seen him before, and her imagination had created many faces and forms for the man she knew only by reputation.

As the men sorted themselves and found their places, Gabria stared wildly about, trying to spot the murderer. He had to be there! Yet there was no one that fit her perception of an evil sorcerer. The only Wylfling she saw were sitting together near the head of the tent, and one, she noticed with surprise, was seated on a litter with a brown blanket wrapped around his legs. She sat down by Athlone, her heart hammering. Maybe Medb was waiting to make an appearance. She clenched her hands and tried to still her trembling.

Lord Malech stood, his broad face sweating profusely, and held up his hand to quiet the talking. "Lord Medb, we have several strangers who have requested to join the council."

Gabria froze. Her eyes raked the assembled Wylfling to find the chief who responded. On the litter, the man with the brown blanket idly waved away a fly and inclined his head.

"So I heard." He turned to Gabria. "On behalf of the council, may I express our delight and relief in the survival of a son of Dathlar. Your father's death was a blow to us all."

Gabria's mouth dropped open. She stared and stared until her head swam and the fury began to boil in her stomach. She had been cheated! The days of humiliation and grief and sweat had gone for nothing! She wanted to shriek at the injustice of it. The last, bitter, blood-soaked laugh had gone to Medb, for now her clan's honor would have to be sacrificed to a cripple. She started to stand, not knowing what she would do, but Athlone slammed her down and gripped her arm like a vise.

"Don't move," he hissed. "Don't say a word."

Gabria could not have spoken if she wanted to. Her breath seemed to be strangling her.

The chieftains looked at her curiously, expecting a response. When she said nothing, Malech cleared his throat nervously and said, "The Corin massacre is a subject we have been avoiding . . . to our shame. Now we discover a Corin has survived. We cannot sidestep this hideous crime any longer. Boy, will you tell us what happened at your treld?" Malech averted his eyes from Medb and waved at Gabria to stand.

Athlone released the girl's arm with a warning squeeze, and she slowly climbed to her feet. Over the heads of the men, she could see Medb clearly, and her hatred fumed. No one had told her the truth. They had let her run wildly into a trap where the only escape was to retreat. She could not duel with a crippled man in any way; there was no other avenue of revenge that would satisfy her weir-geld. She could hire the Oathbreakers to assassinate him, if they would, or she could attack him herself one dark night, but both thoughts were repugnant and would not honorably settle the debt of vengeance.

Gabria could think of nothing else to do. Perhaps, if she convinced the council that Medb was responsible for the heinous crime, they would discipline him. Unfortunately, she doubted the chieftains would do much. It was obvious, even in the first few minutes she had been with them, that the chiefs were afraid.

The realization startled her. As Gabria looked about her and saw the men's grim mouths and tense postures, a small feeling of pride began to grow in her mind. These men who boasted so loudly around the fires at night quailed before a single chief, a man of their own standing, while she, a woman, was a rider of a great Hunnuli and had survived the worst doom a clansman could inflict on another. If she could survive that, she could endure this hideous disappointment.

Keeping her voice low and level, Gabria told the council everything she had told the Khulinin, as well as her vision of the massacre. She disregarded the growing agitation of the men and kept her eyes pinned on Lord Medb as she talked. Her gaze did not waver when she detailed her evidence of his guilt. The Wylfling chief sat motionless through the telling, returning her silent challenge with his gray eyes narrowed like a wolf's. Still, Gabria could see the angry glints in the gray of Medb's eyes and a tic in the muscles of his rigid neck.

Despite his shattered legs, Medb was still a powerful, vibrant man. His energy pulsed in every muscle and made him look younger than his forty winters. He was very different from anything Gabria had imagined and, in other circumstances, she would have thought him handsome. His features were chiseled on a broad face and were framed by a short beard and curly brown hair. It was a face meant to be open and friendly, not twisted into a mask that hid malice and unconscionable deceit.

When Gabria finished speaking, an uproar erupted from the council. The men shouted and gestured angrily. Several leaped to their feet. In the deafening outbursts, it was difficult to understand their arguments. Lord Malech tried to quiet them, but his efforts were wasted in the chaos.

Savaric stood up. "Silence!" he bellowed, and the racket died down. "The Corin have been dead for four months. Why do you show your outrage only now?"

The men slowly quieted.

"Why do you just now bring forth this survivor?" Lord Branth asked, adding a sneer of disbelief to his last word.

"To guard against his untimely demise. He is, after all, the last of the Corin. Now that we all are witness to his existence, we cannot ignore the reasons for the annihilation of his entire clan."

"The evidence I have heard condemns the greed and bloodlust in a few exiles who unlawfully banded together to harry our clans," Branth retorted.

Shouts of agreement met Branth's statement, and Lord Caurus of the Reidhar slammed a horn cup on the ground. "Ten of my best mares were stolen by that pack of jackals and thirty sheep were slaughtered and left to rot."

Lord Ferron of Clan Amnok said immediately, "This has never happened in the memory of our clans. We must deal with these marauders swiftly before they massacre another clan."

"The Corin were not massacred for simple greed," Savaric said.

Branth snorted. "Then why? Because the exiles did not like the color of their cloaks?"

"I should think that would be clear, especially to you, Branth, whose holdings lie next to Dathlar's. And to all of you who have listened to Medb's promises of wealth and power. There is only so much power to go around."

Lord Jol, oldest of the chieftains, said fiercely, "I received no offer from Lord Medb. What is this?"

"Empire building, Jol," Koshyn said.

The chief barked a laugh. "Absurd. No one man can rule the clans; they are too far apart. Mine is almost in the northern forests."

Savaric turned to Medb. "But it is true, isn't it, Medb? Why didn't you negotiate with Jol's Murjik? Are they too distant to be of use . . . or were they next for the sword?"

Jol paled, and the warriors began arguing heatedly about the exiles, Savaric's accusations, Gabria's evidence, suspicions of others— everything but Lord Medb's complicity. Some wanted to believe Savaric was right. Despite Medb's offers, most of the chieftains were appalled by the idea of the clans in the chains of an overlord. They knew in their hearts why Clan Corin had died, but they did not know what to do about it. One of their own had never turned on them in this manner.

Even if Medb did confess to ordering the exile band to massacre the clan, the chieftains were fearful of punishing him. His strength had grown beyond any imagining and, with his mercenaries, he outnumbered every individual clan. The chiefs were also afraid of knowing the truth about his sorcery. If Medb truly had reconstructed the ancient spells, the clans were doomed. There was no one left who could fight him.

But Savaric would not let the chieftains evade the truth forever. He strode to the center of the tent and glared at Medb. "My blood brother died at Lord Medb's order. I cannot challenge him to a duel, but I demand the council take action to punish this most hideous crime."

For the first time since his greeting to Gabria, Medb spoke.

"Fools," he hissed quietly. He held out his hand, palm up, and began to speak. His voice was gently compelling, as if he were speaking to a group of rebellious children.

Gabria looked at Medb in surprise as the noise ended abruptly and every man turned to listen. Their faces were blank and their eyes seemed to yearn toward him. The girl looked at Athlone and he, too, was staring at Medb with rapt attention. Even Medb's own men were craning over his shoulder to hear what he would say next.

"Are you weak-kneed girls who must hang on every word mumbled by a simple boy? For reasons I cannot fathom, I am being unjustly charged with a crime that is most foul. I had no cause to slaughter the Corin. They were fellow clansmen, horsemen like myself. Would I cut off my own fingers?" He sounded aggrieved. "And to what purpose? Their lands lie far beyond the farthest hoofprints of my outriders. It is absurd." He settled back on his litter and curled his lip in a smile. "Yet I can understand how you could be deceived by this boy's fable. You are blinded by the red cloak and an earnest air. The boy was coached well by Savaric, was he not?"

The men murmured to themselves, their eyes still pinned on Medb. His words made sense to them. Gabria's and Savaric's arguments began to melt away like ice in the warmth of the sun. Medb's voice was so pleasant, so logical. He could not have harmed the Corin; it had to have been the exiles acting on their own. Athlone, too, looked puzzled and wondered if maybe his father were wrong.

Gabria felt confused. She knew that Medb was lying, but his words were sensible and his tone was so sincere that she wanted to believe him. Something strange was happening in her mind, and she struggled to find the cause.

"I cannot help but wonder why Lord Savaric is trying to lay the blame at my feet. I have done nothing to him." Medb paused as if in thought, letting the varriors feel his wounded innocence. "And yet if I were to be deposed by this illustrious council, who would care for the interest of my clan? I have no son. Would my considerate neighbor thus feel charitable and watch the Wylfling's holdings while a new chief is chosen?"

Savaric struggled to utter a word, but his voice seemed to be lost. Furiously he stepped toward the Wylfling. Medb lifted his hand and the Khulinin stopped abruptly, as if walking into a wall.

Medb came to his point with slow relish. "I am not the only one who is threatened by Lord Savaric's greed. Even the Turic may fall to his guile. Already he is making plans to overthrow the tribes and steal the southern foothills of the Darkhorns, lands that border mine!"

Suddenly, Gabria laughed. This man, perched on his litter, bloated with his own monstrous arrogance, was daring to sully another man with accusations of deceit and greed? And these warriors, taken in by Medb's spells, were sitting like enchanted frogs, taking in every word. It was more than Gabria's battered self-control could tolerate. The effects of Medb's spell evaporated in Gabria's mind, and she stared around her and laughed again.

The sound of her mockery was bare of humor and sharp with frustration, and it sliced through the clansmen's stupor like a scythe. They started in surprise and looked at each other guiltily. Savaric's body jerked as the spell broke and he nearly fell. Seth reached out and caught him by the arm.

Medb's face tightened unpleasantly. He shot a considering look at Gabria. He gestured to two of his guards, whispered an order, and turned back to the chiefs to continue the thread of thought he had spun in their minds. This time, he set aside his spells and fanned the flames that he hoped would bring the council to his feet. His two guards slipped out of the tent.

"Corin," Medb addressed Gabria. "There were valid reasons for forbidding uninitiated boys into the council; your outburst is one of them. Please contain yourself."

"So, you do recognize my blood," she replied, holding her cloak up in her fist. "And I shall soon know yours." With the sorcerer beyond her reach, her obsession for revenge burned in her head. It warped her common sense into a blind carelessness.

Malech glanced apologetically at Savaric, missing the imperceptible movement of Medb's hands. But Seth noticed it, and he recognized the forming of an arcane spell. He quickly leaned over to Gabria.

"Take this," he whispered and thrust a small ball into her hand. "Keep it with you."

Gabria opened her hand and found a white stone ball, intricately carved. Within its hollow core were three other balls of graduating sizes, one inside the other. It took a moment before she recognized the object and then she nearly dropped it. The Oathbreaker had given her an arcane ward. But when she raised her eyes, she too saw the strange movement of Medb's hand.

The air hummed briefly in the tent; one warrior slapped at an imagined fly, and Gabria felt a slight pressure in her head. Then it passed and she sighed in relief. She should have known better than to tamper with the anger of a sorcerer. Her carelessness had almost cost her. Gabria hid the arcane ward in her tunic and threw Medb a look of pure hatred.

Medb caught her look and pursed his lips in annoyance. He had seen Seth pass something to the boy, and now he knew what it was. He was not surprised the Oathbreakers still had a few of the relics left by the old sorcerers, but he was irritated to see that the priest had given one to an outsider—and that the ward operated so well for the boy. There was something very curious here. The fact that the boy was alive was strange. The exiles had sworn they had killed Dathlar and all of his sons. Obviously they had been careless.

Malech interrupted his musings. "Savaric, keep the boy quiet or he'll have to leave."

The men were still considering Medb's words, and Koshyn asked angrily, "Do you have proof of your ridiculous accusations against Savaric?"

Savaric crossed his arms. "Your arrogance astounds me, Medb."

"Only when the cloak fits," Medb replied. "Perhaps this will convince you."

Suddenly there was a commotion outside the tent and Medb's two guards came in, dragging a young warrior dressed in a tatered, filthy robe that had once been Turic. Athlone uttered an exclamation and jumped to his father's side as the warrior was dumped unceremoniously at Malech's feet. The other men strained to see who the man was. Only Medb watched Savaric to witness his reaction. The young man moved feebly on the carpets, his body twitching as if he were trying to avoid imaginary blows, his hands clenching spasmodically. Moaning, he rolled over and stared wildly at the roof of the tent.

"Pazric," Savaric whispered sadly.

The warrior's face was caked with dried blood and was bruised and haggard; his skin seemed shriveled around his bones. Athlone knelt by his side and tried to lift him to a sitting position. Pazric flinched in terror from the wer-tain's touch and tried to scramble away, but his battered body failed him and he curled up, gibbering, by the fire pit.

Athlone stood up. "What have you done to him?"

"I?" Medb looked insulted. "My men found him like this, crawling in the desert and near death. The Turic left him to die."

"And this is your proof?" Lord Ferron said. The Amnok's face was as gray as his cloak. "This wreck you salvaged from the waste-land? Haven't you a healer in the Wylfling?"

Medb shrugged off the last question. "Don't you recognize him? This is the inestimable Pazric, second wer-tain of the Khulinin. Look at his neck. That is what they do to treacherous filth who are not worth the clean cut of a sword."

Pazric raised his head for a moment and every man looked. A bloodied discoloration encircled his neck like a collar. Purplish flesh puffed out around the edges of the marking and oozing gouges covered his throat like claw marks.

"A leather strap soaked in water," Medb said conversationally. "As the sun dries it, it slowly strangles its victims."

"This proves nothing," said Lord Koshyn.

Medb clapped his hands. "Dog! What was your mission with the Turic?"

Pazric cringed. His eyes bugged and rolled with terror. He forced his voice out of his ravaged throat. "To offer them a treaty."

"What treaty?" Medb demanded.

The other warriors moved nervously, helplessly, and watched Medb, Savaric, and Pazric. The four Oathbreakers glanced at each other knowingly.

"To trade land," Pazric croaked. He hid his head under his arms and cried with the effort of answering.

"What land?" Medb pushed relentlessly.

"Their holy land . . . southern foothills . . . for the Altai Basin."

"That's impossible." Lord Quamar shouted. His clan knew the Turic well, for the Ferganan's treld was in the south by the Altai River. "They would never accept a treaty like that."

"The Altai Basin is Wylfling land," Medb reminded them, knowing they were well aware of it. "Yet Savaric feels it is, or will be, open land for his unencumbered use."

Savaric disregarded Medb's insulting accusations and the growing dissension around him. Instead, he studied Pazric's huddled body. The wer-tain would sooner die than intentionally lie about his honor, his lord, or his mission. It was true that he had been sent to deal with the Turic tribesmen, but only to arrange a mutually acceptable meeting place for livestock exchange, and Savaric doubted that the tribesmen had perpetrated any of the brutal injuries on Pazric. They had dealt with him before and respected his integrity. But Medb, also aware of

Pazric's honesty, must have captured him on his way home and warped his mind into a cringing mass of lies to sway the council. Looking at Pazric's face, Savaric debated how much of the second wer-tain's mind had been destroyed. The warrior's sunken eyes seemed turned to an inner agony that was controlling his every word, an agony that almost certainly came from Medb.

Savaric swallowed. No man doubted the chieftain's courage in battle, but sorcery was a fearsome mystery he had never faced. He shuddered at the recklessness of his idea to goad Medb, and he hated to use Pazric in his ruse, for there was an excellent chance that forcing Medb to expose his powers would result in someone's death. Unfortunately, it was the only chance he saw to terrify the chiefs into uniting against Medb.

"Lord Savaric, did you send this man to the Turic with a treaty offer?" Lord Malech asked unhappily. He was rapidly losing control of the council and he knew it.

Giving his son a warning look, Savaric answered. "Certainly. It is no secret we deal with the Turic."

"For livestock, but what about land?" Ferron asked.

Savaric shook his head. "The southern hills are not fit for a lizard, let alone a horse."

"Yet they have the Altai River and the sparse grass is excellent pasturage for goats like yours," Branth pointed out. "You have not answered the charge. Did you offer to exchange the Altai Basin for the Turic's land?"

"What does it matter if I had?" Savaric said with heavy scorn. He strode to Medb, ignoring the Wylfling guards, and pointed dramatically at the seated man. "Look at him. He is a useless hulk. If he lives to the next wintering, it will be an act of the gods. He cannot move without a litter or survive without aid. He is only a burden to his clan. And he is a chieftain! He must see to the welfare of the herds, the training of the werod, and the survival of his clan. No able-bodied warrior in his clan will tolerate his weakness for long, and before many days, there will be strife in his ranks. If he were truly concerned for the interests of his clan, he would step down and have a new chieftain chosen by the council."

Several men loudly agreed, and Branth blew his nose with scornful rudeness. Patches of color flamed on Medb's pale cheeks and his hands twitched on his lap.

Savaric pushed harder. Medb had been injured within the year, and Savaric sensed the mental wounds had not yet healed. Fighting down his anxiety, he rubbed the salt deeper. "Step down, Medb," he sneered. "You're a legless parasite on your clan. Not even the exiles want you."

Athlone, watching Pazric, abruptly stepped back in alarm. The younger warrior's eyes were filling with hate and his face contorted into bestial rage. He snarled, the sound bubbling and ragged. Savaric heard the warning and knew his ploy was working. Medb's mental control on the man was slipping.

"Admit it, Medb. Give up your clan. They don't want you. You're not fit to rule a feeble clan like the Wylflings, let alone an empire."

Savaric's last word ignited the explosive atmosphere. The clansmen burst out into a tumult of violent shouting, abusive curses, and vehement repudiation.

Medb sat upright in his litter, his dark eyes boring into the Khulinin chieftain. Despite his crippled legs, he seemed to dominate the huge tent as he swept his arms in a command to his guards. Gabria and the Oathbreakers jumped to their feet to defend Savaric, and Athlone, reaching for his sword, leaped in front of his father.

Medb laughed in scorn. "You poor whining fools. You snap at my heels and never see the truth. I am tired . . ."

Medb got no farther. A maniacal scream rose above the noise. Pazric stumbled upright. His swollen lips were pulled back over his teeth; his robe swayed madly around his bruised limbs. With unbelievable speed, he clambered over the fire pit and sprang for Medb.

Athlone grabbed for him. "Pazric, no!" But Pazric's tattered robe fell apart in the wer-tain's hands. The young warrior broke free and snatched at Medb's throat.

Without warning, a brilliant blue light flared in the tent; it smashed into Pazric and slammed him to the floor. Gabria cried with dreadful recognition, for Medb had used the Trymian Force. Everything else came to a horrified stop.

Medb slowly leaned forward and spoke a strange command. A pale, coppery force field began to form around him.

"Now you all know your fate," he said. "The clans will be mine or I will unleash the power of the arcane and destroy every man, woman, and child that bears the name of a clan."

"Gods," Koshyn whispered.

"How?" Malech asked, his voice shaking.

Seth answered, speaking for the first time. It was too late to warn them now. It had been too late the moment they walked into the council tent. "He has the *Book of Matrah*."

Medb turned his dark gaze on the Oathbreakers. "And despite your inconvenient refusal to translate the sections I requested, I have mastered more sorcery than your feeble minds can comprehend. And beware, whip lovers, soon I will have all your books in my possession and your citadel will be rubble."

The translucent dome around the sorcerer was almost finished, and Medb pointed to Pazric's body. "Take your dog, Savaric. He served us both well. Then count your days. By the next gathering, I will be ruler of the clans. This council is over." Medb gestured to his guards and four of them picked up the litter. The dome hovered around his body.

Imperiously, Medb ran his gaze over each man, as if pronouncing his fate with a single look. He gave a negligible nod to Branth. To Athlone and the Oathbreakers, he showed only contempt. At Medb's order the bearers carried him toward the entrance. When he passed Gabria, he snarled, "You're the last of the Corin, boy. Do not hope to continue the line."

The Wylfling left the tent, and the council disintegrated. Lord Ferron left before anyone could stop him. Everyone else rushed to their feet.

"Is Medb serious?" Malech asked weakly.

Koshyn threw out his arms. "Gods, man. You saw him."

Seth said without emotion, "He has gained control of the arcane. What do you think a man like that will do with that kind of power?"

Athlone knelt by Pazric and gently pressed his fingers beneath the fallen man's jaw. "He's dead," he said dully.

Savaric shook his head. "He was already dead when Medb brought him in."

Gabria removed her cloak and laid it over Pazric's body. She was shaking badly, and the scarlet wool quivered in her hands when it settled over Pazric's battered face. The memory of the blue flame burned in her mind. Before, the Trymian Force had only been a word on Piers's lips and a nagging bad dream. Now she had seen it. It was a reality, a force that killed at a man's calling.

Gabria paused. A tiny thought nudged into her despair. It was a wild, frightening grain of an idea, yet it stirred her dead hopes. Perhaps revenge was not totally beyond her grasp.

"You were right, Gabran, weren't you?" Lord Jol said with bitterness. He appeared to have aged rapidly in that short afternoon. "Medb ordered the massacre of the Corin."

Gabria nodded. The clansmen were suddenly subdued, as if they did not want to share each other's despair.

"Yes, he did!" Savaric stated, turning to face them. "To make an example to all of us and to weaken our resolve. If he has succeeded in doing that, then the Corin died in dishonor."

"What do you expect us to do? Fight the monster?" Lord Caurus demanded, his face as red as his hair.

"Yes!" Sha Umar shouted. He was chief of Clan Jehanan and he intended it to remain that way. He stood by Savaric and shook his fist at the other chiefs. "Our survival depends on it. Medb has not gathered his full strength yet. Now is the time to attack—before he marshals his forces."

Branth laughed. "Attack? With what? Lord Medb would destroy you before the first bow was drawn. The only way the clans will survive is to swear fealty to him."

"I will never allow a broken-kneed, murdering *sorcerer* to rule my clan!" Caurus threw his wine cup into the fire pit.

"Then we must join together. We must unite our werods to fight him or we are lost." Savaric felt the chiefs' unspoken resistance, and he fought down a rising sense of despair.

Branth curled his thin lips in a sneer. "And who will command this united rabble? You, Savaric? And after you have disposed of Medb, will you pick up his sword and take his place?"

The Shadedron chief stepped forward. "And what about that band of exiles? We don't dare leave our clans undefended," Lord Malech said.

Caurus agreed. "We do not have a chance against Medb here. I say we'd be safer defending our own holdings."

"Better than putting ourselves between two greedy chieftains," Lord Babur of the Bahedin said with a glare at Savaric. Babur was ill and had said very little at the council meetings.

"I still think it is impossible for him to succeed," Jol said stubbornly. "The clans are too far apart."

"This is getting us nowhere. The council is over." Malech stalked out of the tent, trying not to hurry, followed by his wer-tain and advisors.

The remaining chiefs looked at each other unhappily. Branth strutted to the entrance. "If any of you wish to talk to me, I will be in my tent. Everyone knows where that is." He, too, left with his men.

Koshyn sighed and pulled his hood over his head. "There is little point staying here to argue with the wind, Savaric. The clans will never unite."

"But he wants us to bolt for our holes so he can take us one by one. We must try to work together," Savaric implored.

"Maybe. Maybe not. Good-bye, Corin. Take care of your Hunnuli." Koshyn and his warriors filed out.

Without another word to each other, the remaining men left the council, propelled by shame and shock. They had not yet recovered from witnessing the blatant and heretical use of sorcery in the sanctuary of the council tent. After two hundred years of ingrained prejudice and hatred, they had seen the object of their scorn resurrected before their eyes. For the first time, they were witnessing the bitter folly of their ancestors. The men were also recoiling from the truth of the Corin massacre and Medb's shocking declaration of his intention to rule the clans as overlord. The frightening possibilities of the arcane and the logic of Savaric's arguments were lost in the morass of the chieftains' fears for their clans.

In moments the tent was empty, save for the Oathbreakers and the Khulinin. Savaric stared at the entrance as though trying to draw the others back. His eyes were bleak and his lean body sagged with dismay. Gabria and Athlone carefully lifted Pazric's body and carried it outside, where Nara consented to bear it back to the encampment. Savaric and the four cultists followed behind and stepped out into the hot afternoon sun.

Seth picked up his whip, coiling it carefully in his hands. "Our journey was for nought. It was too late to warn the council."

"I thank you for trying," Savaric replied. "Will your citadel be able to withstand Medb's attack?"

"For a while. Some of the old wards still operate, but our numbers are dwindling. In the end, it will be the same for us as for you, and Medb will have free rein in the archives."

"You could burn the books."

Seth shook his head. "It is difficult to destroy a sorcerer's tome, and we would not do it. Someone else may have need of them one day."

"Then defend them well." Savaric watched the people moving through the camps. Some word of the events of that afternoon had already spread, for no women were in sight and the men moved with nervous haste.

Seth spoke to his companions briefly and turned to his brother. "Take care of the Corin. And yourself."

The brothers clasped hands, then the Oathbreakers gathered their whips and disappeared among the tents.

The Khulinin and the Hunnuli silently bore Pazric back to camp.

12

Time confirmed Savaric's worst fears, for the gathering did not survive the night. He argued desperately with every chief except Branth that evening, trying to weld them together against Lord Medb. Unfortunately, the traditions of generations and the stubborn individuality of every clansman were too ingrained. Most of the chieftains turned deaf ears to Savaric's pleas. The lords vacillated through the night while their clans seethed with emotions. The truth of the Corin massacre and Medb's sorcery was told and retold, and the stories grew with every telling until fact and rumor were tangled in knots. Fear ran rampant through the camps. By dawn, Lord Jol pulled the purple banner from the council tent and moved Clan Murjik north toward home.

Lord Medb watched them go with pleasure. He was angry at himself for losing his temper and revealing his power so early. He had planned to rope the council into his control first, then wait to unmask his sorcery when the manuscripts from the Citadel of Krath were in his hands. Not that it really mattered. There was no man who could dispute his rise to overlord now, and if the clans chose to return to their own holdings rather than fight together, then so be it. It would take longer to crush them, but in the long run it would mean a more final collapse. Each clan would be brought to its knees in its own treld and each chief would have to capitulate alone.

Of the twelve clans, only seven presented problems for Medb. The sorcerer counted the clans mentally: he had regained control of the Wylfling after his accident six months ago with the combined weapons of sorcery and fear; the Corin were exterminated; the Geldring were his thanks to the treachery of Branth; Quamar had given him the Ferganan that afternoon; and Ferron would soon come crawling with the Amnok. That left only the Shadedron, Murjik, Reidhar, Dangari, Jehanan, Bahedin, and, of course, the Khulinin. If all went smoothly, the Oathbreakers would soon be eliminated and, by spring, the council of chiefs would cease to exist.

Of course, several of the chieftains were exceedingly stubborn. Lord Caurus of the Reidhar was a temperamental hot-head, as well as a ferocious fighter and a man intensely devoted to his clan. And while Koshyn of the Dangari was young, he could not be treated lightly. No, what was needed was a demonstration that would break their spirits and bring the chiefs to heel, a demonstration that would also salve Medb's pride and give him intense satisfaction: the destruction of the Khulinin. With Savaric dead and the powerful Khulinin weeded down to more manageable numbers, the other chiefs would soon realize their deadly mistake.

Defeating the Khulinin would also enable Medb to finish the destruction of the Corin. That boy, Gabran, was a nuisance and a loose end. Medb did not like loose ends. He planned to have a word about that with the exile leader as soon as they arrived. Such carelessness was unforgivable.

The next morning, the merchants read the signs of war in the clansmen's faces, packed their goods, and quickly left. That afternoon, the Shadedron gathered their herds to depart.

Lord Malech's shoulders slumped as he brought down his black banner, and he glanced apologetically at Savaric. Without a word or gesture of farewell, he mounted his horse and led the Shadedron south. Lord Ferron only waited until dark before slipping fearfully into the Wylfling encampment and kneeling before Medb, giving the oath of fealty for the Amnok clan.

By dawn of the second day after the splintering of the council, the remaining clans had separated into armed camps, bristling with suspicion and anger. The Khulinin remained isolated on the far bank of the Isin. Only Athlone and Savaric crossed the river to talk with the other clansmen. They tried desperately to convince Caurus, Sha Umar, Babur, and Koshyn to ally with them, for with the addition of clan Amnok, Medb's forces were overwhelming. Already there were rumors that Medb was bringing more men to his camp, including the band of exiles.

But Caurus was secretly jealous of Savaric's wealth and authority. He did not trust the Khulinin to lead the combined forces, nor did he want the responsibility himself. Medb's magic terrified Caurus more than he cared to admit. Eventually he, too, gathered his caravan, and the Reidhar clan sought the familiarity of their own holdings near the inland Sea of Tannis.

Koshyn refused to commit himself one way or the other. He had only recently become chief, and he could not decide what was best for his clan. He listened and watched and waited for the final lines to be drawn.

Lord Babur, too, vacillated between Savaric's pleas and Medb's threats. His illness had grown worse, and he knew he didn't have the strength to fight a long war. But that night he died, some said by his own hand. His young son, Ryne, immediately threw Medb's emissary out of his tent and went to join the Khulinin. Sha Umar, a long-time friend of the Bahedin chieftains, came with Ryne and pledged the aid of the Jehanan to Savaric.

Even with the promised help of two clans, the days were long and bitter for Savaric and Athlone, and the stress began to tell on the whole clan. Pazric was sent to the Hall of the Dead on a funeral pyre, which Savaric lit at night to ensure the entire gathering would witness it. After a violent argument with Athlone about his negligence in telling her about Lord Medb's crippled legs, Gabria spent most of her time sitting on the banks of the Isin River.

Cor, on the other hand, thrived on the tense atmosphere of the camp, and his verbal attacks on Gabria grew vicious and more cunning. Only Nara kept him at bay, and Gabria wondered how long it would be before he gathered enough courage to change his weapon from his tongue to a sword. It would not be difficult to kill her in the night and blame it on an agent of Medb. She kept her dagger close to her side and stayed within Piers's tent after dark.

During the day, Gabria had little to do, and time dragged interminably. She lay for hours on the grassy bank of the river in the hot sun and tried to order her thoughts. The shock and disappointment of losing her chance to duel Medb had not diminished, and Gabria found herself examining more and more the possibilities of sorcery. Half a year ago, she would have been aghast at the mere suggestion of the arcane, but in that short time she had lost her clan and been exposed to more sorcery than she ever dreamed possible. It had gone a long way to changing her views of magic—as evidenced by her willingness to even consider it.

Still, whether or not she had a real talent for sorcery was inconclusive in her mind. Piers had his theories and Gabria had been lucky in guessing the truth of the brooch, but nothing had given her absolute proof. And if she did have a talent, what could she do about it? There was no one to teach her and she did not have the knowledge to use the *Book of Matrah* or the manuscripts in the archives of Krath's citadel. She might have an inherent ability, but if it could not be honed it was useless. Piers could not help her—he knew too little—and Nara was untrained in the rules of sorcery and could only protect her from others. The problem was like a sword in the hands of a woman. Gabria laughed at that analogy: she could handle a sword quite well.

Gabria was still debating the dilemma when she and Nara walked back to the camp for the evening meal. Cor had disappeared, and Gabria was happy for the reprieve as she trudged toward the tents. The camp was unnaturally quiet that evening, and people seemed to move with one eye over their shoulders. Smoke from the cooking fires rose sluggishly and hung overhead in the breathless air. Dogs lay in the tents' shadows and panted.

To the east, in the distance, two massive thunderheads piled against the hills and rose like twin battlements before a wall of steel-gray cloud. The setting sun etched the snowy heads of the thunder-clouds with gold crowns and mantles of rose, pearl, and lavender. Deep in the clouds' cores, lightning flickered endlessly, warning of the violence of the coming storm.

Extra outriders were posted that evening, and the herds were moved closer to the shelter of the valley ridges. Other men tightened tent ropes and checked the stakes. After the evening meal, the fires were put out. As the dusk deepened, the storm front moved closer and the lightning became visible in brilliant flashes or wicked streaks that cracked like an Oathbreaker's whip.

Gabria sat restlessly on the ground before Piers's tent and watched the approaching storm. Piers was in another part of camp, helping a woman in labor; Savaric was with Koshyn; and Athlone rode with the outriders. Gabria wished that she were out there with the men rather than sitting in camp. Anything would be better than her edgy, frustrating loneliness. The wind sprang fitfully and tugged at her hair. Abruptly, the breeze died.

Before long, the thunder became audible. By the time night was full, the explosions were incessant. Lightning flared endlessly through the massive sky, pursued by the incessant rumble. Just then, lightning struck an ancient cottonwood tree by the river, splitting it to the ground. Thunder shattered the night, and the first drops of rain spattered in the dust. Gabria fled for the tent.

She sat in the darkness and listened to the tent heave in the wind, struggling against its ropes, and to the sounds of the storm just beyond the thick material. Usually she loved storms and reveled in the wildness of their passing. Tonight, though, she huddled on a stool, feeling a strange sense of dread.

The fury of the storm made her nervous. She jumped at every clap of thunder and stared wildly around when lightning illuminated the tent's interior. Finally, she crawled onto her pallet, pulled a blanket up to her chin, and lay shivering as she tried to sleep.

Some time later, Gabria woke with a start of terror. Lying motionless and trying to control her gasping breath, she strained every sense to catch what had frightened her: a faint sound or movement or smell that was out of place. She realized that she had been asleep for a while, because the storm had settled down to a steady rainfall and the thunder was more subdued.

Then, in the corner of her vision she saw the half-drawn curtain move, as if nudged from behind. She gently eased her hand toward her dagger, her heart hammering madly in her throat. But before her fingers found the blade, a dark shape sprang from behind the curtain, just as lightning flashed outside. In the instant illumination, Gabria saw a man lunge at her and she caught the flash of steel in his upraised hand. Her immediate thought was of Medb. He was trying to fulfill his promise with an assassin.

"No!" she screamed in fury and tried to roll off the pallet, but she was hindered by her blanket. The knife missed its mark and slashed down her right side, skittering off her ribs. The man grunted in anger and furiously pulled his weapon back for another blow. Gabria felt the wound like a firebrand as she struggled with the blanket and her tangled clothes, and her rage increased with the pain. Medb would not dispose of her this easily. She yanked off the blanket, threw it at the dark figure, and scrabbled for her dagger. The man cursed as the blanket tangled his aim, then he threw it aside.

"I'll get you, you little coward," he snarled and grabbed her shoulder.

Cor. It was Cor, not an agent of Medb. Gabria was so surprised, she missed her dagger and knocked it aside. The warrior dropped his weapon and yanked her around to face him. She fell with her dagger underneath her back. Gabria stopped struggling and stared at Cor's blurred face in the darkness. The whites of his eyes glimmered and his teeth showed in a grimace of hate.

He shook her. "I knew you were a coward deep down; you won't even fight to save your worthless skin. Well, I've waited a long time to do this. You thought you were so smart, turning me into half a man, useless for everything!" He leaned over her, his breath reeking of strong wine.

Gabria squirmed, trying to keep her dagger hidden behind her back. The guilt and pity she had felt for Cor died completely, and she stared back at him, matching his loathing. Cor pulled Gabria to her knees and forced her head back to expose her throat.

"I've been watching you and waiting. Now there's no one to save your neck." He pulled her head farther over his bent knee, until her spine creaked and her neck screamed in protest. "You see, with one quick snap, I could break your back and leave you dead, or better yet, just like that Wylfling."

Before Gabria could react, Cor jerked her up and punched her in the face. His fist exploded into her eye and she fell back on the pallet in a daze of pain and surprise. She closed her eyes and swallowed convulsively. Her dagger lay beneath her buttocks.

Cor slapped her. "Look at me, you pig-faced coward. I want to see you plead before I break you."

Gabria tossed her head up, her pain forgotten in a surge of rage and disgust at the madman who had beaten, ridiculed, insulted, and threatened her once too often. Her green eyes ignited and her hand curled over the dagger's hilt. "Go crawl in a hole, eunuch."

Cor snarled. His dark shape swayed, then savagely he grabbed Gabria's throat with both hands, his dagger forgotten in the urge to kill the Corin with his bare hands. His fingers dug into her windpipe and his nails tore her skin. Gabria felt her breath burning in her lungs as she tried to wriggle her dagger out from under their thrashing bodies.

Moaning incoherently, Cor squeezed harder and grinned maliciously. Gabria tore at his iron grip with one hand. But Cor didn't see her other hand. With desperation and fury, she lifted the blade and rammed it into his stomach. This time, there was no doubt of the presence or the origin of the blue flare.

In the darkness, Gabria saw the aura build in her arm and flow up the dagger into Cor's body. He jerked violently and clutched at the knife, his face a mask of hate and disbelief. His eyes rolled and he sagged on top of her. Gabria gasped and fainted.

The first thing Gabria became aware of was light. A small globe of yellow light intruded through her partly open lids into her darkness and drew her from unconsciousness. The second thing she noticed was pain. Then the pain rushed into her head and down her neck and side, until every bruised muscle and laceration throbbed madly. The heaviness she remembered across her chest was gone, and she heard someone moving around her. Gabria tensed, thinking it was Cor, but someone gently raised her head and a cup was pressed to her lips. She smelled the sweetness of Piers's own wine and relaxed. The wine warmed her bruised throat and settled gently in her stomach, where it spread with a healing heat through her body.

Gabria slowly opened her eyes—or eye since one was so swollen she could barely crack the lid. The orb of light wavered for a moment and settled into focus, revealing a small lamp hanging on its pole. She squinted at the light and looked higher into Piers's face. The healer appeared strangely upset, and Gabria smiled weakly at him. Outside, the wind had died and the rain was falling in a steady drizzle.

Piers let the girl finish her wine and then helped her lie down on the pallet before he spoke. "The evil fortune that fell to your clan does not seem to include you."

"Where is Cor?" she mumbled.

Piers glanced behind him. "He's dead." There was no condemnation in his voice, only sadness and regret that she had been forced to act.

The light and the effort of keeping her eye open was too much for Gabria, and her lids settled shut. She sighed deeply, wondering what Piers was thinking. After sharing his tent for so long, Gabria had come to like the healer and she hoped that the affection was mutual. Her hand groped for his. "I saw it, Piers. This time I saw it. As blue as Medb's bolt that killed Pazric."

Piers's hand caught hers and gripped it tightly. He looked down at the girl's battered face unhappily. She looked so young, too young to bear such burdens. The healer stood up and fetched his supplies from the wooden chest, poured more wine, and carried the things back to Gabria's pallet. Piers carefully moved her tunic and examined the long, ragged tear down her side.

Gabria held the wine cup and listened as he worked. She was puzzled that he said nothing. Maybe this time his disapproval outweighed his acceptance of her, and he had decided not to risk his life to protect her. Gabria would not blame Piers if he exposed her: sorcery was a serious crime to conceal.

Strangely, however, Gabria did not feel horrified any more by the reality of her ability. Now that it was confirmed by her own eyes, she

faced it like some incurable disease that had to be accepted if her
sanity were to be preserved. A small part of her quaked in terror at
the truth of being a sorceress, but she imprisoned that part behind a
wall of desire for self-preservation. Gabria found it difficult to believe
that she could be so callous about such a heretical ability, but perhaps
the months of secret fear and debate had strengthened her for the
final acceptance.

"You're not saying much," Gabria finally said to Piers.

He was cleaning her wound and trying to work gently. "It is one
thing to suspect sorcery; it is another for you to face it."

She sighed again and said, "I am not certain I want to. I seem to
be like Medb. Does this mean I'll be twisted by the powers of magic
into something cruel and depraved? Am I going to become an evil
queen at Medb's side?"

"Magic is not an evil unto itself. It is only as good or as wicked as
its wielder," Piers replied softly.

"That's not what my father's priest delighted in telling us. He used
to recite countless incidents of the corruption of magic."

"Magic can be corrupting. It is a tempting power," Piers said,
trying to be casual. "My daughter was tortured and killed for allegedly
killing the fon of Pra Desh with sorcery."

Gabria gasped, "Why?"

Piers looked away into the distance. "My daughter married the
fon's youngest son, against my wishes. The fon was the ruler of Pra
Desh, but his family was a vicious, backstabbing pack of thieves.
About a year after the marriage, the fon's wife poisoned him and
needed a scapegoat when he died. Her youngest daughter-in-law was
available, so the wife fabricated some evidence and accused my
daughter of killing the fon with sorcery."

Piers explained his daughter's fate quietly, but Gabria could hear
the undying rage still in his heart. "You said I reminded you of her.
Was she a sorceress?"

"No." He spat the denial vehemently.

"But I am."

"So it would seem." Piers said nothing more and finished bandag-
ing her side. She watched him worriedly.

Just then, Athlone burst into the tent, shaking off rain and splat-
tering mud from his caked boots. "What's the problem, Piers?" he
asked. He unwrapped his soaked cloak and did not seem to notice
Cor's body lying to one side of the tent. Then he looked up. "Oh,
gods. What happened now?"

Piers tossed a curved dagger to him. He caught it and turned it over in his hands. A wolf's head was carved on the butt of the handle.

"Cor was trying for a little revenge of his own," the healer said.

"Neat. Kill the last Corin and blame it on the Wylfling. Is she hurt?"

"Not seriously."

Gabria smiled painfully at the wer-tain. "They can't get rid of me that easily."

"What about Cor?" Athlone asked.

Piers nodded to the body on the floor and Athlone moved to examine it. He checked the wound, then rocked back on his heels and stared thoughtfully at the dead man. "Your dagger must carry quite a punch," he remarked.

Gabria tensed. She wondered if Athlone suspected anything. He could accept her wielding a sword and wearing a boy's disguise, but she knew he would never condone sorcery.

"I'm sure it did. So would yours if you were being strangled," Piers said.

"If I were being strangled," Athlone returned, "I would make damn sure of a killing stroke. This underhanded pin-prick wouldn't have killed a goat."

Piers looked irritated. "It punctured his stomach, Wer-tain. It is a slower way to kill, but it's just as effective as a slit throat."

Athlone met the healer's gaze skeptically and was about to reply when he saw Gabria wince and noticed for the first time the extent of her injuries. He changed his mind and nodded before standing up. It had not occurred to the wer-tain until that moment just how close Gabria had come to death. The realization shook him more than he believed possible. Athlone looked away. "I will tell Father what happened," he muttered and hurried out of the tent.

Piers began to wrap hot cloths soaked in salt water around Gabria's neck.

"My dagger did not pierce his stomach," Gabria whispered.

"Athlone would not be pleased to hear the truth."

"Neither would Savaric."

"Then we won't bother them with the truth." Piers tilted his head back and took a deep breath. "Sorcery is a thing little understood in this age, and, despite the clans' efforts to forget it, it will keep cropping up at the most inopportune times to wreak havoc. I believe the time has come to change that."

Gabria's green eyes opened wide. "Are you appointing me?"

"I am merely giving you a chance to do as you see fit." For the first time, Piers relaxed and looked at Gabria fondly. "I don't think you have the makings of an evil queen."

"Thank you," she said, grateful as much for his compliment as his protection.

"Thank my daughter. In a roundabout way, you are my revenge on the stupidity of her judges."

A short time later, Athlone returned with Savaric from the Dangari camp, where the chieftain had been arguing fruitlessly with Koshyn. Savaric's look was grim and his eyes, burning like dark coals, seemed to gaze elsewhere as his mind roved many paths. He glanced at Cor's body and Gabria's injuries and shook his head regretfully, his thoughts obviously already passing on to something else. He gestured to his son and left.

Athlone paused by the entrance and, for a moment, his eyes met Gabria's. To his relief, her gaze was as clear as spring water; the awful brilliance he had seen in them the morning of the council was gone. But her face looked so sad. There was something in the unspoken pain in her eyes that pierced the wer-tain to the heart. Unhappily, he said good-night and closed the tent flap behind him.

After the storm, the morning came on fresh winds from the north. The sky was cloudless and clean, and the rivers flowed high between their banks. The ground was muddy after the rain. Before long, the hot sun dried the foliage and the tents, and the reddish soil returned to dust. The clanspeople recovered their herds from the shelter of the hills and set about repairing the damage caused by the storm.

Savaric made no attempt to return to the other camps. Instead, he stayed in the background and unobtrusively watched the happenings across the river. He judged the wind and eyed the far skyline and kept his own counsel. Cor was quickly buried beneath a cairn of rocks with none of the honor or grief that accompanied Pazric to his grave.

Savaric passed a quiet order that the Khulinin should pack to move under the guise of mending and cleaning. They did so, hiding most of their gear in the covered carts and keeping the pack animals close at hand. They would be ready to leave at a moment's notice.

Across the river, Sha Umar and the Bahedin's new chief, Lord Ryne, quietly prepared their clans to move. Koshyn still kept his clan isolated, while Branth readied his werod for war and Ferron quailed at the terms of his "alliance" with Medb.

Lord Medb, meanwhile, awaited his approaching reinforcements, kept track of the fleeing clans, and counted the days until Savaric's mangled corpse would lie at his feet. He learned of Cor's death from a spy in the Khulinin camp. No one seemed to know how the man died, but it was well known he had intended to kill the Corin. Medb considered this information carefully and filed it away. The boy was becoming more fascinating every day. Maybe he would wait a while before killing the brat. It might prove more interesting to study him.

Overall, Medb thought that events were proceeding well. The only ugly incident that marred his pleasure was the betrayal of the bard, Cantrell. The old singer had lived with the Wylfling for a year and brought status and honor to the clan with his skills. Many chiefs had tried to lure Cantrell away, but he seemed content to remain with the Wylfling.

Medb knew of Cantrell's ability to read men's fortunes; it was a talent the bard little enjoyed and tried to avoid. But after Lord Ferron had come to capitulate, Medb had felt invincible. The night of the storm, he had called for Cantrell to foretell his doom. The bard had reluctantly agreed, and for his pains had been properly punished and cast out. It was regrettable, but no man could threaten Medb with impunity. Not even a master bard.

Later that day, just after noon, the Khulinin were still packing and cleaning their camp. Gabria had slept most of the morning and, after a light meal, she went outside for a breath of fresh air. Her side hurt abominably, despite Piers's medicines, and her throat and head felt worse. To avoid attention, she wore her hat pulled low over her eyes and stayed in the shadows of Piers's tent. She could see Nara standing in the Isin's rapids, pawing playfully at the water. Boreas stood nearby, watching her. For a moment, Gabria thought of calling Nara, then changed her mind. The Hunnuli were enjoying each other too much for Gabria to consider interrupting them.

Besides, Gabria didn't really want company. All morning she had mulled over the tragedy of the night before. She could hardly believe that she had killed a man with an arcane power that she knew nothing about. It was a terrifying truth to face. She could deal with her family's murders, her exile, and her unlawful acceptance into Savaric's werod, because those things were external. Sorcery was far different. It affected her being and nothing short of death would ever change her or take away this heretical talent. Dispiritedly, she pulled her hat lower over her face and wondered what she should do. Medb was so far beyond her reach.

Something caught Gabria's attention just as Nara neighed. She looked toward the other camps and saw an old man working his way hesitantly through the ford in the river toward the Khulinin camp. He almost fell in the water. She walked curiously toward the river bank, thinking the man might be drunk. His head was down, almost as if he were having trouble seeing where he was going, and he leaned heavily on a staff.

Gabria stopped a few paces from the water and called, "Do you need help?"

Startled, the old man raised his head, and Gabria gasped in dismay. A bloody bandage was wrapped around the man's face, covering his eyes, and on either side of his nose, dried blood was caked in patches and matted in his beard. Horrified, Gabria clambered down the bank into the water and caught the old man's arm. He gratefully leaned on her and followed her guidance toward the tents. Several guards came running to help. They led the wounded man into Piers's tent, where he sank thankfully onto a stool.

"Get the healer quickly," Gabria whispered to one of the guards. He nodded, his mouth tight with anger. They all recognized the bard and were stricken by his hideous injury. The warrior dashed out and the other guard stepped outside to watch the tent's entrance.

"Thank you," the bard murmured. "I was beginning to think I would never cross the river."

Gabria looked at the bard unhappily. He was a distinguished man, and he wore a dark blue robe cut in an ornate pattern popular among the Wylfling. He wore no cloak and had no weapons. His hands were long and supple. He carried himself well despite the agony of his wound, but she saw that his skin was gray beneath the dried blood, and he gripped his knees with the effort of hiding his pain.

"Why did you come here?" she asked, kneeling by his feet.

"I was not welcome elsewhere." He pointed to his crude bandage. "I also hope to see your healer."

"Of course. He's on his way." Gabria leaped up to see if Piers was coming.

"Wait. Sit a minute. He will be here soon enough." The old man felt for Gabria's arm and pulled her gently to the ground by his side. "I am Cantrell."

"I know," she mumbled. Although Clan Corin had not been able to afford a bard, Gabria had heard this man many times at past gatherings and had loved his soaring tales and sweeping music. "You were with the Wylfling."

"Until recently. Medb took offense to one of my riddles," he replied calmly.

"Medb did this to you?"

He nodded. "And you are the Corin whom tongues are wagging about?"

"Yes. How did you know?"

"By the inflection in your voice. The Corin always rolled their R's as if they appreciated the sound." He cocked his head in puzzlement. "But you are a woman. That is interesting."

Gabria bolted upright and stared at him. "How—?"

"Don't worry. I know you are trying to pass as a boy, but you cannot hide the telltale characteristics of your voice from a trained bard." He smiled wanly. "I'm sorry. I couldn't help showing off a little."

Gabria moved stiffly away from the old bard, her heart in her throat.

But Cantrell reached out for her. His hand found the girl's shoulder and groped down her arm to take her hand. His skin was cold and clammy, but his grip was strong. "Do not fear for your secret," he said gently. "I have heard a great deal about you at this gathering. I simply had no idea you were a woman. It makes your survival more intriguing. I—"

Without warning, the bard straightened. He gripped Gabria's hand tighter, and his ravaged face grew still. He sat for a long time, quietly rubbing her palm with his thumb, lost in deep concentration. Gabria watched him curiously; Cantrell sighed and his chin sank to his chest. She waited for him to speak. After a while he dropped her hand.

"I was right. You are intriguing. Seek the Woman of the Marsh, child. Only she will be able to help you."

"Who is she?"

But Cantrell shook his head slightly, and, at that moment, Piers and Savaric came into the tent. Puzzled, Gabria moved to the rear of the tent to keep out of the way while Piers unwound the blood-stained bandages. When the dirty material fell away, revealing the slashed, oozing remains of the bard's eyes, Gabria looked away. Savaric blanched at the sight and his face paled under his tan. With gentle hands, Piers tended to the hideous wound.

Cantrell sat like a statue during the operation, as if his face were carved of wood. Only when the healer finished wrapping new bandages around the bard's head did Cantrell allow his shoulders to sag and the breath to escape his lungs in a ragged sigh. The men remained quiet while Cantrell drank a cup of wine laced with a mild dose of poppy.

The bard was the first to speak. He felt for the table by his side and laid the cup down. "Thank you, Piers. You have well earned your reputation as the gentlest of the clan healers."

Piers glanced questioningly at Savaric, then replied, "You are welcome, Bard. You should have come to us sooner."

Cantrell leaned toward the chieftain. "There were many interesting things to hear in Medb's camp. Unfortunately, he wanted to listen to me as well, and he did not like what I told him."

"Which was what?" Savaric asked.

"A riddle."

"Oh?"

The bard tilted his head. "You keep your curiosity in check. That's good because I doubt you will understand the riddle any more than I did. My riddles, like most prophecies, are very confusing. If they were clear to us, they would negate the future they were created for. All I can do is give a man a riddle to accept as he wishes. Medb did not accept his."

Gabria turned her head and stared at the old man's face, engrossed in his words.

Cantrell said softly:

"No man will kill thee,
No war will destroy thee,
No friend will betray thee,
But beware thy life,
When the buttercup bears a sword."

"And for that Medb blinded you," Piers said in disgust.

"He took offense at the implications."

Savaric smiled ruefully. "Is there a meaning in that riddle that holds anything for us?"

Piers said, "I don't like that part about no man will kill him."

"And no war will destroy him," Savaric added. He moved to the tent flap. "Medb has heard his doom and we are well aware of ours. Flower or no, we will have to fight."

Cantrell reached carefully for his staff, "Lord, it would be wise to move soon. Lord Medb is bringing in more mercenaries, and the exile band has been called. He plans to destroy the Khulinin first."

The chieftain and Piers exchanged glances, then Savaric said, "I was afraid of that." He called to the guard outside by the tent entrance. "Tell Athlone, Jorlan, and the elders that I want to see them in my tent. And send for Lord Ryne and Sha Umar. Now." The guard dashed away. "Cantrell, do you feel up to attending me a very short while longer?"

The bard nodded. "I am grateful for your hospitality."

"We are the ones who are grateful. Piers, we will be leaving tonight." With the bard leaning on his arm, Savaric walked out. The healer sat down and stared morosely at the pile of filthy bandages and the bowl of blood-stained water. Gabria came to stand beside him.

"Piers, who is the Woman of the Marsh?"

The healer started out of his musings and said, "What? Oh, a fable, I guess. She was supposed to live in the marshes of the Goldrine a long time ago."

"Is the woman still alive?"

"Still? I doubt she ever was." He looked at her strangely. "Why?"

"Cantrell told me a riddle, too." She stared at the leather chest where her scarlet cloak had been neatly packed away and thought of the gold brooch that her mother had given her many years ago: a golden buttercup, the flower that was her namesake.

13

Late in the night, when the air was chilled and the stars blazed across the sky, the Khulinin, the Jehanan, and the Bahedin gathered their caravans together and struck out southwest, following the Goldrine to the mountains. It was impossible to keep their leavetaking a secret, for the caravans were too massive and the animals were restless in the cool hours before dawn. Still, Savaric hoped to gain an element of surprise by slipping out without warning. A sleepy crowd gathered on the banks of the river to watch the clans leave. By sunrise, the caravans were miles away.

Medb anticipated their flight and immediately sent trackers to follow the clans' trail. It would be several days before his reinforcements arrived and, by the time he marched, it would be too late to catch the fleeing clans on the plains. But eventually they would go to ground, and when they did, Medb knew that he could crush them all.

For three days the clans followed the Goldrine River west toward Khulinin Treld. They traveled quickly, making few stops during the day and walking late into the night. The chiefs knew their time was limited and pushed their people hard. It could have been a difficult trip with three chiefs commanding the huge train, but the leadership seemed to fall naturally on Savaric. Lord Ryne was inexperienced in his new position as chieftain and leaned heavily on Savaric's advice. Sha Umar also bowed to the Khulinin's authority—he was smart enough to know Savaric was the better leader in a drastic situation like this.

So Savaric, almost instinctively, was leading them toward the safety of Khulinin Treld. Yet, as the miles stretched out behind the caravans, he began to have second thoughts. Khulinin Treld was the natural place for them to go; Medb would expect it and plan for battle in that terrain. However, the treld promised no real defense for a large group that contained many women and children. They could be starved out of the hall in a matter of days, and there was no good place for defensive stands. The treld was also close to Wylfling Treld. Too close for comfort.

However, Savaric knew of no other alternatives. They did not dare fight Medb on open ground: the three clans would be massacred in the first rush. There were no natural defensive positions near any of their holdings and no other clan that would give them aid. The Dangari had been Savaric's last hope, but Koshyn was still vacillating when the clans left. The Khulinin, the Bahedin, and the Jehanan were alone, with no hope for more aid, no hope for mercy, and no place to make a stand before Medb's larger, more formidable-army. Savaric racked his brains for a solution. The responsibility of the clans weighed heavily, and, though he rode his stallion to a lather and wore himself into exhaustion keeping the caravans moving, Savaric came no closer to an answer.

The fourth night out of the gathering, the waning moon rose late beyond the grasslands to waken the wolves. The night was breathlessly uncomfortable. The moisture from the recent storm had quickly dried in the arid air, and the heat soared with every passing day. Now, even the nights gave scant relief. There was little wind to keep the mosquitoes at bay, and the dust settled slowly about the wagons. After setting the watch and posting the outriders, the camp fell into an uneasy rest. Savaric, weary of his own thoughts, gathered Ryne and Sha Umar and went to find Piers and Cantrell.

The bard had collapsed with a fever soon after coming to the clan and had been under Piers's care during the trek. To everyone's relief, he was beginning to recover. Savaric hoped he had regained enough strength to give advice. Cantrell was the repository of nearly every song and tale told by the clans for generations. Somewhere in that vast store of clan history and tradition, Savaric hoped to find the key to their survival.

They found Piers and Cantrell in the healer's tent, finishing a light meal. The tent had only been partially raised over several poles and the wagon to give the occupants shelter. The flaps were wide open to catch the fitful evening breeze. Piers had not lit a cooking fire; only a small brass lamp glowed in the dark interior. Even so, the tent was stuffy and hot. Cantrell lay on a pallet near the entrance. His skin was gray with exhaustion, but he had eaten well and his wounds were healing.

Piers welcomed his guests and offered cups of wine. The chiefs accepted and sat down around the bard.

Cantrell's face was unreadable beneath the bandages, but his mouth lifted in a smile as he greeted the men. "Khulinin Treld is far tonight, my lord," he said to Savaric.

"I am weary, Bard," Savaric chided. "We had hoped to hear a song that might help us face the leagues still to go. Not an observation on the distance to the treld."

"My voice lacks its strength and my hands lack an instrument. Would you settle for a tale?"

"I shall listen to your wisdom, master," Savaric said quietly.

Cantrell was still for a moment. He was well aware of the deadly peril that faced them. For years he had traveled among the clans—from the northernmost Murjik Treld on the fringes of the great forest, to the deserts and the towers of the Turic tribesmen. He had seen Khulinin Treld and knew its advantages and its weaknesses, and he had watched the buildup of the massive Wylfling forces. He also knew Medb. The sorcerer would hunt the Khulinin to the grave unless the clan found a way to destroy him.

Cantrell had pondered for many hours what he might tell Savaric if the chief asked his counsel. Advice was a two-edged sword the bard did not like to wield lightly, particularly when his prophetic riddles clouded the issue. Yet, during the long, painful hours of riding in the wagon, he had remembered an ancient tale that had survived the wars and invasions of countless years to be written on a scrap of vellum and buried in the vast library of the Citadel of Krath. A long time ago, he had been allowed to study some of the priceless manuscripts there and had found that tale. It came to his mind now, and in its substance he saw a glimmer of hope.

"Many years ago," Cantrell began, "before Valorian led the clans over the mountains to the vastness of the Ramtharin Plains, other peoples held this land. Short, dark-haired sons of the Eagle, they came from the west, beyond the Darkhorn Mountains, and joined the plains to their vast empire. Greedy for slaves, horses, and the riches of the grasslands, they subjugated the simple tribes that lived here and built their roads with the bones of the fallen. They built many fortresses to guard their mighty domain and garrisoned their armies within. From these walls of adamant, the invaders pinned their conquered realm in a grip of steel. Four of these strongholds were built to guard the steppes. One was located on the eastern flank of the Himachal Mountains, by the Defile of Tor Wrath."

Sha Umar looked startled. "Do you mean those old ruins on the spur of the ridge?"

Cantrell barely nodded, for his wounds still ached.

"I remember that vaguely," Lord Ryne said. His dark blue eyes shifted from one man to another. He was still nervous in such illustrious company, but his self-confidence was growing. "There was another fort near Bahedin Treld, along the Calah River. But that one was razed by the men of Pra Desh years ago."

"That's true," Cantrell replied. "But this fortress still stands. It has withstood many attacks. I believe there are wards set in the gates to protect it from arcane assault."

Sha Umar nodded and the other men looked both interested and apprehensive.

Cantrell continued. "When the western empire began to crumble, the strongholds along the frontiers were abandoned to bring the armies closer to home. After that, the fortress was used by other tribes and a self-proclaimed king or two. In the past years, its only enemy has been time." He stopped for a moment, then his voice began a slow chant.

"Stone and timber, brick and mortar,
Blood for fastness, bones for strength,
Iron and steel and tears of mourning
Built the walls of Ab-Chakan.

Guardian of the Savon River
Fair it stood upon the mount.
Bearer of the Eagle standard
Watcher of the Dark Horse Plains.

Seven towers wrought of darkness
Bound with gold and spells of might.
Swords of steel held fast the ramparts
Strength of heart kept safe the gates.

Distant horns called home the warriors
Empty now lie halls of stone.
Eyeless shadows watch from towers
Only wind walks on the walls."

Cantrell fell silent, letting the images of the song play through the listeners' thoughts. "It's rather archaic," he said after a time. "But that is a fragment of a song I found long ago."

Savaric stared thoughtfully into his cup. Unlike the other men, he had not traveled the eastern slopes of the Himachal Mountains and was not familiar with the ruins or the defile Cantrell mentioned. He was reluctant to remove his clan to lands he did not know, and he had only the bard's reputation to give any value to the consideration of the fortress. "This place—Ab-Chakan—what is it now?"

"Well, the clans never had any use for a fortified garrison, so it has been abandoned for years. But the walls still stand and the defile has many caves that bore deep into the mountains." Cantrell paused, his face turned toward the chiefs around him. "For men with a little ingenuity, it could be an answer to a prayer."

Sha Umar smiled slightly. "The werods will not like it. Fighting within walls goes against the grain."

"So does dying needlessly at the hand of a paid mercenary," Savaric said dryly.

The Jehanan chieftain laughed. "I shall remember to tell them that."

"Lord," said Cantrell. "I do not know if this is sound advice. Ab-Chakan may be useless to your needs, but if it fails, the defile can be defended for months by a mere handful. And Medb would not anticipate such a move. It might give you a little more time."

Savaric looked past the open tent flaps into the distance. "How far is this place?"

Cantrell pondered. "Several days journey north of Dangari Treld . . . perhaps thirty leagues from here."

"I hope that Koshyn doesn't try to get in our way," Lord Ryne spoke up. "We have few enough men as it is."

"I doubt he will," Sha Umar replied. His lean, aquiline face broke into a smile, and he gestured to Savaric with his wine cup. "Koshyn respects you even if he does try to straddle two horses at once. It's that band of exiles I'm worried about."

"Yes. They were called forth five days ago. If they find us before we reach shelter, there will be much blood spilled," Cantrell noted.

"Then we must move fast," Savaric said, suddenly reaching his decision. He felt more hopeful than he had in days. At last there was an objective to reach for that offered a semblance of success. "Are we agreed?" he asked the others. The men nodded. "Then we will turn north and go to this fortress." He paused and added, "Cantrell, if you wish to leave, I will provide a guide, horses, and supplies. Unfortunately, I can ill-afford to send an escort."

Cantrell waved off the suggestion. "I knew what I was walking into when I came for help. I have read the Khulinin's riddle of doom, my lord. Now I want to understand the answer."

Savaric's mouth curled up in a weary smile. "I hope you do not regret your curiosity."

Beyond the rim of firelight, where the herds dozed in the warm darkness, the outriders passed in silent vigil. They rode around the livestock, humming a soft song or stopping to exchange a quiet word with the sentinels around the camp.

On a low knoll near where the horse herd lay, Nara stood, darker than the night itself. Only her large eyes sparkled with faint starlight. Occasionally she swung her head to sniff the breeze or swished her tail at a mosquito. Except for these brief movements, she remained still. On the mare's back, Gabria shoved her bow aside, leaned on Nara's rump, and tried uselessly not to fidget. She was bored with the inactivity of guard duty and too anxious to sit still.

Time and again she remembered Cantrell's strange reaction to her—and his advice to seek the Woman of the Marsh. Gabria had tried to ask him to explain what he'd meant, but the days had been too hectic and at night he was too ill and tired to answer. Piers could not help her, and she didn't know who else to ask.

The marshes, as well as Gabria could remember, were southeast of the Tir Samod, where the Goldrine River, swollen with the waters of numerous tributaries, flowed down into a low, half-drowned land of reed-choked channels, pools, and treacherous mires before filtering into the Sea of Tannis. She had never heard of a woman living in the marshes. If there was such a woman, why was she important? Why would Cantrell tell her to seek this woman? Gabria wondered if the bard sensed her inherent ability for sorcery. Perhaps that was why his response was so odd. Maybe this Woman of the Marsh had something to do with magic.

For the past few days, Gabria had been able to put aside the realization of her power in the frantic departure and the hurried march of the caravan. It was easy to ignore Piers's thoughtful looks and Cor's absence, and it had been simple to keep the truth from Nara. But here, in the darkness, the shadows and distractions were dispelled and Gabria was forced to come face to face with a self she did not know. The girl she once had been, the girl who happily kept a tent for her father and brothers and who ran laughing through the days, had somehow become this short-haired stranger who wielded an unknown power and set herself above clan law. She had tamed a Hunnuli, ridden with a werod, and killed a man with the Trymian Force. Gabria did not recognize herself any longer, and what she found instead was frightening.

It did not matter how Nara might reassure her or Piers might protect her; she could not shake off seventeen years of ingrained distrust of sorcery. To her, magic was a power that corrupted any soul it touched and caused nothing but grief. Lord Medb was exactly what she expected a sorcerer to be: ruthless, deceitful, murderous, lusting for more power. If she were a true clanswoman, she would immediately turn herself over to Savaric and suffer the proper punishment before she became like Medb and threatened the welfare of the clans.

But the sense of survival that had sent Gabria walking out of Corin Treld refused to consider the notion. She would have to find a way to control her talent so she would never use it inadvertently again. Perhaps Cantrell had told her to seek the Woman of the Marsh because he knew this woman could help her deal with this unwanted ability. If only she knew how to find her.

Nara shifted and raised her head. Her ears swiveled forward. *Boreas and his rider are coming*, she informed Gabria.

The girl sat up quickly. She stiffened her shoulders and watched the black figure of Boreas materialize out of the darkness. Noiselessly, the huge stallion stepped up beside them and nickered softly in greeting.

The wer-tain sat silently, watching the dozing horses nearby. Gabria saw the dim sparkle of polished mail under the robe that covered him to his knees, but the glimmer of his helm was hidden beneath the hood of his cloak. She could not see the wer-tain's face in the shadows of his hood, and she hoped he could not see hers.

"Nothing stirs tonight," Athlone said quietly.

"No." Gabria had not spoken to him since Cor's death and she was not certain she wanted to now. She was horribly afraid that Athlone would probe into her actions and discover her power. The old threat she had once thought forgotten reared its ugly head between them.

"My father tells me we are going north,"

"North," Gabria said testily. "Are we going to skulk in the mountains like thieves?"

He sighed, trying to be patient. "This caravan is too big to 'skulk.' We're going to an old stronghold called Ab-Chakan."

"I suppose that will be better than running over the plains like frightened rabbits."

Athlone turned his head and she could feel his cold glance. "If you had a better suggestion, you should have informed Savaric."

"I do not interfere with the councils of the wise," Gabria said huffily. She wished he would go away.

"Fine words for a woman who claims herself chieftain, disrupts an entire gathering, and threatens a sorcerer."

"And what was it worth? You let me delude myself with hopes of vengeance, then sat back and watched me make a fool of myself in front of the lords of the clans."

Athlone shook his head. "This is an old argument. I did not know he was injured so badly until I saw him the first day."

She was silent for a long while. The Hunnuli stood motionless, their ears cocked back to listen, their ebony eyes catching the light of the old moon as it thrust its horn above the hills. Athlone waited. His face was still shrouded in night, and his fingers picked restlessly at the folds of his robe.

Finally, Gabria slammed her fist on her knees. "What do I do now, Athlone? I've waited months to challenge Lord Medb. Now I have no satisfaction to quiet the voices of my brothers or wash away the memories of that day. Medb has slipped out of my grasp."

"There are other ways to gain vengeance. Some more subtle than others," he said.

Gabria whipped her head around and her heart began to pound. She could not see his face to read his expression.

"There are other ways," he added, his voice level. "Some more fitting than others, to seek your revenge against a man like Medb. Sorcerer or no, he is still a man with his own weaknesses. Seek those out. Learn his greatest fears and use them against him."

"How?" she asked sarcastically. "Do I stop him in the middle of a battle and ask a few questions, or do I visit his tent at nightfall?"

"Use your wits, Corin. None of us know how the coming days will unfold. Perhaps, if you're clever, you will have weapons at hand that will be sharper than any sword."

Gabria stared at the wer-tain. Just how much did he know about her? Had he talked to Piers or was he making his own deductions? Or was he simply offering his best advice? "All right, I'll watch. But I doubt it will do much good."

Athlone rubbed his hand down Boreas's neck. "We never know. Wars are terribly unpredictable." He stopped, then said, "I did not tell you, but I was very glad to see you alive the other night. If Cor had succeeded, I would have personally flayed him alive."

"I'm glad you didn't have the opportunity," Gabria replied, surprised and pleased by his remark.

"How long will you continue this charade?" he asked suddenly. "You cannot pretend to be a boy forever."

Gabria shrugged. "I hadn't thought that far ahead. I guess until Savaric finds out or Medb kills me."

Athlone's hand unconsciously gripped his sword hilt. "Medb will not kill you if I have anything to do with it," he muttered under his breath.

"What did you say?"

"Nothing. Tomorrow, you will join the outriders to search for Ab-Chakan."

She saluted. "Yes, Wer-tain." He turned to go, but she held out her hand and stopped him. "Athlone, do you know of the Woman of the Marsh?"

Athlone stiffened. Boreas snorted as his rider leaned forward. "Where did you hear of that?"

"From Cantrell."

"Well, forget it immediately. That woman is evil and dangerous. You have no business with her. I forbid you to mention her again." He kneed Boreas, and they vanished in the dark.

"That was strange," Gabria said, astonished by his vehement reaction.

Nara nickered softly. *The man does not understand yet. He thinks as you once did about magic.*

"Once did?"

Your beliefs have traveled far since you felled Cor the first time with magic.

"The first time," Gabria repeated weakly.

Surely you did not think I did not know. Hunnuli are most comfortable with magic-wielders. We can sense many things about our riders that men overlook.

"Then you know I killed him."

Of course. And now you know the truth.

"That I am a sorceress." Gabria sounded disgusted.

You are not a sorceress yet. Your powers are untrained, but you have much natural talent. That should not be wasted. Especially now.

"Well, what can I do about it?" she demanded, trying to keep her voice down. "Lord Medb would never teach me, and who else knows the forbidden arts?"

Follow the bard's counsel, Nara answered.

"The Woman of the Marsh? I don't even know if she exists!" Gabria said.

The woman is there. In the great marshes. She will help you if she feels your desires are strong enough.

Gabria was stunned. She knew that Nara was telling the truth, and the possibilities of what the Hunnuli was saying were incredible. She sat lost in thought for some time before she broke her silence. When at last she spoke, her voice was filled with sadness.

"Oh, Nara, these are strange days. Legends spring to life, clan fights clan, and our fates hang on the thread of a sorcerer's spell. Now I have a power I was taught to despise and I don't know what to do with it. All I can think about is Medb and magic and the look of death on my father's face." Her words failed, and she leaned despondently on Nara's neck.

The Hunnuli nickered in sympathy. *I cannot always understand men's feelings, but I, too, have felt loss and loneliness. When that happens, you must look for new strengths and the new pastures.*

Gabria listened to the gentle words in her mind. She slipped her arms around Nara's neck. "Will the marshes do?"

That will do very well. I have felt the need for a long run.

Two hours after dawn, Athlone sent his outriders forth as scouts. Riding northeast, they spread out to find the fastest road to the Himachal Mountains and the fortress of Ab-Chakan. Gabria and Nara rode with them. They galloped for leagues over the grassy, level end of the valley of the Hornguard. Gradually the terrain rolled upward and the hills surged toward the feet of the mountains. Ahead, the dark, smoky smudge marking the mountains sharpened into individual peaks.

The Himachal Mountains were not mountains in the rugged, glorious form of the Darkhorns. They were mere vanguards to the mighty range, and their crowns rose only to a modest height above the plains. Yet, despite their shorter, rounder tops, their slopes were steep and difficult and thick with heavy underbrush and timber.

At the southernmost end of the mountains, where a wide valley led a stream out of the forests to meet the Isin River, Clan Dangari had built their treld and ran their studs year round. They were the most sedentary of the clans and were trading their nomadic instincts for the pleasures of horse breeding.

Athlone's scouts cautiously bypassed Dangari Treld and continued north, seeking only the defile and the fortress. There was still no word of Koshyn's movements and nothing had been seen of the band of exiles. The Oathbreakers sent word to Savaric that the army of hired mercenaries had arrived at Medb's camp and the combined forces of the four clans and the hired soldiers were marching after the Khulinin. Medb had also followed through with his threat to the cultists and had sent a large force to besiege the Citadel of Krath.

Time was running out. Savaric turned the clans north after the scouts, and the race began.

The three clans had a five-day lead on the Wylfling and they would need every hour of it to find the fortress in time. The caravans moved much slower than an armed host and had many leagues to travel. It would be close, but Savaric hoped that the clans would make it to Ab-Chakan with a day or two to spare. That hope was a real possibility—as long as the Dangari or the exiled marauders did not slow them down.

The next four days were miserable, but Savaric's pride in his people grew tenfold. With the host of the sorcerer on their heels, the three clans drew together and fled for the mountains. Excess baggage, broken wagons, and sick or weak animals were left behind. They made no stops during the day and at night they only stopped long enough to rest the horses, water the livestock, and eat a cold meal. The clans lit no fires, and the tents remained packed; the people collapsed in the shelter of their wagons and waited for dawn. On the trail, the sun burned on their heads and the dust rose to choke them. Before long, the grueling pace began to tell, particularly on the children and the foals, but the caravan pushed on, knowing it would mean certain death if they were caught on the open plains.

Late on the second day of the journey north, several scouts, including Gabria, returned to tell Savaric that the walls of Ab-Chakan still stood and the caves in the defile were empty. Two men had been left to watch the fortress, and others waited along the way. Dangari Treld was quiet and no news was known of the exiles.

Savaric sighed with relief when he heard the scouts' reports, and he sent several more trackers out to follow the advance of Medb's forces. In secret, he wondered where Koshyn and the Dangari were.

On the tenth day of the trek from the gathering, Savaric got his answer.

14

Footsore and weary, the three clans swung east to avoid Dangari Treld and then north again to follow the Isin River. The Himachals lay on their left hand and the vast, wind-walked plains of Ramtharin lay on their right. Savaric was relieved they had traveled almost thirty leagues in the four days since leaving the Goldrine River—an unheard-of pace for a caravan so large—but the clans were exhausted. Men, women, children, and animals were pushed to the limits of their strength. Only the Hunnuli showed no signs of fatigue as the caravan trudged the last leagues toward the defile.

Along the mountains' foothills, the Isin River flowed south, following the lay of the terrain. Like a boundary line, it separated the rugged hills on the west side from the smoother grasslands that rolled east to the sea. After some debate, the chieftains decided to stay on the east bank of the river. There was very little cover to shield them from hunters and few places where they could easily defend themselves if caught, but their passage would be easier and faster.

The decision proved a wise one. As the caravan traveled farther north, the mountains tumbled down into rough hills, gullies, and sharp-backed ridges that would have been impossible for the wagons. On the east bank, the slopes were gentler and the patchy growths of scrub were easier to avoid. The clans moved faster, hoping that they were almost to the fortress and safety. Only the openness, something they usually loved, made them feel strangely insecure. No one knew when the exile band or Medb's host would sweep down on the slow-moving caravan, so people waited and watched and constantly looked over their shoulders.

Then, just after midday of the fifth day, one of the outriders, scouting to the south of the caravan, wheeled his horse and galloped back to the line. Instantly, the werods herded the wagons together and drew a tight ring around them; swords glittered in the sun and a deadly shield of spears pointed outward from the ring. The outriders galloped in and all the mounted men filled the gaps behind the warriors.

The three chiefs drew their swords and waited as the scout reined to a stop. Savaric's face was stern. Gabria and Athlone waited side by side on their Hunnuli just behind him. The clans were quiet while they waited for the news.

"Lord," the Khulinin said to Savaric. "The Dangari are behind us. They ride swiftly without herds or wagons."

An excited murmur rushed through the listening clans. Their worst fears seemed to be realized.

"We should move back to the river and the shelter of the trees," Lord Ryne suggested.

Savaric shook his head and slammed his sword back into its scabbard. "No. We have no time. We will wait."

No one else moved. They watched warily as a large troop of mounted, mail-clad men swept toward them along the skirts of the hills. The riders carried their painted shields on their arms and in their hands were tall spears of ash. A blue banner floated at their head.

Suddenly they swerved toward the waiting caravan and galloped up with a noise like thunder. The three clans instinctively moved closer together, and the warriors' hands tightened on their swords. A horn cried out, clear and keen, and the company came to a halt not far from Savaric. The two groups eyed each other silently. Then, a lone man rode forward, leading a string of seven mares. A white horsetail flowed from his helm. His blue cloak was thrown back over his shoulders, and his fair face grinned in relief.

"Savaric, you are a hard man to track down."

"Koshyn, what in Surgart's name are you doing here?" Sha Umar yelled suspiciously.

"I could ask you the same, for you are on my holdings," Koshyn replied, ignoring the hostile looks of the clansmen. "But I've come to pay my debt. Seven mares, remember?"

"You choose a strange time to do so," Savaric said.

"The situation demanded it. The exile band is not far behind me."

Athlone, his eyes smoldering, urged Boreas forward. "And you led them directly to us!"

Koshyn's face darkened as though a cloud of rage had passed over him. "They attacked my treld last night and butchered five of our prized stallions and a score of mares before we could drive them off. They're licking their wounds now, but they will return."

Voices burst out in anger and surprise from the watching clanspeople. The warriors kept their spears raised, but their hands relaxed. Every person there understood the Dangari's grief and rage at the loss of their beloved horses.

"Why did the marauders attack your clan?" Savaric asked.

"Because I refused to join Medb. We left the gathering after you. Medb was furious. I think he diverted the exiles from you to take his revenge on us."

"I see. Thank you for the warning and the mares. We must go." Savaric wheeled his stallion and raised his hand to motion to the caravan. Although he desperately wanted the help of the Dangari, he would not beg for aid now—not after days of frantic flight and worry.

Koshyn rode forward and stopped him. The young chief's eyes were bright with anger, and the tattoos on his face faded into a dark flush. "We're going with you, Lord Savaric," he said. "I have been justly punished for my sluggardly courage and now I ask your leave to join you."

Savaric paused and looked at his fellow chieftains. Sha Umar shrugged; Ryne nodded firmly. Savaric stared at the Dangari's face for a full minute and weighed the fury and sincerity he saw in Koshyn's blue eyes. Then he nodded abruptly. "Your help is most welcome, but we must move fast if the marauders are following. Where is the rest of your clan?"

"They are coming. We're driving the herds to secret pastures in the mountains, and the women are gathering supplies. I came to find you and learn your counsel."

"Listen, then. We are going to Ab-Chakan at the Defile of Tor Wrath. Join us there as quickly as possible."

Koshyn stared. "That pile of rock? What for?"

"Piles of rock are easier to defend," Savaric replied curtly.

The younger chief looked over the weary clans and back to Savaric. He still couldn't believe the caravan had traveled this far so fast. When his scouts had told him the location of the clans, he wouldn't believe them until he saw the trail for himself. His respect for Savaric had doubled.

"We will be there," Koshyn said. He handed the lead line of the seven mares to Savaric, spurred his horse around, and cantered back to his men. With a ringing shout, they galloped back toward their treld.

Sha Umar grinned. "Now we will only be *very* outnumbered instead of *desperately* outnumbered."

Savaric leaned on his saddle horn and said, "If only the other clans could be so easily persuaded." He waved to the caravan, and the werod and wagons fell in behind him.

Nara waited a moment and watched the dust settle behind the vanishing company of horsemen. *We will have to go soon. Before it is too late.*

"Yes, tonight, I suppose. I hope we will find the clans still alive when we return," said Gabria.

Since she had made the decision to search for the Woman of the Marsh, a strange reluctance to leave the Khulinin had hindered Gabria. She kept putting off their departure, waiting for a better moment. Gabria realized that the days were pressing close, but every time she considered leaving, a thought like a stinging fly buzzed in her mind: it had happened once; it could happen again. She could return to find nothing left but blood and smoke and rotting corpses. The image terrified her, more, she told herself, than the fear of her power or an uncertain meeting with an odd woman of legends. If she stayed with the Khulinin, she would not have to face the agony again and she could live or die with them.

Nara understood her reluctance. She pawed the ground and snorted. *They will survive for a while behind the wall of that fortress. They do not need you yet.*

Gabria shivered slightly. "Can you promise me they will be alive when we return?"

I can promise you nothing. Just have faith in them.

She rubbed the mare's neck, feeling the rock-hard muscle beneath the velvet hair. "You are always honest, Nara. You give me heart."

The mare looked at Gabria sideways from beneath her long forelock. *That is why I am with you. Pack ample food; I do not know how long we will be gone.*

The afternoon slowly passed into evening. The sky was barred with high clouds and the sun faded to copper as it fell. It was nearly dusk when the scouts found the remains of an ancient road in the tumbled shrubs and weeds of the Isin's valley.

Built long before the horsemen rode the plains, the road had served the fortress of Ab-Chakan as a supply route to other cities and strongholds, places that had fallen to ruin after the demise of the empire. Now, only crumpled patches of paving stone showed through the grass and dirt.

As the clans traveled farther north, the road became more obvious. Its straight flight and level course were clearly seen on the flanks of the hills where it followed the river. Although the grasses and vines clambered over the stone, the road was still passable and the caravan thankfully used it. Even in the dim twilight, the clans could see the skillful handiwork of the men of old in the cut and lay of the stones.

Several hours after nightfall, the clans halted by the river. Savaric spread the word that they were five leagues from the fortress and would reach it the next day. Breathing prayers of thanks to their gods, everyone prepared for the night. Soon the camp sank into the silence of exhausted sleep. Only the sentinels and outriders moved beyond the edges of the encampment. The night was quite black, since the moon would not rise until much later and no fires or lamps were lit. A mild wind hummed over the grass, and the stars reflected on the river's surface like jewels on a black mirror.

Gabria waited until all was still, then she stealthily collected her gear. She took only a bag of food and her dagger. Piers would care for her things until she returned. After a moment's thought, however, she fished out the arcane stone ward and wrapped it carefully in her cloak. She dressed in a dark blue tunic and pants, folded her cloak into the bag, and shoved her dagger into her belt.

Piers and Cantrell were sleeping beside the wagon. She carefully picked up her bag and a water skin, and slid over to the bard. She gently shook him. He woke immediately.

Gabria could not see Cantrell's face, but she felt his body stiffen. "It's all right," she whispered. "It's only Gabria."

He lay still for a moment, listening, then he murmured in understanding, "You are leaving."

"Yes. Please tell Athlone not to worry. I will be back."

He chuckled softly. "The wer-tain will be very busy for the next few days, but I will tell him. Please be careful. My advice is not always commendable."

"The Hunnuli will see to my safety. Farewell." She slipped away.

Piers rolled over. "So she is leaving at last."

"Yes. I only pray it does more good than harm."

"Bard, she had no choice."

Cantrell sighed. "I know. But the Woman of the Marsh can be dangerous, and she may not accept another pupil."

"It is more dangerous to have an untrained magic-wielder in our midst."

The bard relaxed into his blankets. "We will see soon enough," he said sadly.

Piers lay back and looked up at the stars. "The gods give you speed, Gabria," he murmured to himself.

Nara was waiting for Gabria on the edge of camp. As silently as wind-blown shadows, they glided past the guards and disappeared into the darkness. For a short distance, the Hunnuli cantered south along the path the clan had followed, then she veered east and stretched out into a gallop. Like a cloud scudding across the night sky, she swept over the leagues of grass, her legs thrusting forward in an endless rhythm. She ran effortlessly, and the air trembled as she passed. Astride the mare's back, Gabria held fast to Nara's mane and marveled at the speed the Hunnuli held. The girl leaned forward. The wind whipped the mare's black mane into her face.

Nara felt her rider's joy and in answer, she leaped forward ever faster. Her nostrils flared, her ears tucked back, and her muscles flowed beneath her black hide. The immeasurable plains opened before them. Far ahead, a thunderstorm etched the horizon with lightning. Flinging her head high, the mare raced to meet the storm.

They swung wide to the east to avoid running afoul of Medb's army, eventually bending their way south toward the Sea of Tannis and the marshes of the Goldrine. The storm was left behind. After a while, Gabria was lulled by the rocking of Nara's gait and she dozed on the mare's neck, watching through half-closed lids as the land flowed away beneath them in a blur. Imperceptibly the blur began to lighten and tinge with color. Once, Gabria started awake and looked up to see the sun poised on the rim of the world.

The hills flattened somewhat, rising in a slow, easy swell, and their treeless slopes soon were covered with thick grasses that formed a springy cushion under Nara's hooves.

The day quickly grew hot and the wind faded. Above, a hawk circled in the brilliant blue sky, but it was the only living thing that Gabria saw all day. Either the animals were lying low to escape the heat or had fled at the sight of the running Hunnuli. By noon, shimmering heat mirages wavered in the distance. Gabria was stiff and thirsty, and, at last, she could feel Nara beginning to tire.

The Hunnuli found a water hole in a depression between several hills, and horse and rider rested in the shade of a small copse of trees. Gabria and Nara left again a few hours later and the mare galloped south with the wind. At dusk, they came to the edges of the Goldrine Marshes.

It was late in the morning before Athlone knew that Gabria was gone. The realization that he had not seen the girl or the Hunnuli for hours came gradually as he led a company of the werod ahead of the caravan. When he questioned Boreas, he learned that Gabria had left in the night, but where she was going the stallion would not say. Blazing with fury, the wer-tain galloped Boreas back to the caravan. There were only two men who might know where the Corin went, and Athlone intended to find out what they knew.

Piers, walking by the side of his wagon, saw the wer-tain bearing down on him and spoke a soft warning to Cantrell, who was seated on the loaded bundles. The healer clucked to his old mare and began whistling nonchalantly.

"Where is that wretch of a Corin?" Athlone demanded as Boreas skidded to a halt. The clansmen around them stared curiously; Piers tried to look innocent.

"The boy will be back soon, Wer-tain," Cantrell answered.

Athlone's face was livid. "Where is he?" he shouted, almost forgetting to use the masculine term before the interested on-lookers. Boreas pranced sideways under his rider's agitation.

The bard shrugged. His bandaged face showed no expression; his voice was calm and reasonable. "His cause was urgent and he will return. Let us leave it at that."

"I will not leave it at that. That boy is under my care and . . . stop that infernal whistling," he snapped at Piers. The healer gave him an aggrieved look, which Athlone ignored. "Gabran had no just reason to leave alone at this time! It's far too dangerous." His eyes suddenly narrowed. "Unless . . . he's been under Medb's sway all this time!"

"Athlone, read your heart," Cantrell said. "You know that is not true."

"Then why did he leave? And why did you let him go?" Athlone shouted at both men.

"We had no say in Gabran's decision," Piers replied. "But we would not have stopped him."

Boreas spoke gently in Athlone's mind, *Nara went with Gabria, Athlone. They will return soon.*

The wer-tain calmed down a fraction. "I hope to the gods that boy does return," he said with feeling. "Because if Medb or the marauders don't kill him, I just might." Boreas spun around and galloped off, leaving Piers and Cantrell relieved.

"Have you noticed," Piers said, "that the wer-tain appears to care for the Corin more than he realizes?"

Cantrell nodded. "Interesting, isn't it? But the tragic paradox is if she kills Medb to save the Khulinin, clan law will order her death for using magic. Athlone, as wer-tain of her adopted clan, will have to fulfill that edict."

"Is that her doom?" Piers asked sadly.

"Only if she can find the answer to Medb's riddle."

"And if she does not . . ."

Cantrell finished the sentence for him. "None of us need worry about difficulties with clan law."

High, hazy clouds drifted in during the afternoon and obscured the sun with a half-hearted veil. Word passed down through the ranks that the fortress was only a few miles distant, and those with sharp eyes could already discern the black towers like tiny teeth against the reddish bluffs. The caravan was heartened by the news. Forcing their weary legs to move faster, they pushed on, hoping to reach the stronghold by dusk.

Suddenly there was a commotion at the rear of the caravan. It spread up the line like wildfire as a Khulinin, a crude, bloodied bandage on his shoulder, galloped by on a lathered horse. Two outriders rode at his side. Voices raised in consternation, for the Khulinin recognized him as one of the trackers sent to observe Medb's forces. The clanspeople watched as he halted before the chiefs at the head of the caravan. Many heads turned to look behind them, expecting to see the sorcerer's army bearing down on them. Many hands reached for weapons.

The tracker leaned wearily on his saddle and saluted his chieftain. His face was grimy with dust and sweat, and his brow was creased with pain. "They are close, Lord," he said, trying to keep his voice steady. "Three days at the most."

The men broke out in exclamations. Savaric cut them off. "Where?"

"They were moving toward Khulinin Treld, but they turned after us several days ago."

"I see. Have you seen the band of exiles?"

The tracker nodded angrily. "They chased us for a while. An arrow killed the other scout, Dorlan."

Savaric cursed under his breath. "Where are they now?"

"Harassing the Dangari. The blue cloaks are coming behind us, too."

Savaric's smile was dry. "I wonder who will reach us first."

Built during the reign of the eighth Tarn Emperor, the fortress, Ab-Chakan, was the culmination of one architect's dreams and skills. The builder had chosen his site midway in the Himachal Mountains, where the valley of the Isin opened out onto the plains. At the head of the valley, the hills closed in, forming a deep defile that wound inward to the heart of the mountains, where the cliffs rose in impregnable buttresses and the river sprang from the lightless roots of the mountains.

At the mouth of the gorge, where the river flowed out into the valley, the slopes ended abruptly in high bluffs. There, the emperor's architect had built Ab-Chakan on a small ridge of rock that thrust out from the southern cliffs and partially blocked the entrance to the defile.

The builder had constructed an octagonal fortress with black towers at each corner. Walls thirty feet high and so thick two horses could walk abreast along the top united the towers. The battlements had overhanging parapets and crenelations through which archers could shoot. The great stones of the wall were set with such skill that no wedge could be driven between their joints.

Realizing the value of the defile behind the fortress, the men of old also constructed a thick wall from the corner of Ab-Chakan over to the northern cliff, barring the entrance to the gorge. The Isin passed beneath the wall through a culvert. The river's current was too strong to swim or dam, and as it curled around the foot of the fortress, the Isin itself provided another natural defense for Ab-Chakan.

It was nearly dark when the wagons finally reached the crossroads, where a wide, well-paved road intersected their road and went up to the main gates of the fortress. The caravan halted and every eye turned to the hulking, dark mass above them. Its blank walls and windowlcss towers were eerie and seemed to loom over the clans in the twilight.

Even Athlone was reluctant to broach the hidden secrets of the fortress at night, so the clans decided to spend the night in the relative safety of the defile. Another road led to a crumbled gateway in the river wall. The travelers carefully picked their way over the remains of the road and into the gorge. The noise of the tumbling river seemed horribly loud in the canyon, and the wind-haunted walls of rock reared over them like prison towers. The floor of the defile was uneven and rocky. The meager path was often blocked with stony debris, but the clans pushed on deeper into the gorge, until they found a wide, grassy area free of broken boulders. There they set up camp and waited anxiously for morning.

Light came slowly in the deep gorge, but the chiefs and their clans set to work long before the sun rode over the river wall. They found caves near the mouth of the river, and they hid their wagons and supplies. The herds were left under such guard as could be spared. The women went to work gathering what food could be found, baking unleavened bread, filling the water skins, and gathering wood. The armorers set up their small forges to repair weapons and make arrows and spear points. The children were sent to cut fodder for the animals.

Savaric, meanwhile, put the men to work on the river wall. It had stood for centuries, but floods and time had taken their toll. The warriors put aside their horses and swords to carry stone and shift earth. They spent the day strengthening the gate and filling in the ruinous gaps in the stones.

Athlone was still angered at Gabria's disappearance, so he threw himself into the unfamiliar labor. His men watched him and wondered, but they were heartened by his tireless strength and they worked long into the night without complaint or slacking. Above them, the massive shape of Ab-Chakan sat in forbidding vigilance.

When night came, the three clans were pleased with their progress. The women and children had gathered a large store of food, water, and firewood. The river wall was patched and the gate was shored up against attack. Few expected the wall to survive a prolonged siege, particularly if the guardian fortress fell. But while its stones stood and defenders survived, the wall would help protect the herds and act as a last defense if the clans had to retreat into the defile.

The clanspeople went back to their camp bone-tired and, although they had done a major task, they all knew that the primary work had to be done tomorrow on the fortress. So the clanspeople treated their blisters with salves, rubbed their weary muscles, and prayed for more time—time to strengthen Ab-Chakan and to learn its secrets, time for the Dangari to arrive.

Savaric knew that Koshyn would keep his promise to come, but somewhere between Dangari Treld and Ab-Chakan was the band of marauders, and behind the Dangari was Medh's army. If anything went wrong, Koshyn's clan would be slaughtered. Savaric considered sending messengers to the Dangari to urge them on; instead, he settled for posting watchers on the bluffs. It would do no good to tell Koshyn something he already knew.

Nevertheless, Savaric could not keep his eyes from wandering to the south, where he hoped to see the dust of an approaching clan. Or of a Hunnuli. Athlone had told him of Gabran's disappearance and, although he was distressed at the boy's danger, he sensed Gabran had an important reason for leaving. If the gods allowed, the boy would soon return.

The next day, the clansmen broached the fortress. The three chiefs, along with Cantrell, Athlone, and a picked force of warriors, trod the ancient road to the main gates. The stone road that began in the valley crossed the river on a crumbling bridge and climbed the face of the short hill.

When the men reached the top of the hill, they stood on a broad, smooth ramp that led through the wall into the fortress. On either side were two of the eight towers, and, at their base, the walls molded into the natural rock and fell away to the valley floor. Before the men, the main gate stood partially open.

Two bronze doors, now weathered to a dingy brown, hung in the huge archway of the front entrance. Fifteen feet tall or more, they rose above the men's heads to a curved lintel carved with strange beasts and letters. On each door a bronze lion's head glared down at the interlopers. The lions, guardians of the gate, were worn and grimy, but their topaz eyes still glittered fiercely in the rising sun.

Within the gate, the men glimpsed another wall and red-colored buildings, dark doorways and patches of thick weeds. The abandoned walls towered above them, and the wind moaned in the empty towers. The men paused at the entrance and stared nervously inside. The huge, echoing fortress held only shadows, but the enclosed, lifeless confines were almost more frightening to the free-roaming clansmen than all the armies of Medb's host. Warriors with gleaming swords were a tangible danger. These strange, old ruins were beyond their knowledge. Still, the clans' survival depended upon this stronghold and upon learning how to exploit its advantages.

Athlone boldly stepped forward and pulled on one of the doors. Several men jumped to help him. They expected the doors to be heavy, but the massive bronze gates had been cleverly hung so only one man was needed to open them. To the warriors' surprise, the doors swung back and slammed into the stone with a resounding boom. The men started like nervous hounds as the sound reverberated through the courts and battlements. A flock of crows leaped out of a tower and flew overhead, cawing harshly.

Cantrell leaned on his guide's shoulder and laughed softly. "If anyone is here, we have certainly made our presence known."

The men glanced at the bard sharply, and Ryne said, "Who could be here?" His voice was uneasy.

"Only the dead and their memories," the bard replied. "These are only stones, Lord Ryne, hewn by men as mortal as yourself. There is nothing within to be wary of."

Ryne was not convinced, but he did not want the others to see his dread. He stepped through the gateway. Athlone and the others fell in behind him. Before them, the road passed through another, smaller wall and into the fortress proper. At one time, the area between the two walls was kept clear and free of debris, its wide space a vital part of the fortress's defenses. However, years of wind-blown dirt and wild growth had accumulated, and weeds grew profusely among the moldering trash, tumbled rock, and the rotting remains of a few wooden shacks put up by later occupants. While the main wall had only one gate, the secondary wall was pierced with eight, one at each tower and one at the road. Single bronze doors with small lions' heads guarded the gateways.

The clansmen walked into the fortress and gazed about with wonder. Despite the military function of the stronghold, its center was similar to a wealthy city. Inside the eight gates circling the inner wall were the decayed ruins of wooden barracks, stables, kitchens, and servants' quarters. But beyond those were luxurious houses and courts, broad paved paths, verdant gardens now overgrown and wild, and fountains—all built or decorated with skillfully carved granite or local red stone. Only the eight towers were built of ebony marble, a stone that glistened like black ice and was prized by the old invaders.

Savaric and the warriors slowly paced up the main road past the empty houses, toward the center of the stronghold. The clansmen were stunned by the sheer size of the fortress and the work that had gone into its creation. The men had never seen anything like it.

In the light of early morning, the shade among the buildings was still heavy and a chill lurked in the silent stones. There was no sound except for the men's footfalls. Athlone caught himself staring and listening for a voice in the halls, or a footstep on the side streets, or a face in the embrasures. Instead, all he saw were barred or broken doors, rotting roofs many of which had fallen in—and eroding masonry with weeds and grass growing in every chink that could hold earth. Year by year, Ab-Chakan was falling into ruin, yet it surprised him how many walls still stood.

The warriors passed out of the buildings' shadows and saw in front of them, in the center of the fortress, the graceful rooms and terraces of the palace built for Ab-Chakan's general. A wide courtyard curved away on either side of the palace. In its center stood a fountain with a carved horse of black marble. Stained and pitted, the statue reared elegantly over a dried pool. Athlone strode to the horse's side and put his hand on the raised hoof.

"I'm beginning to admire these strange people," he said. "They certainly knew horses."

"And knew how to build," Savaric replied. His face was creased with worry, and he inspected everything closely. He was certain he had made the right decision to bring the clans here, but he was overwhelmed by the immensity of the fortress they had chosen to defend. No one in their group had any experience in this kind of warfare, while Medb would possibly have several advisors in his mercenaries who knew how to plan a siege.

"Now it is time for work," Savaric continued. "Ryne, you worked well on the river wall yesterday. Would you bring the werods and examine the walls and towers? Be sure there are no breaches or weak places."

The young Bahedin nodded, pleased to have such an important task.

"Jorlan," Savaric said to his new second wer-tain, "I want you to take two men and find the wells. If the water is bad, we will have to bring some from the river."

Sha Umar looked down the road to the great walls. "We'll need plenty of food. I'll start bringing in the supplies."

Savaric agreed. "Cull out the livestock, too. We'll leave the breeding stock and the horses in the defile."

The men left for their tasks. Cantrell and his guide, Athlone, and Savaric were left alone.

"I would like to see this hall," Savaric said, "before we become too busy."

The men walked across the court to the entrance of the great hall that formed the front of the palace. Seven arches graced the front of the building. Behind the middle arch was a smaller replica of the magnificent bronze gate. Athlone gingerly pushed it open, and the doors swung gently aside. The Khulinin looked into the hall.

It was lit by deep embrasures set just below the roofline, and the light of the morning sun poured through. Two rows of tall pillars supported the vaulted roof, which was still in good condition. On the floor, faint traces of gold still gleamed through the thick layer of dust, debris, and bird droppings. No hangings, trophies, or anything of wood or fabric remained. But on every wall were murals of ancient battles and generals long forgotten. The colors had dulled with time and the walls were scarred and filthy, but the figures were still clear and detailed.

Savaric and Athlone were staring, fascinated, at the walls when Cantrell suddenly raised his head. "There are horns blowing at the front gate," he said urgently to Savaric. "Leave me. We will find our own way out."

The two warriors bolted for the door and ran across the courtyard. As they raced down the road toward the main gates, they, too, heard the horns of the Khulinin outriders blowing frantically from the valley below. Other warriors were crowded around the gate and clustered on the walls. Savaric and Athlone charged up the stone stairs, pushed through the men, and stopped on the brink of the parapet.

There, a mile distant from the crossroads, a small company of horsemen was galloping from the south. A blue banner streamed at their head. Behind the troop, a cluster of wagons was following at full speed and a larger group of riders was fighting a running battle in the rear with an unidentifiable company of warriors. The attackers wore no cloaks and were less disciplined than the fleeing warriors, but they kept up a deadly barrage of arrows at the larger force and cut down anyone who fell behind.

Clan Dangari gained rapidly on the fortress, its attackers close on its heels. It appeared to the watching men that the pursuers did not realize the other clans were nearby.

Savaric and his men leaned over the wall to see the chase.

"Come on, Koshyn!" Athlone shouted. "Ride!"

Suddenly a score of horsemen led by Sha Umar left the shelter of the river wall and galloped toward the approaching clan, their horns blowing a welcome. The horsemen and wagons pivoted around the foot of the fortress and hurried toward the river wall. The attackers took one look at the approaching warriors and the clansmen gathered on the walls, then wheeled about and cantered off to the shelter of the woods on the other side of the valley. The weary clansmen rode gratefully into the defile to the sound of horns blaring wildly.

The Dangari had come.

15

Nara stepped carefully onto a sand bar and snorted when she sunk up to her knees in quaking mud. *I am sorry, Gabria. I can go no farther.*

Gabria glared at the river in frustration, but she understood Nara's predicament. The giant mare was coated with mud and had already been mired once, and they were barely into the fringes of the great delta. Since daybreak they had been following the Goldrine as its banks eroded away to mud bars and beds of reeds. The river had quickly sunk into a morass of shallow channels, quicksand, and insecure little islands.

When Gabria and Nara arrived at the river the night before, they had camped in lowlands thick with thorns, brambles, and grasses. But in the morning, as the Hunnuli had traveled deeper into the wetlands, patches of rushes and giant marsh grass with silvery tassels crowded out the thickets. Just a little farther ahead, Gabria had been able to see where the pale gray of the tassels turned to a solid mass of tossing green. Sadly, the illusion of solidity was quite treacherous, for the grass was a shifting quagmire where no Hunnuli or horse of any kind could go.

Nara heaved her front legs out of the silt and lunged to a more solid bank. Her head down, she stood breathing heavily, her massive strength already drained by the leeching marsh.

Gabria slid off the mare unwillingly. She had hoped the Hunnuli would be with her when she faced the Woman of the Marsh, and she had relied on Nara's wisdom to seek a path through the dangerous mires. But it was obvious Nara could not go on.

She sighed. "How do I find this woman?"

The woman will find you.

The girl yanked her hat off and thrust it in her bag, then she crossed her arms, feeling very disgruntled. "And how can I be sure she'll help?"

She will help you. She is a magic-wielder. Like you.

Gabria looked away. Until that moment, no one had told her the woman was a sorceress. But her intuition had already informed her of that possibility long ago.

Nara's eyes glittered like black crystal. She nudged the girl gently. *I will wait nearby.*

Without another word, Gabria fastened the food bag to her belt, gritted her teeth, and stepped out bravely. The mud oozed to her ankles and water seeped into her boots, but she did not sink like the Hunnuli. She heard Nara plunging away behind her and, for a moment, her resolve almost crumbled. She faltered in midstep and thought of running after the horse. Then her foot slipped and she fell headlong into the river.

The water was warm and brackish and smelled of rotting vegetation, yet it cleared her head. Sputtering, Gabria stood up and looked down at herself ruefully. She was muddy from head to toe and smelled like a swamp; the sleeves of her tunic were black with mud and her bag was soaked. It serves me right, she thought irritably. I've come too far to panic now at the idea of facing my dreads alone.

Her jaw set, Gabria struggled downstream toward the heart of the marshes. The morning sun turned hot, and a smell of moldering vegetation began to rise from the river. Gnats and mosquitoes plagued her. The water spread relentlessly over the land and the ocean of marsh grass loomed closer. She soon found that what looked like one vast fen of grass was really an endless network of pools, quaking mires, and winding, half-strangled channels. Through these a cunning eye and foot could find a wandering, unsteady course over patches of mud, tiny islands, and sand bars. However, as the hours passed and Gabria floundered deeper into the marsh, she began to despair of her cunning.

The journey grew very tiresome. Great reed beds often blocked her path, forcing her to wade or swim in deep, scummy brown water. Thickets of grass towered over her and shut her into a green rustling world. She knew the wind was blowing above, for the tassels rippled in sun-drenched waves, yet nothing stirred the water's surface but the swirl of a fish or the leap of a frog. Soon, Gabria was perspiring heavily, which only drew more fascinated insects.

The day dragged on as Gabria floundered south into the marsh.

She looked for anything that would help her find the woman: a path, a hut, even a footprint or a small item dropped in passing. But the marshes hid their secrets well. She found no sign of any other human being, only water and reeds and herons that watched her with jaundiced eyes.

At last, filthy and exhausted, the girl came to a long, dark mere, where the water was deep and obscure and barred her way on either hand. She stared at the water for a while and wondered if Athlone would laugh if he saw her like this: more mud than sense. It would hardly matter if he did, Gabria decided. She was too tired to care or to swim the mere. Weary and numb, she crawled onto a dry-looking tussock and curled up in the middle of the grass. Her food was ruined, so she drank a few swallows of water, laid her head on the bag, and tried to rest.

Darkness came and with it the noises of the marsh increased to an uproar. Frogs croaked everywhere. Mosquitos hummed. Thousands of creatures that sounded like rusted crickets squeaked incessantly until Gabria was in a frenzy. The biting insects were out in force, too, and they covered every part of her exposed skin. She swatted and squirmed, but nothing would keep them away. She was cold, wet, miserable, and very lonely.

At last she decided she would have to move or go mad. But just as she was about to sit up, Gabria heard a distant noise in the mere. She froze and held her breath.

The noise came again—a soft splash like a creature paddling in the water—or a snake hunting. She had heard of the huge carnivorous snakes that inhabited the marshes, and although they rarely reached sizes capable of devouring a human, she had no desire to meet one. Silently, Gabria's hand crept to her dagger. The moon, an old shaving, had not yet risen and the night seemed utterly lightless. Her eyes strained through the black to see, her ears listened fearfully.

Suddenly a small, lithe animal popped out of the water by her feet. Gabria leaped back like a stung cat and whipped out her dagger. The animal churred and bobbed its head. She stared at it in amazement. It was shaped rather like a short, fat snake with a blunt nose and tapering tail. However, it also had four webbed feet and a whiskered nose. Its round eyes glittered in the starlight. It chirped again in obvious inquiry, and Gabria eased her dagger back into her belt. It was only an otter.

"Hello," she said tentatively.

The otter chittered.

Gabria suddenly felt foolish. It was bad enough to be startled out of her wits by a small, harmless animal, but to talk to it in the middle of the night? She squatted down and shook her head. The marsh was wearing her to rags.

All at once, the otter snapped alert and, before Gabria could blink, it dove into the water and vanished.

Gabria sighed. She leaned back and stared at the stars beyond the walls of grass. The Khulinin would be watching those same stars, and she wondered if they saw them from the walls of Ab-Chakan. She had only been gone three nights and it seemed like years stretched between her and the clan. They were far beyond her reach and time was slipping fast.

A splash interrupted Gabria's thoughts and, to her surprise, the otter bounded back onto her island. It was holding something in its mouth, and it contentedly crunched through its meal before it washed its face and paws and chirped again at Gabria.

"I'm hungry, too," she muttered.

The otter glided to her side, tugged at her pants, and bounced to the edge of the grass. Gabria watched with growing curiosity. It called demandingly and came back to pull at her. Hesitant, she stood up.

The otter ran to the edge of the grass tussock.

A suspicion grew in Gabria's mind; she stepped forward. The otter squeaked happily and moved on. Gabria's suspicion changed to a certainty, and she bent over and followed the animal into the thick growth. It was difficult to see the dark-furred animal, for it seemed to blend into every shadow and shade. The going was exceedingly slow for Gabria, but the otter moved unhurriedly, keeping close in front of her as it chose its way unerringly through the treacherous paths of the marsh.

For hours, Gabria stumbled after the creature, through reeds and fens, around meres and beds of marsh grass, until she was bone weary and sick to death of the smell of stagnant water.

Still, the otter led her on, even when she was floundering in waist-deep water or struggling through grasping mud that sucked at her legs. Occasionally the animal turned around and chirped at her encouragingly before it plunged deeper into the marshes, along paths only it could see.

After a while, the water imperceptibly changed from black to dark pewter to pale gray, and the shapeless masses of night silently regained their form and hue. Gabria blearily glanced toward the east and saw the red rim of the sun ignite as it touched the edge of the sky. The otter saw it, too, and chittered at Gabria.

The girl staggered to a stop. Panting and exhausted, she held up her hand. "I'm sorry, but I've got to rest. I . . ."

Before she could say more, the otter bobbed its head, whisked into the reeds, and disappeared.

"No, wait!" Gabria yelled frantically. But the otter was gone and she was too tired to follow. She sank down on the driest patch of reed and mud she could find and put her head in her hands. She could only hope that the otter would come back. Gabria was not certain the animal was leading her to the marsh woman, but it had a definite purpose, and it was the only guide she had in this dangerous place.

Fortunately, she did not have long to wait. The sun was barely up above the horizon when the otter returned. The animal was swimming down a narrow channel, tugging at a rope floating in the water. Gabria staggered over to help. She pulled the rope and a small, slim boat floated out of the tall grass. The craft was light, flat-bottomed, and the color of a faded reed. The otter climbed into the boat and chattered at Gabria.

"Are you serious?" she asked, horrified. Plowing through the mud was bad enough, but she had never been in a boat and didn't want to try one now.

The otter squealed and patted a long pole lying on the bottom of the craft. Gabria looked aghast, but she climbed gingerly into the boat and sat down. A slow current pulled the craft into deeper water. After a short time, when the boat didn't show signs of immediately tipping her into the water, Gabria relaxed a little. She stood up very carefully, grasped the pole, and pushed it into the water. The pole hit the muddy bottom of the channel and the boat moved forward. Gabria grinned at the otter and pushed the pole in again. Very slowly, they moved down the channel.

"Where to now, little one?" Gabria asked the otter.

As if in response, the animal dove off the gunnel into the water. Its small brown head bobbed up in front of the boat. Gabria followed in the otter's wake.

The sun was well up by that time, and the marshes glowed green and gold in the morning light. The day grew hot. Gabria was tired and her head was heavy with sleep, but she could not relax. Her stomach was twisted into knots of tension and her thoughts kept returning to the look on Athlone's face when she had asked about the Woman of the Marsh. His reaction was born of an ingrained fear of magic-wielders, but Gabria wondered what he would think of *her* when he knew the full truth of her powers. She stared at the water. She wondered, too, what her family would have thought if they had known of her heretical talent. Would they have understood that her obsession for vengeance was leading her to a sorceress to learn the ways of magic?

Gabria felt the tears in her eyes and forced them back. Gabran would have understood. Her brother had loved her unconditionally, and she knew that he would have supported her decision to seek the Woman of the Marsh. Piers and Cantrell supported her, too. She realized now that the bard had sent her to this woman to learn to use her natural talent, not to subdue it. And Gabria finally decided that it was the right choice. Whatever the consequences, she wanted to learn every strength and weakness of sorcery, to find a way to destroy Medb.

The otter chittered.

Gabria started out of her thoughts and glanced ahead. A line of trees blocked her way and, as she followed the otter closer, the line became a dark, heavy wall of mangrove. The strange trees grew close together, their prop roots pushing into the stagnant water. Under their branches, the air was stuffy, and very little light forced its way through the dense foliage.

Gabria poled her boat with care through the tangled roots of the mangroves, following a twisted path only the otter could see. The trees grew close together, and open spaces of water became fewer and farther apart. The air was stifling and fetid.

At last, the otter crawled onto something solid and came to a stop. Gabria glanced up in surprise. They were at the foot of a huge framework of roots. In the center, the prop roots merged into a mangrove unlike any other. It was tremendous; its roots delved deep into the waters of the river. Its branches spread out in a vast, gloomy canopy.

The otter waved a paw at the tree and chirped.

"There?" Gabria asked in disbelief.

Reluctantly, the girl climbed out of the boat and teetered on the slippery roots. Before she could protest, the otter whisked away into the water and vanished. Gabria was left alone. She looked around. There were no insects or birds or frogs, and the gloomy swamp around her was completely silent. Gabria shivered. She would have given anything to be safe and dry in Piers's tent, instead of wet, filthy, and clinging like a snail to a slimy mangrove root in the heart of a sorceress's domain.

Gabria gathered her courage and clambered over the roots to the main trunk. The tree was incredibly wide; compared to other trees, its trunk was a massive column in a forest of sticks.

Where would a sorceress live in a thing like this? Gabria looked up into the branches, around the roots, even into the water, but there was no sign of any life, human or otherwise. The girl was beginning to think the otter had deceived her, when she saw a narrow, horizontal crack in the side of the tree. It was barely wider than a handspan and ran several lengths above her head. Gabria peered in. Although it was completely dark within the tree, she sensed it hid a cavity large enough to enter.

There was no other possibility. Gabria squeezed through the crack into pitch darkness. The air was stifling. It seemed quiet within the tree, but as Gabria's senses sharpened in the darkness, she became aware of a soft rasping and, even softer, a creaking rustle like tiny whispers. Gabria waited—for what she was not sure.

After several moments, a single shaft of red light struck down from somewhere above and illuminated the sorceress. The old woman sat on a chair, which in turn rested on a platform that hung from an unseen ceiling. She was more like a corpse than a woman, hunched and wizened and incredibly pallid. Her unblinking eyes shone red in the light. She had a beautiful, mad-looking face, and she stared down at Gabria with a triumphant sneer.

"So, you have come at last," she said, her voice harsh from disuse. "I have waited too long for a magic-bearer to find me."

"I—," Gabria started to say.

The woman cut her off. "You have come to learn. I know who you are . . . but I do not know if you are ready to pay my price."

Gabria stared up in fascination. She was both horrified and awed by the feverish power that blazed in the woman's red eyes.

The sorceress met Gabria's gaze, and her face contorted into rage. "I know what you're thinking," she cried. "You think I am only an old hag hiding in a swamp, tripping through my ancient skills and feeding on old grudges. Well, I was a powerful sorceress once, a Shape-Changer. My power brought men to their knees. Behold!"

She threw her arms wide and sang a chant in a strange tongue that reverberated to the rootlets and twigs of the great tree. Gabria pressed back against the wood. The interior began to waver and fade; the air hummed like a harp string. The woman's voice rose to a cry of triumph as a vision formed in the chamber. To Gabria's gaze, the tree was transformed to a palace where gold gleamed on mirrors, water sprang from a thousand fountains, and the walls shimmered with the silk banners of a noble house. Before Gabria stood a woman, a sorceress as she had always imagined one to be: fair yet dangerous, lovely and fell, clothed in gowns of velvet and bejeweled like a queen.

But as quickly as the vision formed, it dissipated to a thin mist and vanished in a puff. The woman, diminished to an ancient crone, sagged back in her chair with a groan of exhaustion. "My strength is almost gone," she whispered.

Gabria stared about bemused, half expecting to see the dark-haired woman still standing nearby. But the vision, whether the truth of the past or the dream of an aging hermit, was gone. The girl leaned back slowly and tried to keep her face expressionless. It was obvious the woman was a sorceress, and though she had lost the strength to wield her powers, she still had knowledge.

"It takes more wisdom than strength to use magic," Gabria said, trying to placate the old woman.

The sorceress glared at her irritably. "Foolish. What do you know of sorcery? I have watched you since the massacre of the Corin. All I saw were your paltry attempts to discourage a few overenthusiastic men."

"Discourage!" Gabria cried. "I killed a man."

"You see? Discouragement would have been better. But you bungled it. You know nothing of magic."

Gabria forced her anger back and said, "That is why I came to you."

"I take no more neophytes."

"Not even for a price?" asked Gabria after a moment's hesitation.

The woman looked down at her. "What price are you willing to pay?"

"Whatever you ask that is within my means."

"Your means. That is limited indeed." The sorceress waved her hand through the red light and her platform descended slowly to the floor of the tree chamber. Her hand, spiderlike, crept over Gabria's wrist and pulled her down to sit on the platform beside the chair. Gabria flinched at the dry, dusty touch, but she did not withdraw her hand.

"What is it you seek from sorcery, clanswoman? You know the practice is forbidden on pain of death."

Gabria could feel her blood pulse beneath the woman's grip. She knew without question that it would not avail her to hide the truth. "I seek vengeance for the murder of my father, my brothers, and my clan."

"Ah, yes. Is that your only reason?" Her eyes pierced Gabria's like needles, dissecting every layer of thought. "Vengeance is a dangerous motive for sorcery; it can warp your will and turn on you like a snake." The woman turned her nose up and her eyes slid sideways to watch the girl. "But it can also precipitate one's learning." She paused. "This Medb you wish to destroy, he has grown powerful of late and will require much cunning and will to overcome."

"He is also overconfident. He thinks he is the only sorcerer in the clans."

The woman nodded in agreement. She had studied Gabria for some time and was pleased with what she saw. "At the moment, he is. But the man is a savage. It is because of sorcerers like him that the people rose up against us and purged magic from the plains. Now, only I remember the bright days of grandeur and wisdom, when magic was a glory and its wielders were worshiped with honor." Her voice began to rise in fury. "But, now . . . Now, I hide my power from the eyes of men in the reek and mire of this foul swamp."

The woman's face twisted with rage, and her words screeched in her throat. Suddenly she began to laugh—a rude, maniacal sound that terrified Gabria. "A just punishment he shall have for doing this to me. We will topple this self-satisfied malefactor into the muck."

Gabria straightened and asked breathlessly, "You will help me?"

"Did I not just say that?"

The girl nodded, uncertain whether she was pleased or frightened. "Thank you."

"Do not thank me yet." She released Gabria's hand and sat back, her rage still embedded in her ancient face. She studied the girl for a moment and a sharp gleam, like a hungry rat, lurked in the sorceress's red eyes. Oh, yes, she would teach the girl the secrets of using magic. She would give Gabria enough knowledge to defeat that upstart, Medb. Then, if all went well, the girl would pay the price of her training. The Woman of the Marsh smiled, a slow, wicked twist of her lips, and cackled with anticipation.

16

Athlone stood on the graying walls of the river gate and watched the exiles' guard fires burning like a fiery noose in the field before the fortress. In the gathering gloom, he could barely see the marauders clustered around their fires. The exiles thought they had little to fear. The trapped clans would not waste the time or the men to chase down an enemy that would scatter and flee at the first sign of strength.

It tested Athlone's tolerance to see the outcasts taunt and posture beyond arrow range, but he could do nothing about them. Savaric had ordered no shots fired or sorties made—yet. Let the exiles think the four clans were cowering in the depths of the defile.

Since the arrival of the Dangari that morning, Savaric and the other chiefs had made plans to bring the four clans out of the defile to the fortress under cover of night. One of Jorlan's men had found a hidden stairway leading from a storage room in the back of the fortress, down the back of the ridge, and into the gorge behind the river wall.

The stairs made it easy for Savaric and the others to slip down to the defile, but the way was too narrow and steep for a large group with pack animals. The clans could only enter the fortress by the front gates. However, a move like that was too dangerous during the day, for the exile band could wreak havoc on the women, the children, and the wagons of supplies. At night, the clans could slip into the stronghold in relative safety. Particularly if the marauders were busy elsewhere.

Athlone grinned to himself. He would not have to wait much longer. The wer-tain sensed someone come up beside him, and he turned to see Koshyn lean against the parapet.

The young chieftain's face was unreadable in the deepening twilight, and his tattoos were almost invisible. "For men who are dead to our eyes, they are making a nuisance of themselves."

Athlone made a sound deep in his throat. He shifted restlessly. "They think we can only sit here on our pretty wall and show our teeth."

Koshyn glanced over his shoulder and studied the fading light in the west. "Let them be ignorant a little while longer. It will be dark soon, and we'll be able to ride." He turned around and stared up at the black, hulking mass of Ab-Chakan. The walls and towers of the old fortress rose above them in a massive silence, its stones hiding secrets and echoing with memories that were beyond the knowledge of the clansmen.

"I feel like a mouse scurrying around some unholy monolith," Koshyn said softly, as if afraid the stones would hear. "What are we doing here?"

Athlone's strong face twisted in a grimace. He, too, felt the weight of the old walls. "Trying to survive."

"In an inhospitable place that was never meant for us. We aren't used to stone beneath our feet and walls before our eyes. We fight with muscle, bone, and steel." He gestured to the fortress. "Not with crumbling, old masonry."

"Would you prefer to face Medb's fury on the plains below? It would be a glorious way to die."

The Dangari grinned and shook his head. "And fruitless. No, Athlone, I am not stupid—only afraid."

Athlone lifted his gaze to the west, half-hoping to see a Hunnuli mare galloping out of the night. But only the wind rode the grass; only the muted hooves of the horses waiting in the defile echoed in the night. "We all are," he muttered.

Abruptly Koshyn pushed himself away from the parapet and slapped the sword at his hip. "We are too gloomy, Wer-tain. While there are weapons at hand and an enemy to fight, let us ride as warriors are meant to."

Athlone smiled grimly. "You're right, my friend. We will be in paradise before this fortress falls. Come, we'll show the exiles our teeth."

They linked arms and strode down the stone steps to the gate, where Savaric and a large group of mounted warriors were waiting for full darkness. Behind the riders, in the depths of the gorge, stood the massed ranks of the four clans. The men, carrying packs on their backs, looked uncomfortable and edgy. The women and children stood in a large group in the center of the ranks, their arms full of bundles and their eyes downcast to hide their fear. Loaded pack animals, oxen and cattle that could be eaten later, waited patiently among the lines. Not a torch flickered or a fire burned. It was almost totally dark in the defile. Athlone could feel the anxiety of every person about him.

A shiver charged the wer-tain's nerves like the touch of a ghost. He had seen Ab-Chakan in the daylight and even then its empty chambers and ancient silences had unsettled him. He knew what his people were feeling now as they waited to enter the fortress in the depths of the night.

Another group of warriors taken from all four clans stood along the wall, watching Savaric. They were the volunteers who would remain behind to guard the river wall and the herds that had been driven deep into the defile. Athlone frowned. There were so pitifully few men to guard the crumbling, old wall. There was little choice, however; the remainder of the fighting men, nearly three thousand, were needed to protect the fortress.

The light of the sunset had died and night was upon the clans. The roar of the river seemed unnaturally loud in the quiet, crowded gorge. Despite the breeze from the rushing water, the air was sluggish and heavy with a damp chill.

Athlone pulled his cloak tighter around his shoulders as he and Koshyn went to greet the mounted warriors. Boreas came to join the wer-tain. In the darkness, the black horse was almost invisible. Only his eyes, glowing like moons behind a thin cloud, and his white mark of lightning could be seen. Eagerly he snorted and butted his nose on Athlone's chest. The wer-tain vaulted to his back.

Savaric came to the Hunnuli's side and looked up at his son. The chief's hood was drawn over his nose, hiding his sharp features, but Athlone's gaze reached through the darkness to touch his father's in a wordless moment of understanding and sadness. In a passing breath, their thoughts and concerns became one and each gave to the other the strength that they would need for the coming days. Savaric nodded once. He squeezed his son's knee, joined his hearthguard, and in a low voice gave the warriors his last-minute instructions.

"Ride safely, Athlone," Jorlan said, coming up beside the Hunnuli.

Athlone greeted the other man. "I'll see you soon in the fortress."

"Hmmm," said the second wer-tain. "I can hardly wait to hole up in that monstrosity of stone."

"Think of the pleasure Lord Medb will have when he fully realizes the size of the nut we are giving him to crack. He will be quite surprised."

Jorlan's face broke into a malicious grin. "That's an image worth savoring."

"Athlone," Savaric called. "It's time."

The chieftain's command was passed down the lines of clansmen, and the tension immediately intensified in the defile. The ranks of men shifted forward in a press of armor, swords, and packs; the women drew closer together. At the end of the lines, Sha Umar and the rearguard waited impatiently to go.

Jorlan saluted Athlone as the mounted men moved to the river wall. Koshyn joined Athlone and the gate was eased open.

"Remember," Savaric whispered loudly, "we need time!"

On soundless hooves, Boreas passed out of the defile, and the company of riders fell in behind him. All were mounted on black or dark brown horses, and in the thick night, Athlone doubted the marauders would see them until they were on top of the fires. He urged Boreas forward until they reached the foot of the ridge beneath Ab-Chakan, where the river curved south. In the defile, the main ranks of the clans waited breathlessly, tight with tension, with only a long walk to a cold, dark ruin before them. But Athlone and the warriors with him could ride like clansmen were born to: with horns blowing, swords in their hands, and an enemy to fight face to face.

Athlone could wait no longer. An excitement and fury roared within him that was fired by days of frustration and running. He drew his sword. Koshyn caught his feeling and cried to the horn bearer with them. "Now, let them hear the song of the hunt."

The horn burst in the quiet night like a thunderclap. It rebounded through the hills, ringing clear with the victory of a quarry sighted and the joy of the coming kill. Before the last note left the horn, Boreas reared and neighed a challenge that blended with the horn's music and forged a song of deadly peril. In unison, the other men drew their weapons with a shout and spurred their eager mounts into a gallop toward the fires.

The exiles were taken by surprise. As the riders swept down on them, the outcasts broke out of their stunned lethargy and frantically ran for their horses. The Hunnuli burst among the largest group. Two men fell to Athlone's sword and one to Boreas's hooves. The rest scattered in all directions, the clansmen on their heels.

A few exiles were caught by the riders and immediately put to death. The remainder fled to the sanctuary of the rough hills, where they could easily lose their pursuers. Thus it was that the marauders did not see the files of heavily laden people and animals toil up the road to Ab-Chakan, nor did they hear the thud as the massive gates were closed.

At dawn, the horn bearer again sounded his instrument to welcome the sun and to gather the riders. Exhausted, their fury spent, the warriors rode back, pleased with their labors. They had suffered only a few minor wounds while nine of the exiles had been killed. The troop rode to the gates of the fortress, and the men who greeted them and took their lathered horses were relieved to have the riders back. The big bronze gates closed behind them with a thud of finality.

It was not long before the exiles edged back to their cold fires and took up their watch of the fortress.

As soon as it was light and the women were settled in the palace and surrounding houses, guards were placed in the towers to watch the plains for signs of Medb's army, and the chiefs and their men set out to explore every cranny of the stronghold. The men spent all morning poking and digging and opening things that had not been opened in generations. By the time they returned to the palace's hall to confer, even Koshyn was admiring the handiwork of the men of old and the most reluctant clansman was realizing the capabilities of the fortification.

The outer walls and the towers were still in very good condition. The inner walls were crumbling but defensible, and many of the stone buildings in the fortress's center were sturdy enough to shelter the clanspeople and the livestock. The cisterns, buried deep in the rock, were full, since the water was constantly refreshed by seasonal rains.

As soon as the chiefs had planned their defense of the stronghold, everyone set to work to prepare the old fortress for what it had not seen in centuries: war. The walls were patched, the trash and rubble were cleared out of the space between the two walls, and the gate was secured with logs and chains. Wer-tains and children alike began to grow confident in their new refuge. It would take more than Medb and a few clans to rout them out of this hill of stone.

The clanspeople were still working desperately when a horn blew wildly from one of the towers. The people looked up at the sinking sun in surprise. It was too early for the sunset horn. Then the realization dawned on them all, and the chiefs came running to the wall from every part of the fortress. The men close by the main wall crowded up onto the parapet.

There in the valley, the exiles were galloping their horses about and the vanguard of the sorcerer's army was riding up the old road.

As planned, horns blew from all the towers and five banners—one gold, one blue, one maroon, one orange, and one dark red—were unfurled above the main gate.

Savaric's hands gripped the stone. "Medb is here," he called to the people crowded into the bailey below him. "You all know your duties."

Silently, the warriors dispersed to seek their weapons and take their places along the battlements. Athlone ran up the stone steps to join the chiefs, and without a word, Lord Ryne pointed down to the valley.

Once again Medb timed his arrival to create the greatest impression. The sun was already behind the crown of the mountains when the sorcerer's army arrived at the Defile of Tor Wrath and the valley was sinking into twilight. A sharp wind blew the grass flat and swirled about the foot of Ab-Chakan.

Heralded by the wind and cloaked by the approaching night, the sorcerer's vanguard crossed the bridge and stopped at the foot of the hill just below the fortress. They waited in ominous silence.

Behind them, the main army marched to the command of drums. They came endlessly, countless numbers obscured by the dim twilight that hid their true form. They came until the valley was filled and the army spread out along the mountain flanks. There were no torches or lamps or voices or neighs of horses to break the monotony of the terrifying black flood. There was only the sound of the drums and the remorseless tread of feet.

The clansmen watched the coming host in dismay and disbelief. Never had they imagined anything like this. The force that marched relentlessly toward the defile was no longer Wylfling or Geldring or Amnok or foreigner lured by gold. It had become a faceless, mindless mass driven by the single will of one evil man.

The wind eased and all movement died in the valley. The night-shrouded army gathered its breath and waited for its master's signal. But the sorcerer held them firm. He let the troops wait, allowing them to see their goal and the clansmen to see their doom. In the fortress above, Savaric and the clans looked on with dread. Still Medb held back his army. The tension burned until it became almost unendurable.

Then a lone horseman rode out of the vanguard and up to the gates of the fortress. He was cloaked in brown and a helm hid his face, but nothing could hide the snide, contemptuous tone of his voice.

"Khulinin, Dangari, Bahedin, and Jehanan. The rabble of the clans." He snorted rudely. "My master has decided to be merciful to you this once. You have seen the invincibility of his arcane power and now you see the might of his host. Look upon this army. Weigh your advantages. You will not survive long if you choose to oppose Lord Medb. There are still other choices: surrender to him and he will be lenient."

Savaric struggled to find his voice. Furiously, he shoved his hands over the edge of the stone wall and gripped it tightly for support. "Branth, I see you have lost your cloak." His voice was harsh with derision.

The Geldring made a broad sweep with his arm to indicate the army behind him. "Brown is such a strong color, fertile with opportunities."

"So is dung, but I wouldn't trade my clan for it. How do the Geldring feel about forsaking the green?"

Branth's words were clipped with anger. "My clan obeys."

"*Your* clan!" Savaric forced a rude laugh. "No longer, Branth. Your clan is Medb's and it is he they obey. The Geldring no longer exist. Go away from here, traitor."

Branth sneered. Behind him, in the valley, the army shifted restlessly. "Bravely spoken, chieftain. Soon, you, too, will see the wisdom of wearing brown. Only do not take long to decide. The army has already smelled blood." With a harsh cry, Branth spurred his horse back down the road.

Medb, in his enclosed wagon, nodded to himself in satisfaction. He forced his restive army back, away from the fortress. Anticipation would put a keen edge on the fear he had honed in the stronghold; when at last he released the attack, the clansmen would not survive for long.

Their fates were sealed as surely as Medb's victory was assured. The Khulinin and the others would cease to exist; their chieftains would soon be destroyed. Even if Savaric and his allies did surrender, Medb certainly did not plan to be lenient.

* * *

The first attack came before dawn, in the cold hours when reactions are slowest and muscles are chilled. It was only a probe to test the strength of the defenders and the clansmen easily beat back the attack. Still, the men found it was a relief to fight. After the long, interminable hours of waiting through the night, the screaming horde of mercenaries that swarmed up the road to the wall was a blessing. The chiefs knew it was only a test, and they quickly repaired their defenses to meet the next onslaught.

This time they had a long wait. After the mercenaries fell back beyond the river, the army's encampment was quiet for a few hours. Savaric posted guards and allowed the rest of the defenders to stand down, but few of the warriors left the parapets. They watched and waited to see what Medb was going to do next.

Around noon, the activity in the huge camp suddenly increased. Wagons were seen moving to the hills and returning with stacks of cut logs. Hundreds of men clustered together and appeared to be working on several large things the clansmen could not identify. The noises of wood being cut and hammered sounded long after dark.

In the fortress, Savaric and the clansmen continued their vigilance through another long, unbearable night.

At dawn the next day, the labors of Medb's army became clear. Three large objects were wheeled out of the encampment, across the old bridge, and set up at the base of the hill, out of arrow range but as close to Ab-Chakan as possible. The clansmen were in position on the fortress walls, and those in the front ranks watched curiously as the strange wooden devices were prepared.

"What are those?" Lord Ryne asked, voicing everyone's curiosity.

Savaric called to one of his men. "Bring Cantrell here."

The bard was quickly brought and carefully escorted up the stone steps to where the chiefs were standing on the parapet. "I hear Medb has been busy," Cantrell said after his greeting.

"There are three wooden things just below the fortress," Savaric answered. "They're heavy, wheeled platforms with long poles on top. The poles are attached at one end of the platform and have what looks like large bowls fastened to the other end."

"Look at that," Sha Umar added. "The men put a rock in that one device and they're pulling down on one end."

Cantrell's face went grim. "Catapults."

As if in response to his word, the device below snapped loose and a large rock sailed up and crashed into the wall just below the parapet. The defenders instinctively ducked.

"Good gods!" Savaric exclaimed. The men peered over the walls just as another rock was flung at the fortress. The missile hit the bronze gates with a thundering boom. The clansmen were relieved to see there was no damage to the wall or the gate, but as the morning passed, the men on the catapults found their range and the heavy stones began to rain down within the front walls of the fortress. Several clansmen were killed when a huge rock landed in their midst, and the old parapet sustained some damage. The other men were thrown into confusion as the boulders continued to crash down around them.

Then, just before noon, Athlone glanced over the wall and saw the army forming across the river. "Here they come!" he shouted. A horn bearer in the tower by the gate blew the signal to warn the defenders along the walls.

In the valley below, men rushed forward and set up make-shift bridges over the Isin River, and the sorcerer's army launched its full fury at Ab-Chakan. Under the cover of a deluge of missiles and arrows, the first ranks of soldiers with ropes and ladders charged up the road and the sides of the hill to the front walls. All the while, the army's drums pounded relentlessly and a roar of fury echoed through the fortress.

In the first frantic minutes, Athlone was too busy to appreciate the strategic advantages of his position, but as his men fought off the attackers, it dawned on him that the old strong-hold was easy to defend. Not only did the swift river prevent a large attack force from crossing all at once, but the ridge's steep slopes slowed down the advance of the enemy and left them open to the deadly fire from the battlements. The clansmen cheered when the first wave fell back, and a glimmer of hope returned to their hearts.

The second wave came, more enraged than the first, and nearly reached the top of the walls before they were repulsed. Attack after attack was thrown at the walls and each was pushed back, foot by bitter foot, until the ground was heavy with dead and wounded, and the surviving defenders were shaking with exhaustion.

It doesn't matter, Athlone thought grimly as he threw away his empty quiver, how easy it is to hold this fortress. Medb has the greater numbers and the advantage of time. Eventually the fortress will collapse from the lack of men to defend it.

In mocking reply to Athlone's thoughts, the enemy's horns bayed again and a new attack stormed to the wall. This time the onslaught scaled the defenses. The clansmen drew their swords and daggers and fought hand to hand as the fighting swayed frantically over the battle-

ments. Blood stained the old rock, and yells and screams of fury echoed around the towers. Time and again Savaric rallied the men and
fought off the wild-eyed attackers from the parapet, only to face more
of them with fewer men at his side. Desperately, he brought the men
on the back walls around to the front and prayed the river wall and its
defenders were enough to protect Ab-Chakan's back.

The clansmen lost all sense of time. The battle raged through the
afternoon in a seemingly endless cycle of attacks and repulses. Sha
Umar went down with an arrow in his shoulder. Jorlan was slain defending Savaric's side. The catapults continued to hurl missiles over
the wall and at the gate, damaging the fortress and distracting the
defenders. All the while, the drums pounded incessantly in the valley.

Then, without warning, the enemy withdrew. They fell back to
their encampment and an eerie silence fell over the valley. In the
tower by the gate, the horn bearer sounded the call for sunset.

The clansmen looked around in surprise as darkness settled down
around them. They had won the day. But as the chiefs began to count
their dead and wounded, they wondered if they would be so fortunate
tomorrow.

Across the valley, in Medb's tent, the sorcerer's rage burned hot.
His powers had doubled since leaving the Tir Samod, and he had
healed his crippled legs. However, there were no spells to bolster his
energy and he was near collapse from sustaining his army's rage during the long battle. He had suffered heavy losses. Finally, Medb realized he had underestimated Savaric. The four clans were backed into
a stone burrow from which only something unexpected could flush
them. There was nothing left to do but hold off further attacks until
new plans could be made.

The sorcerer allowed his army to return to its encampment, and
he went into seclusion to rest and ponder. Ab-Chakan would fall if he
had to crumble it with his bare hands.

Shortly after midnight, Athlone mounted Boreas and joined a
small troop of volunteer riders waiting by the front gate. Several men
carried torches and bags of oil.

Savaric was waiting for Athlone and came to stand beside the big
Hunnuli. The chief's face was deeply worried. "I don't like this,
Athlone," he said forcefully. "It would be better to forget those cat-
apults. They're too heavily guarded."

The wer-tain's eyes met his father's and he nodded. "I know. But those machines are wreaking havoc on us. Besides, it would do the clans some good to see those things burn."

"But if you get trapped outside the gates, we might not be able to help you."

"It's not too far, Father," Athlone replied. "We'll burn those things and get back as fast as we can."

Savaric sighed. He hated the danger his son was riding into, but he, too, wanted those catapults destroyed. Finally, he nodded reluctantly.

The wer-tain saluted him. Then, without warning or reason, a deadly chill touched Athlone's mind and a shade seemed to pass over his father's face. Alarmed, Athlone sat back on Boreas and rubbed his hand over his chin. The feeling of malaise was gone as quickly as it came, leaving in its place a dull, aching hollow and a newly planted seed of fear. He shook his head slightly and wondered what was wrong.

Savaric did not seem to notice. He bid farewell to his son and stood back out of the way. The bronze gates were opened.

The first inkling of disaster came with a flare of torches at the fortress gates, then a storm of horses' hooves thundered down the road and swept with gale force into the midst of the guard around the catapults. Led by a rider on a flame-eyed Hunnuli stallion, the horsemen surged into the stunned enemy. The riders' weapons ran red with blood, and their eyes gleamed in the joy of battle.

While Athlone and his men pushed the enemy back, the men with the torches rode to the catapults. They doused the devices with oil and threw their torches onto the wooden platforms. The catapults burst into flames and the riders began their retreat.

But Lord Branth was expecting a possible attack on the siege weapons, so he was waiting with his men in the encampment. At the first sign of attack, he charged across the bridge to meet Athlone's men, before the riders could escape.

The clansmen on the walls of the fortress watched in horror as Athlone and his riders were surrounded and the fighting grew bitter. Savaric shouted frantically for more warriors to ride out and rescue the men, but he knew that it was already too late.

Inexorably, the Wylfling and Geldring pulled down the riders. Athlone and his men were forced into a tighter and tighter circle. They fought back ferociously, anxious now only to survive.

Then, without warning, a spear was hurled over the warriors' heads into Boreas's chest. The great Hunnuli bellowed in pain and fury. He reared and his hooves slashed the air. He tried to leap over the fighters and carry his rider to safety, but the spear was buried too deep. The stallion's heart burst, and his ebony body crashed to the earth.

Athlone felt his friend's dying agony in every muscle of his body; his mind reeled in shock. He held on blindly when Boreas reared and sprang, but as the Hunnuli fell, he was too overwhelmed to jump off. The horse's heavy body collapsed beneath him. Athlone saw the ground rushing toward him just as unconsciousness dimmed his searing grief.

A triumphant shout roared from the attackers. They pressed forward and quickly slew the last surviving Khulinin who tried in vain to defend Athlone's body. Lord Branth shoved his way through the crowd to the corpse of the Hunnuli. He gleefully grabbed Athlone's helm, wrenched it off, and raised his sword to cut off the wer-tain's head.

"Hold!" The command stilled the chief's arm. Furiously he looked up and saw Lord Medb standing by the bridge, his face illuminated by the burning catapults. A second spear was in his hand. Branth quaked.

"I want him alive," Medb said. "I have a use for the son of the mighty Savaric."

On the wall of the fortress, Savaric watched as his son and the big Hunnuli fell. He saw the enemy swarm over their bodies and he saw Lord Medb standing straight and strong on the river's bridge. The chief's eyes closed. Slowly his body sagged against the stone wall and he gave in to his grief and despair.

17

Gabria lost track of time. The hours she spent with the Woman of the Marsh seemed to spring from an eternal wellhead and flow endlessly beyond her memory. The girl and the sorceress had descended to a large, round chamber that lay beneath the tree. They sat together around a small wooden table, the woman hunched over her words and gestures like a jealous priestess and the girl watching with a pale face and a fascinated light in her eyes. Slowly, as the uncounted hours passed and the rasping voice muttered unceasingly in her ear, Gabria began to understand the depths of her power.

"Will is at the center of sorcery," the woman said time and again. "You have no time to learn the complexities, the difficult spells or gestures that govern the proper use of magic, so beware. You are attempting to impose your will on the fabric of our world. Magic is a natural force that is in everything: every creature, stone, or plant. When you alter that force, with even the smallest spell, you must be strong enough to control the effect and the consequences."

Gabria stared into the sorceress's remorseless black eyes and shivered.

The woman's dark gaze fastened on her. "Yes! Be afraid. Sorcery is not a game for half-wits or dabblers. It is a deadly serious art. As a magic-wielder, you must use your power wisely or it will destroy you. The gods are not free with the gift and they begrudge any careless use of it."

"But can anyone use this magic?" Gabria asked.

"Of course not," the woman said irritably. "People are born with the ability. That was the reason for the downfall of the sorcerers so long ago. A few magic-wielders abused their powers and those people without the talent grew jealous and resentful." The woman coughed and shifted in her seat. "But that time is past. As for you, your potential for sorcery is . . . good. Your will to survive is a facet of your strength. And that strength of will is the most essential trait of a magic-wielder."

Gabria nodded. "I understand."

The sorceress's face twisted into a mass of wrinkles. "You understand nothing! You have no conception of what it is to be a sorceress. You are a child. Do you know yourself at all? You must know every measure and degree of your own soul or you will not recognize when your sorcery has begun to leech strength from your being."

The woman sighed and leaned back in her chair. "Not that it matters. You will not have the time to learn, if you wish to defeat that worm-ridden Wylfling any time soon."

"Then what am I supposed to do?" Gabria shouted in frustration. "If I cannot learn my own abilities, how in Amara's name am I supposed to control this power?" Gabria discovered that she was shaking. She clamped her hands together and stared at the table.

The woman laughed, a cackle edged with arrogance. "You do not need superhuman knowledge or control for this task, only desire and concentration. The critical ingredient in any spell, no matter how simple, complex, or bizarre, is the will and strength of the wielder. Those, at least, you have plenty of. I am merely warning you, should you overextend yourself—particularly in an arcane duel." She paused and her eyes lit with a strange, greedy light. "I do want you to succeed."

The girl was puzzled by the odd look in the old sorceress's face, but before she could think about it, the woman hurried on.

"You need to know what you have become a part of, so listen." She jabbed her finger at Gabria. "The other trait you need for spells is imagination. Not all spells are rigidly defined. It is often better to create your own. On this we will proceed."

The old woman stood up and fetched a stub of a candle. She set it down in front of Gabria. "The reason you need to use spells is to formulate your intent. The words elucidate the purpose in your mind and help you focus your power on the magic.

"When you used the Trymian Force before, it came as an unconscious reaction to your will to survive, and so it was very weak and uncontrolled. But if you had used a spell, you could have changed the intensity of the force and used it at will."

"But how do I learn these spells?" Gabria asked.

"Sorcerers experimented with spells for years. They worked out many spells that were formulated for the greatest clarity and efficiency. But you do not always need to use them. Magic spells can be worded any way you wish." The woman suddenly snapped a foreign word and the candle in front of Gabria popped into flame. The girl started back, her eyes wide with surprise.

The sorceress snuffed out the flame. "You try. Concentrate on your purpose and speak a command."

Gabria gazed at the candle. She tried to picture a flame in her mind, then she said, "Light, candle."

A tiny flame puffed and died out.

"Concentrate!" the sorceress ordered. "Focus your will on that candle."

The girl tried again. She closed her eyes and demanded, "Light, candle." This time the candle's wick flickered once and lit in a gentle, yellow flame. Gabria opened her eyes and smiled.

"Good," stated the sorceress. "You are beginning to understand. You must know *exactly* what you are trying to do or the magic will go awry. That is why we use spells." She snapped another strange word and the candle's flame went out. "Now," the woman continued. "It is possible to do almost anything you desire with magic. But it is vital to know exactly what you want to do before you begin."

Gabria nodded, fascinated by the old woman's teaching. "What are some things you cannot do with magic?"

"You cannot create something out of empty space. You have to use something that is already there. See." With a brief word, the sorceress changed the candle to an apple. "You can alter form or change an appearance, but you cannot create."

"But what about the Trymian Force?"

"The Trymian Force, like a protective shield or any kind of visible force, is formed from the magic within you. That is why it is important to know your limits; you must not weaken yourself so much that you cannot control your spells. Remember that if you duel Medb."

The old sorceress brought other small items to the table and had Gabria practice basic spells: changing the object's form and altering its image, even moving it around the chamber.

As Gabria's confidence grew, her skill developed in leaps and bounds. She learned how to form the intent of a spell into the words that would trigger the magic and how to dismantle a spell before it went awry.

The sorceress, surprised by Gabria's rapid progress, taught her other spells of healing and shape-changing, and the rituals for the arcane duels. She also taught the girl the best spells to control the Trymian Force, call it at will, and most important, to defend herself against it with protective shields.

At last, the old woman nodded in satisfaction, and her wrinkled face creased in a smile. "You have learned all that I can teach you. Now you must teach yourself. Practice what I have told you, learn your limits and your strengths. Remember the dangers if you lose control of the magic." She went to an old battered chest by the wall, pulled out a small silk bag, and brought it to Gabria. "Go back to the clans. When you are ready, open this bag. Inside is the last item you need to become a full sorceress. The item will help intensify your powers and mark you as a true magic-wielder."

The old sorceress sank into her chair and was silent. Gabria leaned back feeling numb. The girl looked about her, amazed, for the time with the sorceress seemed so unreal. She wondered how long they had been in the chamber.

Gabria began to stand up, but immediately her exhaustion caught up with her. Her body sagged, and she caught the chair to keep from falling. She took a weak step toward the stairs that led up to the entrance. What day was it? How long had she been there?

"I must go," she mumbled.

The sorceress raised her hand and a spell caught the girl before she fell. Gently, she laid Gabria down on the floor. The girl was already asleep. For a moment, the woman stared down at her with glee in her heart. Never had she known an ability so strong. This girl had strength, will, and talent, and if she did not lose her wits, she had a good chance of defeating Medb. The old woman rubbed her hands together and cackled with pleasure. Once Medb was dead, Gabria could return to the marsh and pay her price, a price the girl did not need to know about. The sorceress's hands moved over the girl and she muttered a spell, one of the few complex incantations she still remembered.

She was stunned when the spell failed. She knew that her powers were weak, but the girl's natural defenses were not that strong. There had to be something else. The woman quickly searched Gabria's clothes until she found the small stone ward. Her eyes flew wide when she recognized it, for she thought all those wards had been destroyed. She shrugged, pocketed it, and recreated the spell; this time it worked perfectly. Chuckling to herself, she went to rest. It had taken the last remnants of her strength to force the spell on the girl, but it would

ensure the payment was made if Gabria had to crawl from the edge of
the grave to deliver it.

Gabria came awake and sat up in confusion. She was lying on a
pallet in the chamber beneath the mangrove and there was no sign of
the sorceress. Daylight glimmered through the hatch that led up to the
tree trunk.

"Oh, gods," she whispered. "What day is it?" She jumped up in
frantic haste and gathered her belongings. Her cloak and food bag
were lying nearby, already replenished, and her water bag was full.

Something scratched at the wood outside, and the otter peered
down through the hatch. It chirped when it saw Gabria was already
awake.

Gabria flung her cloak over her shoulders. "I have to go," she
muttered to herself. "I have been here too long." She climbed the
steps, crawled through the hatch into the tree trunk, and peered
through the crack in the tree. She remembered that it had been sunny
when she arrived at the mangrove, and now the rain was falling in
sheets and the clouds were low and heavy above the trees.

Gabria grasped her bag and followed the otter down the tangled
roots to the small boat that bobbed on the tugging tide. The wind
whirled past her head and yanked at her cloak, but she ignored it just
as she ignored the rain. Only one thought prayed on her mind: How
long had she been gone?

The journey back through the marshes was long and tedious.
Gabria poled the boat with quiet desperation while the otter led her
through the labyrinth of reeds and channels. Unerringly the animal
found the river's main current and followed it laboriously upstream.
The rain fell incessantly; the clouds moved sluggishly inland, pushing
the tide ahead.

Fortunately, the otter had taken a shorter route through the
marshes to find solid ground. Gabria had approached the marshes
from the north, where the delta encroached farther inland. By following one of the main channels west, the otter cut off many miles of
their journey.

A few hours after sunset, the rain stopped, and, for the first time,
Gabria saw an end to the rushes and marsh grass. The river had swung
away from her to the north in a great loop that eventually turned west
again. Not far from Gabria, the marshes ended abruptly in a bold
scarp of arid hills that were the last bastion before the great plains.

Gabria poled the boat ashore near the fringes of the reeds. The channels had dried to shallow pools and stagnant meres, making it difficult to travel by boat. The girl tugged the craft up onto the bank and stood gratefully on solid ground.

The otter glided to her feet and sat up, its round eyes glistening. It chirped and waved a paw at her. Then, with a flick of its tail, it dove into the water and was gone.

"Wait!" Gabria lunged after it, but the otter had vanished. The girl slid to a stop before she fell in the water and looked dolefully at the marsh. She had hoped the sorceress's guide would lead her back to Nara.

Water dripped into Gabria's eyes as she scanned the marshes to find her bearings. Although the rain had stopped, the impenetrably inky clouds were a solid, sinking roof. She was cold, wet, and miserable. Gabria knew vaguely where she was, for the hills that began near her feet stopped the southern encroachment of the delta. However, she had to go north. Nara waited for her on the northern edge of the marshes; now, between them, lay the silt-laden Goldrine River.

Gabria started walking. It was very difficult going; since she could only see a few paces in front of her, she could not choose the best path through the heavy brush and boggy ground. Several times, Gabria tripped over unseen roots or fell into a sink where the mud stank and the water was slimy. She struggled on for hours until her muscles were limp and her nostrils were deadened to the rank smells.

Finally Gabria stopped. It was still quite dark and she bleakly looked around and admitted to herself that she was totally lost. She had no idea which way to go and precious time was being wasted. She needed Nara.

The Hunnuli had told her once to whistle if help was needed. Gabria knew that it was impossible for the mare to hear her, and yet, she thought that, maybe if she used her new powers, she could reach the mare with her need. A slim chance at best. Gabria decided to try it. There was nothing to lose by whistling in the dark. She closed her mind to everything but Nara, inhaled deeply, and whistled, bending her will to the mare with all the urgency she could muster.

The night was silent for a long moment, then, astonishingly, Gabria heard a horse neigh, as if from many miles away. She whistled a second time and hoped desperately she had not heard amiss. The call came again, joyfully and much closer this time.

"Nara!" she shouted. The Hunnuli was coming. Gabria turned to face the direction from which she heard the sound of hoofbeats, and the giant black horse burst out of the darkness. The mare skidded to a halt in front of the girl and reared, her head thrown back and her mane flying.

Gabria gasped, "Nara."

The mare settled down and her breath steamed in a snort. *Truly you have learned your art well.*

The girl's mind whirled in happiness, confusion, and wonder. "How did you come so fast?" she blurted.

The sorceress sent a message to tell me to come south, but your call led me here.

"How long have I been gone?"

The sun has set four times since we parted.

Gabria mentally counted the days. That did not seem right. If Nara was correct, she had only spent two days with the marsh woman. It seemed like years. She leaned gratefully against Nara's warm shoulders and ran her hand down the livid white streak.

"Let's go home," Gabria said.

With the girl on her back, Nara trotted westward through the failing edges of the marsh, toward the hills where the ground was firmer for a horse's hooves. Once on the dry slopes, she ran with the speed of the wind. Behind them, an orange glow fired the east as the clouds broke before the rising sun.

Gabria and Nara came to Ab-Chakan before sunset, riding in from the south along the flanks of the foothills, in the shelter of the trees. Nara eased silently through the undergrowth to the edge of the broad valley. In the thickening darkness they saw the fires and torches of Medb's army. Gabria's heart sank. She had seen the Wylfling werod in full array, but even the tales of added forces had not prepared her for the vast fields of tents, wagons, horses, and piles of supplies she saw. She would never make it through that camp to the fortress. Medb's forces were spread out in a semicircle at least a half-mile wide. Not even a Hunnuli could bolt through those ranks alone.

Gabria dropped her head. She was too late. It had not occurred to her that she might not be able to reach the Khulinin, and now that possibility was all too real.

Suddenly a horn sounded on the walls of the fortress. Clear and proud, its notes soared over the valley. Gabria stared at the fortress with pride and she felt her crumbling will revive. Behind those alien walls of stone, the four clans were still adhering to tradition with the horn call to sunset. She noticed angrily that the sorcerer's army had not bothered to reply. They had sunk so deeply into conquest that they had abandoned the traditions of the clans.

She was leaning over to say something to Nara when the mare's ears swiveled back and her nose turned to catch the breeze.

"What is it?" Gabria whispered. Her hand crept to her dagger. Without her other weapons, she felt ill at ease, and she wished that she had brought her sword.

Men are behind us. The whip carriers. They are seeking us.

Gabria drew her dagger and hid it in a fold of her cloak. If the Oathbreakers were seeking her, they would find her. When they did, no weapon—save, perhaps Nara—would save her if the men of Krath wanted her dead. But the cold, hard feel of the knife under her hand steadied Gabria as she waited quietly for the men to come.

Gabria wondered why the Oathbreakers were trailing Nara. The last she had heard, the cult was besieged in their towers by Medb's forces, and no man among them would desert his post. She shuddered. If the Citadel of Krath had fallen, Medb would have all the arcane tomes, manuscripts, spells, and artifacts in his grasp. He would be able to bring the clans to their knees in a matter of days.

Just then, out of the twilight, a shrouded figure on a dark horse rode into the trees. The figure raised his hand in a sign of peace as ten other riders rode up behind him. The man threw back his hood, revealing his thin, cruel face. He nodded and said, "Hail, Corin, and well met."

Gabria inhaled sharply. It was Savaric's brother, Seth. She stared at the bloodied gash on his forehead and at the weary, blood-stained men behind him.

Seth nodded, his fury barely contained. "Yes, we are all that is left. The citadel fell yesterday. Now we ride to the fortress. Do you wish to go?"

Gabria could only nod. Seth motioned for his men to dismount. "We will go at midnight," the Oathbreaker said curtly. Then, without another word, he withdrew with his men and sat down to wait.

It was an hour after midnight when Gabria and the Oathbreakers started. Hundreds of campfires burned in a broad swath across their path. Guards and squads of men patrolled among the tents. Somewhere a drum beat endlessly, as if marking the single heartbeat of the enemy camp. Medb had not bothered to fortify his flanks, for he expected no attack from behind.

Gabria and the men, leading their horses, were able to slip past the sentries to the outskirts of the encampment unnoticed. They gath-

ered behind several wagons near the old road and waited for the path
to clear.

They only had to wait a few minutes before Seth nodded to his
men. As they mounted their horses, Gabria shot a glance down the
road and saw that it was clear. She mounted Nara and closed her mind
to everything but the road ahead, the road to safety and the clan.

Gabria's eyes began to gleam. She leaned forward over Nara's
mane and the Hunnuli instantly sprang forward. The mare's ears were
flattened and her head stretched out. Her hooves rang on the stone.
Behind them, Seth and the cultists galloped in a tight group, their
whips uncurled and the wrath of their goddess revealed on their faces.

Horns suddenly bellowed around them; men began shouting and
running toward the road. The stone path still lay empty, but through
the tents came soldiers to cut them off. Nara screamed a challenge as
a mass of dark-skinned Turic warriors surged toward her. Gabria answered with the Corin war cry and hung on as the Hunnuli tore into
them.

Snapping and kicking with hooves deadlier than any sword, the
horse plunged into the attackers with ferocious speed until the men
fell back in terror. The Oathbreakers followed the mare closely, their
whips cracking with killing force. Arrows rained down among them,
and one of Seth's men fell. Still they raced on behind the fury of the
Hunnuli.

Before Gabria realized it, they had passed the main camp and
reached the fields and front lines. Startled, enraged faces turned
toward the riders and the horns blared again. Then Nara raced past
the defenses and toward the old stone bridge. Before the mare lay the
dark, littered, bloody ridge and the road to the fortress gate.

Gabria prayed fervently someone would open the gate. Already
she could hear the sounds of hooves as enemy riders galloped in pur-
suit. The fortress remained ominously quiet. Nara neighed imperiously as she ran over the bridge and up the road, but the gate still
remained closed. Gabria glanced back and, seeing the pursuing riders,
she closed her eyes and gritted her teeth. Open the gates, her mind
cried.

A war horn sounded from the tower. As the ancient wall reared
up in front of the riders, the gate was thrown open and Nara and the
Oathbreakers' horses galloped through. Shouts of anger came from
behind as the gate crashed shut and was barred. Gradually the yells
and hoofbeats dwindled away and a tense quiet fell over those in the

fortress. Gabria lay on Nara's neck, panting. The Oathbreakers wearily dismounted.

From out of the black shadows by the wall, a figure walked through the men to Nara's side. The Hunnuli nickered a greeting, and Gabria looked down into Savaric's face. She was stunned by the haggard lines on the chief's face and the weariness that dulled his movements. She slid off the mare and saluted.

"Lord, I beg your forgiveness for leaving without your permission. I only know I felt my reasons were important and that I had little time."

Many of the other warriors were staring at Gabria; Koshyn crossed his arms. Savaric remained quiet and deliberately examined her from head to foot, taking in her filthy, tattered clothes, her thin body, and her lack of a sword. At last, he returned her salute. "I'm certainly glad to have you back," he said, then his eyebrow arched in disapproval. "The next time you decide to leave, tell me first."

"Yes, Lord." She was relieved to find that he was not angry with her, but she still had to face Athlone. And Gabria knew *he* would have a few things to say. She glanced around and wondered where he was.

She and the men were standing by the front gate, in the bailey between the two walls. A few torches flickered on the parapets, casting a dim light on the exhausted faces of the defenders and on the battered walls of the old fortress. Everywhere Gabria looked were signs of a hard-won battle. Broken weapons littered the ground, huge rocks and fallen masonry lay between the walls, blood stains marred the parapets. Gabria suddenly shivered. Where was Athlone?

Seth and his men walked to Savaric's side, and the brothers greeted each other.

"Does your presence here mean the citadel has fallen?" Savaric asked.

"For now."

"What of your library?"

Scth shook his head. "We had time to hide the most important books where Medb will never find them. But—" Scth paused and pointed to his men. "We are all that are left."

Savaric glanced around. "There are not many left here, either. If Medb tries one more all-out assault, we'll not be able to hold the fortress. I'm afraid you picked a poor place for a sanctuary."

Seth shot a look at Gabria. "Not necessarily." He looked back at his brother and for the first time noticed something in the chieftain's face: the lines of crushing grief. Seth leaned forward and asked, "Where is Athlone?"

Gabria stiffened.

For a moment, Savaric stared into the night, his face frozen. "Athlone is dead," he finally answered. "He took some men out last night to burn the catapults and I did not stop him. Medb's men overwhelmed them."

Gabria stepped back as if struck by a blow. She started to shake and her heart caught in her throat. Without a sound, she turned and fled into the fortress.

18

In the heated darkness of his tent, Lord Medb stirred on his couch. His eyes slowly opened like a bird of prey disturbed by the movement of a coming victim. A cold smile creased his face. So, he thought with satisfaction, all the prizes are gathering in the same trap. It made things much easier. Medb was not surprised that a few rats from Krath's citadel had escaped; that warren was so full of bolt holes, even he would have had a difficult time finding them all.

What did surprise the Wylfling lord was the return of the Corin and his Hunnuli. He thought that the boy was long fled, cowering in some hole. Instead, the Corin had broken through his lines to the safety of the fortress. Medb chuckled to himself. He knew the outcome of this siege. While it was true he had been surprised by Savaric's move to the fortress, it would still not avail the fool. The fall of the clans was inevitable. He had let his mercenaries try their hand at cracking Ab-Chakan, and the ruin still stood. Now it was his turn. He would let the clans stew a little while longer, then he would attempt another method of breaking them that would be faster and more efficient.

A new, delightful possibility had fallen into Medb's lap and he was pleasantly contemplating his choices. He chuckled and glanced at his unconscious prisoner, bound hand and foot to the tent poles. Medb had in mind a simple trade, after which the clans could go free with their beloved Athlone returned. They would not realize until too late that the man was not the same independent, fiercely devoted leader he had been. But by then Athlone would be chieftain and the Khulinin would be solidly in a Wylfling grip. Of course, if the clans refused to barter, Medb would still have the pleasure of forcing them to watch as

Athlone died a particularly nasty death. He leaned back on his couch and laughed.

Morning came quickly on the wings of a rising wind. The night chill fled and the heat of the sun seeped into the earth. The clansmen and the Oathbreakers stood behind the walls and watched the sun illuminate the sorcerer's camp. There was no sign of the bodies of Athlone, the Hunnuli, or any of the men who had gone with them. Throughout the fortress, the clansmen gripped their weapons and waited in the mounting heat and dust. They knew Medb would not hold off his attack much longer.

In the general's palace, Piers was attending the wounded in the great hall. He had heard of Gabria's return, but he had not seen her and was beginning to worry. By midmorning, there was still no sign of her and Lady Tungoli offered to go look for the Corin.

She found Nara first, in the shelter of a crumbling wall near the main road. Gabria was curled up asleep in the mare's shadow. Tungoli gently shook her.

"Gabran," the lady said gently. "Morning is almost gone. Piers is pacing the floor waiting for you."

Gabria stretched her stiff muscles and looked up at the lines of grief etched on Tungoli's face. Her own sadness tightened her throat and her heart ached. She stood up and the two of them walked slowly back toward the palace.

"I'm glad you're back," Tungoli said after a few steps. "Athlone was very fond of you. He was terribly upset when you left."

The girl felt her tears burning in the back of her eyes, and she fiercely fought them back. She could not weep yet. "I'm sorry," she said, not knowing what else to say.

A small smile touched Tungoli's face. "I may be a foolish, wishful mother, but I don't believe he's dead."

Gabria stared at the chieftain's wife.

"It's only an intuition, I guess," Tungoli went on. "But I feel he is still alive. For now." Her mouth trembled and tears sparkled on her eyelids. "I would give almost anything to have him safe."

A small seed of hope stirred in the girl's mind. "If you're right, Lady, I will do everything I can to save him."

Tungoli took her arm. "I believe you, Gabran. Thank you." They walked on in silence to the palace.

Piers was delighted when Gabria came into the great hall. He waited beside the warrior he was tending and watched gladly as the tall, sunburned girl strode through the crowd to him. She moved with a subtle grace and wore an air of self-assurance most clanswomen tried to hide.

Piers clasped her with honest warmth. "Welcome back, Gabran. Your journey was successful." His words were a statement, for he could see the truth in her eyes.

Gabria nodded, touched by the unspoken concern in Piers's gesture. "For what it's worth."

The healer understood much of what she did not say. "Choices are often hard," he said softly. "But don't you think yours was already made?"

"I guess there never was a choice. I ride the only way left open for me." She smiled a little weakly. "Sometimes though, it seems to me I am very unfit for this task. Why would the gods lay so careful a trail and spend so little time preparing the one who must follow it?"

"That is the paradox of some of our best tales, Corin," Cantrell said behind her.

Gabria turned and greeted the blind bard. "I doubt anyone will sing tales of my deeds. Everything I've done has been unlawful."

"It is the ending of the tale that often decides that," he replied.

Seth came through the palace doors and saw Gabria. He came to join them. "Corin, I need to see you. Are you done here?"

Piers looked at the cultist in obvious distaste. "Go ahead, Gabran. We'll talk later."

Seth strode out the doors, expecting Gabria to follow. She hesitated. Her eyes met Piers's, and she saw his unmistakable support and affection. Comforted, she ran to catch up with Seth.

The silence was the first thing Gabria noticed when she and Seth passed the last building and came into sight of the inner wall. They slowed and Gabria stared around with a growing suspicion that something was wrong. There was no one by the inner wall, so they walked through the first gate to the bailey.

On the battlements above, Savaric, Koshyn, Ryne, and a crowd of warriors were leaning against the stone parapets, staring down at the fields. No one moved. Beyond the fortress wall everything was quiet. There was no sound or sense of movement in the valley below.

Following Seth, Gabria picked her way over the trampled dirt and tumbled stone to the stairs. They joined the chiefs on the parapet and looked over the wall to the fields. The sorcerer's army was in full array; the men stood in stiff ranks in a large crescent around the mouth of the valley. Everything was totally still.

Lord Koshyn suddenly stirred and pointed. "Look."

A large wagon carrying a number of men and pulled by four horses rolled out of the ranks of men toward the fortress. The defenders watched in growing suspicion as it crossed the bridge and stopped by the remains of the catapults. It turned ponderously around, and the men on board heaved off something large and black. As the wagon pulled away, a gasp and a moan of anger rose from the watching warriors. It was Boreas, the spear still protruding from his chest.

Mcdb did not give the clans long to recover from their shock. Horns suddenly blared from all corners of the field and four horsemen, bearing the banners of stark white, trotted out of camp. They halted by the dead Hunnuli. The horns continued to sing until the fortress echoed with their music. A second wagon rolled slowly down the road. Behind it came a procession of Wylfling warriors; in their midst rode the sorcerer on a large white horse.

Gabria stared at the sorcerer in amazement, for she had not known he had healed his crippled legs.

Medb's brown cloak had been discarded for a long robe of white—the color of death, the color of magic-wielders. He raised his hand and the procession stopped. Medb motioned a second time. Three Wylfling soldiers dragged the stumbling body of a man from the wagon to Boreas's body. They stepped back and Athlone fell to his knees. The horns stopped.

The clansmen immediately recognized the wer-tain, and a cry of rage roared out of the fortress.

Lord Medb laughed and spurred his mount forward. A Wylfling warrior seized Athlone's head, yanked it back to expose his throat, and poised his dagger inches away from the jugular. The clans grew quiet and waited.

"Khulinin. Dangari. Bahedin. Jehanan. Hear me!" Medb shouted. "I wish to congratulate you on your success thus far. You have held off your defeat quite admirably. However, your luck will not carry you forever, and I am afraid that when you fall, I will not be able to control my men. They are growing impatient and very angry. Most of you will not survive. But I do not wish to lose four clans, so I have a proposal for your consideration. Is there any man who will listen?"

After an angry pause, Savaric, Koshyn, and Ryne climbed to the top of the parapet and stood side by side. With a blade at Athlone's throat, they had little choice.

Lord Medb leaned forward like a snake eyeing its prey. "The terms are simple. For the safe return of Athlone, I want the Hunnuli, the Corin boy, and the four chieftains turned over to me. If these hostages are given quickly, I will withdraw my army and allow your clans to go in peace."

The chiefs exchanged glances. "What if we refuse?" Koshyn shouted.

Medb snapped a word. The Wylfling stepped back from Athlone. At another word, an invisible force yanked Athlone to his feet and held him spread-eagle in the air. From out of the ground, pale flames of red and gold flared up and around his body. Athlone writhed in agony, but Medb's magic held him mercilessly fast.

"Athlone will die very slowly before your eyes. And then your clans will follow," the sorcerer replied.

For a heartbeat, Savaric wavered. He would give anything to save his son from death. He would gladly surrender himself to Medb if he thought that Athlone would live. Unfortunately, he was certain of only one thing: Lord Medb could not be trusted to keep his word. His treachery was as plain as his heresy. Without a twitch of remorse, the sorcerer would slay his hostages, massacre the clans, and destroy Athlone anyway. In a voice that belied the tearing grief in his heart, Savaric shouted, "Your terms are intolerable. We cannot accept them."

Lord Medb threw back his head and laughed. "Don't jump into your fate so fast, Savaric. Give yourself time to think. You have one hour. At the end of that time, you will surrender the fortress or die."

Without warning, Medb raised his hand and pointed to the great bronze gates of the fortress. A blue fire sprang from his fingers. It struck the gates in a brilliant flash, searing along the edges of the bronze doors and scorching the stone arches. The ancient arcane wards in the entrance held for a few moments, then they cracked under the tremendous power and the gates crashed to the ground.

The clansmen stared down in horror as the dust slowly settled around the broken gate.

"One hour," Medb called. "Then Athlone dies." He stopped the flames around the wer-tain and waited as the Wylfling planted a post and hung Athlone up by his wrists. Then Medb reined his horse around and rode back to his army.

Gabria watched Athlone. From where she was standing on the parapet, she could not see his face, only his body hanging limp on the pole. She felt someone move beside her and turned to see Savaric staring down at his son. The chief's hands clenched the edge of the stone wall as if he wanted to tear down the parapet.

"Are you going to do anything to save him?" Gabria asked, although she knew what his answer had to be.

The chieftain shook his head, not even looking at her. "There is nothing we can do. Medb will not free him and I will not sacrifice the clans."

The girl nodded in understanding. Silently, she left the parapet and walked up the road toward the palace. Nara was waiting for Gabria in the big courtyard and came to join the Corin as she sat on the rim of the fountain.

For a long time, Gabria ignored the people passing by and stared at the mare waiting patiently by her side. The glorious Hunnuli, Gabria thought, they are as intelligent as humans, telepathic, impervious to sorcery, stronger and swifter than any other creature, and totally devoted to those few humans lucky enough to befriend them. They were creations of magic.

Everything Gabria had learned in her life had taught her to reject magic in any form, yet the clans did not reject the Hunnuli. In fact, Gabria began to realize how much magic was still a part of clan life. The magic was hidden behind different names, but the power was everywhere. It seeped in the rituals and traditions of the priests and priestesses; it was guarded by the Oathbreakers; it was sung of by the bards; it was embodied by the Hunnuli; and the talent to wield magic was still passed on from generation to generation.

Yet the clans, in their fear and ignorance, turned a blind eye to the power in their midst. Even after two hundred years, their prejudices had not allowed them to see the truth. Magic was not an evil, corrupting power. It simply was a force that existed, a force that could be formed into something as lovely or as hideous as its wielder desired. For the first time in her life, Gabria recognized how foolish her people had been to ignore magic.

Just then, Nara turned her head and her ears pricked forward. Gabria followed the mare's gaze and saw Cantrell walk carefully down the steps of the palace. He had a bundle under his arm.

Nara neighed and the bard called, "Gabran, are you there?" Gabria walked over to him and took his arm.

"Come," he said. "Walk with me a moment." They walked slowly around the courtyard, out of earshot of any casual listeners. The Hunnuli stayed close behind.

Gabria finally spoke. "Will the clans never learn to accept magic for what it is?"

"Not as long as Medb lives," Cantrell replied.

She sighed. "Then perhaps they need to see magic as something positive as well."

The bard gripped Gabria's arm tightly. "I heard Medb's ultimatum. There is not much time left."

They came to the front of the palace again and Gabria stopped walking. She knew what she had to do to free Athlone and save the clans—the conflict had stood at the end of her path since the day she left Corin Treld. But the very idea terrified her. She was no match for Lord Medb and she knew the consequences of her failure. Unfortunately, there were no more alternatives.

Cantrell held out the bundle he had been carrying. "I thought you might need this."

She opened it and found her scarlet cloak with the buttercup brooch, and a long, pale green tunic.

"The tunic was the closest I could find to white," the bard joked with a faint smile. He embraced her quickly. "The gods go with you, Gabria." He turned and left her.

Gabria wound her fingers in Nara's mane, and they went back down the road toward the main gate. Behind a ruined wall, Gabria stripped off her clothes. The rags that bound her breasts, the filthy tunic, and the Khulinin cloak were tossed aside, though she hesitated taking the gold cloak off. The Corin kept only her leather hat, her boots, and her pants. She tucked her father's dagger into her boot, then pulled the green tunic over her head and belted it with her sash. She thought about using her power to change the tunic's color to white, but she changed her mind. It was time magic-wielders had a new color. Gabria laid her red cloak over her shoulder and sighed with relief. Never again would she have to play the boy. Soon the clans would know her for exactly what she was.

Gabria took a slow breath and opened the sorceress's bag. A long, needle-thin diamond splinter fell glittering into her hand. Gabria stared at it, puzzled. The sorceress had told her this thing was the sign of a true magic-wielder, but she had not said what Gabria was supposed to do with it.

"You will need an assistant to help you complete the rite," someone said behind her.

Gabria nearly jumped out of her skin. Nara snorted, but it sounded more like an agreement than a warning.

Seth walked around the wall and joined her. "It is too difficult to insert the splinter alone."

"How do you know?" she gasped.

"The men of my cult have guarded the knowledge of the magic-wielders for years in hopes someone would need it."

"But how did you find me?"

His eyebrows arched. "I followed you."

Gabria studied him for a long time before she gave him the diamond. Seth took her arms and extended them, palms up. His weathered face was impassive. He spoke the words of the ancient rite as if he had spoken them every day of his life, without hesitation or distaste. The words were still hanging in the air when he raised the diamond splinter to the sun to capture the heat and light. The sliver glittered in his hand. Then, with a skill as deft as a healer, he pierced Gabria's wrist and slid the splinter under her skin.

The pain lanced through Gabria's arm, and she could feel the heat of the diamond burning under her skin. Immediately the splinter began to pulse with the pounding of her heart. A tingling spread through her hand and up into every part of her body. The sensation was warm and invigorating. Gabria looked into Nara's wise eyes and smiled.

Seth turned her wrist to look at the splinter pulsing under her skin. "Use this wisely, Corin. You are the last and the first, and it would be best if you survived."

"Thank you, Seth."

He grunted. "Go."

The girl mounted the Hunnuli, and the horse trotted toward the main gate. The one-hour reprieve was over. Medb had returned.

The Wylfling lord rode arrogantly up to the fortress. His army was ready to attack; his face was alive with triumph. "What say you, clansmen?" he shouted to the defenders.

Lord Savaric, Koshyn, and Ryne leaned over the parapet. "We will not deal with you," Savaric called.

"But I will!" a strange voice shouted below him. Hoofbeats clattered over the stone road and the Hunnuli galloped forward. The mare reached the entrance and went up and over the fallen gates with a terrific heave of her hind legs. Gabria's scarlet cloak flared like wings. The horse landed lightly and cantered a few paces forward to a stop.

Savaric shouted, "Gabran! Come back here!"

Gabria ignored him and calmly faced Medb. Her hat and her

cloak still disguised her femininity and the embedded splinter that pulsed in her wrist. "I will make you an offer, Lord Medb," she said coldly.

"I do not deal with mere boys," Medb sneered. He snapped a word and magic fire flared around Athlone. The wer-tain jerked in agony.

"Gabran!" Savaric cried.

Gabria was silent. With deliberate slowness, she raised her hand and the ruby light of the splinter gleamed on her tanned skin. The flames around Athlone snuffed out, the cords binding his wrists parted, and his body sank to the ground. The wer-tain shivered once and his eyes opened. A Wylfling warrior, his sword drawn, jumped toward the fallen man. A blue flare of Trymian Force surged from Gabria's hand to the warrior's chest, flinging him backward into a smoking, lifeless heap.

The silence on the field was absolute.

"Oh, my gods," Koshyn breathed.

Medb stared at the Corin thoughtfully. So that was the answer to those many, puzzling questions. He parted his thin lips in a twisted smile. "What is your offer, boy?"

"You may have me and the Hunnuli in exchange for Athlone's life. But you must fight me to win your prizes."

He shrugged. "A duel? That is impossible. A boy cannot fight a chieftain."

"I am chieftain of the Corin, thanks to you. But I do not wish to use swords in this duel."

"An arcane duel? Against you?" Medb laughed. "If that is what you want, I will humor you." The sorcerer knew his strength was low. He was not fully recovered from the battle two days before, and he had expended a great deal of energy shattering the fortress gates. Still, he thought it would take little effort to crush this upstart. Smiling, Medb ordered his warriors back. He dismounted on the level space by the fallen gates.

"You are a fool, boy. Did the bard not tell you the riddle of my doom?" the Wylfling asked.

Gabria looked down at Medb. Standing straight and tall, he was a powerful, handsome man. "It is a riddle no longer."

"Oh?" He fixed her with a cold stare.

"*I* am the answer to your riddle, Medb, for I am no boy and my name in the northern dialect means buttercup." Before her stunned audience, Gabria peeled off the leather hat and shook her head until the loose curls fluffed out and framed her face in gold. Then she unpinned the cloak and let it drop over Nara's black haunches. The wind molded the green tunic against her breasts and slender waist. The sun glittered in her eyes, as hard and as bright as any sword.

"Gabran is dead these many days. I am Gabria, his sister, and daughter of Lord Dathlar."

For the first time since his hands touched the *Book of Matrah*, Medb was deeply afraid. This girl had come out of nowhere with a knowledge of sorcery and the emblem of a magic-wielder burning in her wrist. Where had she gotten her knowledge? And the splinter. He had not been able to find one, but this girl had not only attained one but had it properly inserted. For a moment, Medb's heart quailed and the hairs rose on the back of his neck.

Then he steadied himself. She was a difficulty he had not anticipated, but he had not struggled this far to be overcome by a girl and a riddle. She might be the "buttercup," but she was not bearing a sword. With a silent curse, Medb swore he would end the riddle once and for all.

The girl slid off the Hunnuli and the mare backed away, leaving her alone. Gabria pushed away every doubt that might distract her, closed her eyes, and concentrated on the ancient spell the Woman of the Marsh had taught her. She lifted her right hand and pointed behind Medb. "I, Gabria, daughter of Dathlar, challenge you, Lord Medb, and by my challenge set the first wards."

Medb's voice purred. "I, Lord Medb, accept your challenge and, by my acceptance, set the second wards."

Gabria opened her eyes. The spell had worked. Four scarlet pillars of light stood equidistant from each other, forming a square that enclosed Gabria and Medb in an area only twenty paces wide. A pale mist glowed between the pillars and arched overhead. The two were now surrounded by a protective wall of power that shielded the spectators. Gabria could see the clansmen watching with horrified fascination from outside the wall.

"You have unwisely challenged me," the sorcerer sneered. "But the question is not who is stronger, but by what means I shall prove it to you."

Medb lifted his hand and launched a sphere of Trymian Force. It was only a test, and the Corin dodged it easily The blue ball exploded on the ward shield. He fired more at her, faster and faster, and she swayed and dipped around the bright, deadly fires as if dancing with them. The girl did not try to retaliate; she only avoided his assault and waited for his next move.

At last, Medb grew weary of playing with her. He had to be careful, for his strength was waning and he did not know how great this girl's powers really were. He studied the Corin for a moment, then he spoke a command.

Suddenly Gabria felt a tug of wind at her feet. The strange little wind whipped abruptly into a whirlwind of vicious intensity and wrapped around Gabria in a swirling, shrieking maelstrom. Dirt and grit flailed through the dark wind, tearing at her hair, her skin, and her clothes. She tried frantically to escape the maelstrom, but the force of the whirlwind tossed and buffeted her, ripped the breath from her body, and wrenched every bone and muscle.

Then, as quickly as it had begin, the wind died away. Gabria fell to the ground, panting and crying with pain. Her tunic was shredded and her skin was raw and bleeding.

"See how easy it is?" Medb said. "Let me show you another. You have survived the tragedies in your life well, but do you really know the terrors of your mind?"

Before Gabria could defend herself from it, a paralyzing chill froze her. She threw her hands across her face. Images crowded into her mind: her brother falling, his skull crushed by a battle axe; her father hacked by a dozen swords; Nara torn alive by wolves; Athlone hanging by shredded ligaments from a bloody pole. From a dark gray patch of earth, the rotting corpses of Clan Corin staggered out of their graves and pointed accusing fingers at her. Gabria stumbled into a desert of searing thirst and unendurable loneliness. A scream tore at her throat. Desperately she tried to rise, only to pitch forward when her legs would not respond.

Beyond the shield, Athlone struggled to his feet. He leaned against the pole, his eyes on the girl. "Fight him, Gabria," he cried.

"Do you understand now?" Medb chuckled appreciatively. "You should have stayed at your place by the cooking fires and left the wars to those capable of handling them."

Gabria tried to stop the chaos in her mind and bring her thoughts back under her control. She realized the visions that plagued her were fears she had known before. There was nothing that she had not already faced. A little at a time, she forced the images out of her mind and finally broke Medb's spell. She tottered to her feet.

The Corin knew now that she could not defeat Lord Medb in a confrontation of expertise. He had been studying and conditioning his talent too long. She lacked the skill necessary to destroy him outright. Gabria had only one hope, a slim one at best: to catch him off guard. If she could survive just long enough to take him by surprise, perhaps her untried powers would be enough. Quickly she rapped a spell that exploded underneath the sorcerer's feet and threw him to the ground in a sprawling heap.

Medb jumped up, enraged. "Enough of this!" he shouted. The Wylfling decided to use a killing spell he had already perfected. He spread his arms wide, his lips formed the harsh words, and slowly he began to bring his hands together.

For a moment, Gabria stood warily. She began to feel a pressure on all sides. There was no pain or distress, only a mild discomfort, as if she were wrapped in a heavy fur. She braced herself and tried to fend it away, but the pressure increased. Her head began to throb and her chest hurt. She was having trouble breathing. Straining to escape the pressure, Gabria clenched her teeth and used her power to form a protective shell about her body. The arcane grip grew stronger. She fought to maintain her shield, but Medb's grip contracted with a jerk, once and then again. Her protective shield cracked and the pressure closed in around her. The pain worsened, and the Corin's bones began to creak under the stress. Gabria moaned and her hands tore at her head.

Medb pushed his hands closer together and struggled to break the girl's resistance. He could feel his strength beginning to ebb, but he disregarded his growing weakness in his effort to kill the last surviving Corin.

Unseen by Gabria and Medb, Athlone began to stagger toward the arcane shield. He knew he should be horrified by what Gabria was doing, but instead he was strangely drawn to the arcane duel and his only lucid thought was to help his friend. He could not bear to see her die.

Gabria cried as Lord Medb strained harder. The pain in her body was almost overwhelming and her consciousness began to close in around her. In desperation, the girl gathered her last shreds of strength and courage into one final core of resistance. She clung tenaciously to one thought: she would never submit. Her last awareness flickered and she screamed her defiance.

Lord Medb tried desperately, but he could not crush the girl's last opposition. Her defiance was fueled by fury and righteousness and by a will that Medb sensed was greater than his own. Surprise and a seed of doubt crept into his mind. He felt his power weakening rapidly.

All at once, Athlone shouted furiously, "Medb, no!" The wer-tain stood by the arcane shield, his face dark with rage and helplessness. He put his fist through the shield and, to Medb's horrified surprise, the arcane wards shattered. The shield abruptly disintegrated, slamming Athlone to the ground.

Gabria felt Medb's power fade, and in that moment, she remembered the last line of Cantrell's riddle. Summoning every ounce of will, she wrenched loose of the sorcerer's arcane grip. The blackness vanished and the pain eased. Her vision returned with startling clarity. She had just enough energy left. Before Medb was aware of what she was doing, Gabria snatched her father's dagger out of her boot and transformed it into a silver sword. The splinter in her wrist flared red with her blood as she hurled the sword at the sorcerer. It soared in a glittering arc across the space between them and plunged into Medb's chest.

A great cry shook the fortress. Medb jerked, contorted by pain, and his cruel mouth shaped one last curse. Then he collapsed backward, impaled by the silver sword.

Gabria shivered uncontrollably. The world fell away and she sank to the ground. But as the edge of consciousness darkened, a vision came of a hollow tree and an old woman who waited for her. Before the pain finally drowned her, Gabria clawed the air, trying to answer to the strange summons that beckoned her to the marsh.

19

Lord Savaric did not hesitate after the sorcerer fell. With a wild shout he called to his warriors and raced through the gates toward Medb's army, which stood in stunned silence in the fields. The Khulinin were fast on their chief's heels. Lord Koshyn, Lord Ryne, and the clansmen raised their voices into battle cries that shook the towers, and the four clans sprang after the enemy.

Clan Amnok broke immediately. They had wanted no part of Medb's treachery, but had been swept along by Lord Ferron, their cowed chieftain, and trapped by the sorcerer's tyranny. Now, without Medb's arcane goad to force them on, they turned and ran. The Geldring, too, were reluctant to fight; despite Branth's ravings, they fled with their wer-tain to the camp. The Ferganan simply threw down their weapons and refused to fight. Only the mercenaries, well paid and eager for battle, the exiles, and the Wylfling drew their swords and faced the charging clans.

The four clans roared joyfully. The sorcerer was dead, the enemy forces were cut in half, and Athlone had been saved. Now they were running to something they understood. As they charged across the fields, they beat their shields with their weapons and shouted their challenge across the plains. Their running feet raised clouds of dust, and, through the thick air, the sunlight glistened on their helms and their swords. With one will, both sides met in a deafening crash.

The tumult rattled through the fortress. Seth, from atop the wall, watched the battle for several minutes before walking down to the ground. His icy, remote eyes revealed no feelings as he felt Athlone's wrist and laid the unconscious man in a more comfortable position.

Then he turned to Gabria. She was lying in a heap, her face pale and her golden hair dirty with sweat and dust. The Hunnuli stood over her.

"Tell her we still guard the most treasured books of the old sorcerers. She may have need of them one day."

The Hunnuli did not answer, as he expected, but she flicked her head in understanding. Gabria stirred as the noise of the battle finally drew her awake. Seth put a skin of water to her lips; she drank thirstily and struggled to her feet. He watched her impassively.

The girl looked around at Medb's body, at the furious fighting that raged in the fields, and at Athlone lying nearby. For just a second, her gaze softened as she looked at the wer-tain. At last she met Seth's eyes.

He nodded to acknowledge her. "It was said in tales long ignored that sorcery would one day be found in the hands of a woman."

Gabria didn't answer. She was tired beyond exhaustion, but she could not rest. The strange image of the Woman of the Marsh remained in her mind, compelling her to come. She hauled herself up onto Nara's back and put on her cloak.

Seth kept his stare pinned on her. "You are leaving?"

"I have to," she said curtly.

At Gabria's command, Nara wheeled and cantered south down the old road. The girl did not watch the fighting as they passed or look back at the fortress. The noise of the battle receded, and before long they were alone.

"Please take me back to the marshes, Nara," Gabria said, her voice indistinct and empty.

Nara's thoughts were worried. *What have you left to say to this woman?*

"Don't be concerned. I need to see her."

Nara asked Gabria nothing else, but a foreboding chilled her. Her rider was so remote. The girl's unresponsiveness could not be explained simply by weariness or distress. There was something different, an unnatural sense of urgency that precluded everything else. The mare settled into a gallop. There was little she could do but comply until they reached the marshes and she could learn the real purpose behind their journey.

Like a wild tide, the four clans swept through the remaining forces of the sorcerer's army, until the ground was littered with dead and the earth was stained with blood. The Wylfling and their mercenaries fought bravely, but by the close of day they were defeated. Most of the exiles were cut down, except for a few who escaped to the hills. The Geldring, Ferganan, and Amnok clans had already surrendered, preferring the punishment of the council to annihilation by the enraged, triumphant Khulinin, and they stood aside while Savaric tore down Medb's banner.

The fighting was still going on in the valley when Athlone regained consciousness. For a moment, he thought he had drunk too much, because his stomach was queasy and his thoughts were a jumble of bad dreams and unfamiliar pain. Then he opened his eyes and saw that he was lying beside several other wounded men by the gates of the fortress. Piers was tending a warrior close by. The memories flooded back with all their griefs and furies.

The wer-tain's moan brought Piers to his side. The healer helped him sit up, then forced a cup into his hands. Athlone stared numbly down the hill at the body of Boreas while he drank the liquid. Whatever Piers had given him burned in his stomach with revitalizing warmth, and, after a few minutes, he was able to stand. When he saw Medb's body, his jaw clenched.

"Why did she have to do that?" he groaned.

Piers said quietly, "Gabria had no choice, Wer-tain. She had to use the weapons at hand."

"The weapons at hand," Athlone repeated ironically. He could remember using the same words to Gabria. "Where is she?" he asked after a while.

Piers's face clouded with worry. "She and Nara went south. I think she is returning to the Woman of the Marsh."

"Returning!" Athlone cried. He threw the cup to the ground and ran for the nearest horse.

Piers yelled angrily, "Athlone! You'll never catch a Hunnuli on that."

The wer-tain ignored him, grabbed the bridle of an escaped mount and swung up in the saddle. He savagely reined the animal around and kicked it into a gallop.

A day later, Athlone's horse fell and did not rise again. No Harachan could catch a Hunnuli or even keep pace with one, yet Athlone, his heart sick with fear and confusion, had urged the horse on until it had dropped. Now he was on foot and farther from Gabria than ever. In the hours he had ridden like a madman, he had given no thought to anything but keeping to Nara's trail and finding Gabria.

But that day, as he trudged southeast in the hot sun, he had too much time to think and his emotions twisted inside him.

Athlone could hardly believe Gabria had killed the sorcerer with magic. He guessed she had learned sorcery from the marsh woman, but why had the girl decided to use magic as her weapon against Medb? Gabria had never shown any sign of using sorcery . . . or had she? As Athlone jogged along, he began to remember things that had seemed odd to him: her fight with Cor and the man's strange illness; Cor's later death at her hand; and even the fight Gabria had had with him at the pool, when she had felled him with a mere shoulder wound. Athlone vaguely recalled how he had called her a sorceress, but how could he have known? She was nothing like what he expected a magic-wielder to be, nothing like Medb. Gabria rode a Hunnuli and she had saved the clans. She had saved him. Where was the evil in that?

Athlone groaned and ran faster. He had to find her before she was lost in the marshes. Suddenly, to his relief, he heard a Hunnuli neigh a strident greeting. Nara galloped down a long hill to meet the wer-tain. She was drenched with sweat and caked to the knees with dried mud. And alone.

Come. Gabria has met the Woman of the Marsh. She sent me away.

Athlone was nearly overwhelmed by the force of the mare's distress. Gabria would never have ordered Nara away if she were planning to return. He vaulted to the horse's back without hesitation and held on as Nara burst into a dead run back the way she had come.

It was early morning when the Hunnuli reached the western fringes of the marshes. Nara worked her way down the river as far as she could go before she was forced to stop and let Athlone slide off.

"How will I find her out there?" he demanded, glaring at the marshes around him. Weary, hungry, and feverish, he was starting to feel ill.

Nara neighed. *The marsh woman came to meet Gabria in a boat. They went downstream past that bend. Gabria is nearby. I can sense her.*

Athlone threw up his hands and plunged into the mud. Before moving off, he stopped and, without turning around, asked, "Nara, if Gabria is a sorceress, why do you stay with her?"

Nara snorted. *The Hunnuli were bred to be the guardians of the magic-wielders. It is only evil we cannot tolerate.*

Athlone nodded and trudged on. The full meaning of the Hunnuli's words did not come to the chief's son until much later.

* * *

At the same time Nara was racing away to find help, the Woman of the Marsh was leading Gabria ashore on a small, overgrown island, not far from where the girl had left the Hunnuli. The woman had thought about waiting for the girl in the tree, but when she had learned Gabria was coming, her anticipation grew too strong. The sorceress had brought her things in her boat and met the girl at the edges of the marsh.

The old woman clicked her tongue as she laid Gabria on a mat under a makeshift shelter and unpinned the red cloak. The girl was in dreadful shape, but she had come and she was still alive—that was all that mattered. It would take a little more time to build up the girl's strength and tend to her most dangerous hurts, or neither one of them would survive the transference. Still, the sorceress gloated, after waiting two hundred years, another day will make little difference.

By nightfall, Gabria was sleeping heavily. She had been fed and drugged with poppy. While she slept, the sorceress pored over her musty manuscript to memorize the best possible incantation. The transference would have to be perfect and would require a great deal of strength and skill, but the results would be worth the effort.

The old woman cackled with glee. She would be young again! She could look in a mirror and see a beautiful, smooth-faced woman instead of an ugly shell. Best of all, she could return to the world. That fool, Medb, had accomplished that at least: he had broken the clans' centuries-old complacency and had opened the door to sorcery once more.

It was a shame the girl had to die, for she would make an excellent ally. She had incredible will and a natural talent. Nevertheless, the price had to be paid and the transfer of youth left little life in the donor. The woman laughed to herself and set aside her manuscript. She would not have to wait much longer.

Morning was streaming into the shelter when Gabria awoke. She roused slowly, heavily dragging herself through a drug-induced fog to awareness. When she finally opened her eyes, she wondered vaguely where she was, then she wished she could go back to the peace of sleep. Her body hurt abominably, and even more painful was the empty, aching loss in her heart. What had begun at Corin Treld had at last reached its completion, leaving her life in ashes. Medb was dead, Athlone was beyond her reach, Boreas dead, and Nara gone. And now, because of her duel with the sorcerer, she was condemned to death or exiled to a life of emptiness. There was nowhere she belonged but the grass-covered barrow at Corin Treld. Her clan was at peace now; perhaps they would welcome her.

When the sorceress came in, Gabria stared at her apathetically. "Oh, it's you."

The woman put on a smirk of false sympathy. "Come, my child. It is time to pay your debt."

"What debt?" Gabria mumbled. She tried to rise, but the crone pushed her down.

"Thanks to me, you have destroyed a powerful and dangerous sorcerer. But now there is no life left for you. You do not sacrifice anything by relinquishing your youth to me. It is a fair deal for us both." The sorceress held up a small, lighted oil lamp.

Gabria glanced at the lamp, wondering what the old hag was talking about. Before she realized what was happening, her gaze was captured by the light of the flame and the sorceress mesmerized her into a mild stupor.

The old woman sat beside Gabria on the mat. She set the oil lamp between them, took the girl's hand, and started the spell. The magic began to build around Gabria, and the Woman of the Marsh grew absorbed in her task.

Suddenly, without warning, a commotion on the edge of the little island disturbed the woman's chant. She looked up worriedly just as a large and angry warrior burst into the shelter. He was flushed with fever and his body trembled with rage.

The woman screeched, "Stay away! Your magic can't hurt me!" and jumped to her feet. She pulled Gabria's stone ward out of her pocket and thrust it in the man's face.

Athlone knocked the ward out of her hands. He took one look at Gabria and pounced on the sorceress. "What have you done?" he bellowed, shaking her like a rag.

"She must pay," the old woman screamed. She clawed at his fists, but it was like scratching steel.

Athlone dropped the old woman and leaned over her. "Pay what?"

The woman hesitated, reaching into her sleeve.

"Pay what!" he demanded again.

She snatched a slim dagger. "The price for my help," she cried. "Her youth is mine now!" She stabbed upward toward Athlone's stomach, a faint blue aura cloaking the blade.

The wer-tain saw the knife coming too late and tried to twist away. The knife struck his belt, slithered sideways, and sliced into his left ribs. The crone's feeble Trymian Force was doused. Athlone roared in pained fury, and the woman screeched in real terror. She tried another stab, but Athlone hit her with his fist and knocked her to the ground. He heard a sickening crunch as the woman's head struck a large rock. She jerked once and lay still.

Athlone stood for several breaths, staring at the hag's body on the ground as if he could not believe she were dead. Then he wiped the sweat off his forehead, and a grim smile spread over his face.

Gabria cried out. Athlone whirled around and stared at the girl in horror. The marsh woman's half-finished spell had ruptured and the forces of magic she had gathered and not used abruptly coalesced into livid red clouds that swirled around Gabria in a gathering tornado. The oil lamp spilled and flames spread around the Corin, setting her cloak on fire. Gabria screamed again over the rising shriek of the unspent power.

Athlone was filled with terror at losing her. Without thinking, he leaped at Gabria through the wild forces and ripped her cloak off. The magical aura engulfed him.

Even as the uncontrollable power raged around him, the wer-tain was stunned by the natural, familiar feel of the magic. In a brilliant flash, he realized that magic and sorcery were not a perversion or an evil threat, simply a natural power inherent in his world—a power that could be tapped only by those born with a talent. At that moment, he knew without a doubt that he, too, had that talent.

The revelation shook him to the core. He understood a part of what Gabria must have felt when she had learned of her power. It was a bitter lesson to realize he had been wrong about something so vital.

As quickly as his acceptance took shape, Athlone noticed Gabria was doing nothing to escape the maelstrom. His skin was tingling and his ears ached in the rising shriek of energy amplified to an explosive crescendo.

"Gabria!" he yelled, pulling her close to him.

The girl hung against the warrior. Her eyes were closed and her body was limp.

Athlone held her tighter. Oh, gods, he wondered, has she given up? "What do you truly want?" he shouted at her.

Gabria was still for so long that Athlone thought he had lost her, then she stirred. Her answer was nearly lost in the roar of the whirlwind, but he heard it.

"I want to be myself."

She wrapped her arms around Athlone and forced her will into the center of the whirling magical vortex. Then, to her everlasting joy, she felt Athlone's mind tentatively reach out to her and offer his strength. Together, they slowed the wild whirl of broken sorcery and spread the destructive force apart until it dissipated into a mist on the morning breeze. The angry red light faded and the fire died down.

Gabria gritted her teeth against a wrenching nausea as the remnants of the spell vanished and the day snapped back to familiarity. It was over. Then she saw the burning remains of her scarlet cloak and the pent-up tears of five months flooded her eyes. She leaned against Athlone and sobbed.

For five days, Gabria and Athlone camped in a hollow by the river, spending their days along the banks and their nights in the warmth of each other's arms. It was a time of healing for them both and, under Nara's watchful eye, they slept a great deal and talked very little. Neither of them wanted to broach the subject of sorcery or the future until the time was right. For now they were content to be together for as long as they were allowed.

On the afternoon of the sixth day, Nara neighed a greeting to a horseman who appeared on a far hill. Athlone and Gabria exchanged lingering looks and reluctantly walked to their camp to wait for the intruder.

The young clansman, wearing a Khulinin cloak, reined his sweating horse to a halt and slid to the ground. His gaze slid past Gabria, but he saluted Athlone in undisguised relief and pleasure. "My lord, we have been looking for you for days."

Athlone turned cold at the title. His nostrils flared and he took a step forward. "Why do you call me that, Rethe," he demanded.

Rethe bowed his head. "That's why we had to find you. Lord Savaric is dead."

"How?" Athlone demanded.

"He was stabbed from behind . . . just after the fight for the camp. We think Lord Branth is responsible."

"Where is Branth now?"

The warrior looked up unhappily. "We don't know. The book of that accursed sorcerer is missing, too. Lord Koshyn and the Geldring's wer-tain believe Branth took it after he murdered Lord Savaric."

Athlone felt his grief well up. "Thank you for the message. Please leave us."

Rethe nodded but he did not move. "My lord, Lord Koshyn has

called for an immediate reconvening of the council. He asks that you bring Gabria to the council."

"Why?" Gabria asked.

The messenger glanced past her nervously.

"Answer her," Athlone said sharply.

Startled by Athlone's tone, Rethe involuntarily looked at her. Gabria smiled briefly, and he relaxed a little. He and the other Khulinin could not fathom the realities of Gabria's true sex or her ability as a sorceress. She had spent five months in close companionship with them and no one even suspected. The clan owed its life to her and everyone knew it. Unfortunately the debt would not erase her crimes. Rethe had no idea how the clans would react if Gabria returned with Athlone, but he doubted few people would be pleased.

"I don't know," Rethe answered. "I was only told to pass on the message."

Athlone and Gabria looked at one another for a long time, their eyes locked in understanding. Finally, Gabria nodded.

"We will come," Athlone said.

Rethe accepted the dismissal, saluted, and rode away. Athlone watched him go as Gabria slowly began to obliterate their camp and gather their meager belongings.

Athlone stood for a long while, his face blank and his back sagging. He walked out of camp and disappeared into the hills. Gabria sighed. She knew the grief he was suffering and she, too, grieved for Savaric. Nara lay down, tucking her long legs underneath her and Gabria cuddled into the haven of the mare's warm sides.

Gabria was asleep when Athlone returned at dusk. He gently ran his finger along her jaw. His heart jumped when her eyes opened, filled with love and welcome.

The wer-tain's voice was harsh with grief, but his hands were warm and steady as he wrapped his golden cloak around her shoulders. "I have no horse worthy to give you as a betrothal gift, so I hope you will accept this instead."

Gabria sat for a long time, gently rubbing the gold fabric between her fingers and thinking about her family and her clan. Finally, she replied, "The Corin are dead. It is time to let them rest." She looked up at him and smiled radiantly. "I accept your gift."

Athlone was delighted. The smile she gave him was worth the uncertainty and difficulties of the days ahead. The warrior had no idea if the council would allow him to marry the girl, but now that he was chieftain of the Khulinin, the other lords would have to tread carefully.

"You don't mind being with a known heretic?" Gabria asked. It was the first time either of them had spoken of the subject, and, though she remembered the Khulinin's shocked recognition of his own talent, she was not certain how he was dealing with it.

Athlone smiled faintly. "Boreas did not mind."

Nara snorted and nudged the new chief.

"Did you know," Gabria asked as Athlone settled down beside her, "that Nara is carrying Boreas's foal?"

Athlone's smile grew as wide as the sky.

20

Two days later, just before noon, Nara paused on a high hill overlooking the valley of the Isin River. From the crest, Athlone and Gabria looked down on the army encampment spread out before the defile. Sections of the big camp had been destroyed in the battle, but other sections were teeming with people and three new camps had sprung up displaying the banners of the Murjik, the Shadedron, and the Reidhar clans. Even as Gabria and Athlone watched, an outrider galloped among the tents toward the fortress and clanspeople began to swarm to the edge of the camps.

"They seem to be expecting us," Athlone said dryly.

Gabria nodded. Athlone gently twisted her around to face him and looked into her eyes. "Are you certain you want to do this?"

She leaned against him. "I have nowhere else I want to go. I belong to the clans."

"Even if the council passes a death sentence?"

Gabria smiled nervously. "Then I may change my mind."

Nara trotted down the slope to the valley. By the time she came to the edge of the encampment, a huge crowd had gathered. The clanspeople were strangely silent, for they did not know how to deal with the heretical sorceress who had saved the clans. No one cursed or reviled Gabria, but no one welcomed her, either.

The Hunnuli stopped, her path barred by the throng. Koshyn, Ryne, and Jol of the Murjik walked through the crowd and came to stand in front of Nara.

"Greetings, Lord Athlone," Koshyn said. "I am glad to see you are safe. Greetings to you, Gabria."

Athlone dismounted and gave his hand to Gabria. She slid off the mare and faced the chieftains, her back straight and her eyes proud.

Athlone was about to return the greeting when Lady Tungoli came running through the clanspeople and past the chiefs. She hugged her son fiercely, laughing and crying in turn, then she turned to Gabria and without hesitation embraced the girl with the same joy and relief.

"You did everything you could to save my son," she said softly in Gabria's ear. "Now I will do what I can to save you."

Gabria hugged her with gratitude.

"Athlone," Koshyn said, "word of your coming has forewarned us. If you are willing, we are ready to convene the council in the palace."

"My lords," Tungoli's clear voice rang out. "A favor. Gabria's fate affects all the clans. I ask that this meeting be held in the open so all the clanspeople may attend."

Koshyn looked at Ryne and Jol, then Athlone. They all nodded. "So be it," the Dangari said. "We'll meet in the courtyard." A murmur of approval swept through the watching crowd.

With one hand resting on Nara's neck and the other hand on Athlone's arm, Gabria walked up the stone road to the fortress. The crowd parted before her and followed close behind, as the girl, the Hunnuli, and the chiefs went through the fortress and gathered in the wide courtyard before the general's palace.

The remaining chiefs had already arrived and were waiting on the palace steps. Lord Sha Umar leaned shakily against a pillar, his arm in a sling from his arrow wound. Lord Caurus of the Reidhar and Malech of the Shadedron stood side by side, looking ill at ease, but there was no sign of Medb's old allies, Ferron and Quamar.

Koshyn quickly explained the change of the council to the other lords, and they, too, agreed. Seats were brought for the chiefs and they made themselves comfortable at the top of the steps, under the arched portico.

Athlone held Gabria close for just a moment before he went to join the lords. The girl stayed at the foot of the steps, her fingers twined in the Hunnuli's mane. Tungoli stayed with her. The other clanspeople crowded into the courtyard until the area was packed.

Lord Koshyn rose. As the oldest, healthiest surviving chieftain of the four triumphant clans, he had assumed some authority the past eight days. He stood now and took control of the council. "Lord Athlone, we welcome you. We are deeply stricken by the death of your father."

Athlone nodded his thanks, for he did not trust himself to speak at that moment. He was still not used to the title of 'lord' or the aching grief that filled him whenever he thought of his father.

Koshyn went on. "I will tell you now what has happened since you left." He gestured to the five other chiefs. "We are all that is left of the original council. Branth has fled, as you know. Lord Ferron killed himself shortly after the battle, and Lord Quamar of the Ferganan has already stepped down. Of the sorcerer's army, the exiles and the mercenaries are either dead or scattered. The Wylfling await the punishment of the council.

"As for the three clans that joined Medb, they did so at the instigation of their lords and they did not fight in the final battle. Only the werods came with the army, their families still wait at the Tir Samod for some word of their fate. If you agree, Athlone, we have decided to suspend their punishment. We believe it is the only way to begin reuniting the clans."

Athlone rose from his seat. "I agree with the council's decision. There has been enough hatred and bloodshed."

Koshyn nodded once, then he looked down at the young woman standing quietly beside her Hunnuli. He was dismayed by the closeness he had seen between Athlone and Gabria. He had no idea what this council would decide, but he did not want Athlone to be forced to kill someone he obviously loved.

"Now we have to face the most difficult decision of all. Gabria, you have saved our clans and our way of life from destruction. For that, we owe you endless gratitude. But in doing so, you used a heretical power that is forbidden on pain of death."

"You have thrown us into quite a quandary," Sha Umar spoke up. "If we follow our laws and put you to death, we bring dishonor on the clans for rejecting our debt of gratitude, but if we ignore our laws and allow you to live, we open the door for any magic-wielder who wants to practice sorcery."

"Perhaps it's time we did," a voice called from the palace. The crowd stirred and muttered among themselves, for everyone recognized the rich voice of Cantrell.

The blind bard walked out of the palace doors accompanied by Piers. Cantrell's step was firm and unhesitating as he came to stand beside Koshyn. "We have tried to ignore magic for two hundred years, and look where our fears took us. The clans were nearly destroyed by a man who abused the arts of sorcery. If our people had learned from their mistakes and regulated sorcery instead of turning their backs on it, this war with Medb would not have happened."

"But magic is a perversion!" a priest shouted from the crowd. He was supported by yells of agreement.

"That is what our ancestors wanted to believe, and they stuffed their lies down our throats in every tale, prayer, and law. But I tell you," Cantrell said as he rose to his full height and spread his hands out to include every person there, "magic is as natural as the air we breathe. It is only as dangerous as the person who wields it. If Medb had not had magic at his use, he would have simply used other weapons to conquer us." The bard pointed to Nara. "Look at the Hunnuli. We all believe in the inherent goodness of such horses. They were gifts to us from Valorian. A Hunnuli nearly killed Medb, yet another stands here beside Gabria. If magic were evil as we have been taught, would the Hunnuli stay with the girl?"

The large crowd began talking and arguing amongst themselves. They had never heard or seen anything like this.

Lord Jol stood up. The old chief was shaken by Cantrell's words, but he did not like change and stubbornly clung to the safety of the laws. "This girl broke clan law!" he shouted, "She impersonated a warrior, joined a werod, attended a council meeting, and claimed herself chieftain. For those crimes alone she should be put to death."

Athlone came to his feet, his face dark with anger. "Those crimes occurred while Gabria was with my clan. As her chieftain, it is *my* responsibility to deal with her punishment. This council need only concern itself with her use of sorcery."

Koshyn nodded in agreement and held up his hands to calm the two men. "Today we only need to decide what to do about Gabria's sorcery. We have to remember," he said with an ironic twist of his mouth, "if we have her put to death, we are killing the last of the Corin. Another great dishonor for our clans."

The lords were quiet for a time, some of them looking at Gabria, others looking anywhere else but at the girl. The onlookers continued debating loudly with each other. Gabria remained still, her stomach twisted in knots. She was terrified of this meeting, but she had known from the moment she broke the Woman of the Marsh's magic that she would have to face the council.

Cantrell took a deep breath and walked with Piers to the edge of the steps. "My lords," the bard said, his voice ringing through the courtyard, "if you kill the girl, Gabria, for using magic, then you shall have to put me to death, too, for I, also, have the talent to use magic."

The noise around the palace abruptly stopped as every person stared at the venerable bard in shock.

Cantrell cocked his head at the silence. "I try not to use my talent, but it inadvertently comes out in my riddles."

Piers looked at the stunned faces around him and said, "My lords, you will have to kill me as well. I, too, have used magic. I do not have the talent to wield it, but I have a stone of healing that works by a magic spell and has healed several people in my clan."

Athlone shook his head. He should have known Piers was mixed up somehow with Gabria and the sorcery. He glanced at the other lords. Lord Jol was slack-jawed and Malech of the Reidhar was looking distressed; Koshyn had a faint smile on his face. Sha Umar simply looked fascinated.

Slowly, Athlone stood up and his movement drew everyone's attention. He motioned toward Cantrell and Piers. "I seem to have a talent to wield magic, too. I have only known for a few days, but in that time I have learned a great deal." He went down a step and held out his hand to Gabria. Proudly she walked up to stand beside him.

"I believe it is time to change the laws," Athlone continued. "Not only to save Gabria, but to save ourselves. Even if we kill her and wash our hands of this incident, another person with the talent will come forward, perhaps to destroy us. For our own survival, we need to learn the ways of magic again and to regulate it. I beg you, lords, change the laws. I do not wish to die, but I will stand with Gabria."

The other six chieftains stared from Piers and Cantrell to Athlone and Gabria. Before they had time to really think, Koshyn drew the lords together and began talking heatedly to them. Lord Jol continually shook his head, and Lord Caurus looked doubtful, but at last they seemed to reach some sort of agreement.

Lord Koshyn stepped forward. He said to Gabria, "I suppose it is too much to demand that you never use your sorcery again."

Gabria held tightly to Athlone's arm, her heart pounding. "My lord, I cannot promise that," she replied, trying to keep her voice steady. "There may come a time when I will need my power. Lord Branth is still missing and the *Book of Matrah* with him. But I will promise this, I will never use magic in any way that will harm the clans. I swear on the honor of the Corin."

The Dangari chief glanced back at the other lords. They merely nodded.

"Then listen to our decision. The council frees you, Gabria, from the punishment of death in gratitude for your courageous rescue of our clans. But the law forbidding magic must stand until such time as the council can decide what to do about this issue. Lord Athlone, you are to be held personally responsible for your actions as well as those of Gabria, Piers, and Cantrell. If at any time they break the laws that are decided upon, they and you will be put to death. Is that acceptable?"

The watching crowd broke out in an uproar of mixed relief and anger. They had no choice but to accept the chieftains' decision, but many of the clanspeople, especially those who had not been involved in the battles with Medb, were not pleased.

But at that moment, Gabria did not care. Athlone swept her up in a joyous embrace and Tungoli ran to embrace them both.

Athlone went up the steps with Gabria and faced Koshyn. The younger chief grinned broadly at them both.

"We accept your decision," Athlone called to all the chiefs. To Koshyn, he said quietly, "Thank you, my friend."

Koshyn's blue eyes twinkled. "Just don't make me regret it." He turned to watch Gabria as she went to embrace Piers and Cantrell. "I can see now the laws must be changed, but it will take a great deal of time and persuasion."

"Thanks to you, we have the time."

"How will you handle Gabria's punishment with the Khulinin?" Koshyn asked curiously.

Athlone grinned. "I will make her marry me."

Koshyn burst out laughing. He clasped Athlone's arm, and the two men went to join the other lords.

The evening light lingered softly in the sky as Athlone and Gabria walked alone by the Isin River. They followed the grassy banks past the encampments to a place where a burial mound had been built on a small hill overlooking the fortress and the valley.

There had been many dead to mourn after the battle with Medb's army. The bodies of the exiles and mercenaries had been burned and buried without ceremony. Medb's body was burned and dumped in the river. The dead of the clans were buried in a large mound near the fortress. Savaric, though, had been sent to the Hall of the Dead with every honor. His body rested now in the large mound crowned with a ring of spears.

Athlone and Gabria stood by the mound as the quiet twilight dimmed. Overhead, a hawk soared in the cool evening breeze.

"Do you think he was terribly disappointed with me?" Gabria asked, looking up at the spears silhouetted against the sky.

"I doubt it. Surprised, maybe. But he would have been proud of your courage," Athlone replied.

She laid her head back on his shoulder. "Do you suppose he would have put me to death for joining his werod?"

Athlone chuckled. "Father would probably have considered marriage to me punishment enough."

"But what . . ."

He tilted her head up. "Enough questions." Then he gathered her close and kissed her.

High above them, the hawk cried once and swept away into the darkness.

Lightning's Daughter

To Jeannie,
one good dedication deserves another!

Prologue

Lord Branth slid into the shadowed entrance of a storage tent just as several enemy warriors dashed by. He drew a long, ragged breath and, for a moment, savored the warm darkness of his shelter.

Events were happening so fast. He could hardly believe he was hiding in the middle of this huge encampment —a camp that up until a little while ago had been the center of a victorious force of clan warriors and mercenaries under the ironfisted command of Lord Medb. Now, the camp was nothing more than a place of chaotic retreat.

Branth cocked his head to listen to the sounds outside the tent. He could still hear the clash and yells of battle from the broad valley beyond the camp. His fingers curled tighter around the dagger he held.

The fools! he thought to himself. The Wylfling clan was still fighting. Didn't they realize the day had been lost when the sorceress had destroyed Lord Medb? Had they missed that stunning duel of magic?

Even now the forces of Medb's enemies, led by the Khulinin chieftain, Savaric, were sweeping over the valley into the big camp to destroy the army.

Branth shrank back into the tent while more clan warriors ran by. Their gray cloaks identified them as Amnok. The Amnok had been Medb's allies until the fury of the Khulinin and their forces had fallen upon them. Branth curled his lip. Cowards, all of them! His own clan, too, had betrayed him, laying down their weapons and leaving him alone to face his doom.

He had not stood idly by while that doom strove to catch him, however. Branth was Medb's second-in-command and would be executed without question if he were captured by Savaric's men. He was also practical and self-serving, a man who did not believe in wasting energy and blood on a lost cause.

No sooner had his clan abandoned him in the valley, than Branth had decided it was time to grab what he could and leave. He had already packed a saddlebag with his own gear and two bags of gold taken from another chieftain's tent.

There was just one more thing Branth wanted before he left, a thing that would ensure the prosperity of his future. He wanted Lord Medb's *Book of Matrah*. The book was an ancient compilation of two hundred years of arcane study. The knowledge contained on its pages was priceless. Lord Medb had kept the book under close guard, but Branth knew where it was and he wanted to get his hands on it before it was discovered by anyone else.

Branth had a strong feeling that he had the inborn talent to wield magic, and, with the tome, he could learn the forbidden arts of sorcery. He would then exact his own revenge on the clans and the sorceress, Gabria, for the defeat and dishonor he had suffered this day. All he had to do was get the book and escape before anyone found him.

Escaping was not going to be easy. He shifted an eye cautiously around the edge of the tent flap. The way was clear for the moment, so he ran, zigzagging between the black felt tents toward the biggest dwelling in the encampment.

More enemy warriors raced by, and several groups of Medb's mercenaries ran past, heading for the horses picketed at the east end of the camp. Branth avoided them all and kept moving until he reached the circle of tents around Lord Medb's big shelter.

He stopped abruptly and swerved behind an open tent flap. Five warriors were standing by Medb's tent, watching another man take down the chieftain's brown banner. Branth swore furiously in a barely controlled whisper. The warriors wore the gold cloaks of the Khulinin.

One of the men turned sideways, and Branth recognized the handsome, hawk-nosed profile of Lord Savaric, the man who had stood up to Medb's unlawful bid for rule of the Ramtharin Plains.

Branth's curses died on his lips as he studied the chieftain and the tent where the book lay hidden. Savaric obviously felt the victory was his, for his sword was sheathed and only five of his hearthguard, his personal bodyguard, were with him. Branth could not see anyone else close by. He pressed back into the shadows and wondered what to do. There was very little time left.

Suddenly a great roar of victory resounded through the valley. Branth glanced out toward the mountains where the ruins of the ancient fortress of Ab-Chakan sat on its hill, overlooking the valley of the Isin River and the encampment of Medb's army. He could not see the valley floor, where the battle was being fought, but he could make out the remnants of the four clans, who had taken refuge in the ruins, standing by the walls and cheering. He glanced back at the six Khulinin and saw that they, too, were watching the spectacle. One man, a respected warrior named Bregan, was standing close to Lord Savaric.

At that moment, a commotion snared the warriors' attention. Several mercenaries were riding furiously through the tents toward Lord Savaric. It was unclear if they meant to attack or surrender, for their swords were drawn, but the blades were behind their backs. The hearthguard took no chances with the riders' intentions. They drew their own weapons and ran out to head off the mercenaries, leaving Savaric temporarily alone.

Branth did not waste a second. As soft-footed as a stalking cat he ran across the space between the tents and slipped up behind Savaric.

The Khulinin chieftain sensed his enemy's presence too late. As Savaric started to turn, Branth rammed his dagger into the man's back and up into his heart.

The chieftain grunted, a hard, surprised sound, and sagged to the ground. Branth jumped over the body, ran into the tent, and snatched the book from its hiding place. He was out and running before the other warriors realized what had happened.

His pleasure in the murder was confirmed when he heard Bregan's agonized cry, "Lord Savaric!" In a matter of moments, Branth found a saddled horse and was galloping out of the valley toward the east. A vague idea formed in his mind as he rode. He would leave the plains for a while, until the clans' emotions cooled and the events of this battle were mere memories. Maybe he would go to the city of Pra Desh in the kingdom of Calah. There he could study his book and perhaps sell his services to wealthy Pra Deshians willing to overlook the laws forbidding sorcery.

In time he would return to the Ramtharin Plains and remind the clans that their troubles had not ended with the death of Lord Medb.

1

Gabria stood motionless on the hard-packed floor and watched the faces of the clanspeople crowded in front of her in the chieftain's hall at Khulinin Treld. Many she knew had come to the trial, and some of those she loved. Piers Arganosta, the healer of the Khulinin; Cantrell, the great bard; and Lady Tungoli, widow of Lord Savaric and mother of the new chieftain, were seated in the front rows, their faces creased in worry. Sadly, too many other faces in the crowd did not show worry. They wore looks of confusion, hostility, and unhappiness.

To her left, Gabria could see eight men and women seated on benches against the whitewashed walls of the hall. Their expressions were deliberately blank as they attempted to watch the proceedings with open minds. Thalar, priest of the god Surgart, stood before the Khulinin and exhorted the chieftain and the people to reject the foul heresies of magic and to cast the evil sorceress out.

"Sorcery is an abomination!" he shouted. The priest was a short, squat man who made up for the inadequacies of his height with the volume of his voice.

Thalar had been shouting for some time now, and Gabria could sense Lord Athlone's mounting rage and frustration. Unfortunately the chief was behind her on his dais, and she was forbidden by the laws of the *getyne* to look at him. She must face her accusers and leave the chieftain free to act as an impartial judge.

Gabria sighed and shifted her weight a little to ease her stiff back. The doors of the huge earthen hall were closed, and the heat from the crowd and the fire in the central hearth was growing uncomfortable. The smell of resin from the numerous torches overwhelmed the smells of leather, wood smoke, and sweat that usually permeated the meeting hall. Gabria badly wanted a drink of water, but she was not permitted to speak during the *getyne*, so she tried to ignore her thirst and concentrate on the faces before her.

This ordeal is all too familiar, she thought. Half a year ago, at the start of spring, her clan had been massacred by followers of Lord Medb. Without family or friends, she had come to Khulinin Treld and stood before the chieftain to ask for acceptance into the clan. Instead of revealing her identity as a woman and risking rejection, she had disguised herself as a boy and brought with her a legendary and rare Hunnuli horse she had rescued from wolves. The Khulinin had reluctantly chosen to take her in on Lord Savaric's recommendation.

Now, months later, the Khulinin had to choose again, but this time they knew the full truth of Gabria's identity and her powers as a sorceress. Under normal circumstances, clan law prescribed death for a woman found guilty of hiding her sex in order to join a werod, the tribes' fighting units. The penalty for practicing the heretical arts of sorcery was also death. Yet in Gabria's case, the circumstances were far from normal. She had been the only person in the eleven clans able to face Lord Medb's sorcery and she had saved them all from annihilation or slavery. In thanks, the council of chieftains had released her from the punishment due a sorceress, but only under the condition that she not use magic again until the laws were revised. However, they did not release her from punishment within her new clan for her other crimes.

The new chieftain of the Khulinin, Lord Athlone, had made his feelings for Gabria known to his clan and had already paid the bride price to the priestess of the goddess, Amara. The Khulinin knew they could not anger their chieftain or ruin the honor of the clan by putting Gabria to death. Nevertheless; the ancient laws could not be maintained if Gabria was allowed to go unpunished. Some penalty had to be meted out to calm the anger and resentment of the clanspeople. Many of them, incited by Thalar, wanted Gabria exiled. Others wanted her tongue cut out so she could not speak the words needed to cast spells. Still others, though only a minority, felt she deserved a mild sentence. The controversy raged through the Khulinin during their trek home and continued even as they prepared the treld for the coming winter.

The emotions grew so high, Lord Athlone had finally stepped in to put an end to the furor. As chieftain, his powers were bound by the limits of clan law. He could have simply released Gabria from any judgment, but he was the son of a chief and had been wer-tain, commander of warriors, for several years. He knew when it was time to acquiesce to the demands of his people. Reluctantly, he had agreed several days past to hold a *getyne*, a form of clan trial in which a *tyne*, or jury, of eight decided the accused's guilt and punishment.

To Priest Thalar's fury, Lady Tungoli had insisted that the *tyne* be composed of four men and four women. Women did not usually serve on a *tyne*, but the lady reasoned that, since Gabria's crimes encompassed so many issues, it was only fair that clanswomen should help judge her. Lord Athlone had agreed. And so four men—two elders, a warrior, and a weaver—and four women—the priestess of Amara, two wives, and a grandmother—gathered on a chilly autumn afternoon to decide Gabria's fate.

The sorceress shifted her weight again and pushed a strand of flaxen hair out of her eyes. The heat was growing worse. Beads of perspiration gathered on her forehead, and her long skirts hung on her like a heavy blanket. She wished the people would hurry and get this over.

Particularly Thalar. The priest's voice was still ringing loudly through the hall. With a small frown, Gabria tried to concentrate on what he was saying.

"I do not condemn the council of chieftains for releasing this woman from her justifiable execution," he cried, his voice thick with righteousness. "The chiefs were overcome with joy and relief at their release from the evil ambitions of Lord Medb. But they did not see then that they had only traded one evil for another. *This* magic-wielder—" he pointed a finger at Gabria "—still lives! The responsibility of wiping out this heretic has now fallen into our hands. We have a gods-given opportunity to show the clans of the Ramtharin Plains how we deal with magic-wielders. We do not tolerate them!" Thalar's voice rose to a thundering shout. "Khulinin, we must blot out this stain of sorcery before it spreads. Fulfill the penalty of death. Kill the sorceress!"

The words were barely out of the priest's mouth when the healer, Piers, leaped to his feet and demanded the right to speak.

"No! I am not finished," Thalar shouted. He had the crowd's attention and wanted to press home his point.

Lord Athlone, however, had had enough of Thalar's rantings. "We have heard you for some time, Priest. Give the right to someone else. Piers, you may speak."

The healer, ignoring Thalar's infuriated glare, turned to face the *tyne*. His pale skin and light, graying hair looked almost colorless in the dim light of the hall, but there was nothing lackluster about his speech. The old healer loved Gabria like a daughter and would have done anything to save her. "Khulinin, I realize that I am not a blood member of this or any other clan. I am a foreigner to your ways and laws. Yet in the eleven years that I have been with you, I have never seen you act with anything but honor, courage, and loyalty. This young woman who stands before you has those same qualities in full measure.

"When Medb's men massacred her clan, Gabria did not crawl away in fear to die. She took the only way open to her to seek justice for the murder of her people. When she learned she had the talent to wield magic, she did not hide her power, she used it to save all of us. Gabria's methods were wrong by the strictures of your law, but they were the only methods available to her and she acted on them with courage and honor. The council of chiefs has released her from death for her use of sorcery. Can we now turn our backs on their wisdom and justice and kill her for striking back against an enemy stronger than even the warriors of this clan? She does not deserve death for that, she deserves our respect."

For a moment the healer looked at each member of the *tyne* as if to seal his words in their thoughts, then he smiled at Gabria and sat down.

The watching clanspeople shifted and murmured among themselves.

Lady Tungoli rose next and claimed the right to speak. As widow of Lord Savaric and the mother of Athlone, Tungoli held one of the highest positions of status and respect among the Khulinin women. Everyone listened quietly as she nodded to the *tyne* and began to talk. "I would like to speak for myself and for several witnesses who are not in this hall today," she said. She did not raise her voice, yet her firm words were heard clearly throughout the hall. "For myself, I will only note that I agree wholeheartedly with the beliefs of those I am here to represent.

"The first is Lord Savaric. I knew my husband well enough to say with complete confidence that he would never have ordered Gabria's death under these circumstances. He respected her for her courage, her intelligence, and her determination. If he were here today, he would examine her deeds, her motives, and her strength of character, as well. He would want you to do likewise.

"The other witnesses I wish to include are the Corins. Gabria's clan did nothing to earn their fate. They were pieces in Lord Medb's game, pieces he discarded when they would not turn against their fellows. Gabria did not accept that fate. She fought back to redeem her clan's memory and to win justice for the murder of her family. The Corins would not have expected anything less, and neither should we."

"Perhaps there is another witness we should take into account," added a man from the crowd, the Khulinin herd-master. He looked toward lady Tungoli, who nodded and relinquished the right to speak. "I mean the Hunnuli mare, Nara. Clanspeople have always loved and revered the ancient Hunnuli breed. We believe that Hunnuli cannot tolerate evil in any form. And yet, if that is true, why does Nara love Gabria and stay with this admitted sorceress? Does the horse know something we do not about the quality of magic? I think the mere fact that a Hunnuli horse trusts and obeys Gabria says more for her heart than any of the guesses we can make." The herd-master quickly sat down.

Finally the bard, Cantrell, stood and turned his sightless eyes toward Gabria. His rich bass voice rang through the hall, capturing everyone's attention. "The herd-master has brought up an interesting incongruity. For years we have been told in song, story, and decree that magic is heretical. We have believed in its ultimate evil and in the despair and grief sorcery can cause. In that we were right: Sorcery is evil." Many of the onlookers gasped and stared at the bard in shock. He smiled, and his fingers lightly touched the strings of the harp at his side. A soft melody lifted on the air and enticed the peoples' imaginations.

"But what we forgot was that magic could also be as beautiful as a Hunnuli horse, as good as a healing stone, as intricate as an ancient riddle, and as strong as true love. Magic is only what people make of it. It has been a part of the plains since the birth of the world, and it was said, before the Destruction of the Sorcerers, that the ability to wield magic was a gift of the gods. It is time we accept our heritage once again. I ask you to accept Gabria. She has a great gift that should be protected, not destroyed." He turned toward the *tyne* and lifted his harp toward them. "Be fair in your decision, Khulinin. We may need Gabria again some day."

The clanspeople stared at the old bard as he sat down, and his words hung in their thoughts. When no one else moved to speak the members of the *tyne* huddled together and discussed their problem. Gabria stood alone in the space before the chief's dais and waited. A heavy silence fell on the watching people.

Sweat dripped in beads down Gabria's forehead as she remained still, her head up and her face calm. How would they decide? she wondered. All she really wanted was peace, rest, and time to build a normal life again. This past year she had suffered more than most people would in a lifetime. Gabria wanted fervently to get through this trial so she could put the memories behind her.

She glanced down at the splinter of the Fallen Star gleaming under the skin of her wrist. It was too bad she could not put away her sorcery as easily as her memories. The talent to wield magic was an integral part of her, as natural as breathing. It was not a power she had wanted, but she had learned to use her talent to survive. She knew now she would never be able to ignore or forget the magic. Neither would anyone else in the clans.

At last Gabria heard Athlone stand. The edge of his sword clanged against his stone seat, and the sound rang through the quiet hall. The members of the *tyne* left their benches and stood.

Athlone, his feet planted on the stone dais and his arms crossed, searched the faces of his people. A golden torque of rank glittered on the chest of his leather shirt, and gold bands encircled both of his arms. He had recently cut his hair, and Gabria thought the shorter, dark brown locks and thick mustache enhanced the clean lines of his features. "What is your decision?" the chief asked without preamble.

The elder, a gaunt, silver-haired man, spoke. "We have heard the accusations against Gabria. We all know the truth of her deeds and her courage. Because she has given us our lives and our freedom to be Khulinin instead of Medb's slaves, it is our decision that she be freed from the penalty of death and exile. She has earned a place among the Khulinin."

Thalar sprang to his feet, his face dark with anger. "Never!" he shouted.

Athlone raised his hand to still the priest's outraged interruption. "Continue."

"However," the man went on. "We feel the laws of the clans cannot be put aside even for this. Therefore, we order that Gabria be pronounced dead for a period of days equaling the time she spent in her disguise—a passage of six months, by our reckoning. During banishment, no person may speak to her or acknowledge her in any way, and Gabria must retire to the temple of Amara beyond the treld. There she will serve the goddess in penance. At the end of six months, Gabria may return to the clan and be accepted as a permanent member."

Surprised, Gabria gripped her hands together to still their trembling. The sentence was harsh, for she would be alone and unaided through the winter. Most women would die under such difficult straits. On the other hand, Gabria knew—as Athlone must—that she stood a good chance of surviving the ordeal. Unlike other clan women, she could handle a bow and a sword. She might go hungry now and then, but she would not starve.

Thalar stepped forward, his expression wild, his eyes burning into Gabria with all the hatred of a priest for a heretic. "This is outrageous! That woman is profane! A creature of evil. If she is allowed to enter the holy temple of the Mother Goddess, our whole clan will be cursed!"

At that Piers jumped up to protest. The healer, the herd-master, and several others crowded around Thalar and began to argue. Others joined in until the entire hall was filled with shouting voices. The noise crashed around Gabria like an avalanche. She gritted her teeth and silently watched the uproar.

"Silence!" Athlone bellowed. "Enough!" He crossed his arms as the shouting ceased, and every face turned toward him. "Priest Thalar has a valid argument. Perhaps the members of the *tyne* could explain their decision and put the clan's mind at rest."

This time the priestess of Amara stepped out of the group. Her long green robes were a bright contrast to the more somber colors of the men. She was an older woman, past forty-five summers, and equal to Lady Tungoli in the honor and respect of her clan. Her gray hair was swept back in a long braid, and her startling green eyes seemed to pierce through Thalar. "It was I who made the suggestion to the *tyne* to send the sorceress to Amara's temple."

"You!" Thalar exclaimed in surprise.

Gabria, too, was startled and watched the woman as she paced forward in the light of the lamps and torches to face the priest.

"I believe I know more of the goddess's ways than you do, Thalar. A man who follows the god of battle and death cannot begin to comprehend the power of life and birth. It is my belief that Gabria has the favor of Amara. Her survival and her success against overwhelming odds are indications to me that the goddess is watching over her daughter. If this is the case, then Cantrell's arguments for magic are more than the artful words of a skilled bard." She paused as Cantrell chuckled.

"I suggested sending Gabria to the temple," she continued, "to learn the truth of the goddess's will. If the sorceress is blessed with

Amara's grace, then she will live and thrive to return to us. If she is not, the mother goddess will punish her as no mortal can imagine."

For a long moment the Khulinin stared at Gabria. No one moved or said a word. At last, Lord Athlone raised his hand. "So be it. Lady Gabria's sentence begins at moonrise tonight. She may return to the clan in six months, marked by the rise of the full moon." He turned on his heel and strode to the chieftain's quarters in the back of the hall. The tapestry fell closed behind him, signaling the end of the *getyne*.

Thalar snorted in disgust and stamped to the entrance. As the guards pulled the doors open for him a cold gust of wind swirled into the hall. The chilly air seemed to rouse the crowd from their astonishment. In ones and twos they averted their eyes from Gabria and left the hall until only the sorceress and Cantrell remained.

The young woman took a deep breath and stepped away from the fire. She sank down on the dais steps. "We have been back in the treld but ten days and already they are getting rid of me," she said with bitter sadness.

The old bard did not answer her immediately. Instead he gently strummed the strings of his harp. Cantrell had lost his sight the previous summer, when Lord Medb had slashed his face in a fit of rage during an ill-fated clan gathering. The bard had fled the sorcerer's camp and found sanctuary with the Khulinin. Since then, Cantrell's ancient harp had rarely left his hands. His eyes were gone, but the music of his harp and his songs had kept his life full.

He played his instrument now, letting the notes flow into the new ballad he was creating about Gabria. The clans loved heroic tales, and it would not hurt to remind them of the courage in Gabria's deeds. For a while he simply played to her, knowing the music would say more than his voice. He brought the tune to an end with a strong flourish and listened as the notes passed into silence.

Cantrell stood and laid his harp carefully by his stool. "I am pleased you will not be far away. We will be waiting for you to come home."

"Home," Gabria repeated sadly. "I am a sorceress. The only home I had is now a ruin. I doubt I'll ever be allowed to find another." She climbed to her feet and looked miserably at the door through which Athlone had disappeared. She hadn't even been given a chance to say good-bye to him.

Cantrell felt for her arm. He pulled her close and held her tight. "You will survive this, child. And more to come. Be ready."

Gabria smiled into his blind face. "Is this one of your prophecies, Bard?"

"No. It is something I feel—like the coming of night. It will be moonrise soon. You had better go."

Gabria picked up her golden clan cloak from the steps, threw it around her shoulders, and walked toward the big double doors. Behind her, the bard resumed his seat and ran his fingers along his harp. The soft music followed her toward the doors. Just as she was about to leave, a familiar voice called to her. Gabria turned and saw Athlone hurrying to her with a bundle in his hands. The emotions of the past few hours swelled within her, and she ran to meet him before the fears and angers could tear apart her flimsy control. She wrapped her arms around him and buried her face in his neck.

The chieftain hugged her fiercely. "I could not let you go without a word."

As he held her is his arms, she looked up and said forlornly, "Six months is a long time to be away." She dropped her eyes again. "I have never been alone for so long."

"I don't like it either," Athlone replied, "but the law must be upheld or we will never have peace." He looked down into her deep green eyes. "Besides, you will not be totally alone. Nara will be with you, and while I cannot visit, I'll watch and guard you as much as I can."

His face suddenly lit with laughter and he added, "The goddess must look after you, too. I have already paid the bride price. Will you marry me when you come back?"

She looked away. "You may change your mind in six months."

Athlone cupped her chin in his hand and gently turned her head to look at him. "I'd sooner change my clan. I will be waiting for you. In the meantime, take this." He thrust a bundle in her hands, then kissed her deeply. "And take my love." A final hug and he was gone, striding back to his quarters.

The sorceress watched him go, her heart heavy. Finally she stepped past the entrance and looked down through the deepening twilight at the wintering camp of the Khulinin. The chieftain's hall was built into the side of a large, treeless hill overlooking a broad valley in the foothills of the Darkhorn Mountains. To the north, the Goldrine River tumbled out of a deep canyon and spread out to water the fertile valley. Here, in this natural shelter, the Khulinin spent every winter, caring for their herds and gradually losing their nomadic habits.

From the promontory where she stood, Gabria could see the entire encampment of black felt tents, corrals, and scattered permanent buildings that dotted the banks of the river. Beyond the Goldrine, large herds of horses and livestock grazed on the lush grass of the foothills. The Khulinin were a large, wealthy clan, and Gabria had hoped to make a home with them. Now she was not so sure. Two hundred years of hatred and suspicion of sorcery ran too deep in the beliefs of the people to be put aside in a few months. Gabria doubted the clans would ever completely accept magic—at least in her lifetime.

Even Lord Athlone could not help her cause. He had admitted at Gabria's trial before the gathered chieftains that he, too, possessed the talent to wield magic—but only because that admission would help sway the council in its deliberation of her crimes. Yet he had never used sorcery before his people, and they seemed content to ignore his talent so long as he never utilized it. Gabria, on the other hand, was not only the sole survivor of a massacred clan, she had the audacity to train as a warrior and the temerity to openly display the forbidden powers of magic. She was too different to be acceptable.

There was but one creature who totally accepted Gabria for everything she was: Nara.

The woman raised her fingers to her lips and blew a piercing whistle. The guards on either side of the doors ignored her, but they could not ignore the magnificent mare that neighed in response to the whistle and came galloping up the main road through the treld.

The mare was a Hunnuli, a rare, wild breed of horse that had once been the steeds of the ancient sorcerers. Like all Hunnuli, Nara was larger and more intelligent than other horses and impervious to magic.

Gabria's sad face slowly broke into a smile as the huge black horse galloped to the hall and slid to a stop. The young woman knew every clansperson nearby was watching the beautiful mare, and her heart warmed with gratitude and joy as the Hunnuli reared before her rider in the timeless obeisance of respect and honor.

Gabria pulled herself onto Nara's broad back.

Are we leaving? Nara asked in Gabria's mind. The Hunnuli's telepathic thoughts were gentle, and full of love.

"I am to go to the temple of Amara. The Khulinin want me out of sight for a few months," Gabria replied irritably.

The mare dipped her head. *It is better than death.*

Gabria's lips twisted in an ironic smile. "Yes, I guess you're right." She paused to secure Athlone's bundle to her belt, then said, "I must

leave by moonrise, but I would like to stop at Piers's tent first. They
did not say I had to go empty-handed."

*We'd best hurry, then. The moon has already reached the mountain-
tops.*

Nara trotted down the path to the edge of the treld and the spot
where Piers kept his shelter. The healer's tent had been home to
Gabria for the past six months. Piers had discovered her hidden identity shortly after she had joined the Khulinin, but he had kept her
secret despite the danger to himself. He had offered her sanctuary,
security, and friendship when she needed them most.

Gabria slid off the mare and walked into Piers's tent. The large,
dark shelter was quiet and empty; only a small lamp burned on the
table. The girl looked around in relief. Piers was not there. By law, the
healer would have to shun her if she came near him, and she knew
neither one of them could bear that.

She found her old pack, the one she had salvaged from the ruins
of her home at Corin Treld, and began to gather her belongings.
There was not very much: a few tunics, a leather jerkin, boots, a
blanket, a small wooden box with her precious flint and steel, and a
sheath for her father's dagger, though she had lost the weapon itself.
She borrowed a cup, a pot, and a few cooking utensils from Piers's
hearth. Last of all she collected her bow and sword.

When Lord Medb had fallen at Ab-Chakan, Gabria thought she
was through with the pants, the sword, and the skills of a warrior. Now
she realized she would need them again to survive her banishment.
She took off her full skirts and put on a pair of heavy winter pants,
which would be warmer and more practical than a skirt. Then, reluctantly, she belted on her short sword. She would be alone through a
long, cold winter, and even though she would be near a treld, wolves,
bears, cave lions, and other creatures were known to prowl the valley
and the hills. She would feel safer with a weapon at hand.

Gabria was about to leave when she noticed a full leather sack
lying near the coals of the hearth fire. A red cloth was fastened to the
sack—red for Clan Corin. She peered into the bag and smiled. Piers
had found a way to say good-bye. The bag was packed with food: dried
meat, beans, horsebread, dried fruit, and a flask of Piers's own favorite
wine. There was enough food to satisfy her for many days. Gratefully
she took the bag and gathered her loose belongings into two bundles.

Outside the tent Nara waited patiently. When Gabria appeared
and began arranging the bundles over the mare's withers, Nara nickered softly. *The priest watches.*

Gabria surreptitiously glanced around Nara's chest and saw Thalar standing in the shadows of a nearby tent. He was watching them with obvious anger and disgust.

"He does not obey Lord Athlone's command," she replied, annoyed.

He is not the only one who watches.

The sorceress sprang onto the horse's back and tightened the golden cloak around her neck. "Then let's show the Khulinin how a Hunnuli and her rider leave camp."

Nara trotted back to the main path. She paused for a moment to sniff the chill evening breeze, then lifted her head and neighed a challenge that rang throughout the camp. The unexpected noise brought people running out to look. The stallions in the far pastures answered with their own clarion cries, and the dogs in the treld barked furiously.

Nara proudly neighed again and reared, her powerful front legs pawing at the pale stars. Gabria felt her own joy soar to meet the Hunnuli's. She drew her sword and answered Nara's call with the Corin's war cry.

The mare leaped forward. Her eyes ignited with a golden-green light as she galloped down the road through the treld. Her hooves pounded the hard ground.

Gabria clung to the mare and raised her sword above her head. "Farewell, Khulinin!" she shouted to the dark tents and the people who stared after her.

From the hall's entrance high on the side of the hill, Lord Athlone smiled as he watched them go. He should have known Gabria would not slink out of the treld. He raised his fist in a silent salute, which he held until the horse disappeared into the deepening night.

It was fully dark by the time Gabria and Nara passed the Khulinin burial mounds and found the tiny stone temple of Amara nestled in a copse of trees atop a hill. Because the temple was used only a few times during the year, it was small and very plain. A rectangular stone altar sat across from the only door, and above the altar a large circular window faced the east and the rising moon.

Gabria left Nara outside to graze, carried her bundles into the temple, and built a small fire in one corner away from the window. Chewing on a piece of dried meat, she curled up in her blanket and cloak. For a long while she stared at the fire and tried not to shiver. A cold draft blew through the window and made the fire dance.

Though Gabria was apprehensive, she was not frightened or worried about Amara's reaction to her presence in the temple. Despite Thalar's warnings, she had always felt secure and accepted by the Mother Goddess. Nothing had changed that, but this temple was so quiet and strange! She could hear Nara grazing among the trees, and she thanked Amara with all her heart for the black mare. Gabria was used to noisy, bustling camps and the constant company of people. This silent solitude was frightening. She could not imagine being alone for a long period of time, and without the Hunnuli for company, Gabria doubted she would be able to bear this banishment for six months.

It would be six very long months without Athlone, too. Gabria cuddled deeper into her blanket and let her thoughts wander to the Khulinin lord. When they'd first met, Gabria had hated Athlone. He was a wer-tain then, commander of the Khulinin warriors, and his father's most trusted adjutant. He, too, had befriended a Hunnuli, a stallion named Boreas who later died at Lord Medb's hand. Gabria quickly learned that Athlone was a forceful, commanding, sometimes impetuous man whose sole loyalty lay with his clan. He had been immediately suspicious of Gabria's disguise, and when he discovered the truth of her identity, he nearly killed her. It was only through the unexpected help of magic and the support of Nara and Boreas that Gabria was able to fight him off and eventually convince him to help her. What had begun as mutual animosity and distrust, grew to respect and love.

Unfortunately, their love was not being given much of a chance to blossom. The deep feelings they shared were very new to both of them and had not been fully explored. Gabria worried that a six-month separation might prove too rocky for the tenuous roots of their new love.

Thinking of Athlone reminded Gabria of the bundle he had given her. She had not yet opened it. Quickly she pulled the wrapped parcel out of her pile and untied the leather thongs that held it together. Several small items tumbled onto her lap, each one hastily wrapped in large pieces of woolen fabric.

The young woman was pleased to see that each scrap of fabric was large enough to cut for mittens or to piece together for a small blanket. Best of all, a packet of bone needles was tucked into one of the parcels. Gabria began to unwrap the packages and found a little stone oil lamp, its wick hole plugged with wax to hold the oil, a pair of mittens lined with rabbit fur, a hatchet, and a warm cap.

Last of all, she found a long, narrow package bound with a golden armband. The band was small and solid, traced with an interwoven design of fanciful horses. It slipped over her hand and settled comfortably on her wrist. Armbands were a favorite gift among betrothed couples, and Gabria sensed the band was Athlone's way of reassuring her of his love. The thought pleased her.

Finally she uncovered the narrow package. The gold wool fell away, and a dagger slid into her hand. Gabria gasped. The dagger blade was forged from steel, a rare, valuable metal crafted only in the city of Rivenforge in the kingdom of Portane. The handle was braided silver, formed to fit the hand and inset with small rubies and topaz. Red for the color of the cloaks of the Corin clan, gold for the Khulinin.

Tears formed in Gabria's eyes as she turned the dagger over in her hands. The weapon was a priceless gift given from the heart. Women did not usually carry such weapons, but she had owned another dagger once. It had been a gift to her father from Lord Savaric, and she had found it in the smoking ruins of her home. It had been her only physical rememberance of her dead father. Unfortunately, on that afternoon when she faced Lord Medb in the duel of sorcery, she had transformed her father's dagger into a sword to slay her clan's murderer. The weapon had been destroyed with Medb's body.

She realized then that Athlone understood how much the old dagger had meant to her. The armband was his gift of love, but the jeweled weapon was his gift of hope that she could build a new life.

Gabria wiped the tears from her eyes with a scrap of wool and carefully laid the gifts aside. She found her empty sheath, slid the dagger in, and fastened it to her belt. The weight of the weapon felt good on her side. She curled up in her blanket once more and watched the fire die to embers.

As the coals' glow dimmed, Gabria promised herself that she would endure this exile. She would go back to Khulinin Treld in the spring and do everything in her power to build a good relationship with the clan *and* with its chieftain. She owed herself nothing less.

2

Gabria did not realize how much the events of the previous summer had drained her emotionally and physically until she had time to relax. After only a few days at the temple, she caught a cold and came down with a fever and racking cough. For days she stayed in the small temple, curled up on her crude bed, lost on the paths of her thoughts. She had barely enough strength to eat or fetch water and firewood. Nara kept watch over her and waited worriedly for the illness to pass.

One cold night as Gabria tossed in a feverish, restless doze, she thought she heard the sound of Nara's hooves galloping up to the temple. There was the soft thud of footfalls, then she sensed another person close by. She struggled to wake until a cool hand soothed her forehead and a familiar voice spoke softly to her. A cup filled with a warm herbal drink was brought to her lips. She drank without opening her eyes and settled down into a peaceful sleep.

Piers stayed with her through the night and slipped away at dawn, leaving behind a stack of wood, a filled water jug, and a simmering kettle of soup. He did not come back after that night—he did not need to. His herbal drink eased Gabria's symptoms and his brief, comforting presence revived her interest in survival. Gabria was not sure how he'd known of her illness. She could only thank her goddess that the healer cared enough to risk the visit.

The food Piers had given Gabria sustained her through the days of her malaise. However, as her illness eased and she regained her strength, she realized the supply of food was dwindling rapidly. She would need more than a few beans to keep herself alive. One cold, cloudy afternoon she forced herself to take her bow, mount Nara, and hunt in the hills for meat. To her pleasure, her skill with the bow had not diminished. She brought down a small deer, and that night she feasted on venison.

The exercise and the meat were just what she needed, and Gabria felt stronger than she had in days. After that she went out every afternoon to ride Nara, or to hunt, fish, or gather food in the hills. Her health and her good spirits returned in full measure. She was pleased to notice that, as she grew stronger, her intense grief for her family began to ease, taking with it the bitterness and anger that had burned within her during her struggle for revenge. She was left with a growing sense of contentment and release.

As the last days of autumn passed, Gabria began to enjoy the solitude of the little temple, the peace of her thoughts, and the quiet companionship of the mare. She felt closer to Amara in this place, and each day she knelt by the altar in the light of the rising sun to give thanks to the Mother Goddess for sustaining her.

Nara, too, seemed to thrive in the peace of the temple. The foal within her, sired by Athlone's Hunnuli stallion, Boreas, grew steadily and filled out Nara's sides as she grazed contentedly on the dried winter grass of the hills.

Although no one came to visit them, Gabria often saw Athlone at a distance, keeping a watch on her. His vigilance meant a great deal to Gabria, and she always acknowledged him with a wave.

The only thing that began to bother Gabria as the time passed was boredom. She spent many hours every day gathering food and turning the stone temple into a more comfortable dwelling. But there were times when she had nothing to do. Then loneliness would creep in, and she would long for the distractions of a busy treld. She wanted to find something that would keep her busy during those lonely, dull times.

Then one rainy, cold night she found the answer. An autumn storm had blown in suddenly as Gabria was collecting firewood. By the time she'd made it back to the temple, she was soaking wet and chilled to the bone. She dumped the wet wood in a corner to dry and quickly laid some kindling in the small hearth she had built. To her annoyance she realized she had not banked the morning coals, and the fire was dead. Gabria tried to light the kindling with her flint and steel, but her hands were trembling with cold and she could not draw a spark. Her frustration grew with every failed attempt.

All at once, an idea flashed in her head: she was a magic-wielder. She could use a spell to start a fire. All it would take was a single word.

Gabria hesitated for just a moment. She had promised the council of chiefs that she would not practice sorcery, and under normal circumstances she would have kept her vow. Now, however, she was banished from the clans and dead in the eyes of her people. What she did during the time of exile was her own concern.

She spoke the word of her spell, and a warm, cheerful flame leaped out of the pile of kindling. Gabria grinned like a mischievous child. At that moment, she decided to use her time to practice her sorcery. She had only learned the basic skills and rules of wielding magic from her teacher, the Woman of the Marsh, and had found little opportunity to use her powers since then.

Gabria decided to begin her practice by perfecting one spell. After some thought, she chose a spell of transformation. Magic could not be used to create something out of nothing, though it could alter forms or change appearances. Gabria had used a wild version of a transformation spell to transform her father's dagger into a sword during her fight with Medb. That experience had taught her how powerful that enchantment could be.

When her evening meal was over, Gabria found a pinecone and began to practice changing its shape. Her teacher had stressed that a spell had to be perfectly clear in the magic-wielder's mind or disaster could result. Gabria was a little clumsy at first. Her concentration would waver, the image of the spell would not focus in her mind, or she simply did not try hard enough. At those times, the pinecone would warp and twist from the image she had chosen for it. Sometimes she could not make it change at all.

That night and for many days after, she practiced her spell until she was able to change the pinecone into any shape, size, or color she desired. In the process of her learning, a deep respect and curiosity for the endless powers of magic were awakened in her soul. Delightedly she took the next step in the progression: to transform the essence of an object, not just its appearance, into something different. Once again she chose a pinecone and began to try transforming it into her favorite fruit, a sweetplum.

It was a few days before the end of the year when Gabria began to notice the gifts.

The year, and three months of Gabria's banishment, would end on the night of the winter solstice. By clan reckoning the new year always began on the day when the sun resumed its journey back to the north. During the last days of the year, it was customary to present gifts to the clan priests and priestesses as thanks for special blessings that had been received during the year. Women usually gave gifts to the priestess of Amara in gratitude for a healthy child, a pregnancy, a loving husband, or a fruitful herd. The gifts were small—food or hand-made items that were given from the heart. The priestess used these gifts as part of her livelihood.

One evening Gabria came back from checking her snares and found a bowl of eggs and a beautifully wrought leather belt lying on the threshold of the temple. Curious, she picked them up and looked around. The clearing and the temple were empty. She carried the things into the stone room and laid them on the altar. She could only imagine someone had brought the gifts for the goddess and had been afraid to enter the temple because of her. It's strange, Gabria thought as she cleaned a rabbit, gifts such as these are usually given to the priestess in person, not left in front of the temple.

To Gabria's surprise more gifts were left by the door the next day while she was gone: a jug of honey, a pair of wool slippers, and a loaf of bread. Gabria gazed hungrily at the honey. She had not had any-thing sweet in months, but she placed the gifts on the altar by the others and ate her meal of rabbit soup.

Seeing the gifts gave Gabria an idea. She owed her goddess a huge debt of gratitude for preserving her life and sheltering her these past few months. There was very little she could give as a gift, but as she stared at the pile of furs and skins on her bed, an idea formed in her head.

The next night was the Night of Ending, the last night of a very eventful year. Snow fell heavily that day, so Gabria spent much of it working on her gift for Amara, cutting pieces of soft leather and stitching them together into the shape of a horse. She worked late into the night to sew a mane and tail, stuff the little body, and color it black with soot from her fire.

When she was finished she set the horse on the altar and knelt to voice her thanks. It had been a very long year, and she hoped the next one would not be as difficult. As she raised her hopes to Amara, a cold gust of wind swept through the window, setting Gabria's fire leaping. She shivered. Hurriedly she banked her fire and crawled into her warm coverings. At dawn the priestess would be coming to the temple to perform the ceremony of prayers for the new year. Gabria did not want to make the situation uncomfortable, and she planned to be away before daybreak. She fell asleep to the sound of the wind humming around the temple.

Gabria had only been asleep a few hours when Nara's thoughts brought her bolting awake. *Gabria, the priestess comes.*

The sorceress frantically leaped to her feet and grabbed for her boots and cloak. Outside she heard Nara neigh a greeting to the Khulinin priestess and her acolytes. Gabria saw through the window that a faint golden light rimmed the hills to the east and glimmered on the snow that blanketed the ground. She stuffed her feet into her boots and shoved her belongings into the corner. She was about to dash out when the priestess and two young women entered the temple.

The women's eyes widened when they saw Gabria. The priestess's gaze was turned only to the altar and the window facing the rising sun.

Gabria knew she should slip out now, for most priestesses did not allow the uninitiated to attend this ceremony, let alone a woman under banishment. Yet she hesitated, drawn by the grace and beauty of the priestess at her altar.

At that moment the priestess, without turning around, said, "Stay."

The acolytes looked shocked when they realized who she was talking to, but the priestess had already begun the prayers and they did not dare interrupt.

Gabria was pleased. She pressed back into her corner and knelt as the acolytes knelt.

Softly at first, like the light that began the morning, the priestess chanted her prayers to Amara the Mother, goddess of love, life, and birth. As the light intensified and the stars dimmed, her chants grew clearer, more joyful. The priestess's green robes glowed in the morning light and swayed gently with her body while she sang. Her long grizzled hair flowed loose to her waist, like a maiden's.

The fiery rim of the sun edged over the plains, and its pure light poured directly into the stone temple. The priestess's voice rose to a song of greeting, and the acolytes' voices joined hers with triumph.

Although Gabria did not know the words of the prayers, she felt their meaning sweep through her mind and carry her to the heart of her feelings. As the light of the sun warmed her face, she raised her hands and hummed the tune of the invocation, sending her own thoughts of gratitude to the goddess who nurtured her.

The prayers came to a last song of hope when the sun parted from the far horizon. Only then did the priestess lower her arms. Standing in the blaze of sunlight, she turned to face the other three women, her wise face still glowing with her joy. She gave a slight nod to the sorceress kneeling in a corner lit by the sun.

"Thank you, sisters, for your help," she said to the acolytes, then added, "Lady Gabria, Amara shines her light upon you."

The acolytes gasped, and one said, "Mistress, remember the law."

The priestess lifted her hands to the sunlight. "Here in Amara's temple I am the law. Please go outside and wait," she told them. "I will join you in a moment."

The two women walked out, keeping their gazes firmly on the ground.

Gabria slowly stood. "Thank you for asking me to stay."

"I'm pleased you did. This only confirms my belief that you hold the goddess's favor." The priestess paused to study Gabria from head to foot. "You are looking well."

"I am feeling fine," Gabria said eagerly, "although I was ill for a while. It was miserable. I didn't have the strength to leave my bed. I think I remember Piers coming once, but that time is rather blurred." She broke off, and her eyes went to the round window where the light was pouring into the room. "It's strange. It seems more than just a fever was healed within me. I feel as if a great weight has gone from my mind."

The priestess nodded. "Your experiences last summer would have exhausted a seasoned warrior. I knew you were worn thin when you left the treld. Your voice was full of bitterness and defeat. I do not hear that any more."

"I don't feel it. It's ironic. The time I've spent in the temple was supposed to be a punishment. Instead, it has been the best healing I could have had."

"Lord Athlone will be pleased to hear that," the woman said, her eyes were warm with pleasure. "He has worried constantly about you and misses you sorely."

Gabria smiled to herself. "And I him." She colored slightly and said, "I'm sorry. I didn't mean to talk so much. It's just nice to see another person."

"There is no need to apologize. I am glad to listen."

"Before you go, could you tell me how the clan is faring?"

The priestess caught the faint note of loneliness in Gabria's voice. "The clan does well. This mild weather has been a blessing. The herds are healthy and everyone is keeping busy." She paced to the window and looked out at the snow.

"I haven't seen much of Lord Athlone lately," the priestess went on. "He has been working with Lord Koshyn of the Dangari and Lord Sha Umar of the Jehanan to restore clan unity." Her wise face looked troubled. "Lord Medb did more damage than he ever imagined when he tried to conquer the twelve clans. Our people were not meant to be ruled by a single overlord. We're too different from one another. Now the people who sided with Medb are fearful and defensive, the ones who fought against him are angry and resentful, and those who ran are ashamed. Lord Athlone is worried that all of this will tear the clans even further apart. He has been communicating with every chieftain on the plains to help sooth the angry feelings. It has kept him quite busy."

"I hope they can resolve some of these problems before the clans gather this summer at the Tir Samod," Gabria said.

"So do I. We do not need another war." The priestess stopped as something else occurred to her. "There was another piece of news I heard. It's only a rumor, but Branth may be in Pra Desh."

"Branth!" Gabria spat the name. "That murderer. I had hoped he was dead."

"Apparently not."

"Has Athlone said anything about Branth's whereabouts?"

The priestess replied, "Not that I know of. He might be waiting for more reliable information."

Gabria shook her head absently and stared at the floor while she pondered the priestess's news.

After a moment, the priestess went to the altar and studied the gifts lying to the side. A knowing smile touched her mouth. She picked up the little black horse. "Yours?"

Gabria looked up. "Nara is pregnant."

"Indeed. Then I shall take this and add the mare to my prayers."

The sorceress walked over to the altar. "Aren't you going to take the other gifts?"

"Those, young woman, are for you."

"Me!" Gabria gasped.

"There is a small but growing belief among the women that you are the blessed of Amara. There have been five births this season and all have been successful. Some women attribute that to your continued presence in the temple. They have brought these gifts to you."

Gabria was amazed. "But you are Amara's priestess. These gifts should be for you."

The woman's smile widened, and she shook her head. "I do not need them." She paused, her eyes boring into Gabria's. "But the clan needs you whether it knows it or not. Stay in the light of Amara's grace, and you will weather all the hatred and suspicion the unbelievers throw at you." She came to stand in front of Gabria. The girl tensed, waiting for the rest of the warning.

"Step out of the light," the priestess continued, her voice low and adamant. "And I promise you, the goddess will destroy you."

Gabria nodded once in understanding. The priestess examined her face for a long moment before she stood back, satisfied with what she saw.

"You will be home in three months, in time for the celebration of the Birthright. I will look forward to your return."

The Birthright was the ceremony of thanksgiving to the goddess, Amara, for a fruitful birthing season. It was a vital part of the clan's duty to the Mother of All. Gabria could not help but wonder if the rest of the Khulinin would look forward to her return at that time.

The priestess strode to the entrance. "If the Hunnuli needs help at the time of her birthing, call for me."

"Thank you, Priestess," Gabria said with gratitude. She went to the door and watched the three women walk down the path until they disappeared among the trees.

For many days after the priestess's visit, Gabria mulled over her words. After so many months of rejection and suspicion, she found comfort in the knowledge that a few clanswomen were beginning to accept her basic goodness and her loyalty to the gods. Sorcery was believed to be a heretical evil and a perversion of the gods' powers. Gabria had believed that herself until she came to understand her powers. Perhaps now the clanspeople were beginning to question their old beliefs, too. That was an encouraging thought.

The only part of the priestess's news that worried Gabria was the rumor about Branth. She wondered if he really was in Pra Desh and if he had the *Book of Matrah*. She turned cold at that possibility. Everyone believed the Geldring chieftain had stolen the book of spells, so it was very possible that he could be trying to use the knowledge captured within its ancient covers. Gabria hoped with all her heart that he was not, because Branth was as cruel and ambitious as Lord Medb. The gods only knew what kind of trouble the Geldring could devise with his power.

Gabria wondered, too, what Athlone might do when he learned where Branth was hiding. Clan law granted Athlone every right to seek Branth and exact justice for the murder of his father. But Athlone had responsibilities to the clan to think of. Besides, if Branth had become a practicing sorcerer, Athlone would not have a chance against him.

Gabria finally shook herself and set aside her disturbing thoughts. She still had several months left of her banishment, and it seemed senseless to waste her time worrying about a rumor she could not confirm. She brought out her pinecones and returned to her practice of sorcery.

As the winter days passed, Gabria grew more adept at her spells. Her first attempts to turn the pinecone into a sweetplum were dismal failures. Her plums were either too hard, too sour, or too strange to eat. Finally, one evening, she envisioned exactly what she wanted, spoke the words of her spell, and changed the prickly brown pinecone into a perfect sweetplum. She laughed with delight when she took a bite and the delicious juice ran down her chin.

The sorceress practiced a few more times until she had a bowl of different kinds of fruit, then she went on to the next step: changing an organic substance into something inorganic. By this time her senses were more attuned to the process of bending magic to her will. In only a few days she was able to transform the pinecone into stone or any object she desired.

Gabria was so busy hunting for food and practicing her magic, she did not notice immediately that winter was giving way to spring. The weather had remained dry and mild so the changes came gently to the land. The fifth full moon of her exile had come and gone before she realized that the air was not as chilly and the days were growing longer. She had less than one month left before she could return to Khulinin Treld.

To her surprise, Gabria had to admit that she was not completely happy about going back. She had grown to like the freedom to use her magic. It would be difficult to give that up—even with the possibility that the council of chiefs would change the laws forbidding sorcery when the various clans gathered later that summer at the Tir Samod.

But that was not the only reason she was reluctant. As much as Gabria liked Khulinin Treld, she did not feel at home there. The only home she knew in her heart was a broad meadow far to the north, where the Corins had once made their winter camp. She had not been back since that day of the massacre, almost a year ago.

One night, when the half-moon rose above the plains, Gabria lay on her pallet in the dark, cramped temple and thought about her family long into the night. After a while she dozed, drifting in and out of sleep. Her dreams crowded in and jostled with her memories of her father and brothers. She tossed and turned as the dreams grew more vivid, and the phantoms of her old terrors gathered like shadows in her mind.

In the blink of an eye, her thoughts cleared. A vision came to her then, as real as the first time she had experienced it. It was the same vision she had dreamed that previous summer, just before her first meeting with Lord Medb.

Gabria saw herself standing on a hill, looking down at the ruins of a once-busy camp. The sun was high and warm, and grass grew thick in the empty pastures. Weeds sprawled over the moldering ashes and covered the wreckage with a green coverlet. A large mound encircled with spears lay to one side, its new dirt just now sprouting grass.

Gabria jolted awake. The vision faded, but the image of the burial mound remained clear in her thoughts. She had no idea if the mound was real. When she found Corin Treld after the massacre, she had been alone and unable to do anything but leave her people where they had fallen. It was all she could do to save herself.

Gabria mulled over the vision for several days, and in that time her desire to see her home again became a powerful yearning. The more she thought about it, the more important it became for her to see for herself if her clan had really been buried. There had been no chance to say good-bye to her father and brothers on that horrible day. Perhaps now, while she still had about eight days of exile remaining, was a good time to go. On Nara she could cover the distance to the treld in three or four days and be back before anyone missed her. No one would have to know she had left the temple.

When Gabria told the Hunnuli mare of her idea, Nara agreed. *To see your home once more will give you strength*, the mare told her. *We will go*.

They left the next morning in the cold, misty hour of dawn. Nara cantered east beyond the foothills to the plains and gradually swung north to avoid the Khulinin scouts. By sunrise they were well to the north of Khulinin Treld and following the Sweetwater River. Nara settled into an easy, flowing canter that would carry them for hours over the open leagues of grass.

Gabria relaxed on Nara's broad back. It felt wonderful to be on the plains again, away from the temple, the hills, and the people who would not come near her. Here on the wide, treeless grasslands she could see from horizon to horizon, feel the wind that tugged at her hair, and rejoice in the eternal blue sky that arched over her head. She threw her arms wide and laughed happily at her freedom.

Nara neighed in reply. The black horse stretched out into a gallop, her muscles moving effortlessly as she raced the wind for the sheer joy of running. Her black mane whipped into Gabria's face. Her hooves pounded the hard ground.

Gabria laughed again. She felt the power of the Hunnuli flow beneath her as quick and hot as the lightning that marked the horse's right shoulder. All at once she was overwhelmed by love, gratitude, and wonder. As long as she had Nara, she knew she would never be alone. She would always have an empathetic companion who would stand by her no matter how often her own people rejected her. She flung her arms around Nara's neck and pressed her cheek against the soft hair.

The mare slowed to an easy canter. *Are you all right, Gabria?*

The young woman sat up, smiling, and rubbed the horse's shoulder. "Stay with me, Nara, and I will be."

Always, the Hunnuli replied.

Silently they went on. There was no need to say more.

They traveled north for three days through the wide, grassy Valley of the Hornguard. To the west, the snowy peaks of the Darkhorn Mountains towered into the sky, their white mantled heads crowned with clouds and their gray ramparts hidden behind veils of wind and snow. To the east, the smaller range of the Himachal Mountains bordered the valley like an old, crumbled fortress wall. The valley was a fertile, green land where antelope, wild horses, and small game flourished. Both the Geldring and the Dangari hunted in the Hornguard, and, since Gabria had no desire to meet anyone from the clans, she and Nara stayed to the western side of the valley among the foothills of the Darkhorns.

To Gabria the journey felt strange, yet half familiar. They were traveling back the way they had come almost a year ago. The mountains and hills looked much the same: barren, gray-brown with winter, and patched with snow. Only Gabria was different. She felt a lifetime older and wiser; she was no longer a simple, terrified, girl. The realities of war and magic had changed her.

Her problem was that her experiences had not erased her memories. The closer they came to Corin Treld, the more nervous Gabria became. Time and again she remembered that hideous day when she had stumbled into the ruins of her home and found her murdered family. She had thought that she would be calm and able to deal with the memories, but the feelings of terror, grief, and confusion boiled out of her mind like a turbulent flood.

As hard as she could, Gabria fought down the turmoil within her and pushed on, refusing Nara's suggestion to stop and eat or rest. The Hunnuli was not bothered by the constant traveling, but she grew worried about her rider. Gabria was obviously lost in her own thoughts. She was no longer alert or attentive to her horse and their well being.

On the third day from Khulinin Treld, Nara cantered over a hill and down into a bowl-shaped gully. She paused at the edge of a half-frozen, muddy pool.

Do you remember this place?

Gabria stared down at the dark pool. "Very well. I still have the scars on my hands." She ran her hand down Nara's neck. "A small price to pay for the gift of a friend."

In one motion, they both looked up to the top of a nearby hill where a small cairn of rocks could still be seen on the crest. It was there that Gabria had buried Nara's first foal.

She had come across the wild Hunnuli trapped in the mud and fighting for her life against a pack of wolves. Gabria had driven off the marauders and spent two days digging out the pregnant mare with her bare hands. She had tried to save the foal, but it had died during birth. She had laid it to rest among the rocks.

Thinking of the foal, Gabria belatedly remembered Nara's current condition. The mare was almost ten months into her pregnancy. Shamefaced, she ran her hand down Nara's silken neck. "I'm sorry," she said softly.

Nara nickered. *There is no reason to be so.*

"Let's camp here tonight," the young woman suggested.

The mare tilted her head and looked at Gabria with her wise eye. *There are still several hours of daylight left. We could be in Corin Treld by nightfall.*

Gabria shook her head. "We need to rest. Besides, I want to face the treld in the light of day."

They found shelter in a shallow overhang in the side of one of the hills. Nara went to graze while Gabria built a small fire, ate her meal, and lay down on her blankets. Darkness came quickly, for the sky was overcast and the air was heavy with the threat of snow. Gabria closed her eyes and tried to sleep.

She was very tired, and she knew tomorrow would be a trying day, but her thoughts could find no rest. Her mind kept returning to the reality of the massacre and the dream-images of her clan's grave mound. What would she find tomorrow? Had her family been buried with honor or were the bodies still there, rotting into the grass? She tossed and turned as her imagination envisioned every possibility, then jumbled the imaginings together with the real memories of the carnage. Phantoms drifted through her mind with half-remembered faces and voices silenced by death.

Outside Gabria's meager shelter, Nara came to stand against the cliff wall. The horse's eyes reflected the firelight, glowing like gems against the darkness.

Gabria remembered lying in the dark that night long ago, watching the eyes of the wild, trapped mare and wondering what would become of both herself and the horse. She never imagined the incredible events that were to follow. Now, she and Nara were going back to the place where the chain of events had begun.

Gabria sat up and leaned back against the rock. No, that's not quite true, she thought. The chain of events led back to Medb and his greed, and even farther back to the generations of clanspeople who had zealously avoided magic. It went back to the Destruction of the Sorcerers, to the blossoming of the magical city of Moy Tura, to Matrah who compiled his great tome, to the early magic-wielders who had experimented with magic, and as far back as Valorian, the hero-warrior who had first used magic to defeat the evil gorthlings of Sorh. Gabria was only a small part in a story that actually had begun centuries before and would continue long after she was dead.

The woman laughed. Seen in that perspective, her worries and inner turmoil were merely threads against a vast tapestry of clan history and human events. All of her frightened imaginings would change nothing about the treld or her dead clan. What was done, was done. She would simply have to wait until morning to settle her personal fears. She lay down again, pulled her cloak up to her chin, and let her thoughts relax. This time she drifted off into a peaceful, dreamless sleep.

Snow was falling the next morning when Gabria awoke. It was a light, fitful shower that patterned Nara's dark coat with tiny stars and dusted the ground with powder. The mountains were completely obscured behind a wall of cloud. Gabria shook the snow off her belongings, ate a quick meal, and mounted Nara. They left the gully without a backward glance and trotted slowly north through the swirling snow. Corin Treld was not far by horseback, but Gabria did not want to miss it in the billowing storm.

Fortunately the snow shower did not last long. A little before noon, as Nara crested a ridge near the treld, the snow stopped and the clouds began to break.

Gabria felt her heart pounding. "It's not far," she said. "It's just across that stream and up the next hill."

Nara broke into a canter. She went down the ridge, leaped the stream without missing a stride, and ran up the slope of a long, tree-less hill. Suddenly the sun broke through the clouds and poured down on the land. The Hunnuli reached the top of the hill and stopped.

For a breathless moment, Gabria wondered if they were at the right place. The area looked similar to the home she remembered: the broad meadow surrounded by trees on two sides and backed by the dark, tree-clad mountains; the small stream that clattered along its stony bed; and the pile of boulders by the copse of trees where chil-dren used to play. With a stab of pain, Gabria realized this was the same meadow, it just looked different without its once-thriving treld.

Gabria flung up her hands and cried with relief and joy. Her vision had been right; there, in the broad field, stood a new mound, crowned with spears and shining with a dusting of snow in the morn-ing sun. She slid off the Hunnuli and ran down the hill. Halfway down, she unpinned the Khulinin cloak and dropped it in the grass, then she drew her sword and shouted the Corins' cry of victory. Her voice sang through the empty meadow. The young woman raced up the slope of the mound and through the ring of spears to the very top. She bran-dished her sword high.

"Corin!" she shouted. "I did it, Father. You are avenged!"

The silence of the ruined treld rose to meet her. Head thrown back, she listened to the wind in the grass, the cry of a hawk overhead, and the music of the stream. It almost seemed as if beloved voices would sound then, acknowledging her heroic feats, but there was no one left to answer her. She looked around, half expecting to see her father, her brothers, or someone standing by the mound.

The meadow was empty, and only the wind walked in the treld.

Gabria's joy died within her as quickly as it had come. Beneath her feet lay the hundred-odd members of Clan Corin; her father, Lord Dathlar; her three older brothers; and her twin brother, Gabran. They were long gone, beyond the earthly lands they had once walked. Her family was in the realm of the dead now, in the presence of the gods. They might know of her victory over their killer, Lord Medb, and the price she had paid to earn her revenge, but they could not share in her glory. They were gone, forever beyond her reach.

Gabria's eyes filled with tears as she looked down. The new

growth of spring was beginning to cover the mound; the earth was gently settling down around the buried bodies. The girl noticed the spears were already sagging, so she walked around the circle and straightened each one. When she was finished, she climbed down from the mound.

For most of the afternoon Gabria wandered around the treld, remembering the places she had loved so well: the site of her father's tent, the chieftain's hall they had proudly built with logs, the pens and corrals, the tents of her brothers and her friends. Everything had been burned by the marauders during the attack, but Gabria found many traces of what had been. The foundation of the hall sprawled in the weeds, its interior crisscrossed with a few charred logs. Bits and pieces of personal items lay in the grass. The charred remains of the tents stood rotting into the blackened earth.

At last Gabria came to a level place by the edge of the treld. There was only a broad, burned patch on the ground to mark the spot, yet Gabria would never forget this place. She had dragged her father's body from the front of his hall to this open ground and laid her brothers beside him. Then she had built a makeshift pyre and burned them as was befitting for honored warriors. It was all she could do alone.

Whoever had come later and buried the clan had also buried the remains of Dathlar and his sons, leaving no trace of the pyre. It was as it should be, and Gabria gave thanks to the unknown benefactors who had worked so hard to honor her people. She stared at the ground for a long time, remembering the faces of her family. This time her memories brought her warmth and peace. The anguish was gone. At long last her old terrors had been laid to rest.

She walked back through the treld a final time. Near the ruins of the hall she paused and looked around. Except for the burial mound and the scattered, decaying ruins, the meadow looked much like it must have before the Corins came to winter there. She smiled with bitter sweetness. That was the wonder of it: no matter how much blood was spilled on the grass, the plains remained constant and unchanging. This land could not be altered by human feelings.

"Farewell, Corins!" she called. "Rest well."

Sadly she walked back up the hill to Nara. She pinned on her Khulinin cloak and mounted the Hunnuli. "We can go. There is nothing here for me now."

The mare turned to face the burial mound in the meadow below and, with a trumpeting neigh, she reared high in the Hunnuli's gesture of honor and respect. When her feet touched down again, she and Gabria looked at the treld for one last time. After that, Nara turned south and cantered away.

3

Two days later, Nara and Gabria came to the hot springs in the foothills of the Darkhorn Mountains near Wolfeared Pass. They had stopped there the year before to rest and bind the wounds gained both from the wolves and during Nara's rescue from the mudhole. Once again Gabria gave in to the temptation of warm water. They found a warm pool among the bubbling springs and twisting vapors, and both woman and horse spent the afternoon soaking away the dirt of their journey. It was delightful. By the end of the day, Gabria felt more relaxed and peaceful than she had in a year.

As she dried herself she thought of Athlone and the Khulinin, suddenly realizing she was excited to see them all again. Her banishment would be over in two nights, and she could rightfully return to the clan. For the first time she felt as if she were going home. Smiling to herself, she put on her pants and tunic and fastened her golden cloak. In two days she would be home—at last.

Gabria made camp that night at the edge of the springs, upwind of the mineral-laden pools. Nara stayed close, grazing on the sweet grass. The woman was just settling down to sleep when the mare threw her head up and sniffed the night breeze.

The young woman sat up. "What is it?"

Do not worry, Gabria, Nara told her. *I will be back soon*. Without another word, the horse galloped into the darkness.

Surprised, Gabria shouted, "Wait!" She jumped to her feet and ran after Nara, but the mare was already gone.

The girl stood perplexed, staring into the night. What had gotten into Nara? The mare did not usually go off alone without an explanation. Surely she could not be going into labor. It was too soon, and she would have told Gabria. Neither did Gabria think there was any immediate danger lurking in the night. Nara never would have left her rider unprotected.

Gabria returned to her blankets and tried to put her concern aside. Nara had said not to worry, but the sorceress found that that was impossible. She could not close her eyes, and sleep stayed far away through the long night.

Just before dawn, Gabria heard Nara's hoofbeats pounding into the little valley. She bolted to her feet and ran to meet the horse. She could barely see the black mare as Nara materialized out of the darkness.

Nara snorted. Her flanks were heaving from her exertion. *We must go*, she demanded.

"Go!" Gabria shouted. "Go where? Why did you leave?"

I must take you to the mountain. To the Wheel. Someone wants to see you.

"Who?"

The mare stamped her hoof, clearly agitated. *Gabria, please! You will see.*

Gabria stared at the horse in astonishment. If the demand had come from anyone but Nara, Gabria would have insisted on an explanation before she went anywhere. Instead she shrugged, gathered her belongings, and silently mounted the Hunnuli. She would trust Nara to keep her safe wherever they were going.

Nara galloped out of the valley of the hot springs and headed deeper into the mountains. The night was still quite dark, but the Hunnuli raced over the rough terrain as if her path was lit by the sun. Gabria held onto the horse with every ounce of strength she had as Nara lunged, jumped, and twisted higher and higher into the heart of the Darkhorns over a trail only the mare could see.

"Nara, slow down," Gabria cried.

The Hunnuli flattened her ears and ran faster. *We must be there by dawn.*

"Be where?"

The Wheel, was Nara's only reply.

The Wheel. Gabria had never seen that strange place. She had only heard it mentioned in the old tales told by the bards. The Wheel had been built in the mountains by Valorian, somewhere near the pass where he had led the first clansmen from the west to the grasslands. No one knew where the Wheel lay or even what it was; the tales had grown vague with time, the pass forgotten as the clansmen had turned their lives to the plains and let go of what had gone before.

Gabria gritted her teeth and clung to Nara. It took all her concentration to stay mounted against the jolting violence of the Hunnuli's gallop. She would find out soon enough what this place was and who wanted to see her.

Nara continued to run ever higher up the steep, rocky valleys, through forests of pines and dark spruce, and around thickets of heavy underbrush. She plunged over rock falls, raced past high alpine meadows where deer grazed, and galloped over the rough clearings left by avalanches or forest fires. The dry winter was especially evident this high in the mountains. There were only a few feet of snow where normally the drifts would have stood over Gabria's head. Nara was able to find her way through the low patches of snow without much difficulty.

By dawn they were high in the mountains, nearing the twin peaks of Wolfeared Pass. There were fewer trees on the upper slopes, and the undergrowth was thin and sparse. Nara finally slowed to a trot. Her breath came hard and fast, vaporizing into clouds in the cold, thin air. Her body was steaming from her efforts.

Gabria patted the horse's neck. She was worried, for Nara should not be running like this in her condition. Wherever we are going, she thought, it is important enough to Nara to endanger herself and her unborn foal.

We are close now, Nara told her.

The sorceress sighed with relief. She was surprised to see the early morning creep into the mountains with a soft light that dimmed the stars and revealed the peaks' rugged faces.

Nara struggled up a rocky incline, past a few stunted pines and clusters of boulders, to the edge of a broad plateau. There she stopped and snorted in satisfaction.

Mystified, Gabria looked about. The plateau lay like a huge plate on the side of the northernmost of the two peaks, its bare, flat ground swept clear of heavy snow. It seemed empty at first, and Gabria asked curiously, "This is it?"

Nara lifted her head to the peaks. Gabria followed her gaze and saw the distant pass that cut between the two pinnacles.

The Wheel is here. Go see. They will come soon.

"Who are 'they'?" Gabria demanded.

Nara did not respond. She remained gazing at the peaks as if waiting for something to appear. Her ears were perked, and her nostrils flared in the cold air.

Gabria shook her head and slid off the mare's back. Her legs and hands were stiff from clinging to Nara; it felt good to stretch her muscles and walk on her own feet. She took a deep breath of mountain air, savoring the sharp, rich smells of frost and alpine trees. For a moment she stood at the edge of the plateau and looked down to where the land fell away into the rugged highlands of the Darkhorns. Her eyes followed the land downward over the slopes as the sun rose higher and spread its light over the distant plains below. The endless leagues of the Ramtharin Plains were slowly revealed to Gabria in lightening hues of indigo, purple, and lavender. From her high promontory she could look far to the east, where the grasslands of her people rolled beyond the horizon.

A smile lit Gabria's face. It was no wonder Valorian's people had looked down on those lands and rejoiced. The plains were vast and beautiful and held everything the clanspeople needed to survive. Whatever they had left behind could not have compared to the grasslands.

Gabria turned away from the edge and studied the big plateau around her. At first glance it seemed strangely empty. There were no trees or shrubs or large boulders to break up the tableau, only a few scrubby, tough plants and some blotches of lichen on the flat ground. The only thing that caught her interest was a low pile of rocks lying in the center of the plateau. She was perhaps thirty paces away from the pile when she saw something else. On the ground in front of her were two lines of smooth, round, grayish stones. One line curved away to the right and left in a huge arch; the second line intersected the first and ran directly to the pile of rocks.

Gabria followed the straight line of stones to the rock pile. She saw immediately that the pile was a cairn, carefully shaped into a circle about two paces across and as high as a horse's knees. Radiating out from the cairn were other equally spaced lines of stones. Gabria followed a second line out; the curved trail of stones circled the cairn and united each straight line into—Gabria nodded her head—into the shape of a giant wheel. She walked around the entire circumference of the huge design, marveling in the perfect curve of the circle and in the arrow-straight lines of the spokes. It was a remarkable creation.

If this is Valorian's Wheel, Gabria thought, it has to be over five hundred years old. Despite weathering and time, the Wheel was in very good condition.

She shook her head in wonder at the dream behind the Wheel. Lord Valorian was a man known to many civilizations, for tales of his deeds had spread far beyond the limits of the plains. He was a hero-warrior and a chieftain, a man believed to be half-god. He traveled to Sorh in the realm of the dead to fight the gorthlings for Amara's crown; he bred the Hunnuli from his own stallion and taught them to communicate with magic-wielders; he was the first human to tap into the powers of magic, and he led his people out of the miseries of their old land to a new home beyond the mountains. After his death, his twelve sons spread out across their new land and formed the twelve clans of Valorian, preserving their father's heritage and passing on the talent to wield magic.

Gabria smiled and thought Valorian might be pleased to find one of his descendants had come back to see his wheel.

Without warning Nara neighed a cry of welcome. *They come!* she trumpeted.

Gabria turned in astonishment. She had never heard Nara sound so joyful. Her eyes followed the horse's gaze to the high pass where the light of morning was streaming onto the mountain face. A herd of dark horses galloped down between the peaks, their manes flying and their tails raised like royal banners. Snow flew from their hooves, and the thunder of their coming rumbled over the plateau.

With the sun reflecting off the rocks and the snow, it was difficult for Gabria to clearly see the horses; then she rocked back in astonishment. She clambered up to the top of the cairn for a better view. As they drew closer, she recognized them immediately, for the horses were huge and black. They were all Hunnuli.

They galloped onto the plateau where Nara pranced to join them, and the entire herd neighed their welcome to the mare and the woman. They flowed into a circle around Gabria, following the curve of the wheel.

She tried to count them, but there were too many and they raced by her in a boisterous, wild run. Their black coats gleamed in the sunlight, and a blazon of white lightning marked each horse at the shoulder. Her mouth slightly open, Gabria stared at the magnificent mares and stallions. Her heart sang with their delight.

At last the Hunnuli slowed down and stopped. They wheeled to face the woman, their breath billowing in clouds around them. A stallion broke away from the ring, trotted forward, and nodded his head to Gabria.

He was huge. Even on the cairn of stones, the woman's head

barely reached his nose. She realized immediately he was the King Stallion. His great strength was molded in the muscles of his neck and legs; his eyes glowed with a deep, abiding wisdom. White hairs of age covered his muzzle, yet his step was powerful. A regal courage showed in his every movement and toss of his head.

We greet you, Sorceress, he told Gabria. The stallions thoughts to her were proud but kind.

She swept back her cloak and bowed low to the majestic horse.

We have waited a long time for the magic-wielders to return, he continued. *The Hunnuli were bred and born to be the companions of humans with the ability to use the powers of magic wisely. We have missed them. You are the first in a long time to return to the arts. For that we are greatly pleased.*

Gabria stared at the stallion, her eyes huge. She had no idea what to say to him. Sensing her confusion, Nara left the circle of Hunnuli and came to stand beside her.

The King Stallion turned his dark eyes to Nara. *Serve her well,* Gabria heard him tell the mare. *She must continue her work if sorcery is to return to the clans.*

The mare agreed with a neigh.

Gabria spoke up, "Nara has been my friend beyond all imagining. She has served me very well indeed."

And so shall her sons, the stallion replied. Then he dropped his head down to Gabria's height, arching his massive neck, and looked at her through the long hairs of his forelock. *Sorceress, we have asked you to come to Valorian's Wheel so we can warn you. Someone, some human, is tampering with magic beyond their control.* He shook his mane angrily.

You know the Hunnuli cannot be harmed or altered by magic, but we are innately sensitive to it and to any change in the forms of magic. Lately, we have sensed strange vibrations emanating from the east. These frighten us, for we believe the powers of magic are being abused.

Gabria looked away, her eyes thoughtful.

The stallion snorted. *You know who it is?*

"Possibly. An exiled chieftain may be in Pra Desh. We think he has the *Book of Matrah.*"

Then, Sorceress, you must go. Find the source of this tainted magic before something terrible happens that you cannot challenge or reverse.

Gabria paled. "Do you know what he is doing?"

The Hunnuli lifted his head to the east, his nostrils flaring. *That is unclear to us. The only thing we know is this magic-wielder is unskilled in handling the powers he is trying to use. He must be stopped.*

Gabria felt her heart sink. Oh gods, not now, she cried to herself. To the stallion she forced her reply: "I understand."

Good. The stallion neighed a command, and a smaller, younger male broke away from the herd and joined Nara. The stallion bowed his head to Gabria.

It would be wise if you took other humans with you, the king told her. *Particularly the chieftain, Athlone. He would be a great help to you. Eurus will go with you. Lord Athlone will need a mount befitting his talent.*

Gabria eyed the young stallion doubtfully. "I don't mean to be ungrateful, but Athlone is very reluctant to admit his powers. Now that his stallion, Boreas, is dead, he may not accept another Hunnuli."

The King Stallion snorted, a noise that sounded much like laughter. *We will let Athlone and Eurus work out their own relationship. I'm certain the chieftain will come to his senses.*

The woman's mouth tightened, for she knew Athlone's stubborn nature. "I hope so," she muttered.

With a toss of his head, the king signaled his herd. The horses neighed and pranced forward.

Farewell, Sorceress, he said to Gabria. *We will come if you need us.* Then he wheeled and galloped back up the plateau, the other Hunnuli falling in behind him.

Before Gabria could draw another breath, the horses were gone. The thunder of their hooves echoed on the peaks and faded. An empty quiet fell on the plateau. She gazed at the twin peaks, wishing the Hunnuli would return, wondering if she would ever see their like again.

Nara nickered to her softly. *When Valorian brought the clans over that pass and built this wheel to celebrate their journey, they had over two hundred Hunnuli in their midst. Now our herd has barely thirty. Our numbers are dwindling rapidly, Gabria. Without magic and magic-wielders to give us purpose, our mares and stallions do not always mate. Our breed will disappear.*

Eurus snorted in agreement.

"May the gods forbid that ever happening!" Gabria said vehemently. She vaulted onto Nara's back. "Let's go home."

The two Hunnuli fell in side by side and made their way down the mountain at a more careful pace. By late afternoon they had reached the foothills and turned south toward Khulinin Treld.

* * *

Two days later Gabria and the Hunnuli arrived at the Khulinin camp, just as the horns were blowing to send the evening outriders off on their duties. She rode Nara past Marakor, the tall summit that guarded the entrance to the valley, and waved to the startled outriders standing guard nearby.

She smiled to herself as one of the guardians galloped toward camp to warn Lord Athlone. Nara trotted placidly along the path to the treld, Eurus close by her side. By the time the two Hunnuli reached the training fields by the camp, Gabria could see activity at the chieftain's hall. A moment later a horseman came galloping down the hill to meet her. It was Athlone.

Even from a distance Gabria could see his anger. His body was rigid on the horse, and his face was dark with fury. He reined his stallion to a halt in front of Nara.

"In the name of all the gods," he shouted, his eyes on Gabria. "Where have you been?"

Before the startled woman could answer, Eurus came around behind Nara and snorted at the chieftain.

Athlone stared at the second Hunnuli, his anger retreating a little before his surprise and curiosity. "Who is that?"

I am Eurus, brother of Boreas, the young Hunnuli replied.

By this time the members of the hearthguard and the other warriors had caught up with their lord. They gathered close by him, their faces interested but wary. Other clan members clustered around, staring and pointing at Gabria and the two Hunnuli.

Casually, Gabria glanced at the clanspeople to gauge their welcome. She was relieved to see they showed no overt hostility, only curiosity. The priestess of Amara stood at the back of the crowd, a wise smile on her face as she nodded a welcome. Athlone seemed to be the only one disturbed by her return. This time, however, she was not troubled by his reaction. The chief was a volatile man, and Gabria sensed his anger was fed mostly by concern. Instead of rising to meet his rage, she merely askcd, "How did you know I was gone?"

Athlone tore his eyes away from Eurus. "Piers went to find you five days ago. He told me you had left. There was no sign of where you were going, when—or even if—you would return."

She smiled. "You should have known that I would return."

Athlone nodded once, sharply, unwilling to give up his anger that easily. "Where did you go?"

"Heretic!" someone suddenly shouted from the edge of the

crowd. Thalar shouldered his way through the people and planted himself in front of Nara. "Be warned. Your exile is over, but this clan will not tolerate your evil magic!"

Nara snorted menacingly, but the furious priest ignored her and shook his fist at the young woman. "Your presence curses us, Sorceress, and your foul heresies bring our doom. Leave us in peace!"

"Thalar!" the chieftain said sharply.

Nara, however, had had enough. Her head snaked forward, and she snapped at the priest, her teeth coming dangerously close to his head. The crowd gasped as Thalar stumbled backward, his eyes wide with shock.

"That will be enough," Athlone demanded.

Thalar started to say something, but the Hunnuli mare flattened her ears, and he stepped hastily back. Glaring ferociously, the priest withdrew to the edge of the crowd.

The sorceress ignored him. She patted Nara and said to Athlone, "Please, Lord, could we go to the hall? The Hunnuli are hungry, and I am very tired. I will tell you everything over a hot meal."

The chieftain nodded and said with genuine relief, "Welcome home." He glanced back at the hall with a strange expression of regret. "There is someone else who has been waiting for you."

"Oh?" Gabria asked. She felt a tug of foreboding, but Athlone dismounted without a reply and handed his reins to a warrior. Gabria, too, slid off her horse. The mare gently nudged her rider before she and Eurus trotted back to the meadows.

Gabria watched them go. Standing beside her, Athlone studied the sorceress's features and marveled that a face capable of showing such love could also have such strength.

The crowd began to disperse to their own tents and cooking fires. Athlone, Gabria, and several hearthguard warriors walked up the hill to the entrance of the hall.

Twilight was settling into the valley. Once inside the open doors of the hall, Gabria noticed the lamps were lit and a fire was burning in the central hearth. A haunch of meat had been set to the side of the fire, ready for the chieftain, his family, and any other warrior who wanted to eat in the hall. Lady Tungoli and her serving girls were setting up the trestle tables before bringing in the meal.

Gabria said softly, "It's good to be home."

The chieftain overheard her, and the quiet pleasure of her words evaporated the vestiges of his anger. He offered her his arm, and they walked into the hall together.

As Gabria and the men ate their meal and talked, Piers, Cantrell, and a stocky, ruddy-skinned man Gabria did not recognize came to join them. Other clanspeople sat close by, listening. Lady Tungoli organized her serving girls and also joined the group to hear the talk. No one bothered to introduce Gabria to the stranger in their midst.

Sitting beside Athlone's dais, Gabria told them all about her vision, her journey to Corin Treld, and the burial mound she had found there. She did not mention her own catharsis, but those who knew her well sensed the new peace and assurance in her manner. She went on to describe the Wheel and her meeting with the Hunnuli. Her listeners sat spellbound as she told of the black horses and their king.

When she repeated the King Stallion's warning about Branth, the stranger sucked in a breath through his teeth. "Lord Athlone, I—" he began.

The chieftain waved him to silence. "A moment, please, Khan'di." He turned back to Gabria. "You haven't told us yet why you have a second Hunnuli."

Gabria lingered over her cup of wine for a moment before answering. "The King Stallion sent him."

"Why?"

"He thought you needed a mount befitting your abilities."

Athlone looked up at the ceiling, the lines on his face taut. "I have a good mount. One befitting a chieftain."

The warriors around him stared at their chief in surprise. Any among them would have traded their swordarms for a Hunnuli to ride, but Gabria looked into Athlone's face and understood his refusal. She sipped her wine and let the subject drop. The King Stallion's advice was wise. She would let Athlone and Eurus work out their difficulties.

Athlone, meanwhile, settled back into his seat and acquiesced to her silence. He had no wish to push the subject further. Instead he poured more wine into his cup and passed the silver ewer to the stranger. "Khan'di Kadoa, now you know why we have been unable to find Lady Gabria," the chieftain said with a twist of wry humor. "Perhaps now you would tell her why you are here."

Gabria finally got a good look at the stranger when he rose from the table and bowed to her. She guessed he was about fifty years old, for his short-cropped hair was gray and his heavy face was deeply lined around the mouth and forehead. He was dressed simply in a pair of leggings and a knee-length hooded shirt, but there was nothing simple about the massive gold seal ring on his index finger. He met her scrutiny with a sharp, interested gaze of his own, and Gabria recognized immediately that this man was no fool.

"Lady, I am Khan'di Kadoa, a nobleman and merchant from the great city of Pra Desh, capital of the kingdom of Calah," he said smoothly. "I have come to talk to you about this exile, Branth. As I have told your chieftain, Branth has been in Pra Desh over six months now and has been causing nothing but trouble."

Gabria shifted in her seat. "What has he been doing?"

"He has an old book of spells and the ability, however feeble, to use them." The man leaned forward, his dark eyes piercing under a line of bushy eyebrows. "When he first arrived, he ignored our laws forbidding sorcery and tried to sell his services. Then, he simply stole or conjured what he wanted. Before long he had the entire city in an uproar. He became such a problem that the city guards tried to arrest him. He killed them all. Then the ruler of our city, the fon, captured him."

A note of suppressed rage hardened the nobleman's voice. "The fon is an ambitious woman. She not only wants to rule Pra Desh, but Calah and the other Five Kingdoms, as well. She has already laid her plans to take over the rest of the country and invade our neighbor, Portane, in just two months' time. Somehow, she has coerced this Branth into serving her. She uses his book and his power to strip our fine city, all to build her armies. She will lay waste to Pra Desh just to satisfy her insatiable lust for power." Khan'di paused. When he spoke again his voice was calmer.

"Lady Gabria, Branth's presence has become intolerable. I beg of you, please come to Pra Desh and remove this man before the fon fulfills her plans. I know I am asking a great deal, but if you could just take him away, the people of Pra Desh—nay, of all Calah—would rise up and deal with the fon themselves."

The hall went very quiet as the clansmen waited for a response. Gabria looked at Athlone's stony face, then at the splinter of the Fallen Star, the mark of a magic-wielder, glowing redly just under the skin of her wrist.

Sadly, she touched the bright spot. After the Hunnuli's warning and this news from the Pra Deshian, Gabria felt that she had no choice. She would have to try to find Branth before he wreaked havoc on the city or returned to the clans to take Medb's place. She knew, too, that she would have to postpone her marriage to Athlone. It wouldn't be right, beginning their life as husband and wife under such difficult circumstances.

"Athlone," she said into the silence. "He's right. I must go to Pra Desh as soon as possible."

At first the chief did not respond. He sat and stared into the fire for several long moments, his expression showing no trace of the conflict that warred within him. Finally he seemed to reach a decision, for he tossed out the dregs of his wine and slammed his cup on the arm of the stone seat. He did not notice that the horn cup split from the force of the blow.

Rising, he said tersely to the men around him, "It is late. We will make plans for the journey tomorrow. Gabria will go to Pra Desh."

His companions were startled by the abruptness of his dismissal. They stood and began to leave the hall.

"Bregan," Athlone called to one of the warriors. "Stay. I need to talk to you."

Gabria gazed at the chief's back, trying to hide her hurt. He had accepted her decision without a word; perhaps he didn't care after all. Since her return from the temple, she had found Athlone to be angry, irritable, and interested only in the news she could give. She began to wonder if she had misread him earlier. He was not worried that she was missing, simply angry that she had disobeyed his command by leaving the temple to go to Corin Treld. Perhaps in six months he had already changed his mind about her. She rose to go, her heart heavy. She looked up when Piers touched her sleeve.

The healer read the look in her eyes and understood. "Don't take his rudeness to heart. The responsibilities of a chieftain weigh heavily on him tonight," he said gently.

She looked up at her old friend and squeezed his arm. "It's not very often you defend Athlone."

The healer's pale eyes met hers with sympathy and caring. "I'm fond of you both. Don't worry. Athlone will come around as soon as he straightens out his own thoughts."

Wearily she nodded, more hope than conviction in her heart, and the healer took her arm. "Come," he said. "I have your old sleeping place ready for you."

He led Gabria out of the hall and down the path toward his tent. She looked back at the hall entrance, hoping Athlone would call to her, but the lord was talking to a warrior and did not even seem to notice she had left. She bowed her head and hurried on with Piers.

In the hall, Lord Athlone paced back and forth by the fire pit. The hall was momentarily empty, save for Bregan. The warrior was standing silently by the dais, waiting for his chieftain to speak.

Bregan was twenty years older than Athlone and a handspan shorter. His dark hair, worn short, was graying, and a black and silver beard trimmed his square face. He was dressed in a warm tunic and pants with none of the ornamentation or gold jewelry that was the privilege of a warrior of his experience. His features were well-defined, but in the past winter a deep sadness had left permanent lines on his forehead and face. Bregan watched his lord despondently, for he knew what Athlone was going to ask him and what he would have to answer.

Lord Athlone finally stopped pacing and said, "Bregan, I have asked you twice to be wer-tain and both times you refused. I have to ask you again. I need you as commander of my warriors."

Bregan shifted uncomfortably. "Lord, you know I can't."

Athlone held up his hand. "Before you refuse again, hear me out. I am going to Pra Desh with Lady Gabria."

The warrior did not look surprised. "Good. Branth must die," he said flatly.

"And Gabria must not," Athlone muttered. He put his hands on the older man's shoulders. "I understand how you feel, but I am chieftain now and I must leave this clan in capable hands. The journey will take months. You have the wisdom to rule in my stead, and you still hold the respect of the werod. There is no one else I trust as much."

"Lord, you do me great honor, but please choose another! I cannot go back on my vow."

Athlone studied the man before him and saw the adamant refusal in Bregan's eyes. Of Lord Savaric's five hearthguard warriors who had been with him the day of his murder, only two still survived. Two of the warriors had chosen suicide instead of facing the shame and dishonor of their failure. One warrior had died of an illness on the way back to Khulinin Treld—some said he had lost the will to live. The fourth withdrew from the werod and each day drank himself into a stupor. Only Bregan remained a warrior. After Savaric's death, he voluntarily stripped himself of his status and the gifts he had won for distinguished service, then placed himself in the bottom rank with the young warriors in training. He would begin again, he had told Athlone, and work to regain his lost honor.

The chief shook his head. He could respect Bregan's choice, but it did not help him solve his dilemma. He had not yet chosen a wer-tain for the clan in the hope that Bregan would eventually accept. Now he had to decide on someone else quickly. He dropped his hands from Bregan's shoulders and resumed pacing.

"Do you have any suggestions?" he asked.

"Guthlac would serve you well."

"He's too young."

Bregan's mouth lifted in a slight smile. "He is several years older than you were when you became wer-tain."

Athlone stopped pacing, his face thoughtful. "I will think about it."

"He is a good warrior, and the others approve of him. He has been an excellent mentor for the younger men."

"Isn't he also your cousin?" Athlone asked, his eyebrow arched. The older man smiled, then the chieftain found himself mirroring the expression. "I will think about it," he repeated.

Bregan stepped forward. "Lord, will you consider something else?"

Athlone turned slightly, surprised by the note of pleading in the warrior's voice.

"Allow me to come with you," Bregan said. "I failed your father, but I swear by my life I will not fail you. You will need guards. Let me be one of them."

"This will not be an easy journey. Gabria goes to face a sorcerer."

"I know that. Lady Gabria will need protection, too."

"Pack your gear," Athlone ordered.

"Thank you, Lord." Bregan saluted the chief and withdrew, leaving Athlone in the chaos of his own thoughts. The young lord paced for a few more minutes, then left the hall and walked up a path to the top of the hill overlooking the camp. A large, flat rock lay among some scrubby bushes at the edge of the slope. It was Athlone's favorite place, for it afforded a view of the entire valley.

He gathered his cloak close against the night wind, sat on the rock, and studied the glorious clouds and patterns of stars breaking the monotony of the black sky. In front of him, a full moon sailed high above the plains. He looked down on the encampment. The black tents melted into the darkness, but here and there pools of firelight gave shape to the sleeping camp.

Usually this view of Khulinin Treld gave Athlone solace and strengthened his sense of purpose. Tonight, it only made his confusion more acute. Duty to his clan had always been his sole obligation. When his father had been alive and Athlone was only wer-tain, that duty was clear and simple: defend the chieftain and the clan with his strength of arms and his battle-wit. Now he was chieftain and his sense of duty was split. He still had to care for and defend the Khulinin, but he also had to avenge his father's murder, sustain the honor of the clan, and struggle to maintain peace with the other clans on the plains. To make matters more complicated, he loved a heretical sorceress more than life itself and feared for her safety. He was still ambivalent about sorcery, especially his own talent, yet his love for Gabria was undeniable.

Athlone looked up at the deep black firmament and prayed he had made the right decision to go to Pra Desh. He would choose Guthlac to serve as wer-tain while he was gone. Hopefully the clan gods would watch over the Khulinin until he could return.

The chieftain shook his head and stood up. The decision was made; nothing could be served by worrying the matter to death. There were problems to settle, plans to make, and a journey to begin. For good or ill, he was going to Pra Desh with Gabria.

Calmer now, he strode back down the hill and returned to his quarters in the hall. He thought about going to Piers's tent to see Gabria, but the night was late and she had suffered from the long journey. He decided to wait until morning, when she was rested. He knew he hadn't given her a very pleasant welcome that evening; in the morning he would apologize and make up for his bad temper.

With a yawn, Athlone laid his sword by the bed and settled down on the wool-stuffed mattress. He was asleep in moments, dreaming of Gabria.

4

Gabria was glad to be back in Piers's tent, lying on her own pallet and listening to the familiar sounds of the sleeping camp. Her body was tired, and her thoughts were weary of spinning over the same paths. She wanted to sleep, but she could not. A strange restlessness coursed through her mind and kept her tossing and turning. The girl could not identify the cause of her uneasiness. It did not seem to spring from her own worries. It was a vague anxiety that stirred the deepest levels of her consciousness and kept her on edge throughout the night.

It was near dawn when Gabria was brought upright by a pain that lanced through her abdomen.

"Nara!" she said aloud.

Gabria! The call came clear in her mind. *Please come. It is time.*

The woman paused only long enough to pull on her boots and grab her belt and dagger. She bolted from the tent and ran down to the pastures. Nara was waiting for her by the river. Gabria recognized immediately the signs of approaching delivery. The foal had dropped down toward the birthing canal, and Nara's sides were wet with sweat from her labor.

Without a word, the two walked out of camp and into the hills. They found shelter in a small glade at the bottom of a wooded valley.

Gabria rubbed the black horse's neck and spoke quietly to her as the labor progressed. "The baby is early," the woman said after a while.

Nara breathed deeply before replying, *By a turn of the moon. I should not go running in the mountains before my time.* She trembled while a long contraction rippled through her body.

Gabria's fingers tightened on the black mane as the tremors of pain reached her. "Is it all right?" she asked.

I think so.

They lapsed into silence again, waiting for the natural progression of life. Just before the sun lifted over the hills, Nara lay on the ground. Unlike her first pregnancy, there was no difficulty with the birth. A small, black colt slid neatly out of his mother and lay squirming in his wet sac. Gabria cleared the birthing sac away from his body, wiped out his nostrils, and cut and tied the umbilical cord. Nara climbed to her feet and began to lick him vigorously.

Gabria stood back, tears streaming down her face, and watched in sheer delight as the black foal began to struggle to his feet. The sun rose over the hill, and sunlight poured through the trees. Its warmth invigorated the baby Hunnuli. He tottered to his feet and nuzzled close to his mother for his first breakfast.

Gabria cleaned the glade and went away to bury the remains of the birth and to give Nara time alone with her baby. She smiled to herself as she worked. The baby was alive and Nara was well! The words sang in Gabria's mind. She had not realized how strong her worry had been until it was gone. Happily she returned to the glade. She was so tired, she decided to lie down for just a moment. The woman was asleep in a heartbeat.

In the treld not far away, the hornbearers blew their welcome to the morning sun and the clanspeople began another day. Athlone, dressed in his finest shirt, overtunic, and pants strode down the path to the healer's tent. He jingled the small bells that hung by the entrance.

"Come!" Piers shouted from within. The healer was struggling with a pan of fresh bread when the chieftain entered. Muttering, Piers fumbled the hot pan to the table and dumped a heavy, flat loaf onto a wooden plate. The bread tipped off and fell to the floor.

Laughing, Athlone picked the loaf off the carpet and dropped it back on the plate.

"Thank you," Piers said. He poked at his handiwork. "Look at that. It would break teeth. I will never learn the knack of baking."

Athlone sat on a stool, still chuckling, and said, "You need a woman of your own."

The healer grimaced. "I've had one. They're more trouble than baking my own bread."

The younger man nodded vaguely as his eyes searched the tent for Gabria. Piers took one look at Athlone's gaze and the finery he wore, and realized immediately that this was not a casual visit. He turned back to his hearth and tried to appear natural as he spooned some porridge into a bowl.

"Where is she?" the chief asked.

Piers cast a worried glance at the chief. He poured two cups of ale, brought his bowl to the table, and sat down before he answered. "I don't know. She left in the middle of the night."

Athlone slammed his fist on the table. "Someone is going to have to nail that girl's foot to the ground!"

Piers picked up a spoon and dipped it in his porridge. "Her gear is still here."

"Well, maybe she'll come back for *that*," Athlone replied, glaring at his ale.

Piers glanced up at him. "She always comes back."

"Hmmm. I just wish she'd tell me once in a while where she was going." He sat morosely and watched Piers eat his meal. He was always fascinated at the neat, almost ritualistic way the healer consumed his food. His eating habits and his social manners were the only two things that Piers had not left behind when he had fled Pra Desh eleven years ago. Athlone had never been to the great city, and he had the feeling there was a lot to learn about the people and their customs before he arrived there.

Piers looked up and caught Athlone's eyes. Deliberately he put his spoon down and straightened his thin shoulders. "I have a favor to ask," he said with some effort. "I would like to go with you."

The chief was astonished. "You have sworn more times than there are hairs on a horse's back that you would never return to the city."

Piers nodded. "I know. However, I think your gods would forgive me if I changed my mind. Gabria may need my help. Besides . . ." He shrugged and looked away. "She has taught me a thing or two about facing memories. It is time I go back."

Athlone leaned forward, stunned. As far as he knew, Piers had never told anyone, except perhaps Savaric, why he had left Pra Desh. He had appeared at a clan gathering one summer and followed the Khulinin home. They had been happy to have the skilled healer in their clan and had not pried into his past.

"What about the clan? They will need a healer while you are gone," Athlone said.

"I will ask the healer of the Dangari to send one of his apprentices. He has a man ready to pass his rites."

Athlone stood and rubbed his chin thoughtfully. "All right. You are welcome to come with us." He paused. "How did you know I was going?"

"You could not do otherwise."

Athlone snorted. "And what of the clan I am leaving behind, O wise sage?"

"They will be fine," Piers replied. "It is us I would worry about."

The chieftain laughed without humor and went to the entrance. "We will leave in two days . . . provided Gabria returns in time." He turned and strode out.

Piers watched him go. He missed his friend, Savaric, very much, yet through Gabria he had found some common ground with Athlone. Now the son was becoming as good a friend as the father. The old healer sighed to himself. He could hardly believe he had asked to go to Pra Desh. Even after eleven years he was not certain he was up to facing the old memories and emotions. At least Gabria and Athlone would be with him. He would not have to endure the ordeal alone. He forced down his rising apprehension and went to find a rider willing to take a message to Dangari Treld.

In the meantime, Athlone returned to the hall and the business of planning for the journey. He met with the elders and warriors and told them of his decision. A few were concerned about his leaving, but the majority understood the necessity of finding Branth and avenging the murder of Lord Savaric. Quite a few men volunteered to go with him. He chose Bregan and three other seasoned warriors as an escort and ordered the remainder to stay and obey Guthlac, whom he named wer-tain.

As the meeting continued, Athlone and the elders discussed clan problems. They made plans for the approaching birthing season, when the herds would be having their young, and for the Khulinin's departure for the Tir Samod. Guthlac made several astute suggestions, and Athlone was relieved to see the elders and the warriors listened to the new wer-tain with respect. At least, the chieftain thought, I can feel secure about leaving the clan in Guthlac's capable hands.

By late afternoon, the entire clan knew that their lord was going on a long journey and that Gabria was missing again. Everyone was buzzing about Pra Desh, magic, Branth, and the absent girl. The priest, Thalar, stole from group to group, trying to convince the clanspeople that Gabria's evil was spreading and that she was going to destroy their chief. But the priest's lies were overshadowed by the tale of Gabria's meeting with the King Stallion. Those who had heard the tale the day before spread it all over camp, embellishing the story with every telling. People flocked to the meadows to stare in awe at Eurus, who contentedly grazed before his audience. The speculation grew that Gabria had left to see the Hunnuli herd again. Perhaps, the people said to one another, she would return with more of the horses.

The truth became clear late that afternoon in a way no one quite expected. The clanspeople had not known of Nara's pregnancy before Gabria was banished and had seen little of the mare since her return, so they had not noticed her bulging sides. Thus it was that the news of Gabria and Nara's return swept through the camp like a whirlwind.

Athlone was the first to know of their coming. He was talking to Piers about supplies for the journey when he suddenly stiffened. "Eurus?" he gasped. His eyes went wide, and his handsome face broke into a grin.

"Piers," he cried in delight. "She's coming back. Eurus told me. Nara has had her foal!"

The two men ran through the camp just as an outrider came from the edge of the treld, shouting the news. Clanspeople gathered in the fields to see Gabria, Nara, and the long-legged foal come out of the hills and cross the meadows. Never in the recent memory of the Khulinin had anyone seen a baby Hunnuli.

The foal stared wide-eyed at the crowds, his small ears perked and his whisk-tail twitching. He trotted forward to sniff noses with Eurus. The stallion nickered gently; the foal whinnied in reply. As the three Hunnuli gathered around Gabria and walked with her to the camp, the clan watched, caught up in the wonder of the moment.

Athlone met them on the training field. He swept Gabria into his arms and kissed her soundly. "Don't ever leave me again without telling me where you're going."

Happily she hugged him. "Hello to you, too."

"And you!" the chieftain said, turning to Eurus. "Why didn't you tell me where they were?"

The stallion tossed his head. *You did not ask*.

Gabria laughed. "You'll have to get used to having a Hunnuli around again, Athlone."

The chieftain chose to ignore her remark. He stood with Gabria as the three Hunnuli trotted off to the river and the crowd of excited clanspeople slowly dispersed.

"We're going to leave in a day's time," Athlone said after a while. "Is the foal strong enough to travel?"

Gabria looked at him sharply. "We?"

"I am going with you. So is Piers."

"Piers, too? Blessed be Amara!" She grinned, the relief plain on her face. "Thank you, Athlone. I was afraid I'd have to go alone."

"You've been alone long enough," Athlone replied.

"But what about the council this summer?"

"If Branth and the fon do not cause too much trouble, we'll have enough time to return for the gathering at the Tir Samod." He hesitated, then he drew Gabria close. "Will you marry me before we go?"

She leaned into him, her eyes almost level with his. Her finger gently traced the strong line of his jaw. She had been dreading this question. "Not yet, Athlone. I love you so much. But this journey will be long and dangerous. I'd rather begin our marriage on happier omens. Besides, I want you to be certain of your choice. You are chieftain of the most powerful clan on the plains. I am a convicted sorceress. This journey may give you a chance to know who I really am." Gabria felt her fingers trembling, and she clasped them together tightly behind Athlone's back. "You might change your mind by the time we reach Pra Desh. You should have that chance."

"I know who you are," he protested.

"Are you certain you can spend your life with magic and all of the uncertainty, hatred, and suspicion that go with it?" Gabria asked quietly. Her face was pale and set.

Athlone hesitated, and in that moment Gabria saw the faint shadow of doubt in his eyes. Although she hated to wait, she was glad now she had made that decision.

He looked away, aware that she had seen his doubt. "All right," he said. "I'll wait. If only to satisfy you."

She hugged him again, and the two walked through the camp toward Piers's tent. "What about the colt?" Athlone asked when they stopped by the tent flap.

"I wondered about that, too. He is premature, but Nara says he can easily keep up with your Harachan horses. She insists on going with me."

Athlone glanced away, trying to be casual. "What about Eurus?"

"Oh, he's coming, too," Gabria said, hiding a smile.

"Good. He can help look after that foal. Does the colt have a name?"

"Not yet. Nara told me the foal will name himself when he is ready."

"A son of Boreas," Athlone said with a proud grin. "I can hardly believe it."

The woman looked up into his smiling face, and her hand reached out for his. They went into Piers's tent for the rest of the afternoon.

Clouds were moving in from the northwest and the wind was freshening on the morning Gabria and her party left Khulinin Treld. They gathered in the training field just after day-break to bid farewell to the clan. Khan'di astride his chestnut arrived first, then Piers on his favorite brown mare and Gabria with the three Hunnuli. The chieftain and his four hearthguard warriors came last with the pack horses. Bregan rode his gelding, Stubs, and Athlone was mounted on his gray Harachan stallion.

Every member of the party was dressed in plain, unadorned clothing and cloaks of undyed wool. Khan'di had stressed the importance of secrecy, warning the chief that the fon's spies must not learn of Gabria's journey to Pra Desh. Athlone agreed, for he knew how fast news could travel on the plains. Even the golden banner that usually went with the chieftain whenever he ventured from the treld was left behind.

When the travelers were gathered together, the entire clan came to see them off. Only Thalar was conspicuous by his absence, though the priest of Sorh and the priestess of Amara came to bless the people leaving the treld.

Lord Athlone rode before the Khulinin and raised his arms until the crowd fell quiet. In the customary speech to the clan, he reminded them of Savaric's murder and his duty as Savaric's son to seek wiergeld, or blood money, for the murder of his father. Since he wanted to minimize the taint of sorcery on his journey and leave his people in a propitious mood, he told the clan only of the fabulous city he would be visiting and of the tales he would have to tell when he returned. No mention was made of the *Book of Matrah* or Branth's more recent crimes.

Cantrell stepped forward and sang a boisterous song of leave-taking that had the Khulinin singing and clapping as the party rode out of the valley. Many of the men rode with them for a time, calling out their farewells, while the rest of the clan stayed behind and cheered them on their way.

Before long, the travelers passed the last of the foothills and came out into the open country. A light rain began to fall, and the accompanying riders turned back for home. The party pushed on in single file, their cloaks pulled tight against the cold wind and rain. The pleasant leave-taking was behind them, and each person was lost in his or her own thoughts of the journey ahead.

By afternoon the rain eased, and the clouds raced south across the sky. Gently sloping hills, clad in gray-green grass, unfolded under the horses' hooves and rolled endlessly beyond the horizon. The riders shook out their cloaks and relaxed a little on their mounts.

They were riding northeast, following the Goldrine River. They planned to parallel the Goldrine as far as its junction with the Isin River, then strike east to intersect the old caravan route that ran north along the Sea of Tannis.

The caravan route ran north and south, and dated back to the days before the clans roamed the plains. It had been made by the invading armies of the Eagle, the same men who had built the fortress, Ab-Chakan. It was still used as a major overland route between the clans' trelds, the Turic tribes in the south, and the Five Kingdoms in the north. At the end of the road lay the golden city of Pra Desh.

Gabria had never been to Pra Desh, though she had heard about the city from her father, who had visited there once, and from Piers. She knew that Pra Desh was the capital city of Calah, one of the Five Kingdoms in the Alardarian Alliance and that a person titled "the fon" ruled the city's government. She knew little else.

Piers had told Gabria once that the latest fon had poisoned her husband and had pinned the blame on Piers's daughter. His daughter had been tortured and executed as a sorceress. Sick at heart, Piers had turned his back on Calah and Pra Desh. He had never returned to his homeland or the city of his birth, and his sense of rage and injustice had been deeply buried behind a facade of resigned sadness.

Gabria studied Piers's back as he rode ahead of her. Then she nudged Nara forward to walk beside the healer's horse. The old brown mare nickered pleasantly to Nara, who towered over her, and the Hunnuli answered in kind.

Piers smiled wanly at Gabria. He hated getting wet. "I suppose it is too late to change my mind."

"Not if you don't mind a long ride back to the treld."

He glanced over his shoulder to the dark line of stormclouds and rain that could still be seen behind them. "I don't think so. It's drier here."

"For now." Gabria studied her friend for a moment before she asked, "Piers, what is the city like?"

He grimaced, surprised by her question. "What, Pra Desh?" He gestured to Khan'di ahead of them. "Ask him."

The old anger and grief were very clear in his voice. Gabria was startled by the intensity. "Do you know him from before?" she inquired.

"Yes, and he knows me." Piers glared at the man's straight back. "He is the son of one of the wealthiest merchant families in Pra Desh. He was a courtier and my good friend. He is also cunning, ambitious, and clever. He was supposed to be the fon's taster, but on the night the fon was poisoned, Khan'di fell conveniently ill. I was nursing him instead of dining with the fon." Piers's fingers tightened around the saddle horn. "I could have saved the fon if I had been there." He shook his head sadly. "I've always wondered if Khan'di deliberately feigned his illness."

"I'm sorry," Gabria said, knowing how useless that sounded.

The healer shook himself and laughed. "Why? It is I who should be sorry. I came on this journey to face those people, to remember my daughter, and to banish my inner hatred. I am off to a poor start." He fell silent.

Gabria thought Piers had forgotten her question. She was about to repeat it when he drew out a small wineskin and took a long swallow. He slammed the stopper back in and looked up at Gabria. His pale gray eyes were twinkling.

"You asked about Pra Desh?" His hands flew out in a grand gesture. "The queen of the East. There is no other place like it in the world. It is huge, sprawling, magnificent! It is a city of incredible squalor and unbelievable wealth; of palaces, teeming wharves, markets, bazaars, and tenements."

Gabria stared at the healer, surprised by his sudden change of mood. She rarely saw Piers so animated.

"Pra Desh is the center for all trade and commerce in the East, you know," he noted. "Every road, caravan route, and shipping lane leads to Pra Desh. You can find anything available in the known world in that city. There are schools of great learning, libraries, academies of art, and theaters. The city is rich with artisans, philosophers, explorers, merchants, seamen, teachers, noblemen—and overflowing with slaves, peasants, and criminals." Piers laughed. "Gabria, you have never seen anything like it."

The girl tried to form a picture of this incredible place in her mind. "It sounds so . . . big," she said lamely.

"You have nothing to compare to it, nothing that could help you fathom its size. The entire population of the eleven clans would be lost in the old part of the city."

Gabria's mouth went slack. It suddenly occurred to her that, not only was she riding into a hornet's nest, it was much bigger than she expected. How could *she* do anything useful in a city so big? "Well, if they have all of those people, why do they need me?" she asked, exasperated.

"Ask him," Piers replied, pointing at the nobleman again. "He's the one who made the demands."

"Khan'di!" Gabria shouted. The other men looked around in surprise, but the Pra Deshian pretended he had not heard.

Piers looked annoyed. "I'm sorry. In Pra Desh, women must always address a man by his full name. To do less is to show a lack of respect."

Gabria gritted her teeth. "Khan'di Kadoa, may I please speak with you?"

At that, the nobleman half-turned and nodded once.

While Nara trotted forward to join the other rider, Gabria tried to put on a pleasant and sociable expression. She knew very little about this man, and what she did know she was not certain she liked. He was of medium height with a stout figure turning to fat. A mustache hid his thin mouth, and his shrewd eyes were almost lost in the folds of his ruddy skin. He was often polite to the point of arrogance and had the confidence of a man who was used to being obeyed.

Gabria could not help but wonder what his true motives were for asking her to come to Pra Desh. Was he setting an elaborate trap, vying for his own power and influence, or was he truly concerned for the welfare of his city? His hidden motives would not change her decision, but Gabria would be happier if she knew what to expect from him.

Since Gabria did not know how to salute the emissary and it was difficult to bow on horseback, she inclined her head politely to the man. Khan'di looked up at the sorceress on the huge black horse and returned her greeting.

She threw her hood back and let the wind tug at her hair. "I was talking to Piers a moment ago," she said. "He told me how big your city has become."

"It is the largest city in the Five Kingdoms, perhaps in the world," Khan'di answered proudly. "I've heard that Macar is bigger, but that was several years ago, before their tin mines began to decline. Since then their trade has fallen slightly. Pra Desh, of course, has widened its influence throughout the Sea of Tannis. Our merchant fleet is the largest and . . ."

Gabria sighed to herself as he talked on. It was the most she had heard him say in four days. She smiled and held up her hand. "Khan'di Kadoa, excuse me, but you are speaking beyond my experience. I know little about Pra Desh or its shipping."

"Oh, of course. Forgive me," he said. "Was there something in particular you wanted to know?"

"I was curious," Gabria continued. "Why, in a city so large, could you find no one to remove Branth? Why did you ask me?"

"Because," Khan'di said, irony edging his words, "sorcery is forbidden in Pra Desh just as it is on the plains. We do not have the clans' intense hatred for the arcane, but it was more convenient and safer to outlaw it. To outlaw such practices keeps magic-wielding foreigners from coming into the city and disrupting the trade."

Gabria straightened and gazed at the man in surprise. "Foreigners? I thought your people could use sorcery, too."

"No. Only the clanspeople or those with clan blood in their ancestry have the power to cast spells. Many wise men have studied this unusual inherited trait, but no one has discovered why only the clans have such power." He lifted his hand eloquently. "To put it bluntly, you were the only one available."

"Wonderful," Gabria muttered. "All right. If I am to go to Pra Desh as a sorceress, what guarantees do I have for a safe passage? Will I face Branth with my magic, only to be put in prison if I win?"

Khan'di reached into his saddle bag and pulled out a scroll sealed with the stamp of his family. He held it up. "The fon rules the roads of Calah, but within Pra Desh *I* am patron of the powerful merchants' guild and head of the most respected and influential family in the city. If you are successful in routing Branth, you will be paid handsomely from my treasury and escorted with honor back to the borders of Calah. I give you my word as a Kadoa."

Gabria was skeptical. "What of your fon? She will not be pleased to lose her personal sorcerer."

Khan'di laughed once, a sharp, bitter bark. "Leave her to me."

Gabria studied him for a long moment. It was still possible the Pra Deshian was leading her into a trap. If not for the warning of the King Stallion, she might not have accepted Khan'di's plea so readily. Now, as she examined his fleshy face and watched the way his hands tightened around the reins in suppressed anger, she thought that he was probably telling the truth, at least as he saw it.

"That will have to do," she finally answered. "Do not go back on your word." She plucked the scroll out of his fingers, nodded once again, and turned Nara away.

The man watched her go, his mouth pulled tight. The woman was ignorant, but she was not stupid. He would have to tread carefully with her. And her Hunnuli. Khan'di could not swear to it, but just before the big mare turned, he thought he saw an almost human glint of warning in her dark eyes.

5

For five days the party followed the Goldrine River as it flowed northeast then east across the grasslands of Ramtharin, toward its junction with the Isin River. Ignoring the cold winds and incessant rains, the riders traveled fast from dawn to dusk, stopping only at noon to eat and rest the horses. True to Nara's word, the foal had no trouble keeping up with the other horses and seemed to thrive on his mother's milk and the constant exercise. The people slowly settled into the routine of the trail, too, as their muscles adjusted to the long hours of riding and their minds grew accustomed to each other's constant company.

Gabria divided her time between Athlone, Piers, and Khan'di. Although she did not care for the nobleman from Pra Desh, he enjoyed talking to her and was a fountain of information and advice. While Piers told her about Pra Desh's history, culture, and society, Khan'di filled her in on the changes that had been taking place in the government, economy, and politics during the past few years.

"The kingdom of Calah is ruled by a king," he explained one afternoon, "but the capital city, Pra Desh, is ruled by the fon."

"The king allows that?" Gabria asked in surprise.

Khan'di chuckled. "He usually doesn't have much choice. The fon controls the vast flow of goods to and from the Five Kingdoms, so he or she holds more wealth and power than the king. It is not the easiest of situations. There has been constant feuding between the king and the fon for generations."

"Where is your king now?"

The nobleman's brow lowered in anger. "About eleven years ago, the king of Calah died in a mysterious accident, leaving a son too young to rule. Fast on the heels of that disaster, the fon was poisoned. His body wasn't even cold when his wife snatched control of the city *and* the kingdom. She still holds them both—in the name of the young prince, of course."

"Why hasn't the prince reclaimed his throne?"

"No one knows where he is. The fon held him prisoner for a few years, but we have not seen him recently. I'm afraid she may have disposed of him."

The nobleman fell silent after that and rode with his expression frozen and his eyes as hard as rock.

The next day, during another talk, he told Gabria more about Branth's arrival in Pra Desh.

"The man was a fool," Khan'di said in disgust. "He ensconced himself in a big house in one of the wealthiest districts of the city and began flaunting himself in the highest social circles. He made no se-cret of his talent as a magic-wielder, but he was smart enough not to use his power openly. Then odd things began to happen. Gold was stolen out of locked safes, gem shipments disappeared, and ships sank in the harbor for no apparent reason. Men who angered Branth were financially ruined." Khan'di shook his head. "By the time someone tied the crimes to Branth it was too late. The fon sent a detachment of her own guards to arrest him, but he'd had plenty of time to set up his defenses. His house was fortified and his power too great to over-come. He blasted the captain of the guard with a strange blue fire."

"The Trymian Force," Gabria said softly.

"The what?"

"It's a force drawn from the magic-wielder's own energy." She grimaced. "It can be very deadly."

Khan'di nodded. "It certainly was. Branth wiped out an entire company of heavily armed men with it."

"How did the fon finally capture him?"

"The way she takes anything—through guile. She played on Branth's vanities and lured him to the palace with the promise of an alliance." The man broke off and surprised Gabria by glancing over his shoulder at Piers riding behind him. She thought for just a moment there was a flicker of regret in his dark eyes.

"I suppose the healer told you," Khan'di continued, "that the fon is an expert at poison?"

"He mentioned it," she replied carefully.

"Well, she used a special poison of her own concoction to gain control of Branth's mind and render him helpless. He still has his talent, but she has the book and controls his actions."

Gabria looked pale. She despised Branth, but it was hard to imagine the powerful, ambitious chieftain trapped in the grip of an insidious poison. It gave her the shivers. "Can she make him do anything?"

"The man is a total prisoner."

"What will happen to him if we take him away from the fon and her poisons? Will he regain his will?"

"I don't know or care. Just remove him or kill him." Khan'di twisted his mustache, a habit that showed when he was agitated. "We *must* get him away from the fon before she invades Portane. If she attempts that, the entire Alardarian Alliance will shatter. Pra Desh will be ruined! I—"

Nara suddenly tossed her head, interrupting him. *Gabria, someone comes.* The mare whirled and faced a hill they had just passed. Eurus neighed a warning to the men, and the party drew in close to Nara and came to a halt.

At that moment, a lone horseman appeared on the crest of the hill and waved to them in apparent excitement. He was too far away to recognize, yet they all saw he was not a clansman. He was a Turic tribesman from the southern desert. Gabria glanced worriedly at Athlone, and the hearthguard gathered around their lord, their hands resting on their swords.

The horse came toward them at a full gallop, his ears pinned back and his tail flying. The man leaned back in his stirrups and greeted the party with a wild, high-pitched ululation. The afternoon sun glittered on the great curved sword by his side, and the burnoose he wore flew out behind him like a flag.

He reined his horse to a snorting, prancing stop directly in front of Nara and Gabria and swept off his hood. "Sorceress!" he cried. "I have been looking everywhere for you!"

Gabria was so surprised she could only stare down at the man. He was young and lean, with the dark skin and brown eyes common to Turic tribesman. His black hair was worn in an intricate knot behind his head. His face was clean-shaven, revealing the strong, narrow lines of his jaw and cheekbones. Gabria thought he was compellingly handsome, and he met her confused stare with a bold, masculine look of pleasure.

He ignored the other men, who were watching him with varying degrees of curiosity and wariness, and dismounted from his horse. He came to stand by Gabria's foot. "You are Gabria of Clan Corin," he stated, looking into her face. "I know it. I am Sayyed Raid-Ja, seventh son of Dultar of Sharja. I, too, am a magic-wielder. I would like to travel with you and learn your sorcery."

Gabria felt her jaw drop.

"Absolutely not!" Athlone thundered.

"Why not?" Sayyed asked reasonably, turning to the chief for the first time. "Lord Athlone, forgive me. I was so pleased to find the sorceress that I forgot my duty to you. Greetings!"

Athlone nodded curtly. He had taken an instant dislike to this man, and he did not appreciate the way the Turic was looking at Gabria. "Good day to you, son of Dultar. Please stand aside. We must be on our way."

"That's impossible," Gabria mumbled.

"What?" Sayyed and Athlone said at once.

The woman quickly gathered her wits and turned to the tribesman. "How can you be a magic-wielder? Only clan blood carries that talent."

Sayyed flashed a grin at her. "My mother was of Clan Ferganan. She was captured one day near a waterhole by my father. He sought a slave to sell in the market that day, but it was he who became a slave to a wife and twelve children."

"You are half-clan?" Piers exclaimed.

Khan'di shrugged. "It is enough."

"How do you know you are a magic-wielder?" Athlone demanded.

A mischievous twinkle danced in Sayyed's glance. He stooped down, picked up a handful of dirt, and tossed it into the air. The earth and stones flew high, then exploded into a cloud of shimmering blue butterflies.

The unexpected fluttering startled Khan'di's gelding. It snorted in fear, spun around, and slammed into Athlone's stallion. The Harachan horses picked up the gelding's panic and leaped into a frenzied attempt to escape.

"Of all the stupid things to do," Athlone yelled from the back of his bucking stallion. "Get rid of those things!"

Sayyed spoke a command and the butterflies vanished. He tried to look contrite as the riders calmed their mounts.

He is a magic-wielder, Nara told Gabria, *though how much use butterflies will be against Branth I cannot say.*

"All right," Gabria said, trying not to laugh. "You are who you say you are. Why do you want to come with me?"

Sayyed threw his arms wide in excitement. "To learn! My father has enough sons to bother with, so I can do what I want. I want you to teach me about sorcery."

"It looks like you know enough already," Khan'di remarked dryly.

"Only a trifle I have learned by accident. I want to know more."

"No," Gabria said. She was thoroughly taken aback. "I can't teach you, I hardly know enough myself."

"Well, then, I might help you. They told me at Khulinin Treld that you are going to battle another sorcerer. Let me come. If you can't teach me, maybe I can help."

"I don't think . . ." Gabria began.

"Isn't sorcery forbidden by the Turic?" Athlone interrupted in annoyance.

Sayyed locked his gaze with Athlone's and said, "Yes. And since I have been outlawed from my people, I decided that I should die doing what I was born to do."

His words and their obvious sincerity touched Gabria to the core, stirring the similar feelings she had about magic. To hear another person state a desire for sorcery so honestly was all she needed to win her trust. The King Stallion had advised her to take other humans with her. Why not another magic-wielder?

She held out her hand palm up. "Come, Sayyed Raid-Ja. If you're so certain, maybe I can use your help."

"No!" Athlone snarled, but his protest was lost in Sayyed's shout of glee as he clasped Gabria's hand to seal the deal.

Nara began to move, and the whole party fell in beside her, leaving Athlone fuming on his mount. The chieftain kicked his horse forward and caught up with Gabria. To him, her expression looked maddeningly pleased.

The chief gritted his teeth. Unless the Turic changed his mind and left, it looked like they were stuck with him. The man had already swung his horse in behind Nara and was whistling a tune to himself. Short of driving him off at sword-point, there was nothing Athlone could do about him.

"What possessed you to invite him along?" Athlone said coldly to Gabria. "You don't need his help. And we don't have time to molly-coddle an irresponsible boy."

Gabria was stung. Her eyes flashing dangerously, she leaned over and snapped, "The King Stallion told me to bring others with me. I am following his advice."

"Why him? He's a Turic. He'll just be in the way," Athlone replied, his fury mounting.

Gabria glared at him, hurt and angry. On this journey she needed
all the support and trust Athlone could give her. She could not understand why he was being so vehement about this stranger. "Because he
sought me out. Because he cares about what he is. Because he is a
magic-wielder and I may need him!" Her last word broke off sharply,
and she lapsed into silence.

Athlone studied her for a long time, watching the way her blond
hair curled around her ear, how her small nose turned up slightly at
the end, and how the freckles on her cheeks stood out when she was
angry. She was so lovely it made his heart sing and yet, sometimes she
was so strange and distant to him; he did not know how to reach her.
All he could do was try to understand, but that hardly seemed enough.

The chieftain let out a long breath. "Perhaps you're right," he told
Gabria, his voice still sharp with anger. "Not all magic-wielders are
willing to use their powers. One like the Turic might be useful."

"You have the talent, too, Athlone," she said quietly.

"And no desire to use it." The chief shifted his weight and kicked
his horse forward. For the rest of the afternoon he rode the point, well
ahead of Gabria, Sayyed, and the others.

Gabria and Athlone had little chance to bridge the rift over the
next few days. Gabria felt she was in the right in their dispute over the
Turic's presence and did not try to approach the chieftain with apologies or contrition. Athlone, in turn, had few opportunities to talk to
her. Every time he tried, he was called away by the warriors or interrupted by Piers or Khan'di.

Sayyed did not help matters, either. The young Turic made himself at home with the company. He laughed and joked with the warriors—Secen, Keth, and Valar; helped Bregan hunt for meat; talked
medicine with Piers; and discussed the merits of fabrics and spices
from the South with Khan'di. But he saved the best of his attentions
for Gabria. He used every chance he had to be near her, whether
Athlone was there or not.

The sorceress was resting upon Nara's back one afternoon while
the mare paused for a drink. Seeing an opportunity to talk to Gabria
alone, Athlone waved his men on and went to join her and the Hunnuli on the riverbank. She looked at him curiously and a little warily,
as if expecting the outbreak of another argument.

"Gabria, I—" he began. Then he stopped, for it dawned on him
that he really did not know what he wanted to say to her.

"Lord Athlone!" Bregan yelled. "Secen is signaling."

The chieftain cursed under his breath and looked for the warrior, who was riding the point. Secen was atop a far hill, signaling the presence of other riders. Athlone left Gabria and hurried to investigate. By the time he checked the two riders Secen had spotted and made sure they had not seen his party, Gabria had joined Sayyed.

The chief's face darkened with anger as he watched the two of them together. Sayyed had found some early wildflowers and had made a crown for Gabria. They were talking and laughing like old friends as she fastened the ring of flowers in her hair.

Athlone spurred his horse away so they could not see the doubt and anger on his face.

On the evening of the twelfth day, Gabria and her companions reached the Tir Samod—the name given to the holy joining of the Goldrine and Isin Rivers—where the clans of Valorian had gathered every summer for countless generations. They arrived before sunset and made camp in the grove of cottonwood trees near the place where the council tent usually stood. To the clansmen the meadows looked empty and strange without the big camps, the bustling market, the huge council tent, and the throngs of people, dogs, and horses that crowded the site every year. Except for the ripple and rush of the two rivers and the wind sweeping through the bare trees, the place was quiet and peaceful.

For the first time in several days the sky was cloudless and the sun set with the promise of another clear day. After the evening meal, the warriors settled down by the fire to clean their weapons and tack. Piers examined his medical supplies to see if any had been spoiled by the intermittent rains of the past twelve days. Khan'di sat on his cushion and cleaned his nails.

For a short time, Gabria watched Nara and her baby as the colt frolicked in some shallow water. Beyond the horses, the gold light of sunset illuminated the circle of standing stones on the holy island of the gods in the middle of the rivers. Gabria looked at the island and then beyond to the far banks.

Every year when the clans gathered, each one encamped on the same site. The Corins had always made their camp to the north of the island on a wide, grassy bend of the Isin.

With little thought, Gabria took off her boots and waded across the gentle rapids of the Isin to the opposite side. She climbed the low bank and meandered slowly toward the trees that identified her clan's ground. As in the treld far to the north, there was little here to mark the passing of the Corins: a few old fire pits, a refuse pile that would last only until the next flood, and some cut trees. Like the Corins' meadow, there was also a burial mound. It had been left by the Khulinin when they camped on the Corin ground the previous summer.

Gabria wandered to the mound and stood gazing at the one spear and helmet that still adorned the single grave. The rustling of the grass alerted her to the presence of someone else in the campsite. She turned, smiling, thinking it was Athlone.

"Someone you know?" Sayyed asked.

The woman shook her head and pushed her disappointment aside. She had wanted Athlone, but Sayyed was good company, too. In the few days she had known him he had already become a close friend, someone with whom she felt comfortable and happy. She crossed her arms and said, "I didn't know him except by name. He was Pazric, second wer-tain of the Khulinin. He was the first to be deliberately murdered by sorcery in over two hundred years."

"Oh? I hadn't heard about him. Tell me."

"Lord Medb killed him during a council meeting of the chiefs last summer. It was the first time Medb displayed his powers."

Sayyed stared down at the mound. "That must have been terrible," he said with sincerity.

Gabria turned away. All at once she was overwhelmed by memories of that harrowing, event-filled day—the day Pazric had died; the day she had attended the council to accuse Medb; the day Savaric had forced Lord Medb to reveal his sorcery. Her throat tightened, and she blinked as the light of sunset blurred and shimmered through sudden tears.

Quickly Sayyed put his arm around her waist. He was rather short for a Turic and Gabria was tall for a clanswoman, so their heads were level as he pulled her close. She leaned against him and drew solace from the comfort of his strong arms and the warmth of his presence.

Her sadness slowly disappeared until her mouth curved up in a faint smile. "You remind me of my brother, Gabran."

Sayyed masked a grimace with a chuckle. "Why?" he asked, hiding his disappointment. "Was your brother handsome?"

She laughed. "Yes, and kind, as strong and cunning as a wolf. He could also make me laugh." She sighed softly. "I loved him very much."

He tightened his arm around her. They stood for a long while in the afterglow of twilight, silhouetted against the pale gold luminescence that hung in the western sky.

From his place by the fire, Athlone watched the two distant figures and felt his heart grow heavy. The Turic was intruding deeper and deeper into Gabria's life. He had only been with the travelers for seven days and already she was fascinated by him, this energetic tribesman who plainly worshiped her. A boil of jealousy erupted in Athlone's mind, fed by his pride and uncertainty.

To the chieftain, the most frustrating thing was his own confusion. His relationship with Gabria was still new to him—they never seemed to get a chance to let their feelings develop without something getting in the way. Now this Turic was with them, and Athlone was no longer sure where he stood. Worst of all, he didn't know what to do about it! Gabria was intelligent, self-reliant, and determined. She had proven her courage and worth ten times over. If she wished to give her love to Sayyed instead of him, then Athlone felt she had earned that right. Gabria had suffered enough heartache and pain without being forced into a relationship she no longer desired. Of course, that did not mean Athlone had to like being put aside.

He slammed the sword he was cleaning into its scabbard and strode out into the darkness. It was easy to tell himself that he could let her go if she chose to leave, but the thought of losing her was tearing him apart. Without thinking, he wandered to the small field where the horses grazed. There he stood, staring into the night, searching for the familiar shape of his old friend, Boreas.

The search was futile, and Athlone knew it; Boreas had been slain in the final battle with Medb the previous summer. That didn't lessen the chieftain's need for his old steed, though. Just as Nara was Gabria's friend and confidant, Boreas had been his companion and advisor.

Athlone frowned and readied himself to return to camp, but something moving in the darkness stopped him. It was the great black bulk of a Hunnuli, a stallion like Boreas. The chieftain's heart leaped with hope and fear. *His ghost, perhaps, returning from the dead to aid me when I most need his advice?*

The Hunnuli came to his side, but it was not Athlone's long-dead steed. An unfamiliar pair of wise eyes gleamed at him, and a deep, soothing voice said, *I am not Boreas*, Eurus told him. *But I am here.*

Thankfully the man leaned against the big horse and ran his hand through the stallion's long, thick mane. He stood, stewing over his problem, his mind working like a boiling pot with bits of thought and feeling bubbling to the surface faster than he could follow them. He loved Gabria and did not want to lose her, yet he did not know how to win her back.

On the heels of those thoughts came the guilty notion that, perhaps, it would be better if he didn't win her back. She was a sorceress. She should be with other magic-wielders, people like Sayyed who would appreciate and support her talent. Athlone was chieftain of the largest and most respected clan on the plains. Even if Gabria survived this journey and the clan chieftains changed the laws forbidding sorcery, there would always be suspicion, distrust, and hatred for magic-wielders. He was not completely sure he was ready to accept the controversy and the constant battle for acceptance.

With that thought, a bubble of remorse boiled out of his mind. *He* was a magic-wielder, too. But it was so much easier to ignore that truth, to let Gabria go, and to live peacefully as a mere chieftain with his clan—like his father and his father's father before him.

Athlone twisted the black mane into his fingers. He knew full well he couldn't take that path and live with himself. No, winning Gabria's heart was the important thing; somehow he would have to find a way to reconcile himself with his talent. If only he knew what to do.

He shook his head in frustration and pushed himself away from the Hunnuli.

The black horse nudged Athlone's chest. *Sometimes the heart speaks clearer than the mind, lord chieftain.*

Athlone laughed humorlessly. "And sometimes they argue unmercifully." He patted the horse and went back to the camp. After a word with the sentry, he retired to his small traveling tent. For Athlone, it was a very long night.

6

Gabria and Nara stood in rippling grass on the point of a high bluff and looked down on the green plains below. The woman shielded her eyes from the noon sun and peered downhill to the caravan trail that wound over the rolling grasslands like a giant snake. The route was not like the stone road near the fortress of Ab-Chakan. It was really nothing more than a dirt path worn into the ground by years of constant use. Nevertheless, it was wide and well marked, and the hooves of countless pack animals had pounded the surface to a rock-hard consistency. In some places the wagons and traders' carts had cut wheel ruts several handspans deep.

Even now, as Gabria looked up the road, she could see the dust kicked up by a distant merchant caravan heading north toward Pra Desh. She glanced toward the south. The semi-arid high plains had gradually dropped down in elevation as Gabria's party had journeyed east, and the rough grasses and shrubs had given way to lush meadows, scattered copses of trees, and small sparkling streams.

Coming up beside her, Bregan sat back in his saddle and stretched his legs. "It's good to see that road," he commented. "We should be about half way to Calah."

"We are," Khan'di noted as he joined them. "But we need to be closer. We've got to get to Pra Desh within twenty days."

"Are you tiring of our journey already?" Piers asked in an icy tone.

Gabria glanced irritably at the healer as the rest of the men came up the hill. Piers and Khan'di had remained bitterly polite to each other, but their poorly hidden animosity was beginning to annoy her. She sighed and leaned her arms on Nara's mane. After twenty days of constant traveling they all needed a change—especially Athlone. Gabria shot a look at the chieftain.

It was obvious something was bothering him. He was cool and distant to her, spoke to Sayyed only when he had to, and was short to everyone else. Gabria had tried several times to talk to him, but it was difficult to find time for privacy on the trail, and Athlone seemed to avoid her in night camp. After days of being ignored, Gabria was hurt and confused. It was much easier to deal with Sayyed. He was always there, warm and comforting with his ready smile and his easy wit.

Gabria could not help but wonder if Athlone had decided at last that he did not want her. The thought made her half-ill with dread. She had given him time to make up his mind, but deep in her heart she had always believed he would finally come to accept her for everything she was. Now she was not so certain. She fought down the queasy feeling in her stomach and tried to dredge up some hope.

The one good thing to come out of the journey was Athlone's friendship with Eurus. Little by little, the man was spending more time with the horse, grooming him, feeding him special tidbits, or just talking to him late at night. The special bond between a Hunnuli and its rider was beginning to form. Gabria was pleased for Athlone's sake. She decided it would be better if she did not interfere. Eurus knew what he was doing.

She pulled her cloak closer about her shoulders. The sun was shining, but the early spring winds were cold and damp with approaching rain. For to the northwest a gray line of clouds was forming along a storm front that would bring rain by nightfall.

Piers looked at the clouds and shivered. He had a bad cold, despite all of his precautions. "I wish we had time to stop at Jehanan Treld. I would like to be under a real tent before that rain hits," he muttered.

The company urged their horses downhill and joined the great caravan route to the north. With luck, Gabria thought, we will be in Pra Desh in another fifteen to twenty days.

A few hours later, the party was riding through a narrow creek bed lined with eroded gullies and budding trees. Bregan suddenly held up his hand and brought the party to a stop. Athlone cantered his horse forward. The others stayed back and watched as Bregan pointed to a far hill where a group of horsemen were coming down the slope.

The chieftain rode back, smiling for the first time in days. "We have visitors," he told them cheerfully.

Bregan trotted ahead to meet the seven riders cantering toward the road. They were led by a horseman holding aloft the dark red banner of the Jehanan chieftain, Sha Umar.

The two groups met along the road. Sha Umar and Athlone greeted each other like old friends while the Jehanan warriors accompanying their lord saluted the Khulinin and stared in surprised awe at the three Hunnuli.

Lord Sha Umar grinned through his neatly trimmed beard at Gabria and saluted her. "Greetings, fair lady. I see you have increased your number of black horses."

The sorceress returned his smile. She had always liked the Jehanan chief, for he had been one of the few lords to support her at the chiefs' council after Medb's death. She noticed his arm was still stiff from the wound he had received in the battle at the fortress, but his strong, tanned face was as healthy as ever, and his robust voice left no doubt as to his power and authority.

"Athlone," he boomed. "You should have sent word you were coming! When one of my outriders told me he had spotted you on the road, I didn't believe him. I had to come out here to see for myself."

Athlone laughed. "My apologies, Sha Umar, but we're traveling fast. We hadn't planned to stop."

"At least stay the night. The treld is not far. Besides—" he pointed to the sky "—there's a storm coming."

The Khulinin chief followed his gesture to the dark clouds. "I suppose we could use some supplies and a good night's sleep."

"Done!" Sha Umar exclaimed. He beamed with pleasure. "We don't have time for a feast, but I can promise you a good meal and a dry tent. Come."

The two chiefs rode ahead, side by side, and the others fell in behind.

Sha Umar lowered his voice so only Athlone could hear. "You are riding fast and without your cloaks. Your mission must be important."

"Yes," Athlone stated flatly.

"Would it have anything to do with Branth?"

Athlone assessed his friend for a moment before he answered. "Perhaps. But we do not want our journey to become common news."

"That's what I thought. Good. We can't leave Branth loose with Medb's old tome."

Athlone agreed. "The clans couldn't stand another war."

"Exactly. What can we do about that blasted book?"

"What do you mean?" the Khulinin asked carefully.

Sha Umar slapped the horn of his saddle. "That tome! It's caused nothing but trouble from the day it was found. What if you take it away from Branth and someone else gets his hands on it?" He paused as if embarrassed. "What would Gabria do if she had it?"

Athlone froze. "What are you implying?" he demanded, his voice harsh.

"Magic can corrupt, Athlone. It's simply a fact of human nature. That much power could lead even the purest to stray into greed, self-ishness, cruelty, or vanity. Gabria is controlling her powers now, but what if that book of knowledge fell into her hands? How would she react? What would she do?" He looked at his friend. "More to the point, what would *you* do?"

Athlone was silent for a long while. When he finally answered, his voice was deeply troubled. "By the gods, I don't know."

"You'd better think about that on your way to find Branth," said Sha Umar.

The Khulinin chief looked away, and the two men, without another word, left the road and led the party east toward Jehanan Treld. The winter camp of Clan Jehanan was only a few leagues away, sheltered in a wide, green valley not far from the Sea of Tannis. The Jehanan numbered several hundred, and their clan was rich in pride and tradition. Although their treld was close to the sea and they often fished and gathered food in its waters, they remained stock breeders and horsemen who followed their herds across the plains in the summer. They were fiercely loyal to their chieftain, devoted to each other, and hospitable to guests.

The Jehanan happily greeted Athlone and his companions, and they recognized Gabria from the summer before. Because of their gratitude to her for their survival, they stifled their fears and suspicions of her powers and welcomed her as befitted the lady of Clan Corin. They gave her the finest guest tent and a serving girl to tend to her needs. A bag of the clan's best oats was their gift for Nara. They were all amazed by the black colt and clustered around him in a distant but admiring circle.

Gabria was pleased by their efforts and, for her part, she hid her weapons, put on her skirts, and tried to blend in with the jovial crowd.

That night the travelers joined Sha Umar in the chief's big hall, a long, low building crafted of local stone and driftwood. The Jehanan chieftain was still unmarried, so his sisters served as hostesses and skillfully supervised the serving girls and the food.

The lord stinted nothing for his friends and had his finest wine brought out and the best of his remaining delicacies set before his guests. Because it was early spring, there was very little fresh food to offer. Still, the larders and storerooms of the treld yielded dried fish, sugared fruits, honey, bread, cheese, pickled gulls' eggs, and shellfish brought from the sea that day.

Gabria was delighted with the fare. Her clan had never traveled near the Sea of Tannis and had no access to seafood. She happily feasted on clams, crabs, and gulls' eggs and washed her meal down with the fine white wine.

As soon as the chief's meal was cleared away, other clan members gathered in the hall. They pushed the benches and trestle tables aside and cleared a space in the center of the hall. The clan's bard brought out his pipes and invited several other men to join him with their drums. The torches and lamps were lit as the dancing began.

For a while, Gabria watched the dancers and clapped her hands to the music. For the first time in days, she felt comfortable, warm, and full. She drank wine freely, nibbled on the sweet cakes and dried fruits that were being passed around, and relished every note of the exciting, happy music. Then, before she realized what he was doing, Sayyed pulled her to her feet and whisked her into the boisterous dance. She barely had time to be surprised at the Turic's knowledge of the clan's dances before he whirled her away to the rhythm of the pipe and drums.

From his seat by Sha Umar's dais, Athlone leaned back and watched the pair dance the intricate steps. He had been drinking the Jehanan's strong wine steadily and was unaware that his pain and his feelings were plain on his face.

Sha Umar glanced at his friend and followed Athlone's stricken gaze to the fair young woman moving through the crowd of dancers. The Khulinin had been closed-mouthed and irritable all evening. Now Sha Umar was beginning to understand why.

"You have not married the Corin yet," the Jehanan chief said bluntly.

Athlone shook his head and drained his cup to the dregs. He held the horn cup out for more. "She was banished from the clan for six months. When she returned, we left for Pra Desh," he replied.

Sha Umar filled the cup. "You picked up that young Turic pup along the way, I hear. He seems pleasant enough."

"Huh," Athlone grunted. "A half-breed."

"If he bothers you," the Jehanan commented, "you should send him on his way."

"Gabria asked him to come."

"Ah." The truth became abundantly clear, and Sha Umar smiled. "Athlone, as a warrior there is none better in the clans than you. As a lover you have a lot to learn."

Athlone glared at his friend, his brown eyes rock hard. "What is that supposed to mean?"

"Look at her! Is that the face of a girl madly in love with her dancing partner? She likes him, yes, but she has been watching you all night. Her heart is as plain as day when she looks at you." Sha Umar leaned over and slapped Athlone's shoulder. "Don't worry about her! Let her dance and enjoy. Come, talk with me while we have a quiet moment. When we are finished you can sweep her off her feet."

The Khulinin stared at the older man for a long moment. Sha Umar's words made sense. Maybe his friend could see the problem clearer; he could understand what Athlone could not. For just a heart-beat the Khulinin lord almost accepted the truth of Sha Umar's words, then he saw Sayyed pull Gabria into his arms. The smile that lit Gabria's face brought Athlone's doubts pounding back. But before he could react to his anger, Sha Umar took his arm and pulled him away to the chieftain's quarters, where the two men talked long into the night.

By the time they were finished discussing the problems of clan unity and their plans for the upcoming gathering at the Tir Samod, the music had stopped and the main hall was quiet. In the dim light of the dying fire, Athlone saw only some bachelors without tents of their own asleep on pallets along the walls. Piers and a few companions were still deep in their wine cups in a far corner. Gabria was nowhere to be seen.

Swallowing his disappointment, Athlone walked with Sha Umar to the entrance and looked out over the camp. The wind had begun to gust around the tents, and the first drops of rain splattered on the ground.

The Jehanan chief put his hand on Athlone's shoulder. "I'll have your supplies ready for you at first light, my friend."

Athlone nodded his thanks. Sha Umar bid him goodnight and returned to his chamber. The Khulinin drew on his cloak and stepped into the wind and rain.

The treld was quiet and dark; only a few dogs and the night out-riders would be out on a stormy night like this. Ducking his head to the wind, Athlone made his way toward the men's guest tent. Just as he reached the entrance he paused, pleased to see Eurus, Nara, and the colt standing nearby, sheltered from the wind by the canvas. He was about to go inside, then changed his mind and made his way toward the smaller tent that had been set aside for Gabria. It was very late, but he could see light shining through the tent flap. Perhaps he would have a chance to talk to her. In private, he could learn the truth of her feelings.

Athlone was about to call to her when he heard a sound that froze his heart: Sayyed's voice. The man was in Gabria's tent. They were talking very softly, so softly that Athlone could not hear their words, but he did not need to. Their low, private tone was enough to breathe life into every dread he had imagined.

The chieftain clenched his hands into fists. Sha Umar was wrong; Gabria had indeed turned to another man. It took every ounce of his will to turn around and walk quietly back to his tent. Like a man half-dead with cold, Athlone lay down on his pallet and clenched his eyes shut. Although he tried to sleep, nothing he could do would erase the memory of those seductively whispering voices from his mind.

The rain began to fall harder.

Gabria raised her head and stared toward the tent flap. "Did you hear something?"

Sayyed half-closed his eyes and leaned out of the lamplight into the shadows. " 'Tis the wind and the voices of the dead as they ride the steeds of Nebiros," he said in a low, dismal voice.

The sorceress smiled lopsidedly. "Oh, good. It might be the Corins. They would love to be out on a night like this."

Shaking his head, the Turic chuckled. He rose and fastened the tent flap tight against the wind. "I forget sometimes that you have already had your life's share of death and pain. Your next life should be one of ease and happiness. Perhaps as the spoiled wife of a wealthy man?"

Gabria wrinkled her nose and leaned back against one of the cushions strewn on the floor. "Why do you Turics delight in punishing yourselves with talk of many lives? I like our clan belief of paradise. I would rather go to the realm of the dead, a place where you can ride the finest horses and feast with the gods."

She filled her cup from a wineskin, drained it, and filled it again before passing the skin on to Sayyed. Her head felt light with wine and music, and the heat of the dancing still burned on her cheeks. She was delighted by the joy of the evening and by Sayyed's attentive company. Tonight she wanted him more than she cared to admit, and yet, even as her body yearned for the young, handsome Turic, her thoughts wandered to Athlone. She had waited all evening for the chieftain to

dance with her, but he had disappeared with Lord Sha Umar. Only
Sayyed had remained.

For his part, the Turic was well aware of the effect he was having
on Gabria, and that made his heart surge with hope. Smiling, he sat
down on the floor beside her, poured his wine, and picked up the
handful of polished stones they were using for a game of Rattle and
Snap. "Reincarnation is difficult for some to understand, but it seems
clear enough to me. How else can a soul attain perfection? One lifetime is not enough to learn the grace and wisdom of the One Living
God."

Gabria sipped her wine and laid her head back on a cushion.
"And what does your god have to say about magic-wielders?"

"Our holy men preach against magic for the same reasons yours
do," Sayyed said. "Magic and sorcery are an abomination of the Living God's power."

"Do you believe that?"

"No. My father does, though. He was the one who banished me.
Now I am like you. I have no tribe. No family." He waved his hands in
the air in a mock spell. "Only magic."

Gabria shifted a little on her cushion so she could see his face.
Her eyes were not focusing very well. "And you still want to learn?"

"I cannot ignore what I am as long as there is a chance of doing
something good with my talent. I believe magic is a gift of the Living
God." He held a finger up. "Or gods, if your people are correct."

"I think it's a gift, too," she whispered.

"That's why I sought you out. You are the only one who can teach
me the laws of sorcery." He glanced at her and caught her watching
him with a slightly puzzled frown. "What is it, fair lady?" he asked, but
she only shook her head and looked away. He was surprised to see
tears sparkling in the corners of her eyes.

Quickly Sayyed leaned down beside her. He cradled her face in
his hands and tilted her head up so she had to look at him. The tears
brimmed and spilled down her cheeks.

Gabria touched his jaw and smiled blearily at him. She was about
to pull his head down to kiss him when suddenly her vision blurred.
The lightness in her head turned to a dark, heavy fog, and she slowly
sank back into the cushions. "Sayyed, I can't . . ." she began to say
when her eyes closed. She was asleep before she could finish the sentence.

The young Turic looked down at her for a long while and the need
for her rose in him like a tide, pulling at him with an almost irresistible

force. Yet he fought it down. He had fallen in love with Gabria that first afternoon, when he saw her sitting on the back of that magnificent Hunnuli mare. Since then he had come to realize that Gabria was a woman to be won, not conquered. He also knew full well that she had not yet given up her love for Athlone. The Khulinin chieftain had a hold on this woman that was not easily broken.

Sayyed sighed and sat back on his heels. He prayed to his god that someday she would choose him over the irritable lord. In the meantime, he had sworn his undying loyalty to her and he fully intended to fulfill his oath—no matter what.

Gently he pushed the curls off her face and traced the line of her cheek with the tip of his finger. Then he covered her with a woolen blanket and went to the tent flap. Outside the rain came down in torrents, blown into sheets by a powerful wind. Sayyed looked out toward the tent where he was supposed to sleep and shook his head. This tent was just as comfortable and did not require a long walk through a heavy storm.

He found an extra blanket and lay down on the rugs across from Gabria. Just before he fell asleep, a grin lifted the corners of his mouth as he imagined what Athlone would think if he knew who was keeping Gabria company in the dark hours of the night. The Turic went to sleep with the grin still on his lips.

Sayyed had slept only a few hours when a strange sound brought him instantly awake. His hand went to his dagger as he leaped to a crouch and poised, waiting for a repetition of the noise. It came again, low and terrified, a moan of pain and sorrow.

"Gabria?" Sayyed cried. He sprang to her side and laid his hand on her cheek. Her skin was as cold as ice.

She moaned again, and the sound tore at his heart. He had never heard such despair. He shook her carefully to waken her, but she seemed to be trapped in the depths of a hideous dream. Her face was contorted by terror and her hands clenched around his arm with maniacal strength.

"No!" she shouted suddenly. "You can't! Don't do it." Her cry rose to blood-chilling screams that tore out of her throat in uncontrollable terror.

"Gabria!" Sayyed shouted frantically. He shook her hard, but she shrieked and struggled, still locked in the visions of her dream. Finally he slapped her. The stinging pain seemed to rouse her, so he slapped her again and again until at last her screams stopped and she fell sobbing into his arms.

Voices called outside the tent, and people crowded into the entrance. Athlone was the first one in, his face ashen. He took one look at Gabria in Sayyed's arms, at the crumpled blankets and the empty wine cups, and his mind went numb. He wanted to step forward and comfort Gabria himself, but he could not force himself to move.

Just then Piers pushed his way in through the onlookers. He took a quick, speculative glance around before hurrying to Gabria. Her look frightened him. She was shaking violently, and her face was deathly white. She let go of Sayyed and clung to her old friend. Neither of them saw Athlone by the tent flap or the look of pained fury on his face.

Slowly Gabria calmed down enough to speak, and the haunted look faded from her eyes. "By the gods, Piers," she gasped. Her voice was hoarse from screaming. "They're really trying to do it!"

"Who is?" he asked, confused. "Do what?"

She grabbed the front of his tunic. "Branth! That woman! I saw them. In some dark room Branth was forming a summoning spell around a golden cage. Something was there for just a moment. I saw it, Piers. It was hideous! I looked into its eyes!"

The onlookers gasped and edged away. Gabria scrambled to her feet, her face wild. "The King Stallion is right! Branth is trying to summon something horrible. We have to go now!"

Outside the tent the three Hunnuli neighed in response to Gabria's emotional summons.

The strident calls broke Athlone's numbness, and he strode forward, relieved to be able to do something. "It is almost dawn. Sayyed, tell the men to saddle their horses. Piers, stay with Gabria until we are ready to go. I will tell Sha Umar that we are leaving."

Gabria's fear galvanized them all and everyone leaped to obey Athlone's commands. In a matter of moments, the company gathered their gear, mounted, and bid farewell to the surprised Jehanan. In the darkness and pouring rain, they urged their horses after Nara as she cantered northwest once again to meet the caravan road.

7

In the darkness of the dank palace storeroom, Lord Branth sank down on a stool and tried to light the oil lamp on the table beside him. His hands were shaking so badly that it took several attempts before he could bring the fire to the wick. When the flame leaped up, he leaned forward and rested his head on his arm.

The tall, thin woman behind him crossed her arms and stared at him in disgust. "You fool," she hissed.

The spell had failed. They had been so close this time. Branth had performed the opening ritual flawlessly, and they had even seen the creature begin to appear in the small, specially reinforced cage. The summoning had been going well until Branth had hesitated in the completion of the spell, and, in that vital moment, the creature had slipped away.

The fon paced around the table in fury. Branth had practiced the spell dozens of times. He had all of the proper tools—the oil lamp, the golden cage, the collar of gold to put around the creature's neck—yet he had still failed. The woman's deep-set eyes narrowed to slits, and she wondered if he had deliberately spoiled the incantation. She had noticed of late that his body was becoming resistant to her mind drug. He tried to disobey her occasionally, and his eyes showed brief flashes of willfulness. She decided to increase the drug to ensure that Branth remained her slave.

Unfortunately the man was too exhausted to try the spell again tonight. It was infuriating to have to wait, but the fon realized she should not force Branth to attempt the incantation a second time until he was fit and rested. He had to be at his utmost strength to control the being she sought.

The fon calmed down as she thought about this creature. Gorth-lings, as some named them, were quite tiny in stature and rather mild in appearance. Nevertheless, they embodied great evil, and, according to Matrah's book, their essence greatly enhanced the powers of a sorcerer strong enough to capture one and pull it from the realm of the dead to the world of mankind. More importantly, to the fon's mind, gorthlings could impart the power to wield magic on a human who did not have the inborn talent. In his tome, Matrah had explained the dangers inherent in summoning a gorthling, but the fon paid little attention to that. There would be no danger, because she was certain she could control the creature.

The fon smiled to herself. Once the gorthling bowed to her command, she could take the next step in her plan. She would use her sorcery and the armies of Pra Desh to quell any unrest in Calah and conquer the other four kingdoms of the Alardarian Alliance. From there it would be an easy step to conquer other realms to the north and the east, and with the might of the East in her grasp, she could swoop down on the barbarian clans and add the rich Dark Horse grasslands to her domain.

All at once, the fon threw back her head and laughed. An empire would be hers—not a mere city, but a world! She sobered as her glance fell on the exiled clansman staring blankly at the floor. She would have to watch him closely after this failure. When the gorthling was hers, Branth would go to the deep, natural pit in the dungeon where she often rid herself of inconveniences.

The only threat the fon could imagine was the other clan magic-wielder. One of her spies had picked up a rumor in court that Khan'di Kadoa had secretly sent for the sorceress to rid the city of Branth. The woman snorted. She hoped the sorceress would come, though she had not decided whether it would be more beneficial to kill the clans-woman or capture her for her power. She wanted to study that prob-lem a while longer, but there would be time for such pondering later. Her primary concern now was to capture a gorthling.

Irritably, the fon put away the makings of the spell. She hid the golden cage and the *Book of Matrah* in a secret compartment she had constructed beneath the floor of the old storeroom. The room was forbidden to the palace inhabitants on pain of death, but she was taking no chances with her precious book or the golden cage.

As soon as Branth was completely rested they would try again. Until then, she would have to tighten her security and continue to lay her plans for the invasion of Portane, the first of the neighboring kingdoms that would fall to her might. With a snap of her fingers, she ordered Branth to move to his pallet of straw by the wall, where his chains hung. The man ignored her, and she was forced to yank him to his feet. For just a moment, his eyes flashed hatred.

"Branth!" she said, her words cold and deadly. "Go to the wall."

The emotions snuffed out of the man's gaze. He shuffled to his place like a whipped dog. The fon chained him with the shackles, left him some food and water, and locked the heavy door of the store-room.

Although it was night and the palace inhabitants were probably asleep, the fon took the precaution of using hidden passages to reach her private rooms on the third floor of the palace. With a chuckle of pleasure, she stepped out onto the balcony of her bedroom and looked down on the sprawling city of Pra Desh. The harbor was a silver crescent in the moonlight. Her glance found the reflection of the Serentine River and slowly followed the water's path north through the city and beyond into the rich farmlands of Calah. The river's trail vanished in the darkness, but the fon followed it onward in her imagination, past the borders of Calah to Portane and the other lands of the Five Kingdoms.

"Soon," she whispered to herself. "Very soon."

"Gabria!" The shout came from a long distance behind her, its urgency clear over the sound of galloping horses.

The young woman tried to ignore the call. She knew what the shout meant: they had been riding for hours and the men wanted her to slow down. But the memories of her dream still burned in her mind and urged her on. She had to keep going. She had to get to Branth before it was too late.

The call came again. "Gabria!"

Gabria, this road is treacherous. We must slow down, Nara said in her thoughts. *The others cannot keep pace with us.*

"Then leave them. I don't need any of them," the woman cried. Although Nara continued to run, Gabria could feel the mare's reluctance breaking her smooth stride.

I know the men are causing you confusion, but you cannot leave them. You need them with you.

Gabria's hands tightened on the horse's mane. She had a wretched headache from both the wine and the vision, and her thoughts were a whirlwind of frightening, half-seen dreams and tangled memories of Athlone, Sayyed, and the night before. She was angry, confused, and in no mood to be reasonable. "No. I don't need them. They're making me crazy."

Nara nickered, the sound like gentle laughter. *So I have noticed. Still, we cannot go on like this. My son cannot keep up.*

Gabria turned to look back and saw the small, black form far behind, struggling gamely through the mud to catch up with his mother. Eurus was staying with him, and farther behind were the seven men and the other horses. She said, "Oh, Nara, I'm sorry."

The Hunnuli immediately slowed to a walk, and in a moment, Eurus and the colt cantered to her side. Their black coats were spattered with reddish mud, and their hooves were caked with the stuff. The colt was so tired he could not even nicker his relief.

The men caught up shortly. Their horses were muddy, too, and sweating heavily. Atop his steed, Piers looked thoroughly miserable.

Athlone, who looked much less put out by the hard ride, started to say something, but Gabria glared at him, turned her back on the company, and rode ahead up the trail—this time at a more manageable pace. The men glanced at one another, yet no one spoke their thoughts. They were a very silent group as they followed the road north in the wake of the sorceress and her Hunnuli.

The rain ended shortly after midday, and a warm wind from the south pulled the clouds apart and cleared the huge sky. By late afternoon, the green-gold hills basked in the warm sun, and a verdant smell of herbs and grass rose from the damp earth.

The comfortable heat of the spring sun dried the travelers' cloaks and hoods, their packs and horses. It also warmed their spirits. Gabria slowly felt her tension and frustration melt away in the mellow sunshine. Although her dream still bothered her and urged her on to Pra Desh, she slowly realized that much of her inner turmoil was caused by the men. They *were* making her crazy.

She was already worried and nervous about a confrontation with Branth and the fon. Now her emotions were being torn apart by the two men she cared for more than anyone. She still loved Athlone, but he did not seem to want her. Sayyed, on the other hand, obviously adored her, but she did not know if she wanted him. She was being pushed and pulled in too many directions.

The other men were not much help, either. Piers, her usual counselor and supporter, was either miserable with his cold or arguing with Khan'di. For his part, the merchant was constantly urging the party to keep moving toward Calah as fast as they could go. Bregan never let

Lord Athlone out of his sight long enough for Gabria to talk to the chief, and the other three warriors never said a word to her.

This journey would be enough to try the patience of Amara, Gabria noted silently. Nevertheless, she knew Nara was right. She did need the men to help her reach Pra Desh and find Branth. Without them she would be lost. The young woman took a deep breath and let it out in a long sigh. It would do little good to antagonize her companions with her bad temper. She would have to calm down and find a way to deal with her tangled feelings.

By the time the company stopped to camp by a watering hole, Gabria had rejoined the men. Her earlier frenzied anger was apparently put aside. She laughed and talked with Sayyed and Piers, chatted with Khan'di, and teased Bregan about his short-legged horse. She tried to talk with Athlone, without much luck. The chief was taciturn all evening and seemed to have his thoughts a thousand leagues away.

For the next several days the company continued on their northern route, riding fast on the heels of Gabria and the Hunnuli. She pushed them all hard, for the sense of urgency that had awakened during her dreams grew stronger by the day. They were losing precious time. They had to reach Pra Desh before Branth attempted his spell again.

Although Nara and Eurus tried to keep a pace the smaller Harachan horses could tolerate, the constant, hard traveling began to take its toll on the weaker horses.

One afternoon, four days from Jehanan Treld, Bregan's horse tripped in a rodent hole at the side of the road and fell heavily on his head. Gabria, riding beside the warrior, heard a sickening crack as the horse went down and saw Bregan thrown violently to the ground. She slid off Nara immediately and went to the warrior's side. His head was bloodied, and his eyes held a vague, dazed look. He tried once to get up before he fell back in her arms.

The other men dismounted and came running. Piers examined the injured warrior, then looked up at Athlone with obvious relief. "He's cut and bruised. He might even need stitches, but he should be all right."

"Stubs won't be," one of the other warriors said glumly.

They turned to look at Bregan's gelding, still struggling on the ground. The three Hunnuli were standing beside the stricken horse, their muzzles close to his to quiet and comfort him. Everyone could see the shattered, bloody end of his foreleg.

Athlone cursed. He knew how much Bregan loved his horse. Silently, Athlone drew his sword and knelt beside the gelding.

"No! Wait!" Bregan pulled himself painfully to a sitting position. Blood poured down his face from the deep cut on his forehead. He struggled to focus on his horse and, as the realization hit him, tears mingled with the blood on his face. Slowly he crawled to Stubs and cradled the horse's head in his lap.

The gelding nickered once and relaxed in Bregan's arms. Without a word, the old warrior gently pulled the horse's nose up until the base of the throat was exposed. Athlone drove the point of his sword through the soft throatlatch, deep into the brain. Stubs died instantly.

Bregan, blinded by blood and tears, closed the gelding's eyes and passed out.

They removed the bridle and saddle and erected a cairn of rocks over Stubs's body. Piers and Secen gently lifted Bregan onto the healer's mare. It was almost dark by the time they rode on, so they soon stopped in a sheltered, wooded valley only half a day's travel from the winter camp of the Reidhar clan.

While the other hearthguard warriors set up the small traveling tents and Gabria started a cooking fire, Piers tended to Bregan's injuries. The warrior had roused from unconsciousness and was muttering between his clenched teeth as the healer gently cleaned the wound on his forehead. That done, Piers began to stitch it closed with a tiny bone needle and horsehair thread. Athlone and Khan'di came to sit beside them.

"The blow to Bregan's head is serious," Piers said without preamble. "He's going to need at least a day of rest."

The chieftain glanced an inquiry at Khan'di. The nobleman rubbed his mustache and said, "There is not much time left. If the fon stays with her original plan, she will invade Portane in fifteen days."

"My lord, I . . . Ouch!" Bregan flinched away from Piers's needle.

"That's what happens when you move! You're worse than a child," the healer admonished. He pushed Bregan's head around so he could see the gash better in the firelight.

"If you were about to say that you don't need the rest," Athlone told the old warrior, "forget it. All of us could use a respite from the road." A look of concern crossed his face. "We could also use several new horses and some supplies."

Piers looked sharply at the chieftain. "Do you intend to stop at Reidhar Treld? Is that a good idea?"

"No. But they're close, and we have little choice."

Khan'di asked, "What is wrong with the Reidhar?"

"There's nothing particularly wrong with the clan," said Piers, tying off a stitch on Bregan's forehead. "The trouble is their chieftain, Lord Caurus. He hates sorcery, and he's suspicious of the Khulinin's wealth and influence. Last summer, when Medb threatened the clans with war, Lord Caurus would not side with Medb, but he wouldn't side with Lord Savaric either. He took his clan back to their lands and waited to see what would happen."

"I don't know what he expected to do there," Bregan commented. "His clan would never have survived an attack by Lord Medb if the sorcerer had survived the battle at Ab-Chakan."

Athlone chuckled. "Caurus still can't believe my father and Gabria destroyed Lord Medb without his help."

"He won't be happy to see us," Bregan said, frowning.

"He will abide by clan hospitality," Athlone stated flatly. "We will receive the supplies we need to continue."

Piers finished the stitching and began to put away his tools. "Will he include Gabria in that hospitality?" he asked carefully.

Khan'di turned to watch the sorceress as she helped Sayyed fix the evening meal. "She travels with us. Doesn't clan law make it clear that she must be included?"

"Caurus might not pay attention to the details of the law, but I don't intend to give him a choice." Athlone replied.

Bregan and Piers exchanged glances at the stone-cold tone of the chieftain's voice. "I hope you're right." Piers said. "Gabria needs rest more than any of us."

There was a pause. The chief shifted slightly and said, "Why?"

"I think this confrontation with Branth is affecting her more than we realize. She has been pushing herself too hard."

Athlone's eyebrows went up. His cold, dark eyes softened a little, and he nodded once to himself. "We have all been pushing her," he said quietly. He slapped Piers on the shoulder and went back to work.

After the meal, Athlone passed the word of their destination to the rest of the party. Gabria's heart sank. She did not like Lord Caurus. He was loud, arrogant, and very unpleasant to anyone who annoyed him. He had also made it clear last summer that he despised sorcery—an attitude he had impressed upon his clan.

While the men settled down for the night, Gabria went for a long walk beside the creek that meandered through the valley. She took only her thoughts with her and tried to find solace in the solitude of the spring night. She did not have much success.

On her way back to camp, she passed the meadow where the horses grazed and saw Athlone standing in the grass with Eurus. The chieftain was brushing the Hunnuli's ebony coat with a steady, unconscious stroke.

For a time the young woman stood in the shadows and watched the chieftain. She wanted to talk to him, to ask him what was wrong, to learn if he still loved her. But an uncomfortable reluctance to know the truth made her hesitate.

Her heart pounding, Gabria finally walked out of the trees to Eurus's side. The big horse nickered a welcome, and Athlone started, dropping his brush. To hide his nervousness, he slowly leaned over to retrieve it, then took the time to clean it of dirt.

Nara came to join them, and Gabria leaned gratefully against the mare's warm side. "Athlone, I . . ."

The chief did not seem to hear her. He resumed brushing Eurus and immediately said, "Tomorrow, when we ride to the Reidhar camp, I want you to wear your skirts. Put your sword away and keep quiet."

Gabria straightened and felt her face begin to burn. "I had already planned to do so," she replied, her words frosted with anger.

"Good. We need the Reidhar's cooperation. And another thing," he went on, "all of us have been expecting a great deal from you. Too much, I think, and our feelings have only been getting in the way. We need to remember the priorities of our journey."

Athlone glanced at her form in the shadow of the Hunnuli. It was too dark to see her face or the hurt confusion in her eyes. "Gabria," he said, brushing Eurus harder, "I came on this journey to help you, not get in your way. From now on I will stand behind you and allow—"

Gabria pounced on the last word. "*Allow!*" she cried, coming around beside Eurus. "Don't patronize me with your pride-riddled speeches, Athlone. I don't deserve it!" She glared at him. "What are you really talking about?"

For days Athlone had been wondering what he would say if he had time alone with Gabria. Now he had that time, but nothing was coming out as he had planned. He wanted to gather her in his arms and feel her warmth and love. Instead all he could see in his mind was her slim, strong body in Sayyed's embrace, and the more the image played in his head, the greater his anger waxed. The jealousy grew until all of his rehearsed speeches and truest desires were burned in its heat. His days of frustration, anxiety, and confusion suddenly crested in a flooding wave of anger and confusion that came sweeping out in a reckless torrent.

"I'm talking about Sayyed!" he shouted at her.

"Sayyed!" Gabria gasped in surprise. "What does he have to do with this?"

"Everything. You love him. You had him in your tent the other night. All right! If he's the one you've chosen, then take him. I will not hold you to our vow."

Gabria was shocked. She did not know whether to laugh or cry. Of all the things that had gone through her mind in the past few days, she had never imagined Athlone could be jealous. How could she have missed it? She stepped toward him, raising her hands to implore him. "My tent. Yes, I did—"

But he was angry beyond reason. "No. I've heard enough. Our betrothal is broken." He turned his back on her and strode swiftly into the darkness. The wind swirled his cloak like a gesture of farewell, and he was gone.

Gabria started after him. "Athlone! Wait! You haven't heard anything," she cried, only she was too late. Her hands clenched into fists. "The gods blast that man!" she shouted with frustration and hurt. For just a moment, a pale blue aura glowed around her hands in the darkness.

Gabria, Nara warned softly.

The sorceress glanced down and saw the telltale glow, the first sign of the Trymian Force building within her. The force was a powerful spell that fused the energy within a magic-wielder into one destructive force. It could sometimes appear as an instinctive reaction in times of strong emotion. Gabria had learned well the idiosyncracies of the Trymian Force when she'd accidentally killed one man and almost killed Athlone the summer before.

Quickly she hugged her arms around herself and forced her emotions to calm. The blue aura faded and, with it, her anger. Gabria shook her head. She should have known better than to approach Athlone when he was tired and worried about their stop at Reidhar Treld. Now their situation was worse. Athlone had exploded in one of his rages and broken their vow of betrothal. Gabria felt cold.

She pulled her cloak tightly about herself and glared at the night, toward the spot where Athlone had disappeared. She could not go on like this, with her emotions in constant turmoil. For the sake of her survival she would have to put her life in order. She would concentrate on her journey and the confrontation with Branth, and deal with Athlone and Sayyed later. As much as they meant to her, they would simply have to wait. Her survival came before the demands of her heart. Perhaps afterward, if she was still alive, she would have the freedom and the time to settle such affairs of the heart. Until then, she would avoid close confrontation with the two men. There was no other way.

With a heavy step, Gabria walked alone toward the creek. The sheltering shadows of the night gathered around her like a suit of black armor.

Piers was still awake, sitting alone by the fire, when Gabria came back from her walk. She knew the healer was waiting up for her, but this night she did not want to talk. Instead, she bent over his shoulder, gave him a quick hug goodnight, and slipped away to her tent.

Piers watched her go. He understood the fears she faced and the uncertainties with which she wrestled. He knew how much her love for Athlone and her friendship for Sayyed were troubling her. He just wished she would talk to him about all of it. He might not have the right advice—how could you advise a sorceress? Yet he could listen and be a friend if she needed one. He knew more about her than anyone else alive.

Piers shook his head and began to bank the fire. Perhaps he had been foolish sitting out here in the damp, waiting for her to come back to camp and talk to him. As much as he knew about Gabria, there was so much more he did not know. In the strange, difficult year since her clan's massacre, she had learned the skill of reticence, to keep her own counsel, and to do as she decided on her own. Those were traits she had acquired to survive.

The healer went to his tent and crawled into his warm coverings. No, he decided, the waiting was not wasted. His gesture told Gabria he was there if she needed him, and he knew her well enough to realize she would be grateful for that.

The travelers broke camp the next morning in a haze of golden sunshine. High clouds dotted the deep blue sky, and a light wind whisked the leafing trees.

Bregan had had a restless night. The old warrior was stiff and aching from his fall, and he grumbled under his breath as he helped load the packhorses. He tried not to look grief-stricken when the other men brought in their mounts to be saddled.

Athlone watched stonily from the back of his gray stallion. His dark eyes were ringed from lack of sleep, and his mouth was drawn tight with a hidden sadness. The shadow of his morning beard made his face look gaunt.

Gabria watched him with mingled sadness and regret. The pain of their argument still ached in her mind. Yet when Sayyed, who deftly read the expression on her face, winked at her, she could not help but smile.

She looked over the rest of her companions as they mounted. The group was heavily armed, dirty, travel-worn, and weary. They looked more like a rabble of thieves and exiles than a nobleman and the finest of the powerful Khulinin clan. Gabria hoped the Reidhar were in a generous mood that day.

She pushed down her nervousness and rode Nara in behind Piers's mare. Keth, carrying Bregan behind him, and the other riders fell in line with Athlone. The travelers left the caravan road and struck northeast at an easy canter. If all went well, they would be at Reidhar Treld by midday.

8

The day blossomed into a glorious, warm spring afternoon as the travelers followed the faint trail that led to Reidhar Treld. The land was much like Clan Jehanan's holdings: gently rolling hills, patches of woods, open meadows, and lush valleys. Like the Jehanan, the Reidhar had their winter camp near the sea, but unlike their neighbors to the south, the Reidhar had given up many of the ancient nomadic ways and were turning more often to the water. Year by year their herds of horses dwindled and more and more of the clanspeople chose to stay at the treld during the summer to fish the teeming waters of the inland sea or mine the rich veins of copper in the hills nearby. More than any other clan, the Reidhar had lost the ways of Valorian.

Evidence of the changing social patterns were quite visible to Gabria as Nara crested a ridge that looked down over the Reidhar settlement. She had never visited the Reidhar clan at their treld, so the differences between her own clan and this one were startling. The Corins had been a small group and one of the most nomadic of the twelve original clans. The Reidhar clan was larger, and its roots went deep into the place they called home. A huge, ornately decorated stone hall graced the center of the treld, and many stone buildings replaced the usual tents. There were permanent structures housing the clan artisans, as well as storehouses and barns. A wide, shallow stream meandered down the valley's center, past the meager herds of stock animals, and flowed a short distance to the sea.

From her vantage point, Gabria could look down the valley to where the creek flowed between two gentle bluffs and tumbled out to a white beach. Even from the ridge, she could see the boat sheds, drying racks, and docks that crowded the sands. Beyond those, the small fleet of tiny fishing boats bobbed on the sparkling water.

"No wonder their horses are such poor beasts," Keth, the warrior in front of Bregan, said aloud. "The clan is nothing but a bunch of fisherfolk."

"They can still fight, so keep a civil tongue in your head," Athlone reminded him sharply.

"They couldn't last summer," the warrior muttered.

Lord Athlone ignored him. Fisherfolk or no, the Reidhar were still clan and kindred in blood and spirit, and despite Lord Caurus's refusal to fight Lord Medb the year before, Athlone felt that the Reidhar still deserved the respect due any clan. Lord Caurus was a great warrior and fiercely devoted to his people. It was not cowardice that had forced him to leave that disastrous gathering, it was his own independent nature and an unfortunate distrust of the Khulinin.

Athlone nodded to his companions, and the party rode downhill toward the busy treld. On a rise nearby, an outrider drew a horn and sounded a warning to the camp below. At the edge of the treld, another rider left his post and galloped down the valley to find the chieftain. By the time Gabria and her party reached the fringe of the encampment, Lord Caurus and his hearthguard were gathered on horseback in the middle of the path. Behind them clustered other warriors and clansmen, until the entire way was blocked. Their faces were wary as Athlone and Bregan spurred their horses forward to meet Lord Caurus.

The Reidhar chieftain was obviously startled by Lord Athlone's sudden, unexpected arrival at his treld. Caurus made no attempt to hide his suspicious, angry expression, but he remembered enough of his manners to greet Athlone first. He raised his hand. "Hail, Khulinin. Welcome to Reidhar Treld."

"Greetings, Lord Caurus," Athlone replied evenly. He eyed the heavily armed men around the chief. "This doesn't look like much of a welcome. Were you expecting someone else?"

"We were expecting no one. Least of all you."

Athlone shrugged. "I did not have time to send messengers. Our mission is urgent. We had not planned to stop, but we are in need of supplies and extra horses."

"We have no extra horses," Caurus said belligerently.

The Khulinin chief clicked his tongue. "Lord Caurus, do I need to remind *you* of the dictums of clan hospitality? Just last spring you were rumored to be the most generous host in the clans. Have you forgotten in one short year?"

"I have not forgotten." Caurus shifted in his saddle, his ruddy face wary. "You are welcome, Lord Athlone, but we cannot allow that sorceress to enter our treld."

With difficulty, Athlone swallowed his rising anger and stared coolly at the red-haired chieftain. "Why not, Caurus? She has been welcomed by other clans. We will not leave her at the edge of camp."

"We are about to celebrate our Birthright ceremony. If that heretic were to enter our treld, Amara would curse our clan forever."

The other Reidhar warriors muttered in agreement. The clan wertain kicked his horse forward and deliberately dropped his hand to his sword hilt.

Inwardly, Athlone groaned. He had expected reluctance and suspicion, but not outright refusal. It was their bad luck to have arrived so close to the clan's Birthright ceremonies.

"Gabria," Athlone called over his shoulder. "Come here and bring the foal."

The startled Reidhar fell back a step, and a hint of fear passed over Caurus's face as Gabria rode Nara forward to stand by Athlone. The colt and Eurus came with her.

A long moment passed before anyone spoke. The men of the Reidhar stared in open amazement at the fair woman and the magnificent black horses.

Finally Athlone asked. "Would Amara bless Gabria and her Hunnuli with a healthy colt if she were displeased?" His tone was deceptively pleasant.

This possibility stunned Lord Caurus. His face grew as red as his hair as he struggled to find a solution to the dilemma Athlone had thrust on him. He never imagined the sorceress could be anything but evil. And yet, if that were true, how could she now have three Hunnuli, one a baby? The Hunnuli despised evil and avoided it at all costs. Still . . .

Caurus suddenly threw up his hands in disgust. "The sorceress and her Hunnuli may stay. But—" he glared at all of the party "—only for one night."

Athlone barely nodded in reply. "Your generosity is over-whelming."

The Reidhar wertain slammed his fist on his sword. "Lord Caurus, you cannot allow this!" he shouted. "That . . . female is a magic-wielder! I don't care how many Hunnuli tag after her, she's a profaning heretic. The goddess will never forgive us for bringing her into camp."

"Gringold," Caurus said in annoyance, "I have made my decision. Abide by it!"

"As wer-tain of this clan, I cannot let her evil endanger our people."

"And as chieftain of this clan, it is *my* decision to make," Lord Caurus thundered. "I will not dishonor the Reidhar by refusing aid to another chieftain."

With a snarl on his lips, the wer-tain backed down, but he savagely reined his horse over to Nara and leaned forward, his eyes blazing like a wolf's. The wer-tain was a big man with heavy muscles and the overbearing attitude of a bully. He bore the scars of many battles and carried a full array of warrior's weapons.

Nara pinned her ears back and snorted a warning. Gabria remained still, her expression cool and unruffled as the wer-tain shook his fist at her.

"Lord Caurus has given you one night, Sorceress. If you do anything that reeks of magic, I'll slit your throat."

"Thank you, Wer-tain Gringold, for your gracious welcome," Gabria said with all the politeness she could muster.

"Gringold," Caurus snapped. "Return to the treld and prepare quarters for our guests."

They all breathed a sigh of relief when the wer-tain saluted his lord, spurred his horse away, and disappeared into the treld.

A very dangerous man, Gabria thought to herself. Her mouth tightened to a thin line, and she sadly remembered the Jehanan. She knew full well the Reidhar would never offer her companions a welcome like the one Sha Umar's clan had provided.

She was quite right. Escorted by Lord Caurus and the warriors of the clan, Gabria and her party were led through the treld to the stone huts at the edge of the camp that were used to house guests. The huts were cold, damp, and sparsely furnished with a few cots and a fireplace. As soon as the party reached the huts, the Reidhar left them for the rest of the afternoon. No one came to talk, offer wine, or bring food or firewood, and no one brought blankets or the barest necessities due to a guest. The Reidhar blatantly ignored them all.

After a while, Piers found the clan healer and talked him into giving them enough firewood to light a fire in one of the huts. Two warriors, Secen and Keth, filled the water skins at the stream, and Gabria and Sayyed unpacked the bedrolls. After a great deal of trouble and effort, Athlone and Bregan found a trader willing to deal for several horses.

The trader was from Calah and spent his time traveling the plains and dealing in horseflesh. He had stopped at Reidhar Treld for a few days and had been disappointed with the trade so far. He was pleased to barter with the Khulinin for their pure-blooded Harachan.

Several hours later, Athlone and Bregan returned to the guest huts with three new horses. Lord Athlone was pleased with the deal, for the trader had taken the three Khulinin pack horses in an even exchange for three Calah horses. Athlone knew the trader had gotten the best deal, because the clan horses had better breeding and training and only needed a little rest and food to be back in shape. Still, the Calah horses were sturdy, strong, healthy, and available. Even Bregan had not been displeased. He had chosen a black gelding with long legs for his mount.

It was dusk by the time Athlone and Bregan had settled and fed the horses and made their way to the huts. Both of them were hungry and looking forward to the evening meal. By the unwritten clan code of hospitality, it was the chieftain's duty to feed his guests. If the guest was a visiting lord, then he and his escort were always invited to share the host chief's meals. Thus Athlone fully expected an invitation to Caurus's evening meal awaiting him when he returned. But when he inquired about it, Piers shook his head.

"My lord," the healer replied, "there is neither food nor a message from Caurus. We are as good as forgotten."

"This insult shall not be ignored," Athlone snarled. He slammed his sword and scabbard on a cot beside him. "Remove your weapons," he told his men. "We are going to the hall to eat with Lord Caurus. All of us." He waited impatiently while Sayyed and the warriors left their swords, bows, and daggers on the cots. Slowly the chief brought his temper under control. It would not help their problems if his fury got the best of him.

When everyone was ready, he nodded once to his men and turned to Gabria. She was standing by the fire dressed in her long skirt and over-tunic. He was surprised to see she was wearing the armband he had given her and carrying her jeweled dagger in a scabbard under the sash of her skirt.

"Caurus may not feed you if I come," she said. Her words were spoken half in jest, but her eyes were shadowed with worry.

"Caurus will have no choice," Athlone retorted. He crossed his arms, and his lips curved upward in a harsh smile. "I'm sure he has done this deliberately to show his anger at me for bringing you to his treld. The clans will never learn to accept magic-wielders if we let chieftains like Caurus get away with these insults."

Gabria looked at his face, and for a moment she saw something there she had never noticed before. That cold, calculating smile was exactly like his father's. Lord Savaric had been a deliberate, controlled, cunning man who had often harnessed his anger to fire his actions. He had always sought for ways to turn difficulties to his advantage.

Gabria sighed to herself. Athlone was going to need every scrap of his father's wiles and self-control tonight.

The treld was peaceful as the travelers left their hut and walked down the path toward the hall. The sun had dropped below the hills, leaving the plains to the approaching night. The smells of cooking food and wood smoke mingled in the treld with the usual smells of animals and people.

As the party approached the chieftain's hall, Bregan took the lead and the other hearthguard warriors gathered around their lord. Piers, Khan'di, and Sayyed drew close to Gabria. Without asking to enter, they walked past the startled guards and strode under the flapping yellow banner above the doors into the large stone hall.

Lord Caurus, his wer-tain, a few hearthguard, and several bachelors were grouped around a long, wooden table near the center of the hall. Caurus's wife, Lady Maril, and two girls were busy serving the men from a platter of roast meats and a kettle of stewed vegetables.

The entire group fell silent as the Khulinin chief and his companions entered the hall. Lord Caurus, for once, went very pale.

"Forgive me, Caurus," Athlone said, his voice amiable. "We seem to be late."

There was nothing for the Reidhar to do, short of openly insulting the Khulinin, so he accepted the party's presence. With an ill-tempered look and a grudging gesture, Lord Caurus ordered the bachelors to another table and had places cleared for Athlone and his party. Lady Maril hastily set eating knives and plates for the guests and poured wine. The Reidhar warriors did not utter a word.

The serving girls brought more meat and vegetables and laid out baskets with thick slabs of bread. Gabria thought the meal would have been quite good if the silence and tension had not been so palpable. As it was, she found it very difficult to ignore the hostile looks of her hosts. Even Lady Maril, who sat beside her lord to eat her meal, remained grimly quiet.

Finally, the silence became too much for Lord Caurus. He pushed away his platter and said to Athlone, "I heard you found some spare horses."

Athlone continued to eat for a few minutes before he answered. "Ah, yes. A trader from Calah had a few strong horses he was willing to part with. Unfortunately, he only had three. The rest of the stock we saw was quite poor." He took a bite of bread and did not bother to look at Lord Caurus.

Caurus colored slightly and leaned back in his carved chair. "Your horses seem weary. You have been traveling fast?"

Athlone nodded. "As fast as we could." He was not going to give this ill-mannered boor the satisfaction of an easy answer. He gestured to a girl for another helping of meat.

"Your business must be urgent."

"Yes," the Khulinin chief replied casually.

"Where are you going?" Caurus pressed.

"Hunting."

At the other end of the table, Sayyed choked back a laugh, and Caurus turned fiercely on him. "And you, Turic, what are you doing with clansmen?"

The young tribesman stood up and bowed. "I am Sayyed Raid-Ja, son of Dultar of Sharja. I am traveling the Ramtharin Plains to compare the hospitality of the clans."

"And you, Pra Deshian," Caurus rapped at Khan'di. "Where are you going?"

The stocky nobleman raised and lowered his eyebrows as if he had just been asked a stupid question. "With them," he said, waving his hand at the table in general.

"I see." Caurus twisted his mustache in anger. His expression was thunderous, and white showed around the edges of his mouth. He felt it was bad enough that the Khulinin had come without warning, stampeding through his camp with their sorceress in tow, and now they wouldn't even tell him about their journey.

"By the way," Athlone broke in pleasantly, "we still need a few supplies. Trail food. A new water bag. Grain. Some leather to repair our tack."

"To go hunting," Caurus said sarcastically.

Wer-tain Gringold suddenly slammed his eating knife on the table. "Lord, I wouldn't give them a used horseshoe."

"We don't need horseshoes," said Bregan as reasonably as he could manage.

The wer-tain turned to the Khulinin beside him and studied Bregan for a moment until a flicker of recognition lit in his narrow eyes. He curled his lip. "It's a good thing your chief is only going hunting. With you as a guard, he's going to need better luck than his father."

"Bregan!" Athlone's voice cut like a whip across the silence and stopped the warrior in mid-lunge.

The wer-tain chuckled as Bregan forced himself to sit down again.

"Now," Lord Athlone said to Caurus, "about those supplies."

Caurus scowled. "We have little to spare. This has been a bad winter."

Khan'di looked amazed. "A bad winter? We didn't know. I'd heard you had a prosperous summer last year, since you weren't involved in that unpleasantness with Lord Medb. Besides, the weather has been quite mild this season."

Athlone raised his hand to forestall the Reidhar chief's angry retort. "Caurus, look. We need those supplies badly. I cannot tell you exactly why or where we're going because your treld is too close to the caravan road. Word can spread fast, and we need the element of surprise. Just know our mission is very important. If we had not needed new horses so badly, I wouldn't have bothered you."

Caurus's anger subsided a little, and he shifted his heavy frame in the chair. For the first time he looked directly at Gabria and asked, "And what of the sorceress? Is she a part of your important mission?"

Gabria had been quiet during the meal, trying to stay out of the conversation and not exacerbate the raw emotions in the room. At Caurus's question, she looked up and met his stare with a cool expression of her own. "I am only a part of this troupe, Lord Caurus, and I can promise you that I have controlled my sorcery and kept my vow to the chiefs."

"Huh!" Gringold said harshly. "What is a vow to a magic-wielder? They twist and turn their promises like nests of snakes until no one knows where the words begin or end. Remember Lord Medb and his silky promises? You are just like him, treacherous and evil."

"She saved your clan, you miserable slug," Secen, the Khulinin warrior, snapped.

Gabria, amazed by the warrior's quick defense, smiled at him with gratitude.

"Since none of you had the guts to fight," Bregan added.

This time it was Gringold who leaped to his feet. His golden wer-tain's belt glittered in the firelight as he reached for his eating knife.

"Gringold!" Caurus shouted as the other warriors jumped up. "Sit down."

The big wer-tain was too angry to obey. He snatched a heavy platter from the table and brought it down hard on Bregan's head. The older warrior slumped sideways on the table, dazed and bleeding from his reopened head wound. Without a pause, Gringold slashed at Secen with a knife and caught a third Khulinin warrior in the stomach with the platter. Then, before anyone could stop him, he lunged across the table and grabbed Gabria's wrist. "Viper!" he shouted at her. "You saved nothing but your worthless neck."

Athlone, at the end of the table, snarled a curse and leaped toward the wer-tain. Before the chief could get there, Sayyed desperately grabbed for Gringold's knife arm, and Bregan tried to block the wer-tain's body on the table. To their dismay, Gringold was a powerful fighter. He swept them off and tried to wrench Gabria over the edge of the table.

However, he had forgotten Gabria's past and her own training as a warrior. Instead of being the screaming, struggling female he had expected, the woman fought back. She snatched a heavy goblet from the table, smashed it into his face, and twisted her wrist out of his grasp.

Swearing, Gringold covered his bleeding nose and looked up to see the sorceress poised in front of him, her dagger drawn and her green eyes blazing. At that moment, Athlone reached him, and a furious blow to the jaw sent the wer-tain reeling. Even that did not stop the man. He staggered upright and went after the chieftain.

Lady Maril abruptly jabbed her husband in the ribs, jolting him out of his shocked inactivity.

"Gringold, that's enough!" Caurus shouted belatedly. "You men hold him."

The Reidhar warriors, who had not moved during their wer-tain's attack, now scrambled after Gringold and pinned his arms to his sides.

"My apologies, Lord Athlone," Caurus said with some sincerity.

"No!" Gringold yelled. "No apologies. I demand the right to defend my honor by battle."

"A duel?" Caurus exploded. "Whom would you challenge?"

The wer-tain glanced at Bregan and the other Khulinin warriors, then he shook off his men and pointed at Lord Athlone. "I challenge you, Chieftain. To the death."

Caurus looked aghast. "Don't be a fool, man," he gasped, rising from his seat.

Gringold disregarded him. "What do you say, Khulinin?"

For a moment, Athlone did not answer. If he accepted and was badly wounded or killed, his loss could jeopardize their mission. On the other hand, if he did not accept, his refusal to duel with a man of lower status would seriously harm his influence in the clans and cloud his own honor. He looked about him—at Bregan leaning against the table while Piers tried to staunch the blood on his forehead; at the other warriors, one nursing a cut on his arm and one bent double over his bruised abdomen. Athlone glanced at Sayyed and Khan'di, and finally he looked at Gabria. The woman had sheathed her dagger and was standing quietly nearby.

The sight of her ignited a powerful mix of feelings within Athlone. He knew he still loved the sorceress in spite of their arguments, and he was furious with Gringold for assaulting her. If that was not enough to fuel his temper, his anger, jealousy, and hurt pride from the past days still hammered at his patience and self-control. He felt ready to explode.

Lord Athlone grinned wickedly to himself. He would never admit it aloud, but what he really wanted was someone to vent his rage upon. Gringold had just volunteered. "Your challenge is accepted," he murmured. "You have been rude and insolent. You have insulted and attacked my men. Worst of all, you assaulted a woman of our clan. For the sake of our honor, I will meet you in the morning. May Surgart bless my sword."

Lord Caurus groaned and sank back in his seat. Without another word, Athlone gathered his people and left the hall.

By dawn the next day, word of the duel had spread through every corner of the treld. Because the sky was clear and the sun shone with the promise of a warm, comfortable day, the clanspeople began to gather early around the chief's hall. Duels were exciting to watch, but rarely were two such excellent antagonists matched in a battle to the death. Wer-tain Gringold was big, heavily muscled, and well-trained with the short sword, while Lord Athlone, although lighter, was reputed to be the finest swordsman on the plains. The clan could not wait to see the outcome.

While the Reidhar gathered by the hall, Lord Caurus paced in his quarters and cursed the rashness of his wer-tain. Individual dueling was a common clan practice used for settling arguments, ending blood feuds, or claiming weir-geld, and its rules were strict and rigidly adhered to. Combatants were required to fight with only a short sword and without a shield or mail for protection. A man needed every advantage of strength and ability to survive, so challenges were restricted to the initiated warriors of the werod.

Normally Lord Caurus would not have objected to a duel. The battles were usually fought until one opponent surrendered, and he would have enjoyed seeing Athlone taken down a notch or two. A battle to the death, however, was an entirely different matter. Athlone's death could have serious repercussions throughout the clans. The other chiefs would be furious with Caurus and blame him for the killing. The powerful Khulinin would be without a chieftain and *they* would be enraged. And that sorceress . . . Caurus shuddered to think of the problems she could cause.

As for the other possibility, he would hate to lose his wer-tain. Gringold was a hot-tempered fool at times, but he was an excellent leader to the clan's warriors. He was Caurus's cousin, too.

All in all, the outcome of this duel looked grim to Caurus.

Unfortunately, not even a chieftain could call off a challenge if the combatants were determined to fight. Caurus had tried to talk to Gringold that morning to no avail. The wer-tain was adamant; the duel would be fought.

On the other side of the treld, as Caurus paced back and forth in his hall, the travelers joined Athlone in the meager hut to help him prepare.

Gabria watched the men for a short while, then slipped outside. Athlone had all the help he needed, and she wanted to be alone to compose her feelings. She was very worried. Athlone was an experienced, highly trained swordsman who could easily hold his own in duel. But Gringold was a brutal, powerful fighter, and battles between two well-matched antagonists were often unpredictable. Gabria swallowed hard to banish the nervous flutters in her stomach.

For a few moments she paced anxiously by the door until, finally, to take her mind off her worries, she retrieved the horse brushes from the baggage and carefully brushed the dust off Nara and Eurus until their ebony coats glistened. She combed their manes and tails and brushed the colt's scruffy coat. When she was finished grooming the horses, she leaned against Nara and tried to be patient.

Abruptly the wooden door of the hut swung open and Athlone strode out, followed by his four hearthguard, Piers, Sayyed, and Khan'di. Gabria stared at the Khulinin lord with pride. He wore only a pair of tight-fitting breeches, and he carried his sword in one hand. His muscles, while not as bulky as Gringold's, were well-formed and as dangerously sleek as a mountains lion's. His skin had been rubbed with oil to make it difficult for his opponent to hold him; his hair was tightly bound.

Gabria recognized the concentrated look of resolution in his eyes. He had withdrawn from everything but the battle at hand. "My lord," she said softly. "Your mount is ready."

Athlone looked at her, then at the great Hunnuli stallion that stood watching him with those deep, intelligent eyes. He hesitated for a breath while his reluctance to ride a sorcerer's steed gave way to his common sense. He and Gabria knew the horses only accepted magic-wielders, yet the rest of the clans only knew that a man who could ride the magnificent horses was a man to be honored and respected. His appearance on Eurus would make a valuable impression on the minds of the Reidhar and hopefully unnerve his opponent.

Athlone vaulted to Eurus's back, raised his sword, and shouted, "Khulinin!"

The four hearthguard warriors repeated his cry, and their shouts reverberated through the valley. They immediately took their positions beside their chief, and the others fell in behind. Nara walked with Gabria, for the sorceress did not want to distract the Reidhar's attention from Lord Athlone. To her relief, Piers laid her hand on his arm and walked beside her while Sayyed stayed close behind.

On Eurus's back, Athlone looked out over the Reidhar camp and saw the clanspeople swarming to the path to watch his approach. He grinned with pleasure and held his sword, blade down, as a gesture of peace to the Reidhar clan. The people cheered their approval. They did not care if he was an opponent to their wer-tain. All they saw was a proud clan warrior astride a great Hunnuli, his sword gleaming in the sun, his body ready for battle. In that moment, Athlone became a thrilling embodiment of the clans' hero, the legendary warrior, Valorian.

They cheered as the group approached the hall, then fell silent and gathered in a ring around the wide, open space before the building. Lord Caurus and the wer-tain were waiting by the entrance. Gringold's body was oiled like Athlone's and laced with scars from many fights.

Athlone paused for a moment to run his hand down Eurus's neck. He felt so alive, so natural, sitting on the back of this Hunnuli. He was as comfortable and at ease with this horse as he had ever been with Boreas. It was like coming home to an old friend.

Eurus twisted his head around and looked at Athlone through his long forelock. *His reach is longer than yours, but he only uses his sword in his right hand.*

The chieftain chuckled. "You know him well?"

Merely observant. Keep your head down.

With a laugh, Athlone slung his leg over Eurus's withers and slid to the ground. He saluted Caurus.

The Reidhar chief returned the salute, as one lord to another. He tried to appear calm, but his face was grim, and his red beard fairly bristled with his agitation.

"Lord, a moment," Gringold said. "I must ask a favor."

"What is it?" Caurus asked impatiently.

The wer-tain turned and pointed to Gabria. "The sorceress. She must not interfere. Keep her at sword point."

Before anyone else could move, Sayyed drew his long curved blade and planted himself before Gabria. "Do not try it," he said flatly.

Athlone caught Sayyed's glance, and the chief gave a slight nod of approval. Sayyed grinned.

The Reidhar warriors edged forward, waiting for their lord's command until Caurus waved them back.

"Lord Athlone, tell her she is not to interfere."

"I do not need to, Caurus. She would not do so."

"So be it. Begin the duel."

The Hunnuli and the travelers withdrew to the edge of the ring of people as Athlone and Gringold approached each other. The two men faced off silently and raised their swords above their heads until the two points touched. Gringold's anger had hardly abated from the night before. His rugged face was twisted into a sneer of rage. Athlone was almost expressionless, and his eyes watched the wer-tain with the calculating calm of a hunter.

Into the silence stepped the clan priest of Surgart. He raised his arm. "God of war, god of justice," he shouted. "Behold this contest and judge these men. Choose your champion!" At his last word, the priest swung his arm down and the two men brought their swords clashing together.

Eurus's observation was right; Gringold held his sword only in his right hand, but he used his left to punch, gouge, and grab, and his reach was several fingers longer than Athlone's. His strength was greater, too, and he bore down on the chieftain with the power and fury of a bear.

Athlone met Gringold's sword attack blow for blow. He soon realized, though, that without a shield, he could not keep up his guard against the brute strength of the wer-tain. He ducked to avoid a punch to his head, slipped under Gringold's arm, and, switching his sword to his left hand, nicked the man in the ribs. The wer-tain roared in rage and doubled his attack.

The sounds of clashing swords rang through the treld as the men fought in wordless fury. Time and again Gringold tried to beat down Athlone or crush him with his greater strength, but the chieftain was faster, more agile, and used his sword with either hand. Neither man could force a killing blow on the other, so they both struggled to wear the other down and catch a weakness or a fatal slip.

Before long, the men were sweating heavily. Gringold was bleeding from several cuts and nicks from Athlone's sword. Athlone's jaw throbbed from a well-landed punch, and his muscles were aching. He drew back a moment to wipe the sweat from his eyes.

"Too much for you?" Gringold sneered. "Would you care to kneel here and let me end it? I'll kill you swiftly."

Athlone jeered with contempt, "You couldn't hit a dead horse, you lumbering oaf."

Gringold charged the Khulinin, his sword swinging in a vicious arc. Athlone dodged and slashed at the man's legs as he passed. The blade caught Gringold's right thigh and cut deep into the muscle. The man staggered.

At that moment, Gabria heard Sayyed mutter a strange phrase, and she saw Gringold pitch forward to land heavily on the ground. To everyone else the wer-tain appeared to have fallen because of his wounded leg, but Gabria knew better. Her hand clamped around Sayyed's arm.

"Stop that, now!" she hissed.

The Turic shrugged like a boy caught in mischief. "Do you want Lord Athlone to lose?" he whispered.

"Of course not. But he has to win this alone. He would not tolerate our help."

"All right, but if you change your mind . . ."

They turned back to the duel in time to see Athlone press his attack on the fallen man. Gringold barely avoided the chief's sword by rolling under the blow and deliberately tripping Athlone with his legs. The chief fell on top of him, and Gringold took the opportunity to land several punches on Athlone's face.

The Khulinin chief, his head reeling, struggled out of the way and climbed to his feet. He faced the wer-tain with his sword in both hands. He could taste blood in his mouth, and his eye was beginning to swell. He drew some deep breaths as the wer-tain staggered to his feet. They glared at each other through their blood and sweat.

Swinging his sword in short, wicked, slashes, Athlone feinted toward Gringold's wounded leg just enough to force the man's sword down, then he cut upward for the throat. The Reidhar's reflexes were not fast enough to parry the jab, so he slammed his fist into the chief's stomach. The blow deflected Athlone's arm just enough to throw off the blade. The sharp edge cut the skin of Gringold's neck and slid by.

The heavy punch threw Athlone off balance, and he stumbled, gasping for air. Instantly the wer-tain jumped after him and jabbed his sword toward the chief's upper body. Athlone saw the blade coming. He tried to twist out of the way, but the point caught him in the hollow of his right shoulder. He snarled in pain, wrenched away from the blade, and fell heavily on his side. His sword was jarred out of his hand. It landed in the dirt a few feet away from his outstretched fingers.

Gringold shouted in delight. The wer-tain, his neck and leg running with blood, slashed his blade down at Athlone's head. The Khulinin twisted away from the blow and reached for his weapon.

"Oh, no, you don't," Gringold cursed. Unable to reach Athlone's fallen sword himself, he tossed aside his weapon and jumped on the chieftain. He wrapped his hands around Athlone's throat and grinned at the delight of killing a man with his bare hands.

"Gabria, please!" Sayyed whispered fiercely.

The sorceress clenched his arm. "No."

Athlone's world suddenly closed in around him in a red vise of pain. He struggled desperately to dislodge the heavy wer-tain sitting on his chest and to pull off the hands that were slowly strangling him. He might as well have tried to move a mountain. Inexorably the agony increased. The blood roared in his ears, and the used air burned in his lungs. His strength drained away.

Unbeknownst to him, the power of his sorcerer's blood began to build in every fiber of his being. In his last moments of lucid thought, he remembered his sword lying only inches away from his fingers. He gave a frantic, tremendous lunge that brought him close to the weapon. He stretched every muscle and tendon in his arm to reach the hilt.

Gringold paid no attention to the heaving of his victim. He was too certain of victory. The Khulinin would be dead in seconds. He closed his eyes and bared his teeth as he squeezed harder.

All at once, Athlone's fingers touched the cold leather wrapping the hilt of his sword. In that moment, his rage and desperation fused with the magic within him into a furious surge of power. A faint aura of blue, so dim it could not be seen in the morning sun, glowed around his fingers as he clamped onto the sword. The energy burst outward from every muscle and nerve ending, and galvanized into one mighty effort. He brought the sword up and over, hacking into the curve of Gringold's unprotected neck. The blade cut into muscle; blood splattered over both men. Unseen, a pale burst of blue sparks exploded out of Athlone's hand as the magic power seared into the wer-tain's body.

Gringold died instantly. He jerked once and slowly toppled over Athlone, his dead face twisted in a grimace of surprise and rage.

Athlone gasped a lungful of air. He felt the pain and roaring in his head recede into darkness. A blessed quiet stole over him, and, as his sword fell from his hand, he passed into unconsciousness.

9

A shocked silence hung over the crowd for several moments while everyone stared at the two men lying in the dust. Then the quiet was shattered. The clanspeople broke loose in excited talk, sporadic cheers, and wailing from Gringold's relatives.

Gabria drew a long, ragged breath and slumped against Nara. She tasted blood in her mouth where she had bitten her lip.

He lives, Eurus told her, and she nodded gratefully.

Piers and the Reidhar's healer stepped out of the crowd at the same time and hurried to their men. They pulled Gringold's heavy body off Athlone and checked the two warriors. The clan healer glanced at Lord Caurus and shook his head.

Caurus gritted his teeth. The duel was over. Surgart had chosen his champion.

The ring of clanspeople began to break up. Several men approached the wer-tain's body and bore him away to his family. The travelers gathered around Athlone.

"He's not badly hurt," Piers assured them. "He has mostly bruises and flesh wounds."

"Then why do I feel like a stampede just ran over me?" Athlone croaked. The chieftain opened his eyes and squinted at the anxious faces around him.

Sayyed flashed his bright grin. "A stampede did run over you. A very large and ugly one."

Carefully, with Piers's help, Athlone sat up. "He's dead?"

They all nodded.

"I had the strangest feeling when I struck him. I thought I . . ." Athlone stopped and looked at his hand.

Piers and Gabria exchanged wondering glances.

"Most men have strange feelings when they're being strangled," Bregan said.

Piers quickly stanched the bleeding in Athlone's shoulder, and he and Bregan helped the chief to his feet.

Athlone breathed deeply in the warm spring air. "Saddle your horses. We're leaving." His words were hoarse from his bruised throat, but his tone was adamant.

"My lord," Piers protested, "you can't possibly ride."

At that moment, Lord Caurus joined them. Most of his belligerence was gone, replaced by a modicum of concern and regret. "Lord Athlone, surely you will rest here tonight."

The Khulinin chieftain glared at him. He was aching, his shoulder was on fire, his face was battered and bruised, and he was utterly exhausted. He was in no mood to placate this bad-mannered lout. "You said one night, we stayed one night. I will *not* remain in this treld another hour."

Caurus's face flamed bright red. He started to say something, but Athlone straightened, let go of Bregan, and walked away without another word. The others followed. Caurus made no effort to go after them.

While Athlone sat on a stool and Piers fussed over him, Gabria and the men packed their gear, saddled the horses, and prepared to leave. When they were ready to go, Athlone turned his gray stallion over to Bregan and mounted Eurus. Gabria hid a smile of joy and relief. Since none of the Reidhar came to bid them farewell, the party left the treld without fanfare and rode west up the valley to rejoin the caravan road.

They had traveled only a few leagues from the treld before Piers took a close look at Athlone's pale face. He called an immediate halt and ordered the chieftain to rest. Ignoring Athlone's protest, the party stopped and made camp along the banks of a small stream. Gabria arranged the chief's blankets on a soft mat of leaves and grass; Piers gave him a mild concoction of poppy extract and wine. Athlone decided he was too weary to argue further. He drank the wine and was asleep in moments.

Bregan, too, lay down to sleep in the warm sun, and Valar and Keth went hunting. The others stayed near camp and relaxed.

Gabria changed from her woman's skirts back into her pants and warm tunic, which were more practical and comfortable than skirts on a journey like this. She had learned to enjoy the easy movement and the lighter weight of pants. She pushed back her hair and went to start a cooking fire. She hoped the hunters would find something. The supplies were dwindling fast.

"Rider coming," Secen shouted. The travelers drew together and watched warily as a horseman, leading a pack animal, came up the valley. The man, who wore the yellow Reidhar cloak, stopped at the edge of camp and saluted respectfully. He did not seem surprised to find them so close to the treld.

"Lord Caurus ordered me to bring you these supplies and to offer his apologies. He hopes that when the Khulinin visit again he will be able to prove his hospitality."

"I hope so, too," Secen muttered.

Piers stepped forward to take the packhorse's lead rope. "Thank you, rider. Please take our greetings to Lord Caurus."

The man nodded civilly and left the way he had come.

Gabria, Piers, and Sayyed unpacked the horse, and after hobbling him with the rest of the string, examined what Lord Caurus had sent.

"For a man who claimed to have had a bad year, he certainly was generous," Gabria said, holding up a nutcake.

Sayyed looked over the parcels and bundles. "He sent everything Lord Athlone asked for."

"And then some," Piers remarked. "Oh, look at this." He held up a carefully wrapped cask of Reidhar's famous honey wine. "I could almost forgive him his rudeness."

"Do you suppose the man is feeling a little guilty?" the Turic asked in heavy sarcasm.

"Guilty as a horse thief," Gabria replied with satisfaction.

She and Piers repacked the extra gear while Sayyed fed the horses. Next they laid out the delicacies and set about preparing the evening meal. Shortly before sunset, the two warriors returned with several rabbits and a small deer. The plain, meager meal Gabria had expected was transformed into a feast.

The smell of roasting meat awakened Bregan and Athlone and lured both warriors to the fire. The chieftain sat down and leaned back against a fallen tree trunk while Gabria poured a cup of wine for him.

"You're a sight," she said, studying his battered face. She wanted to say more, to tell him how relieved she was that he was alive, but the words stuck in her throat. She had made her vow to avoid further difficulties with Athlone and Sayyed until later, and she was going to stick by her decision. She handed him the wine cup and watched as he drained it, then she filled it again.

Athlone tried to grin, but the pain of his swollen face made him wince. He said nothing, for talking still bothered his throat, and watched Gabria return to the fire. The wine warmed his stomach, and the evening breeze was pleasant on his face. An unexpected contentment stole over him. For the first time in many days, he did not worry or grow angry or morose. He was too happy to be alive and in the company of these companions. Even Sayyed.

The young Turic was sitting nearby, keeping an eye on the roasting meat and repairing some tears in the sleeve of one of his robes. Athlone noticed that even though Sayyed poured his attention on Gabria, she was keeping her distance from both of them. She had hardly spoken to either man in two days.

Perhaps there was some hope, Athlone thought to himself, that Gabria's relationship with Sayyed was not what he imagined. Perhaps he had jumped to conclusions too soon. Already he regretted his precipitous ending of their betrothal the night before last. He had not planned that, and he had not given Gabria a chance to talk. Now she might never tell him how she felt out of injured pride and hurt. Athlone sighed. He had made a serious mistake by getting so angry; he had set their relationship back almost to the beginning. If he ever wanted to let her go, now was the time to do so. However, Athlone knew he could not give her up so easily. Even if she loved the Turic, the chieftain wanted to try to win her back. He slowly drank his wine and watched Gabria as she helped prepare the meal.

When the food was cooked, the travelers gathered around the fire to enjoy a hot meal and the gifts sent by Lord Caurus. They ate so much stewed rabbit, roast venison, cheese, fresh bread, winter squash, and nutcakes that no one bothered to move after the meal was over. Everyone lounged by the fire, redolent with food and wine. Athlone was still weak from loss of blood, but the bone-deep exhaustion was gone, and he propped himself by the tree trunk and relaxed in the tranquil evening.

Keth brought out a wood whistle he had made and piped tunes to the rhythm of the dancing flames. Sayyed uncovered his gaming stones to take his chances with Bregan. Gabria stayed by Piers, watching and listening to the men around her.

Sayyed, sitting across the fire from Gabria, played the stones and smiled at her with barely concealed hope and yearning. He was not the least upset by her sudden withdrawal from their increasing intimacy. She had not shut him out completely, and the caring that still lurked in her smile and her eyes fed his hope. He would simply bide his time.

A pale moon hung over the camp, and the night was cool with a mild breeze. An owl hooted nearby. Athlone was about to return to his blankets when all at once, Gabria sprang to her feet.

"Athlone, someone is near the camp!"

The chief sat up, and the men jumped to their feet, their hands reaching for their weapons. Beyond the firelight, Nara neighed in the darkness. Her call sounded to Gabria more like a greeting than a warning.

They peered into the darkness around them, until Bregan pointed to an indistinct, pale form on the edge of a grove of trees near the camp.

"Come forward," the old warrior shouted.

A cloaked figure shuffled hesitantly into the farthest reaches of the firelight.

"Are you the Khulinin party?" a muffled voice called.

Athlone struggled to his feet. "Who wants to know?" he answered.

"I am looking for the Corin girl. The one they call 'sorceress,' " came the reply.

Before Athlone could stop her, Gabria stepped forward. "I am here." She sensed no danger from this person, but she was glad when the three Hunnuli appeared out of the night and gathered around her.

The shrouded figure gasped and stepped back at the sight of the huge, black horses.

"I am Gabria of Clan Corin," the sorceress said gently. "Don't be frightened. What is it you want?"

The stranger seemed to take courage from Gabria's calm voice and edged into the firelight. "I saw you at the treld, but you left before I could talk to you." With trembling hands, the stranger pushed back the hood of the bright yellow Reidhar cloak and revealed the face of a woman. She was not a beautiful woman and never had been. Years of toil and living out in the dry wind and sun had taken a hard toll on her thin, angular face. She was well past middle age, gray-haired, and she wore no jewelry or ornaments to mark her as a member of the higher social ranks of her clan.

"How did you know we were here?" Bregan demanded

"I overheard the outrider who brought the supplies tell Lord Caurus where you were camped." She glanced warily at the men and turned back to Gabria. "I have something I must give you, Lady," the woman said nervously. "It is very important." She pulled at something hidden behind her. "Come on!" she cried and yanked harder. A small grubby girl stumbled out from the folds of the yellow cloak. The girl tried to clutch her companion's skirts, but the woman thrust her toward Gabria.

"This is Tam. She is ten summers old. My sister died giving birth to her," the clanswoman told Gabria desperately. "She is a magic-wielder like you. Please, take her with you. With you she will be safe. I can't hide her talent much longer, and if Lord Caurus finds out he will kill her."

Gabria was astounded. She looked speechlessly from the little girl to the clanswoman.

"We can't take a child with us," Khan'di began to say, but Athlone cut him off with a gesture.

"How do you know she can wield magic?" the chief asked.

The woman gestured nervously. "She can! She does things. She . . . she's different."

Gabria laid her hand on Nara's neck. "Is the child a magic wielder?" she asked the mare.

Yes. The mare answered. Her foal whinnied in agreement.

The sorceress knelt down to look Tam in the face. The child was dirty and disheveled. Her ragged clothes were obviously hand-downs from a larger child, but her features were pretty and her unkempt hair was thick and black. Her enormous eyes had an intense, wary gaze that seemed much too old for her years.

Gabria felt her heart melt. Khan'di was right, they did not need a child along. This journey would be long and dangerous, and the chances of survival were questionable. Still, as Gabria studied Tam's troubled face, she felt no doubt. This little girl was a kindred spirit, a magic-wielder, and as such she should be nurtured, protected, and taught, not left to the questionable mercy of someone like Caurus.

"Would you like to come with us, Tam?" Gabria asked.

"She can't talk," the woman cut in.

"Can't or won't?" Piers inquired.

The clanswoman shrugged. "She hasn't spoken since her father died five years ago. My husband says she's a weakling."

Gabria gently pushed a strand of dark hair away from Tam's eyes. "Did your husband also say how she got this?" She turned the little girl's head toward the firelight and pointed to a large, purplish bruise on her temple.

The woman sidled back, her expression a mixture of fear and

sadness, and said, "That's why you've got to take her. She won't last much longer with me."

"I don't know how safe she'll be with us," Gabria said.

"At least she'll have a chance," the woman pleaded. "Tam's your kind. You'll take care of her. I can't!" Before anyone could stop her, she tossed a small bundle on the ground, turned, and fled into the darkness.

The warriors started after her, but Athlone stopped them. "Let her go." They came back, sheathing their weapons.

Khan'di, his heavy face frowning, came forward. "Lord Athlone, I must protest. This is no journey for a child. We can't lose any more time by dragging her along."

Piers knelt beside Tam and ran his long fingers over the bruise on her head. "She seems healthy, if undernourished. She should be able to stand the journey."

"Besides, we can't just leave her here," Sayyed said.

"Or take her back to Lord Caurus," Keth added.

Athlone quirked an eyebrow at the sudden rush to defend this little girl. He agreed with Khan'di's protest, but at the moment, they did not have much choice. "She'll have to go," he decided. "The Hunnuli can look after her, and we can spare enough food for one more small mouth."

Gabria smiled at Athlone gratefully and, for a moment, the pain in his heart receded under the warmth of her relief and pleasure.

Tam had not budged during the departure of her aunt or the exchange between the men. She stood as if rooted to the ground, too frightened to move. Gabria was surprised by her total silence. The little girl did not cry or speak or even whisper. She just stayed in the place where her aunt had left her and stared fixedly at the sorceress in front of her. Gabria slowly held out her wrist where the jewel splinter glowed red under her skin.

"Tam," she said softly. "I am Gabria. I am a magic-wielder, too."

Tam did not respond. Her small face was pale under the dirt, and her hands were clenched at her sides.

The sorceress cast a glance at the men. Only Piers, Athlone, and Sayyed could see what she was doing, so she picked up a stone the size of her fist. She smiled at Tam. "Watch." The months of practice in the stone temple came to Gabria's aid, and with just a single word, she transformed the stone into a perfect sweetplum.

Tam's eyes grew huge. The men around her started in surprise.

"How did you do that?" Sayyed asked eagerly.

Gabria looked up at Athlone, the hint of a smile in her eyes. "Practice." She pressed the plum into Tam's hand and watched as the girl tasted it.

Tam tried a tentative bite, and her body seemed to relax a little. Plum juice ran down her chin as she devoured the fruit.

Lord Athlone said nothing at first. He was not sure what he should say about Gabria's display of sorcery. To be honest with himself, he had to admit her skill at changing the stone to a fruit intrigued him. It looked so simple, so useful. He watched Tam wipe her hands on her tattered skirt and, for the first time, the chief smiled at her. "Now that you have her attention," he said to Gabria, "why don't you give her a real meal. She looks famished."

Tam suddenly nodded eagerly, and she held out her hands imploringly.

Piers smiled. "There's certainly nothing wrong with her hearing."

All at once, Tam's eyes widened. Whirling around, she put her fingers to her lips and blew a piercing whistle. To everyone's surprise, a dog barked far down the valley. Gabria's mouth opened, and Athlone and Sayyed started in disbelief.

"Did you hear that?" Gabria gasped incredulously.

Bregan glanced around. "What? The dog?"

"I thought I heard—" She stopped.

"What?" Piers asked, puzzled.

The dog barked again, closer this time, and Gabria, Athlone, and Sayyed heard the words in their heads. *Tam! Tam! I'm coming. I am free, and I am coming!*

Suddenly the Hunnuli neighed, and a huge, mottled dog charged into the firelight, barking with frantic joy. A frayed rope dangled from his neck. He leaped on Tam and knocked her flat, licking her and whining with delight. The girl hugged him fiercely.

Gabria stared at the dog in amazement. "I can understand him!"

"The dog?" Khan'di frowned.

"Yes!" Sayyed agreed excitedly. "He is barking, but in my head I can hear his meaning."

Piers said, "Well, I don't."

"I do," Athlone said, astonished. He sank back down to his seat.

Khan'di crossed his arms. "That's ridiculous. It's just a dog. A scruffy looking one at that."

"It's a Tesser," Bregan told him. "A hunting dog from the northern forests. The Murjik breed them. These dogs are white in the winter and brown in the summer. He's shedding."

"Tesser or not, it's still a dog and dogs do not talk," Khan'di insisted.

Gabria shook her head. "No, he doesn't talk as we do, but something is translating his voice to us. I don't understand it. I've never heard of anything like this."

The dog in question sat down beside Tam and wagged his plumed tail. His lips pulled back in a wolfish grin. Carefully, Gabria held out her hand to let the dog sniff it. He woofed.

Hello, the magic-wielders heard. *I am Treader.*

"Treader," Gabria repeated in wonder.

Tam's pale face lit with a brilliant smile as if someone had just discovered her most wonderful achievement. Silently she tapped her chest then touched the dog.

"Ah," Gabria muttered, studying the child and the dog together.

Athlone caught her thought. "Tam did it?"

"She must have. Somehow she has put a spell on him to translate his voice, and because she used magic . . ."

"We can understand him, too," Sayyed finished.

"So why can't *we* hear this remarkable dog?" Khan'di asked.

"Tam's magic must be limited," Gabria answered. "Her spell was probably intended to translate Treader's voice only to a magic-wielder. She didn't know she was going to meet more of us." Gabria fingered the frayed end of the rope tied to the dog's collar. "I wonder whose dog it is?"

Secen said with a smirk. "Lord Caurus's, maybe?"

Tam shook her head and pointed to herself.

"I doubt it's hers," Bregan remarked. "It's a valuable dog. Should we take it back?"

At that, Tam leaped to her feet and flung herself on the dog's shoulder. Treader rose, barking furiously.

Athlone smiled lopsidedly. "Ah, no. He says he goes with Tam whether we like it or not. Besides, we don't have the time to go back."

"Think they'll come looking for it?" Sayyed asked.

The chieftain shrugged. He was exhausted again and ready for his blankets. "Probably not tonight," he muttered. "And we'll be leaving at dawn." As Piers came to help him, he waved a hand at Tam. "Feed the child." In a moment, he sank into his rough bed with deep relief and was asleep before the others returned to the fire.

Khan'di grumbled something about troublesome children and retired to his tent. The rest of the group gathered around the fire and brought out the remains of their meal. The Hunnuli foal tagged along.

Sayyed grinned as he watched Tam dive into a bowl heaped high with bread, meat, and cheese. "She's so small. Where is she putting it all?"

"She acts as if she hasn't eaten in days," Valar said.

Bregan nodded. "Maybe she hasn't. She certainly doesn't look well cared for."

"Her kinswoman didn't even say good-bye," Gabria said.

"No," agreed Piers. "But Tam doesn't appear to be upset about it."

The little girl listened to them all and kept her thoughts hidden behind her bright eyes. When she was finally finished, she laid her plate down and smiled her thanks.

The night was late by that time, and one by one the men went to their beds to sleep. Gabria collected the bundle of Tam's meager belongings and nestled her down in a small traveling tent. Nara and Eurus returned to grazing, but the foal stayed near Gabria's tent.

Early the next morning, in the dim moments before the sun rose, Gabria awakened and found Tam's bed empty. Hastily she donned her pants and tunic, and ran outside, only to stop and smile with relief. Tam had not gone far. She slept curled up beside the Hunnuli foal, her head pillowed on his warm side, her hand resting on his leg. The dog lay at her feet, and Nara stood protectively over them all.

The mare turned her dark eyes to Gabria. *The child will do well. She has already tamed her Hunnuli.*

Gabria was pleased to agree.

The travelers prepared to leave their camp soon after sunrise. Athlone was much stronger after a night's sleep, and he swore he could ride Eurus with no difficulty. Piers tried to convince him to rest another day, but the chieftain knew that they should not waste any more time. Although Gabria had said nothing, Athlone sensed her restlessness and recognized the way her eyes constantly turned to the north. Khan'di, too, was growing impatient. The danger in Pra Desh would not wait.

So they packed their gear, obliterated their camp, and rode out of the Reidhar's valley. If anyone from the treld missed a dog, they did not bother to chase the Khulinin party.

As they trotted over the line of hills marking the valley, Gabria glanced back at Tam riding behind her on Nara, and she wondered if the little girl was unhappy to be leaving her home. To her relief, Tam did not seem to be upset. The girl wagged her fingers at the Hunnuli foal trotting by her foot and stared out over the plains with a shy look of delight. Whatever Tam was leaving behind would not be missed.

In the days that followed, Gabria had no reason to change her mind about Tam or regret that she had accepted the little girl. Tam was an intelligent child who tried to be helpful. She learned quickly not to annoy Khan'di, and she was wary of Athlone and the warriors, but Sayyed could bring a shining smile to her face and Gabria held her trust. She settled in to the difficult routine of the journey, and the steady food and attentive care soon filled out the hollows in her cheeks and erased the dark circles around her eyes.

The humans in the party quickly discovered Tam would be no trouble for them. True to Athlone's word, Nara and Eurus guarded the little girl like one of their own offspring. One or both of them were always close by to keep her from harm. Nara's colt helped in his own way, for he tagged after Tam constantly, making it easier for his elders to guard them both. The dog, Treader, stayed with his mistress most of the time, but he liked Sayyed, too, and once in a while the Turic would take him hunting. Treader's catches helped supplement their supplies and more than made up for what he and Tam ate.

For all these happy achievements, Gabria could not overcome the little girl's silence. She never made any noise at all. Even if she was a mute, Gabria thought Tam should be able to make some sound—a cry, a groan, or a whimper. But the girl was totally silent. She was so still the men often forgot she was there. When someone spoke, she sometimes flinched before she realized who was talking to her, then she would look at the ground and nod politely. Only when no one seemed to be paying attention to her would Tam lift her eyes and watch everyone with her grave, fascinated gaze.

While Tam liked Gabria and seemed to be happy, she did not become deeply attached to any of the people in the party. Gabria thought the little girl had been so neglected in her past that she had withdrawn into the sanctuary of herself, a place where only pure and gentle creatures like the dog and the Hunnuli were allowed. Gabria could not help but wonder if any human would ever be able to draw her out from behind her walls.

10

Several days after leaving Reidhar Treld, the travelers abandoned the caravan trail and struck across country for Calah. The traffic on the caravan route had increased with every passing league until the party found it impossible to avoid detection. At Khan'di's urging, they left the easy trail and sought a faint, seldom-used path that was shorter and much rougher than the caravan route. Here the grasslands and meadows gave way to higher hills, rock-strewn valleys, and thicker woods of oak, juniper, and pine. The tall prairie grass was replaced by brambles, brush, and vines. The Ramtharin Plains had come to an end in the Redstone Hills, the boundary between the grasslands of Valorian's clans and the rich farmlands and forests of the kingdom of Calah.

The travelers pushed on as fast as they could, the warmer winds of advancing spring coming swiftly on their heels. The closer they drew to Pra Desh the more Khan'di urged them on. He knew if the fon stayed with her original plan for the invasion of Portane, the party would arrive in Pra Desh with very little time to spare. There was also the possibility that the fon had changed her plans or plotted some new outrage for the city. Khan'di had been gone from Pra Desh for over two months, and he was frantic to get home to lay plans of his own.

Gabria, too, felt the urgency of the passing days. The memory of the terrible vision played in her memory time and again, driving her on toward Pra Desh like a goad in the hands of an unseen but brutal taskmaster.

One afternoon, as she rode Nara along the rugged slopes of the Redstone Hills, Gabria thought again about her confrontation with Branth. She was not looking forward to that encounter. With luck and some cunning of their own, the company might be able to find the renegade chieftain and slip him out of the city before the fon realized he was gone. Unfortunately, Gabria could not pin her hopes on things going that easily. Branth's magical powers were not only the fon's greatest weapon, but her greatest peril, as well. She was certain to have him imprisoned and guarded like a dangerous animal.

Gabria allowed herself a sigh. She was not ready for this confrontation. She had learned the basic skills of sorcery from the Woman of the Marsh in a hurried lesson that had lasted only two days. There had been no time to practice or prepare before she'd met Lord Medb for the duel, and her victory over him had been founded on tenacity and luck. Since that time she had only been able to practice during the months of her banishment—months that now seemed brief indeed. To all intents and purposes she was still an apprentice. Yet everyone expected her to face a sorcerer who was better prepared and had the *Book of Matrah*.

She shot a look at Athlone and Sayyed on the trail ahead of her. It was too bad she did not feel ready to teach them the rudiments of sorcery. Athlone had the strength to wield his talent well. Gabria did not know about Sayyed's natural abilities, but if his determination and personality were any indication, he could be as powerful a sorcerer as Athlone. If only she felt capable enough to teach them!

Her thoughts were still on sorcery and the future when the party crossed over a high, craggy ridge into the kingdom of Calah and looked down on the valley of a broad river.

"There is Pra Desh," Khan'di told his companions, pointing down the valley to the south. The city was still leagues away, but from their vantage point, the travelers could make out the high towers, the white walls, and the vast harbor of the huge city.

The river in the valley, the Serentine, flowed from the forests far to the northwest. It ran east across the northern plains, past Amnok Treld, Bahedin Treld, and three of the Five Kingdoms, gaining substance and changing from a tumbling stream to a wide, majestic river. At the end of its long journey, the Serentine swept past the feet of the Redstone Hills and into the finest natural harbor in the Sea of Tannis.

Here, at this propitious meeting of river, land, and sea, the people of Calah built their capital and nourished it into the richest and most powerful maritime city on the Tannis. Their fleet controlled the northern and western coasts and roved the sea to its farthest reaches. The merchants of Pra Desh traded everything in the known world from raw materials such as grain, timber, and ore to livestock, slaves, and finely wrought crafts. They shipped silk, wool, and cotton, jewelry, spices, wines, pottery, weapons, and carpets. They brought anything that could be bought to the marketplaces of Pra Desh and filled their coffers with the gold coins of many realms.

After a moment, Khan'di pointed to the right, and the travelers saw where their path wound down out of the hills to the valley and joined the caravan route as it paralleled the river to the city. They rode on to the last heavily wooded hill before the path dipped down to the open farmlands. There, Khan'di led the party into the shadows of the trees.

He turned his horse around and addressed the others. "Pra Desh is only three leagues away, and I want to get you into the city unnoticed. The fon's spies are on every street of Pra Desh and at every gate. They have orders to report *anything* unusual."

Gabria sadly ran her hand down Nara's neck. She knew what she was about to say would be painful, but she had thought about it for days and there was no other way to maintain the party's anonymity. "We will have to leave the Hunnuli," she said quietly.

Khan'di bowed his head to her in mixed respect and relief. "Lady Gabria, you have saved me the pain of asking that favor. Unfortunately, there are no other Hunnuli in my country, and as far as anyone knows the only one in the clans belongs to the great Corin sorceress. You would not be safe for long on the streets of Pra Desh."

The young woman nodded unhappily. Although she had made the suggestion, the thought of leaving Nara behind made her very uncomfortable. "Do you mind?" she asked the black mare.

Of course I do, Nara answered. *Leaving you goes against everything I am. But you are right. It must be done.*

If you really need us, we will come, Eurus added.

"Thank you," Gabria replied.

"All right," Khan'di said. "Listen. We will separate here. I should not be seen with clansmen. It might also be best if you split up and enter the city in small groups." He dismounted, found a stick, and drew a detailed map in the dirt.

"This is the Serentine River," he explained to his listeners, pointing to the relevant marks with his stick. "This is the harbor, this the Redstone Hills. Here is the old city wall on the west side of the river. It extends around the fon's palace here on Second Hill, the temple of Elaja on First Hill, and the older residential districts, warehouses, and merchant offices. This is the arsenal where the fon's guards live and the weaponry is stored.

"The city, of course, has long outgrown these walls, and you will find the markets, the auction houses, and the shipwrights' yards here, here, and here." He pointed to each spot on his map. "The rest of the city spreads out this way to the north along the river and up the slopes of the hills. The land to the east is swampy and often floods. Only the poorer peasants, criminals, and runaway slaves live there. Do you understand so far?"

The fascinated clanspeople nodded in unison.

"Good. Now, there is a row of warehouses here in the old city. Follow this caravan road through the gate called the Sun Door. If you look for the tall buildings with the different colored flags on their towers, you will find the warehouses. Go to the fifth one in the row. It is a wool house and will be flying an orange flag. There is a wooden sheep hanging above the doors. Go there and wait for me. Do not wander around. Do not ask questions."

"What will you be doing?" Athlone demanded.

"Seeking information." Khan'di's heavy face broke into a scheming grin. "I have spies on every street, too."

"Whose warehouse is it?" Piers asked coldly.

"My cousin's. He pretends to be a supporter of the fon, but he has been helping me." The Pra Deshian actually rubbed his hands together and chuckled. It was obvious he was delighted to be back in the midst of the intrigue and political scheming.

"What do we say if we meet anyone at the warehouse?" Gabria asked.

"Say nothing." He glanced at the sun through the tree branches. "By the time all of you get there, the warehouse will be empty except for my cousin. He usually works late. He will know who you are."

Athlone grunted. "Do you trust this man?"

"Totally. His daughter is my son's wife. He knows what I will do to her if he betrays me."

The travelers were quiet for a time as they studied Khan'di's map. The Pra Deshian mounted his horse. "Remember. The fifth warehouse." He spurred his horse back to the path.

"Be careful, Khan'di Kadoa," Gabria called after him.

He glanced back, hiding his pleasure at the concern in her voice. "You, too, Sorceress."

Reluctantly Athlone, Gabria, and Tam dismounted from Eurus and Nara. The chieftain wiped out Khan'di's map with a leafy branch while the others unloaded one of the packhorses and secreted most of the traveling gear and tents in a dense thicket.

Gabria was wearing her riding skirts that afternoon, so she brought out a long, cotton scarf and wrapped it like a veil over her head and across her mouth and nose. In her travel-stained garments, she would pass as a simple clanswoman. While she gathered a few belongings out of the packs for herself and Tam, someone bumped into her. Gabria turned and came face to face with Athlone.

The chief was as dirty and travel-worn as she and still bore the evidence of his recent battle. His face had lost its swelling, and he could see out of both eyes, but the bruises were colorful shades of blue, green, and yellow.

Gabria decided his bruises and his newly sprouted beard gave him a raffish look. Hesitantly she touched his arm. "You look like a border ruffian," she teased.

For a moment, he almost gathered her in his arms. He turned toward her, lifting his hands to caress her face, then he saw Sayyed standing close behind her with a strange glint in his black eyes. Athlone's impulse faltered in a rush of renewed doubts. His hands fell back to his sides.

To hide his confusion, he patted Eurus, then swung up on his gray stallion. "Mount up, you motley plains rats. Let's ride." His warriors grinned at him and sprang to obey.

"Bregan, you and I will ride with Lady Gabria. Piers, you go with Tam, Sayyed, and Secen. You two," Athlone said to the last warriors, "are on your own. Go first. Don't get lost and don't stop to chase the women." The two warriors saluted and trotted out of the woods.

Gabria threw her arms around Nara's neck. The world suddenly shimmered through the blur of her tears. "By Amara, I am going to miss you," she whispered to the mare.

Nara gently pressed her head against Gabria's back, enfolding the woman in the curve of her neck. *And I you.*

"I don't want to do this. It doesn't feel right."

I will be close. You only have to call.

Gabria sniffed and smiled lopsidedly. "Like in the marshes?" she asked, remembering that awful day she'd been forced to leave Nara behind to seek the Woman of the Marsh alone.

Yes, but this time you have friends with you. Trust them. They love you. I will be waiting when you are ready for me.

Gabria nodded. Lovingly she traced the white lightning mark on Nara's shoulder before she patted her again and stepped away. A sharp nudge almost knocked her over. She twisted around and found the foal nearly stepping on her feet, Tam hanging onto his wispy mane. Treader sat beside her, his ears drooping.

"Good-bye to you, too, little fellow," Gabria said.

The colt whinnied shrilly in reply.

Gabria was about to take Tam's hand, but the girl's stricken expression made her pause. The child's dark eyes were huge, and a trail of tears had blazed tracks through the dirty smudges on her cheeks.

She doesn't want to leave us, a light, childlike voice said in Gabria's mind.

The sorceress started in surprise; this was the first time the colt had sent his thoughts to her. She knelt by Tam. "You must understand," she said to the girl, "we are going to a big city. We cannot take the Hunnuli. It would be too dangerous for them, and for us, as well."

Treader barked. *She thinks she'll never see the horses again if she goes away.*

"They will wait for us," Gabria explained patiently. "When we return from the city, they'll come down from the hills and greet us." She took Tam's chin and lifted her head up until the girl had to look at her. "All you'll have to do is whistle and they'll come." She smiled. "You can whistle, can't you?"

The little girl grinned through her tears and nodded.

She wants to know if we will be gone long, Treader growled.

"No. Only a few days. All right?"

The colt bobbed his head, Treader woofed loudly, and Tam let go of the Hunnuli's mane to take Gabria's hand.

"That was some conversation," Athlone remarked as Gabria settled Tam on Piers's horse.

"Do you know what's really amazing? Tam never once opened her mouth. She can send her thoughts to these animals just like the Hunnuli do."

"Good gods," Athlone exclaimed. "Is that a natural part of her talent or something she learned to do?"

"I don't know," Gabria said. "I hope we can find out one of these days. It certainly is a useful ability."

The little girl sniffed loudly and wiped her nose on her sleeve, then she waved good-bye to the Hunnuli and settled comfortably against Piers's back.

Gabria touched the healer's knee. During their preparations he had sat on his horse without speaking or moving. Now, as he glanced down at Gabria, she was startled by the haunted expression on his face. His normally pale skin was deathly white; his thin features were pulled tight with tension. His hands were clenched around the saddle horn.

"Are you all right?" Gabria asked worriedly.

He nodded and drew a long, ragged breath. "I did not expect to feel my memories so sharply."

Gabria understood completely. "Face them," she whispered, "and you will find they are only ghosts." She waited while the healer considered her words, then he relaxed a little and took his hands off the saddle horn.

He squeezed her hand. "I'll see you at the warehouse." He reined his horse around, and he, Tam, Sayyed, and Secen took the two remaining packhorses and rode off through the trees. Treader ran ahead of them.

Reluctantly Gabria threw an extra saddle blanket over the withers of the pack mare and mounted. It felt so strange to sit astride such a small, thin horse. She gathered the reins and cast one last look at the Hunnuli, then she followed Athlone out of the trees and back to the path without a backward glance.

Before long, they trotted their horses over the last rise and down into the fertile Serentine Valley. Here, this close to the sea, the valley was so wide that the travelers could barely make out the hills on the opposite side. The land was so fertile almost every square acre was used for crops, pasturage, or vineyards. Huts, cottages, barns, sheds, farmhouses, and outbuildings of every kind were scattered on both sides of the river. The closer the riders drew to the city, the more numerous the cottages and houses became. Inns, hawkers' stands, and shrines appeared along the road. The caravan trail soon changed to a stone-paved road as other trails and paths met and joined it.

The flood of people, carts, wagons, and animals on the road increased with every step closer to Pra Desh. Gabria and her companions had seen several caravans and small groups of riders on their journey, but they were not prepared for the crowded, swarming populace that lived in Pra Desh. The clanspeople had never been to a city this size, and the largest group of people they had ever seen in one place was at their own clan gatherings. This city was mind-boggling. Even Piers, who was a native Pra Deshian, had lived on the open plains long enough to be taken aback by the throng that rushed purposefully back and forth. They crowded into the markets, crushed into the streets with a seemingly endless tangle of animals, pedestrians, and conveyances, and shouted, sang, talked, and bellowed in every known language.

Gabria tried not to let her mouth hang open as they followed the road into the city, but she could not hide her wide-eyed amazement at everything she saw. There were so many new things to look at!

Pra Deshians were fervent in their worship of their one god and his prophets, and built shrines and temples at every wide spot by the road. There were also open markets, shops, tenements, stables, and huge houses all along the great caravan route.

The road passed through the outskirts of Pra Desh, past a guard post at the official city limits, and into the city proper. Customs officials were checking loaded wagons and collecting taxes from irate drivers. A squad of five guardsmen in purple tunics helped enforce the collection. They were too busy to notice the small groups of dusty clanspeople that rode by. Gabria breathed a sigh of relief as she, Athlone, and Bregan passed the guard and were lost to sight in the crowded streets.

They stayed close together in the streets, following the road as Khan'di had instructed. It still paralleled the river into the heart of Pra Desh's market district. They passed the huge fish market, the meatmongers' street, and the livestock market. One street seemed to be dedicated to the leather trade and another was obviously for bakers.

Along one particularly busy street, Bregan reined his horse closer to Athlone's and leaned over. "Lord, I don't think this city is at war yet." he said over the noise of wagons and pedestrians.

Athlone glanced around. He had come to the same conclusion. "You're right. But have you noticed the number of armed men in the crowds? The city looks like a fortified camp. The fon's invasion must be coming soon."

"So we have come in time," Bregan replied.

Gabria, riding close by, said, "I don't think there's much time left. I've been watching the people and they seem to be in an ugly mood. They don't like all the soldiers in their midst."

"I wonder how much cooperation the fon is getting from the Pra Deshians," said Athlone.

"We'll find out tonight from Khan'di," Gabria said.

The chieftain nodded once. "If he comes."

The travelers rode on in silence. After a while, the road curved away from the river and left the busy market streets behind. The riders passed through an entertainment district of theaters, libraries, and a huge amphitheater to a quieter residential area. The houses here were two-story stone and wood edifices set back from the streets behind privacy walls. The houses were older and showed signs of age, but most of them were well-maintained and their gardens overflowed with flowers.

The road began to rise up a gradual slope until abruptly the riders reached the old city wall. There was a wide gap between the houses and the towering wall, and Gabria felt vulnerable as she rode across the open space to the gate. The Sun Door was a high, arched entrance with two tall gatehouses to either side. A rising sun was carved on the huge wooden door that stood open to allow traffic to pass. More soldiers, these wearing the red of the fon's own guard, stood on both sides of the entrance and carefully scrutinized those who passed through. They ignored the glares and the ugly remarks hurled at them by the city people who went by, but they kept their hands on their swords at all times.

As unhappy as she was to leave Nara, Gabria was glad now the Hunnuli mare had stayed behind. The guards would have noticed the huge black horse instantly. As it was, they still paid more attention to Gabria and her companions than she cared for as she and the two men rode by.

Athlone nodded to one guard and passed under the arched gateway as if he'd done it all his life. Bregan and Gabria were quick to follow. The road led them deep into the maze of crowded, crumbling houses and dark alleys of the old city. Then, unexpectedly, the road split. The right hand way led uphill, and the left gradually dropped down toward the harbor.

Athlone reined his horse to a stop in the middle of the fork and studied each road.

"Which way, Lord?" Bregan asked, coming up beside him.

"Khan'di said to look for the tall buildings with the flags," said Gabria. "But I don't see any."

The three gazed at the city around them. To their right and atop a huge hill sat the temple of Elaja, its white columns and facade shining in the late afternoon sun. On a neighboring hill to the south was the magnificent palace of the fon. Even from a distance the riders could see the palace's multi-storied wings and the crenelated wall that surrounded the huge edifice.

Several buildings close by seemed to be barracks, and Athlone thought there was a dangerously large number of soldiers about. The presence of so many armed men around them alarmed him, so thinking quickly, Athlone spurred his horse to the left fork and trotted downhill. To his relief, the way opened up after a block or so, and he saw the full expanse of the busy harbor. At the bottom of the hill, just outside the city walls, were rows of tall buildings, each flying a different colored flag. Beyond those were the teeming wharves and the great crescent-shaped harbor.

Athlone allowed himself a grin of relief. He had not fancied the idea of asking a guardsman for directions. By the time the riders reached the rows of warehouses, the sun had sunk below the tops of the hills, the sign for laborers and workers to end their day. Athlone, Bregan, and Gabria found Keth and Valar loitering in the shadow of an alley between two warehouses. From there they watched the wool house and kept track of the workers as they left.

"Where's Piers?" Athlone asked when he dismounted.

Keth shrugged. "I don't know. We haven't seen him or the Turic."

"You don't think he's lost," said Valar.

Athlone scratched his beard. "I doubt it. Piers knows this city better than any of us."

"Maybe he went to find old ghosts," Gabria said, as if to herself. The men glanced at her in surprise.

"Well, we can't look for him. He'll have to make it here on his own," the chieftain noted. He took his place in the alley and waited for the remaining workers to leave the warehouse.

Twilight settled into the streets of Pra Desh, and the warehouse workers slowly filtered out and left. No one noticed the five riders waiting in the heavy shadows between the buildings.

At last the street was empty. Athlone was about to approach the warehouse when three horses, two packhorses, and a dog jogged down the street. The chief stepped out to meet them.

"Where have you been?" Athlone demanded.

"Gathering information of our own," Piers answered. He helped Tam down from the horse.

Athlone crossed his arms. He had been more worried than angry. "You could have been betrayed to the guard."

"Not by the people I talked to."

"You really don't trust him, do you?" asked the chieftain.

"Khan'di?" Piers's shoulders shifted slightly under his healer's robes. "Yes and no. I trust him only as long as we are useful to him."

Athlone agreed. "All right. Listen to him tonight and tell me afterward what you think."

The healer nodded with satisfaction. He had dreaded the possibility that Gabria was walking into a clever trap set by the fon, a trap that sported Khan'di Kadoa as bait. Two magic-wielders would be an invincible weapon in the fon's hands. But after what Piers had heard this afternoon from old friends and connections in the Healers' Guild, he doubted Khan'di was planning to betray Gabria.

It was common knowledge around the city that the Kadoa family had suffered severe financial losses because of the fon. Khan'di's wife and son were in hiding, and several other family members had been arrested and had subsequently disappeared into the depths of the palace. The powerful Kadoa family had no reason to love the fon and every reason to dispose of her. Several contacts had even hinted to Piers that Khan'di, as the most influential nobleman left in Pra Desh, stood a chance of assuming the coronet of the fon if she were removed. Piers knew his former friend well enough to know that possibility alone would be enough to ensure Khan'di's trustworthiness. The healer patted his mare thoughtfully. He would be very interested in hearing what Khan'di had to say tonight.

At a word from Athlone, Piers handed his reins to Sayyed and followed the chieftain toward the fifth warehouse. The others stayed behind to wait.

The huge timbered building loomed above them, dark and strange in the deepening twilight. The warehouse's big wooden sign creaked in the night breeze. Athlone stifled a shiver as he looked up at the building. Its unfamiliar size and blank walls made him distinctly uncomfortable.

He was about to knock on the warehouse entrance when the door was whisked open and a short, portly man rushed out. The man was going so fast he did not see Athlone and slammed full force into the big Khulinin. Both men grunted and staggered back. The stranger would have fallen if Piers had not caught him.

The man gasped at the sight of the two strangers at his door and threw his hands up in alarm. The hand lamp he was carrying swayed wildly.

"It's all right," Athlone hastened to explain. "Khan'di sent us."

The sound of that name seemed to reassure the man, for he straightened up and looked closely at the two men in the light of his lamp. When he saw the healer's face, he lit up in amazement. "Piers Arganosta! I thought you were dead!"

Piers grimaced. "I've heard that a lot today."

"You probably don't remember me," the Pra Deshian said with a grin. "I was quite a bit thinner in those days."

The healer studied the other's face for a moment, then he smiled in recognition. "Lord Athlone, this is Sengi Kadoa, Khan'di's younger cousin and a page to the fon."

"The old fon," Sengi corrected, his voice edged in anger. "Today I am a wool merchant and—" a devious look flashed across his features in the lamplight "—a spy. That woman on the throne looks to me for mercantile advice." Sengi looked around and ushered the two men into his warehouse. The door opened into a room obviously used as an office. He lit another lamp, and in the increased light the two men were able to get a closer look at their host.

Sengi bore a strong resemblance to Khan'di in the shape and density of his body frame, the heavy lines of his features, and in the ruddy coloration of his skin. But where Khan'di's eyes were sharp and calculating and his expression readily showed his cunning intelligence, Sengi's face was placid and his eyes were framed by skin crinkled from laughter.

The merchant straightened his rumpled robes with nervous hands and flicked his eyes from one man to the other. "Did Piers say 'Lord Athlone?' " he asked after a hesitant pause. "You are a clan chieftain?"

"Of the Khulinin," Athlone replied shortly.

The Pra Deshian's expression melted in obvious relief. "Did you bring the sorceress? Is she here?"

Athlone jerked his head toward the door. "Outside."

"Ah, praise Elaja!" Sengi clapped his hands. "Please, bring her in. The warehouse is empty. She will be safe."

"What about our horses?"

"There is a closed shed in back I use for the dray horses. There is enough room and grain for yours. Grain, ah!" He smacked his forehead. "I'll be back." With that, he bustled from the office, deeper into the warehouse.

Piers met Athlone's eyes and shrugged slightly. "He's always been like that. Busy. But he's an honest man to his friends. He'll do what he can."

In a short time, the travelers settled their horses in the shed behind the warehouse and gathered in the office to wait for Sengi. He came back carrying a bottle and a tray of food. His eyebrows went up at the sight of all the people, their gear, and the dog.

"Goodness. I did not expect so many." He looked over them all, especially Sayyed and the little girl, and was rather puzzled. "Is the sorceress with you?"

Gabria stepped forward to meet him. She untied her scarf and lowered the veil from her face. "I am Gabria."

Sengi blinked at her, then he smiled with welcome and relief. "Your disguise is good, Lady. It hides your fairness like a leather bag can hide a jewel. Please, come."

The merchant, still carrying his tray, led the party into the main warehouse. Even in the darkness they could sense the vast size of the room and hear its echoing emptiness.

"My stock is low at the moment," Sengi said, directing them toward the building's rear. "The fon has not interfered with my business as she has with Khan'di's, but she has imposed heavy taxes on all of us to finance her plans for war. I expect more wool soon from the north country." He shook his head. "But that bloodthirsty woman will suck up all of my profits. If we do not act soon, she will destroy the economy of this city, and without the merchants . . ." He let his sentence trail off, then ducked into a narrow gap in a pile of big bales. The pile reached up out of the range of the lanterns, into the darkness that clung to the high ceiling.

From the smell, the clansmen realized the bales were wool fleeces packed and tied together. One by one, the travelers followed the merchant through the gap and into a narrow space as wide as two men side by side and twenty paces long. The wool bales and the warehouse wall surrounded them.

Sengi set the tray and his lamp down on a wooden crate. "I created this space two months ago after Khan'di left for the plains. I thought it might be useful. My workmen will be here tomorrow, but if you are quiet and stay out of sight during the day, you can stay here as long as you need to. I will care for your horses."

The men looked around the space dubiously. "Is all of this secrecy really necessary?" Bregan asked.

The wool merchant glared at him. "If the fon hears even a rumor that the sorceress is in the city, she will tear Pra Desh apart to find her."

Athlone nodded once and set his gear down. The others followed his example. Sengi looked around to be sure all of his guests understood his warning. "Now then, I must get some more food." Again he rushed away into the warehouse.

While the merchant was gone, the travelers piled their weapons and packs out of the way and settled down to wait.

Piers picked up the bottle, uncorked it, and sniffed the contents.

"Andoran Wine," he said in delight. He found his own horn cup and poured a full measure.

The wine was being passed around when Sengi returned. More bread, cheese, sugared dates, and another bottle of wine filled his arms. Khan'di followed in his wake.

The others stared in amazement at the nobleman as he stepped into the lamplight. His travel-stained knee-length robes and leggings had been replaced by resplendent robes of brilliant blue and gold, trimmed with white furs and embroidered with gold threads. Rings clustered on his fingers, and a heavy gold chain with the dolphin emblem of the Kadoa family hung about his neck.

Khan'di smiled at their reaction. "I've been to court this afternoon to pay my respects to the fon. That is only right, since I am newly risen from my sick bed."

Athlone cocked an eyebrow. "Sick bed?"

"Before I left Pra Desh I had my seneschal spread the word that I had fallen ill with a contagious disease. My healer has convincingly kept up the lie for all these weeks. Now, at last, I am well. The fon seemed disappointed."

"Was it wise to reveal your return to health now?" Piers asked.

"It was the only way I could learn what I needed to know." He rubbed his hands together. "We have come just in time." He waited for a few minutes while Sengi bustled around, bringing a jug of water, a couple of leather stools, and another lamp.

When the wool merchant was satisfied, he nodded farewell to his guests. "Until tomorrow. And, Piers, I hope you will tell me how you came to be among the clans. Good night."

When he was gone, Khan'di lifted the hems of his robes and sat down on a stool. The travelers helped themselves to the food and wine and gathered around him.

Khan'di hesitated another moment before he began. "The fon has accomplished a great deal while I was gone," he said. "The entire kingdom of Calah is now completely in her grasp. No one has seen the young prince for days. It is rumored she had him thrown in the pit beneath the dungeon. She has either beggared, bribed, or destroyed many of the old noble Pra Deshian families, and the merchant guilds are almost bankrupt."

There was a deep undertone of anger and sadness in his voice, and as Gabria listened to him, she began to understand that Khan'di's motivations were not totally selfish. He truly cared for his city and its well-being. He wanted to protect his power, influence, and wealth, but he also wanted to protect Pra Desh. Perhaps Khan'di had earned Piers's distrust those many years ago in the old fon's court, but now he was striving to save his city—not just himself—from the ravages of a merciless ruler.

Khan'di went on. As he talked, he restlessly employed his hands to emphasize his words. "As you may have noticed, the fon has not yet begun her invasion of Portane. She has delayed in order to gather more draftees and mercenaries for her army. I haven't heard yet when she plans to strike."

"In about four days," Piers said quietly.

"Where did you hear that?"

"In a tavern. It was full of soldiers. They were complaining about leaving home."

Khan'di drew a deep breath. "Four days. That doesn't give us much time."

"Does the fon still have Branth?" Gabria asked.

"As far as anyone knows. No one has seen him, and there has been no sign of any sorcery."

"He's preparing," she said, her voice strangely distant. The memory of her dream-vision flared up in her mind, and she shuddered.

Athlone set his cup down and leaned back against a bale. "Preparing for what?"

"The strike against Portane?" Bregan suggested.

"Quite likely," said Khan'di. "I have arranged a meeting for tomorrow with the masters of the city's guilds. I am going to try to stage a distraction that will help you enter the palace unnoticed. There you should begin your hunt for the exiled chieftain."

Athlone looked at Gabria. Her face looked so pale, it worried him. "How do we get into the palace?" he asked the nobleman.

"I am working on that, too," Khan'di replied. "I have an idea, but I need to locate someone whose help we need."

"So what do we do in the meantime?" Athlone demanded.

"Wait. A day or two at most. We must move before the fon attacks Portane. If she breaks the alliance of the Five Kingdoms, the whole region will go to war. But we have to lay our plans well. The fon is no fool." He rose to go, his fine robes gleaming in the lamplight. "I will be back tomorrow if I can." He hesitated, his dark eyes on Gabria's face. "If I don't come back within two days, please try any way. We cannot leave a sorcerer in the fon's hands."

Wordlessly Gabria held out her hand, palm up. The nobleman

nodded and placed his hand, palm down, atop hers. They locked fingers in the clan gesture of sealing a vow.

Khan'di, satisfied, left their hiding place.

Athlone waited until he heard the warehouse door shut before he turned to Piers. "Is what he said true?"

The healer put his empty cup down and spoke with regret. "Unfortunately, yes. Perhaps even worse than he told us. The city is on the verge of open rebellion. The people here are terrified, but they've been abused as much as they're likely to stand. One spark will set them off."

Athlone looked thoughtfully at the gap where the Pra Deshian had disappeared. "Do you think Khan'di is about to provide that spark?"

"Undoubtedly."

"I just hope we don't get caught in the flames," Bregan muttered. The others could only nod their agreement.

11

They waited for three days in the wool merchant's warehouse, a wait that quickly became difficult. The stuffy confines between the wall and the bales reeked of lanolin, and the narrow, enclosed space was like a prison to the roving plains people. They could not talk or move around during the day for fear of attracting attention. At night they had to stay within the confines of the warehouse. Sengi brought them food and water, told them what news he knew, and gave them what he could to make them comfortable, but he could do little to ease their anxiety and restlessness.

Khan'di sent a message saying he was safe and still working on his plans. However, he could not come himself. Gabria worried about him and about all of her companions. The tension was wearing everyone thin.

She was particularly worried about Piers. The old healer spent most of his time drinking Sengi's wine and speaking to no one. He sat against the wall, his eyes staring at a place far away and his body sagging with the sadness of his memories. For his sake, Gabria prayed that their wait would soon end.

On the evening of the third day Khan'di finally returned, soon after the last laborer had left the warehouse. He brought with him a map of the palace and an old, ragged man wearing only a goatskin tunic and rough leggings.

Once again the travelers stared at Khan'di when he came into their hiding place. His rich court robes were gone, replaced by a shirt of chain mail, leather pants, greaves of steel, and a bright blue surcoat embroidered with his dolphin emblem. His normally controlled features were alive with anticipation. He held out his arms and cried, "Tonight, we go to war!"

The travelers gathered around him, everybody talking and asking questions at once. Piers rose from his place at the wall and came to join them.

"Please! I will explain," Khan'di called over the noise as he waved them to silence. Concisely, he told Gabria and the warriors of his plan to attack the palace and free Branth from the fon's clutches. When he was finished, they stared at each other and then at him in shock at the sheer audacity of his plan.

"Are you serious?" Gabria asked.

"Absolutely. The pieces have all fallen into place."

"You are relying on a great many pieces," Piers remarked dryly.

Khan'di's eyes blazed. "This plan will not fail."

"Can you trust him?" Athlone demanded, pointing to the old man who had been standing silently through the discussion.

"He is a hillman from one of the ancient tribes that live in the Redstone Hills. He has given his word that what he knows is true and that he will lead you where you need to go. He will die before he breaks his vow," Khan'di replied.

Athlone rubbed his chin. "Fair enough." He paused. "Will you give us your vow, as well?"

The nobleman locked eyes with the chieftain. "I swear to you before my god," Khan'di said, "and upon the honor of my family, I will raise the people and create the biggest riot this city has ever seen."

The chieftain studied Khan'di's face and was satisfied with what he saw. Gravely he responded, "Then I swear before our gods that we will follow your plan and do our best to find Branth."

"And kill him if you have to," Khan'di added. "Do not leave him in the fon's hands."

Athlone nodded. "Agreed."

"What about the fon?" Gabria asked.

"If all goes well, you won't have to worry about her. She'll be too busy fighting an uprising."

Piers looked dubious. He was the only one who completely understood the risks Khan'di was taking by trying to bring a city like Pra Desh into an armed revolt. "Are you so certain the army will mutiny?"

Khan'di slapped the hilt of the sword hanging at his belt. "Enough will. The fon's regulars won't, but the mass of the army is conscripted and they want no part of a war with the other kingdoms."

Piers shook his head. "My old friend, your audacity is astounding. Elaja be with you this night."

"And you, Healer." Khan'di looked around at them all. "Tomorrow we will meet again. Until then, good luck, my friends." He started to leave, then turned and squeezed Gabria's arm. "Thank you, Sorceress," he murmured.

When he was gone, the clanspeople gathered their weapons and their gear. They packed everything they did not need and stacked the bundles by the wall.

Piers exchanged his long healer's robe for a tunic and a pair of Athlone's woolen pants. He strapped his healer's bag to his belt. He was standing, staring at the floor when Gabria touched his arm. He nearly jumped out of his skin.

"Are you all right?" she asked, for his face was sickly pale. He seemed to have aged ten years the past three days.

The healer licked his dry lips. "I never thought I'd go back there. To the palace. Did I tell you my daughter died in that dungeon?"

Gabria's heart went out to him. "You only told me the fon had killed her."

"Tortured her," he corrected bitterly.

"We have Khan'di's map. You don't have to go."

Abruptly Piers's head snapped up. "Yes, I do, for both our sakes. Besides, a guide works better than a map."

"I am glad you think so, too," she said with relief and gratitude.

"What about Tam and Treader?" Sayyed asked. "Do we leave them with Sengi?"

The words were barely out of his mouth when Treader started barking madly. Tam sprang forward and wrapped her arms around the Turic's waist. Gabria, Athlone, and Sayyed clamped their hands over their ears to stifle the racket, but they could not silence Treader's frantic pleas ringing in their heads.

"He's trying to tell us that Tam is terrified to be left alone," Gabria cried over the barking.

A strange, sympathetic look came over Sayyed's face, and he bent down to pry Tam from his side. The girl transferred her grip to his neck, and he lifted her easily, whispering something in her ear. Treader's barking immediately stopped; the big dog's tail wagged. Sayyed glanced at Athlone and shrugged. "When I was small, I did not like to be alone either. I'll keep her with me."

The chief agreed, and Tam shyly smiled her thanks.

When they were ready to go, Athlone signaled to the hillman to lead the way. The old man could not speak their language or even the polyglot language of the wharves and streets. He merely grunted and loped out of the warehouse, expecting the others to follow.

The moment the travelers stepped out of the warehouse, they sensed something was different in the warm spring night. The city seemed to crackle with the tension of a coming storm. A strange brightness from thousands of torches glowed in the market streets and guild houses. An angry murmur was heard in the distance—the blending of thousands of feet marching on stone, the shout of angry voices, and the clash of weapons. On the hill above the warehouses, horns blared from the barracks and the palace.

The company had to hurry to keep up with their guide. Although he was old enough to be Athlone's grandfather, the hillman was as wiry and agile as a mountain goat. He led them down into the dark maze of warehouses, wharves, and custom houses. Several times the travelers had to press back into the shadows as groups of shouting, angry people, brandishing knives, pikes, or homemade weapons, marched past. Khan'di's uprising had begun.

Before long, however, the noise and activity were left behind. The hillman led his charges out of the harbor district and up into the hills behind the old city wall.

Gabria glanced up as they hurried through the darkness and was surprised to see the sky was clouding over. Lightning flickered far out over the sea. She hesitated. A strange feeling teased the edges of her senses, but whatever it was, it was too faint for her to recognize. Putting the feeling aside, she hurried after Athlone.

The hillman was leading Gabria and her companions up the southern end of the Redstone Hills, a place where the steep slopes were weathered by harsh seas. Deep gullies slashed down between the hills, and rock-strewn crags reared up over the stony vales. Not many people came up into the hills, for the inhospitable slopes made traveling difficult. Only the ancient tribes lived in the rugged lands, raising their half-wild goats, unimpressed by the vast city that lay at their feet. And only the hill tribes knew the extensive honeycomb of caves and passages that riddled the heart of the hills.

The night was completely dark by the time the party came to a narrow ravine about half a league behind the city wall. Clouds had totally obscured the moon and stars; the only illumination came from the distant lightning and from the torches and fires in the city below. The travelers turned to look back at Pra Desh and were surprised to see rivers of torchlight flowing up the streets toward the old city. The mobs were on their way to storm the gates.

Gabria knew the success of this part of Khan'di's plan depended on the fon's army; if enough men mutinied, the gates could be seized and held open, and the citizen mob would spend their rage against the palace. It was too difficult to see what was happening around the barracks and walls, but it seemed obvious from the noise and the blowing horns that there was a great commotion going on. Gabria could only pray that Khan'di's plot was proceeding as hoped before she followed her companions down into the night-dark ravine.

They stumbled along the rocky bottom for a time before the hill-man came to a stop in front of a huge fallen boulder. The massive piece of granite was half-buried in the side of the ravine and camou-flaged with brush and rock debris. Without a word, he began to pull the brush away to reveal a narrow, black hole behind the boulder. Quick as a squirrel, he darted in, leaving the others standing outside.

"Is this it?" Gabria asked suspiciously.

The old man poked his head out and waved angrily for them to follow him. One at a time, the warriors, Gabria, and Treader squeezed through the hole. Tam kept her hand glued to Sayyed's, but she followed without a complaint or a whimper into the pitch-black cave.

The party crowded together. The cave was barely high enough to allow them to stand upright and so lightless they could not see the walls, the floor, or each other's faces. No one dared to take a step.

Suddenly a tiny light flared in the back of the cave, where the hillman crouched over his flint and steel. To everyone's relief, he lit several rush torches and passed them on to the men, then he gestured again and vanished into the darkness.

"I think I'd rather be back in the warehouse," Bregan said, staring up at the low-hanging ceiling.

Athlone gripped the warrior's arm as he started after the old man. "So would I," he said. "So would I."

In single file, with Athlone in front and Bregan bringing up the rear, the party followed its silent guide down into the depths of the earth.

Not far away, in a small, dark room beneath the palace, the fon stood with her back against a wall, watching Branth through narrowed eyes. She was not certain he was ready to attempt the spell again. She would have preferred to wait a few more days to summon the gorth-ling and launch her army at Portane, but only a short time ago she had received word that a mob had risen in the streets and was marching toward the palace. The army, the soldiers she herself had levied, had betrayed her and opened the city gates to the rabble.

She gritted her teeth, and a snarl of hatred twisted her thin mouth. Oh, heads will roll for this treason! The streets will run with the blood of traitors, she swore to herself. Already the mob and the rebellious factions of the army were fighting the guards still loyal to her. The battle raged in the streets near the palace, too close for complacency.

The fon slammed her palm against the wall. It was that damned Khan'di Kadoa's doing. She could sense his hand in this treachery. She should have disposed of that conniving vermin before this, but he had the support of the powerful merchant guilds and she had not been ready to face them in an outright confrontation.

Well, after this night the Kadoa family would cease to exist and the merchant guilds would come groveling. This night she would have her gorthling.

In front of her, Branth leaned over the big, leather-bound tome on the table and emotionlessly recited the words of the spell. An aura of power was building around him. Even the fon could see the faint greenish glow. Yet the man seemed unaware of anything but the book and the small golden cage on the table before him.

His voice intoned unceasingly through the long, complicated spell. In the light of the small lamp the fon could see a sheen of sweat on his forehead, and a faint trembling begin to shake his frame. Then, to her delight, a tiny pinhole of light appeared, hovering in the center of the cage. She knew from reading the book that the pinhole was an opening to the immortal world of gods, dreams, and powers unlimited. Slowly Branth straightened and began the second part of the spell: to widen the door and call a gorthling out of his realm.

The fon watched impatiently. She wanted to rip the hole wider with her own hands and snatch the gorthling into her domain, but she had learned enough to know the evil creatures were dangerous and had to be handled with care and cunning. She curbed her frustration and watched as the hole began to open bit by bit. When the hole was a handspan wide, Branth suddenly stopped.

"What's the matter, you fool?" hissed the fon. "Go on!"

Branth appeared to struggle within himself, ready to say something. His mouth worked, and his hands tightened into fists. "No," he groaned between clenched teeth. "Not this."

The fon stepped forward, her eyes blazing. "Do it!" she screeched.

The exiled chief blanched. The days of drugs and mind control slowly destroyed the feeble vestiges of his will. Like a living corpse, he turned back to the tome and the cage.

As he resumed the spell, the green aura grew brighter. The magic about him increased, widening the hole of light in the cage. The light grew so dazzling that the fon had to shield her eyes.

She blinked once before she saw it.

A small, wizened face peered through the hole. The fon held her breath. Branth had lost control of the creature at the same point during his previous attempt at the spell. This time, however, he did not fail. He chanted the incantation, slowly drawing the gorthling out of his world and into the cage.

The creature came cautiously. He climbed out of the hole one limb at a time and finally crouched, snarling, in the corner of the cage. Branth said a command, and the hole of light snapped shut.

The fon's eyes took a moment to adjust to the faint light, then she stared in horrified fascination at the thing in the golden cage. The gorthling resembled a small, incredibly ancient monkey with long, twisted limbs and the face of a mummified child. The fon suppressed a shudder as the creature turned his inhuman eyes toward her. Before he could look her in the eyes, she turned away and snapped to Branth, "Put the collar on the thing."

This was the most dangerous part of the spell, for the sorcerer had to put a collar of gold on the gorthling in order to properly control him. However, the tome stated in no uncertain terms that the gorthling could not be touched by human hands. The fon did not know why, and she did not want to find out.

Branth reached for a long-handled clamp and the golden collar. He had practiced many times with the clamp upon various small animals; he was now quite deft at snapping the collar around creatures in the cage. But neither he nor the fon had counted on the cunning and agility of the gorthling.

He zipped around the small cage, avoiding the collar and Branth's best efforts with ease. Time and again the sorcerer almost had the collar about his neck only to have the gorthling slip away. The fon grew wild with frustration. "Collar the thing!" she screamed.

At that moment, the collar dropped off the clamp and fell to the cage floor by the edge of the bars. Branth, his consciousness numbed by the fon's poisons, simply reacted. He stuck his fingers through the bars to retrieve the collar.

"No!" the fon shrieked.

Even as she sprang to grab the man's arm, the gorthling pounced on Branth's fingers and sank his teeth into the man's skin. Branth howled in agony and tried to yank his hand through the bars, but the gorthling clung to his fingers, ripping off chunks of flesh and gulping them down.

The taste of blood drove the creature into a frenzy. He screeched and clawed and tore Branth's hand to shreds. The man writhed and screamed so violently, the fon could not get near to help him.

All at once, the gorthling fell quiet. The fon stepped back, her eyes wide in dread, for the creature was beginning to grow. His body pulsed with a lurid red light and blood dripped from his mouth. In just a moment he was as big as the cage.

Appalled, the fon backed to the door, leaving Branth to his doom. She hoped the creature would remain confined in the cage, yet even as her hands fumbled for the latch, the gorthling burst the bars of the gilded prison. Branth and the fon froze.

Still clinging to the sorcerer's bloody hand, the gorthling turned his eyes on the fon. Across the room, the fon caught his gaze and was drawn into the black depths of his eyes. She found herself gazing into an evil she never knew existed, an evil so powerful and destructive it swallowed her rational thought and emptied her mind of everything but total terror.

Her shriek filled the small room. Somewhere in the shreds of her consciousness a tiny spark of self-survival remained and guided her hand to the door latch. The gorthling reached his clawed hand for the oil lamp on the table. Instantly he flung the lamp at the woman as she wrenched the door open with a desperate heave and fled screaming down the corridor.

The oil lamp smashed against the wooden door, its oil bursting into flames on the wood and running in fiery rivulets down to the floor. The gorthling curled his lips in malicious glee, then he turned his eyes to Branth.

The clansman had not moved. His face was racked in fear and pain; his hand and lower arm were in bloody shreds. Still he could not force himself to move against the horror of the gorthling.

The creature stopped growing the moment he burst out of the cage, and now he crouched like a big cat on the table, clutching

Branth's arm. "Where did you learn your spell, Sorcerer?" the gorthling rasped.

Branth shook violently at the sound of the dry, vicious voice. He
gasped an answer and pointed to the book on the table.

The gorthling looked. "The *Book of Matrah*? No wonder you
failed." He cackled. "Who are you?"

The sorcerer forced himself to answer, "Lord . . . Branth of
Clan Geldring."

"A clansman. You would be. Only clansmen have ever called for
my kind." He sank his claws deeper into Branth's arm. "Where are
we?"

Branth whimpered. "A palace. In Pra Desh."

"You are not in your own land. Why is that, little chieftain?"

"I was exiled."

"Oh ho!" the gorthling sneered. "Your people have banished you.
How sad. Perhaps I shall change that. It might be interesting to visit
your clans." He laughed, the sound as bitter and raw as acid.

The creature's laugh was more than Branth could bear. He collapsed to his knees, sobbing and shrieking for mercy.

"Mercy!" the gorthling screeched. "I know nothing of mercy. But
I know that you, little chieftain, are mine!"

Without warning, the creature sprang for Branth's face. The man
fell over backward onto the stone floor, gibbering in terror and clawing at the thing on his head. The beast clung with grim determination.
Smoke swirled about them, and the gorthling's eyes blazed in the light
of the fire.

The gorthling's body began to pulse again with a lurid red glow.
The being forced Branth's mouth open. The Geldring shrieked one
last time in despair before he fell deathly still. Inch by inch the gorthling worked his way into Branth's mouth. The creature looked out
once from between the chieftain's teeth and chuckled with satisfaction, then the man's mouth snapped shut and the gorthling disappeared from sight.

The room was quiet except for the crackle of the fire on the
burning door. The fire had spread across the floor and now touched
the pile of straw on Branth's pallet. The flames leaped higher. Smoke
swirled out into the corridor.

Within Branth's body, the gorthling began his metamorphosis.
Swiftly the creature melded his form into the sorcerer's body, joining
his life to Branth's heart, muscle, and bone in a symbiosis that could

be broken only by death. Once the union was complete, the gorthling had total control of the man's body and brain.

In the process, Branth's soul was destroyed. The gorthling stripped his victim's mind of all thoughts, memories, and dreams and inserted his own cunning and intelligence. As Branth's brain was emptied, the gorthling retained a very superficial knowledge of the chief's memories and emotions. One emotion in particular caught the gorthling's interest: hatred. There was a vestige of a very powerful hatred and resentment for one particular magic-wielder. Unfortunately, the gorthling could not clearly understand the jumbled human memory. Perhaps in time he would learn the identity of that magic-wielder. For now the gorthling had other things to think about.

Branth's body flinched and jerked upright. The gorthling opened his eyes. Branth's normal arrogant gaze was gone, consumed with his mind and soul. In its place was a glint of inhuman evil.

The gorthling stood up, slowly testing the muscles of the new form he had invaded. Other than the injured hand, which the gorthling could heal over time, the body was basically fit and healthy. The creature grinned. In his normal shape, the gorthling had no power of his own, only the ability to enhance other forms of power. However, once he tasted blood, he was able to inhabit a mortal body and add his powers to the new host's own abilities. This body had potential, especially with its inherent ability to wield magic. A great deal of damage could be done to this world before anyone became aware of his true identity.

First, though, the gorthling had to find out more about the people who lived here. In the immortal world beyond the realm of the dead, he had been distantly aware of this world and the human beings who trampled the earth. He had noted the course of their history in a faint, disinterested fashion, paying only slightly more attention to the clanspeople who had the unique ability to wield magic—a talent granted to them by Valorian, the Hero-Warrior and rumored half-human son of the goddess, Amara. Only a magic-wielder could have called the gorthling to the mortal world, and only a magic-wielder could send him back. If he was going to stay here in this big, powerful body, he would have to find all of the clan sorcerers and destroy them. Particularly the one that caused his host, Branth, such hatred. That magic-wielder had piqued the gorthling's curiosity.

Something crashed behind the gorthling, causing him to whirl around. The wooden door was lying on the floor, consumed in flames. The gorthling looked around at the spreading fire. Usually fire did not bother him, but this body did not like it; the creature coughed and drew back from the heat.

Then he remembered the woman. She had been standing by the door and had seen him arrive. She knew what he was. There was no other option; he would have to find her. Gleefully snatching a torch stub from a bracket on the wall, the creature lit it. Branth's ruined hand was painful, but the gorthling had experienced worse pain before. He grabbed the *Book of Matrah* from the table, darted past the burning door, and sprang out into the corridor.

A staircase lay ahead. Laughing aloud, he ran up the stairs and through the corridors of the lower palace levels, setting fire to everything that would burn.

"Oh, gods," Gabria gasped. "Did you hear that?"

At the sound of her voice, the party stopped dead in the black tunnel. They had lost track of how long they'd been stumbling, crawling, climbing, and scrambling after the old man through the endless maze of crevices, tunnels, and caverns. The cold, damp blackness was wearing on them all. They looked around nervously.

"Hear what?" Piers whispered.

They remained frozen, their ears straining through the impenetrable darkness. The old man looked back impatiently.

Gabria clamped her hands over her mouth to stifle a scream as a wave of terror engulfed her. She sagged back against Piers, trembling and light-headed. She heard Tam begin to whimper.

Sayyed and Athlone said together, "What was that?"

"What was *what*?" Bregan said too loudly.

Gabria felt her heart thudding in her chest. She was breathing heavily from the shock, but the unknown terror was subsiding as quickly as it had come. "I don't know. Something happened. Close by. Something horrible."

The chieftain held up the wavering torch. "Did you hear a sound just then, Sayyed?"

The Turic shifted nervously. "I sensed it rather than heard it. It was hideous!" He bent down to reassure Tam and to hide the tremor of fear in his face.

Gabria drew herself up and tried to shake off the terrible remnants of her horror. "Athlone, we'd better hurry. I think that may have been Branth."

The party went on, faster now, driven by the urgency of Gabria's fear. The old man led them through another narrow passage, around a rock fall, under a stone ceiling so low they had to crawl on their hands and knees, and into a tiny, rough chamber that seemed hardly more than a wide crack in the earth.

The hillman said several incomprehensible words and pointed to the back of the cave, then he turned and disappeared into the darkness before anyone realized what he was doing.

"Wait!" Athlone yelled, springing after him, but the man had already ducked down another crack and was gone.

"By Surgart's sword, I'm going to strangle that little rat if he left us lost down here," Athlone cursed. He strode to the back of the chamber to the spot the hillman had indicated and found another slender fissure on the rock wall. Carefully he squeezed through. There was a long moment of silence before his voice came back to the others.

"Come this way."

Gabria and the others pushed through the narrow crack, came around some boulders, and found themselves in what seemed to be an enormous cavern. They could not see very much of the lightless space, for their feeble torchlight was swallowed by the towering blackness. A cold silence surrounded them. With great care they edged out across the floor. Only Piers remained frozen to his place, his eyes staring sadly into the dark.

Although she did not have a torch, Gabria walked forward a pace to see what she could discover. Her shin abruptly slammed into a very sharp rock. "This is ridiculous," she snapped. Raising her hand, she called out a command and a ball of bright light formed over her head.

Every man there jumped like a stung horse.

"Good gods, Gabria," Athlone yelled. "Don't startle us like that!"

The four Khulinin warriors stared at the light and at Gabria in mixed disbelief and alarm. She looked back at them apologetically. She regretted being so precipitous with her spell, but the frustration of near-blindness and the pain in her leg drove her to act without thinking of what anyone's reaction might be. They were not used to her sorcery, and the sudden ball of light had been a shock.

Bregan finally shook his grizzled head and tossed his torch to the ground. "Have you got any more of those lights, Lady Gabria?"

Her smile to him was dazzling, and in just a few moments four balls of light hung in the air over the mens' heads. Their glow revealed the details of the entire cavern.

Their first impressions had been right; the cavern was huge. As they looked around, it became obvious that, while most of the cavern was natural, a great deal of human labor had been spent smoothing the floors and enlarging the walls. Some un-natural features had been added, too: cages, stocks, chains on the walls, a huge wheeled rack, a forge, and several other unidentifiable machines—all thankfully empty.

"Gods," Athlone shuddered. "It's a torture room."

Without warning, Piers gave a grief-stricken moan and ran forward. In the center of the cavern was a hole, and the healer stumbled to the very edge. He fell to his knees and leaned precariously over the rim.

"Oh, Diana," he groaned.

"Piers!" Gabria cried. She ran to him and tried to draw him away. The hole appalled her. It was a smooth-sided pit that fell away into a terrifying blackness. A faint, putrid odor rose from the unseen bottom.

"She's down there," the healer said, his voice sinking in despair. "The fon's executioner took great delight in telling me. Diana wouldn't confess to poisoning the old fon—even when they tortured her. They condemned her anyway and threw her down there. My poor Diana." He leaned against Gabria, covered his face with his hands, and wept. "All these years," Piers cried. "All these years. I never truly believed she was dead . . . until I saw this pit."

Gabria finally understood. So many things he had said and done fell into place: his flight from Pra Desh, his refusal to talk about his family or his past, his abiding sadness. She knew how he felt. For the healer, looking into the pit must have been like standing on top of a burial mound and saying good-bye to those buried there. She held onto her friend and let him cry.

"There's nothing down there any more," she said softly. "Diana is gone."

He wept until the worst of his grief had waned, then he was quiet for a very long time, his gaze lost in the depths of the pit. Gabria could hear the others moving around and searching the cavern for an exit, but she stayed with Piers while he faced the phantoms of his past.

When at last he wiped his eyes on his sleeve and stood up, Gabria knew his grief was under control. The slow, painful process of healing his old wounds had finally begun.

"Was this why you went back to Corin Treld?" he asked, offering her his hand.

She nodded, took his hand, and rose to her feet. "The dead must lie in peace."

"And so they will," Piers answered wearily. Then he added, "Now, let's seek the living. I would still like to face the fon."

"Do you know the way out?" she asked.

"Yes. I was here years ago as a healer, but I've never had to stay in this place of torment."

Piers led her around the pit and headed for a wall where a rack of tools and instruments hung. The others followed. He found the door latch, which was cleverly hidden in the stone, and pulled the rack aside to reveal the door. They filed out, with Gabria's lights bobbing overhead, and found a staircase leading up to the next level. When the last warrior left the torture chamber, Piers looked once more into the black cavern and gently shut the door.

The party went upstairs to the prison level and paused to wait for Piers to take the lead. The travelers stared about them in horror. There were two corridors, one on either side of the stairs, lined with lightless stone cells. The walls were wet with moisture, and the floors were ankle deep in muck and excrement. The smell was horrible.

The noise was even worse. The sight of the lights had excited the prisoners, and they screamed and cried and shouted behind their bars in a hideous cacophony of misery and fear. Surprisingly, there were no guards.

Piers slowed as he came up the stairs, and his eyes widened. "I know some of those people," he exclaimed. "They don't belong here!"

Secen started toward a door, but Athlone stopped him. "Not now. We don't have time."

They hurried on, leaving the dungeon and its tormented prisoners behind, and ran up to the next level. Khan'di's map did not include the deep underground levels of the palace, only the fon's wing, where Branth was supposed to be. The party had to rely on Piers's eleven-year-old memories of the extensive storerooms, wine cellars, and cold storage rooms underneath the main floors.

The healer was surprised by how much he remembered. Released of his grief, his memories flowed out as clear and sharp as yesterday's hours. He was able to lead his companions up through the levels to a corridor just below the fon's wing of the palace.

Khan'di had told them that, according to spies, Branth was being held in one of the fon's personal storerooms. The healer took his companions through a large room full of vats and up a winding staircase. At the top, a solid oak door blocked their way. Piers reached for the door handle, but Treader began barking furiously and shoved himself between Piers and the door.

"Piers, be careful!" Gabria cried. "Treader says there's fire."

The healer looked skeptical, but he stood back from the stout oak door and very carefully opened it just a crack. A dark cloud of smoke billowed out, and the voracious roar of a fire out of control sounded clearly through the slight opening. Piers slammed the door shut.

"By the gods, what happened?" Athlone exclaimed.

Piers glanced around worriedly. "I don't know, but we'll have to go another way."

The travelers raced down the stairs and through the storage room. From there they took a different corridor, one that led up the main stairs to the palace's banquet hall. There they stopped and gazed about them in frightened astonishment. A few torches were still burning in the sconces on the walls of the ornate room, giving off enough light so the party could see the expanse of the entire hall.

The banquet hall was in the central block of the palace along with the waiting rooms, the fon's throne room, and audience chamber. To the north was the fon's wing of private apartments, chambers, and servants' quarters. Already the fire from below was spreading through the first floor of that wing. It was eating through the timbers and the north wall of the banquet hall. As it climbed to the floor of the second story, the blaze consumed everything in its path. Even as the travelers came to a stop and Gabria banished her lights, the banquet hall was filling with smoke. A muted roaring echoed through the room.

Palace guards, servants, and courtiers ran back and forth, carrying items out of the fon's wing; some were running in panic, others screamed or yelled orders. No one seemed to be doing anything to control the fire, and no one paid attention to the clanspeople in the hall.

"Lord!" Keth called. "Look at this." He was standing in a deep embrasure looking out a rare glassed window.

Athlone and the others joined him and crowded into the space. They followed Keth's gaze out to the high wall that encircled the palace. The fon's guards were struggling to keep the mob from the massive wooden gate that blocked the entrance. But while the travelers watched, the gate was forced open by a well-disciplined troop of men who pushed through and attacked the guards. A huge group of people flooded through the breached gate behind them. A roar of triumph rose outside, then the mob came to a stunned halt. A pale flash of lightning illuminated the hundreds of faces staring at the burning wing of the palace.

Thunder and a distant crash reverberated through the building. The smoke grew thicker.

Gabria turned back to the dim, smoky hall. A boy rushed by her carrying an armload of jeweled goblets. The sorceress coughed and stared through the open double doors into the fon's wing, where the dancing red and yellow glow of fire revealed more and more people fleeing with the fon's valuables.

Athlone drew back from the window. "Where is the fon in all of this madness?" he yelled above the noise.

"And where is Branth?" Gabria shouted.

12

Piers." Athlone grabbed the healer's arm. "What are the chances Branth could still be alive if he is in those lower storerooms?"

The healer tore a strip off his shirt and tied it over his nose and mouth to filter out the thickening smoke. "None, Lord. The whole corridor was on fire."

"If the fon had moved him, where would she have taken him?" Athlone had to shout over the noise of the people and the increasing roar of the fire.

"If there was time?" Piers lifted his hands. "He could be in her apartments or in the guardrooms of the other wing. He could be anywhere."

The chief thought fast. "Then we'll have to split up. Search what you can, then get out fast. If anyone finds Branth, either bring him or kill him. Everyone understand?" They nodded. "Piers, you know this place. Take Gabria and Keth. Look where you think he is the most likely to be. Bregan, you come with me. We'll go upstairs to the fon's rooms. Secen, Valar, and Sayyed, you take Tam and the dog and check the other wing."

They hurried into their groups and started to leave. Only a few of the fleeing palace inhabitants glanced their way before rushing on.

"Don't wait too long to get out," Athlone shouted after the men. Gabria was about to follow Piers when the chieftain took her hand. He wanted to say something to her before they parted in the smoke and fire, but sensible words failed to come to mind.

Gabria looked into his face, still bruised, bearded, and smeared with mud and dirt. She pulled off the strip of cloth tied over her nose and mouth and lightly kissed his cheek. Then she ran after Piers and vanished into the smoke.

Athlone looked after her in surprise before a quirk of a smile touched his mouth. He gestured to Bregan and left the banquet hall to find the stairs leading up to the next floor.

As Athlone and Bregan disappeared in one direction, Piers led Gabria and Keth through a set of doors, down another dim corridor, and into the audience hall where the fon usually held her large public festivals, court functions, and celebrations. A few lamps were lit in the room despite the late hour, and Gabria looked around in amazement at the rich furnishings. The walls of the vast room were covered with tapestries, colorful banners, and hangings of silk embroidered with the ship emblem of Pra Desh. Padded benches and chairs lined the walls, and a huge fireplace dominated one end of the room. Gabria noticed the big room was empty and was already filling with smoke.

Piers came to the center of the room and slowed down to get his bearings.

Gabria grabbed his sleeve. "Where are we going?"

The healer continued to study their surroundings as he answered. "The fon should know where Branth is. If we can find her, maybe . . ." He paused as another crash reverberated through the palace. Screams echoed down the corridor. "Floor gave way," he muttered. He glanced at the stone walls. "It won't be long before enough floors collapse to bring down all the walls."

"Then let's hurry," Keth suggested nervously.

"Do you know where she might be?" Gabria asked.

Piers curled his lip. "If I know that woman, she's in the vaults trying to save the treasury." He hurried his companions out of the audience hall and into the first of the fon's two waiting rooms. These rooms, where supplicants waited for personal interviews with the fon in her throne room, were even more luxurious than the hall. They were filled with precious rugs, wallcases of delicate porcelain, handsomely carved furniture, and shelves of valuable books.

This room was empty of people, so Piers walked through to the next. That room was much like the first. Here, her personal secretaries usually screened the people who would be allowed in the fon's presence. At that moment, the only people in the room were two noblemen and one palace guard. The courtiers were older men in various stages of night dress, and they were shouting and frantically pounding on an arched wooden door. The guard was beside them, trying to hack at the door handle and frame with the point of his sword.

Piers came to a quick halt and cursed under his breath. The men had obviously been there for some time, because the door handle was splintered from the guard's blows.

"What is it?" Gabria whispered behind the healer.

"The vaults are behind the throne room and that door is the only way in."

The guard shouted angrily at the clanspeople, "What are you doing here?"

"Quit yelping and *help* us," one of the noblemen ordered, ignoring the newcomers.

The guard gave a sharp laugh. "You'll never get that door open. She's barred it from inside."

"She?" Piers demanded. "The fon?"

The guard glared at him. "Who else? Now, get out of here!"

Piers shoved past the guard, ignoring his sword, and shouldered into the group of noblemen. "I'll help," he said, adding his weight to the door. The courtiers looked startled but they wanted badly to reach their ruler, so they moved over to include him. All three threw their strength at the door, but the wood did not budge.

One of the noblemen sagged against the door. He was breathing heavily, perspiration dripping down around his round face, and his eyes were wide in fear. "I can't believe this!" he cried. "A riot in the streets, a fire in the palace, and she hides in her throne room. What are we going to do?"

More crashes sounded upstairs. Cries and screams filled the corridors beyond the audience hall, and the distant rumble of thunder sounded outside.

The frightened nobleman shoved himself away from the door and ran for the other room.

"Wait!" His companion shouted after him.

"You save the shrew," he cried and dashed out.

The other men looked at one another. The courtier gave Piers an odd glance before turning away.

"There is no other way in?" Gabria asked.

They shook their heads and bent to try again.

"Look out!" the guard bellowed, leaping sideways as a smoldering chunk of the ceiling collapsed where he had been standing. Smoke billowed through the hole, and the room was lit by the lurid glow from the flames in the timbers above the false ceiling.

"We'll never get this door open this way," the old nobleman shouted over the crackling of the fire.

"Arc you sure she's in there?" demanded Piers.

The guard replied, "She ran by here a little while ago, before we knew of the fire." He shivered and gripped his sword. "It was strange. She looked wild! Just slammed the door and barred it."

Gabria stared at the door while the guard was talking, and in her mind she formed the words of a spell. "Piers, get out of the way," she ordered.

Before the two Pra Deshians could argue, Piers hustled them aside. Gabria raised her hand and concentrated on focusing her magical energy. In that moment she sensed again the strange feeling of growing power, and this time she recognized what it was: the latent magic in the area was increasing. The phenomenon was still not strong enough that she could identify the cause of the increase, so Gabria set the puzzle aside for now. She spoke the command for her spell. In a breath, the door collapsed into a heap of splinters and wood dust.

"Oh, Elaja!" the guard wailed, and he, too, took to his heels out of the room toward the audience hall.

"Nicely done, Gabria," Piers said thankfully.

"The sorceress?" the remaining nobleman gasped.

Gabria tried to reassure him. "We're here for Branth, nothing else. Do you know where he is?"

"Dead, I hope," the man snarled. He thrust his body into the open doorway and blocked their path. "I thought I knew you from somewhere," he shouted at Piers. "You're the healer whose daughter was condemned for sorcery! Well, you helped kill one fon, but you won't get this one."

Keth leaped past Gabria and lifted his sword. Piers held him back. He finally recognized the man. "Ancor, I had nothing to do with the poisoning and neither did my daughter."

The courtier would not listen. "Her own husband admitted it!" he yelled.

Piers shouted fiercely in reply. "And where is he? Keeping the prince of Calah company in the bottom of the pit?"

The old man blanched as if that thought had occurred to him in the past. "The fon told us his ship went down with no survivors," he said defensively.

Another chunk of burning ceiling crashed to the floor, setting rugs and a tapestry alight.

"Healer," Keth called, "we've got to get out of here."

"Not without the fon," Piers answered harshly, and he tried to push past the nobleman.

The danger of the fire and the anger on Piers's face made the old man frantic. "No! Leave this place," he shouted. "You are a traitor and your daughter was a murdering heretic!"

Gabria was watching her friend and saw something break in the normally quiet, gentle man. All of the fury, the guilt, and the sense of injustice he had been carrying within him for eleven years had been stirred up by the sight of the dungeon and by the flood of memories that engulfed him. That this insulting old man would dare call his beloved daughter a murdering heretic was more than Piers could bear.

With a roar of fury, the healer balled his fist and hit the nobleman in the face. The man fell like a poleaxed cow. Piers sprang over his body and dashed into the throne room with Gabria and Keth close on his heels.

No sooner were they through the door than they all skidded to a halt. Their attention was drawn to a large, canopied throne that sat on a wide dais against the opposite wall. The fire had already reached this small, opulent room through the ceiling. Sparks and flaming chunks of wood were raining down, starting more fires on carpets, tapestries, and on the red canopy over the golden throne. Beneath the flaming canopy sat the fon of Pra Desh, her eyes staring horribly at the intruders.

Piers's fury still burned in his blood. Without a conscious plan, he snarled a curse and ran toward the fon, ignoring the smoke and flames.

"Piers, no!" Gabria shouted.

The healer lifted his hand as he raced up the marble steps of the dais, and he was about to grab the fon when she looked up at him.

The healer faltered. He hardly recognized the woman. Her face was twisted into such a mask of horror that he realized instantly she had slipped beyond the edges of sanity. Her eyes were empty of reason and filled with insensible fear. When she saw him, the fon cowered down into her seat, moaning and trembling in terror.

Piers stared at her with pity and astonishment. What had happened to turn this strong-willed woman into a crazed, fearful wreck?

He was about to take her arm when a large piece of the ceiling crashed down to the floor behind him. Piers whirled around and cried out. The wreckage had fallen on Gabria and the warrior. Frantically the healer ran back, dodging small fires, and dragged Gabria's body out from under the smoking chunks of timbers and paneling. Keth was still conscious and able to move. He crawled out by himself and dazedly helped Piers smother the smoldering sparks on Gabria's clothes and drag her to the slim protection of the stone doorway.

Piers breathed a silent prayer of thanks as he examined the sorceress. She had a bump and a cut on her head and was dazed, but she was already coming around.

"Piers," Keth yelled, steadying Gabria. "If we don't go now, we'll never get out."

The healer agreed. The rooms behind them were already burning, and the throne room was almost intolerably hot.

"I'm going to get the fon," he called. He started forward, when something caught his eye. He half-turned, and a man burst through the doorway, slamming into Keth and knocking the warrior sideways. Gabria cried out and fell. The man rushed past Piers, his eyes hooded in smoke and shadow and his mouth twisted in a maniacal smile. He had a large book under his bleeding arm.

There was something familiar about that man, Piers thought, then all sensibilities fled from his mind. Horror-struck, he stared at the fon. She had risen from her throne and was watching the stranger, terror warping her face into a hideous grimace. Just as the man reached her, she screamed a heart-tearing wail of despair. Piers saw the flash of a dagger blade in the man's hand. Before the healer could move, the man had grabbed the screaming fon by the hair, hauled her off the dais, and slashed her throat. Laughing gleefully, he flung her bleeding body to the floor.

In the waiting room behind the clanspeople, the Pra Deshian nobleman regained consciousness. He gazed at the body of his ruler for one horrified second before he fled.

The murderer saw the movement and raised his head.

"Branth!" Piers whispered, shocked to his soul.

The exiled clansman ignored him. Still clutching his bloody dagger, he bolted past Piers for the door. Keth tried to block him, but the man slashed wildly, cutting through Keth's tunic into his arm. The warrior fell back, and Branth ran, laughing, out of the throne room.

Piers pulled himself together. There was nothing more to do but get out fast. He and Keth took Gabria's arms and helped her out of the room. Behind them the blazing canopy collapsed over the golden throne.

Gabria was still woozy from the bang on her head, but she was able to walk. With the aid of Keth and Piers she hurried past the fires in the waiting rooms and into the audience hall. The hall, too, was hot and filled with smoke. They rushed through the hall and entered the corridors. The roar of the fire in the fon's wing assailed their ears.

"This way," Piers said, and he led them away from the sweeping flames. There was no sign of Branth or anyone else. The people had long since fled that part of the palace. Bending low, the two men and Gabria ran, coughing and gasping, along the dark corridors to the spacious front entrance hall in the center of the palace.

The huge double doors were open, and a strong draft blew in through the hall. Outside, Gabria could see hundreds of people milling around the gates and the wall, watching the great fire.

She and the men were about to go to the doors when a new sound caught their attention over the roar of the fire and the crack and groan of the dying palace. They heard a thud and a clash of blades by the opposite wall in the shadows of a broad staircase.

"Branth!" someone shouted in fury.

Gabria's heart froze. It was Athlone's voice.

The sorceress and Keth leaped forward at a run to find the source of the noise. They dashed across the wide, dark hall and found three men locked in battle in the shadows at the foot of the stairs.

Just as Keth shouted the Khulinin war cry, one figure broke away from the other two and raced for the door. What looked like a large book was tucked under his arm. A pale flash of lightning filled open doors, and the light revealed the man's face for only an instant. In that instant, Gabria recognized him.

"Branth!" she hissed furiously. Her hands rose instinctively, and she fired a bolt of the Trymian Force at the fleeing man. The blue bolt seared toward him, but Branth dodged around the door. Gabria's arcane force exploded on the wooden frame.

The gorthling's step hesitated when he realized a magic-wielder had attacked him. Unfortunately, it was too late to do anything about it. The gorthling's new powers were untried and there were too many people around. He had to get away from this place as quickly as possible.

By the time Gabria reached the door, Branth had already disappeared into the crowd of onlookers.

"Gabria!" Sayyed shouted behind her. She turned to see the Turic and his group running into the hall from a corridor in the south wing. She went to join them, and the whole party converged at the base of the stairs.

Gabria took one look at Athlone and Bregan and stifled a cry. Bregan lay on the bottom step, a bloody dagger buried to the hilt in his chest. Lord Athlone was leaning against the wall, coughing and groaning. No one said a word. Sayyed and Valar picked up Bregan, Secen put his arm under Athlone, and the whole party fled the burning palace.

They crossed the courtyard and took shelter on the far side of the wall. Somewhere in the north wing, a section of the roof collapsed and a huge portion of the front wall slowly crashed into the raging inferno. Sparks and flames soared high on the night wind.

For a moment, Gabria leaned gratefully against the cold stone and gulped in the clean night air. She was sick, dizzy, and utterly exhausted. Her head felt as if a stone mason was pounding on her temples. She ignored the curious onlookers and wished desperately for a drink. Tam pressed against her, trying hard not to cry.

Beside her, Athlone had sagged against the wall and was taking deep racking breaths to expel the smoke in his lungs. She reached over and clasped his hand.

"What happened?" she asked.

For a long time he could not answer. Finally, he croaked, "We searched upstairs as far as we could and found nothing. The palace was a bonfire."

Gabria took a close look at him and winced. His face was black with soot, his clothes were riddled with burns, and the soles of his boots were charred.

"We came down the stairs to get out and saw Branth in the hall." The chief struggled to stand straight. "We tried to stop him, but he was . . ." Athlone tried to find the right word. "Wild. He just leaped at us like a mad wolf. Bregan saw his dagger and threw himself in front of me." The chief's voice cracked, and he shook his head in grief and anger.

Gabria glanced at Piers, who was bending over the old warrior. The healer caught her eyes and shook his head. Gabria wanted to weep.

At that moment, Khan'di came through the crowd. The nobleman's clothes were spattered with blood, and his face was strained with worry and weariness. His smile lit up when he saw the travelers by the wall. "Praise Elaja, you are safe," he cried. His expression fell when he saw Bregan, but he had little time for sorrow then. Urgently he turned to Gabria. "Sorceress, we desperately need your help."

Gabria groaned. She did not feel well enough to help herself, let alone Khan'di. Nevertheless she stood up, hanging on to Tam for support, and followed the noblemen back around the wall to the entrance gate.

For a long time they simply stood and stared at the monstrous fire that was consuming the fon's magnificent palace. The city's fire brigade was frantically trying to protect what was left of the central block and the south wing, but the blaze was too much for their bucket lines.

Khan'di cleared his throat. "Sorceress, the fire is far beyond our control. Is there any way you can put it out?"

Gabria was stunned. The fire was so big, so powerful, she had never considered such a thing. It was easy to form globes of light or make a door turn to dust, but to quench such a vast inferno? She doubted that she had the skill or the strength.

Lightning flickered overhead, and she looked up at the sky. "There's a storm coming. The rain will put it out."

Khan'di followed her gaze. "I know," he said, "but it's moving too slowly. Right now the wind is whipping up the fire." He pointed to the burning roof where a strong gust swept sparks and burning debris into the air. "If any of that lands in other parts of the city, it could start more fires. Some areas are so old and full of wood that a single spark could start a conflagration that even a hurricane could not put out."

Gabria understood his fear, but still she hesitated. "Isn't sorcery still against the law in Pra Desh? What will all of those people do if I start using magic?"

The nobleman tapped his sword. "You still have my promise of protection. No one will dare touch you as long as you are under my care."

Gabria was silent. If there was only something she could do! She pushed her weariness and headache aside and tried to think. How does one put out a fire? Water was the obvious answer and water was coming, but not fast enough. She knew from her teacher, the Woman of the Marsh, that human magic-wielders were not strong enough to control something as powerful and unpredictable as the weather, so she could not manipulate the storm. Nor did she think she should try to direct the tremendous fire itself. What she needed was a spell that was uncomplicated and foolproof that she could keep under control, even in her weakened state.

The sorceress rubbed her temples with one hand and held on to Tam with the other. What was another way to put out a fire? Blow it out with a great wind. Dump dirt on it to smother it. . . .

Her mind focused on an idea. She knew fire needed air in order to burn. If the air was cut off by dirt or a wet blanket, the fire died out.

Gabria realized she did not need dirt, all she needed was an airtight, arcane shell over the fire. The flames would fade, the sparks could not fly, and the city would be protected. All she would have to do is hold the shield until the storm broke.

The storm.

Gabria stared up at the black sky, and the strange feeling of growing power that she had sensed earlier burst into understanding. The thunderstorm was enhancing the powers of magic!

Magic existed in every person, animal, and thing. It lay everywhere to be tapped by a human with the talent to utilize the power. Gabria realized, as the thunderstorm bore down on the city, that the magic around her was intensifying as if the vast forces of the storm were heightening the magical energy already present.

She looked back at the walls of the palace and wondered if she could make use of this increased power. She would need a lot of strength to hold a shield so big—strength she did not want to needlessly waste with Branth still on the loose.

"All right," she said forcefully and dropped Tam's hand. She heard Athlone and Sayyed come up behind her as she faced the palace and concentrated on the enhanced magic around her. The splinter in her wrist suddenly blazed with a ruby light from the power that coursed through her body. Slowly Gabria formed her spell.

She began her shield on ground level, at the corners of the two four-story wings on the north and south sides of the palace. Using every fiber of her skill and concentration, she created a protective arcane ward at each corner and carefully lengthened the wards up until they resembled glowing pillars of red light. She raised them higher—past the first floor; past the second; up to the eaves of the palace. Gradually the wards arched upward and joined over the center of the roof. Their red light was almost lost in the fiery glow of the inferno.

The crowd behind Gabria stood in amazement and watched the scene in awe. Sayyed's mouth hung open, and Tam stared wide-eyed in fascination.

Lord Athlone stood transfixed by the spell Gabria was creating. He knew she could draw on the invisible magic around her and shape it to her will, but this was the first time he could clearly see and understand what she was doing. To his amazement, none of his old fears and superstitions rose to hinder him. Instead, he was filled with a budding fascination and a desire to reach out and test the magic with his own hands. He could feel the power around him and within him; it coursed through his veins as naturally and cleanly as his own blood. The Khulinin chieftain stared at the sorceress and felt the grip of his doubts and reluctance for his own talent begin to weaken. Without intending to, Athlone edged forward until he was standing just behind Gabria.

Meanwhile, Gabria spoke quietly to herself to fix her intent in her mind. She raised her hands to complete the spell. The red pillars of energy began to glow brightly. They spread out, wider and wider from top to bottom, rapidly stretching out to encase the entire palace in an airtight, glowing veil of magic. In a matter of moments the shell was complete. The edges joined, overlapped, and sealed, and suddenly the noise of the fire was gone. The shell began to fill with smoke.

The courtyard, streets, and gardens around the walled palace erupted with noise as everyone began talking and gesturing at once. Ignoring the uproar, Gabria fought to concentrate and maintain her spell. Even with the help of the increased magic of the storm, she could feel her strength slowly draining away. She held on and prayed the rain would come soon.

Time dragged by. Although the trapped smoke made it difficult to see within the shield, it soon became obvious that Gabria's spell was working. No sparks or burning debris escaped, and, without fresh air to feed its monstrous energy, the fire was dying. Little by little the flames sank down and went out as the air within the shield burned away.

Gabria closed her eyes and forced her concentration to hold steady. She was growing weaker by the moment; the red light of the splinter in her wrist wavered.

Lightning burst overhead, and the thunder boomed only a heartbeat later. The wind gusted, the smell of rain heavy upon its blast.

"Here it comes," Khan'di said with a quiet note of triumph.

A raindrop spattered on Gabria's nose. More drops fell, and lightning seared the sky. The sprinkle soon turned to a deluge. Khan'di shouted in glee and raised his fist to the pouring rain.

Slowly, so as not to restart the fires with a burst of air, Gabria dissolved her shield, allowing the rain to wet the red-hot stone walls. Steam boiled out of the wreckage where the rain drenched the remains of the fire. The light and the intense heat were gone. Gabria took a deep breath of the cold, wet night air. She did not care if she was soaking wet, she was only thankful to be cool and alive.

All at once her dizziness and exhaustion caught up with her. She sagged into Khan'di and felt his arms catch her. She heard Sayyed and

Athlone around her and managed a weak smile before her eyes closed and she sank into welcome sleep.

Gabria woke up suddenly and bolted upright on the bed. Something was wrong. Her heart was racing, and her eyes stared wildly around the room. Nothing about this place was familiar. It was big and airy and comfortably full of dark furniture, elegant wall hangings, and thick rugs. An embroidery stand sat by the far window, where sunlight poured into the room. A table near the bed was covered with bottles of perfume, combs, and boxes of jewelry. Even the big bed Gabria was in was different from anything she was used to. This room was obviously not in a treld.

Gabria took a deep breath. Wherever she was, she could not help herself by panicking. She tried to think. The last thing she could remember was the storm. She had no idea how she came to be in this strange place or how long she had been there.

She was about to get up when a small girl and a large dog burst through the door. They saw Gabria was awake and threw themselves at the bed in delight.

Gabria, laughing with relief, grabbed them both in a hug. "Hello, you two! Where is everyone?"

Treader barked, *They're eating. They say if Gabria awakens, she should come eat, too.*

Gabria thought that eating sounded like a wonderful idea. She hopped out of bed and looked down at herself in surprise. Her dirty, burned, wet clothes had been replaced by a soft nightdress, and her body and hair had been washed.

Tam bounced off the bed and twirled around to show Gabria the blue dress she was wearing, then she danced to a chair where a red outfit was draped over the padded leather arm. She brought the dress back to Gabria.

The woman was astonished. "For me?" She ran her hand down the fine, soft red wool. The dress was fashioned in a style she had never seen before: it laced at the sides so the bodice fit tightly over her figure, then fell from her hips in a loose, swirling skirt.

Delighted, she slipped the dress over her head and pulled the lacings tight. The dress fit her well. When she was ready, she followed Tam and Treader along a passage past more rooms and down a staircase to the main hall.

Unlike the fon's palace, which had a separate dining hall, most of the houses in Pra Desh were built with a large central room that was used for dining, entertaining, and family gathering. At that moment, Khan'di, Athlone, Sayyed, two of the hearthguard, Sengi, and several members of the Kadoa retinue were sitting at a large table, eating what Gabria guessed was the midday meal. Everyone sprang to their feet when she came down the stairs. She was secretly pleased to see Sayyed's grin of pleasure and Athlone's open look of relief and admiration.

Tam and Treader ran over to join Sayyed, while Khan'di strode forward to escort Gabria to his table.

"Gabria, I am pleased to welcome you to my house."

She could not help but twirl around to display her dress. "Do I thank you for this? It's lovely."

Khan'di smiled in paternal appreciation. He had not realized until now how pretty this woman could be. "We had to throw out your singed clothes. I merely replaced them. It was the least I could do." He led her to a chair and heaped her plate with spiced meat, cheeses, fruit, and fresh bread. Sengi poured a cup of light, fragrant wine.

Gabria waited until she had eaten her fill before she asked any questions. The men were glad to answer.

"Much has happened the past two days," Khan'di began.

"Two days!" Gabria exclaimed. "I slept two days?"

"A day and a half really," Sayyed corrected. "It was almost dawn when the storm came. You slept yesterday, and it is noon now."

The sorceress was amazed. She had not known the spell would exhaust her so much. "What about the palace?"

Khan'di said, "The fire is out completely. The north wing is totally destroyed. The south wing has smoke and water damage, and the roof has been burned in places, but it is salvageable. We plan to rebuild."

Gabria caught a note of suppressed excitement in his voice. "We?" she repeated pointedly.

Athlone replied for his host. "Khan'di Kadoa has been chosen by the guilds and the noble families of Pra Desh to be the new fon."

Gabria's face lit with a smile. "That's wonderful!"

Khan'di's satisfaction showed in every movement of his body and in every line of his face. "We are going to rebuild the palace as soon as the economy of the city has recovered. The fon's army has been disbanded, and her supporters are in prison. Luckily, her treasury was still intact in the vaults. We have already sent peace delegations to the other kingdoms. And—" he leaned forward and his hand slapped the table in glee "—we found the prince of Calah unharmed in the dungeons."

"How is that possible?" Gabria asked in surprise.

"The fon must have been too cautious to kill him immediately, so she kept him handy."

"But what about the fire?"

"The fire did not reach down very far. The doors protected the underground levels and enough air leaked in from the cracks and fissures in the dungeon to keep all the prisoners alive."

Sengi added proudly, "The prince will be restored to his rightful throne."

"And the feuding will begin again," one of the other noblemen chuckled.

Gabria took a sip of her wine. "What about the fon?"

"The courtier, Ancor, and Piers told us what happened." Khan'di curled his lip in distaste. "The remains of the fon's body were found in the throne room. She and her monstrous tools of torture were dumped in the pit. The dungeons have been emptied and sealed."

"What of Bregan?" she asked softly.

Athlone frowned. The loss of his friend still pained him deeply. He could hardly believe the old warrior was gone. "He will be buried this afternoon. He has won back his status and honor as a Khulinin warrior."

She nodded and looked away to hide the blur of tears in her eyes. "Has anyone found Branth?"

There was a long silence; Gabria guessed the answer.

"The city guard did not recognize him in time," Khan'di said heavily. "He stole a horse and slipped out of the city. He was seen riding north."

The sorceress leaned back in her chair and stared at the far wall. Her responsibilities to Khan'di and Pra Desh were fulfilled with Branth's departure from the city. Everyone would have preferred to have him in chains and ready to face the city's judges, but despite their best efforts, the man had slipped away.

Gabria chewed her lip as she thought. She had two choices now: she could let Branth go and return home in time for the clan gathering, or she could pursue him and run the risk of missing the important council of chieftains. Her first inclination was to let Branth escape. She was tired of traveling and ready to go home. She wanted to settle her problems with Sayyed and Athlone, then attend the council and persuade the chiefs to change the laws against magic. The clan gathering was the only time in the year that all eleven chiefs met to create or change the laws that governed the clans. If she was not at the gathering this year, the chiefs could easily ignore the matter of sorcery or even vote against it.

Unfortunately her better judgment disagreed with her first inclination. The King Stallion had warned her that someone was experimenting in evil magic, and her vision had confirmed it was Branth. Back in the caves two nights ago, when she had sensed that great terror, she felt Branth had done something horrible. But what? A fearful, nagging doubt pricked her mind, and she remembered the look of bestial cruelty on his face in the throne room. The exiled chief was gone from Pra Desh, but he still had the *Book of Matrah* and was still very dangerous.

Gabria swallowed her disappointment. She rose and said to Athlone, "My lord, I have to go after him."

For a moment, the Khulinin chief did not answer. He had already guessed how she would choose. Although he was proud of her determination and courage, a small cloud of foreboding darkened his thoughts. The feeling of terror he, too, had sensed in the cave had lodged in his mind, and he was badly frightened for Gabria. Worse, he knew that the only way he could help her against Branth was to learn sorcery himself.

To Athlone's surprise, the idea did not unsettle him. When he had watched Gabria standing alone, smothering the fire and protecting Pra Desh, he had realized that he had made a mistake. Athlone had known for a year that he had the talent to wield magic, a talent that could be used for great good, and he had ignored it.

The chieftain stood and bowed slightly to their host. "Thank you for your earlier invitation, but we will be leaving as soon as possible."

Khan'di's shrewd glance went from the chief to the woman as he said, "I did not expect anything less."

They buried Bregan that afternoon in the hills above the city. The travelers and the new fon escorted the warrior's body up the steep trail to a high peak that overlooked the grasslands far away in the purple haze.

They built a bier of logs and arrayed the warrior's body in his mail shirt, his golden clan cloak, and his finest clothes. The hearthguard laid his weapons by his side; Lord Athlone put a gold armband on his forearm as a symbol of Bregan's restored honor, and Gabria and Tam brought the bag of salt, the loaf of bread, and the water bag that the warrior would need for his journey to the realm of the dead.

They doused the bier with oil and set it ablaze. As the flames climbed toward the sun, Gabria sang the women's prayers for the dead. It took several hours for the fire to die to embers. Only then did they cover the ashes with a high mound of dirt and mark the grave with a spear and helmet as befitting an honored clan warrior.

It was almost dark when the party rode back down through the hills, leading Bregan's horse. Halfway to the city, they paused while Gabria slipped off her horse and walked ahead a few paces into the twilight. She put her fingers to her lips to whistle a piercing call, but Tam's shrill call sounded before Gabria had drawn a breath.

The little girl's whistle was enough. Three Hunnuli cantered out of the darkness. They gathered around Gabria, nickering their pleasure, then Eurus went to greet Athlone and the colt trotted to Tam.

"It is safe to come to the city," Gabria told Nara. "Khan'di has granted us safe passage." She clambered up onto the mare's back and threw her arms around her neck. "I missed you," she murmured.

And I you, Nara replied. *But it's not over, is it?*

"No," Gabria answered sadly. "Not yet."

13

Two days later the travelers rode with Khan'di and an escort through Pra Desh to the outskirts of the city. They passed the guardpost at the city limits just after daybreak and stopped in front of an inn to make a final check of their baggage and to bid farewell to Khan'di. Everyone was rested and ready to go. The packhorses were fully laden, and all of the gear had been retrieved, cleaned, and repaired.

When Piers dismounted to tighten his saddle girth, Khan'di approached him.

The new fon looked ill-at-ease, but he came straight to the point. "I should have asked you this before, Piers. Now is my last chance. I would like you to stay in Pra Desh. I need a healer in the palace. Please come back."

Gabria and Athlone, overhearing the fon, looked at one another and held their breath.

The healer did not answer immediately. He was startled by Khan'di's offer and, for just a moment, he was tempted. He had spent his three days in Pra Desh in the houses of healing, helping with the wounded from the fighting and the injured survivors from the fire. In that time he realized he missed the big city and all it had to offer. He had much to learn of the new medical advances the Pra Deshian healers had made in the past eleven years.

Then he thought of the clan that had become his family, of the lovely valley where his own tent overlooked a shining river, and of the sorceress who had helped fill the aching loss left in his heart by his daughter's death. He settled his clan cloak over his shoulders and shook his head. "I can't."

Khan'di gripped his arm. "Piers, I know you're angry with me, but I did not know what the old fon's wife was planning that night. Please believe me! I found out later that the woman had given me something to make me ill in order to get you out of the way. By the time I learned of this, you were already gone from the city. I'm sorry!"

Piers clasped his old friend's hand in his own. For eleven years he had been plagued by uncertainties about Khan'di's deliberate involvement with the old fon's murder. Hearing the truth at last healed a few more of his lingering scars. "It's not that," he said, his thin mouth smiling. "I have finally put my daughter to rest. It's just that I have made a new home with the Khulinin. I want to go back."

Khan'di searched the healer's face, judging the sincerity of his words, then he nodded. "A few years ago I would have called you a fool to leave Pra Desh for the barbarian outlands." He shot a glance at Gabria and Athlone mounted on their Hunnuli. "Now I know better. Long life, my friend. Come visit when you can."

The nobleman stood back as the healer mounted. The clan horses shifted restlessly, pawing and sidestepping with excitement. They knew it was time to go.

Khan'di strode over to Gabria. He laced his hands behind his back and looked up at the woman with fondness. "I promised you a reward. Are you sure you won't take it?"

"We have no need of it. Your generous supplies are enough." She gestured to the hills beyond the city. "Just watch over Bregan's mound, will you?"

"With pleasure, and thank you, Sorceress. May Elaja go with you."

The woman nodded sadly. In spite of her earlier reservations, she had come to know and like this man in the two months they had traveled together. She would miss him. "And with you, Fon Kadoa."

Khan'di went to stand with his escort. "Don't forget," he called. "Take the north fork two leagues from here. My scouts said Branth is following the river."

Athlone raised his fist in salute to the fon, then he waved his arm to his own party. Eurus half-reared and leaped forward. His huge hooves pounded the paving stones. Nara and the other horses fell in behind, following the stallion down the caravan road. Khan'di raised his hand in farewell and watched until the horses disappeared,

From the shadows of a deep copse of trees, the gorthling watched the farm through Branth's eyes, his anticipation growing with each passing moment. It was one of the large communal farms that were common throughout the Five Kingdoms. Early morning sunlight washed the three white-walled cottages and their outbuildings in a pale golden light. Smoke rose from the chimneys, and chickens clucked around the yard.

As far as the gorthling could see, all of the men had gone to the fields, leaving four women, a girl, and several children in the houses. He licked his lips. For five days now he had avoided human contact while he learned the uses of his new body and studied the basic spells in the *Book of Matrah*. His ruined hand still bothered him, but it was healing well. Now he was ready to try out his new skills.

The door opened in one of the cottages, and a slender young woman walked out, carrying a bucket. The gorthling felt the bloodlust stir his thoughts and his body. He avidly watched the woman carry her bucket to the well and lower it down to fill it. The stirring grew to an urgent desire, and he stepped out of the shadows. His eyes began to glow with a vicious red gleam as he slid his dagger into his sleeve and began to walk toward the farm.

Gabria watched the plumes of smoke rise from the smoldering ruins of the farmhouse and tried not to look at the scorched bodies lying in a row under the apple tree. She was horribly shaken by this destruction. This was the third communal farm along the river that she and her companions had found in this state. The first farm in Calah had been appalling. There had been four men and a boy murdered by what Gabria immediately recognized was the Trymian Force. The horribly mutilated body of a woman was dumped in a wagon, and neighbors located the remains of the rest of the three families in the burned and gutted cottages. Even the outbuildings had been put to the torch.

Since that afternoon six days ago, the travelers had tracked Branth out of Calah and through neighboring Portane from one destroyed farm to another. They had ridden as fast as possible, but Branth stayed tantalizingly out of reach. Secen, one of the best trackers in the Khulinin, estimated the exile was only a day in front of them. However, Branth stole a horse whenever he needed a fresh one, and he never stopped long enough for anyone to catch up with him.

Gabria leaned forward to rest her arms on Nara's mane and let her head drop. She was tired and felt wretched. She could hear Athlone nearby, talking to the farmers who had found the smoking ruin earlier that morning. Piers and Tam were waiting by the road, while Sayyed, Treader, and the warriors searched the surrounding fields for some sign of Branth.

The woman let her eyes wander toward the charred cottage. It looked so hideously incongruous against the backdrop of the flowering orchard and the warm, bright spring day.

Athlone returned to her side. "It's the same as the first two," he said grimly. "No one saw anything. They think it happened late last night, but they don't know how or why. There is sign of only one man, and no one can believe only one man could do all this." The chief began to pace angrily between the two Hunnuli. "That's what I don't understand. I can believe Branth would steal a horse, food, or gold, and he would kill a man or two who stood in his way. He is a vindictive, arrogant brute, but he never did anything violent that did not serve his own ambitions." Athlone gestured at the ruins. "This kind of cruel, senseless destruction is not like him."

Gabria agreed. "Something happened to him in Pra Desh," she said. "Something changed him."

"Any ideas?"

"I wish I knew."

Athlone turned on his heel and mounted Eurus. "We'd better find him before he burns every farm in Portane."

Just then they heard a shout, and Secen came running toward them from the fields north of the burned barn. "Lord Athlone," he yelled, "we found his trail."

"Still heading for Rivenforge?"

"No, he's turned west. He's going toward the river."

"Sacred gods," Athlone cried, "please lead him to the plains!"

Branth's move away from the heavily populated farmlands was what the chieftain had been hoping for. Branth was exiled from his people and condemned to death for the murder of Lord Savaric and the part he had played in Medb's war. Nevertheless, Athlone thought the familiarity of the plains and the lure of home would lead Branth away from the Five Kingdoms. Athlone had no authority in the kingdoms or any experience with their laws and customs. He would prefer to be in clan territory when they caught up with the renegade.

Gabria, however, accepted Branth's move west with mixed feelings. She wanted him out of the Five Kingdoms, but if he entered the Ramtharin Plains and clan jurisdiction, her use of her arcane powers would again be problematic. She could not use her sorcery without breaking her vow to the clan chiefs. If she and her companions caught up with Branth and he fought them with his magic, she would have to dishonor her vow and face the wrath of the clan chieftains. It was not a pleasant prospect. With a sigh, she grasped Nara's mane and sat back while the big mare trotted after Eurus to find the other riders.

The travelers found Branth's trail and followed it across the farmlands and vineyards of Portane. The trail remained clear—Branth was making no effort to hide his tracks—and it continued west to the Serentine River. At the riverbank, the tracks turned north, parallel to the river, then, at the first ford, the tracks vanished into the water. Secen checked and found the trail on the far bank. Branth had crossed the river into the plains.

The travelers forded the wide, muddy river easily, struck the trail, and hurried on. Gabria looked out over the rippling plains with pleasure. The season was ripening to summer, the time when the plains were the most beautiful. The grass that clothed the treeless hills grew thick and green. Wildflowers of yellow, red, and white bloomed on every slope and in every hollow. The few trees close to the creeks that wandered here and there were in full leaf, and arching above it all was a clear, glorious dome of azure.

For five days Gabria and her companions trailed Branth, drawing no closer to the elusive exile. To Secen's annoyance, the trail remained clear, but it meandered all over the region. Branth backtracked, circled around, and wandered back and forth as if looking for something.

At one point he skirted very close to Bahedin Treld before turning northwest. Most of the Bahedin would have left for the gathering at the Tir Samod by this time of year, but the elderly and the very young often remained behind. Athlone pushed his party on without rest; they could not afford to lose Branth's trail.

After a day of running west, Branth angled north. His trail did not falter from that path, as if he had finally decided on a destination. The pursuers followed, but the farther north they rode, the more nervous they became.

"I don't like this, Lord Athlone," Secen said as he knelt to study the tracks left by Branth's horse. "If he keeps on this way, he'll ride straight into—"

"I know what lies to the north," Athlone interrupted sharply. "Moy Tura."

Just the name of the infamous ruined city sent a shudder down the chieftain's back. He looked north over the open plains, as if he could see across the leagues of grass to the ancient city of the sorcerers. He had heard many tales of the fabulous metropolis, and those tales were enough to keep the heartiest of clan warriors away from the place.

"How far is Moy Tura?" Sayyed asked uneasily.

"Seven leagues, perhaps. Enough distance that Branth might veer off and miss the ruins," Secen replied.

"I hope so," said Keth. "I don't want to find out if the tales about that place are true."

"Maybe we'll be lucky, Lord," Secen said as he remounted. "Maybe one of those legends will eat Branth for an evening meal."

The others laughed, and they set off again on the exile's trail, everyone hoping that the man would go anywhere but Moy Tura.

Far to the north of the Khulinin hunting party, a lone rider kicked his weary horse into a trot and rode up the slope of a high tableland. "It has to be here somewhere," the gorthling hissed. He had been searching for days for the sorcerers' city and so far, had not even seen a road that might lead to it.

He cursed his vague memory. The gorthling knew Moy Tura was the center of arcane learning. All of the clan magic-wielders went there to study their craft. If any man knew who and where all the magic-wielders were, he would be in Moy Tura. The only problem was the gorthling did not know exactly where the city was located, and Branth's memories strangely did not include anything about Moy Tura.

The gorthling curled a lip. He was growing tired of this fruitless search over empty land. He wanted to find Moy Tura and its sorcerers and destroy everyone who could possibly ruin his plans. He still wanted to locate those clans who had exiled his host's body—there would be perverse pleasure in wreaking revenge on them—and there was also the mysterious magic-wielder who had kindled such hatred in Branth's memory. It would be interesting to track that one down, too. But first, he wanted to find Moy Tura.

The gorthling urged his horse on, faster and faster, until it finally reached a decent vantage point. He reined the animal to a stop and sat looking at the view before him. There was not much to see. The huge, treeless plateau stretched away for leagues without features or landmarks to break its level expanse. The gorthling rode on. His instincts told him the city was close by, but he could see nothing that looked like a well-populated metropolis. There was only grass and sky.

A little while later the gorthling rose in his stirrups and caught sight of something rising out of the plain far ahead. He rode toward it.

As he drew closer, he saw more details and features. There was a high, crumbling wall, and behind it he could see buildings, towers, and parapets, but they were all in ruins. What was this place?

It was not until he rode to the enormous entrance and saw the two huge stone lions lying in the rubble that he realized where he was. They had guarded the city since its birth, or so the stories said.

Viciously he reined his horse to a stop. What had happened? The gorthling could see now that Moy Tura had been destroyed. The entrance gates had been shattered by a tremendous explosion and most of the buildings had been razed. The streets were full of rubble, wind-blown debris, and weeds. As far as he could see the only life here was a rat, some magpies, and a swarm of flies. Even the land around the city was empty and barren. Where were all of the magic-wielders?

The gorthling cursed and urged his reluctant horse into the ruins. There was still time to search the place before dark. Perhaps he could find some clue to the whereabouts of the sorcerers. There had to be a few left to pass on the inherited talent or his host body could never have summoned him. The gorthling rode forward and disappeared into the dead city.

"Are you sure he went in there?" Gabria asked as she stared at the broken walls casting shadows in the early morning light.

Secen nodded, his face pale under its tan.

The travelers were silent as they gazed about them in nervous curiosity. They had arrived at the plateau late the night before, but they had not tried to enter the city for fear of losing Branth's trail in the dark. Now it was the dawn of a warm, breathless day, and Branth's tracks led directly into the old ruin.

Just in front of the riders, the entrance lay open, its gates in pieces. A stone lion crouched nearby, cracked in two, resting on the rubble.

Piers studied the lion curiously. "I thought there used to be two," he muttered. "The stories always mentioned a pair."

Athlone took a deep breath. "Let's go," he called. Eurus, his ears pricked and his nostrils flared, walked warily into the city. The others came behind, keeping close together as they passed the fallen lion and the piles of rubble at the gateway. The ruins closed in around them.

The party silently followed the tracks of Branth's horse through weed-choked streets, around crumbling houses and wind-torn towers, past empty shops and decaying walls. Grass grew in every available chink, and piles of broken stone lay everywhere. Here and there a few fallen statues or shattered fountains could be seen in the ruins, attesting to the grandeur of the once-proud city.

Gabria was amazed by the remnants of beauty that still survived in the desolation. Moy Tura had not been a large city, even by the standards of two hundred years ago. It had been a close community of people dedicated to the art of sorcery. They had built what they thought was the greatest, most magnificent city in the known world.

That was the tragedy, Gabria thought to herself. All of their beauty, wisdom, and power had not protected their homes from the jealousy, greed, and anger of the outside world. The sorcerers who had lived here had been too isolated from their kin. They had put themselves on a pedestal and had ignored the warning signs when the pedestal started to crack.

According to legend, the city was betrayed by a sorcerer, a bitter man who had told the clans of the secret ways into the city—ways that skirted Moy Tura's deadly magical defenses. The man was, in turn, betrayed by a chieftain. He, along with all the other sorcerers, was massacred. It took the gathered clans only one day to destroy the city. For two hundred years it had lain, slowly sinking into dust, hidden behind a shroud of fear and terrifying legends.

Gabria's thoughts were still on the past when Sayyed rode close beside her and drew her out of her reverie.

"I hope all the tales about this place aren't true," he said. His horse snorted at a rat that scurried past.

Gabria shivered and watched Treader chase the rat into a pile of stones. "So do I. There are some particularly nasty ones: ghosts, a guardian, a sorcerer's curse, hidden traps for unwary looters, and evil beings that lurk in the city at night."

"That guardian," the Turic said, looking nervously around. "Even the Turic tell the story of Moy Tura's guardian."

"The Korg?" Piers said behind them. "No one has proven that it exists."

"What's the Korg supposed to be? Doesn't that word mean lion?" Gabria asked.

"Yes, it was an ancient breed of large lions that once lived on the plains. That lion at the front gate was supposed to be a korg, one of two that guard the gates," Piers explained. "But the guardian of the legends was a sorcerer originally—a shape-changer. He altered his shape to avoid the massacre and remained here after the city was destroyed. It is said he went mad and lost the power to revert to human form."

Gabria thought of the desperate sorcerer and stared sadly over the ruins around her. Living here would drive anyone mad. Even in the sunlight the shattered city was bleak and desolate. So much wisdom gone to waste.

The riders fell quiet again. Their voices seemed jarring and unnatural in the dead city. It was better to ride in wordless haste and get through there as fast as possible.

Before long they found the remains of Branth's night camp in an empty house. His tracks, still clear in the dust, continued from there deeper into the city.

The travelers were over halfway through the ruins when Nara and Eurus threw up their muzzles and tested the air.

Branth is close, the mare told Gabria, *and so is something else.* She sprang forward.

"What is it?" Gabria cried. All the horses broke into a canter along the road.

I do not know. It is strange. It is near Branth.

Treader suddenly erupted into a furious barking, *Ahead! The man is close.* He bolted into the arched entrance of a courtyard. The riders followed him at a run. They burst through one of four gateways into what had once been a spacious, stone-paved courtyard in front of a multi-columned temple. Now the court was full of debris, and the temple was a pile of collapsed walls and shattered columns.

"There!" Athlone shouted, pointing toward a horse and rider in the shadow of the temple.

The rider glanced back at them in surprise, then he whipped his head around and stared at something in the temple ruins. His horse reared violently.

The travelers raced across the courtyard, led by Treader and those riding the Hunnuli. They saw Branth more clearly now. He was trying to regain control of his terrified horse. He savagely yanked its head around and whipped it forward into a frantic lunge just as a strange, fearsome beast sprang out from the fallen stones of the temple. A huge paw swiped at the horse's rump and missed. Branth wheeled his horse around a pile of stones, screeched in triumph, and sent his mount bolting out of the courtyard through another gate.

Snarling with rage, the beast turned to face the oncoming riders. Its body was half again as large as a Hunnuli's, but it had teeth like curved daggers and a great, tangled mane tumbling about its hideous face.

"The Korg!" Piers cried. "It's the missing stone lion."

Athlone reacted instantly. "Split up! Get out of here!"

The riders obeyed, for everyone could see that no weapon of theirs would make a dent on the stone flanks of the huge lion that faced them. They turned and rode desperately for the several gateways behind them. The beast roared in fury; its eyes glowed with an uncanny yellow light as it raced after the fleeing horses.

Before Gabria realized what he was doing, Sayyed slowed his horse and turned in the saddle. His hand raised, he fired a very pale blue bolt of Trymian Force at the lion. The feeble energy bounced off the beast's face, stinging it into a greater frenzy. It leaped forward faster.

"Sayyed, get out of here!" Gabria screamed.

The Turic's expression turned to horror, and he fled after the others. The warriors and Piers were already riding through the entrances. Gabria and Tam on Nara, Athlone on Eurus, Treader, and the colt were together in the courtyard when the lion finally caught them.

Gabria immediately created a wall of magic around her companions. The lion slammed into the invisible barrier and rocked back on its haunches. For just a moment, its yellow eyes blinked in stunned surprise, then it roared and paced along the front of the barrier, looking for a break in the wall.

In the brief respite provided by the shield, they made a dash for the gateway from the courtyard. In that time, Gabria also made up her mind to stop the creature, but without endangering Athlone. Quickly she told Nara what to do. "Hang on!" she yelled to Tam. The girl's arms tightened around Gabria's waist.

Just as Eurus reached the edge of the courtyard, Gabria dissolved the wall of force. Nara swerved sideways with Treader and the colt beside her, and Eurus galloped through the arch before Athlone realized what had happened.

The stone lion did not hesitate. It turned after the mare and followed her as she galloped back toward the temple. Gabria fired a powerful blast of Trymian Force that exploded on the lion's chest. The energy knocked the beast back, but it did no real damage. The lion was up and after the horse in a heartbeat.

Nara lured him on. She dashed out of the courtyard through the arch where Branth had gone and led the stone lion on a frantic chase through the ruined city, farther and farther away from their companions. Gabria kept the beast enraged with arcane blasts, but she could not kill it.

At last, the colt and Treader began to tire, and Nara looked for a place where they could hide and rest. They ran faster to put more distance between themselves and the lion, then they ducked into a maze of tumbled buildings and clogged streets. They lost sight of the lion for a moment, but its roar of frustration echoed behind them. Nara kept going until they saw another, smaller temple. The place was half-buried in the rubble of the fallen building beside it.

"In there!" Gabria cried. "The gods will protect us."

Nara stopped at the entrance to let her riders dismount, and the little group hurried into the cool shadows of the temple's interior just as the lion bounded into the street behind them. It snarled furiously, a grating sound that overwhelmed the silence of the ruins.

Tam and Gabria held their breath. They and the animals pressed back into the shadows of the small room while the hideous lion stalked by. The beast's weight made the stones of the temple tremble. It hesitated near the entrance to the ruined building, yellow eyes staring malevolently, then passed on down the street. The thud of its footfalls slowly faded out of earshot.

Gabria threw her arms around Tam and hugged her tightly. They settled back into the dim, dusty temple, their ears straining to hear any more noise from the Korg. Time passed slowly. Now and then Gabria heard the lion roar in the distance, and she prayed to Amara that her companions had made it out of the city safely.

While they rested, Gabria had a chance to look around their little shelter. The temple was bigger than the one in which she had spent the winter, but it, too, was simple and unadorned. The only real difference between the houses of worship—apart from their state of repair—was a magnificently carved stone altar. Even under the dirt and cobwebs, Gabria could see the detailed design. One large figure on the front of the altar caught her eye in the pale light filtering through the doorway. She scraped off the dirt from the stone and smiled to herself.

"Look at this," she whispered to Tam and Nara. The girl and the mare picked their way to her side. She showed them her find—a large relief of a man mounted on a Hunnuli stallion. From the lightning bolt in his hand, Gabria knew the man was supposed to be Valorian. The clans' Hero-Warrior had used the power of the lightning to give the Hunnuli their remarkable resistance to magic.

Nara moved around Tam to get a better look. As the mare did so, her hind hoof slipped on a loose slab of rock. She lost her balance, fell sideways, and crashed into the altar.

"Nara!" Gabria cried in alarm. To her immense relief, the mare staggered to her feet and shook herself ruefully.

I am bruised but unhurt, the mare reassured her. *I should watch where I am stepping.*

Tam grabbed Gabria's sleeve and pointed to the altar. The big stone altar had appeared to be a solid chunk of white marble, but the Hunnuli had knocked one side loose. With an exclamation, Gabria scrambled over to look. The whole side of the altar was a cleverly hinged door.

Gabria pulled the door open and peered inside. At first she saw nothing but dust in the dark interior. She reached gingerly into the cavity, feeling the cold stone and dirt beneath her fingers. She lifted the only thing hidden in the altar's interior with great care and laid the object on the floor. Whatever it was, it was heavy and wrapped in a stained piece of fine linen.

Gabria looked at Tam and the two grinned at each other like children with a present. The colt pushed close for a look.

Nara snorted. *Are you going to unwrap it?*

Her fingers trembling slightly, Gabria pulled back the fabric to reveal a mask of solid gold. She dropped the linen and stared. It was the face of a man, beautifully wrought and polished to a brilliant shine. In wonder she reached out to touch it. A strange tingling tickled her fingers, and she froze, her fingertips still resting on the golden surface. A faint pulse of power vibrated out of the mask into her hand. She had sensed power like that in the healing stone Piers sometimes used and in a brooch Lord Medb had once given Lord Savaric. It was the power of magic.

Without a second thought, she wrapped the mask back in its linen cover and tied it to her belt. "It's time to go," she said.

Do you know what the mask is? Nara asked as the little group moved to the door.

The sorceress shook her head. "No. But it is a prize too precious to leave here."

They slipped outside, and, after Treader and Nara made sure the area was safe, Gabria and Tam remounted. They tried to head back the way they had come. It was not long, though, before Gabria realized they were completely lost.

Gabria glanced worriedly at the sun. The day had passed to late afternoon. She did not relish spending the night in the old city with a living stone lion, Branth, or any other evil creature that might be loose

She was lost in thought, pondering their unsettling situation, when Tam tapped on her shoulder. The little girl pointed to a magpie flapping overhead. She closed her eyes and raised her hand toward the bird.

To Gabria's amazement, the magpie fluttered down to Tam's hand. It squawked loudly. *Go to the next street. Turn at the broken statue*, the bird said in her mind. The sorceress turned to the little girl and grinned proudly before she passed the information on to Nara.

They followed the magpie's instructions and wound through the ruins to a broad avenue. Far ahead they saw a high wall with an open arch. There was no sign of the Korg or Branth, but to Gabria's endless relief, she heard a shout and saw two riders come out of the shadow of the wall. A few moments later three more riders, Athlone among them, came out of the ruins and galloped toward the mare, whooping with relief. The entire party met near the wall and greeted one another in joy.

Secen, who had been scouting the area, came riding in through the open arch. The warrior beamed with pleasure when he saw Gabria. "You're safe! Praise Surgart." He turned to Athlone. "I've found him, Lord. Branth left the ruins through another gate. The trail leads west."

"Let's be after him," Athlone said. "I have no desire to stay and see that Korg again."

The others wholeheartedly agreed, and they thankfully rode out of Moy Tura behind Secen. Somewhere in the ancient ruins, the lion roared a cry of anger and hopelessness. Gabria glanced back in sadness for the magic-wielders who had been lost in blood and violence. She prayed that such a thing would never happen again. Tightening the knot that held the mask to her belt, she followed her companions as they resumed their hunt for the renegade chieftain.

14

Gabria did not show the mask to her companions until the next day, when they were away from the desolate ruins of Moy Tura. The party stopped at noon to eat and rest the horses, and she brought out the stained linen bundle and laid it on the grass in front of her. The men and Tam gathered around to watch as she peeled the fabric away.

Gabria's heart pounded. She could hardly believe the beautiful, magical object was real until she could see it again in the light of day. She lifted the last linen fold aside to reveal the golden mask. Drawing a deep breath, she held the mask up to the sun. It sparkled and shone as brilliantly as it had on the day it was made.

"What is it?" Athlone asked in a hushed voice.

"It looks like a death mask," Piers said.

The sorceress ran her finger over the mask's cheek. Piers was right, it did look like a death mask. If that was the truth, then this man had been very important. The clanspeople only made death masks of those they deeply revered.

It was a handsome face, Gabria thought. Even in the rigid lines of the metal she could see the character of his features. There was strength in the planes of his jaw and forehead, stubbornness in his long nose, and humor in the lines around his mouth. When she looked closer, she could see the cleft of his chin, the trace of a scar on his forehead, and the arched lines of his eyebrows. The eyes were closed, but Gabria fancied the irises would be brilliant blue if they were open.

"It's magnificent," Piers said.

"What are you going to do with it?" Sayyed inquired.

Gabria shrugged and turned the mask over in her hands. "I don't know. It holds some kind of arcane power, but I can't tell what the spell is supposed to do."

The Turic rose to his feet and flashed his grin. "Too bad it can't talk."

The young woman nodded absently. She studied the gold mask while the others ate their meal and watered the horses, yet she discovered nothing that was useful. There were no inscriptions, etched designs, or markings of any kind on the metal. It was simply a man's face with an enigmatic expression. Finally she wrapped the mask back in its cloth and packed it with her belongings. For the rest of the day she mulled over the puzzle of the mask and still could find no answer.

The party trailed Branth for seven days after leaving Moy Tura and drew no closer to the elusive exile. He was moving faster now that he knew someone was following him, and the travelers were hard pressed to keep pace with him. To their dismay, he seemed to be pulling ahead of them as he trekked south across the plains. All of them wondered where he was going and what he would do next. On the eighth day they found part of their answer.

That morning dawned clear and warm, hinting of the hot afternoon to come. A light breeze blew about the hills, and meadowlarks dipped and fluttered after grasshoppers. The party was riding south, following Branth's trail along the flank of a long, low ridge, when the Hunnuli abruptly stopped and neighed an alarm.

Gabria, deathbirds! Nara warned her rider.

The sorceress saw the birds then—a large flock of black vultures circling low over a place beyond the hills ahead. "Look," she cried, pointing them out to everyone.

They galloped urgently toward the place, rode to the top of a high hill, and looked down upon a small valley lined with trees. The birds were swinging over a clear space not far from a meandering creek.

"Oh, gods," Athlone breathed.

Gabria bit her lip to stifle the sick feeling that rose in her stomach. The scene in the clearing below looked hideously familiar to her.

"Keth, stay here with Tam and the horses," Athlone ordered. The warrior was glad to comply.

The rest dismounted and walked down the long slope to the clearing by the creek. Several vultures squawked and flapped into the trees.

Twelve people lay scattered in huddled, lifeless heaps—five men, four women, and three children wearing the orange clan cloaks of the

Bahedin. Their carts and belongings were torn apart and thrown carelessly among the bodies. The horses and other animals were gone.

Piers hurried to examine them, but as he turned the mangled
bodies over and checked their pallid faces, it became very clear they
were all dead.

While the healer was occupied with the corpses, Athlone and the
others looked for signs of Branth. They had little doubt that he was
responsible for the massacre.

"They were traveling with full carts and their tents. They must
have been latecomers trying to catch up with their clan on the way to
the Tir Samod," Athlone said bitterly as he examined the wreckage of
a cart. This slaughter sickened him. The Bahedin had long been allies
of the Khulinin, and they had stood with Athlone's father against Lord
Medb at Ab-Chakan.

Gabria's face was pale under her tan. "On their way to the gathering." She turned away from the body of a young woman and swallowed hard. Flies were swarming around the dead girl's face, and
vultures had been pecking at her eyes.

Secen joined Athlone and said, "Lord, I can only find sign of one
man other than the Bahedin. It is as we suspected."

The chief cursed. "Branth."

"The hoof prints are from the same horse we have been following,
and the boot prints seem to match the ones we saw in Moy Tura."

Piers hurried over, his face strained and white.

"They're all dead," Athlone stated rather than asked.

The healer nodded. "Yesterday. They were tortured."

Secen looked sick. Athlone raised his fist and brought it down on
the side of the cart. "Why! Why is he doing this?" he shouted.

Treader began to bark furiously. *Come! I am at the creek!* his barks
told the magic-wielders.

At the same moment, Sayyed yelled, "Gabria, Lord Athlone, over
here. Quick!" Something in his voice spurred Gabria and the men into
an instant response. They ran toward the sound of the Turic's shouts
and Treader's excited barking. As they passed beyond a copse of trees
sheltering the riverbank, they came to a sudden halt.

Sayyed stood on the bank, holding the frantic dog by the scruff of
the neck. In shocked silence, he stared at a corpse that had been
impaled on a sword against the trunk of a tree. The man's body hung
so high his feet did not touch the ground, and they could tell his death
had been painful by his wide, staring eyes and the hideous grimace
twisting his features. He was an older man, with a lined, weathered

face. His filthy, bloodstained tunic had a golden horse, the emblem of a herdsman, embroidered on the left breast.

"I tried to loosen the sword," Sayyed said, his voice tight with fear and wonder. "But he . . . moved."

"That's impossible," Athlone snapped. "He's dead."

The chieftain reached out to grasp the sword pinning the dead Bahedin. He yanked at it several times, then, as Sayyed had warned, the man jerked to life. As Athlone fell back in horror, the hersdman lifted his head. His lifeless eyes stared down at the travelers, and the pain-racked mouth groaned a horrible, bubbling sound of agony.

The warriors backed away, their eyes wide with shock. Treader cowered down against Sayyed's feet. Only Piers stepped forward. He reached up to find the man's pulse.

"By the holy gods," Piers exclaimed, snatching his hand away. "This man *is* dead. His skin is as cold as stone. He has no heartbeat. Look, he's not even breathing."

"Greetings, hunters. I know you are following me."

They turned back to the corpse, who spoke again, his voice raspy and hollow. "I have left this message for you so you will know with whom you are dealing. If you are smart, you will turn back while you are still able."

The dead man looked from one clansman to another. "I was brought here from the realm of Sorh by one of your kind—Lord Branth. I intend to remain here. I have learned from the people who lie dead nearby that there is only one magic-wielder left in the clans, and only she *might* possess the power to challenge me. I intend to seek her out."

Gabria gasped, and Athlone moved closer to her.

The corpse added, "If you wish to find me, I am going to the gathering of the clans." The dead man emitted a harsh, hideous laugh. "I have plans for the people of Valorian."

Abruptly the herdsman's head jerked, his voice stopped, and his body sagged against the sword. There was a long, silent pause before Piers tentatively reached up and closed the dead man's eyes.

"Good gods, what was that?" Secen murmured.

"A spell," Gabria replied, her voice as hollow as the dead man's. She was staring at the corpse. Her skin had gone deathly pale, and her knees were weak. "Branth, or whatever he has become, put a spell on this man to speak that message."

"Whatever he has become," Athlone repeated. "What do you mean?"

Gabria's shoulders sagged. "It claims to be from the realm of Sorh. I'm not sure, but I think there is only one such creature that can be summoned by sorcery: a gorthling."

"What's a gorthling?" Sayyed demanded.

When the woman did not answer, Athlone said, "They're monsters from our ancient stories. They're supposed to be creatures of immortal evil."

"They're not just stories. Gorthlings exist," Gabria whispered. "The Woman of the Marsh warned me about them." Her eyes held a faraway look. She crossed her arms over her chest and took a deep breath.

The men were silent as they tried to absorb the meaning of what they had heard. Athlone and Piers moved to the tree to take the dead Bahedin down. This time when the chieftain yanked at the sword, the man remained lifeless, his soul forever lost to death. They pulled the sword free and gently lowered him to the ground.

They carried the dead herdsman to the spot where his fellow Bahedin lay. A vulture squawked as they approached the bodies, and a few others that had landed nearby sidled away from the Khulinin.

"What do we do with them?" Sayyed asked, indicating the dead clanspeople.

"Bury them," Gabria said flatly.

"We don't have time. That will put us farther behind Branth," Athlone reminded her.

She looked down at the dead herdsman. "Someone buried my clan when I could not. Maybe it was the Bahedin. We could at least burn them. Someone else can build their mound."

The chief nodded. As badly as he wanted to catch up with Branth—or the gorthling that had sided with him—he knew she was right. They could not leave the slain clanspeople to the scavengers.

The task took Gabria and the men the rest of the morning. Using wood from the Bahedin's carts, dead tree limbs, dried brush, or anything that would burn, they built a bier and laid the thirteen men and women side by side with their tools, weapons, jewelry, and the necessities for their journey out of man's world. Keth and Tam brought the horses down, and the little girl watched solemnly as Gabria sang the songs of the dead and lit the fire under the bier. The smoke rose high above the plains, its acrid smell driving the vultures away one by one.

By noon the party was on Branth's trail again, heading south. They rode hard, their anger and worry following at their heels. They found a place to camp at sunset in a hollow between two hills. Gabria built a fire, and everyone gathered around the bright warmth. No one felt like talking.

It was Gabria who finally broke the silence. She lifted her head and stared up at the brilliant stars overhead. "Athlone, I want to go see the Oathbreakers."

The men started in surprise.

"No," the chief said automatically.

Gabria continued to look at the sky, her mind busy behind her eyes. "I will go without you if I have to."

Athlone closed his eyes and swallowed the anger he felt at her defiant tone. "Why? Why them?"

"They may be the only ones who can help me."

"Help you what?" he demanded.

Gabria lowered her eyes and shook her head. "They have a few books from the days of the old sorcerers in their citadel. I think Seth might be able to help me find something I could use to fight the gorthling."

"How can you be sure this *is* a gorthling? All you have are the magic words of a dead man," Athlone said angrily.

"I'm not certain, but everything fits. Branth summoned something evil and now he is slaughtering every human in his sight. He has changed, we have all sensed that. I think he has been overcome by a gorthling. That's how they work; they possess a host body and wreak havoc using it as a tool."

"So why don't we kill its host body?" Sayyed suggested.

"We could do that, but a gorthling is immortal. It would simply take another body as host."

Athlone leaned forward. "Then how do we destroy it?"

Gabria threw her hands up in the air and cried, "I don't know! The gorthling is a creature of magic and must be fought with magic. That's why I must see the Oathbreakers."

The Turic gestured to himself and Athlone. "*We* are magic-wielders. We can help."

The woman shook her head wildly. "I can't teach you enough to fight something as powerful as a gorthling. Look at what it did to all of those people. It would slaughter you. I couldn't bear that."

"And what if it kills you?" Athlone said. "Who will fight it then? Do you expect us to just stand by and watch you face it alone?"

Gabria felt her heart leap. This was the first time Athlone had spoken to her about using his talent. Nevertheless, she forced her excitement down and shook her head. She did not want him learning sorcery just so he could die at the hand of a gorthling. "Athlone, let's start by learning how to fight this creature. Then we will worry about who will destroy it."

Athlone drew a deep breath. "All right. We'll go talk to the Oathbreakers. Just you and I. The others will follow Branth so we won't lose his trail."

The hearthguard warriors protested. They feared the Oathbreakers, as did any sensible man of the Dark Horse Plains, but they were equally intent on fulfilling their duty to protect their chieftain.

"That's an order," Athlone told them. "There's no sense angering Seth and his fellow cultists by bringing all of you. Gabria and I will be all right. You'll have enough to worry about just keeping up with Branth."

The three warriors agreed reluctantly, and Gabria nodded with relief. She knew Sayyed was not happy to be left with the other warriors, but he, too, had to accept the decision.

Later, as she packed the death mask in the small bag of belongings she would take with her, the sorceress wondered if Seth could tell her something about the golden artifact, too. She dismissed that hope immediately; it was possible that the Oathbreakers would refuse to talk to her at all.

The Khulinin left their camp shortly after sunrise the next morning. Secen led his group south on Branth's trail while Athlone, Gabria, and the three Hunnuli turned west to seek the citadel of Krath in the northern tip of the Himachal Mountains.

Athlone estimated it would take almost four days to reach the citadel, talk to Seth, and catch up again with the rest of the party. He hoped with all his heart that this trip to see the Oathbreakers was worthwhile. He had his doubts. The cult of Krath guarded their secrets jealously. They had gained the title Oathbreakers by forsaking their vows of fealty to clan and chieftain and shunning their own people for the desolation of their mountain temple. Even if they had the information Gabria sought, they would not help her out of loyalty to the clans.

Athlone could not stifle a cold feeling of dread at the thought of the Men of the Lash, as the cultists were known. A cloak of suspicion born of whispered rumors and stories of heinous deeds hung on the Oathbreakers' shoulders. Unlike the men of the clans, who worshiped two male gods, the Men of the Lash worshiped Krath, the dark sister of Amara. But where the goddess Amara embodied the positive aspects of femininity, her sister represented the dark, less predictable facets. Krath was the ruler of unbridled passion and violence, of secrecy and jealousy. Her power to destroy lay in ways that were either slow and subtle or sudden and unexpected.

Accordingly, Krath's followers became highly trained killers whose religious goals were to perform perfect murders in the service of their bloodthirsty mistress. The men used no metal in their arts. Their only weapons were their bodies, their whips, and their finely crafted killing instruments of leather and stone. It was said an Oathbreaker could snap a man's neck with his bare hands or remove a head with a flick of a vicious black whip.

The clanspeople looked on the cult with aversion and fear. It was not the Oathbreakers' bloodlust that the clans despised, but the subterfuge they practiced. Their silent, furtive, deliberate style of killing was incomprehensible to the men of the clans. The cultists, for their part, preserved their secretive ways. They had scorned the clans for generations and held themselves aloof in their secret stronghold.

As he approached that stronghold, Athlone missed Bregan's strong, solid presence more than ever. The loss of the warrior was a real blow. Athlone would have appreciated Bregan's level head and experience when the time came to deal with the Oathbreakers. The chief's hand tightened unconsciously around his sword hilt. If he had to, he would tear down the citadel of Krath stone by stone to get the help Gabria needed to destroy Branth. That murderer had too much clan blood on his hands to remain in this world.

The next day, Gabria and Athlone saw the gray-blue humps of the Himachal Mountains rise above the horizon. The Himachals were a much smaller mountain range than the mighty Darkhorns. They did not have the tall peaks and snow-covered summits, and they rose only to a modest height above the plains, yet their slopes were steep and rugged with an almost impenetrable wilderness of heavy timber and underbrush.

Fortunately Gabria and Athlone did not have to enter the wildness of the mountainside. The citadel of Krath was located in the northern end of the range, in the foothills not far from Geldring Treld. The citadel was not hard to find, but almost impossible to enter.

The weather had been clear and warm for several days, but that afternoon the wind shifted and began to pile clouds together. The horizon to the north turned iron-gray, its line edged with towering, white-capped clouds. Gabria and Athlone did not need to urge the Hunnuli faster to avoid the storm. The animals sensed the coming rain and picked up their pace. By late afternoon the riders spotted the citadel of Krath on a promontory a few leagues to the south in the tree-clad flanks of the mountains. They altered their route and hurried south ahead of the rain.

Before long, they came to an old stone road that paralleled the mountain peaks. Gabria and the chieftain recognized the stonework immediately as that of the ancient men, the Sons of the Eagle, who had conquered the plains long before the clans had arrived. The men from the west had also built the fortress of Ab-Chakan, which lay only a few days' journey to the south. The road ran past Ab-Chakan and the Isin River, then vanished somewhere near Dangari Treld in the southern end of the mountains.

For much of its length, the road was very old and concealed beneath a net of grass and shrubs, but it was clear and easy to follow in the rough foothills. Gratefully the Hunnuli took to the road and hurried on.

Gradually they drew closer to the citadel. The horses came to a stop at the foot of the mass of rock upon which it rested, and Gabria and Athlone looked up in dread at the black towers. The two riders could not help but shudder. Neither of them had ever been there before, for the clanspeople avoided the stronghold like a plague camp. Few men who dared enter the confines of the citadel survived to tell of the adventure.

The citadel sat on top of a rocky promontory overlooking a wooded valley. A trail forked off the main road and wound up the precipitous slope to the only visible entrance into the closely guarded stronghold. As far as the travelers could see, the citadel consisted of a massive central keep topped by needle-sharp towers of black granite and surrounded by a high, crenelated wall of the same dark stone. The whole edifice crouched like a brooding, malevolent beast over the road and cast its shadow into the valley below.

The riders stared up at the citadel silhouetted against the lowering clouds until the colt grew restive. The wind suddenly swooped out of the north, whipping the trees and snapping at the riders' gold cloaks. The sun disappeared behind the heavy gray clouds.

The Hunnuli started up the trail at a trot. As they made their way along the winding path, Gabria looked closer at the towering citadel and realized it was not as finished as it appeared from a distance. Part of the keep was still under construction and scaffolding surrounded several towers. She remembered that Lord Medb had sent an army to destroy the stronghold the previous summer, when the Oathbreakers had refused to give him their books and manuscripts on magic. The citadel had fallen, and the high priest and his surviving followers had fled to Ab-Chakan to join Savaric. After Medb's death, they returned to rebuild their home. Gabria was impressed despite her nervousness. The men of Krath had accomplished a great deal of work in a short period of time.

The sky was completely overcast by the time Athlone and Gabria reached the top of the rise. The mountains before them were lost in gloom, and the two riders could see dark curtains of rain hanging from the clouds to the north and west. Gabria shivered and pulled her cloak tighter.

The Hunnuli trotted up the narrow path to the massive front wall of the citadel. A single, round-arched gateway, barely wide enough for a wagon to pass through, was built into the wall. It was blocked by a thick oaken door and an intricately carved stone portcullis. The Hunnuli stopped; Eurus pawed the ground.

The citadel loomed over them, silent and menacing, but no one challenged the riders from the walls. In fact, the stronghold seemed strangely lifeless. There were no banners or flags on the towers, no smoke from cooking fires, and no lights or torches. There did not seem to be any guards on the battlements, and there was no sound of life within the walls.

All the same, Gabria sensed she and Athlone were being watched. She looked up at the high walls. "They know we're here," she said.

"What are we supposed to do, knock?" Athlone made a sound of irritation deep in his throat and slid off Eurus. He found a chunk of rock and strode to the gate. "Seth!" he bellowed, banging the rock on the portcullis. The noise rang around them, but nothing stirred behind the gates or on the walls. A few drops of rain spattered in the dust.

After shouldering the sturdy door, Athlone shook his head and returned to Gabria's side. "Those doors have the same type of arcane wards as Ab-Chakan—you know, those small inscribed tiles. We couldn't batter them down if we had one hundred men." He shrugged and added facetiously, "Maybe they're not answering because they're hiding from the rain."

Gabria jerked her head angrily. "Seth!" she shouted at the walls. "The sorceress seeks your help."

Still there was no response from the citadel, and the rain began to fall heavily. Gabria's expression grew angry. She knew that the Oathbreakers were there and that they were aware of her presence, but she had no time to waste on playing their games. She leaned over Nara's shoulder and said to the chieftain, "They're testing me. If we want in, we shall have to invite ourselves."

Athlone cast one last look at the walls and nodded. Only the gods knew how the Oathbreakers would react to two outsiders breaching their door, but if the cultists would not answer, there was no other real alternative. As an afterthought, he removed his weapons and put them in the meager shelter of the wall. No need to seem too antagonistic.

Gabria saw the sense of his move and handed him her dagger. The Oathbreakers despised metal, so it would be best not to insult them by carrying steel into their stronghold. Besides, Gabria knew full well that if the Oathbreakers wanted her dead, no weapon—save magic, perhaps—could protect her.

She waited while Athlone remounted, then threw her hood back and stared intently at the heavy stone portcullis. It's too bad there is no thunderstorm, she thought, since mere rainstorms did not seem to enhance magic. She could have used the added power to help shatter the arcane wards. Gabria wondered briefly if any of the cultists were magic-wielders. Someone had to have set the wards.

But as she studied the small tiles inset into both sides of the gateway, she realized the wards were very old. Seth had told her once that the Oathbreakers had a collection of old spells and relics left by the ancient sorcerers. These wards were probably from that collection. They would work well against normal humans, but they were too old and weak to withstand a full arcane attack.

Ignoring the heavy rain that soaked her neck and shoulders and plastered her hair to her head, Gabria raised her hand and began her spell. Once again the diamond splinter glowed under her skin. She did not notice that Athlone was watching her with a fascinated intensity. She spoke a command, pointed to each ward, and concentrated her magic on them. They held for only a few moments, then the old wards cracked and the tiles fell out of the wall. Gabria spoke a second command, and the heavy portcullis began to slide up in its grooves. There was a cracking noise behind the oak door and, suddenly, the entire door fell back and crashed heavily to the ground.

Gabria glanced back at Athlone with a faint smile of satisfaction. She was pleased when he nodded with approval and gestured to her to enter first.

Nara snorted and stepped carefully over the fallen door. Eurus and the colt came close behind. The three Hunnuli walked into a dark, empty courtyard that lay before the keep. Gabria held her arm high so anyone watching could see the glowing splinter in her wrist. She and

Athlone strained every sense to catch any movement or hidden danger.

Though no attack came, a tall, black-robed figure did emerge from the deep shadows of the keep. A long hood hid his face, and a black whip hung at his belt. He stopped on the steps in front of the Hunnuli and slowly pushed back his hood. In the fading daylight the two riders recognized the gaunt, hawk-nosed face of Seth, brother of Lord Savaric and high priest of the Cult of the Lash.

"Welcome, Sorceress, to the citadel of Krath," he said coldly.

The woman nodded in reply. She did not dismount at once, but sat on Nara and returned Seth's deadpan scrutiny. It was said of the followers of Krath that they could look into a man's heart and find the hidden evils that were buried there; they pried into secrets and opened guarded emotions that were secreted behind masks. Because of this, few men dared to look an Oathbreaker in the eye, but Gabria was different. She had faced horrors and tragedies, trials and triumphs, until the facades of her life had been worn away, and she had learned to face herself for what she was. She had no fear of what Seth would find in her heart. She knew herself well and had nothing to hide.

After a moment, the high priest seemed to reach the same conclusion, for he nodded once, pulled his hood back over his face, and gestured for them to follow. Gabria tied the bag with the golden mask to her belt, then she and Athlone dismounted and hurried after the priest. The Hunnuli went to stand in the shelter of a nearby shed.

The priest led his visitors up the stairs of the keep, through a wide door, and into the central hall. The big room was dark except for a fire burning in the large fireplace against the opposite wall.

The flames gave off just enough light for Gabria and Athlone to see around the empty room. Unlike the rich luxury of the fon's main halls, this one was stark and barren. There were no rugs or wall hangings, just bare stone. The only furniture in the room was a long, stone table set before the fireplace. On the right wall, a staircase went up to a gallery that ran the length of the hall and half hid a series of arched doorways.

A huge, painted statue, the height of several men, sat in the shadows against the far wall and leered down on the visitors. Gabria recognized the red-painted face and the multi-armed body of the goddess, Krath. The goddess was in a sitting position with her six arms reaching out. Her tongue lolled out of her mouth, and her eyes were wild and malevolent.

Gabria stifled a shiver and turned away. Praying silently that Amara would come into this house of Krath and protect her, the sorceress hurried on after Seth.

The priest moved to the fireplace and stood before the flames for several minutes. He did not offer his guests food or drink. When he spoke again, he simply said, "Your need must be urgent for you to break our door."

"If you had answered us in the first place, Uncle, she wouldn't have had to do that," Athlone snapped.

The high priest turned toward the chieftain. The man's face was still hidden by the hood of his robe, but his eyes burned in the firelight. Athlone gritted his teeth and met his uncle's stare. He had turned away from Seth's merciless eyes once, a year ago, but he would not do it this time. He forced his eyes to remain steady on the unblinking, penetrating glare. It was like looking into the eyes of a cobra.

Seth suddenly threw back his hood. Athlone and Gabria were surprised to see a sardonic smile twist up the corner of his mouth.

"You have grown stronger since last summer, Nephew," Seth stated. "Now, why are you here?"

"We think Lord Branth used the *Book of Matrah* to summon a gorthling," Gabria stated flatly.

To her dismay, Seth's emotionless, hard-lined face actually blanched. "How do you know?"

Gabria described her vision, the events at Pra Desh, and Branth's subsequent actions. When she repeated the message spoken by the dead man, Seth's mouth tightened.

"From what we know of gorthlings, I believe you are right," he said. "The creature has invaded the man's body."

The sorceress nodded. "I was hoping something in your library could help us. We have to find some way to destroy it."

The high priest was silent, as if caught up in some internal debate. Then, without a word, he took a torch from a bracket, lit it in the fire, and strode toward the stairs. Athlone and Gabria hurried after him.

The woman glanced up at the gallery overhead and gasped; shadowy forms stood in the arched doorways. The figures melted back into the darkness as the high priest walked up the stairs, and by the time Athlone and Gabria reached the top, the gallery was empty. Nevertheless, the two clanspeople sensed the wary, watchful presences that lurked just out of sight in the lightless corners.

Seth paid no heed to his men nearby, but walked on through a maze of halls and corridors, past closed doors, down stone stairwells, and deep into the heart of the citadel. Everywhere they went, Athlone and Gabria felt, rather than heard or saw, the constant attendance of the unseen watchers.

At last Seth came to a stout door that was bolted with a brass locking mechanism. The two clanspeople watched in fascination while the priest drew a key from his sash and deftly undid the myriad bolts. He pushed open the door and walked in. Athlone and Gabria stepped inside and looked about in wonder. The large room was lined with shelves. Though many of the boards were empty, about one hundred books and manuscripts lay piled in various places around the room.

Books were a rarity to the clans, for they were difficult to obtain and a nuisance to move from place to place. Normally only healers, priests, and clan chieftains could read, although occasionally the wertains, the chieftains' families, or the priestesses of Amara learned the difficult skill. Gabria had never been taught, and as she looked over the Oathbreakers' precious volumes, she thought she would one day like to learn.

"I thought Medb's men destroyed your books," she said to Seth.

"Some of them, yes. But we were able to hide the most important ones." He set his torch in a bracket on the wall and gestured to a table and benches in the middle of the room. Silently he searched through the priceless collection of books.

"I'm afraid there is very little here that will help you," he said, studying the tomes.

Gabria's heart sank. She had hoped desperately that the Oathbreakers would have some useful information. She did not know where else to turn. "Do you know of anyone else who might know?" she forced herself to ask.

The high priest pulled out several volumes and shoved them back. "I've read all of these. They are just general essays on magic. The problem is that there was never much written about gorthlings. All we know is that they are easy enough to summon, but they are treacherous, cunning, and vicious. If they taste blood, they can inhabit any body they choose. Once that happens, it becomes extremely difficult to send them back."

"Send them back where?" Athlone asked.

"A gorthling cannot be destroyed or killed, it must be sent back to Sorh in the realm of the dead."

"How?" Gabria cried in exasperation.

Seth's reply was chilling. "I don't know how. The only ones who ever summoned a gorthling successfully were Matrah and Valorian. Matrah's spells are probably in his tome."

Gabria sighed. "That doesn't help us much."

"What about Valorian?" Athlone suggested.

"Valorian never wrote anything down. He did not wish those spells concerning the gorthlings to be remembered."

The chieftain threw his hands up and paced restlessly to the shelves. "So now we are stuck with a bloodthirsty creature bent on destroying Gabria, and we have no hope of getting rid of it."

Seth turned his basilisk stare on his nephew. "I did not say there was no hope. The gorthling's human body is vulnerable like any other flesh, and its ability to use sorcery is limited by its own knowledge and its body's weaknesses. It can be destroyed, but you will need strength, ingenuity, and courage."

"A few words of instruction would be better," Gabria muttered. She half-turned to say something to Athlone when the heavy weight of the bag banged against her leg. She remembered the mask. "Perhaps you could tell me what this is," she said, unwrapping the mask and laying it on the table before her.

Seth's cold expression did not change, but he reached out and touched the gold surface. "Where did you get this?"

"I found it in Moy Tura."

The priest's head snapped up, and he stared at Gabria. "You were in Moy Tura? Is the Korg still there?"

"Yes," she replied with a half-smile. "It was because of him that we found the mask. It was hidden in a temple."

"The gods were leading your steps," Seth declared.

"Do you know what that is?" Athlone asked.

"It is the death mask of Valorian." The high priest studied the gold mask on the table. "If anything could help you fight the gorthling, this mask might."

"How?" Gabria demanded.

"The mask was once a powerful talisman. It was used in secret ceremonies for the worship of Valorian. When the clans destroyed Moy Tura and the magic-wielders, the mask and everyone who had used it disappeared."

Athlone crossed his arms. "How do you know about it?"

Seth gestured to the books. "It was described in those several times."

"But you don't know how to use the mask's power," Gabria said.

"Unfortunately, no. That was a secret that was only passed on to the priests of Valorian. Nevertheless, if the magic is still viable, you might be able to discover the artifact's purpose and put it to your own use."

Gabria nodded halfheartedly. She was very disappointed. The high priest had not given her much useful information, only puzzles, hints, and more questions.

Seth, sensing her frustration, wrapped the mask in its cloth and gave it back to her. "I am sorry I cannot be much help, Sorceress. Yet you should not abandon your quest. The gorthling is powerful, even more so housed in a human body endowed with magic. It must be sent back or it will wreak havoc in this world."

The sorceress nodded again, without reply. There was nothing more to say. Silently the priest led his two guests back to the main hall and escorted them to the front door. Despite the rain and the darkness he did not invite them to stay, and they did not ask.

Before Gabria walked down the steps toward the waiting Hunnuli, the high priest stopped her.

"If you are successful in defeating the beast, sorceress, come back. We have other books and relics from Moy Tura. They belong to the heirs of magic. I will teach you how to use them."

"Thank you, High Priest," she answered. "I will."

Under the wary gaze of the hidden cultists, Gabria and Athlone mounted their Hunnuli and rode out of the citadel to rejoin the hunt for Branth.

15

Athlone and Gabria did not stop after leaving the citadel of Krath. They rode through the night, letting the Hunnuli follow the old stone road that ran south along the flanks of the Himachal Mountains. The man and woman traveled silently, each lost in his or her own thoughts and weariness.

At sunrise the Hunnuli came to the Isin River and the fortress of Ab-Chakan sitting on its ridge at the opening of the defile of Tor Wrath. The riders paused for a brief time at the edge of the valley, and their eyes turned to the crumbling old fortress and the two burial mounds nearby. The larger mound contained the bodies of the fallen clan warriors; the smaller mound was the grave of Lord Savaric.

Athlone was very quiet as he looked on his father's mound. The memories of many words and deeds passed through his mind. When he and Gabria were ready to go, the chieftain raised his fist in salute to his dead father and rode on. For a long while after leaving Ab-Chakan, Athlone's expression was very thoughtful.

The horses continued to follow the old road south beside the Isin River. The Isin was a natural guide to the Tir Samod and the clan gathering, and the two riders hoped to find their party somewhere along the banks. At midmorning the three Hunnuli stopped for a drink of water from the shallows under a shady tree.

Gabria and Athlone dismounted and stood staring at the water rippling by. They had not said much to each other during the journey to the citadel. Now they realized their time alone would soon be over.

They looked at one another self-consciously. They did not want to waste this precious time, but neither of them knew what to say. Athlone cleared his throat; Gabria hugged her arms to her chest.

Finally the sorceress broke the silence. "Whatever you may think of me, Athlone, I want you to know that I did not break the vows of our betrothal. Nothing happened in my tent at Jehanan Treld between Sayyed and me."

Athlone's heart was pounding like a drum. He put his hands behind his back and clenched his fingers hard. He felt in the core of his being that she was telling the truth. "Sayyed makes it easy to jump to conclusions," he said. "I'm sorry. I should have trusted you more. I should have listened."

The woman was quiet again. She remembered her vow to avoid confrontation with Athlone or Sayyed until after her quest was complete, but she could not let this chance for reconciliation go by. Athlone meant too much to her. "We still have a lot to offer one another," she replied hesitantly, turning her armband on her arm. "I don't want to give that up."

He watched the sunlight glint off the gold band, and he marveled that she was still wearing his gift. "Neither do I. Your friendship is too precious to lose."

"Perhaps if we start over again . . ."

He grinned. "If the gods will give us some time."

Gabria glanced up at him. "Is it worth a try?"

"What about Sayyed?"

"I don't know. He is my friend, too."

"Then we will see what happens. Many things may change in the days ahead."

Smiling, Gabria held out her hand, and he clasped it tightly. She felt the strength of his fingers and the warmth of his skin; her heart sang with pleasure and relief.

They mounted their Hunnuli and continued south beside the rippling water. At noon Eurus and Nara saw the rest of the party on the riverbank far ahead. The Hunnuli neighed their greetings.

Sayyed, with Tam behind him, rode out to meet them. Tam jumped off the horse before Sayyed brought it to a stop and threw her arms around the colt's neck. He whinnied in delight. The girl happily waved to Gabria and Athlone, then, to Gabria's surprise, Tam did not reclaim her usual seat on Nara but climbed back on behind Sayyed. The Turic ruffled her hair.

"While you were gone, I acquired a new partner," he told Gabria as the group trotted on to rejoin the other men.

The sorceress smiled. "That's wonderful. How did it happen?"

"I'm not sure. She's been staying close to me since I took her through the caves in Pra Desh, but I think she really needed someone while you were away. She seems to have stuck to me."

Gabria looked at the girl who was hanging on to Sayyed's waist. "Just be careful with her feelings," she warned the Turic. "Tam has lost a lot in her short life."

He nodded once just before they reached the other men, and any further conversation was lost in a storm of greetings, questions, and answers.

"You were right, Lord," Secen said to Athlone after the welcomes were past. "Branth has followed the river for two days now. He's still heading south, about a day ahead of us."

"Toward the gathering," Athlone said. He shivered slightly. The thought of the gorthling loose among the unsuspecting clanspeople was appalling. The chief turned to see Gabria come up beside him. He gestured downstream. "I don't suppose we could use magic to catch up with him or to move ourselves to the gathering ahead of that beast."

She was startled that he would ask such a question, and it took her a moment to answer. "Unfortunately, no. It is too dangerous and uncertain to transport people by magic. Too many things could go wrong. Besides, we could lose Branth's trail. There is no real promise that he is going to the gathering. And—" she stopped to pat Nara's neck "—we could not move the Hunnuli. I will need Nara when I face the gorthling."

The chieftain shaded his eyes and looked toward the south, where the green plains rolled beyond the horizon. He knew Branth was far out of sight, but an irrational hope still made him study the hills for any sign of the gorthling. At last he pulled his gaze away and ordered everyone to their horses.

The company rode for the rest of the day as fast as they could go. It was late into the evening when they finally stopped to eat and rest.

Immediately after their hurried meal, Athlone took Gabria a short distance away from camp to a sandy bank beside the river. For a while he said nothing, but stared thoughtfully into the water. The night gradually settled down around them, warm and comforting, rich with the sounds of crickets and the rush of the river.

At last Athlone drew a long breath and released it in a rush. "You asked me once," he said to Gabria, "if I thought Father would have been disappointed in you and your power."

The woman tilted her head to look at him, touched by the sadness and regret in his voice.

"And I told you that he would have been proud of your courage." Athlone hesitated. He wanted to touch her badly, to bring her close and draw on her wonderful inner strength, but he could not do it. He knew he had to face the reality of his decision by himself or he would never be able to wield magic with the honesty and power of his own will.

He had decided in Pra Desh to use his talent, but it was not until he had passed his father's grave at Ab-Chakan that he had fully accepted his irrevocable choice. He sensed now some of the fear and dread Gabria must have faced when she had made her decision to use her talent. Yet, even as he tried to still the cold trembling in his hands, he felt an effusive glow of elation pour out of his mind and release the heavy weight of guilt and remorse that had hung over him from that first moment when he had known of his power and had been ashamed of it. At last he was accepting the truth of his being.

"Father would have been disappointed with me," he went on. He held up a hand to stop Gabria's protest. "Savaric always taught me to use my strengths and abilities to my utmost." Athlone's teeth flashed with a grin in his dark beard. "Once he got over the shock of having a magic-wielder for a son, he would have been furious at my refusal to use my power. I want to change that, Gabria," he said forcefully. "I am a magic-wielder. I am going to learn to use my power."

Gabria gasped. Her breath was taken away by the conviction in his voice. Her thoughts leaped with a jolt of mixed emotions, and she clasped his hands in hers.

He held on, interlocking his fingers with hers. "I need your help, Gabria. Teach me your sorcery."

Her fingers tightened their grip, and she swallowed hard. "No," she replied, her voice firm.

"I have the talent. I only need to know how to use it."

She stared at him, torn between delight and fear. She knew why he was asking now as clearly as if he had said the words; he wanted to help her fight the gorthling. Her mind cried out in protest. If she tried to teach him and Athlone battled a gorthling with untried, poorly trained powers, he would be slaughtered. On the other hand, the chieftain was a stubborn man once his mind was made up. If she did not teach him something, she knew he would try to learn on his own and probably destroy himself in the backlash of a poorly controlled spell.

"Athlone," she cried in exasperation, "please wait! I can't teach sorcery. I don't know enough yet, myself."

He let go of her hands and stepped back. "Then I'll figure it out by myself. Is it like this?" and he snapped a command, the same words Gabria had used in the dungeon to form a globe of light. To her surprise, a soft ball of light did begin to glow just over their heads. In seconds, though, it went out of control and blazed into a furious sphere of brilliant, hot white light that hummed with unleashed magic. The two people shrank back from the heat.

Gabria heard shouts from the other men, but she ignored them and kept her attention fastened on the light. "All right," she cried. "I'll teach you what I can."

"Good," he yelled. "Then would you show me how to put this thing out?"

The woman sighed. She could put it out herself, but if he really wanted to learn, this was as good a time as any to start. "Concentrate on your spell," she shouted to him over the rising noise of the globe. "Fix your purpose in your mind, then speak the words of your command." She watched the chieftain while he closed his eyes and lifted his hand toward the sphere. The blazing ball wavered, dimmed, then it flared again brighter than before.

"Concentrate!" Gabria demanded. "Feel the power within you. Bend the magic to your bidding."

Athlone tried again. A sheen of perspiration glistened on his forehead, and his face went rigid from his effort. This time, instead of thinking about the sphere and wishing it would go out, he concentrated on the feel of the power that surged within him. He had felt that power before, when he had rescued Gabria from the Woman of the Marsh and when he had fought the duel with Gringold. However, in those two instances, the magic had flowed through him uncontrolled and unconsciously. Now he drew it forth willingly and shaped it. When at last he stopped and opened his eyes, the light was gone and Gabria was smiling.

"I did it!" He grinned like a small boy and picked up Gabria by her waist and whirled her around.

The other men appeared out of the darkness, their swords drawn. "What's going on? Are you all right?" they asked as one.

The chieftain waved his men to a stop. "We're fine."

"What was that light?" Sayyed demanded.

Athlone did not hesitate. He had made his decision to wield his power no matter how his clan would react, but he badly wanted his companions' support. The healer and the warriors were his first and most important test of the clan's willingness to be ruled by a chieftain-sorcerer. He cocked an eyebrow and said, "I tried a spell to create a globe of light. It went a little wild."

Piers did not seem surprised. He nodded in approval. The three warriors looked at their lord speechlessly. Secen glanced at Gabria, then back at Athlone. Both his and his fellows' jaws hung slack.

Valar cleared his throat and said slowly, "But Lord, the laws forbidding sorcery have not been removed. What if you are exiled or put to death?"

The Khulinin chieftain replied, "I have thought about that and about many things. I realize I am endangering my position as ruler, but I can no longer turn my back on this power I was born with. The time is coming when we will have to face the gorthling's threat to the clans, and swords will not be enough."

The three warriors stared at him for a long, painful minute until, one by one, they sheathed their weapons and turned back to camp.

Athlone watched them go. They had not jumped into an instant acclamation of his decision, but they had not condemned him, either. He released his breath in a long, silent sigh. It was one thing to demand obedience from a warrior on the field of battle, but Athlone could not in good conscience order his men to accept his talent as a sorcerer. He could only hope their loyalty and respect for him as a chieftain would eventually win them over. Their acceptance would mean a great deal to the rest of the clan.

Sayyed had been watching the exchange with deep interest. He was very aware of the significance of Athlone's decision to wield magic. He slid his sword back into its leather scabbard and stood arms akimbo, his body tight with anticipation. "Good! Gabria, you can teach us both to use our powers."

"Not now," she said hastily. "The night is late."

"This is as good a time as any to start," Athlone said.

Gabria groaned inwardly. She could hardly bear to teach Athlone for fear of what he wanted to do. Now she had to include Sayyed. The men were watching her expectantly, so she gritted her teeth and marched back to camp. Athlone and Sayyed were not going to let her wiggle out of this; it was clear she would have to teach them something—a few of the basic premises she had learned from the Woman of the Marsh. Perhaps if they knew more of the dangers of wielding magic they would have enough sense to leave the gorthling alone when they found it.

Gabria settled down by the fire and waited while Sayyed and Athlone came to join her. Tam came, too, and curled up beside

Sayyed, her large eyes glittering in the firelight with a strange excitement. The other men went to their own tasks, but Gabria noticed they stayed close enough to hear her voice.

She paused briefly and cast her mind back to the mangrove tree in the swamp and the ancient sorceress whose rasping voice still spoke clearly in her memory.

"Will is at the center of sorcery," Gabria forced herself to say. "With every spell you create, you are attempting to impose your will on the fabric of our world. Magic is a natural force that is in every creature, stone, or plant. When you alter that force, even with the smallest spell, you must be strong enough to control the effect and the consequences. The forces of magic can destroy you if you cannot control them," she told her fascinated listeners. "The strength of will is the most important trait of a magic-wielder. Therefore, you must know yourself, every measure and degree of your own soul so you can recognize your limitations and know when the sorcery has begun to leach strength from your being."

"Is that what happened to Branth?" Athlone asked.

Gabria nodded. "I think so. I think the fon pushed him too far and his mind was not clear enough to recognize his danger. All magic-wielders must be very careful not to overextend their powers."

"What else does a magic-wielder need?" Sayyed demanded.

"Desire, concentration, and imagination," the sorceress continued. "Not all spells are rigidly defined. You can often create your own. The reason you need spells is to clarify your intent in your mind. The words help you focus your powers on the magic. You must know exactly what you want to do or the magic will go awry."

"Like my sphere," Athlone said.

"Exactly."

Sayyed leaned forward. "What about the Trymian Force?"

"The force is drawn from the power within the wielder. You can use it at will and change its intensity, but you must be careful not to overuse it or it will seriously weaken you."

"Can you show us how to control it?" he requested, his excitement sparkling in his eyes.

Alarmed, Gabria shook her head. "No. It's too soon. You nearly got us killed when you tried to use the force against the Korg."

"But Gabria," Sayyed protested. "How can we help you fight the gorthling if you don't show us how to use our power?"

All at once, Gabria's fear and reluctance broke loose, and she rushed to her feet. "Don't you see?" she said forcefully. "You can't help me. There isn't enough time to teach you to defend yourselves, let alone fight something as powerful and evil as the gorthling. You will be killed if you try. So don't learn. Don't try. Let me fight it, and if I win, I will teach you later, when there's time."

"And if you don't win?" Athlone asked quietly.

"Then you'll have to find another teacher."

Sayyed sprang to his feet, his long black hair flying like a stallion's mane. "Gabria, you are being unreasonable! You can't fight that thing alone."

"I most certainly can," she cried. "I won't be responsible for your deaths."

Athlone looked up at her, his voice cold with anger. "You will jeopardize the clans and endanger yourself."

"I'll endanger myself far more by taking two unskilled sorcerers into an arcane battle they have no chance of surviving. Without you, I won't be distracted, worried, or terrified for your safety. No! No more. Stay out of this, all of you." She swept her cloak onto her shoulders and strode out of the firelight.

Athlone and Sayyed looked at one another, and for once their thoughts were in perfect accord.

"She is not going to fight it alone," Sayyed muttered.

"No." Athlone arched an eyebrow. "If we work together, perhaps we can learn enough to surprise her."

Sayyed held out his hand, and the Khulinin clasped it to seal the vow.

Tam watched them with her bright, eager eyes and, unbeknownst to the men, she made her own vow to herself. They were not going to leave her out of this.

Meanwhile, Gabria hurried into the darkness. The night was warm and dry, so she went to sit on a nearby hill. Long after the distant campfire had burned out, she sat on the grassy slope while her thoughts spun through her mind. She was frightened of meeting the gorthling alone, but she was terrified of losing Athlone or Sayyed to the beast through their lack of skill or hers. She knew she could never forgive herself if they died in a situation they had no business being in at all.

"No," Gabria whispered to the stars, "they must not fight. It is my duty, not theirs." Within her heart she vowed to fight alone, even if it meant leaving her companions and seeking the gorthling herself. Athlone would be furious, but at least he would be alive.

At one point a doubt crept into her mind: what if they were right?

Was she being arrogant and selfish to think she could handle the gorthling alone? What would the clans do if the creatures did kill her? Gabria immediately banished those doubts. She could think of no other way to destroy the gorthling. The creature had to be fought with magic, and she was the only one who had any hope of succeeding.

16

Day followed day and league after endless league fell behind the small party of riders as they pushed south on the trail of the gorthling. They traveled as fast as possible, for they were desperate to catch the creature before it reached the gathering. They pushed themselves and their horses hard and stopped to rest only when necessary. To increase their speed, they dumped most of their gear, using the pack horses as spare mounts.

Gabria worried at first that Tam or the Hunnuli colt would wear down under the rigors of the rough travel—the journey had already been a long, hard one for everyone. To her relief, the Reidhar girl and the colt managed very well. Tam stayed close to Sayyed, riding with him and keeping him company in the evenings. She still had not said a word, but she smiled more and pampered Sayyed with her constant attention. The Turic, for his part, was pleased to have her friendship and treated her with the humor and affection of a protective big brother.

As for the Hunnuli colt, the months of travel had strengthened him as no time in a pasture could have. He was as big as a Harachan yearling, well developed and feisty. He remained inseparable from Tam.

Five days passed, and the travelers gained very little on the gorthling. Secen estimated they were still about a day behind him. Although he was moving very fast, he still made no attempt to hide his tracks. He seemed to be deliberately luring the hunters after him.

On the fifth day the company passed close to Dangari Treld, so Athlone sent one of his warriors to check on the camp. The Dangari had grown sedentary over the years and left many of their people at home during the gathering. They bred and trained superb horses and usually took their breeding stallions and brood mares to cooler pastures in the mountains for the summer. Athlone prayed the gorthling had not found any of the Dangari.

To his relief, the warrior returned with some gifts of food and greetings from the Dangari in the treld. They were unharmed and had seen no sign of Branth. Lord Koshyn and the main body of the clan had left many days before and were probably already at the gathering.

The travelers rode on beside the Isin River as quickly as they dared go. They managed to draw a little closer to the gorthling until he was perhaps only half a day ahead, but he remained infuriatingly out of reach. The pursuers did not dare force their Harachan horses any harder for fear of killing them and losing all hope of catching the gorthling in time.

The long, hard days of riding were frustrating to Gabria. She spent the endless hours studying the death mask of Valorian and trying to think of ways to destroy the gorthling. Unfortunately the mask gave her no answers, and her knowledge and experience were so limited that she had very little idea of what she might have to face when she finally confronted the creature.

The only two things of which she was certain was that she *had* to fight the creature and that she would do it alone. Athlone and Sayyed had not brought up the subject of sorcery again since that night, and Gabria did not care to remind them. Nevertheless, she knew the two men well enough to realize they had not put aside their eagerness to use their powers. At any other time she would have been overjoyed to help them and would have done anything she could to learn more and teach all her companions, including Tam. But not now. Not so they could face a gorthling.

If only she knew how to convince them of the deadly folly of their desire to help. She sensed they had not given up their wish to learn. Athlone and Sayyed were spending an unusual amount of time talking together out of her hearing. For two men who barely spoke to each other only a month ago, they had suddenly become very friendly. Gabria did not know what they were up to, but it only increased her determination to slip away at the best opportunity and confront the gorthling herself.

If she was going to succeed in leaving the men, she knew she would have to plan her departure just right. She was not a good tracker and she did not want to risk losing Branth's trail. It was possible that he could detour from the Isin and not go to the gathering at all. Therefore, she wanted to stay with the men until they were close enough to the gorthling for her to find him, yet far enough away so the men could not easily catch up with her. Nara was not going to like the idea, but Gabria trusted the Hunnuli mare to help her.

The woman sat on Nara's broad back and forced herself to be patient. The waiting was difficult. It gave her imagination ample opportunity to run wild—an exhausting luxury she could ill afford. They were still many leagues behind the gorthling and had a long way to go. She clenched her jaw. It was time to find the gorthling and finish the ordeal. Branth was not going to slip away from her again.

As the gorthling and its pursuers headed south, the eleven clans of Valorian were making their way across the grasslands to the Tir Samod. For as many years as the clanspeople had inhabited the Ramtharin Plains, the clans had gathered together each summer at the junction of the Isin and the Goldrine rivers to renew their ties and worship their gods as one.

The gathering gave the chieftains the opportunity to meet in council and establish the laws that governed the clans. Through their efforts, they carried on the traditions handed down from their fathers, maintained clan unity, and enhanced their own authority.

While the chiefs met in council, their people were also strengthening clan unity. The gathering gave everyone a chance to renew old acquaintances, visit family members in other clans, strike up new friendships, and arrange betrothals. It also gave the clanspeople an excellent outlet for competition and entertainment.

One of the most popular attractions of the gathering was the huge bazaar and livestock market that sprang up even before the last clan arrived. Merchants and traders from the Five Kingdoms and the Turic tribes came early and set up booths to trade with the enthusiastic clanspeople. Along with the foreign merchants, the clan artisans added their own specialties to the market, so the people had a wide and richly varied supply of goods from which to choose. They loved to trade and barter, and they pitched into the haggling with great delight.

The days of a gathering were usually wild, noisy, and exciting. This year, however, the people were restrained. Too much had happened at the gathering the summer before for the clans to reunite peacefully. Clan had fought against clan in a bloody war that was still fresh in people's memories.

With that danger in mind, Lord Koshyn of the Dangari and Lord Sha Umar of the Jehanan made certain that their people arrived at the gathering first. The two lords, the Khulinin's oldest allies, made it a point to welcome every arriving clan and chieftain as if all the troubles of the past year had been forgotten. Their attitude spilled over onto their people and helped soothe the barely suppressed anger many still harbored. Unfortunately, they could not make the clans forget everything.

When the remnants of Lord Medb's old clan, the Wylfling, came on the fourth day, the whole gathering nearly shattered in rage and old grief. Only the Wylfling's new chieftain, Lord Hildor, held his clan together and forced them to stand their ground before the anger of the other clans. His courage and the timely arrival of the Khulinin helped defuse a potential tragedy. The Khulinin wer-tain, Guthlac, remembered his orders from Athlone and had the entire Khulinin clan come forward to greet and embrace the Wylfling. Gradually the heated emotions cooled down, and the clans warily got down to the business of the gathering.

The chiefs then discovered another real problem: Lord Athlone was missing. The Khulinin chieftain had not been seen or heard from since he had left Reidhar Treld almost two months before. The Khulinin reported that he was going to Pra Desh with Lady Gabria to find Branth, but they did not know when he was coming back.

The chieftains were alarmed. They did not want to start the serious proceedings of the council without him, yet they could not wait all summer for him to appear. Lord Sha Umar finally suggested postponing the council for at least five more days and offered to send scouts out along the clan trails to try to find Athlone.

The other chiefs readily agreed, and Lord Koshyn and Wer-tain Guthlac sent their scouts out as well. While the chiefs settled back to wait for some word of Athlone, speculation ran rampant through the camps about his disappearance. Rumors spread like flies. Some people whispered that Gabria's sorcery had destroyed him, while others thought perhaps Branth had killed him. No one knew what to believe.

On the evening of the fifth day, there was still no sign of Lord Athlone or his party, and the clans were growing tired of waiting.

Lord Koshyn tried to curb his own impatience during the day, without much success. Immediately after his evening meal, he retrieved a flask of redberry wine he had left cooling in the river and walked downstream along the bank to the camp of Clan Jehanan. He found Lord Sha Umar relaxing on a rug under the awning of his tent. The chieftain's maroon banner flapped idly overhead. The Jehanan

leader welcomed the young Dangari gladly, and they sat down to enjoy the cool wine.

For a while they rested in companionable silence, watching the
evening activities of the clan. The women were cooking over campfires
while the children tumbled in the dirt with the dogs. Some warriors
lolled in the shade of the trees. A piper was playing nearby, making
his music light and capricious to match the fitful wind that blew
through the camp, swirling the dust and tugging at the tents.

Koshyn suddenly sat upright. "That man is a nuisance!" he said in
annoyance.

Sha Umar followed his friend's gaze and saw Thalar, the Khulinin
clan priest of Surgart, talking vehemently to a crowd of onlookers at
the Bahedin camp just across the river. The priest had been using his
time to preach against sorcery to all the clans. He knew, as well as
everyone else, that the chieftains were going to discuss magic during
their council and debate on the possibility of altering their laws.
Thalar took full advantage of his lord's absence to try to influence the
other chiefs and their people against sorcery.

"He has certainly been making his opinions known," Sha Umar
replied dryly.

Koshyn looked away, his blue eyes vivid with anger. "And too
many people are listening to him. If Athlone doesn't get here soon, he
may find the entire gathering ready to exile Gabria and turn against
sorcery forever."

Koshyn had fought beside Athlone at Ab-Chakan and was his
close friend. He liked the young woman, Gabria, too. He recognized
the truth of her arguments to reinstate sorcery in the clans and did
everything he could to forward her cause. The fact that his friend
Athlone had the talent to wield magic only increased his determination to rescind the law that forbade the use of sorcery on pain of
death.

"We can't put the council off much longer," Sha Umar said, his
tanned face lined with worry.

"What do we do if he does not come at all?"

The Jehanan chief scratched his beard. "If he and Gabria both
disappear, the people will think the problem of sorcery will simply
vanish."

"No, it won't," the Dangari said vehemently. "Too much has happened for everyone to forget." He gestured to the teeming camps
along both rivers. "Somewhere out there are other magic-wielders
who know of their talents and are afraid, or those who will learn of

their powers by accident and will be killed or exiled. Those people are not freaks. There is a reason some clanspeople can wield magic. We can't keep turning our backs on that power."

Sha Umar's mouth widened into a grin, and he held up his hand. "All right! You don't need to convince me." He passed the wine flask to Koshyn. "We should push to change the laws whether Athlone is there or not."

"Absolutely. We don't need another tragedy like the one Medb brought down upon us."

"Agreed."

Koshyn leaned back on a cushion and stared out beyond the camps to the far hills darkening in the purple of twilight. "I just wish I knew where Athlone was."

"And Lady Gabria. Without her, our task will be much harder," said Sha Umar.

"They must have run into trouble."

The Jehanan chief snorted. "Probably Branth. That fool has been nothing but trouble. I wonder where *he* is."

"Dead, I hope," the Dangari said honestly.

Sha Umar raised his cup to that hope.

At that moment, in the low hills at the edge of the river valley, the subject of the chieftains' annoyance was lying on a flat rock and looking out over the busy gathering. Branth's eyes glowed red with satisfaction and anticipation. The gorthling had not known the clans were so numerous, but that did not bother him. To the contrary, he was delighted. The clanspeople he had found days before had told him there was only one sorceress left on the plains. He had realized then that she must be the hated magic-wielder in the memory of his host body. All he had to do was destroy her and an entire population would be his to do with as he pleased.

The gorthling laughed to himself. There were such fascinating possibilities for revenge against the people who had been so harsh to Lord Branth. With his arcane powers, he could destroy these people one by one, slaughter them all at once or, better yet, enslave them and keep them for his own use.

He studied the gathering carefully. The sorceress was supposed to be at this place, but it was quite large and he did not know exactly where to look for her. The individual clans were camped on their traditional sites along the banks of both rivers. The huge market was on the east side of the Goldrine River, and to the south of the camps was the wide, flat stretch of the valley used for racing and competitions. On the point of land between the two rivers was an open tent crowned by the colorful banners of the ten chieftains present at the gathering. The holy island of the Tir Samod and the temple stood empty in the middle of the confluence of the two rivers. There was nothing anywhere to indicate the presence of a magic-wielder.

The gorthling finally shrugged. The light was fading, making it difficult to see. Besides, at this distance he could not distinguish one woman from another in those busy camps. He moved back into the shelter of a rocky outcropping and settled down to wait for daylight. He would simply go down to the gathering in the morning, when the clanspeople were the most active, and find the sorceress. Even in those sprawling camps, she could not escape him for long.

A few hours later that same night, Athlone brought Eurus to a halt in the shelter of a small copse of trees beside the river. The two Hunnuli were still fresh and willing to go on, but the Harachan horses stumbled to a grateful halt and stood drooping under their saddles. Their riders were just as exhausted. The Hunnuli colt pressed close to his mother, and Treader flopped on the ground and panted. Although they were only half a day's ride from the gathering and everyone wanted to keep going, even Gabria knew they had to stop and rest.

Wordlessly the travelers dismounted, rubbed down their horses, and hobbled them to graze. No one lit a fire. The men dug into their packs for some nuts and dried meat, and they ate a cold meal. Before long, Tam and the men were wrapped in their blankets and sound asleep under the watchful guard of the Hunnuli. Only Gabria remained awake.

The time had come to leave. Athlone had hoped the gorthling would wait a while before starting trouble with the clanspeople—at least long enough for the weary horses and riders to catch up with him. Gabria did not want to give the gorthling a chance to be loose among the clans. She wanted to stop him immediately.

She lay in her blankets for a time to let her body rest. Staring at the stars, she listened to the subdued sounds of the sleepers around her. She was thankful for the nervous, queasy feeling in her stomach and the cold clamminess of her hands, for without those to keep her awake, it would have been very easy to fall asleep in the warm summer night.

Just after moonrise, she slipped out of her blankets, tied the golden mask in its bag to her belt, and went to Nara. The three Hunnuli gathered around her in the darkness and listened as she told them what she was going to do.

Nara's reaction was immediate. *Gabria! You can't fight that monster alone. It is too strong for you!*

The sorceress reached out and laid her hand on the Hunnuli's neck. "I have to try. Are you coming with me?" As she had suspected, the mare could not refuse. Nara would never betray her rider or let her go into such danger alone.

Gabria turned to Eurus. "Please, do not wake Athlone. Let me go alone or he will follow me and die at the gorthling's hands."

You do not know that, the young stallion replied.

"I know enough to not take a chance. Please, Eurus."

The Hunnuli bowed his head. *I will do as you ask.*

"Thank you," she said gratefully. Then she turned to the colt. "Don't worry, little one, your mother will be safe." Gabria sprang to Nara's back and pinned her cloak tightly around her shoulders. For just a moment, she looked back at the sleeping forms under the trees.

While the woman was occupied with her own thoughts, Nara turned to Eurus and sent her message only to him. *We cannot stop her. She is too determined for her own good sometimes.*

What do we do? the stallion asked.

My son can wake the men in a short time. That will allow you to keep your word to Gabria. Bring them as fast as you can. She will not be able to avoid them if they join her at the gathering.

Eurus tossed his head, and his nostrils flared.

Nara turned to her colt. *I must give you a mighty task, my son. Are you willing to try?*

Yes, Mamma!

You are strong enough to carry the girl. After you have awakened the men, take Tam toward the mountains and seek the King Hunnuli. The two of you together can call him. Ask him to come. The sorceress needs his help.

The colt nickered softly in reply, his broom tail whisking in excitement.

Unaware of the Hunnuli's thoughts, Gabria bid farewell to Eurus and the colt. Like a shadow, Nara moved out of the trees and turned south toward the Tir Samod. As soon as she was out of earshot from the camp, she broke into her smooth canter, and she and Gabria vanished into the darkness.

Athlone stirred in his blankets. A strange feeling of alarm disturbed his exhausted sleep, and he tossed and turned. Something was not right; he could sense it even in his sleep, something was missing. He was on the verge of waking when something warm and soft nudged his face. Athlone bolted upright with a yell, grabbed his sword, and came nose to nose with the Hunnuli colt.

Gabria is gone, the young horse told him.

Athlone was on his feet and yelling for Eurus before the other men awakened and realized what was happening.

"Where is she?" the chief demanded when the stallion came to his side.

She left to find the gorthling alone.

"Why didn't you stop her?"

The other men were climbing to their feet, looking confused. "What is it, Lord Athlone?" Sayyed asked. He looked around. "Where is Gabria?"

Athlone snarled, "She's left without us. I'm going after her." He sprang to Eurus's back.

Before the Hunnuli could move, Sayyed ran in front of the big horse. "Not without us, you're not."

"Get out of the way!" the chief yelled. "I've got to get to her before she attacks that beast alone."

"I'm going with you!"

"Your horse can't keep up with a Hunnuli."

"He can try! You cannot go alone," Sayyed insisted.

Piers stepped forward, his demeanor calm. "Athlone, he's right. You and Gabria will need him. Take him on Eurus, and the warriors and I will follow."

Athlone looked down at the old healer, and something in his friend's quiet, reasonable voice calmed his wild impulse. Some of his father's cool, deliberate cunning surfaced in the chief's mind, and he nodded. "All right, Sayyed. You ride with me."

The Turic whooped with relief and went to collect his weapons and burnoose.

As the Turic and the chief were about to leave, the three hearthguard warriors stepped up to Eurus. They were not happy about being left behind, even though they understood the reasons. Nevertheless, they looked up at Athlone and gravely saluted. There was a short pause as they glanced at one another, then Keth said, "Be careful, Lord. The clans need you back."

Athlone said nothing. His hand tightened on Eurus's mane in expectation.

Secen, his strong, plain face clear in the moonlight, said quietly,

"We were afraid at first when you told us that you were going to wield magic. But Lady Gabria's mask reminded us that Lord Valorian had once been a chieftain and a sorcerer. If his people could accept that, so can we."

"We'll support you before the clans, too," Valar added.

Lord Athlone raised his fist and returned his warriors' salute. He was proud of his men and vastly relieved for himself. Their acceptance would give him strength in the days of controversy ahead—provided, of course, that he survived until then. "Come as fast as you can," he ordered.

With Sayyed behind him on Eurus's back, Athlone yelled the Khulinin war cry and urged the Hunnuli into a canter. The two men and the stallion were gone from sight in the blink of an eye.

During that moment of departure, no one noticed that Tam quietly slipped onto the colt's back, and she, the colt, and Treader trotted away into the night.

17

The sun rose orange above the plains into a cloudless sky. Its early heat baked the dust, stirred the flies, and gave the promise of a hot day ahead. In the camps of the eleven clans, the people rose early to take advantage of the cool morning before the day turned uncomfortable.

The food vendors selling meat pies and fruit rolls did a thriving business. The bazaar merchants pulled aside their curtains and opened their booths to the women who came early to haggle. Several bards in the camps brought out their instruments to practice for the storytelling competition to be held before the clans that evening. Children ran and played among the tents. Some of the older boys went out to hunt, while others rode their horses along the river. Five of the chieftains met under the trees by the council tent to enjoy a cup of ale and discuss the possibility of starting the council without Athlone.

No one paid attention to the lone man, wearing a Bahedin cloak, who walked across the fields past the empty site where Clan Corin once camped, and sauntered into the market. For a while he walked aimlessly about, simply looking at the women and the booths. His hood was pulled up to hide his face—a common enough practice on a hot, sunny day. He did not stop to talk to anyone, and no one bothered him.

After a time, the stranger wandered over to the river. Every year the clansmen and the merchants erected a simple, temporary bridge across the shallows of the lower Goldrine River to simplify the crossing from many of the camps to the bazaar. The stranger crossed the bridge easily and walked up a path between the Bahedin and the

Dangari camps, heading toward the shady point of land where the council tent stood.

He was about to pass the Bahedin camp when he realized someone was behind him. He walked faster, but the clansman caught up with him and put a hand on his shoulder to stop him. The stranger's fingers curled in anger.

"Excuse me," a man's voice said. "Have you seen . . ." The speaker hesitated as the stranger turned and looked down at him. The man, an old weaver from the Bahedin, felt a strange shiver run down his back. "Oh, I thought you were someone else." He looked curiously at the tall, silent man, then took a closer look. His eyebrows drew together with consternation. "That cloak. Where did you get it? The embroidery on the hem looks like my son's."

The stranger did not answer. He shoved off the weaver's arm and started to walk away.

"Wait!" the Bahedin called loudly. Alarmed now, he caught up again with the man and yanked him around. "Answer me! You're not Bahedin. Who are you?"

The stranger clamped his hand around the weaver's neck and snarled, "The sorceress. Where is she?"

The old man's eyes bugged out in fear. He tried to pull away, but the merciless grip only tightened around his neck.

"Where is the sorceress?" the stranger hissed. He lifted the struggling weaver into the air with one hand. The Bahedin's face went red, then blue.

Someone screamed close by. All the people in the vicinity turned to stare and several came out of their tents. A short, elderly woman charged up the path, flung herself at the stranger's back, and pummeled him with her fists. She was screaming with fright and fury, and her cries brought people running.

The gorthling cursed. He was not ready yet to draw so much attention to himself or his powers. He wanted to find the sorceress first. Annoyed, he threw the weaver to the ground and backhanded the woman with a stunning blow that sent her reeling into a wicker corral. His violent motion knocked his hood off, and the sun shone full on his face. He paid no attention to the shocked clanspeople who gathered around the fallen couple. He ignored the shouts of the people behind him and continued walking down the path. Close by, a voice cried in stunned disbelief, "Branth! That's Lord Branth."

Other clanspeople stared at the gorthling in open disbelief as he strode by. A loud, angry commotion was building in the two camps and spreading outward in ripples of outrage and disbelief as word of Branth's arrival flew from tent to tent.

The gorthling's lips curled in a wicked grin. Let them yap, he thought. Perhaps the uproar would attract the sorceress and bring her to him. He was growing impatient. Although he studied every female he saw, he did not see any that matched the description of the clan's only magic-wielder. He passed the fringes of the Dangari camp and went down to the banks of the Goldrine.

He glanced back and saw armed men advancing on him from the Dangari camp, sunlight glinting off their blades. Across the river, where the council tent stood in its grove of cottonwood trees, several clansmen were attracted by the loud commotion and gathered on the bank.

Branth hesitated, looking up and down the river where other camps were clustered along the shores. Several women were standing in the shallows nearby, staring at him, their washing hanging from their hands. He was about to turn and head for another camp, when the armed warriors jumped him.

Jubilantly they bound his hands behind his back and searched him for weapons. To their surprise, all they found was a heavy, leather-bound book in a pack slung on his shoulder. A huge crowd gathered, and many of the people shouted threats. Here at last was a scapegoat for some of their pent-up anger, grief, and resentment for the previous summer's blood-shed.

The gorthling watched them with an ugly sneer on his face. He would go along with this farce for a little while longer, just to see if these noisy humans would take him to those who commanded their tribes. Their leaders might know where the sorceress was hiding.

The Dangari warriors shoved Branth down the bank and hauled him across the river to where their chieftain stood, framed by the open entrance of the council tent. Much of the crowd followed, trampling through the water like a herd of horses. The Dangari brought their prisoner to stand before Lord Koshyn, Lord Sha Umar, Lord Wortan of the Geldring, old Lord Jol of the Murjik, and Wer-tain Guthlac. Together, the men faced the bound prisoner while the crowd pushed around in a shouting, gesturing ring.

Lord Koshyn held up his hand for silence. The onlookers gradually fell quiet as their curiosity got the better of their hostility.

Koshyn studied the man before him and tried to quell a growing uneasiness. He did not like Branth's strange arrival. No exiled man under penalty of death just wanders into a clan gathering without a

powerful reason. Then, too, if Athlone went to Pra Desh to find
Branth and Branth appeared at the Tir Samod—what did that say of
Lord Athlone's fate? The Dangari narrowed his eyes. There was a
strange aura of menace about the prisoner that made the hairs rise on
Koshyn's neck. Something about Branth was very different.

The chieftain turned to his men. "Was he armed?"

"No, Lord. He only had this with him." One of the warriors
handed the leather bag to the chief.

Koshyn felt his hands grow cold when he looked in the bag. "The
Book of Matrah," he said aloud. His uneasiness boiled into full alarm.

Lord Jol drew a sharp breath and edged away from the book. The
other chiefs looked at one another with mixed expressions of suspicion and confusion.

After he handed the bag back to his warrior, Koshyn squared his
shoulders. "You are under penalty of death," he said to Branth. "Why
did you come back?"

The gorthling sneered. Death? That was a joke. He drew himself
up to Branth's full height and stared out over the crowd, looking for
the sorceress. He still wanted to find her before he blasted these an-
noying mortals to burned bits.

"Branth," Sha Umar said sharply, "you are condemned to die for
conspiracy, treason, and murder. You can choose your own manner of
death if you answer the question. Why are you here?"

The gorthling had had enough of their questions. He turned his
inhuman glance on the chieftains. "To be your master!" he said with
cold, deliberate malice.

The clanspeople reacted immediately. They surged closer, jostling
and grabbing at the prisoner. The Dangari warriors struggled to keep
them away until the chiefs could decide what to do.

Koshyn's face flushed with rage. Yet even as his fury mounted, a
warning cry sounded in his head. Branth had had the *Book of Matrah*
in his possession for almost a year—plenty of time to learn sorcery. If
that was the case, then the only way they could render him defenseless
was to kill him, or at least knock him unconscious. While he could
think, he could cast spells; someone would have to deal with him, and
quickly.

Everyone's attention was on Branth, and the gorthling's attention
appeared to be on the Dangari warriors that crowded around him.
Without warning, Koshyn snatched a battle axe from the belt of a
warrior beside him and brought it swinging toward Branth's head.

It never landed.

The gorthling saw the blurred movement out of the corner of his eye, then barked a spell that froze the chieftain in mid-motion. The clanspeople around them fell still, their eyes strained wide, their faces caught in expressions of disbelief and shock. The silence spread outward into the crowd until the entire council grove was quiet.

The gorthling laughed and snapped the bonds around his wrists. "Now, worthless little man," he hissed to Koshyn, "perhaps you can tell me where the sorceress is." He raised his hand and sent a powerful burst of energy sizzling into Koshyn's body.

The excruciating pain ripped through the young Dangari. He screamed and fell to the ground in a writhing heap, unable to fight the torturous magic.

The sight of the vicious arcane spell broke the crowded clanspeople's stunned lethargy. They backed away to put a wide space between themselves and Branth. The chieftains, even Lord Jol, drew their swords, and they and the Dangari warriors leaped in to try to save the young lord. The gorthling blasted them aside as easily as swatting flies, killing three of the warriors. He continued to torture Koshyn.

"The sorceress!" Branth shouted furiously. "Where is she?"

"She's not here," Lord Sha Umar answered desperately. He picked himself up from the ground, his eyes pinned on Koshyn's writhing body.

The gorthling's face twisted into a frightening mask of delight, hate, and rage that sickened the watchers. "Where is she?" He made a jabbing motion with his hand, and Koshyn screamed in agony.

Sha Umar stepped forward, his hand raised in a pleading gesture. "We don't know. She went to look for you."

"She went to Pra Desh to find you," Lord Jol cried. The old chief was on the verge of panic. "But she'll be here soon."

Branth pounced on Jol's words. "Soon? When!"

Wer-tain Guthlac spoke up. "No one knows."

"Tell me, you worms, or this man dies!" Branth screamed. "I want the sorceress."

"Then look behind you," a new voice called from the edge of the grove.

The men started in surprise.

The gorthling whirled around and saw a young woman sitting astride a great black Hunnuli. He forgot about the men around him. His cruel mouth laughed in triumph, and his eyes began to glow red as the horse slowly paced toward him.

Without hesitation Sha Umar and Guthlac grabbed Koshyn's

arms and dragged the chieftain's body out of sight, behind the council tent. The other clanspeople fled hastily out of the way. In the chaos, no one remembered the ancient tome in its brown leather bag lying in front of the council tent among the fallen stools, the scattered personal belongings, and the three dead Dangari warriors.

The gorthling sneered. "I've been looking for you, Sorceress."

"And I you," Gabria replied. Nara stopped twenty paces away, and the woman and the gorthling studied each other. Even in the warm morning Gabria felt a chill. The man before her looked like Branth physically: tall, brown hair, muscular build, everything perfectly normal and human. Only his presence was different. There was a cold glint of merciless cruelty in his eyes and an aura of hostility in his every move.

"We don't want you in this world," Gabria said.

The gorthling smirked. "Some people did."

"Go back to your own realm," she retorted. "You don't belong here."

"It's too late, Sorceress. I am here to stay." Even as the words left his mouth, the gorthling fired a bolt of the Trymian Force at the woman.

It came so fast Gabria was taken by surprise. However, the Hunnuli had been waiting for just such a move, and she reared high to protect her rider. The blue bolt struck her full on her chest, burst in a cloud of sparks, and evaporated harmlessly in the air.

The mare snorted.

Shaken, Gabria patted Nara in thanks and quickly formed an oblong clan battle shield with her arcane power. The magic shield was not as effective as a full force field, but it needed much less energy to maintain and would provide some protection. The gorthling came at her again and fired another bolt. This time she caught the force with the shield. Again and again Branth attacked, his barrage of sizzling blue blasts almost constant. He circled the Hunnuli to catch the woman from every angle, but either she or the mare blocked each blow.

In the back of her mind Gabria prayed that a stray bolt would not hit some of the clanspeople hiding among the trees of the council grove or any of the onlookers across the rivers. The uproar of the battle had brought people running from all directions. They were crowding on the banks of both rivers and watching Gabria and the gorthling with mixed amazement and horror. Many of them had never seen an arcane battle before. Fortunately for Gabria, no one dared cross the river to the council grove, and those people who hid among the trees and around the tent stayed very low.

Gabria made no move to take the offensive. She knew the gorthling's ability to enhance human powers would make him a formidable opponent, a sorcerer far stronger than Lord Medb. She hoped that by letting him expend his strength in this attack on her, she could wear him down enough so her powers would have an effect on him. Until then, she and Nara had to stay alert.

Strangely, the gorthling had so far only used the Trymian Force against her. Either he was too arrogant to bother with other spells, or he had not had enough time to study the more complicated spells in the *Book of Matrah*. Gabria prayed his reason was the latter.

The gorthling hurled bolts of the Trymian Force at Gabria and Nara, but he soon grew weary of the attack. He seemed to realize Gabria's intent was to simply avoid him, for he suddenly changed tactics. Instead of bolts that the woman could easily deflect with her shield, he threw balls of fire at the mare's feet that set the grass ablaze. Then he launched a spell that wrenched deep, wide cracks in the earth all around the horse.

Nara was forced toward the gorthling while Gabria frantically tried to put out the fires and seal the cracks. Before she had time to snuff out all the flames, the gorthling fired at her again with the Trymian Force.

Nara reared and caught one blast, barely avoiding a huge crack at her feet. The second hit Gabria's shield at a bad angle and nearly blew her off the mare.

Out of desperation, the sorceress formed a complete protective shield around herself and Nara just long enough to recover her seat and get the mare away from the fires. To Gabria's relief, the gorthling did not try immediately to shatter her defense. He had hesitated and seemed to be breathing heavily. Gabria wondered if he was tiring at last.

"What do I do?" she whispered frantically to Nara. "I can't hold this shield much longer."

The big mare leaped over a crack in the ground and angled around Branth to safer ground. *He is immortal, but his body is human. He is most vulnerable there*, the mare suggested. *He may not know all of his weaknesses.*

Gabria thought fast. Perhaps she could use his human frailties to destroy the gorthling's human body. If he was separated from Branth, it might be easier to trap or banish him. When the gorthling raised his arm to attack her again, she dissolved the arcane shield and formed her spell.

Not knowing the intricacies of the human body, the gorthling had no defense against her magic. Black boils suddenly erupted on his flesh. The gorthling hesitated; a peculiar expression came over his face. His skin faded to a bilious yellow, and he doubled over in excruciating pain. "Sorceress," he bellowed. "What is this?"

Gabria did not answer. She breathed deeply to relax and regain her strength. Now it was her turn to use the Trymian Force. She drew the power from within herself and fired a searing blow at the gorthling.

He was so sick and weakened by the unfamiliar fever that he barely avoided her blow. Time and again Gabria carefully attacked him with the Trymian Force and other missiles—daggers, fire, rocks—anything she could think of to make him move and react and use up his strength.

Finally the gorthling understood the sickness she had given him and cured his symptoms one by one. He staggered to his feet, his human face full of wrath.

Gabria hesitated. She did not think another sickness spell would be effective, because the gorthling was beginning to understand how the illness affected him. He would be better able to defend himself against a second attempt. But now she was at a loss over what to do next.

During that brief pause Gabria and Branth faced each other. The creature curled his lip and said, "You are better than I believed, Sorceress. You have withstood the usual battle spells I use." He raised his hands. "Now try this one."

Gabria stiffened to face the blow, but when it came, it took her completely by surprise. Her mind went abruptly blank. Then the world seemed to explode into a fiery maelstrom of whirling winds and searing heat. She felt herself being pulled helplessly into a giant vortex of tornadic winds and swirling fire.

She rolled and tumbled in the funnel of air and fire, screaming in pain, helplessness, and beneath it all, fury. The heat charred her skin, the winds flayed her face and limbs. Somewhere in the winds she heard wailing voices of other humans in torment, but she could see nothing in the yellow and orange fires. Gabria felt herself drawn deeper into the storm toward a place where the funnel fell into a mindless chasm of madness and everlasting emptiness. She fought back against the winds, clawing and writhing with a desperation strengthened by her powerful will to survive.

Suddenly, out of the roaring chaos she heard a beloved voice reach out like a lifeline to her mind. *Gabria, hear me! It is only a vision. Come back!*

The words rang like a sweet bell in her thoughts and awoke memories of another time and of another sorcerer, Lord Medb, who had also tried to defeat her with visions. She closed her eyes to the winds and fire, and out of the depth of her soul, she laughed.

The roaring winds abruptly ceased. The heat and the pain vanished. When she opened her eyes, she saw the glorious blue sky, the green cottonwood trees, and the muddy brown rivers. Her skin was whole, her arms and legs healthy, and the magnificent Hunnuli still carried her across the council grove. Gabria felt weary to the bone, but she was alive and still able to fight.

She jerked her head up and saw the gorthling standing near the council tent. A flicker of surprise crossed his face. His arcane shield was down, and he was sweating. He looked as tired as she felt.

Gabria knew she did not have the strength at the moment to call upon the Trymian Force, yet there were other spells she knew well that did not need as much effort. She snapped a command, and the bits of rock and gravel around the gorthling's feet were transformed into a swarm of wasps.

The insects buzzed around the gorthling, stinging his human body and infuriating him. He felt his strength waning. He had seriously misjudged this sorceress. She had taxed his power with her unexpected human diseases and her determined counterattack, then he had foolishly drained his own strength to destroy her mind only to have her rescued by the Hunnuli at the last moment. She surprised him with her intelligence and self-will. The gorthling knew he was too weary to continue the fight at the present time. He needed a short time to rest until he could think of a way to destroy this woman and take his revenge on the clans. He vowed he would never leave until he had fulfilled his lust for their blood.

With a furious word, he dispelled the wasps into dust and looked around for some means of retreat. His eyes found the ring of stones on the holy island. For the first time, he noticed the clanspeople clustered on the far banks, and an idea took shape in his mind. Humans had a weakness for the safety of other humans. This woman was likely no different.

A furtive movement out of the corner of his eye caught Branth's attention. Before Gabria knew what he was doing, he ran a few steps toward the council tent and pounced on two men trying to peer around one wall. Both men carried swords, but the gorthling stunned them into immobility with a spell and disarmed them.

Gabria choked back a cry when the gorthling shoved his prisoners in front of him. They were Lord Wortan of the Geldring and Wer-tain Guthlac.

"Do not come near me, Sorceress," the gorthling shouted. "Or these men will die . . . horribly!" He slowly edged around the tent and began to back toward the river, keeping Wortan and Guthlac between himself and Gabria. Nara paced his movements step by step.

At the water's edge he grabbed the two men and hauled them in with him. Both were dazed and could barely stumble through the shallows. He forced the men on through the Goldrine toward the holy island. The Hunnuli and her rider stood on one shore following his every move; the clanspeople stood along the other banks watching what was happening.

The gorthling raised a hand. A lurid red glow ignited over his body, and before everyone's horrified gaze, he began to grow. His body grew taller and larger until he towered higher than the trees and his shadow fell on the people on the west bank. His face warped into a huge mask similar to the gorthling's original wizened features. The beast roared his fury and reached toward the nearest crowd of people. Those by the water's edge screamed in panic and tried to flee, but the press of people blocked their way.

Gabria screamed a warning. She tried to block Branth's hand with a spell, but she was too late. The gorthling grabbed seven people with his enormous hands and dragged them, struggling and shrieking, into the river to join his other hostages. As a diversion, he sent several blasts of the Trymian Force into the fleeing crowd.

Gabria was able to destroy all but one of the blasts. The last searing bolt struck a group of clanspeople, killing six and injuring many more.

"Stay back, Sorceress!" the gorthling bellowed. "Or I'll kill all of them."

Wordlessly, Gabria watched the gorthling shove his hostages together. Even as she racked her brain for a useful idea, the gorthling took his nine prisoners into the circle of stones and sealed the ring with a protective arcane shield, then he shrank back to normal size to conserve his strength.

Gabria gritted her teeth. She had failed. On the far riverbank, screams, wails, and cries of grief and pain blended into a lament that cut Gabria like an accusation. This disaster was her fault. She had not been strong enough to defeat or even contain the gorthling, and now the problem of fighting the creature was worse than ever.

She lifted her gaze to the island, her eyes glittering like cold gems. The gorthling had out-maneuvered her this time. She swore she would not let that happen again. Somehow she would find a way to defeat the beast and send it back where it belonged.

18

"Gabria!" someone shouted. "What's going on?"

Lord Sha Umar ran to Nara's side and stared at the holy island where the gorthling had retreated.

"What is Branth trying to do?" he asked.

"That isn't Branth any more," Gabria replied wearily. "Lord Branth summoned a gorthling in Pra Desh, and the creature invaded his body."

Sha Umar was horrified. "What's he doing here?"

"Trying to kill magic-wielders."

The chieftain looked over at the woman for the first time and noticed how wan and tired she appeared. "Where is Athlone?" he asked.

"North of here. Half a day's ride." She glanced at the sky and saw with surprise that the sun had barely risen to its mid-morning height. Her battle with the gorthling had seemed interminable to her, but it had taken little time.

The island was quiet for the moment. Gabria could make out the group of prisoners huddled together in the center of the stone circle. Branth was sitting on a flat rock nearby, watching his hostages and resting. Of course, Gabria knew he was not resting completely. He was still using power to maintain the faint red force field that glimmered around the circle of stones.

On the opposite banks of the two rivers the camps were in chaos. More people gathered on the banks, their horrified curiosity getting the better of their fear. Relatives and friends grouped around the dead and wailed their grief. Others carried the wounded to the clan healers. No one was entirely certain what was going on. There was a cacophony of frantic shouting, crying, yelling, and excited talking as everyone tried to learn what had happened.

Four other chieftains came running toward the council grove and forded the river. They met Sha Umar and Gabria with a barrage of questions.

The Jehanan chieftain deftly maneuvered them away for a moment to let Gabria collect her thoughts. The woman slipped off Nara and rested thankfully against the mare's strong shoulder. Her moment of quiet was over in a heartbeat.

Lord Caurus pushed past Sha Umar and shook his fist under her nose. "I knew it! I knew you'd be trouble. It was only a matter of time. Two of my people are dead, and it's your fault."

Gabria let his anger wash around her like a wave. She understood his rage and fear, and in part, he was right. She had let the gorthling snatch the hostages and slip away.

Lord Bael, the new chieftain of the Ferganan, butted in past Caurus. "What is Branth doing here?"

"And where is Lord Athlone?" Young Lord Ryne called over the noise.

"How did you get here? I thought you went to Pra Desh?" Caurus added.

The Shadedron chief, Lord Malech, demanded, "What are you going to do about this disaster?"

Gabria answered their questions as best she could and hurriedly explained her long journey to and from Pra Desh. The men's anger and confusion cooled somewhat as they listened. Gabria was pleasantly relieved that the chiefs heard her out with a measure of respect and concern.

The only question she avoided was Lord Malech's. She did not know what to do about the gorthling or his hostages. Even after their battle, she was no closer to sending it out of the world than when she had started. All she had succeeded in doing was tiring herself and forcing the gorthling into a strong defensive position.

She was still trying to explain the battle to the men when Lord Jol pushed through the group and took Gabria's arm. "Lady Corin, would you come and look at Koshyn?"

Koshyn! She had forgotten about him. She broke off and hurried after the old Murjik chieftain. The others followed silently in their wake.

Sha Umar and Jol had laid the Dangari in the big council tent after the gorthling had left the grove. The chief was resting, unconscious, on his blue cloak. Three of Koshyn's hearthguard were dead, but two others stood by their lord, their faces showing their concern. Gabria knelt down beside the wounded chieftain. Koshyn had suffered no obvious external injury from Branth's torturous spell, yet everyone could see there was something dreadfully wrong within him. He twitched and writhed and moaned in pain; his muscles jerked spasmodically, and his hands were clenched in knotted fists. When Gabria touched him, his skin was hot with fever.

"There is nothing I can do," Gabria said sadly. "Only our healer, Piers, can help. He has a stone of healing that will remove the harmful magic from Lord Koshyn's body."

The Dangari exchanged glances. "Where is your healer, Lady?" one of them asked.

"He will be coming soon, I hope." She glanced out the open tent flap. "Lord Koshyn is not the only one who will need the stone of healing. There are other people who were sorely injured, too."

At that instant, Nara spoke gladly in her mind. *Gabria, the men are coming!*

To the chief's mutual amazement, the sorceress jumped to her feet and dashed outside. She ran out to the edge of the trees and saw them coming. Athlone and Sayyed were doubled on Eurus, and the Hunnuli was galloping across the valley toward the gathering.

At that moment, Gabria did not know which of her emotions was stronger, her dismay that they had come when the gorthling was still a danger or her joy at their arrival. She knew she had disappointed them by leaving, but they had come to her aid anyway.

Gabria yelled and waved. They saw her and veered toward her. Athlone nearly fell off the big Hunnuli in his haste to reach the woman. His anger and worry were abruptly doused in the flood of relief that swept through him when he saw her alive and well. He caught her in his arms, crushing her close.

She said nothing, just wrapped her arms around him and held tightly.

Athlone did not say anything, either. He let her go, and she turned to greet Sayyed. The Turic, too, hugged her fiercely.

"I'm glad you're safe," he said, somewhere between laughter and tears.

"Where are Piers and the others?" she asked.

"On their way. The other horses could not keep up with Eurus." Sayyed flashed his charming smile. "I was nearly left behind, too."

The other chiefs caught up with the three just then, and they greeted Athlone with undisguised relief. They immediately bombarded him with questions and several versions of the events of the morning. He talked with them just long enough to hear them out and answer a few of their questions, then he excused himself and went to join Gabria and Sayyed.

As Gabria looked into Athlone's eyes, she could not trust herself to speak. She had tried to decide the men's fate by leaving them, convinced that the fight with the gorthling was hers alone. She knew now that she had been wrong. The creature was too strong for her to face by herself. She had to admit that she needed the help and the support of these two men. However, the decision to use their untrained sorcery in a battle against a much stronger foe was theirs to make. She was still desperately afraid for them, but she had to let them choose their own path.

"I will say only one thing before we talk about the gorthling," Athlone said. He cupped his hands around Gabria's face, and his brown eyes bored into hers. "Don't ever leave me like that again."

The intensity of his quiet words meant more to her than anything he could have said in anger or any statement of his concern for her safety. Warmed to the center of her being, Gabria raised her hand palm up and said, "I promise."

His fingers interlaced with hers, and the vow was made.

They stood in the shade of the tree near the council tent, and Gabria told the two men what had happened from the moment she arrived. They could hear the noise still going on in the camps; the voices of some of the chiefs rose above the cacophony as they tried to assess the damage and calm their people. The council grove bustled with activity, but Gabria, Athlone, and Sayyed were left strictly alone.

Suddenly they heard a voice close by. "I demand to see Lord Athlone. My right as a Khulinin cannot be denied."

The chieftain groaned when he saw Thalar, the clan priest. Lord Sha Umar was trying to distract the priest, but Thalar grew louder and more insistent by the moment.

"I will not leave," Thalar shouted, "until I speak with my chieftain!"

Athlone nodded to Sha Umar, and the Jahanan stood aside. The priest came striding over. "What is it, Thalar?" the chieftain asked, the irritation clear in his voice.

The priest ignored his tone and planted himself before his chief. "Lord Athlone! You have finally come. I'll have you know that the gods-cursed heretic, Branth, has invaded the holy island, destroyed the sanctity of the gods' temple, and slaughtered people of our clans. I *demand* that you remove him from the sacred ring before the gods curse us for allowing this sacrilege to occur."

Lord Athlone tried to hold his temper. Although the priests and priestesses of a clan did not have as much authority as the chieftain, even the chiefs did not deliberately insult or antagonize a representative of the gods. Thalar, however, made self-control difficult.

"We're trying to—" Athlone began, but Thalar turned away before he could complete the sentence.

The priest faced Gabria, and his color turned as red as a beet. "As for her," he shouted, pointing a trembling finger at the woman, "that evil-tainted sorceress has destroyed this gathering! The moment she appeared, all the fury of Sorh broke loose."

Gabria tried to stifle a smile. Thalar did not know the truth of the gorthling's identity, so he had little idea how close he was to the truth.

Unfortunately the priest noticed her half-hidden expression and misread it for ridicule. "See how she laughs? Does she care that six people lie dead, that many more are injured, that nine are hostage, including a chief and your own wer-tain? Does she care for the sacrilege that is being done to our holy temple? Lord Athlone, that woman is a menace, and I demand that you banish her from this camp before she destroys us all."

"No," Athlone replied simply.

Thalar rose to his full height and bellowed, "Then kill her! Root out her evil!" His voice thundered across the grove. Anyone nearby who was not already listening to the harangue turned to watch. "Put an end to this vile stain of magic or by Surgart, I swear I will bring down the wrath of the gods upon this clan. I will—"

He went no further. Lord Athlone had had enough. The chief raised his hand, spoke a single word, and the priest's voice caught in his throat. Thalar's face turned from red to a sickly white, and his eyes bulged as he attempted to speak. Sha Umar and Sayyed grinned; the other chiefs looked stunned.

"No," said Athlone calmly. "As you can see, the stain of magic is spreading."

Thalar gasped and gagged with a mighty effort to say something, but the words would not come.

"You will listen now," Athlone ordered, a bite of steel in his tone. "I am a magic-wielder, too. I intend to help Lady Gabria as best I can to remove that gorthling."

Thalar abruptly stilled, and his body stiffened.

The chieftain saw his reaction and pushed the point home. "That's right. That creature is not Branth, but a beast of Sorh, and Lady Gabria was trying to save the clans from its evil. Do you understand?"

Thalar nodded, his eyes narrowed.

"Good. If you wish to remain with the Khulinin, I suggest you think about your position on sorcery. There are two sides to every argument." Athlone spoke a second command, and the priest put his hand to his throat. He cleared it a few times to make certain that he could speak again.

"So," Thalar said, his tone low and cold, "you, too, have succumbed to the heresy. Are you here to fight the gorthling or help it?" He glared ferociously at Athlone and stalked away from the group.

The men standing nearby stared at Athlone in amazement. "That was very interesting," Sha Umar said.

Gabria touched Athlone's arm. "You have been practicing," she said reproachfully.

"A little," he admitted. "Enough to get a feel for the way magic works."

She turned to Sayyed. "I suppose you have, too?"

He grinned. "Of course."

"How? You two don't know enough to teach yourselves."

Athlone replied, "By listening and watching you."

"You're lucky you did not destroy yourselves with an uncontrolled spell," she said.

Sayyed lifted his hands and shrugged. "You can't show us a feast and expect us to be happy with crumbs."

Gabria was about to reply when a shadow passed over the council grove. Nervously she glanced up, but it was only a cloud passing overhead, formed by the growing afternoon heat.

The sorceress was still gazing at the sky when an agonized scream tore through the camps. Everyone within hearing froze in their tracks. As the scream died away, Gabria, Athlone, and the others ran to the riverbank and stared at the island where the gorthling was standing. He had dissolved his force field and had dragged a woman out of the circle of standing stones to the graveled bank. The other eight hostages still huddled in the ring.

"Sorceress!" Branth yelled. He yanked his prisoner to her feet and held her out at arm's length. "Come to me or this female dies!" He shook the young woman viciously to make her scream again.

"Let her go!" Gabria shouted. "Let them all go, and I will come."

"You come *now!*" he screamed. "I will not wait." So saying, he shoved the sobbing woman toward the water. She ran frantically to escape, but the gorthling's spell caught her before she had taken five steps. The magic seared through her. The creature did not kill her with a quick, explosive burst of Trymian Force. Instead, he used an agonizing power that arched through the woman's body in a slow, massive, disintegrating wave.

Scream after scream ripped from her throat as she thrashed and writhed in the shallow water. The clanspeople watched, motionless with horror. The woman gave a final shriek, then sagged face-first into the water. The current tugged gently at her lifeless body and swirled her fair hair.

Branth did not give the clanspeople time to react. Instantly he shouted a command, and the nearest hostage in the circle stumbled to his feet and began to walk helplessly toward the gorthling. It was Guthlac, the Khulinin wer-tain.

Gabria's eyes blazed with green fury. "Athlone . . ." she began to say, but something interrupted her.

A man stepped off the council grove riverbank into the water. His robes swirled around his short legs, and his face was red with righteous fury. He held his priest's staff over his head like a spear pointed at the gorthling.

"Begone, foul heretic! Beast of Sorh, leave this holy place!" Thalar shouted with all his rage and indignation as he waded toward the island.

"Thalar!" Athlone yelled. "Get back here."

The priest did not hear him. His mind was focused on driving the evil from the blessed island. The Tir Samod was the gods' holy temple, the sanctuary of the priests and the sacred heart of the clans, not a hiding hole for a creature of profane powers. If no one else was going to rid the island of this evil, Thalar swore he would do it himself.

He raised his staff higher. "Go, you gods-cursed worm. By the power of Surgart, I command you to leave."

The gorthling laughed and, without a word, struck the priest with a brilliant blue bolt of Trymian Force. Thalar shrieked once, threw his arms up, and toppled into the river. The rippling water caught his scorched body and carried him gently downstream.

"That's two, Sorceress," the gorthling yelled. "Do you want more bodies to clog the river?"

Gabria spun on her heel and whistled for Nara. Both Hunnuli

came at her summons. "That beast must be stopped," she said as she sprang to Nara's back.

Athlone immediately mounted Eurus, and the big stallion blocked Nara's way. "We're going with you," the chieftain said calmly.

Gabria looked from Athlone to Sayyed and saw the same look of determination on both faces. She could not leave them behind this time, even if she wanted to. She inclined her head once in gratitude and shoved her fear for them out of the way. Now, however, she hesitated, for she was uncertain how to mount an attack that would use the skills of the two men. Sayyed had no mount, and neither man was very proficient with the Trymian Force.

She was still trying to think of a way when Nara perked up her ears. Eurus lifted his head high, and his nostrils flared. On the edge of her senses, Gabria felt something, a faint vibration like distant thunder, or . . . horses' hooves. She raised herself up on Nara's back and saw a plume of dust on the ridge of hills to the west. The vibrations grew louder. A dark form appeared on the horizon, then another, then many more. Nara and Eurus suddenly neighed a joyful greeting that pealed through the gathering and was echoed by every horse in the valley.

A herd of horses galloped down the hills and across the valley, their black coats shining in the sun. A small rider on a little Hunnuli ran just behind their leader. The clanspeople saw them, shouted in awe and delight, and stood aside to let them pass.

The gorthling, too, stared at the approaching horses, and for the first time since he had taken his mortal guise, he felt a pang of apprehension.

The herd thundered down to the river and plunged in with a tremendous, sparkling splash. They ran through the water as easily as air until the entire herd had encircled the island, cutting off the gorthling from the clans. Then the Hunnuli stopped, their heads turned toward the island. Sunlight glistened on their wet coats; their lightning marks gleamed on their shoulders. They pawed the water and snorted in anger.

Five of the horses charged toward the island, their hooves flashing and their teeth bared. The gorthling clasped his hostage in front of him like a shield. He backed away to the shelter of the temple just as the enraged Hunnuli burst up on the shore, then swiftly revived his protective shield of magical energy. The five horses circled the temple warily and waited for their king's command.

Finally the King Stallion cantered up to Gabria on the riverbank, his deep, wise eyes glowing with a golden light. He bowed his head to her. *Sorceress, you needed us, so we have come.*

For a moment Gabria was utterly speechless. She gazed up at the magnificent old stallion, then transferred her amazement to the beaming, dark-haired girl sitting astride Nara's colt.

"I won't ask now how you did this, Tam," Gabria said softly. "You can tell me later, but I am deeply grateful."

The little girl blushed under her tan, and her shy grin grew even wider. Sayyed strode over and pulled Tam off the colt into a huge hug of relief and pride. Tam wrapped her arms around his neck.

The King Stallion snorted angrily. *Tam has told us a gorthling has been released in the world.*

Gabria gestured to the island where the gorthling was pacing back and forth within his defense shield, studying the new arrivals. "Do you know of any way to send him back?"

Sadly, no. That knowledge was never passed on to us. The King Stallion swung his massive head toward his herd. *His magic cannot affect us, however. We will try to keep him confined to the island so he does not harm any more of your people. The rest you must do yourself.*

Gabria was disappointed that even the King Stallion did not know how to dispel a gorthling, but she appreciated his help enormously. She would not have to worry about the clans with the Hunnuli herd to protect them.

I see that you have one sorcerer unhorsed. That will not do. The King Stallion neighed, and another stallion left the ring of Hunnuli. The new horse came to stand in front of Sayyed. He stretched out his muzzle to gravely sniff the Turic.

This is Afer. He will be your mount for this confrontation, the King Stallion told Sayyed.

For once the young Turic was nonplussed. He was torn between delight and awe as he ran his hand down the big Hunnuli's nose. Gingerly he mounted the stallion and settled down on the broad back.

Gabria nodded her thanks to the King Stallion before she turned to the two men. "Remember, Eurus and Afer are immune to magic," she said rapidly. "Stay on them at all times. If you need protection, form a shield between you and the gorthling." After a pause, she added, "Please try to use spells as little as possible. I will attack the gorthling, but I'll need you two distract him. We will try to wear him down until he is too weak to use his power."

"What about the prisoners?" Sayyed asked.

"If we can cut the gorthling off from them and keep him occupied, maybe they'll escape on their own. Perhaps the Hunnuli will help them."

"Have you tried the mask yet?" Athlone wanted to know.

Gabria shook her head. "I still don't know what to do with it."

"Sorceress!" the gorthling suddenly yelled. "I see you brought some help." He laughed maliciously. "These useless beasts will avail you not. Come. I grow tired of waiting. You or these mortals must die!"

Gabria curled her lip in a feral grimace. "We *will* find a way to destroy him." She turned and called, "Lord Sha Umar, the Hunnuli will try to protect the people from any destructive magic, but please keep the warriors and priests away from the island. Will you also watch over Tam?"

"With pleasure, Lady Gabria," the Jehanan answered, coming forward to stand beside the little girl. "The gods go with you."

Gabria turned away so quickly she did not see the stricken look pass over Tam's face. The sorceress signaled to Athlone and Sayyed, and the three magic-wielders rode down into the river. The gorthling laughed with glee as they came.

19

While the King Stallion rejoined his herd, Gabria, Athlone, and Sayyed separated and spread out so they could approach the island from different angles. Their mounts passed through the ring of Hunnuli horses and carefully waded toward the island. The five Hunnuli on shore held their positions and waited.

The gorthling, wary but confident, watched the riders come. There were three humans now. That was an interesting development. There was only supposed to be one magic-wielder in the clans. Curious, he formed an opening in his defense field and fired a blue bolt at the nearest man. He was amazed when the clansman formed a shield and deflected the energy harmlessly into the air. For just a second, the gorthling felt a twinge of fear. Then it passed, and he snarled. What was another magic-wielder or two? He would simply have to strike fast and kill them before they could wear down his strength with their greater numbers.

He glanced at the Hunnuli, too. They were another problem. He knew the five on the island were only waiting to break through his shield and chase him out into the open. No magic would stop them. What he needed was a spell to frighten the humans and a weapon untouched by magic to drive off the horses.

His eye lit on the tall, upright monoliths of the temple, and a cunning grin curled his mouth. He spoke the words of his spell, and once again his body glowed red and began to grow. Soon he towered over the temple and could straddle his hostages. His defense shield dissipated. With a great laugh, he tore a stone from the sacred ring and swung it like a club at the nearest horse. The animal barely dodged in time.

The King Stallion neighed to call his horses back. Magic was a weapon they could avoid, but the horses had no riders to defend them against stone clubs. The five Hunnuli reluctantly withdrew, leaving the magic-wielders and their mounts to their duty.

Before the three sorcerers reached the island shore, the battle was joined. The gorthling fired at Gabria and the two men with a rapid-fire assault of the Trymian Force and other destructive bolts of power. Fortunately for all three, the gorthling was using so much strength to maintain his tremendous size, his bolts of magic were not as powerful as before. The greatest danger lay in the gorthling's stone club, which he swung at the riders whenever they got too close.

The riders quickly discovered another danger. The land around the temple was uneven and rough underfoot. Rocks, boulders, tough shrubs, vines, and small saplings covered the island and made movement on horseback difficult. The gorthling made full use of the uneven ground, forcing the Hunnuli to constantly maneuver over the stony island.

The gorthling himself did not try to move, for the little group of hostages was clinging together in a terrified huddle between his huge legs. They did not dare run, and neither the Hunnuli nor the magic-wielders could reach them as long as the beast stood over them.

It was not long before the gorthling noticed that only the sorceress was offering any real counterattack. She fired her own spells at him while the men only tried to distract him with awkward feints whenever possible. They were rank beginners, he realized gleefully. That noted, he began to concentrate his attack on Athlone and Sayyed, forcing Gabria to expend more and more of her energy to defend her companions.

As time went on, the battle grew more desperate. Gabria silently thanked the gods for the Hunnuli herd. She knew she and the two men would not have lasted so long against the gorthling if they'd had to defend the crowds. The horses stopped several bolts of magic, and their presence kept the gorthling penned on the island.

But even with the help of the Hunnuli, the struggle was telling upon the three humans. Athlone's and Sayyed's inexperience was beginning to show. Their shields were weakening, and several times the gorthling nearly knocked them from their horses. Gabria's fear for them intensified.

Gabria, too, was tiring. She had faced the brunt of the gorthling's attack, and she knew her strength would not last much longer. She pressed the gorthling harder with the Trymian Force, with fireballs, smoke, and flights of arrows. She tried everything she could think of, yet her magic had no effect. The gorthling's size and greater strength helped him ward off her blows with ease. Gabria was running out of ideas.

Then, in the blink of an eye, everything changed.

Sayyed's Hunnuli, Afer, was near the sacred ring when he abruptly slipped on a mossy stone and his front hoof slid down between a cluster of rocks. The stallion lost his balance and fell heavily to the ground. The snap of his foreleg was heard all over the island.

Sayyed was thrown over the stallion's head into the rocks. The Turic lay dazed while his Hunnuli tried frantically to free his broken leg and defend his rider. The other Hunnuli neighed in strident, ringing calls, and Eurus and Nara sprang forward to help the fallen horse and rider.

The gorthling moved faster, grabbing the dazed Turic with one huge hand. Sayyed was bleeding heavily from a cut on his head and was too stunned to try to escape. Nara and Eurus started toward the giant in the stone circle.

The gorthling laughed, and his eyes glowed red. "Now," he bellowed, brandishing his stone club with one hand and Sayyed's struggling form in his other, "watch one of your own die."

To the watchers' horror, Branth hoisted the young Turic over his head. Sayyed fought back weakly, his face working with fear when he saw the ground far below.

Across the river, Tam stood by the Hunnuli colt and Lord Sha Umar, watching the battle. She had not moved from the riverbank since Gabria had left, and she had ignored Sha Umar's offer of food or drink. Her hand stayed on the colt's neck and her eyes remained on the island.

When Afer fell, Tam stiffened and her mouth opened slightly. She watched in growing apprehension as the gorthling grabbed Sayyed. A tiny whimper escaped her lips. When Tam saw the creature lift Sayyed into the air, she quivered with anger and fear. A fury that she had never known before exploded at the injustice and cruelty of losing another person she loved. No, her young mind cried, not again. No! No!

"No!"

Tam's voice rang out loud and clear across the water. At the same time, she instinctively used her wild talent to project her furious thought into the human brain of the gorthling.

The effect was stunning. The protest burst on the gorthling's unprepared mind like an explosion, sending him staggering back. He let go of the Turic and clamped his hands to his head. His concentration broken, he dropped his stone club and began to shrink back to normal size.

The magic-wielders reacted instantly. Before Sha Umar could stop her, Tam jumped on the small Hunnuli and galloped him toward the island. Gabria broke Sayyed's fall by transforming the stones beneath him into a thick pile of hay, and Athlone fired a bolt of the Trymian Force at the unprotected gorthling. The bolt was weak and uncontrolled, but it was enough to knock Branth onto his back and give Sayyed a chance to escape.

"Get to the other side of the river!" Gabria cried.

The Turic did not listen. Instead of retreating, he flung himself into the group of hostages. The gorthling screeched in rage. He fired a blast at the people huddled together, but Sayyed formed a shield over them all. The Trymian Force bounced harmlessly away.

The gorthling felt his twinge of fear return and grow stronger. He immediately revived his own defensive shield. Now he had no escape route, no hostages for safety, and no place to retreat. He was trapped, and while his enemies were tiring, so was he. He could no longer maintain his gigantic size or the full power of his Trymian Force. The thought occurred to him that he had seriously underestimated these humans. He paused for a moment, breathing heavily, and looked around the island for some means of turning this battle in his favor.

Gabria and Athlone took advantage of the brief respite to regroup. Nara clattered over the rocks closer to Eurus, and their two riders watched the gorthling warily.

"We seem to be in a stalemate," Athlone said between deep breaths. "What do we do now?"

Gabria frowned in frustration. "I really don't know. He can't leave the island, but I still don't know how to send him back to Sorh's realm. Nothing I do works!" She glanced into the temple. "Sayyed, are you all right?"

The Turic answered without his usual humor. "We are safe for the moment."

Tam and the colt trotted up the bank and hurried into the temple to join Sayyed. He seemed relieved to see her, so Gabria merely shook her head and let the girl stay for the moment. Tam was already slipping out of the temple to help Afer free his leg, and several Hunnuli from the herd were coming to join her. Tam would be well protected.

The gorthling saw the Hunnuli coming, too, and his anger rekindled. He could still slaughter these people and drive away the infuriating horses. Abruptly he ended the respite and fired a bolt at Athlone, hoping to catch the chief unprepared. To his fury, the man's big stallion stopped the magic on his powerful chest.

"Give up, you feeble humans. You will never defeat me," the gorthling taunted. "I will be here forever! As long as there are bodies to inhabit. No one has ever conquered the gorthlings of Sorh."

"You're forgetting Valorian," Athlone retorted, "and Matrah." He shot a blue bolt at the gorthling's defense shield.

His blast exploded harmlessly, but his words set off a small spark of thought in Gabria's mind. Like a streak of lightning, the thought burst into an incandescent inspiration.

She slapped the heavy bag at her side. "That's it! Of course. Valorian knows!" she cried. The diamond splinter in her wrist flared from her excited burst of energy.

Athlone stared at her sudden transformation. "What are you talking about?"

"The mask!" she said, trying to keep her voice down. "Quick, Athlone, Tam! Get into the temple and join Sayyed."

The little girl had just released Afer's broken leg from the rocks, so she patted the injured horse and hurried to obey, leaving him with the other Hunnuli.

Athlone hesitated. "What are you planning?"

"If Branth can summon something from the realm of the dead, so can I," Gabria replied excitedly.

"Not another gorthling."

"Of course not. I'm going to try to use the power in the mask to summon Valorian. If I am successful, *he* can tell us how to rid ourselves of that beast."

Athlone was awestruck by the simplicity and audacity of her plan. Valorian. My gods! Athlone thought. Without another word he took Eurus into the temple.

Gabria loosed two quick bolts at the ground by the gorthling's shield. As they exploded in a cloud of dirt and gravel, she and Nara hurried through the ring of stones after Athlone and joined the group of people in the center of the temple.

Before the gorthling could retaliate, Sayyed lowered his shield and renewed it around the entire group, including Nara, Eurus, and the colt.

"By the gods," Wer-tain Guthlac said to his chief, "I'm glad to see you!" He instinctively ducked when the gorthling fired a blast at the shield.

The other hostages stared at Gabria in confusion and hope. She gave them what she hoped was a confidant smile and untied the bag from her belt. The mask felt heavy in her hands. She turned to Athlone and said, "I will not be able to help you maintain the shield while I do this spell. You, Sayyed, and Tam will have to protect us all."

He grinned. "Gladly."

Her green eyes sparkled at his reply. "Two months ago I would never have thought you would say that."

"You've taught me well," the chieftain replied.

He went to stand by Sayyed and Tam, and the three joined their wills together to hold the magical shield around the beleaguered group. The gorthling shrieked in rage. He fired more arcane blasts at the shield to try to weaken it, but for now, the three magic-wielders held it firm.

Gabria slid to the ground and leaned back against Nara. The mare curved her neck around Gabria and nickered softly. *In the memory of my sires, Valorian was a tall man, dark-haired, proud, kind, and fearless. Bend your will toward him through the mask. Perhaps he will hear you.*

The sorceress bowed her head. She did not know a formal spell for summoning a being from the realm of the immortals, so she would have to create one of her own. Nara's suggestion sounded as plausible as any idea she might decide upon. She straightened and turned to face the flat stone altar on the eastern side of the temple.

The hostages watched her in growing amazement. The clanspeople on the riverbanks who could see her muttered among themselves, wondering what was happening.

The sorceress studied the stones still standing around her. Legends said that Valorian dwelled with the gods, beyond the realm of the dead. What better place from which to summon him than a sacred temple? If there was anyplace on the Dark Horse Plains where the world of man touched the unseen realm of the gods, the Tir Samod was it.

"Amara, give me strength," Gabria prayed.

Reverently, she held the golden mask up to the sky. As the sunlight sparkled on the enigmatic face, the mask tingled in her hands.

Gabria closed her eyes. One by one, she focused on the sounds around her—the curses of the gorthling as it struggled to break through their defenses, the murmur of the hostages behind her, the click of the horses' hooves on stone, the ripple of the rivers—and one by one, she shut them out of her mind until there was only a vast silence.

Into the silence she sent her plea to Valorian. She bent her will into the magic of the mask and called him with every fiber of her being. The world around her seemed to recede until she was floating in a limitless, lightless, ethereal realm beyond the bounds of her earthly senses. She went without fear into the darkness and continued to call Valorian with her heart, mind, and soul.

Time passed, although Gabria did not feel it. Her mind was wrapped around the image of a tall, dark-haired warrior with a cleft chin and the look of eagles in his face. She had to find him. The safety of his people depended upon it.

Her summons went on without pause until, far ahead in the horizonless distance, she saw a light appear like sunlight through a crack. Gabria moved instinctively toward it, staring at the brilliant, shimmering golden radiance until its power filled her being and tested the measure of her spirit. A warm sense of comfort and familiarity enveloped her.

The mask shifted in her hands. The light vanished, and the sounds of the world rushed back. Around the island the Hunnuli horses neighed a trumpeting welcome. Gabria was so surprised she opened her eyes and looked at the mask.

The most vivid pair of blue eyes she had ever seen looked back at her.

The death mask twitched, stretched, and the mouth suddenly lifted into a smile. "I have come, Daughter. As you have asked." The golden face spoke in a voice both powerful and kind. Its words rang out over the island and were heard as far away as the riverbanks.

Gabria nearly dropped the mask in astonishment. She had not known what to expect when she tried to summon Valorian. She had only used the mask as a focal point for her spell. She raised the mask up again.

A question formed in her mind, but she could not bring herself to ask if this truly was the Hero-Warrior from the clans' distant past.

The mask glowed with a pure radiance, the same light Gabria realized she had seen in her mind. "I am he whom you have called. I am the essence of the man once named Valorian."

For a moment, Gabria was overcome with joy and awe and an overwhelming desire to cry and laugh at the same time. "I can't believe you have come," she said, trying to calm her shaking hands.

"Your power is strong, my daughter. Your need must be great."

"Forgive me, Lord. I have to ask you something that only you can tell me."

"I will listen. But ask your question quickly. I cannot stay long in this world."

Gabria shot a glance at the three magic-wielders. Sayyed, already weary and injured, was concentrating fiercely on the spell, and it was obvious to her that he was tiring fast. Tam was ashen, and even Athlone was beginning to look strained. The shield was a difficult spell to maintain, even without the added strains brought on by the gorthling's constant barrage of destructive magic.

Quickly she turned back to the death mask and looked boldly into the eternal blue eyes. "My lord, one of the Geldring men has summoned a gorthling."

The mask frowned. "How?"

"With a spell from the *Book of Matrah*."

"Those spells should be stricken from all human knowledge. There are some things best left alone by man. Where is this gorthling now?"

"Here. It possessed the man's body and came to our clan gathering. My lord Valorian, I am the only magic-wielder with any training to speak of, but I don't know how to destroy it."

Valorian gazed at her with compassion. "No human, no matter how skilled, has enough power to force a gorthling back through the portal between the world of mortals and the eternal world."

Gabria turned cold. "It has to be done," she cried. "How do we get rid of him?"

"Only one thing in your world has the power to open a passage and force the creature back through."

"What?"

The mask lifted its eyes to the sky. "The power of the lightning," he said simply.

Gabria's mouth dropped open. She was aghast. "Lightning? But no one can withstand the fury of the gods' thunderbolts."

"You are a magic-wielder, a daughter of my blood. Do you travel with a Hunnuli?"

She nodded.

"Astride a Hunnuli, you will be protected. They bear the mark of the lightning for good reason. Their sire, my stallion, was transformed by the lightning into the first of that noble breed of horses."

"Lord Valorian," Gabria said, trying to stay calm, "I cannot create a storm. Where do I find lightning on a clear day?"

"If there are more than one Hunnuli with you, they can summon a storm and its lightning."

The golden light began to fade from the mask, and the blue eyes dimmed. Valorian's expression relaxed, then stiffened into the one the mask had worn when Gabria found it.

"Valorian, my lord," Gabria begged desperately. "What do I do with the power of the lightning?"

"I must go, Daughter," Valorian said sadly. "Use the lightning to send . . . it . . . back."

A faint echo followed the final words, as if they had been spoken across a great and hollow distance. Then the mask was still and lifeless once more. Gabria stared at the golden face and willed it to speak again, but it was too late. Valorian was gone, beyond her reach.

"How do I wield lightning?" she called in despair to the voiceless stones. There was no answer here, she knew, and now there was no more time. The gorthling was using a fierce blue barrage against the shield protecting the little group. Already the force field was beginning to waver. Sayyed looked ready to pass out, and Athlone's teeth were clenched as he concentrated.

"Hold on!" Gabria cried to her friends. "Nara," she yelled over the noise of the gorthling's attack. "Call the King Stallion. Tell him to summon a storm."

Beyond the island, the King Stallion replied with a strident neigh. *We have not called the lightning in generations of our kind. We will try.*

The ring of black horses abruptly lifted their muzzles to the sky. The Hunnuli on the island, even the colt and the wounded Afer, joined their silent communion with the air. Only Nara and Eurus did not include themselves in the call, deciding instead to keep alert in case their riders needed their aid.

To the Hunnuli's advantage, the afternoon was perfect for a storm. The day's heat and a humid wind had already formed billowing clouds in the blue sky, and several little rain squalls patterned the far horizons. As the Hunnuli herd concentrated their power, darker clouds began to gather overhead; the rain squalls moved closer. The horses strained, but the ability they had inherited from their sires served them well.

Gradually the sky grew dark, and a tremendous thunderhead roared out of the forefront of an angry mass of gray clouds. The sun was blotted out, and lightning flickered in the storm's turbulent heart.

The gorthling looked up, and fear shone clearly on Branth's face. That fear did not distract him long, though, and he did not miss the events unfolding in the circle of stones.

"Gabria," Athlone suddenly yelled. "Sayyed passed out. The shield is failing!"

The sorceress jumped on Nara's back just as the gorthling shattered the magic field. With a wild screech of triumph Branth fired a blast at the chieftain through the breach.

Athlone was too exhausted to defend against it. He saw the bolt coming and leaned into Eurus's side. The stallion reared up and took the blast on his shoulder, but the violent movement of the stallion and the explosion of power slammed Athlone backward. He crashed to the rocky ground where he lay motionless.

Tam, exhausted beyond bearing, mentally called the Hunnuli that stood by Afer, and two of them immediately joined Eurus to defend the fallen men.

The gorthling turned away. He could not get near the fallen chieftain or the Turic as long as the Hunnuli stood over them, but that did not matter. Neither man would be any more trouble.

Gabria had not moved from the temple. She and Nara stood between the gorthling and the hostages. Behind her she heard Lord Wortan and Wer-tain Guthlac trying to calm the terrified prisoners. Gabria kept her gaze pinned on Branth. The wind was starting to roar through the temple, and thunder rumbled across the sky. The herd of Hunnuli stirred from their motionless concentration and neighed their victory to the oncoming storm.

The gorthling began to edge warily into the temple, his cruel eyes fastened on Gabria and her mount.

The sorceress stared at him implacably and made no move to attack. She had only one idea for what she would do with the lightning. If that did not work, she would not have a chance to try anything else. She sat still on Nara, feeling the powerful heat of the Hunnuli warm her legs; her fingers touched the jagged white mark on Nara's shoulder.

As it had in Pra Desh when Gabria had fought the fire consuming the palace, the magic around the sorceress was intensifying with the power of the storm. She knew the enhanced power would help her, but it could also aid the gorthling. Quickly and precisely she began to form her spell in her mind, waiting for the right moment to strike.

The gorthling stepped between two stone pillars. "Valorian was wrong, Sorceress," he hissed. "Nothing can send me back. Get ready to die!"

Gabria did not reply. Lightning flashed overhead, and she felt the split-second surge of power in the air. Lightning happened so fast, she would have to act instinctively. Branth took another step forward and raised his hands to the sky.

Gabria! Nara cried in the woman's mind and leaped sideways not a moment too soon. A sizzling bolt of Trymian Force slammed down on the spot where they had been standing. The gorthling was using the intensified magic to his full advantage.

Gabria threw herself to the right as another of the gorthling's bolts seared past her. Another blast and another. They were so fast, hot, and deadly that Gabria could not concentrate on her own spell; it took her full attention to dodged the wicked bolts. The sorceress did not dare form a defense shield for fear of using too much of her depleted strength. She could only rely on the agility and protection of her mount.

Big drops of rain spattered on the warm rocks nearby. A lightning streak exploded on a tree across the river near the Jehanan camp, followed instantly by a deafening clap of thunder. The storm was moving, and Gabria knew she only had a brief time before the lightning was too far away. Yet the moment to attack was still not right.

The gorthling fired another bolt at her. It struck the ground at Nara's feet, shattering the rocks and sending gravel and splinters flying. The mare reared away, her motion nearly unseating Gabria.

The gorthling began to laugh, a rude, wicked sound that reflected his arrogance. The sorceress would never destroy him, for in a moment she would be dead.

Frantically Gabria struggled to regain her balance. She saw the gorthling draw his hands back. At the same time, a tingling skittered across her skin and the hairs on the back of her neck rose. She felt more than saw the power that surged around her, concentrating its energy on the tallest stone pillar near the altar to her right. This was even better than she had hoped for. The woman closed her mind to all but her spell and let her instincts guide her.

Lightning struck the top of the great stone monolith, its incredible energy searing the very air. The gorthling flinched away, but Gabria put her trust in the natural protective powers of the Hunnuli and reached out for the streaking energy.

In one fluid movement, she snared the lightning bolt and wrenched it from its natural path into her hand. She felt the incredible power surge through every fiber, bone, and hair of both her body and Nara's, and she saw the mare glimmer with a greenish white glow. Surprisingly the bolt felt warm and soft in Gabria's hand. She swung around and threw the lightning like a javelin, using every bit of strength she had left.

The blue-white bolt split the air to the gorthling and struck his body in a blinding explosion of light, sparks, and heat.

Gabria's vision went black and red with pain. She heard the gorthling's high-pitched screech of despair and hatred, followed by a tremendous crash of thunder. At that same instant, the backlash of the lightning's energy slammed into her and Nara. The Hunnuli staggered under the explosive force, and Gabria was flung to the wet, cold ground.

20

The sound of thunder faded from Gabria's ears, and she became aware of a persistent, needle-sharp pain behind her eyes. It brought her out of her state of shock and back to reality. She opened her eyes for just a moment and saw nothing but blackness and red shooting streaks. A tremor fluttered in her chest. She was blind!

She forced down her terror and concentrated instead on a small, calm voice that was speaking softly near her ear. The voice was unfamiliar, but something about its gentle tone was soothing.

"Tam?" she whispered out of the dark. She tried to sit up, but every bone and muscle in her body sent up a painful protest.

The quiet voice replied with intense relief. "Yes, Lady, I am here. No! Don't move yet. Help is coming."

Gabria obeyed willingly. She lay still on the cold, hard ground and felt the rain pounding on her body. Tam had to be shielding her face, but Gabria could not see.

The sorceress reached out for the girl's hand. "Tam, where is the gorthling?"

"He's gone," Tam answered excitedly. "The lightning you threw disintegrated him! There isn't even a finger left."

Gabria could not help but smile. Tam had certainly found her tongue in the midst of all the chaos.

Another person joined them, and a familiar voice said, "Gabria, let me help you." The clan priestess of Amara wrapped a warm cloak around the sorceress and very carefully eased her to a sitting position. "Can you stand?" the priestess asked.

Gabria swallowed hard and shook her head. Pain and nausea

coursed through her head and her stomach. Every muscle she had was trembling. She felt as weak and blind as a newborn kitten.

"Never mind. Sit here a moment," the priestess told her. "I will tend to the others."

Gabria heard her walk toward the place where Athlone had fallen. Nara came to stand upwind of the sorceress to block some of the wild wind and rain that lashed across the island. Tam still held her cloak over Gabria's head.

"Nara, are Athlone and Sayyed badly hurt?"

They are exhausted, but will recover, I believe.

Gabria turned her sightless eyes toward the mare. "Your thoughts are strained. You sound weary. Are you all right?"

I am very weak. The strength needed to protect us from the lightning was almost more than I had.

The woman reached out and felt the mare's strong foreleg. "Thank you, Nara."

The mare nickered like a gentle laugh. *It was a good battle. The gorthling is gone, and we are still here.*

Gabria sighed. "What is going on out there? Is a healer coming to help Athlone and Sayyed? Afer's leg is broken. Is anyone coming to help him?"

Tam answered, her young voice high with anger. "The priests and priestesses will not allow any more uninitiated onto the island, but they won't cross the river themselves to help. Only the priestess of Amara from your clan had the courage to come."

Gabria's anger stirred sluggishly in her thoughts. She and her companions had faced death to save the clans, but now that they needed help, the people would not even come to their aid. Her nausea faded a little, and she sat up straighter, stirred by resentment.

Before she could think of a suitable angry response, an image of what she had done came to her mind. Her anger retreated while she considered how the entire arcane battle must have looked from the clans' point of view. They were probably terrified out of their wits.

Gabria realized she had an excellent opportunity to make a positive impression on her stubborn, skeptical, suspicious people. They had seen the horror of the gorthling's cruelty and the terror of his magic. Now she could show them the other side of magic: the pleasure of victory and the comfort of healing.

Strengthened by her resolve, Gabria painfully pulled herself up Nara's iron-strong foreleg until she was standing, dizzy and gasping, by the mare's shoulder. The cold rain poured down her face, but she did not care. She concentrated on staying upright, gritting her teeth against the exhaustion that rocked her, and held on grimly to Nara's mane.

A strong arm was laid across her shoulders and steadied her. The priestess's calm voice said, "Gabria, please. You need to rest."

The sorceress refused. "Not yet. Where is Athlone?"

"I'm here." Lord Athlone's voice was strained, but steady. It sounded wonderful to Gabria. He walked wearily around the big mare to say something more and hesitated when he saw Gabria and the strange expression on her face. Her eyes were closed tightly, and her head was tilted to one side in a concentrated effort to hear.

"Are you hurt?" Gabria asked the chieftain.

"Just a knock on the head, but I feel exhausted." He rubbed his temples and looked around, bleary-eyed. "What happened?"

Tam replied, "The sorceress destroyed Branth with a lightning bolt."

"Good gods," he exclaimed.

At that moment, the King Stallion cantered through the water to the island and pranced up to the small group. The Hunnuli herd gathered behind him, their black coats glistening in the rain.

"Athlone," Gabria whispered. "Help me up."

Willingly the chieftain gave her a leg up onto Nara's back and stood aside to watch as the tall, slim woman turned to face the huge stallion.

The black Hunnuli shook his mane. *You have done well, Sorceress.*

Gabria gestured to the herd. "Thank you for your help. It means more than I can ever say."

Valorian would be proud. Suddenly he lifted his great nose to her face. His nostrils flared gently. *Are your eyes hurt?*

"I cannot see," she said simply.

Athlone felt his heart grow sick.

The lightning's brightness burned your eyes.

"Will they heal?" Gabria asked with more hope than conviction.

The stallion snorted softly. *Perhaps. In time.*

She nodded once and changed the subject. "What about Afer? Is there anything we can do?"

At that the King Stallion bowed his head. *We Hunnuli can withstand the greatest arcane powers in the universe, but we are as vulnerable to bodily injury as any other horse. Your magic will not affect him, for good or ill, and your healers cannot mend a horse's broken leg.*

Gabria felt her voice choke, and she had to force herself to ask, "Then we must put him out of his misery?"

"No!" Sayyed's cry echoed through the circle of stones. The tribesman, a rag tied to his bleeding head, was trying to put a temporary splint on the stallion's broken leg.

Tam quickly went to help her friend as he stepped forward in front of the horse.

"You can't kill him," Sayyed said forcefully.

"Sayyed, his leg is broken," Athlone said, trying not to be harsh. "You know no horse can recover from that."

"One has! My father's prize mare. She broke a leg in a race, and my father could not bear to kill her. He suspended her body from a sling until her leg healed enough to bear her weight. It's not easy, but it can be done. Please," Sayyed cried, "give him a chance."

They were silent for a long moment as they thought about the enormity of that task. However, to Gabria and Sayyed, the effort was worth the chance if it would save a Hunnuli.

"We'll try it," Gabria said.

Thank you, Sorceress. Then we will gladly leave Afer in your care. The King Stallion lifted his head and neighed a call that rang to the hills and shook the stones of the temple. He lifted his massive body up high to paw the air in a salute of honor to the magic-wielders. The other Hunnuli reared also. Every human watching thrilled to see the majestic Hunnuli at the height of their pride and glory.

As one, the black horses followed the king up out of the river and west toward their home in the mountains. The thunder of their passing faded away into the storm, but the wonder of their presence stayed with the clanspeople for many days to come. Nara, Eurus, and the colt neighed a long farewell.

Gabria's fingers clenched her pantleg, and tears slipped out of the corners of her closed eyes. She could not see the Hunnuli leave, yet she felt the aching loss of their disappearance. Abruptly she shook her head to clear her mind. The pain shot through her eyes, and she gasped.

"What is it?" Athlone asked, the worry plain in his words. "Are you truly blind?"

Gabria tried to push the pain aside and smile. "For the moment. It should pass. Can you ride?"

He looked up at her and was not reassured by her off-hand reply. He decided not to push her and merely answered her question. "Yes."

"Then, come. Tam, Sayyed, you come too. We have to face the clans."

The others obeyed. Athlone quickly understood what Gabria was trying to accomplish, and he helped Sayyed onto Nara's back with no further questions. He mounted Eurus, with some difficulty, and waited while Tam scrambled onto the colt. Afer hopped painfully over the short distance to stand between Eurus and Nara.

"Priestess," Gabria called. "Will you bring the mask?"

The priestess of Amara went to find the death mask of Valorian. At the same time, the eight hostages stopped in front of the magic-wielders. Guthlac saluted his chieftain with respect; Lord Wortan stepped forward and blinked into the rain to look up at Gabria.

"Thank you, Lady," he said with sincerity. "Is it all right if we go?"

She nodded in his direction.

The eight clanspeople gratefully started out for the river. They walked at first, then their joy and relief broke loose, and they ran through the muddy water to the far bank where the crowd of onlookers and their families welcomed them back with open arms.

The priestess of Amara found the golden mask of Valorian lying on the stony ground of the temple, its handsome face still and lifeless. Her hands trembled as she picked up the heavy gold mask. She carried it to where the magic-wielders waited and stopped before Gabria.

"Truly," she said, her voice ringing with gladness and respect, "you are the blessed of Amara. Go now, Sorceress. The clans are waiting." The priestess raised the golden mask high above her head and began to sing a hymn of praise to the Mother Goddess. Her song reached out to the watching people on the riverbanks and stirred their hearts with a strange feeling of reassurance.

The watching clanspeople did not understand exactly what had happened on the island. They had seen and heard many strange things, things both wonderful and horrifying. Now it seemed that Branth, or whatever he had been, was gone; there were four magic-wielders instead of one, all apparently alive and well; the entire Hunnuli herd had honored them before all the clans; the hostages were free; and a priestess of the Mother Goddess was offering her oblation of song to praise their deeds.

The clanspeople did not know what to think. This spectacle of good and evil, courage and cruelty, honor and treachery was hardly what they had expected from magic. Magic was supposed to be entirely evil, corrupting, and heretical. Many people had been willing to accept Gabria as an aberration. Yet here were three other magic-wielders, two men and a child, who had the same decency and courage and the willingness to lay down their lives for their companions and their people. That was not supposed to be the way of magic.

Emotions were mixed as the four riders and the four Hunnuli waded across the river. The group came very slowly, for Nara and Eurus were supporting Afer between them as he hobbled painfully through the water, so the people had ample time to study the strange party. No one knew whether to cheer or throw stones at them.

The crowd silently watched as the horses angled toward the cluster of chieftains gathered at the tip of the council grove. At the edge of the shore in front of the lords and warriors, the Hunnuli stopped. They stood before the wall of men, their fetlocks deep in the swirling brown water and their manes hanging limp with rain.

There was an uncomfortable pause as the chieftains looked up at one of their own peers and at the woman who had captured the lightning. Quiet hung over the camps while the people waited and watched to see their lords' reactions. Thunder rumbled far to the east, the wind slowed to wayward gusts, and the heavy rain faltered to a drizzle.

Gabria saw nothing of the gathering around her, but she sensed the tension and confusion as surely as if she could see the people's faces. She had hoped to influence the clan chieftains to change the laws against sorcery, but she had never thought to go so far.

She heard the men shift reluctantly, then a voice said, "Welcome to the gathering, Lord Athlone. I did not get a chance to see you earlier." It was Lord Hildor, the chieftain of the Wylfling.

His pleasant words and genuine welcome broke the tense standoff. The chiefs stood aside to allow room for the four Hunnuli to pass, and every lord came forward to voice his greetings to the magic-wielders. The crowds of people broke apart, too, into talking and wondering groups that made no move to go back to their camps.

With a sigh of relief, Lord Sha Umar came to Nara's side and helped Gabria dismount. Like the others, he wondered at her closed eyes, but he made no comment. He only put her hand on his arm and led her to the council tent. The others followed.

Secen, Valar, and Keth had already arrived and were waiting at the tent. The three warriors saluted the magic-wielders with obvious pleasure and relief. Secen told Gabria that Piers was already at work with his healing stone.

Athlone watched while his hearthguard raised his golden banner beside the other chiefs' flags above the tent. He had to swallow hard to fight down the strange mix of relief, pride, and nervousness that rose within him.

The battle with the gorthling was won, but the battle for the survival of sorcery would continue. Athlone and Gabria both knew the clanspeople were too stubborn and their beliefs were too ingrained to be wiped out in a short time. They might be grateful for the defeat of the gorthling, but they were not going to forget two hundred years of hatred and suspicion.

At the entrance to the council tent, Lord Sha Umar, the chieftains' council leader for the year, raised his hand and shouted for attention. "Tomorrow, if Lord Koshyn and Lord Athlone are able to attend, we will begin the council of chieftains. My lords, we have a great deal to discuss this year."

A loud murmur of assent met his suggestion.

He continued. "If all of you are willing, I would like to call a special meeting in the afternoon to learn more about sorcery. Lady Gabria, the Turic, and the girl, Tam, should be allowed to attend."

The other chiefs readily agreed, and so it was decided. Gabria felt weak with relief. She curled her arm up around Nara's throat and pressed her face into the mare's warm cheek.

She nearly jumped when someone said beside her, "Lady Gabria? Lord Koshyn asked me to find this and give it to you. He thought you would need it."

She felt a heavy leather bag being pressed into her hand. "He's awake?" she asked, feeling into the bag.

"Only a short time ago. Healer Piers says he will be . . ." The Dangari warrior's voice faded away at the expression of disbelief and rueful dismay that settled on the sorceress's face.

Gabria began to laugh. She did not need her vision to recognize the old, faded smell, the heavy leather binding, or the faint tingle of power that tickled her fingers from the ancient tome. Now, when she could use it the least, the *Book of Matrah* was in her hands.

The chieftains recognized the book, too, and they stared at her apprehensively. That book had been the cause of strife and death. They wondered what Gabria would do with it.

"Thank you," the sorceress said gently to the warrior. "Would you please give this to Lord Sha Umar until the chiefs can decide what to do with it?"

Sha Umar met Athlone's grin with a shrug and a chuckle of relief. He put the book under guard for safekeeping.

*   *   *

Shortly after the *Book of Matrah* had been passed to Sha Umar, Gabria went to find Piers. She found the healer among the people stricken by the gorthling's arcane blow. He had just finished using the healing stone on the last victim and was talking to the overjoyed relatives when he saw Gabria. He took one look at her, bustled her off to his newly erected tent, and put her to bed.

For that night, the next day, and the following night Gabria slumbered in a peaceful, recuperative rest that not even the uproar in the camps around her could disturb. When she woke in the afternoon of the second day, her first reaction was fear. The world was still completely dark. Her hands flew to her eyes and grabbed at a cloth bound around her head.

"Easy. It's all right," Pier's calm voice soothed her panic. His hands took hers and gently laid them aside. "I've bandaged your eyes for now to let them rest."

She drew a long breath and slowly relaxed. "Is it possible my eyes will heal?"

"I really don't know if you will see again," he told her sadly. "I've never had any experience with this kind of blindness." Piers frowned. He did not like being so unsure about something so important. "I have examined your eyes and I can find no damage. We'll just have to wait."

"I hear voices," someone called outside. "Is she awake?" Sayyed sauntered in, bringing in the smells of sun, wind, and horses. He smiled at Piers, then strode over to Gabria's pallet. "I was beginning to wonder if you were going to sleep through the whole gathering," he said, sitting beside her.

"Before you two talk all day, I have something for Gabria to drink." Piers handed her a cup. "Nara said it is for strength and healing."

The sorceress sat up and raised the cup to her lips. She smiled. The cup was full of the Hunnuli mare's rich, warm milk. Gabria drank every drop and felt her energy flooding back. "What has been happening?"

With pleasure Sayyed and Piers told her everything that had occurred the past two and a half days. Sayyed immediately began with Afer, and with delight in his voice said, "No one expected my idea to work." He laughed. "They kept saying no horse would tolerate being slung by his belly for days on end. They didn't take into account the intelligence of a Hunnuli. We have him supported in a special framework under the cottonwood trees. His leg is splinted, and Tam is spoiling him with treats and handpicked grass. He seems to be doing very well. Even your herdmasters are shaking their heads and saying the sling just might work."

Gabria was delighted to hear that news. The men went on, telling her that Lord Koshyn and the clanspeople Piers had treated with the healing stone were doing well. The chieftains' council had met as planned, and Lord Athlone had explained the details of the gorthling's vicious nature to them all.

"I don't think they fully comprehended what we were fighting until Lord Athlone told them about the massacre of the Bahedin," Sayyed told her. "When they came out of the council tent yesterday, every man among them was as white as the moon." He slapped his knee. "I wish you could have been in the camps last night. The tales of Branth, the gorthling, and our journey to Pra Desh spread from one end of the gathering to the other."

Piers chuckled. "Hardly anyone but you slept last night. They were too busy talking."

"And gawking. The Priestess of Amara and Athlone put the mask of Valorian on display. Every man, woman, and child stood in line to see it." Sayyed shook his head. "No one quite knows what to make of all this—a gorthling, arcane battles, Valorian's mask, the Hunnuli herd—your people have enough to keep them thinking for years."

Gabria smiled. "I hope so. What about the council, have they had their meeting on sorcery?"

Piers answered, "Not yet. They're waiting for you."

"Athlone is at the council tent now, trying to convince Lord Caurus that sorcery is not going to destroy the clans," Sayyed said.

"He'll have a tough fight with that man." The mention of Athlone sobered Gabria. She had something important to tell Sayyed, but she was not certain where to start. The young Turic was so dear to her soul, it was very difficult to tell him what her heart had been trying to tell her all along. She loved Sayyed as a brother and a friend, as someone who filled the aching void left by her twin's death. She wondered sadly how he would react when she told him the truth. Would he stay or would he leave in a cloud of hurt feelings?

But Sayyed surprised her. The Turic took her hand. "It is good to have you alive and well, Gabria," he said. "When you left us to find the gorthling alone, we feared the worst. Lord Athlone was like a stallion heading for battle. He would have left by himself if Piers hadn't talked him into taking me. I've never seen a man so wild." He nodded his head. "If you don't take that man for your husband, he will go berserk one of these days."

Gabria inhaled sharply. "You understand?"

Sayyed gently rubbed her palm with his fingers. "I've known for many days. I just didn't want to see the truth because I wanted you so much, but his feelings and yours are undeniable. You are destined to be together."

"Thank you," she whispered. She touched her bandages with her hand, wishing she could see his face. Despite his words, she would hear the sadness and disappointment in his voice.

"I hope this doesn't mean you won't teach me more sorcery," he said.

Her fingers tightened around his. "You'll stay?"

"Gabria," Sayyed said earnestly, "my love for you is undying. I must simply change it so it does not burn so hot. I came to learn sorcery, and if you will still have me by your side, I want to stay."

"So do I," Athlone said from the tent's entrance. The Khulinin chieftain strode in and joined Gabria and Sayyed. Piers quietly withdrew, leaving the three magic-wielders in the privacy of the tent.

Lord Athlone sat down beside Gabria. He was nervous about her reaction to what he was going to say, and it took him a moment to find the words. "Sayyed and I have talked a great deal the past few days," the chief said slowly. "We have settled a few of our differences, and I have come to understand many things about sorcery and myself. You asked me once if I was willing to live with magic and all of its difficulties. Now I can tell you with all my heart, yes, but only if you are with me. Would you consider renewing our vow of betrothal?"

Gabria sat still, her thoughts swept away by her emotions. "If my eyes do not heal, can you live with my blindness, too?"

"I love you for who you are," he answered simply.

There was a breathless pause, then she raised her hand palm up and said, "I give you my pledge from this moment."

His fingers interlaced with hers, and the vow was made.

Athlone shot a glance at Sayyed. The tribesman nodded once in satisfaction, and the chieftain held out his other hand to the Turic. Sayyed grasped it firmly. He knew then that he had lost a woman, but he had found two new friends. Perhaps, he thought, that was a good exchange on the wheel of life.

The next morning Gabria slowly dressed to attend the council meeting. As she sat waiting for Athlone, Piers unwrapped the bandages around her eyes to replace the cloths with clean ones.

To his astonishment, her hand suddenly grasped his arm in an iron grip. The sorceress was squinting at the entrance where sunlight was leaking through the untied tent flap. "I can see the light," she gasped.

Piers was delighted. He quickly checked her eyes and, against her protest, wrapped them again in the cloths. "Your eyes need rest!" he insisted. "Tonight I'll let you try them, after the sunlight is gone."

When Athlone, Sayyed, and Tam came to get her, they found Gabria in a state of euphoria. Her smile was brilliant, and her joy radiated from every line of her face. The four magic-wielders took her healing as a good omen, and they went to the council of the chieftains with hopeful hearts.

Gabria would never forget that council meeting. After listening to her speech in defense of magic, the chiefs debated for hours over the fate of sorcery and the fate of Gabria and her friends. Athlone, Sayyed, and Tam sat around her through the long, often angry speeches and did not move once to defend themselves. The final decision was up to the chieftains now, and no one could say with certainty what their choice would be.

At last, late in the afternoon, Koshyn and Sha Umar won a major victory. Lord Caurus rose from his seat and said grudgingly, "I see I must cast my lot with the rest of you. I agree to remove the death penalty for the use of sorcery. However, I demand that strict limits be set on the use of magic and on the actions of the magic-wielders. The use of sorcery must be contained to those we deem responsible enough to use it!"

Lord Sha Umar raised his hand. "It is done. I suggest that we extend the gathering a few more days and use that time to establish the new laws for sorcery. This is too important to put off for another year."

The chieftains and the magic-wielders agreed. When Sha Umar gave Gabria the *Book of Matrah*, she and Athlone found the dangerous spells of summoning gorthlings, tore them from the book, and burned them.

"There are some things," she said, repeating Valorian's words, "best left alone by man."

News of the council's decision spread through the camps even before the meeting was over. Emotions were widely mixed throughout the clans, but no one was greatly surprised. The clanspeople were beginning to understand that magic was part of their heritage, a part they could no longer deny.

*   *   *

Three days later, on a gloriously clear, warm summer evening, Lord Athlone of Clan Khulinin married Lady Gabria of Clan Corin in a ceremony witnessed by all eleven clans. The Khulinin Priestess of Amara, clad in flowing green robes, performed the rites of marriage and blessed the couple with prayers of harmony and fertility.

Gabria wore the red dress Khan'di had given her and a golden veil from Athlone's mother—the red to represent the clan she was leaving and the gold to symbolize the clan she was finally officially joining. Lord Athlone was resplendent in his finest clothes and his golden torque. Piers and Tam were there to represent Gabria's family, and Sayyed stood as Athlone's witness.

When the ceremony was over, Athlone removed Gabria's veil and tied it around his waist like a sash. He took his new bride into his arms and sealed their happiness with a long and very thorough kiss.

The three Hunnuli beside them lifted their heads to the evening star and whinnied their joy over the vast Ramtharin Plains.

A Short Glossary

THE CLANS	CHIEFTAIN	CLOAK COLOR
Corin	Dathlar	Red
Khulinin	Savaric	Gold
Geldring	Branth	Green
Wylfling	Medb	Brown
Dangari	Koshyn	Indigo
Shadedron	Malech	Black
Reidhar	Caurus	Yellow
Amnok	Ferron	Gray
Murjik	Jol	Purple
Bahedin	Babur / Ryne	Orange
Jahanan	Sha Umar	Maroon
Ferganan	Quamar	Light Blue

Hearthguard: The chieftain's personal bodyguards. These men are the elite warriors of the clan and are honored with this position for their bravery, skill, and loyalty.

Herd-master: The man responsible for the health, breeding, and well-being of the horse herds.

Holdings: Land granted to a clan for its use while in winter camp.

Outriders: Those werod riders who guard the herds and the camp or act as scouts.

Treld: A clan's permanent winter camp.

Weir-geld: Recompense paid to the family of a murdered person in the form of gold or livestock, or by death in a personal duel.

Werod: The fighting body of a clan. Although all men are required to learn the rudiments of fighting, only those who pass certain tests make up the werod.

Wer-tain: The commander of the werod. These men are second only to the chieftain in authority.

About the Author

Mary H. Herbert was born in Ohio and grew up in the worlds of fantasy. She began writing seriously in high school and continued to write at the Universities of Montana and Wyoming, and the Center for Medieval and Renaissance Studies in Oxford, England. She currently resides in Georgia with her husband and two children. Mary's first novel, *Dark Horse*, was a national chain bookstore bestseller. *Lightning's Daughter* is her second book.